BEFORE MIDNIGHT ENDS
THE GLORIOUS VICTORIES OF ELEANOR MACLEOD
VOLUME FIVE
by Ashley Mayers

First Printing: 2019
ISBN 978-1-943918-24-9
First International Print Edition

Grass Roof Publishing
P.O. Box 14908
San Francisco, California, 94114
www.GloriousVictories.com

Also by Ashley Mayers:
THE SITA CHRONICLES:
Red Sapphire
Violet Sapphire
White Sapphire
Golden Sapphire
Cerulean Sapphire
Green Sapphire
Black Sapphire

THE GLORIOUS VICTORIES OF ELEANOR MACLEOD:
The Cursed Baron
Angels in Disguise
Damsels and Demons
Eastward Beyond the Sky
Before Midnight Ends

Notes from the Publisher:

The Glorious Victories of Eleanor MacLeod is a new five-book epic that adds another layer to the rich fantasy world created by Ashley Mayers and first published in 2015-16 in her seven-book modern multicultural epic, *The Sita Chronicles*.

Before Midnight Ends, the fifth and final book of Eleanor MacLeod's story, continues the modern story from *The Sita Chronicles*, in juxtaposition to the last chapter of Eleanor's epic. *Before Midnight Ends* explores the emotional depths of tragedy, while seeking to present a different view on the inevitable cycle of destruction and rebirth than is typically addressed in classic tragedies that end when the heroes die. For readers who have made it to the finish line of Eleanor's epic, there should be no question about if, how, or even when Eleanor will die, but rather, what her life and her death really mean, and what it is like for her to watch as the world moves on in her wake.

Throughout this series, it is the author's intention to give enough background for an uninitiated reader to develop a relationship with the world of *The Sita Chronicles,* while introducing them to several new heroines whose stories haven't yet been told. Both series fit together as puzzle pieces, creating unique insights into characters who are lovingly developed over the combined set of twelve books. All five books of Eleanor's story are intended to be read in order.

This series, like *The Sita Chronicles*, is a completely original, multicultural saga with roots in Hindu mythology. It exists in a world not dissimilar to ours, where Avatars (deities on Earth), Rakshasas (shapeshifting demons originating on Venus), and Yakshas (shapeshifting nature spirits) are real. While knowledge of Hinduism is not required to enjoy this series, a short glossary is provided in the back of the book to offer readers more context on Hindu cultural references.

This is a work of fiction.

Names, characters, businesses, places, events, and incidents are either products of the author's imagination or used in a fictitious manner. While many of the referenced historical events, figures, and places are inspired by fact, their treatment in this work are fictitious and should not be construed as real.

This book is written in American English using the grammatical, punctuation, and spelling conventions therein. The author has taken great care to apply a professional level of editing and proofreading to her works, while intentionally reflecting various accents, idioms, and dialects appropriate to each character's background, including Scots English, Australian Strine, and Indian English. Readers are kindly requested to approach the linguistic diversity of the series with curiosity and appreciation, rather than nitpicking. Anyone who judges Agatha Christie's English by Poirot's grammar needn't read any further.

This book is dedicated to every poor soul who has been blindsided by the tragic mundanity of grief. May this work bring you catharsis and hope, as it has for me.

~Ashley Mayers

TABLE OF CONTENTS

PROLOGUE

Christmas Eve, 2016 – Basingstoke, England

Ellie sat cross-legged on the floor of her father's secret lair in Basingstoke. Sheranee was cuddled up dozing next to her, but she paid her no mind. She was too overwhelmed. She only sat listlessly, staring at her mother's last manuscript. It was the manuscript she'd held onto, dreading for weeks after Supriya had given it to her. She'd finished reading it just in time. She could hear the hubbub upstairs as the loving relatives and allies of the Avatars of Light were gathering for Christmas Eve. She wiped the tears into her skin and took a deep, calming breath.

"Ellie-bean?" Edmund called as he skipped down the stairs. "Are you down here?"

As he noticed her posture, he took a seat beside her on the soft persian carpet. She tried not to think about what had happened there. He glanced down at the manuscript and put his arm around her.

"I'm proud of you for reading it, Ellie-bean. I avoided reading it myself for quite some time after Supriya finished it, but I'm glad I read it. I feel like I know myself better, and, of course, you and

1

your mother too. I suppose how we deal with our darkest moments defines us more than anything else can."

Ellie's eyes glowed the green of Eleanor's presence, but she didn't say anything, she only brought his hand to her mouth and kissed it, and then put it gently back in his lap.

He hopped up and offered her his hand. "Come upstairs. I have a Christmas surprise for you."

"It isn't a bottle of chouchen, is it? Mum thinks it's too sweet. I suppose after all the beans I made her eat, I ought to make it up to her."

"It's better."

She followed him upstairs, and he lifted the heavy Victorian stove that blocked the secret door back into place.

"Come on."

He led her to the library, where a group of familiar redheads were gathered on cushy leather couches before the roaring fire, drinking glasses of fine Scotch. A young redheaded boy was playing with an old wooden toy train that was chugging continuously around the room, and live squirrels were chasing each other through the branches of a very festive Christmas tree that was so tall, it almost touched the painted ceiling thirty feet above them.

"Ellie!" they exclaimed.

"Why, if it isn't the illustrious MacLeods!" Ellie said cheerfully as she greeted them.

"Merry Christmas," Debbie said as she held up a toast with her translucent, wrinkled hand. In the months since Ellie had seen her last, she'd lost the last hint of red in her thin white hair.

Ellie kneeled down to hug her gently. "I'm so glad you were healthy enough to make it. How did you get here? I thought all the Yakshas were busy preparing for Christmas Eve?"

"I drove them!" Edmund declared proudly. "Can you believe it?"

"Hardly!" Ellie laughed. "When was the last time you drove, Dad?"

He scrunched his nose as he thought about it. "It feels like a lifetime ago. It was nice to get back behind the wheel, actually, for old time's sake. Kuveni popped up the old Rolls Royce, and I drove them all the way down from Elphinstone. Angus and Duncan will be down on the train in the morning, though. They were trying to wrap things up at the gallery before the holiday."

"What a fine Christmas it will be with all of you," Ellie said as she poured herself a generous glass of the fine Scotch and took a seat on a chaise by the Christmas tree. As Edmund followed her lead, sitting in a chair across from her and taking a long, savoring sip, she glanced around. "Where's Supriya?"

"She'll be here any minute. She was busy working on a few Christmas miracles of her own."

With a pleasant breeze, Kuveni stood between them. She released Charlie and Grace from her grip, and Grace leaned woozily on the fireplace mantle to catch her breath, while Edmund hopped up in a blur to twirl Charlie around. Charlie squealed with the thrill, and Edmund steadied him as he let go.

"Merry Christmas, Charlie!"

"Merry Christmas, Dad." Charlie hugged him again. "I was afraid you'd be… never mind."

"I'd be what?" Edmund asked.

"Old," Charlie admitted.

"You know me pretty well, don't you?"

Edmund glanced over at Debbie, and then returned his attention to Charlie, relegating a mischievous twinkle in his eye. He sat back down and patted his lap, and Charlie sat down, hugging his father like he had when he was a younger boy. He'd been clingy ever since Edmund had saved Grace from the brink of death nearly a month earlier, and Edmund took it in stride, helping him nestle into his arms.

Kuveni snapped her fingers, handing Charlie a cup of steaming hot chocolate, and then she hugged Ellie.

"Aren't you a sight for sore eyes," Eleanor whispered as she fingered the beaded collar of Kuveni's black silk dress that went perfectly with the short black bob of her Kate Marriner form. "I always preferred you like this. This form gave you an air of authority that you deserved."

Kuveni squeezed her tighter. "Oh, how I love you, Mistress Eleanor." She wiped a tear from her eye, took a deep breath, looked around at their audience, and refocused her attention on her sacred duties. "I'd better get back. Lord Vibhishana will be here any minute, and then the real games will begin. Oh, I can't wait! It's been too long since we've gone all out in the name of Saint Nick!"

As Kuveni disappeared, Grace looked around, and then kneeled awkwardly before Ellie with her head bowed. "Thank you for inviting me, Holy Mother. I hope you can forgive my intrusion tonight. I know I haven't earned the right to be here, but I didn't want to spend the holy night without Charlie."

Ellie blushed with embarrassment as she glanced over at her father and Charlie, and then at the MacLeods.

She means well, Ellie-bean. For the first time in her life, she fully means well. We should encourage her.

But it's so awkward, Mum! Can't I just be normal for one bloody night?!

Sacred duties never cease, my darling.

Then you deal with her.

Eleanor took her daughter's adolescent moment in stride, and coaxed Grace up out of her position of prostration.

"My child, you must channel your repentance into acts of kindness, remember? You must make meaning from the misery."

"Yes, Holy Mother."

"And, Grace, please call Ellie by her first name. It's awkward for everyone when you remind us of our divine burdens.

Sometimes we just need some human cheer to temper the madness of our everyday lives."

"Yes… Ellie."

The front door slammed open and closed, and in a blur, Supriya was entering the library, wiggling her black pants and jacket into a festive green Christmas dress in a vintage style she'd been practicing for months.

She looked around and grinned as she saw Debbie. "Welcome home!"

She kissed Edmund on the top of his head, graciously allowing Charlie his space, and squeezed onto the chaise next to Ellie.

Ellie hugged her. "Were your Christmas miracles a success?"

Supriya smiled. "They were. It was a painful process having to choose which of the prayers to answer, but I just have to keep reminding myself that we can't heal everyone. I'm going back out later, after dinner, but I wanted to be here to say hello to my mom and Vibhi when they arrive."

Grace took a seat on the couch with the MacLeods and poured herself a tall glass of Scotch, nursing it silently.

"Where's Neha?" Supriya asked. "She said she had a surprise for us when I talked to her yesterday. She sounded unusually excited."

"Is that possible?" Ellie laughed. "I didn't know Neha could sound any more excited."

"To be honest, I half expected to find a tropical beach in the yard, or some other similarly outrageous Yakshini feat."

"I'd prefer a hill for sledding this time of year," Ellie said cheerfully as she finally relaxed. Having them all there was pulling her out of her malaise.

"I've always thought we could use a lake," Edmund chimed in. "Think of what a lovely boathouse the carriage house would make."

"My vote is for a polo field," Debbie winked.

"A polo field." Edmund sat back and sighed. "Now *that* is an idea I'm going to have to seriously think about."

He didn't have time to. In a puff of smoke, Vibhishana and Shanti appeared completely naked in the fireplace. As soon as they saw their unexpected audience, they wiggled on the first clothing they could think of with Vibhishana donning his vicar's habit, and Shanti her scrubs. They sheepishly stepped into the room as Supriya and Edmund both laughed heartily.

Shanti glanced at the MacLeods, but addressed her question to Supriya. "I didn't realize you'd be having humans over for Christmas?"

Supriya stood up and hugged both of them in greeting. "They're not just humans, they're MacLeods."

Ellie shivered as a wave of relief washed over Eleanor.

It's time, isn't it? Eleanor asked Uma. She hoped that Ellie wouldn't be able to hear her.

Before midnight ends, my child, our task will be complete. Your lifecycle will finally return to its natural course, and all will be as it should.

I'm ready.

"Merry Christmas, Father Johnson," Debbie said as Vibhishana brushed the soot off of his jacket. "You'd better get going soon. I reckon this Christmas more than most, people'll be hoping and praying for a visit from you."

He took a moment to figure out who she was, and then he smiled and rushed to greet her. He carefully hugged her, and then looked her up and down.

"Debbie MacLeod, it has been far too long."

"Aye, there's no question about that, is there? I'm just glad I lasted long enough to see you all in your full glory."

As Vibhishana moved to introduce Shanti to the illustrious MacLeods, Eleanor made her move. Ellie gasped as Eleanor pushed her way to the surface, taking control of her body for the first time without Ellie's permission.

Mum? Mum what's happening?

Eleanor took a deep breath and closed her eyes.

I'm sorry, Ellie-bean. It's time. I've been waiting your whole life for this.

For what?

It is time to connect Uma with her next incarnation, my darling. It is time to make things how the need to be.

Will we lose Sheranee?

I don't know what will happen to her, to be honest. I suppose she won't be too pleased to be stuck with Shanti, colonizing the freezing rock of Mars with the other Rakshasas.

Maybe she'll want to stay with you?

My darling, I must go too. It is time. You are ready to stand on your own two feet now, and so am I. My lifecycle must continue, just like everyone else's.

But everyone's doesn't! Dad's doesn't, Vibhi's doesn't, most of our immortal family's doesn't! Why do you have to go?!

I was human, Ellie. It wasn't my destiny to live forever inside of you. I was given the extraordinary gift of watching you grow up, but it is time for me to live my own life again. I want this.

No! I just met you! I've wanted to know you my whole life, and now you're leaving! It isn't fair!

My darling, I can't tell you how grateful I am that after ninety years on Earth, you still haven't learned that life isn't fair. I'm sorry that I'm the one who's going to have to teach it to you, but I need to do this. It is my destiny.

You can't go! I won't let you!

Eleanor felt Ellie scratching at her, trying her hardest to take her body back. Eleanor held on steadfast, as she had learned to do during her own lifetime as she'd battled against Uma's urges, until finally, Ellie gave up.

I will always love you, Ellie. Take with you Shakti's blessings.

Eleanor opened her eyes. Everyone in the room was staring at her. Her head was heavy with Durga's crown, and Sheranee was prostrated at her feet. She summoned her trident and stood up. The green flames of Shakti's power burst forth from her palms.

"Eleanor, what is happening?" Edmund asked nervously.

"Don't worry, darling. Ellie will be perfectly fine. The flames are not hot. It is time for me to fulfill my destiny." As he moved to intervene anyway, Eleanor aimed her trident at him and Charlie whimpered. "Do *not* get in my way, Edmund. I've been waiting ninety years for this."

She approached Shanti with her trident poised, but before Uma made any move, Shanti's eyes turned black, and she snatched it right out of Eleanor's hand.

"I have always hated violence on Christmas most of all," Shanti said. "Please state your business here. We have a long night ahead of us."

But, as she stared at the flaming trident in her hand, feeling the familiar vibration of Shakti's energy, the green flames traveled up her arm and into her. She gasped as a burst of intoxicating power engulfed her, and Vibhishana positioned himself to catch her. He did not try to stop what was happening; he only offered Eleanor a subtle encouraging smile.

Shanti stayed standing as the intoxication passed, but the flames still flickered from her palms and her weapon. Her scrubs had transformed into Durga's sari, and Durga's crown was now fully formed on her head. She gripped the trident, watching as the flames reacted to her will. She put them out, and then looked up at the glimmering gold prongs.

"Keep it, my child. It's yours," Uma said as she forced Shanti's free hand into hers. She glanced at Vibhishana. "We've both been waiting far too long for this."

"Vibhi, who is this?" Shanti asked as she tried unsuccessfully to wrench her hand away. She looked back and forth between Vibhishana and Eleanor. "What's happening?"

Eleanor smiled. "Have you ever felt like a part of you was missing?"

Shanti looked around at the wide eyes of her audience. "From time to time," she admitted. "I didn't notice it until the demon Kali left me... and I ascended."

Eleanor smiled reassuringly. "I am that part, my child. I am Uma, Avatar of Shakti. It is time for us to become one, as we were always meant to be. Do not be afraid. This is our destiny."

Eleanor closed her eyes and shivered as the two goddesses' energy connected into a torrential flow, and then, with a burst of heat, the last of Uma dissolved right out of Ellie's fingertips.

Eleanor opened her eyes and smiled. Shanti moaned with pleasure as their consciousness joined. The green flames surged into a momentary bonfire and then dissolved, leaving everything around them unscathed.

Sheranee roared and pounced across the room to bow before her. Shanti opened her eyes. They were green and sparkling, and behind them, Eleanor could see Uma basking in relief.

"Extraordinary," Shanti murmured.

Sheranee licked Shanti's hands, and as Shanti looked up at Durga's divine crown on her head and down at her sari, she dissolved her trident and engulfed Eleanor into a tight hug.

"Thank you, my child. You were the worthiest of allies."

Eleanor hugged her back, but she felt the world dimming as she had once before. This time, as the peaceful darkness beckoned, she didn't fight it.

Goodbye, Ellie.

She let go.

PART ONE
WHAT CALLS

May 25, 1925, Margaret River, Western Australia
In a flash of light, five glamorous women materialized in the parlor of Eleanor's comfortable seaside home just outside the Western Australian hamlet of Margaret River. They leaned on each other woozily as they gathered their bearings after their highly unusual journey through a Yakshini vortex, and then Eleanor laughed, grounding them all with her relaxed cheer.

"Can you believe that tenor was so shrill? Kuveni, you've rescued our mortal hearing from a dire blow!"

"All in a day's work, my dear girl," Kuveni winked.

"Well, I thought the acting was the most shameful part of his performance. What was he doing crawling across the stage like that?" Mae added. "I mean *really*, what's he going to do in Act Four when his operatic love triangle explodes?"

"I didn't think that whole crawling episode in the temple was intentional. I thought he'd fallen and injured his knee!" Shruti joined in with the friendly jabbing. "He was so ploddy, trudging around with all of his weight on his knees before he fell over. If

13

he'd taken dance at my school, he would have known a thing or two about how to be graceful, even at his size."

"Well, beggars can't be choosers," Yvie reminded them. "It's a wonder we have any culture at all down here at the edge of the world. The local bushies can't tell an opera from a cattle fair, no matter how much money Nellie Melba puts into developing their musical taste."

"Do you think it was rude for us to leave at intermission?" Mae asked with only peripheral concern. "They're sure to notice that six women in the third row are missing; the whole audience was staring at us the whole time."

"My darling girls, we were much better to look at than that fat old miser of a Radamès," Kuveni pointed out. "If an ancient Egyptian soldier had looked half as pudgy as that man, he would have been imprisoned for stealing from the pharaoh's pantry!"

Eleanor laughed. "We were also the most overdressed sheilas in all of Australia. Next time we'll have to send Kuveni ahead as a scout to report back on what to wear before we try another little endeavor like this. They must have thought the entire court of the Queen of England had arrived for the show with our glistening jewels and fine silks."

"It was the court of the Queen of Australia," Kuveni corrected her jokingly. "I don't know why any of them were surprised that we looked like royalty."

Yvie sighed. "It really was my fault. We used to always dress to the nines when we went to the Garnier in Paris. I should have realized that the Bunbury Opera wouldn't be the same. It's still a wonder to me that they have a theater at all."

"I rather appreciate their efforts." Eleanor let herself focus on the positive. "If the tenor's voice hadn't been so excruciating, I would've stuck it out to the end. I was the one who chose to stay local, after all. Kuveni suggested several times that we should pop over to the Met in New York or La Scala instead. I thought the novelty of the small-town effort would be entertaining in a

14

different way, but I suppose it was a little bit too amateurish, even for my uneducated taste."

"Well now, we had a fun little adventure, and now we have your lovely house all to ourselves while our beloved baby Neddy keeps our valiant men occupied in Perth all weekend. What would you like to do, Eleanor dear? It's only nine o'clock here, and it's still lunchtime in Europe, if you want to pop up to France for a bite."

Eleanor did find the option alluring, but as she glanced around at the four kind, intelligent, spitfire modern sheilas with whom she could be entirely her real divine self, she made her choice. "I can't think of anything better than being home, chatting honestly with all of you over some champagne… and perhaps some canelés?"

Kuveni clapped approvingly, and then closed her eyes and whispered a quiet mantra. With a pleasant breeze, Mélusine appeared beside them, clad in her standard white medieval dress rather than the sparkling violet beaded gown she'd worn to the opera with them.

"Is everything alright?" Eleanor asked with a hint of nerves. "I expected you to pop into the room with us after you helped us escape from the opera."

"Everything is perfectly fine," she replied. Eleanor could tell she was hiding something, and she stared her down, waiting for a better answer. "I had to see to a minor emergency back at the Sacred Well, but now everything is fine."

"What kind of emergency?" Kuveni asked as she too gave into a moment of anxiety.

"Let's just say you will have your hands full. The Peruvians have procreated again, and this time they made three offspring: two Yakshinis and a Yaksha."

Kuveni laughed jovially. "Well, it's a good thing little Neddy's been giving me some practice!"

Mélusine didn't look amused. "A human child presents no challenge whatsoever compared to a young Yaksha. You'd better start preparing yourself."

"My lady, not even your Puck was too much for me to handle. Don't worry for one moment about it. I've been feeling a bit of an empty nest since Illa graduated out of my care, and perhaps this is just what the doctor ordered."

"Did Oz suggest you gather up some offspring to mother?" Mélusine asked with genuine puzzlement. "I didn't realize he knew you that well."

"I didn't mean the statement literally, Melysium."

Mélusine shrugged. "Well, you'd better enjoy your last days of freedom. You'll be occupied for decades with those little rascals."

"Kuveni, I didn't realize you were signed up to care for all of the children born into our bizarre foreign world," Eleanor said as she contemplated the idea. She'd always subtly assumed that Kuveni's years of caring for Edmund were a special circumstance due to his unique divine destiny and his worthless evil father.

"It is not an obligation, my dear girl. It is a privilege. It is a beautiful destiny for someone like me to be a matrika, with century after century of fulfilling work to keep me busy. Besides, the Yaksha people need someone with millennia of experience to parent our young. Lady Mélusine was not exaggerating. They really are very difficult to manage, so difficult, that almost none of us are willing to procreate at all anymore. The Peruvians are doing our species a great service by keeping at it like they do."

"What was it I overheard about Eleanor wanting champagne?" Mélusine changed the subject.

She snapped her fingers, and a massive ice bucket appeared on a low cocktail table in the middle of the room along with six delicate crystal coupes.

"Oh, I don't need any," Shruti demurred.

Kuveni snapped her fingers, and a brimming carafe of mango juice appeared on the table beside the champagne.

16

"Posh, Shruti dearest. Tippling is not a requirement of celebrating Eleanor's last weekend of her thirties."

Shruti smiled and relaxed. "Thank you, Your Highness."

"Your highness?" Mae asked curiously.

"Kuveni was the ancient queen of Ceylon," Shruti explained.

"Now, now, that was a very long time ago," Kuveni moved the conversation along. She snapped her fingers, producing a massive basket of french pastries, topped off with a mound of freshly steaming canelés.

"That reminds me! My sisters sent a box of Scottish shortbreads for my birthday!" Eleanor exclaimed. "Stay right here and settle in. I'll go grab them from the pantry."

Eleanor had started to find the shortbreads that she'd eaten for years as her only after-work snack to be too dry and pithy, but they still reminded her of her sisters, whom she had been missing more and more as the months passed by and she and Edmund settled into their newly purchased vineyard estate just down the road from Oz and Yvie down under. It was the same estate that Lord Grimby had rented upon their arrival in Margaret River—the place where Yvie gave birth to baby Ned and where Leo took his last breath on the fateful night of Eleanor's defeat of the demon Haranyakashipu. They'd bought it for an excellent price after their Secret Service nemesis had packed up one meager suitcase and high-tailed it for Fremantle before the sun even rose the next morning.

It was a phenomenon that puzzled Eleanor at the time, given he'd missed her conspicuously divine battle, but that she wasn't willing to question, as it got him out of their hair and her out of a particularly stressful web of lies. Most importantly, it indicated that Mac's dying message warning his superiors of the true power of the Avatars of Light had not made it through the downed phone lines before Surpanakha had killed him, which was a silent triumph that had allowed Eleanor to sleep sounder for the eight blissful months since he'd left.

As she and Edmund had settled into their Aussie life together, with Edmund resuming his post as a local magistrate, and Eleanor taking on the role as the head nurse in Dr. Helmsworth's new rural medical office, she'd thought a few times about asking Kuveni to pop her up to Edinburgh to pay her sisters an unannounced visit, but then she'd let her rational mind make the final judgment, recognizing that there was simply no plausible human explanation for her presence there.

They cannot handle how foreign our world is, my child. They do not share the enlightened acceptance of difficult truths that your other allies do.

Eleanor sighed without bothering to make an argument. She knew Uma was right.

She relegated her familiar disappointment and skipped through the kitchen to the pantry. She stood in the massive closet, looking around at its messy state, racking her brain to remember where she'd put her shortbreads, and hoping that Stanley had not accidentally thrown them out.

"*I am the very model of a modern major general...*"

Eleanor glanced up as the silly ditty penetrated through the wall of the pantry from the dining room, booming from the voice of a lyrical baritone who put all of the singers they'd endured at the opera earlier that evening to shame. She thought for a fleeting moment that perhaps she'd gone mad, but the solo continued, gaining speed and confidence...

"*I've information vegetable, animal, and mineral...*"

The mystery singer broke off into uproarious laughter, and then picked up, struggling to contain himself.

"*I know the kings of Englaaaaand...*"

He lost his battle, and the song stopped. She heard Stanley squeal, and then more laughter, and suddenly she realized the exceptionally awkward problem that had just been created by her unexpected decision to return home early from the opera with her entourage.

18

She tiptoed out of the pantry, and then stood in the hallway just outside the closed pocket door of the dining room, debating her options. She could have Kuveni pop them somewhere completely different… perhaps Bombay, but then Ravi Bidkar would be there to dote over her every divine word, or perhaps Yvie's city house in Perth… but then Edmund and Oz were up there with Ned, and she'd have to give up on her girls-only birthday weekend. Yvie's house just across the vineyards was an option, although the smell of her distillation experiments had become rather dreadful. The truth was, Eleanor wanted to be home with her dearest friends enjoying a completely honest weekend, and a little selfish voice reminded her that Stanley was supposed to be on leave for the week, enjoying his holiday however he pleased as long as he was far, far away…

"*And I quote the fights historical…*" The baritone picked up his song again, and Eleanor rolled her shoulders and tapped gently on the door. Neither of them noticed her intrusion.

"*From Marathon to Waterloo, in order categorical…*"

She knocked louder.

"*I'm very well acquainted too with matters mathematical…*"

She took a deep breath, and ripped open the door.

A beautiful, tall, muscular man with skin the color of creamy coffee was standing on her dining room table, which was pushed to the far side of the room, made into a makeshift stage. He wore nothing but the hat from Edmund's military dress uniform.

Stanley, in turn, was sitting in one of their chairs on the opposite side of the room, with his whole face made up with red lipstick, tasteful rouge, dramatic eye-liner, and well-executed lash-lengthening mascara, wearing a pink silk robe bordered with white fluffy feathers, accompanied by a pair of matching white feathered high-heeled slippers that looked better than his original attempts at similar shoes, now that he had taken to shaving his legs and, more importantly, his toes. A brown wig of a cute modern bob with a matching pink headband completed his outfit, making him look mostly feminine, but still, somehow, clearly male.

The baritone took one look at Eleanor and dove off of his stage and under the dining room table, while Stanley screamed with surprise, and then launched himself up from his chair.

"Eleanor... ma'am... *my lady*, I didn't think you would be here! I thought you were spending the night in Bunbury!"

"You should know by now, greenie, that I go where I please, when I please. You should not make assumptions about where I am at any given moment."

He muttered angrily at himself before addressing her. "I'm sorry, my lady. I wasn't thinking straight."

Eleanor raised her eyebrows. "I can see that." She kneeled down to address their guest. "You don't need to hide under the table, my friend. You've been caught red-handed. We might as well get the pleasantries out of the way."

She gestured for him to come on out, and he reluctantly obeyed, pulling Edmund's hat off of his head and placing it modestly over his manhood as he stood up straight before her.

Eleanor burst into laughter. "I suppose you'll be keeping that. I'll tell Edmund to order another one."

The man contemplated momentarily pulling the hat away from its scandalous position, and then he gave up and kept it where it was. "I'm sorry, ma'am. I'll pay for a replacement."

"No need. We have the funds to buy it ourselves. Now, perhaps you can tell me who it is I've encountered in my dining room? You're an opera singer? Are you worthy of my chief handmaiden Stanley here's affections?"

He glanced at Stanley, looking even more bewildered. "My name is Andrew, ma'am. I'm not much of anything. I was in a circus for a while, trying to make my way as an acrobat, but I didn't like the life. It was too lonely."

"Where did you learn how to sing like that?"

"At church, ma'am. My father was a preacher."

"Then, I reckon he doesn't know too much about your life now, does he?"

Andrew glanced at Stanley again. "No, ma'am, I reckon he doesn't."

"Relax, my friend. I'm not going to call your father, and there's no fire and brimstone under this roof. Can you sing other things? You know, other than that Gilbert and Sullivan prattle?" she asked.

"*Credo in un Dio crudel che m'a creato simile a se e che nell'ira io nomo...*"

"Blimey," Eleanor murmured as a voice ten times more powerful burst forth from him as he sang the deep, ominous declaration. "I believe in a cruel god, who created me in his image, and that in anger I name..."

As he continued on with the aria, growing in intensity with every phrase, her entourage tiptoed up behind her.

"Good lord," Mae murmured as she spied his naked state.

"*Mon dieu*," Yvie seconded as her exclamation gave way to giggles.

Shruti peeked in between them, gasped, and then turned right around and relegated herself to the hallway, keeping her innocent eyes protected from the scandalous sight.

Andrew noticed them, but continued on determinedly.

"*Dalla viltà d'un germe o d'un atomo vile son nato. Son scellerato perchè son uomo; e sento il fango originario in me...* I was born from the cowardice of a seed or a vile atom. I'm wicked because I'm man, I feel the original mud in me..."

He sang and he sang, and Eleanor watched as Stanley's expression evolved from surprise to adoration.

Finally, he reached his last booming declaration, "*Vien dopo tanto irrision la morte. E poi? E poi? La morte è il nulla. È vecchia fola il Ciel!* ... After all this irrationality comes death. And then? And then? Death is nothing. Heaven is an old fable!"

He paused for a moment of penetrating silence at the end of his aria, and then Kuveni burst into applause, and Eleanor and her entourage followed.

"*Bravo!*" Kuveni declared.

"*C'était incréable,*" Yvie agreed. "You're better than the Iago I saw at the Garnier in Paris!"

"*C'est vrai,*" Mélusine agreed. "The power of your voice is very unusual, mon chéri."

"Do you speak Italian?" Mae asked curiously.

Andrew was overwhelmed by their praise... and their apparent forgiveness of his nudity.

"I don't speak much of anything," he replied. "I memorized the song from a record my father had back at home."

"Well, I know a production of *Aida* that could use a pinch hitter like you, pronto!" Eleanor exclaimed.

Andrew glanced at Stanley, and then looked down at the floor.

"He can't, my lady," Stanley whispered. "They'll only let whites perform in the opera. Andrew's mum is an aborigine."

Eleanor thought back to the odd makeup the white performers were wearing earlier in the evening as they'd performed the piece that was supposed to take place in Africa.

"Blimey, the world is wretched, isn't it?" Eleanor asked the question rhetorically. "Perhaps, Stanley, you can give Nellie Melba a call tomorrow on my behalf and ask her if she knows any teachers or musical institutions that do not discriminate based on race."

"Most of them do," Stanley humphed.

"He only needs one that doesn't," Kuveni reminded him.

"You know Nellie Melba?" Andrew asked with a hint of hope.

"She and I are very good friends," Eleanor confirmed. "Divas must stick together, after all."

Andrew's posture deflated. "I don't have any money ma'am. I can't pay for lessons... unless..."

"Unless?" Eleanor raised her eyebrow.

"Is there work I could do here? I could be a stable-hand, or I can help out in the vineyards? I'm very strong, and I can do most things I set my mind to. I'm sure it would only take a year or two for me to save up enough money for lessons."

Eleanor smiled. "There's no need for that. What a waste of God-given talent it would be for you to be a stable-hand. Stanley, tell Nellie Melba that the Earl and Countess of Easton will make an arrangement with whichever reputable teacher or school is willing to take Andrew."

"You would really do that, Eleanor?" Stanley asked. "For a person you just met... naked... in your dining room?"

"It is important to share our great fortune when the opportunity arises, greenie, just like we've shared it with you."

Stanley engulfed her into a hug. *Thank you, thank you, thank you, my lady.*

Andrew was speechless. As Stanley pulled away from Eleanor, he looked elated, but then a wave of despair darkened his expression. As Andrew noticed it, his enthusiasm also deflated.

"Unless you want to frolic about as a stable-hand here for a while first?" Eleanor added, but then she re-thought the proposition. "No, I don't think it's a good idea. It's too risky. Stanley, you are walking on eggshells with your father anyway. We don't need to poke the bear."

"You should go anyway, Drew," Stanley agreed with a sigh of sad acceptance. "Making yourself a stable-hand just to be close to a bumbling butler like me is a waste."

Eleanor squeezed Stanley's hand. "You're a good boy, Stanley."

"Well, there's no point in mourning what you haven't lost yet, my boys. Why don't you hop along to Stanley's room to celebrate?" Kuveni suggested. She snapped her fingers. "Don't forget your special stash of champagne, Stanley dear. I believe it is in your closet, and what luck, it is still cold."

She winked, and Stanley hugged her. "Thank you, Kate."

He took Andrew's free hand, while Andrew kept Edmund's hat positioned in front of his manhood with the other.

"Oh, and Stanley, I trust this is the last time you will be borrowing anything from our closets," Eleanor admonished gently.

"Yes, my lady," he agreed sheepishly.

She noticed Shruti's awkward position, leaning up against the wall with her eyes closed. "Oh, and my ladies and I are going to spend the rest of my birthday weekend here together, so you'd better scamper about clothed from now on."

"Yes, ma'am," they agreed in unison.

As soon as they were gone, Eleanor burst into laughter, and her friends joined her.

"Turns out we got all the opera we needed tonight, and then some!" She wiped away jovial tears.

"Those boys must have been horrified when you stumbled in on them!" Yvie exclaimed.

"I should have checked that the house was empty before I popped us back here," Kuveni sighed. "Well, all's well that ends well."

"You aren't worried?" Mae asked less cheerfully. "Isn't it dangerous for you to let them commit crimes under your roof? I mean, they seem like perfectly nice… er… boys, but still…"

Eleanor shrugged. "To be honest, we have so much to hide that it's nice to have something mundane on the list. Besides, Edmund and I both know what it's like to have to hide who we are. I suppose we both understand poor Stanley's plight better than most."

"You really are Mahagauri," Shruti said as she finally joined them back in the conversation.

"Mahagauri?" Eleanor asked.

"She is one of Maa Durga's incarnations. Her name means the fair one. She relieves suffering and offers forgiveness to her followers… no matter what they've done."

24

"I'm not forgiving rapists or murderers, Shruti. Those two boys were just born different, and now they've found each other. It's a beautiful miracle that they can know love when the wider world condemns them, don't you think?"

"If that is what you really think, my lady, I will not disagree with you."

"Your father loved your mother, didn't he? Even though she was a devadasi," Eleanor pushed, as she noticed that Shruti was not convinced.

"He did, my lady."

"And what did Bombay society think of that? What did the priests think of it?"

"They all thought it was wrong, my lady."

"But was it?"

"It was wrong for them to judge her, my lady. She never had a choice, and nothing she did ever hurt anyone else."

"I'm glad we see eye to eye," Eleanor winked. She took Shruti's hand and led the group back into the parlor.

Mélusine put her arm around Eleanor's shoulders and whispered in her ear, "Ma chérie, you never stop surprising me with the depths of your kindness."

"All in a day's work," Eleanor winked. "Now, what do you say we have a little slumber party, just us girls?"

Kuveni clapped excitedly and snapped her fingers, filling the floor from one wall to the other with fluffy mattresses, down pillows, and blankets. It looked strikingly familiar, and Eleanor paused for a moment as she tried to place it. Then she smiled.

"I knew that was you on the Orient Express."

"Guilty as charged," Kuveni winked. She snapped her fingers again, and the gramophone in the corner turned on and began playing jazzy ragtime hits. With the pop of a champagne cork, Mélusine squealed and began hastily pouring the fizz of a freshly opened bottle into the coupes that had already been laid out, and then Eleanor sighed with contentment.

25

She held up her glass. "To life, whatever it brings!"

"To life," her loving entourage agreed as they clinked her glass.

The toast was too fitting.

"Hello? May I ask who you are and what you're doing?"

"I… I… I…"

Eleanor awoke groggily to the sound of Edmund's confused voice echoing into the parlor from the kitchen.

"Mistress Eleanor, you'd better come quickly." Kuveni's disembodied voice whispered into her ear.

Eleanor stood up and stretched, glancing down at the green silk pajama pants and matching kimono she was still wearing from the night before, and then over to her guests, who were still deeply in the thralls of sleep after their very late night of giggling and girly games over endless champagne. Mélusine, however, had already made her silent exit along with Kuveni.

Eleanor scampered down the hall and into the kitchen, where Edmund stood next to Oz, who was holding Ned sleeping in his arms. Andrew was wearing Stanley's pink, feathered robe paired with Edmund's hat (on his head), and he was still stuttering for an explanation for his presence as he stood beside eight plates, each with generous portions of scrambled eggs, canned beans, bacon, and toast with heaping piles of vegemite, a product that Edmund had come to love over the months, but that Eleanor still found decidedly putrid. The counters and the sink were stacked high with dirty cooking vessels and cutlery, as if he'd been working on his plan for quite some time.

"I... I... I... was trying to make breakfast for your wife!" Andrew stammered.

"You were what?" Edmund asked with more puzzlement than jealousy. Eleanor loved him so much for his calm confidence.

"Colonel!" Stanley exclaimed as he stumbled into the room in a panic. He wore the trousers of his butler's uniform without his belt or vest, and his wrinkled dress shirt, which was unbuttoned and open in front, revealed his completely hairless chest. "I can explain!"

Edmund noticed Eleanor as she tiptoed up beside him. "Is there something you want to tell me, dearest? Have I not been fully satisfying recently?"

Eleanor put her arms around his neck and kissed him on the lips. "Sometimes a girl's just got to branch out, darling."

"Colonel, this is Andrew," Stanley stepped in, not finding her little joke amusing. "He's my... er... very good friend. I invited him over because I thought you'd all be away."

"And you're a colonel in His Majesty's army?" Edmund asked, eying his dress uniform hat.

"I'm sorry, sir. I didn't mean to offend you," Andrew whispered.

"I told him to keep it, darling. I caught him last night using it as a prop for a little performance he was putting on for Stanley."

"Good lord," Edmund murmured. "Stanley, my boy, can you not find a better place to do these things? A place... say... other than in our house?"

"I'm sorry, sir," he whispered. "I thought it would be safer here... since no one was supposed to be home, and there's no one around to call the authorities on us."

Edmund's stern posture deflated as he let himself sympathize with Stanley's plight. "Still, my boy. Perhaps you should invest in acquiring a more appropriate wardrobe for gallivanting around in front of my wife."

"I'm sorry, sir. Eleanor told us not to borrow anything else from your closet, and this robe was all I had to loan him. Andrew got his clothes all dirty pulling the car out of the mud yesterday after the rain, and his clothes are still drying on the line outside. He's too tall to wear my trousers."

"I suppose there isn't too much harm done." Edmund's stomach growled, and he eyed the freshly cooked breakfast again. "You made that for my wife, you say? I daresay, my boy, you've overestimated her appetite."

"I wanted to thank her, sir, for her support."

Edmund chuckled jovially. "If only I had the culinary skill to do the same. I reckon she's earned a home-cooked breakfast every morning for the rest of her life with the amount of support she effuses. Don't you, Stanley?"

"Yes, sir," he agreed wholeheartedly.

"Dearest, can you share? We've been driving all night to get down here from Perth."

"Why did you rush down here, darling? Is something wrong?"

Edmund sighed with annoyance. "Nothing, dearest. We just thought... we thought we'd set up a little surprise party for you. We thought you were spending the night up at the B&B in Bunbury with Yvie."

"Crikey, mate, you sure gave up that secret easily!" Oz exclaimed.

Eleanor laughed and kissed him again. "It was a lovely thought, darling." Edmund's stomach growled again. "Eat whatever you'd like. I'm not particularly hungry, but perhaps the girls would like some."

"The girls? Which girls?"

She grinned and took his arm, and he grabbed one of Andrew's steaming plates. Oz followed his lead, while Stanley and Andrew both gathered up the remaining plates and followed them into the hallway.

"Perhaps we should eat in the dining room?" Eleanor suggested as she noticed their precarious position balancing the plates on their arms. "And, perhaps, since it is already a theater, you can treat us to a song while we eat, Andrew. My husband should know what exactly it is I've signed us up to support."

They veered into the dining room and put the plates down on a serving cart in the corner. Stanley led Andrew as they pulled the table away from its position against the wall, and then Stanley rushed to the hutch and began setting the table with silverware and placemats.

Before Edmund could ask her what she was talking about, Eleanor's sleepy friends, still clad in their matching silk kimonos that Kuveni had conjured the night before, joined them in the hallway.

"Shruti?!" Edmund exclaimed. "How on earth did you get here? Mae? It's been too long!"

"You weren't the only one who wanted to help Eleanor celebrate her birthday," Kuveni said as she walked up behind them and pulled Edmund into a motherly hug.

"How lovely to see you, Kate," Edmund said as he hugged her back. "Did you bring Shruti and Mae here all the way from India, just for Eleanor's birthday?"

"It was nothing, Edmund, dear. Percy's plane is such a joy to fly these days. Don't you think, my darling girls?"

"Umm... yes... it was very comfortable," Mae lied.

As baby Ned stretched and scrunched his face, threatening to cry, Oz repositioned him in his arms, and he curled up and went back to sleep.

"You didn't fly with him, did you? I told you it isn't safe," Yvie asked as she kissed Oz and then her son.

"Don't worry, Yvie. I know my marching orders. Our plane is still gathering dust in Fremantle."

"We drove," Edmund added. "That Ford really is quite pleasant for a long journey."

"You drove?! In the middle of the night!" Yvie exclaimed disapprovingly. "But that's also dangerous! No wonder he's asleep!"

Oz shrugged. "Everything is dangerous, Yvie. Edmund drove the whole way. That's gotta count for something, right? With someone as special as him at the wheel?"

Yvie glanced at Edmund and then conceded. "*Peut-être.*"

"Come, my darlings, Andrew has cooked you a feast!" Kuveni guided them into the dining room.

Edmund sat right down and dug into the eggs on the closest plate. "Why, these are delicious! Andrew, have you thought of being a cook?"

"I was a cook, sir. At the Imperial Hotel in Melbourne. They sacked me after I mixed up the salt and sugar, and the Duchess of Cornwall had a fit."

"Well, everyone makes mistakes, my boy. Especially in the kitchen. I've almost set our kitchen on fire three times in the last six months alone."

"Darling, Andrew has other, more impressive talents," Eleanor interceded. "Perhaps you can show the colonel why you were borrowing his hat."

Shruti looked away, while Kuveni and Mae both watched with piqued interest.

"He'll be wearing the robe this time," Eleanor whispered to Shruti, who looked up reluctantly.

Andrew straightened his posture and took his place standing at the head of the table. He took a deep breath and began with an exaggerated salute.

"*I am the very model of a modern major general, I've information vegetable, animal, and mineral...*"

Edmund's eyes lit up, and he stopped his chomping to laugh and clap with his approval.

Andrew continued on more confidently as he noticed his audience's enthusiasm, but just as he was reaching his climax, "*For my military knowledge, though I'm plucky and adventury, has only been brought down to the beginning of the century...*" he stopped abruptly.

"*Gast ahas!*" a familiar voice hissed. Everyone looked over to the open door of the dining room, where Norwenn was standing, wearing a frumpy, wrinkled brown dress and holding a small train case. She looked exhausted and haggard, with dark bags under her eyes, as if she hadn't slept in days. "Are you all bloody mad?!" she exclaimed.

"Maman?!" Stanley squealed as he hopped up from his chair and began buttoning up his shirt. "What are you doing here?!"

"What are *you* doing here?!" she hissed. "Colonel, what is going on?!"

Eleanor's heart raced at the unexpected confrontation, but Edmund addressed her calmly, and Eleanor could not have been more grateful for his even temper.

"I reckon we are enjoying an impromptu musical performance while we eat a scrummy breakfast. Would you like some? It looks like there's an extra plate. Did you just arrive in town on the morning train? If we'd known you were coming, we could have driven you from the station."

Norwenn glanced at Andrew. "You have a deviant cabaret in your dining room, Colonel. Do you know what Chester would do if he saw this?"

Edmund stood up and straightened his posture. "I don't really care what he would do, Norwenn. Why should I? I'm in the civil service now, and it was never the military's style to intrude on the private goings-on of a household. If it were, I reckon Chester would have been disciplined decades ago for his sordid affair in Bretagne and his wife's subsequent suspicious suicide. Don't you think?"

Eleanor was aroused by his aggressive tone and his surprisingly blunt reference to Lord Grimby's unscrupulous past.

Norwenn reeled from the insult, and then turned her attention back onto Stanley, attempting to keep their conversation private by switching into Breton as she buttoned up the rest of his shirt buttons for him and then rustled his messy hair, trying to smooth it out. As she noticed the subtle layers of rouge and eye liner leftover on his face from the night before, she pulled a handkerchief out of her pocket, licked it, and began trying to wipe it all off, while shaking her head with dismay.

"Are you mad, Stanley? Your father's going to kill you for this! He knew that everything wasn't as you claimed it was with Colonel Marriner, and now he's on his way down here right now to check on you himself."

"Check on me? He's coming all the way down from London just to check on me? Surely he must have better things to do."

"You will ruin us, Stanley! Do you know what he had to do to get you your position? He put everything on the line for you, and now you're squandering it with deviant, illegal activities. He can't go out on a limb for you anymore, you understand? His reputation is on the edge of ruin as it is!"

Stanley threw Eleanor a nervous look as he realized the precarious position his mother's lack of awareness of Eleanor and Edmund's linguistic talents had put him in.

"Maman, we should talk about this in private later," Stanley whispered in Breton. "Look at all these people here."

"We will talk about it now, Stanley! I came all the way down to the edge of the world because I knew, I just *knew*, there was something wrong. And what did I find?! You're back to your old queer tricks again, and now you've dragged Colonel Marriner into it!"

"Maman, we really need to talk about this later," Stanley reiterated.

"Why?! Do you think you'll butter me up? This is serious, Stanley. Your father is going to be furious, and I don't know if I can rein him in again! He had half a mind to throw you in jail himself when he boarded the steamer to come down here."

"The steamer?" Stanley gulped. "Then is he on his way right now? Did you sneak onto the boat with him to warn me?"

"I used all of the savings you've sent me to beat him down here by airplane, but he could be here any minute. He was trying to arrange air passage from Rome before he even got on the boat in Southampton."

"The last time I checked, singing a little ditty in one's dining room wasn't a crime," Edmund interrupted their exchange. "Watching someone else do it, even less so."

Norwenn stepped back with a look of horror on her face as he addressed her in perfect Breton.

"Colonel, you are a Breton? How could Chester not mention it?!"

"I have a talent for languages," he explained vaguely. "I suppose I can't blame you for assuming I couldn't understand you, but you have fair warning now."

Norwenn looked around at her audience, landing her attention on Andrew, who was looking nervously at the floor, and she became more agitated as she switched back into English.

"I will eat my hat if my son didn't engage in illegal activities last night, Colonel. I can see it written all over his smug, powdered face. Now, either you are aiding and abetting him, or you are the most unobservant colonel in the world. Neither explanation will do you well in the presence of Chester or God."

Oz finally stepped in. "I reckon you don't need to tell Edmund anything at all about God, Mrs...?"

"Grimby. You may call me Mrs. Grimby."

Stanley's eyes bulged. "You didn't?! Maman, please tell me you didn't marry him!"

"He's your father! Do you like being a bastard?" she snapped.

34

"Being a bastard is highly underrated." He threw a cheeky glance towards Eleanor. "Besides, I'm already going to Hell."

"So you've resigned yourself to breaking the law of Britain and the law of God? Why don't you just go around murdering people!" she exclaimed. "Do you have no moral center at all anymore?!"

"I have enough of a moral center to do what I think is right!" Stanley shot back. "The law and the church said slavery was right! It took greater men to decide that it wasn't! It takes great men to make up their own minds!"

Eleanor shivered with the thrill as he broke out of his adolescent self-castigation for the first time, parroting a phrase that Edmund had mentioned several times throughout their time together.

"And you are a man now, under the supervision of Colonel Marriner? And as a man, your mind has made up that sodomy is perfectly acceptable?! Under the roof of your employer? While there are women and children around? I don't know who you are anymore, Stanley. I didn't think it was possible for you to have any less sense than you used to, but once again, you've surprised me."

Shruti looked down at her plate, while Mae and Yvie glanced around awkwardly for an escape.

"I told you we should talk about this somewhere else," Stanley reiterated. "Andrew, I'll check if your clothes are dry. If my father is on his way, you'd better not be wearing my robe."

"*Your* robe?!" Norwenn exclaimed.

"Come on, Maman. Let's talk outside. These topics aren't for the ears of women and children."

Stanley threw them all an apologetic glance, and Norwenn humphed as she followed him into the hallway and out the back door of the house.

As soon as they were outside, their heated Breton whispers erupted into more shouting, and Kuveni glided gracefully over to the window and closed it.

"Let's give them some time alone, shall we? Now, I'm still famished, and I think this lovely meal is still hot." She snapped her fingers, and each plate began subtly steaming. "Andrew, dear, why don't you join us? I think we get the gist of where the song was going."

They all sat, eating their eggs in awkward silence, until Eleanor finally mustered the energy to reinitiate the conversation. "So, darling, Andrew doesn't just do Gilbert and Sullivan. He is actually quite a talented opera singer, even though he hasn't had any formal training. I'm going to talk to Nellie Melba about helping us set up a qualified teacher for him."

"Sounds like a fine idea, dearest," he said distractedly as he watched Stanley storm across the lawn in tears. After a long pause where Norwenn paced back and forth, growling angrily, she ran after him, and they reengaged in their argument. He finally pulled himself out of his thoughts, and addressed Andrew. "An apprenticeship is a perfect way to start a career. I myself apprenticed as an artist when I was a boy. It taught me as much about myself as it taught me about painting."

"You're an artist? I thought you were a colonel, sir?" Andrew asked timidly as he tried to keep his focus away from Stanley.

"I am many things; a soldier and an artist are two of them. Those paintings there are mine." Edmund pointed to a set of four pastoral vineyard landscapes above the hutch that he'd painted as soon as they'd settled into their new Australian life eight months earlier. "Eleanor helped me paint the two on the left."

"Hardly," Eleanor scoffed. "If by needling you endlessly, you mean that I helped, then I suppose I'm guilty as charged, but I don't deserve any credit for the artistry. That's all you, darling."

Edmund leaned in confidingly to disagree with her. "She offered many valid suggestions that saved me from falling down a rabbit hole of boring, clichéd motifs. I think in another life she must have been an art critic."

"Do you believe in other lives, sir?" Andrew asked. "My mother believed in something like that—some aboriginal ideas about the spirits of her ancestors and hers being one and the same— –but my father wouldn't have any of it. He said it was un-Christian."

Edmund finished up a sausage before offering an answer. Eleanor was genuinely curious about his answer. "I suppose I haven't discounted the possibility. There is a lot we don't know about how these things work, and I myself have often felt strange instincts from time to time that don't feel particularly like they are a core part of me. Sometimes they feel as if they are coming from someone else entirely." He looked up self-consciously to the group as he realized the incredibly personal nature of his response. "Have any of you ever felt that way?"

"All the time, darling," Eleanor admitted truthfully.

"Maybe we were together in a prior life, too, Eleanor. That would explain why we fell in love at first sight."

He leaned over for a kiss, and Eleanor indulged him, licking his lips playfully before pulling away and clearing her throat.

"You are a wonderfully open-minded man, darling. I don't know how anyone could spend a few minutes with you without falling desperately in love."

"Amen to that," Oz declared with a wink.

As Kuveni noticed their lack of beverages to toast with, she hopped right up. "My darlings, you must be parched! Let me go see what I can scrounge in the kitchen for you to drink."

Without waiting for a response, she skipped out of the dining room.

"So have you tried your hand at proper opera as well?" Edmund asked Andrew as he returned to his meal.

"Only in the bathroom," Andrew admitted. "I tried once to convince the ringmaster to let me do an aria, but he wasn't interested. He said I didn't look the part."

"The ringmaster?"

"I was an acrobat. In the South Australian circus."

Edmund laughed. "You're a man of many talents, aren't you? I didn't think you were old enough to have so much life experience!"

"I left home when I was sixteen, sir. When my father told me I was going straight to Hell."

Edmund grimaced. "Well, my boy, I've been told that myself on too many occasions, and it hasn't happened yet. Don't think too much of it; although, I know that that sage advice is easier said than done. Now, tell me, what is your favorite opera? Have you had the chance to see many? I still haven't seen one that can compete with Shakespeare, although I did quite like that Verdi interpretation of *Otello* that Eleanor took me to last summer in Melbourne. Stanley quite liked it as well."

"I only know Iago's *Credo*," Andrew admitted. "It was on a record of famous villains. I learned as many of the arias as I could."

"Well, which was your favorite? Yvie knows a lot about opera, don't you, Yvie?"

"*C'est vrai*," she agreed.

Eleanor sat back and swooned silently as Edmund engaged Andrew and Yvie in an amicable conversation about opera, until she noticed that Kuveni was still conspicuously missing after her quick errand to find beverages in the kitchen. Eleanor got up and squeezed Edmund's shoulders reassuringly as she excused herself from the dining room.

"Is there a problem?" she called as she reached the empty kitchen. "Kuveni?"

Her anxiety kicked up as Kuveni materialized beside her.

"Do the Yakshini babies need help? You really don't have to stay here to help us with our whims, Kuveni. I know you have better things to do."

Kuveni looked like she might cry. "No, that's not the problem, Mistress Eleanor… No, no, no. The problem is much bigger than that, and it's impossible to fix!"

"Blimey, is Lord Grimby on his way? Can't you just conjure new outfits for Stanley and Andrew? I'm sure we can convince him that Andrew is only here as an audition for our new scholarship supporting the arts. We just have to hash out our story now, so we can all be consistent."

"No, my dear, dear girl. It isn't that. It's your mother."

"My mother?" Eleanor was equally confused and concerned at the thought.

"Your mother is dying, Eleanor. Come now."

"Dying?! But she isn't even sixty yet!"

"She has been deteriorating for months, and steadfastly refusing to see a doctor. If I were going to guess based on her horrid physical state, I would say that she has some form of cancer, different than Leo's, but similarly virulent. I debated mightily with myself when I should inform you, but you were having such a lovely time down here, I didn't want to ruin it. Should I have told you sooner? Would you have wanted to intervene?"

Eleanor felt a battle of fiercely ambivalent feelings breaking out inside of her.

"That woman has always done what she wants. If I'd tried to intervene, she would have been even more ornery."

"Should I have at least warned you? I really couldn't decide."

"It's not your responsibility to keep constant track of everyone in my life, Kuveni. You have much better things to do."

"We can agree to disagree on that, my lady. But we mustn't waste any more time. We must go see her before her final breath, which, if my senses are correct, will be any minute now."

"Wait, we can't just leave! They're going to notice I'm missing! That both of us are missing!"

"It doesn't matter, Eleanor. She's your mother. From one daughter to another, no matter how lost she was, you will want this final moment with her. Please trust me."

Eleanor nodded her agreement and braced herself. With a pleasant breeze, Kuveni dissolved around her, leaving the mess of her most recent web of lies behind. It was the first time in her life that she wasn't grateful for the reprieve.

CHAPTER 3 – WHIT'S FER YE

Eleanor shivered as she materialized inside a dark hole of a room with stone walls and only one tiny, deep-set window. One kerosene lamp was dimly lit by the bedside, and it was completely dark outside. The whole set-up felt a bit medieval, and for a moment, Eleanor wondered if Kuveni had accidentally brought them back in time as she'd blinked them across the world.

She blew into her hands to warm them up, and Kuveni tapped her arm, morphing her silk pajamas into a stylish grey wool ladies' suit with a sinfully soft ivory cashmere sweater underneath, which Eleanor particularly enjoyed without one of Kuveni's modern bras to constrain her.

"Blimey, Kuveni. I thought it was almost summer here!"

"It is three degrees centigrade outside right now."

"But it's the end of May!"

"It's Scotland, my darling girl. Isn't it always wretchedly cold here?"

"I didn't used to think so..." Eleanor spied her mother's wrinkled, pale, cadaverous body lying in the bed, tucked up tightly under a mound of faded, tattered blankets. "Good lord, why don't they have the heater on?"

"Your sisters can't afford to pay for the heating bills."

"But I've been sending them a king's ransom every month!"

"It has not been enough for all of their expenses."

"But it's ten times what I used to send them!"

Eleanor's mother stirred and snorted, and Eleanor took another look around the room with more scrutiny.

"Why is it dark? It doesn't get dark until eleven here in summer."

"It's midnight, my dear girl."

"I'm so out of touch," Eleanor murmured. "Where are we? This isn't Martha's or Mary's house."

"My dear, please focus on your mother for now. I will fill you in on all the unpleasant details later."

"Kuveni, I'm a big girl. Just tell it to me straight."

"It is Martha's and Mary's house," Kuveni admitted begrudgingly. "Jimmy and Fergus went in together to use the copious funds you've been sending them to pay for the children's educations and your mother's care to buy this drafty old rock of a castle on Skye. Now they can't afford to keep it up. All of the money you're sending them is going into the astronomical mortgage."

Eleanor felt her fiery Celtic temper working its way to the surface. "I'm going to kill those bloody bassas! How could Martha and Mary let them do that?! What about the private schools?! The tutors?!"

"Those dolts decided the kids didn't need education, now that they're living the good life on the isles."

Eleanor worked hard to keep herself from bursting into the green flames of Durga's wrath at the thought.

"Did you know about this?" She worked hard to keep herself from projecting her rage onto her helpful messenger.

42

"I did not, Eleanor. I only kept an occasional eye on their status so that I could fetch you if something went horribly wrong. Once I realized how dire your mother's decline really was, I started doing a bit of reconnaissance. It made me dastardly regretful of not keeping a closer eye on all of them."

Eleanor pulled her into a hug. "Thank you."

"It is my pleasure as always to help you, my dear. Now, say your goodbyes, and I will pop back down under to explain your disappearance before Edmund goes positively mad with worry."

"What are you going to say?"

"I'll let you know when I think of it."

"Blimey."

"Don't worry about it, Eleanor. I have six thousand years of experience. I will manage your entourage and your husband. You just do what you need to do, and whisper my name when you're ready for me to pick you up and escort you home."

With a pleasant breeze, Kuveni dissolved, leaving Eleanor alone with her mother.

She circled the room, working hard to relegate her rage at her sisters' worthless husbands' terrible judgment. She glanced out the tiny window that made the room feel like a prison cell. The full moon was lovely, casting a silver glistening glow onto the sea just beyond the craggy coastline, and she took a deep breath, trying to let the beauty of the scene quell her nerves.

As her mother snorted again, she pulled herself away from the window and forced herself to take a seat in a plain wooden chair by the bedside. It buckled as she sat down, and she glanced down and relegated another burst of anger as she noticed that one of the legs was broken.

"They're so bloody poor they couldn't even afford a bloody chair. Why not buy a bloody castle?" she muttered.

Her mother opened her eyes and squinted. "Eleanor Mary MacLeod?"

Eleanor reached forward and coaxed her mother's cold hand out from under the covers. She rubbed it with both of hers, trying to warm it up.

"Aye. It's me."

"It's about time."

Eleanor cringed. She hadn't had enough time to mentally prepare herself for a dying lecture from her ungrateful mother.

"I came to say goodbye, Mum. Please don't ruin it with words we'll both regret."

"One should ne'er regret the truth, or so the wise men say."

"Have you ever thought to ask the wise women?"

Eleanor's mother did not look amused at her little quip. "Have ye not lived long enough to know that no one cares one lick about what women say?"

"I suppose I need to live longer," Eleanor shrugged.

"Yer talkin' like a sassanack again, ye know." Her mother wheezed, but then gathered her strength. "Ye've lived a lucky life, Eleanor MacLeod."

"I've made my own luck," Eleanor countered sternly. "No one in their right mind would argue otherwise."

"Whit's fer ye'll no go past ye. Yer a good lass, Ellie. Ye've deserved whit's come."

Eleanor prepared to offer another, more aggressive counter, and then she stopped herself. Had her mother just complimented her? The idea was too foreign for her to comprehend, and her mother took her silence as an invitation to hunker down for a more serious discussion.

"They need ye, Ellie. They need someone with half a lick of sense to keep 'em in line. Look at this foolishness. Jimmy's off his heid, and he's dragged the rest of 'em down into the gutter wit 'im."

Eleanor had not expected her mother to present such a coherent statement. Her mother squeezed her hand and struggled to sit up, leaning in confidingly.

"He's draggin' the bairns down wit 'im, Ellie. Those lads'll ne'er make anything of 'emselves with a bloody bampot like that ruining all their chances at life. It's well shan, Ellie, and it's been bloody awful to watch."

"I can't make their decisions for them, Mum. They're adults."

Her mother looked pained as she untangled her other hand out from underneath the blanket to squeeze Eleanor's. "It's yer money, Ellie. Wield it like the weapon it is."

She wheezed and lay back. Eleanor helped her readjust her blankets as she began to shiver.

"Money is food and shelter, heat and life, Ellie. Yer money'll make good marriages fer Debbie and Ruthy. It'll save Howie's and Charlie's backs from bricklaying if ye can get those dim lads to hit the books instead of skulking about with their bampot fathers." Eleanor didn't have a response to her mother's surprisingly reasonable point. "Don' let yer life in the lap of luxury with yer auld sassanack colonel let you forget what life was like when we weren't makin' end's meat. Think of what we would've done fer a few shillings. Ye've ruined 'em with your generosity, ye know. Ye've made 'em think they're people they're not, and now God is showin' s'all who they really are."

And, there it was. The edge of the sword pointed straight back at her. Eleanor sighed with resignation at the predictable turn.

"I won't apologize for taking care of my family, Mum. If it weren't for me, you'd all still be rotting away in that one-room cottage. Who knows what Martha and Mary would have done to escape? They would have become scullery maids if they were lucky, or they would have discovered how much money they could make in the most ancient profession."

Her mother gasped. "They would've done no such thing! They were tidy, God-fearin' lasses!"

"Because I *let* them be, Mum! *I* went out and made a living so that they wouldn't have to, and I'm still bloody doing it!" She gave into her anger. "And how do they repay all the work I did for decades to make their lives better? By letting those right chancers chore the funds for a fantasy! Do you know how many madmen I bathed, and how many bedpans I changed so that they wouldn't have to lift a bloody finger?!"

Eleanor growled as she tried to rein in her temper, and her mother chuckled until she wheezed.

"Now ye know what I meant, Ellie. It's about time yer back. They only ever listened to you, and now ye need to tell 'em how to be right braw lasses, like ye always did."

It was only at that moment that Eleanor realized that her mother's opening statement hadn't been an insult. It had been a compliment, and even an entreaty. Her mother dug her hand out of the covers again and reached forward to stroke Eleanor's arm, like she had only done a handful of times, when Eleanor had been sick as a dog.

"They need ye, Ellie, more than they ever needed me. Ye've been their mother since I died inside, and they can't make it on their own. They aren't as strong as y'are, and they ne'er have been. Oxen like you only come 'round once in a century."

Eleanor suddenly felt the ball in her throat attack as she struggled to hold back tears. "Why didn't you ever say so? You were so mean to me! Harping on everything I ever did like I was a rotten little scoundrel!"

Her mother wheezed and snorted, and Eleanor spied the tears that she hadn't seen since the fateful day thirty years earlier when she'd ripped the noose out of her mother's hand.

"Because I dunne wanye t'be hurt like I was, Ellie! I cunne watch ye fall from the sky like I did!"

"So you tried to keep me down?!" Eleanor gave into tears. "Bloody brilliant plan that was, Mum. Save me from falling by trampling me down at every turn."

"I kept ye down to earth!"

"I didn't need any help with that, Mum! The rest of the world was cruel enough to keep an angel from taking flight!"

46

Eleanor's mother began wheezing again, but she reached out and grabbed Eleanor's hand as they both cried. She squeezed it, and patted it, and stroked it with more affection than Eleanor had felt in thirty years, and Eleanor finally reached her emotional limit. She snorted and sobbed and her mind went thick like mud as she stopped being able to rationally comprehend what was happening. Never, not once, not even in the line of fire during the war, had she been so thoroughly out of control of her emotions. If she'd had the wherewithal to think, she would have hated it, but she was beyond that. She had reached a state of being in which she just... was, without a coherent thought attached.

Finally, after some period of time that Eleanor couldn't keep track of in the slightest, her mother snorted and sniffled and cleared her throat. "Like it or not, Eleanor Mary MacLeod, ye needed me."

"Of course I needed you! You're my mother!" Eleanor exclaimed. "I needed you to be Martha and Mary's mother, so I wouldn't have to be!"

Her mother shook her head in disagreement. "Ye needed me te show ye who not t'be, Ellie, and I did a tidy job of it. Ye cunne had a better set of rotten parents te show ye who not t'be."

Eleanor felt her fiery temper working its way back to the surface. "Don't tell me for one second that you were doing me a favor every time you called me a bastard or a whore."

Her mother sighed sadly. "I was all I could bear to be, Ellie. The rest was up to you and God. I'm grateful ye two chums worked it out."

Eleanor startled as footsteps approached in the hallway. She wiped her eyes and her nose, and then gave into panic. She hadn't expected her mother to be so coherent when Kuveni had popped her right into the room, and now she was stuck!

"Open the door!" Debbie hissed as a light clunk and scratch hit the door frame.

The door swung open, and Debbie shuffled inside with her arms buckling at the weight of a tray that she slammed down onto the bedside table beside Eleanor. Charlie slinked in behind her and closed the door, and Eleanor let her panic morph into relief that her unanticipated witnesses were two of her most reliable confidantes who had dutifully kept Edmund's secret for years. She tried to relax and let her expertise at wiggling out of similarly awkward situations guide her.

"Fancy seeing you here," she said cheerfully as she looked up at them.

"Auntie Ellie?!!!" they exclaimed as they pummeled her.

She squeezed them as they held on, until she noticed that Debbie was shaking with sobs. Debbie buried her face in Eleanor's shoulder, while Charlie pulled away and cleared his throat as he tried to hide his sniffles.

Eleanor pulled Debbie into her lap, like she had when Debbie was just a wee lass, noting, subtly, that Debbie was too light. Debbie kept sobbing as Eleanor's mother sat up in the bed and reached her gaunt hand out from under the covers to inspect what was on the tray. A bowl of lumpy pea soup with an odor that indicated it was past its prime was accompanied by a crumbling, dried-out hunk of soda bread. She sniffed the bread and then the soup, took one begrudging bite of the unappealing combination, and then broke the bread in half and offered each piece to the children.

"And what wee nip do ye have fer me tonight to warm me bones, Charlie?"

He glanced self-consciously at Eleanor, and then pulled a small flask out of a pocket inside his ill-fitting coat.

Eleanor watched with equal parts confusion and horror as her mother sniffed it and then tasted a small sip. She grimaced, and then shook her head. "It's about time yer here, Ellie."

As the children gazed hungrily at the off-putting soup, Eleanor coaxed Debbie out of her lap and moved from her chair to the edge of her mother's bed to make way for them to eat.

Her mind somersaulted through the puzzling sight, noticing as she tried to make sense of it that both children's outfits were patched with mismatched fabric and were markedly too small. They both looked like they'd just escaped from an orphanage, an effect made more unsettling by their voracious approach to the soup.

"What in god's name is going on?" she murmured as her mother, who hadn't drunk a sip of alcohol in all of Eleanor's life, took another sip from the flask.

"Smell it." Her mother pushed it in front of Eleanor's nose. "Give it a wee nip. Don't pretend ye don't have the taste fer it."

Eleanor braced herself and then took a tiny sip. She knew that flavor. It was the flavor of a perfectly aged, perfectly-peated, top-shelf scotch. Her mother shook her head knowingly as she saw the recognition dawn in Eleanor's expression.

"Now look again at the bairns, Ellie, and tell me ye wunne do the same."

"The same what?"

Eleanor could not remember the last time she'd been at such a loss.

Her mother leaned in. "Tell me ye wunne give 'em yer soup… and plot the clever murder of their wicked fathers as ye felt the heat of a tidy dear whisky in yer limbs. That's the Devil's fire, it is. And it's burnin' me from the inside out, but I'll tell ye one thing, Ellie: I'd do it all again to get you and yer angels on up here to help me."

Eleanor worried that her divine flames might actually engulf the room as she allowed herself to fully consider what her mother was saying. "Are you telling me that my sisters and their bludger husbands are starving their children and dressing them like orphans while they are drinking expensive scotch?" She felt

Sheranee break free from her divine perch as a burst of rage overwhelmed her. *No, my love! Don't come! You must stay hidden!* As she felt Sheranee begrudgingly accept her orders, she stared at her mother again. "Are you telling me that you aren't even sick? You're just subsisting on bites of bread and whisky so that the children can eat your meager portions of old soup?"

Her mother winked. "It gotcha here, dinnit?"

"But you look like death!" Eleanor exclaimed. "You're wasting away!"

Most alarming of all was that Uma's highly attuned morbid talents could feel her mother's life-force fading. Kuveni hadn't been wrong in her diagnosis of the symptoms, only about the ludicrous cause.

"I hadda getcher attention, Ellie. I knew I'd gecha up here one way or another, at my deathbed or my funeral. It dunne really matter which." She smiled weakly. "But I'm glad I dunne have t'wait in Hell te see ye. I reckon there woulda been scores of Catholics and Jews crowdin' the way, waitin' fer their loved ones to join 'em alongside me."

Eleanor's mind raced. Her temper ignited. The scale of her sisters' treachery and greed had blindsided her completely, and her mother, who was just as much the bigoted fire and brimstone biddy she'd always been, playing the role of the selfless savior was too much for her to bear. She pinched herself, but she was still awake.

Her mother chuckled and took another sip of the whisky. "Ye won't be escaping this nightmare that easily, Ellie. Believe me, we've all tried to wake up, but we're trapped here, in a Hell made up by a gaggle of bloody bampots."

"A gaggle of bloody selfish bassas, you mean."

"If the Devil stumbled on by yer Da standing beside those two choring bassas, he'd send yer Da right on up to the Pearly Gates, Ellie." Eleanor's mother reached out and squeezed her hand. "It's me savin' grace that of all me brood, ye're the one who found yerself an angel, even if he is too auld fer ye."

Eleanor reeled from the (albeit slightly insulting) compliment, and as Debbie and Charlie each took their last polite bites, splitting the soup equally onto their last bits of stale bread, Eleanor's mother leaned in confidingly once more. "Now, where's yer sassanack colonel and the vicar? It's gonna take all the angels to outwit the bassas and smite 'em with the proper whip. I'll leave that to ye, since I'm already dancin' with the Devil."

"I'm sorry, what?" Eleanor hadn't thought that the situation could get any more confusing. At first she'd assumed that her mother's backhanded compliment about Edmund had been a reference to his virtue, but now... *now*...

"Aw, dunne pretend anymore, Ellie. The battle's a-bloomin' and our plan needs drawn! Bring in the Lord's soldiers so we can tear the tartan before the bampots notice!"

Eleanor closed her eyes and subtly wrapped her hand around her green sapphire bangle.

D.H.? What does my mother know about us? Does she think you and Edmund are angels? This is urgent!

"It's no time fer a wee cat nap, Ellie! We've got work to do!"

Eleanor opened her eyes and looked around, biding her time as she waited for a response. She returned to the chair and patted her lap for Debbie to come join her, while her mother patted the bed, inviting Charlie to do the same. She offered him a whiff of the flask, and he stuck out his tongue with disgust. She chuckled and took another sip. Debbie settled in listlessly to Eleanor's lap putting her arms around her neck.

"Mum, have you always been secretly tippling? Even while preaching on and on about it being the Devil's drink?"

Eleanor's mother moved to answer and then stopped herself and rethought what she was going to say. She looked Eleanor straight in the eye. "Yer Da and I reeked after a night out on the skite. We were right braw together after a few bevvies. Ye wuddne known us, Ellie. Like two tidy chums. I dunne drink a drop after the day we died, not until these mincey heids made it me only option to keep me own heid. But I'll tell ye something, Ellie, nothin' quite warms the pinkies like a nip of Glenmorangie."

Eleanor? Are you alright? What's happening?

Eleanor shook off her surprise as Vibhishana's voice echoed in her head. She closed her eyes, and subtly maneuvered her arm behind the chair so no one could see her glowing bangle.

I'm with my mother. Kuveni thought she was dying, but there's more going on than meets the eye. Do you know why she's referring to you and Edmund as angels?

Eleanor did not like his long pause.

I paid her a visit after you and Edmund flew off on your honeymoon. She'd witnessed our cricket match, and Mélusine's fairy tricks only confused her. I decided to manage the situation myself with a more mature strategy.

Blimey, thanks for the warning.

I planned to tell you before you saw her, D.W. I didn't tell her everything.

Eleanor almost laughed. *That would've been a ripe disaster!*

I know, Eleanor. I was very delicate. I only told her that Edmund and I, and a few others, are angels tasked with guiding humans, and that Edmund has not fully learned of his fate yet.

Anything else I should know? She doesn't know about me, does she?

She knows nothing of your power. But I did visit her several times, Eleanor. We continued our conversation from your wedding banquet for quite some time. I think I made some progress.

Aye, I reckon you did. I can hardly recognize her. My whole world is upside down.

Do you want me to come? I can ask Monty to escort me.

No. I can handle it. Thank you for the offer.

Summon me any time.

Aye.

"Are ye callin' forth the Heavenly Father Himself?" Eleanor's mother quipped. "Or do ye need a wee tipple yerself te soften the blow?" She pushed the flask at her.

"Kuveni, please come. I need your help," Eleanor whispered under her breath.

She looked up as Kuveni tapped lightly on the door and then came right on in in the form of Kate, clad in a long plaid kilt with a stylish black cashmere sweater and matching tartan tam o'shanter cap.

"Jesus, Mary, and Joseph, ye *were* callin' forth the Almighty!" Eleanor's mother exclaimed.

"Kate?" Debbie asked meekly.

"You remember me!" Kuveni exclaimed. "I'm glad that your recent misfortunes haven't erased your memories of our good times together at Auntie Eleanor's wedding."

Debbie looked like she might burst into tears again.

Kuveni preempted her meltdown by moving the conversation along cheerfully. "Eleanor, dearest, what can I do for you on this fine spring evening?"

Eleanor glanced at her mother, and then sighed with resignation at the thought of what she was about to do.

"Kate, I don't think their dinner was very satisfying. Can you help us conjure something better?"

"Your wish is my command, my darling girl. As is yours," she addressed Debbie and Charlie. "What would you like to eat, my little loves? What have you been fantasizing about as your tummies have rumbled these past few months?"

"There isn't anything on the island at this hour," Debbie informed her. "And the only pubs are too far to walk."

"I see," Kuveni said with feigned stoicism. "That would indeed be a problem for most people in our position. But, my little loves, I am not most people. Now, tell me, if you were writing a storybook, and an angel popped right up beside you and offered you a nibble, what would it be?"

"Fish n' chips," Charlie whispered. "Oh how I've dreamed of fish n' chips, with vinegar and salt and ketchup, just like we used to have by the docks before Da went raving mad."

Kuveni clapped her hands with approval and snapped her fingers. A steaming bunch of golden fish n' chips wrapped in crisp newspaper appeared in her hand, and she handed it straight over to him. He stared at it with disbelief.

"Lord Almighty," Eleanor's mother whispered.

As Charlie offered the fish to his cousin in a daze, Kuveni threw Eleanor a look of melancholy joy at the beautiful gesture of the hungry boy sharing his food before partaking himself. Debbie reached into the bunch and pulled a hot chip out, looking to Kuveni and then Eleanor for permission.

"Eat! Eat all you can stomach, my children! There is more where that came from. But you'd best eat slowly. Empty tummies don't like becoming too full too fast. There will be plenty of food from now on for those who are worthy of God's bounty. For those who are unworthy, we will leave their punishment to the gods of vengeance."

"You mean the *angels* of vengeance," Eleanor's mother corrected her.

"Do I?" Kuveni asked with a disapproving raised eyebrow that put Eleanor's mother in her place. "Now, what will you eat, my fabulously feisty firecracker? We'd better get you back on the up and up now that you've gotten our attention. I must give you credit, few humans have the discipline to mount a hunger strike of this magnitude. I've only ever seen it a handful of times, and never for a cause so wonderfully mundane. I love you more for it, Moira."

"No one has called me that in thirty years."

"Shall I call you Mrs. MacLeod instead? Or perhaps we can use a descriptive nickname like Biddy?"

"Moira is just fine," Eleanor's mother conceded.

"What'll it be?"

"Anything?"

"Anything!"

"That breakfast we ate after Ellie's wedding was well tidy scran."

Kuveni looked very pleased with the choice, and she snapped her fingers, producing two matching, steaming plates covered in heaping piles of fried eggs, bacon, sausage, beans, mushrooms, fried potatoes, and black pudding with toast, butter, and a roasted tomato. She placed one on the bed beside Eleanor's mother, and handed the other to Eleanor. "You didn't eat one bite at breakfast today, Eleanor dearest. You must be famished by now."

"I think Debbie and Charlie should take the first stab."

She handed the plate over to Debbie, who sat down in the chair and began scarfing the mushrooms and then the eggs down with her fingers, while Charlie doubled his speed inhaling the rest of his fish n' chips.

"My loves, stop!" Kuveni exclaimed.

They stopped and looked to each other in a panic, as if Kuveni might take their food away in an intensely cruel joke.

"You may eat as much as you want, my darling bairns. There is an infinite supply. But remember that slow and steady wins the race. As long as I live, you will never starve again, and I will live a very, very long time."

Eleanor did not like at all that all three of them were so hungry that they paid almost no mind to Kuveni's blatant display of Yakshini magic.

"Ye'll slow ye down on that sausage, if ye know whit's good fer ye," Eleanor's mother scolded Debbie. Debbie coughed and choked as she swallowed too big of a piece, but as soon as she coughed it up, she chewed it up and swallowed it.

Eleanor's mother watched her with deep despair. "Ye remember that first Christmas after yer Da met his maker?"

Eleanor did remember it. She hadn't thought of it in almost thirty years. "You brought home the charity goose you'd won at the women's spinning collective. We ate more that night than we'd eaten in six months."

Eleanor's mother gazed at her plate for a moment of remembrance and then didn't look up as she spoke. "I dunne win it."

"Did you steal it?"

"I bought it, Ellie. With money I earned doing the Devil's work."

"What did you do?" Eleanor really didn't want to know the answer.

"That is between me and my maker... and my vicar confessor."

"Blimey."

"Yer speakin' like a sassanack again, ye know."

"I think you're the only one who notices, Mum."

Her mother gobbled down a nest of thin, golden, salty fried potatoes in one bite, followed by a slab of perfectly grilled bacon, and then returned to the more personal topic.

"I don' regret it, Ellie. Not fer one wee minute. Watching yer faces light up as the goose went down on the table that night was the happiest moment of my life after yer Da's demise."

Charlie finished his last chip, and Kuveni snapped her fingers again, morphing his empty, greasy newspaper into a fresh plate of Scottish breakfast. He began eating with his fingers, and Eleanor noticed for the first time that his ravenous style reminded her of Edmund's. She realized in that moment that her husband's vague childhood memories of the orphanage that he described often as "unpleasant" had been much more deprived than he cared to describe.

"Why is the world so bloody cruel?" she murmured as she watched the boy ravage the beans.

"It is not always so cruel, Eleanor," Kuveni replied as she snapped her fingers, producing three glasses of milk. "Drink up, my loves. You need more nutrition from now on so we can make your bodies as strong as your spirits again."

Eleanor's mother sighed sadly. "I was worried I'd have te watch another tragedy before God called me home, but I dunne think 'twould be watching these wee ones starving like we did, Ellie. It's a right bloody shame that they know what we knew. I thought ye'd saved 'em from it. I thought ye'd saved all of us."

"So did I." The tragedy of the truth threatened to overwhelm her.

A soft tap at the door startled Eleanor, but Kuveni only winked. "Come in!"

Howie and Ruthy rubbed their eyes sleepily as a familiar Yakshini, clad in an identical Scottish outfit to Kuveni's, pushed open the door and urged them inside.

"Excellent work, Illa dear," Kuveni praised her. "Did anyone see you?"

"No, Auntie. The villains are all asleep," she reported.

"Excellent." Kuveni wiggled her fingers in anticipation. "Now, what can the angels make for you, my little loves? Breakfast? Fish n' chips? A shepherd's pie, or perhaps a carpenter's pie?" She leaned in confidingly to Eleanor's mother. "That one is the Lord's favorite. It's really worth a taste."

Howie's eyes widened, and Ruthy gasped as she spied the half-eaten breakfast platter on her sister's lap. As Kuveni observed their overwhelmed indecision, she snapped her fingers and made them each a breakfast.

"There's more where that came from, my children. Eat as much as your tummies can take, and when you're hungry again, I will make you more."

She coaxed them onto the bed beside Eleanor's mother, and handed them each a plate.

"Thank you for your help, Illa dearest," Kuveni said cheerfully.

"Shall I remain here for my next command, my lady?" Illa asked, glancing timidly at Eleanor.

"Were you busy doing something else?" Eleanor asked.

"No, my lady. I was visiting my parents in the Andes."

"Would you like to return to them?"

"No, my lady. They are busy with their new brood. I'd rather be here."

Eleanor laughed. "I don't blame you."

"Stay with us, Illa dearest. Your help will be most appreciated," Kuveni suggested.

Illa took her place standing in the corner of the room, and Eleanor smiled. "We don't need a butler, Illa. Join us!"

Illa glanced at Kuveni.

"You heard the woman!" Kuveni reiterated.

Illa snapped her fingers and conjured a wooden chair in a distinctly Peruvian style with a beautiful embossed leather back. She sat down next to Eleanor, and then looked again to Kuveni for guidance.

"I could use a carpenter's pie, now that you mention it," Eleanor suggested.

Kuveni snapped her fingers and handed the pie over to Eleanor.

"Do you know how to make these?" Eleanor asked Illa as Kuveni politely offered her a fork.

"Oh no, my lady. That recipe takes centuries to master, and only Auntie can make it good enough for Lord Vibhishana to eat."

"Well now, Illa, practice makes perfect," Kuveni reminded her. "Besides, we do not all have his exacting standards."

Illa closed her eyes, scrunched her nose, and snapped her fingers. A pie appeared in her lap, with a darker, more grainy crust, and the distinct scent of spiced sweet potatoes wafting up alongside the steam. She sighed disappointedly.

"May I try it?" Eleanor asked. "It smells wonderfully Peruvian, don't you think?"

"Do you really want to?" Illa asked.

"I do!" Eleanor reached her fork into the pie and took a small bite. "It's good! Very unique. I think this recipe is a keeper. Perhaps we can call it Inca pie from now on?"

Illa's eyes lit up, and she offered the whole pie to Eleanor. Eleanor laughed. "I can't eat two pies, Illa."

"I'll take that carpenter's pie off yer lap," Eleanor's mother offered as she finished up her last bite of toast.

Eleanor smiled and handed over her carpenter's pie. Her mother placed it right on top of her completely empty plate, and dug right in with her fingers. Eleanor took Illa's offering, and Illa watched with satisfaction as Eleanor began eating it in earnest.

"Do you like it?" Kuveni asked Eleanor's mother as she noticed her chewing and chewing with an ambivalent look on her face.

"It tastes too foreign," Eleanor's mother admitted. "But I reckon this is what they were eatin' in the Holy Land?"

"It is," Kuveni confirmed.

"That must be what the wise men were doin' with all that frankincense, gold, and myrrh."

"One does not eat any of those things," Kuveni informed her. "But they did like spices much more than the barbarian Scots did, then and now. You don't have to finish it."

"Moira Howard MacLeod has never left a morsel on her plate, and I ne'er will!" Eleanor's mother declared. She placed the pie by the bedside and picked up the glass of milk. "But I've eaten nothin' but bits of bread fer months. I'll finish the pie later, when I've room in me belly again." She drank down the entire glass, and then belched as she wiped her mouth. "I shuddne dunnit like that, I reckon." She paused and looked pained, and then let the feeling pass. "Now, Ellie, where's yer colonel? Times a-tickin'!"

Eleanor braced herself as she committed to which set of lies she was willing to perpetuate in the totally unexpected circumstances. "He's still in Australia. He can't just pop over here. He doesn't know the angels can travel in the blink of an eye, and it's the Lord's will that he only learn that truth when powers beyond our control decide it's time. Speaking of which, I need to get back before he worries too much. I thought I'd only be here a few minutes to say goodbye."

Debbie dropped her empty plate on the floor and flung her arms around Eleanor. "Don't leave, Auntie Ellie!" she begged.

Ruthy looked up from her half-eaten breakfast, and her lip began quivering. "No!" she cried. "Auntie Ellie, stay here! Save us!"

Eleanor's heart broke as she looked into all four children's expectant, waifish faces. She fought back an urge to ask Kuveni and Illa to pop all six of them back to Australia, but surely that would be wrong... surely? Her mind raced for an excuse to follow through on the fanciful plan. She could tell Edmund that they'd called up from the station after running away from home and finding their way all the way to Margaret River, but surely the children would not be skilled enough to support that web of lies, and then, of course, there was the minor detail that the plan involved kidnapping all of her sisters' children in one go, which was probably wrong... But was it? She beat down a wave of dark, vengeful power burrowing its way to the surface. Surely the villains here were her sisters and their foolish, selfish, abusive husbands.

Think of your strategy in stages, my child. We don't need to solve every problem at once.

Eleanor closed her eyes.

You aren't going to tell me this is a terrible idea?

It is a terrible idea. But look at them, Eleanor. Sometimes we must act as our conscience dictates, and let Shakti take care of the rest.

Blimey. I didn't think you were going to agree with me.

Neither did I.

"Illa, do you know how to make a vortex?" Eleanor asked.

Kuveni grinned. "Eleanor dearest, I like where your mind is going, but I know someone who would probably tell us that it is a very unwise thing to do."

"Well, his other half is on our side, so I think we're all going in on this unwise plan together."

Kuveni clapped her approval as Eleanor took a deep breath, readying herself to dive right into the very unwise plan.

"Would you like to come with me and Kate to Australia for a while?" Eleanor asked the children. "Just while we nurse you back to health and knock some sense into your parents?"

"Yes!!!" they all exclaimed in unison.

Eleanor kneeled down to address them. "You have all done a valiant job of keeping Uncle Edmund's secret, but if you come with Auntie Kate and me to Australia, you will need to be very careful. Uncle Edmund is still a young angel. He doesn't know all the many things that angels can do, and you can't tell him, alright? You must be very careful to keep his secrets. Kate and I will tell you what he is and isn't allowed to know. Can you do that?"

They nodded their solemn agreement.

"Can you do it, Mum?"

"Me? Why would ye bring me? I'm at death's door!"

"You just answered your own question," Eleanor replied.

"How else are we going to explain how the children made it to Australia by themselves?" Kuveni chimed in. "You saw what was happening, and you escorted them down to the edge of the world."

"I kidnapped 'em, ye mean?" Eleanor's mother asked.

"Yes, that is the story we're concocting," Eleanor admitted.

Eleanor's mother looked at the children and then smiled. "I'd do it a million times o'er, I would. It'll teach those rotten bassas a lesson they won't forget, and I'll dare any judge in this world or the next to look me in th'eye and tell me I'm wrong."

Eleanor rolled her shoulders and readied herself. "So, that is the story, my loves. Gramma Moira brought you down to me and Uncle Edmund because you were starving and deprived up here with your parents. You took the train down to Southampton and then boarded a steamer that went around the Cape. You finally landed in Fremantle, and you took the train to Bunbury, and then down to Margaret River, where you, Mum, called from the station. Kate answered, and we went to pick you up. Got it?"

The stared at her, unwilling to admit that they hadn't entirely gotten it.

"Don't worry, I'll help you remember," Kuveni offered. "Now come. Gather around Gramma Moira's bed. You will feel very strange for a few seconds, and then everything will be perfectly alright. Illa, follow my lead. We will pop over to the Margaret River train station. Oz keeps a car parked there that we will borrow for our little farce."

"But I've never transported a human in a vortex," Illa said nervously.

"Don't worry, darling! I will be in charge. Just connect your essence to mine, alright? Are you ready, Eleanor dearest?"

"I'm as ready as I'll ever be," Eleanor said determinedly.

And with a pleasant breeze and a moment of lightheadedness, Eleanor embarked upon her very unwise plan. She hoped she wouldn't regret it for one wee minute.

CHAPTER 4 – HOMECOMING

"Lord Almighty," Eleanor's mother murmured as the Yakshini vortex materialized inside the empty Margaret River train station. She braced herself on Eleanor, while Ruthy fell straight to the ground. Kuveni and Charlie kneeled down to help her.

"Are you alright, my little love?" Kuveni whisked Ruthy up into her arms.

"That felt strange," Ruthy whispered. "And my tummy hurts."

At the thought, Charlie rushed into the corner and lost every bite of the food he'd gobbled down too quickly. He looked like he might cry, but Eleanor steadied her mother (who she now noticed was wearing only a thin flannel nightgown) on Illa's arm, and rushed over to comfort him.

"It's normal for your tummy to struggle when you've gone so long with it empty. Let it settle for a bit, and Auntie Kate will make more food for you, alright? You don't have to worry about wasting food anymore. You must focus on doing what feels right to your body."

"But I made a mess!" He burst into tears.

Kuveni snapped her fingers, and all of the evidence of his problem dissolved. "You have nothing to fear with the angels by your side, my bairn. Now, shall we go say hello to Uncle Edmund? We have quite a full house at the moment, with so many wonderful visitors here to celebrate Auntie Eleanor's birthday. They will all be so happy to meet you."

He wiped his eyes and sniffled, not entirely convinced.

"Come on, my good, tidy lad. You're safe and sound now with Auntie Ellie, just like when you were a wee bairn, rockin' in my arms," Eleanor said as she took his hand and led the way out into the pleasant autumn sunlight.

Debbie took Howie's hand to follow Kuveni, while Illa escorted Eleanor's mother.

"Excellent," Kuveni said cheerfully as she spotted one of Oz's dusty Fords parked right outside.

"So this is what the world looks like upside down," Eleanor's mother murmured. "Looks more similar than I expected. Bigger, I reckon, and greener. The way the press goes on and on about it, I thought it'd all be a wicked desert."

"We've had a very wet autumn. It's been good for the land, but bad for the grapes," Eleanor explained.

Eleanor's mother squinted as she gazed around at the karri trees rustling in the breeze, the flowering white roses lining the muddy dirt road, and the twee wooden details slapped onto the square red brick buildings. "Where're the townfolk?"

"It's lunchtime on a Sunday," Eleanor replied. "They're all at home with their families."

"I reckon that's where they belong," she shrugged.

Eleanor straightened her posture as her mother's gaze landed on her. She suddenly felt a wave of self-consciousness as her years of dreading her mother's reaction to her changed measurements came to a head.

Eleanor's mother smiled as she looked her up and down. "I'm glad t'see ye'rnt skin 'n bones anymore, Ellie. It's no wonder with the angels stuffin' ye like a Christmas goose day in 'n day out. It suits ye."

"Thank you, Mum. I prefer it too." Eleanor sighed with relief and pulled open the driver's door of Oz's car. "Pile on in wherever you can fit. It'll be a good twenty minutes to get home from here."

Illa helped Eleanor's mother into the front seat, while Kuveni guided the children into the back seat, helping Ruthy onto Debbie's lap, and then squeezing in beside them as she slammed the door.

"Illa, dearest, why don't you squeeze in next to Moira," she suggested.

Eleanor silently scrutinized the glove compartment for redbacks before she reached her hand in and collected the key along with a pair of Yvie's sunglasses that she was grateful had been left for her. Illa sat down obediently, placing her hands awkwardly in her lap and leaving the passenger door open.

"You need to close the door, Illa darling," Kuveni reminded her.

She blushed. "I'm sorry. I've never ridden in a car before."

"How d'ye get around?" Eleanor's mother asked.

"I fly," Illa replied quizzically. "How else?"

"How else indeed," Eleanor's mother murmured.

"What an excellent segue!" Kuveni exclaimed. "Let's talk about all the things that Uncle Edmund isn't allowed to know about us yet! Illa, darling, you'd best listen in."

Eleanor smiled, grateful that Kuveni was there to help. She sighed with ambivalence as she pulled onto the muddy road, and the reality of what they were doing hit her. She tried to ready herself for the complications that would undoubtedly arise from her hasty, emotional decision to rescue the children with Yakshini magic. She knew that she'd just made a dangerous move, and she prayed that destiny, or Shakti, wasn't about to smite her for it.

"Now, let's start with transportation," Kuveni began. "Uncle Edmund doesn't know that we can fly."

"But you're angels!" Debbie exclaimed. "Of course you can fly!"

Kuveni laughed. "Yes, my darling girl, it does seem obvious, but Uncle Edmund doesn't really know that we're angels exactly. He knows that we're different, and that he is different, and that together we do all sorts of things to help worthy humans, but he isn't a particularly religious man. It will be quite some time, perhaps even a century, before he realizes exactly how much of an angel he is, and in the meantime, we mustn't push him. Alright?"

"Does that mean that Uncle Edmund will be able to fly someday?" Charlie asked.

"It does," Kuveni confirmed. "With beautiful golden wings, just like the ones you see in the stained glass at church."

"Like the vicar's," Eleanor's mother interjected.

Blimey, D.H. You showed her your wings?

I needed to make a point. It made an important difference in her acceptance of truths she didn't want to hear.

No kidding!

I used my godly light, as well.

But she doesn't know about your time in the Holy Land, does she?

NO. She doesn't, and it must stay that way.

Just have to get my facts straight. I can't believe you showed her your wings... poor Edmund. He'll be the only one left on Earth who doesn't know angels can fly.

He isn't ready.

Eleanor sighed disappointedly. *I know.*

"Won't Uncle Edmund be too old to fly then?" Howie asked. "He's already really old."

Kuveni smiled. "He's older than you think, my love. As are we all. And when he is ready, he will be able to choose how old he looks, just like the rest of us do. Let's play a guessing game, shall we? How old do you think I am?"

"Thirty!" Debbie guessed.

"Fifty!" Charlie exclaimed.

"A hundred!" Howie added.

"A million!" Ruthy squealed.

Kuveni laughed. "Well now, I must admit, I didn't think you'd guess too high. Why don't you try guessing somewhere in between Howie and Ruthy's last guesses?"

"Five hundred."

"One thousand."

"Ten thousand!"

Eleanor's bangle glowed, and she was grateful that the powerful noon sun was shining in the open window, masking its otherworldly luminescence.

What is happening, Eleanor? I can feel your nerves resonating inside of me.

I may have just kidnapped all of my sisters' children.

You did what?

I went to say goodbye to my mother on her deathbed, and they were all bloody starving, Vibhi! Literally starving like Oliver bloody Twist! My mother was starving herself to death so that I would come up there for her funeral and stop what was going on!

Good lord.

And you know the kicker?

No, Eleanor. I don't.

My sisters and their bloody bastard husbands were still drinking fine scotch! I couldn't just leave the children to their fate, Vibhi. Kuveni and Illa helped me pop them down to Australia, and now I have to figure out what's next.

This is very, very bad.

I know!

"Six thousand!" Eleanor's mother exclaimed. "Then yer as auld as God's earth itself!"

"I am not, but we will leave that discussion for another time," Kuveni demurred. "Now, my little loves, why don't you try guessing Illa's age."

"Four thousand!"

"Two thousand!"

"Sixteen!"

"Twenty!"

I would have done the same, Eleanor. I've always had a weakness for punishing those who hurt the ones I love.

Uma agrees.

That doesn't mean it's wise...

I think we've all agreed about how foolish our move was. It's just a parade of fools now.

Let me help you. This is going to be very messy.

Let me think. You complicate things, D.H., as much as you help.

I'm sorry, Eleanor. She felt a pang of his sadness resonate deep within her.

"I'm seventy-five," Illa revealed. "In human years, at least. I am much younger in Yak... I mean angel years."

"If you're seventy-five, then Uncle Edmund must be ancient!" Howie exclaimed.

"Is he six-thousand like you are, Kate?"

"No, he is just a babe compared to me," Kuveni explained. "In fact, I raised him up when he was just a babe. I was the first person who had the pleasure of greeting him in this world."

"How are angels born, Kate?" Debbie asked curiously.

Eleanor's mother looked particularly interested in the answer.

"Well, there is not just one answer to that question. Some angels fall from the Heavens, and some angels are born from a womb. Edmund is only half angel, which is why it's taking him so long to grow up. His mother was human, and she died bringing him into this world."

"Couldn't his father save her?" Ruthy asked. "Wasn't he God?"

Kuveni sighed sadly. "There are some things that even angels can't control, my little loves. There are some things that must be left to the greatest almighty, and Edmund's sweet mother's fate was one of them. Now, how old do you think Uncle Edmund is? I'll give you a clue, the king was named George when he was born."

"The king's name is George now!" Howie exclaimed.

"It wasn't this King George," Eleanor revealed.

"I knew he was too auld fer ye." Eleanor's mother poked her in the ribs teasingly. "Yer auld mum isn't as dull as ye think, I reckon."

"Don't tell me you thought he was a century's old angel," Eleanor laughed. "I won't believe it for a second."

"I dunne think anythin' so mincey, but that bow he gave at the banquet was a right auld bow, it was. Like he'd learned it from Queen Victoria herself."

"He did." Eleanor relished the moment of honesty that she never thought in her wildest dreams she'd have with her mother. "Or, more accurately, he learned it so that he could present it to her, at Prince Leopold's first birthday party in 1854. That story I told you about his grandfather being an artist was true, but it wasn't his grandfather. It was him."

"But whit's an angel goin' around paintin' fer? Shuddne be pullin' bairns outta burnin' buildings 'n such?"

"He's done his fair share of that, believe me. You'll meet some of the children he saved from a burning house last summer. They still live in the village."

"We must be very careful about how involved we get in human affairs. It is a natural requirement of the universe for humans to solve their own problems," Kuveni chimed in. "It is exceptionally unusual for us to get involved like we have with you today. We have only done it because we love Eleanor so dearly, and so her love for you we share."

"We love you, Auntie Ellie," Ruthy squeaked.

"More than we love Mammy," Debbie added.

Eleanor sighed with ambivalence as they all descended into contemplative silence. She didn't blame them. But how her sisters had managed to veer so far astray was still a mystery that was disturbing her. Martha had always had a streak of greed and jealousy in her, but Mary... Mary had always been her most trusted ally. She was determined to get to the bottom of it, and in the meantime, naturally she would cut off all their funds, although the timing would need to be delicate, as they would obviously suspect some correlation between their children's disappearance (and their dying mother's), and an immediate loss of the funds... Her mind raced, and then she gave up. First things first. They must be fed. They must be clothed. And Edmund must be brought into the plan without understanding most of the logistical details that got them there. All of her other messy problems would need to be dealt with in good time.

The children gasped and pointed as the road took a turn around a karri-forested bend and then opened up onto a panoramic view of the sparkling blue Indian ocean stretching far out to the vast horizon.

"Lord Almighty, have y'ever seen a sky so blue?" Eleanor's mother murmured.

"It's like Heaven!" Debbie exclaimed.

"I suppose it is," Eleanor agreed.

Kuveni closed her eyes, engaging in a silent conversation, and as Eleanor reached the edge of the Helmsworths' vineyards, she felt her heart begin racing.

"Now, remember, my loves, you came here on a very, very long boat trip and then you came down from Perth on a train. Gramma Moira escorted you. Eleanor, dear, Percy will help support our story."

"Percy? Lord Blakeney? That queer pouf is here?" Eleanor's mother exclaimed.

"That queer pouf is one of us," Kuveni said sternly. "And you'd best pay close attention to the kindness that the angels bestow upon all of humanity, even those humans who are very different from you, Moira. I shouldn't have to remind you what Father Johnson's favorite sermon is."

"Do unto others…" Eleanor's mother mumbled like a chastised child.

"Correct. Now, Eleanor dearest, Percy has made our excuses to your birthday entourage for our absence, but he has not revealed who we went to the station to collect. Stanley is worried out of his mind that we've gone to get his father, but we will just have to let him stew for a bit while we gather our wits."

Eleanor cringed at the reminder of the other big mess that had descended on her birthday weekend. She had no energy left to worry about the familial drama racking the Secret Service's precarious placement in their home.

"Now, my loves, Uncle Edmund also doesn't know that angels can snap their fingers and make all sorts of useful things like clothes and food," Kuveni informed them. "So, we might have to play a little game from time to time, hiding how we got such wonderful things so quickly. This might be your first test, because as soon as we get home, Uncle Percy and I will make you a little feast in the kitchen, and then we'll start work on Auntie Ellie's birthday banquet. She's turning forty tomorrow, you know."

"Forty," Eleanor's mother murmured. "That makes yer mammy right auld."

"Me too," Eleanor sighed. "At least for a mere mortal." She braced herself as they reached her drive. "Here we are, home sweet home."

She pulled up the dirt road through the vineyards until they reached the wide front lawn that was looking especially nice after their wet autumn. Eleanor glanced up at the freshly white-washed wooden house, where her entourage and the men were all gathered amongst the outdoor furniture, waiting for her return with pitchers of iced tea and bottles of red wine and champagne. She took a deep calming breath and threw on the brake.

"That's more folk than I thought'd be here," Eleanor's mother admitted. "Although, I reckon I look better than if t'were my funeral… barely."

Illa helped her out of the car, and Eleanor got out and met Edmund as he approached them curiously, leaning forward and squinting to spy who was in the car. His jovial excitement at the pleasant mystery morphed into concern and then dread.

"What on earth?" Edmund murmured as he watched Charlie help Ruthy out of Debbie's lap, while Howie slinked tiredly out the other side after Kuveni. "Good lord…" He eyed their horrid state, landing his attention on her mother. "Mrs. MacLeod? What in god's name happened to all of you?"

"I'm sure Ellie'll fill y'in wit all the blether, Colonel, but I daresay I'm not dressed fer the party after our long journey. If ye dunne mind, I'd like a wee cat nap."

"Yes… yes, of course!" He rushed around to help her, but as he got a whiff of her decline, he stopped in his tracks, turned around, and began heatedly whispering his mantras as he paced back and forth.

"Come, my little loves, I think Uncle Percy is already in the kitchen making you a feast. Let's join him. Illa dear, help Gramma Moira into the house." Kuveni carried Ruthy and guided the children right past Edmund, up the stairs, and into the house, gesturing for Oz to join her as she went. As he followed her inside, Mae tagged along.

"She can take the room by the kitchen door," Eleanor told Illa. She squeezed her mother's hand, and then smiled and offered Illa a silent 'thank-you.' As soon as they were out of sight, she turned her full attention onto Edmund.

He looked at her with his black eyes and a miserable look on his face. "She's dying, Eleanor."

"I know, darling. But I think we may be able to do something about it this time. She was starving herself to death to get my attention."

"Surely not." He looked for any evidence that she'd just made an incredibly facetious joke. "You said she was mad, but really, Eleanor. Starving herself to death?"

"My sisters and their husbands have become storybook villains, as far as I can tell. They stole all the money we've been sending them for the children's educations and my mother's care and put it into the down payment for a castle that they can't afford. They've made themselves so house poor that they aren't feeding or clothing the children, and so my mother brought them down to the edge of the world for a reprieve."

"Why didn't she just call?!" he exclaimed.

Eleanor couldn't help but laugh, even though the question wasn't funny in the slightest. "When we get everyone settled, I'll have to ask her. I suppose she didn't think I'd believe her, and to be honest, she might have been right. She has always been such a mean old biddy, I'd probably have assumed that she was trying to slander my sisters for some petty reason."

Edmund shook his head as he began pacing with stress. Eleanor knew why she was so overwhelmed by the whole thing, but she wasn't sure what exactly was getting to him.

"Darling, it will all be okay. They're here now, and we can help them get back on their feet."

He paced some more, and Eleanor spied Shruti watching him from the porch with some combination of curiosity and fear.

"It's all our fault!" he finally exclaimed.

"What is?"

"Everything!"

Eleanor approached him and took his hand into hers to stop his pacing.

"Eleanor, they used the money we sent them to get themselves into trouble! We should have known! We should have made sure they were spending it properly! We should have made sure that they were helping the children, not hurting them!"

Eleanor pulled his other hand into hers, more forcefully than she'd intended, and then looked up into his black eyes. "It is not our fault, Edmund. My sisters married two rotten scoundrels, and we did everything we could to help them. Did you ever wonder why I was putting the cheques in their names and not their husbands'?"

"I did wonder," he admitted. "I didn't want to know."

"Well, now we both know I was right. The real question for me is how my sisters let this happen. But it isn't something I can bear to think about at the moment. We need to help the children and my mother recover. They were living on the brink of starvation for months."

"They look like hell, Eleanor. They look how the children looked in Hyderabad during the famine." He shook his head again. "How could we let this happen?"

"Darling, we cannot take personal responsibility for humans misusing the gifts that we give them. In the end, it is always up to them to make their own fate. We must resign ourselves to letting them."

"You speak as if you're just as alien as I am." Eleanor's heart skipped a beat at his astute observation, but Edmund took a calming breath, letting his eyes dissolve back to their human hazel. "I suppose I've dragged you into a very foreign world, haven't I, dearest? It's a saving grace for me that you're here with me, keeping me sane."

Eleanor was too beaten-down to argue. "We keep each other sane, darling. Speaking of which, shall we go check on Kate and the children? I suspect Percy has already whipped them up something delicious in the kitchen."

She guided him past Shruti and Yvie, who held Ned sleeping in her arms, noticing in passing that Stanley, Andrew, and Norwenn were not around.

"Where are the children going to sleep?" Edmund asked as they passed their first-floor guest room and Illa joined them, closing Eleanor's mother into the room. "We have Shruti and Mae, and then there's Percy and Kate, the four children, your mother, and… have we met? You look very familiar but I can't place from where." He finally turned his attention onto Illa.

74

"We have met, my lord. I am on Lord Blakeney's staff. I photographed your wedding," Illa replied, almost correctly if not for the lordly address. He reached out his hand, and she shook it nervously. "My name is Illa, sir."

He held onto her hand for an extra-long moment. "And you are related to Kate and Percy? You're one of us? You do not feel entirely human. You aren't... you aren't Kate and Percy's daughter, are you?"

Illa threw Eleanor a desperate look and then closed her eyes, undoubtedly requesting assistance from Kuveni or Mélusine.

"Edmund, mon chéri, stop interrogating the poor girl," Mélusine interceded with the foppish accent of Percy Blakeney as she rushed out of the kitchen to join them. "I promise, mon chéri, if Kate and I have a child together, you will be the first to know. Now come. Oz is almost done examining the children. We should discuss what to do with them next."

Illa scampered away to the kitchen, but as Mélusine urged Edmund to follow her, he grabbed her wrist and pulled her back. "Tell me this, and only this, and I will stop interrogating all of you: Stanley wishes so dearly that Norwenn hadn't told him who his real father was. I wish it for him. Is our dark family secret worse than his? Is that why you've been drowning me in lies for so long?"

Mélusine couldn't hide her dismay at the question, and then she glanced at Eleanor and sighed as she made her decision. "Yes, mon chéri. It is. Now come. We must decide how we are going to rescue these children from their evil fathers. It is something we have too much experience with."

Eleanor tugged on Edmund's hand to follow her as she made her way into the kitchen. Ruthy was seated on the counter as Oz finished his pediatric examination with a test of her knee reflexes, while Debbie, Charlie, and Howie were all seated on the counter next to her, chomping away with proper forks and table-manners on a surprisingly healthy looking dish of pasta with fresh mozzarella, broccoli and tomatoes. The rich, spicy scent of raw, minced garlic filled the air, and Edmund's stomach growled. Eleanor noticed with curiosity, while Edmund did not, that Illa was nowhere to be seen.

"Would you like some, Edmund dear?" Kuveni asked. "We have more where that came from."

He blushed with embarrassment. "I ate three breakfasts already. I should control myself. Please keep all you have for the children and Mrs. MacLeod. I'm sure she'll be hungry when she wakes up."

"Edmund dear, when have you ever had to ration food in our presence? If you're hungry, you should eat. There's an infinite supply," Kuveni urged.

"Uncle Edmund, have some! It's angel hair!" Charlie exclaimed.

Debbie kicked him. "He means the pasta, Uncle Edmund. The pasta is called angel hair. It's just a silly name, isn't it, Auntie Kate?"

"Indeed, my dearest lass. Real angel's hair is not very tasty at all," Kuveni winked. She reached into the cupboard under the sink and pulled out a steaming bowl that matched the children's. "Eat some, Edmund. We will turn all of our efforts onto Eleanor's birthday banquet after this."

He glanced at the odd place from which she'd just pulled the fresh meal, and then he glanced at Mélusine as he decided not to press her. "Thank you, Kate. I suppose I will have some."

He took the bowl from her and took a position next to the children, leaning on the counter. As he started eating the pasta with his fingers Hyderabadi style, all four children giggled and stopped eating to watch him. Eleanor could not have been more grateful that they were recovering fast enough to notice how he was eating.

As he noticed their attention, he blushed. "This is how I learned how to eat when I was your age. I was a boy in India, and we never used any silverware at all."

"Did they have silverware a million years ago?" Charlie asked.

Debbie kicked him again, but Edmund only laughed. "I suppose my childhood does seem like a million years ago. But, I reckon that when I was a boy, they did have silverware in some parts of the world, just not in my home where I lived with Abdul Barr, a wonderful old painter who taught me everything he knew."

"Was he nice?" Debbie asked.

"Yes. He was one of the kindest people I've ever known," Edmund agreed. "I didn't realize at the time how lucky I was to know him."

Debbie sighed. "I bet he was nicer than Da."

Charlie snorted. "That wunne been hard. All he'd have to do is not box yer ears."

"Or feed you!" Ruthy squealed.

"Don't be a wee clipe!" Howie said as he smacked Charlie's arm.

"One should ne'er regret the truth," Charlie fought back with Gramma Moira's phrase.

Kuveni interrupted them by collecting a final bowl of pasta from under the sink and handing it to Ruthy. She began scarfing it down with her fingers, until Oz took the bowl away from her.

"What did the doctor already say?" he asked sternly.

"Eat slowly, or we'll be praying to the porcelain god," she repeated dutifully.

"Now follow the doctor's orders. The food will do your body no good at all if it comes back on out the top." He smiled and handed it back to her and then glanced at Eleanor and Edmund. "They should only eat healthy food for now, nothing fried or too heavy. Their systems are in shock. They need plenty of rest, and I reckon when the shops open tomorrow, you oughtta get them some clothes that fit. Maybe Percy can fly you up to Perth in his plane, although it would be best for now if the ankle-biters stay here. They've been through a mighty painful ordeal."

He nodded for them to follow him out of the kitchen and into the dining room, where the children were out of earshot. He leaned in. "Now, Edmund, prepare yourself. Are you ready for the bad news?" Eleanor squeezed his hand as he nodded nervously. "All four of them have bruises behind their ears. The girls have it worse than the boys, and they have bruises on their upper arms, as if they've been grabbed and tossed around a bit. Debbie, Howie, and Charlie also have scars from lashes on their backs. They look about a year old."

"A year?!" Eleanor exclaimed. "Then this isn't new?!"

"The starvation has been going on for quite a while, although I'd say that the boys have been fed more than the girls. The girls' hair is thinning, and their bones are becoming more brittle, but all of them were out of breath just climbing up onto the counter. Healthy children of that age should have plenty of energy. Once they've settled in, we should talk to them more about what's been happening. I'll start an official report in case you need it."

"Need it for what?" Edmund asked.

"To keep the children," Mae said as she entered the room carrying a bulky camera, followed by Illa. "I brought my autochrome lumière. Albert Kahn gave it to me last year after a dinner at the maharaja's palace. He asked me to only use it for documenting Indian life, but I think we can make an exception. The color photography should make it clearer what their horrific state is, in case you need it in court. I saw a case like this get very ugly back when I was teaching in Cambridge. The judges were steadfast on keeping the children with their abusive fathers unless there was very hard evidence against them."

Eleanor leaned up against the wall, trying to get her emotions under control. Somehow their perfectly appropriate use of the terms 'abuse' and 'court,' of 'starvation,' and 'scars,' was too much for her. After a lifetime of escaping from her emotions in terminology, she suddenly couldn't stand it.

"Dearest, are you alright?" Edmund asked concernedly. At that moment, she realized full-heartedly that the answer to his question was 'no,' and somehow, being forced to say so was too

78

much. Without looking back at any of them, she ran straight out the door, down the steps, across the lawn, and through the vineyards towards the sea. As she felt Sheranee break free from her divine perch to join her, she didn't protest.

She ran and she ran, until Sheranee found her, and then she hopped on her back, felt the wind in her hair like she had as a lass riding her father's stolen horses, and she let her mind go blank.

For the first time in her life, she simply was.

Eleanor lay on the soft, white sand of a small beach with her head on Sheranee's tummy as she watched the wispy white clouds move slowly across the blue sky. She was grateful that the day had turned out warm enough for Uma's temperament to be satiated, despite the fact that they were just on the edge of austral winter. The irony that it was much warmer than the early Scottish summer was not lost on her, and she let her mind contemplate it, instead of the many overwhelming thoughts that were angrily beating their way to the surface of her consciousness.

She reached up and rubbed the soft fur of Sheranee's chest, and Sheranee sighed with contentment and dropped into a low purr. It had been far too long since they'd had a lazy day alone together, although Eleanor knew that it wasn't going to last. She had the whole world to return to, and so many plates to spin, she couldn't even remember all of them. She focused on the sound of Sheranee's purring instead of letting her brain enumerate them.

She slipped off the wool trousers and jacket of the suit Kuveni had made for her back in freezing Scotland, and ripped open the front of her soft cashmere sweater to laze about, dozing in and out of hazy consciousness with the sun warming her skin for hours as the shadow of the looming cliffs above (that kept the beach nicely isolated from casual passers-by) slowly encroached into her sunlight.

Finally, as the sun approached the horizon and became a deep red, she heard footsteps skipping down the steep, rocky path, and she sat up, hardly cognizant enough to worry about her scandalously unclad state. As Edmund approached, she looked down at Sheranee, and then lay back down with her head on her tummy. She had no more energy for pointless farces.

Sheranee yawned and repositioned herself with her paws straight up in the air like a playful little housecat. Edmund eyed her suspiciously.

"Join us. Sheranee's tummy makes an excellent pillow," Eleanor said without looking away from the magenta sky as the wispy clouds burst into a new shade of flaming orange.

He shuffled around, contemplating his options, and finally gave in and lay down next to her. Sheranee purred as he carefully lay his head on her tummy.

"Tigers are dangerous, you know."

"Really, Edmund? That's how you're going to start out this conversation? I've been avoiding the real world for hours. I don't need you to hit me in the face with it. Besides, Sheranee isn't a normal tiger."

He took her queue and left it alone. "I was worried about you, but Kate and Yvie agreed that I should give you your space. Were they right?"

"Aye, they're both good advisers. You should feel free to turn to them again if you can't understand me. Sometimes I can't even understand myself anymore."

"Do you want to talk about it?"

Eleanor chuckled. "I suppose it's about time you're coaxing me away from an abyss. The tables have turned, Colonel, and I don't like it one bit. I'd much rather be in your shoes right now. I'd know just what to say."

"What would you say if you were in my position?"

"Don't try that psychological mumbo jumbo on me, Colonel. I'm too smart for you. Twenty years nursing mental patients was enough to teach me all the tricks. It makes it dastardly difficult to get myself out of these ruts."

Edmund paused as he thought about his rebuttal. "I love you, Eleanor."

None of the dastardly doctors had tried that one before... she tried to run with it.

"Why does it all have to be so bloody hard!" she finally exclaimed. "All of it! Every time I feel like I'm finally settled, destiny throws an axe right at me! It's a very selfish perspective, I know. My mother practically starved to death to save her grandchildren, and here I am complaining about the inconvenience of it all. I'm a horrible person, and I know it."

"You are *not* a horrible person, Eleanor," Edmund countered.

"All I can think about is how I failed. How could I have let this happen? Really, Edmund. HOW?!"

"You just told me this morning that this isn't our fault."

"But it is!" Eleanor exclaimed. "We wrote the cheques. We let them steal the money. We let them starve their children while they were drinking fancy bloody scotch!"

"You didn't mention that detail earlier."

"My mother brought a flask that Charlie nicked from Jimmy. It's top-shelf scotch, Edmund. They're all bloody monsters."

He thought for a long moment, considering the new intel. "It isn't our fault, Eleanor. You were right. I've been thinking about it all day."

Eleanor reached over, took his hand, and kissed it. "Tell me, Edmund. Please tell me something I'll believe."

"We can't do everything for them. We called the schools, we managed your sisters' children's admissions, we paid the cheques to the people you thought would be responsible. What the hell else were we supposed to do? Show up and drive their children to school? We couldn't have reasonably done more. And yet still, I feel it too. Why in the bloody hell is this our fault?"

Eleanor had never loved her husband more than she did in that moment.

"Because we carry the weight of the world on our shoulders. It is who we are, and nothing we ever do will change that."

"The world is bloody heavy."

"Crushingly heavy."

She looked over, and he looked back at her. "God how I love you, Edmund. Please don't let me ever forget."

He leaned over to kiss her, and then stopped as he eyed Sheranee.

"She's a tiger, darling. I don't think she'll be offended, but perhaps we should take a dip in the sea just in case."

She stood up and guided him to the water that was so clear that she could still see the many fish swimming around in the dim, orange twilight.

"You lost your trousers," Edmund pointed out.

"Then we're uneven, aren't we?" She unbuckled his belt and flung it across the beach. As she unbuttoned his trousers and they fell to the ground, she caught a knowing look in Sheranee's eye, and then her loyal mount turned away from them and humphed her concession.

"It's been a long time since we've been together in the ocean," Edmund said as he helped her wiggle off her panties.

"Too long," she agreed as they waded into the knee-deep water and she wrapped her legs around him.

The gentle waves battered against them, and her open cashmere sweater absorbed the salty water.

"I like this sweater." Edmund licked her breasts. "It's very convenient."

"So do I."

84

She sighed with the first true contentment she'd felt in weeks as he entered her, but this time it felt delightfully honest. She wanted more of it. She wanted it to be as beautiful as it was in that perfect moment, forever and always.

He pulled her tighter against him, and as the breeze whipped up, and the waves pummeled them more and more forcefully, he moved with the power of the churning ocean instead of fighting against it, and she felt his subtle pulsating power grow into vigorous thrusts, infusing her not only with his human warmth, but with everything else—everything dark and complicated and powerful that made him who he was.

More, you want more, all of the voices inside of her sang.

In that moment, they were finally and truly one, and the vivacious energy of their divine power connected like it never had before. She gasped as a burst of overwhelming ecstasy infused her, and then she went limp, letting him catch her and hold her in his arms.

"Darling, that was… divine."

He guided her to the edge of the water and lay down beside her, and she curled up into the nook of his arm and sighed as the water gently lapped up their bare legs.

Edmund kissed her forehead and intertwined his fingers with hers as they relaxed under the dark starry sky.

"It's hard to believe there was so much tragedy here, isn't it?" she finally let her mind go to the many places she'd been avoiding.

"It's easy to see why they couldn't get away from the tsunami. These cliffs are steep. I wish we'd been here to help, but I suppose there are tragedies like that unfolding every day somewhere. I hate that the cruel universe imparts such suffering."

"I know, darling. If I think about it too much, I won't be able to function." Eleanor nestled deeper into his arms. "This place is beautiful otherwise, though. Like our own little world."

"Do you want to sleep here all night?"

Eleanor sighed. "We shouldn't. We have far too much to do."

"We have a lot of help at the moment. Kate and Shruti are watching the children, Percy's in the kitchen, and Mae has offered to stay with us for the next few months to tutor them so they can get caught up to go back to school. She's on leave for monsoon holidays in Baroda anyway."

"That's so kind of her…" Eleanor felt the ball in her throat that she'd been battling all day returning. "How could I not have known? I've always been such an excellent judge of character."

"You knew not to trust Jimmy and Fergus."

"I suppose there was a reason I didn't want to get married, and watching my sisters deal with their bludger husbands didn't inspire me. But I didn't realize it was anywhere close to this bad! Lashings and starvation? How could my sisters let that happen?!"

"Maybe they didn't. Could Jimmy and Fergus have stolen the money without their agreement?"

"The cheques were in their names. They must have been complacent. With just one of the cheques, my sisters could have skipped out of town in the middle of the night with all the children in tow if they'd wanted to. Hell, they could have made it all the way down here in first class!"

"Whatever class your mother took with the children seems to have been lacking food and water. You don't think… you don't think they stowed away, do you? Perhaps that's why they're so hungry."

"No. I'm sure that it started when they were back home in Scotland. Oz was right. They wouldn't have these physical symptoms if they hadn't been starving for months."

Edmund sighed. "I suppose we should have learned our lesson in Paris about what too much money can buy."

"It does corrupt the wrong people. I suppose I assumed that since marrying the Earl of Easton didn't corrupt me, that sending my sisters a small percentage of what we have at our disposal wouldn't be a problem. Or maybe it never occurred to me at all. I held each of those babes in my arms when they were born. Money or not, it didn't even cross my mind that my sisters would let their children suffer like they have."

"The Earl of Easton?" Edmund protested.

"Do you prefer being the Emperor of India? Or perhaps a Martian prince?"

"Or the bastard son of the King of England? Isn't that what Percy thought at first? Or perhaps it wasn't. That was just an excuse, I suppose. Another lie to keep me in ignorance."

"Well, whatever title you want me to use to describe your situation, darling, you're about as different as a man can be from the bricklaying blokes my sisters married."

"I am just as ordinary as you are, Eleanor. Watching the children scarfing down their meals reminded me of when I was them. Of when I was so hungry at the orphanage, I thought my stomach might collapse in on itself and take me with it."

"I know, darling. I could see the similarity today when I watched them eating. It helped me understand a bit more about where your voracious hunger comes from. But I didn't know how humble your origins were when we met. Your lifestyle with a grand estate and a butler at your beck and call was completely foreign to me. You were living a life meant for people who weren't anything like me at all—for someone born with a silver spoon in her mouth."

"I'm glad you weren't scared away."

Eleanor brought his hand to her mouth and kissed it. "So am I. And I mean that, darling, from the bottom of my heart, despite all of the unusual trials we've been through. It was the greatest fortune of my life that I let myself sit with you that night in the Baron of Heathfield's library. It was a very unusual thing for me to do."

"It was a privilege I never thought would be mine, to sit there sipping cognac with a woman as beautiful as you, Eleanor. You were so fiery and full of life, and that peacock dress was so alluring… it made me want to see what was under it."

"I'd saved for months to buy it. It felt very selfish at the time, because I knew the money could go to the children instead. I suppose I should rest easier knowing that the money shouldn't have gone to them after all, at least not to their bludger parents. If I'd worked harder and made more money to send them, they just would have been ruined faster." She sighed with resignation. "Sometimes I forget who Eleanor MacLeod used to be. My life was hard, Edmund. Day in and day out. It was much harder than I realized at the time; I just had nothing to compare it to."

"I know what you mean. I did not have familial obligations, but I was so bloody lonely, Eleanor. So desperately lonely. I had no idea what my life could be like with you. After Alice left me in the way that she did, I'd resigned myself to being alone, and then I had a few more rather unpleasant experiences when I was a fresh young lieutenant on Lord Curzon's staff that only reiterated how alone I really was."

"Really?! You never told me that!"

"To be honest, I find the stories embarrassing. Suffice it to say, the expertise that you have found so pleasurable was a bit too foreign for my partners, whether they were British or Indian."

"So that's how you know how to drape a dupatta!"

"I hope it's not disappointing? I promise I wasn't a cad about it. They were all... er... experienced women."

Eleanor leaned over and kissed him gently on the lips. "I love you, Edmund. I have no doubt that you were as gentlemanly as they come."

He pulled her closer and kissed her deeper, but as a wave crashed against them, he jumped up in a blur and pulled her into his arms. "I suppose we should have paid closer attention to the tides, lying on the beach in the dark."

"I had you to rescue me, darling." Eleanor kissed him again. She gave into one final romantic moment, and then she sighed with resignation. "I'm not ready to parent one child, let alone four. We don't even have room for them."

"We already worked it out while you were away. Kate, Percy, and Illa will stay with Oz and Yvie. The boys will share a room, the girls will share a room, and Mae and Shruti will share a room. Your mother will stay in the room by the kitchen, although we've decided not to tell her that it was intended for the cook. It will be a wonderfully full house. Oh, and Stanley sent Norwenn away, so we will not need to host her."

"He didn't need to do that! She could have used Sheila's room at Oz and Yvie's. I don't think she'll be back from Perth anytime soon. Oz said that she was avoiding us, and he wasn't going to argue with her."

"That wasn't why he sent her away. He told her that if she couldn't accept him as he was, he didn't want to see her anymore, and so she left."

"Good on him," Eleanor murmured. "I hope that doesn't come back to bite him, though. Lord Grimby can be a thorn in the side… but I can't think about it. We have too much to do."

She squinted, looking around for her clothes in the dark, and Sheranee's green glowing eyes approached. Edmund sighed with unspoken disapproval, but Eleanor only laughed and patted Sheranee's head as Sheranee presented Eleanor's trousers and her jacket in her mouth.

"See, darling. She isn't a normal tiger. Kate and Percy would not bring her anywhere near us if she were dangerous, don't you think?"

Edmund didn't argue as he hunted around in the dark for his clothes, but as she finished wiggling on her trousers and buttoning the jacket in a way that still remained very scandalous without anything but her open damp sweater underneath, he returned triumphant, but with a confounded look on his face. Eleanor didn't like the wheels turning in his head.

"Dearest… You don't think this could be the same tiger that helped us on our honeymoon? The one who killed that worthless American bastard who tried to attack you?"

"Why do you ask, darling?" Eleanor knew her tone was a bit too sweet as she tried to hide her panic.

He looked Sheranee in the eye, and she bowed regally before him.

"Blimey," he murmured. "That means that Kate and Percy were there. They were following us on our honeymoon, even after we left the steamer. No wonder they were there to help after that madwoman kidnapped us. Don't they have anything better to do?"

Eleanor smiled. "Darling, I'm sure they have plenty of important things to do, but they love us. And sometimes we need a little bit of extra help. After all, our trials are harder than most, don't you think?"

"I suppose."

She hopped up onto Sheranee's back and then patted the spot behind her. "Shall we return to the real world, darling?"

"Dearest, we shouldn't ride a tiger. It will be bad for her back to carry our weight."

Sheranee humphed her disagreement as she repositioned and nuzzled Edmund's hand with her nose.

"Darling, she's a very special tiger."

He reluctantly threw his leg over her back, and he grabbed onto Eleanor as Sheranee bucked with a happy roar. Eleanor giggled, and gave into the thrill of a moment she had fantasized about for years.

"Onward, Sheranee! Back to the real world we go!" Eleanor declared.

And with a leap, Sheranee tore up the path to the top of the cliffs, carrying the gods back to the next phase of their complicated destiny.

CHAPTER 6 – SOME OF BOTH

"My loves, you look wonderfully relaxed!" Kuveni exclaimed as they reached the outer edge of their long driveway. "But, I daresay that we will have trouble explaining to the children why your damp sweater is on backwards, Eleanor dearest. And Edmund, darling, you missed a few buttons on your trousers… and all of the buttons on your shirt. But I'm glad that the beach was as romantic as always on this fine autumn evening. We are quite lucky that the water is still so warm. Don't you agree?"

Edmund looked down sheepishly at his scandalous state, and brushed the remnant dried sand off of his stomach.

"Don't worry, my darlings. I have placed appropriate clothing for you in Sheila's bedroom at Oz and Yvie's down the road. Sheranee will take you there, and when you are ready, we will have a nice little family dinner. The children have been napping all day, and now they are ready for a little cheer."

She winked as she slapped Sheranee on the bum, and the tiger took off at a trot.

"I suppose we'll have to be more careful to be fully clothed from now on," Eleanor sighed. "I'm not ready for this."

"We'll take it one step at a time," Edmund reassured her.

She sighed as she felt him lean up against her and wrap his cool arms around her waist. She'd dreamed of that feeling so many times—of them riding Sheranee together half naked on a pleasant evening—that she almost felt guilty about the reality, as if living it was throwing the gauntlet down to destiny. She'd managed to scrape by with a lie about Sheranee that managed to keep her divine status the secret that destiny demanded it to be, but somehow, she feared the technicality wouldn't be enough. She pushed back her anxiety, as she often did, and leaned into Edmund's arms.

As they arrived at Oz and Yvie's door, the lights were on, and Ned's screeching cries were echoing from the warmly lit interior. Sheranee bowed, and Eleanor hopped off, offering Edmund her hand like a gentleman.

"We'll just be a few minutes, my love," Eleanor said as she scratched Sheranee's ears and kissed the top of her head.

"Should I be jealous, dearest?" Edmund teased.

"A girl can have multiple loves, darling. Besides, I've heard you use similar monikers more often than not with our dogs. Speaking of whom, have you seen them today? I swear they wander a little bit farther each day. If they weren't both male, I'd half expect that they'd set up a home in the karri forest with a brood of pups."

"They were lounging in the stables earlier this afternoon when I was feeding the horses."

"They do like the horses. I'm glad they have someone other than us to give them attention. They're going to need it now that we'll be distracted constantly." She sighed with stress. "Come on. Let's get ready. There's a brood of bairns waiting for us."

She skipped up the stairs into the house, and Yvie was pacing back and forth in the hallway, trying to coax Ned out of his hysterical state.

92

"He's too tired!" she exclaimed with a hint of desperation. "Edmund, you must keep my husband in line from now on! No keeping our boy awake all night, no matter how noble the cause, *d'accord?*"

Edmund reached forward and offered to take Ned. As Yvie passed him over, Edmund whispered into Ned's ear, and held him against his cool chest. Ned's sobs dissipated, and he nestled into Edmund's arms.

"He's yours!" Yvie exclaimed. "Can you keep him for now? I need to change for dinner!"

Edmund smiled. "Take your time. We'll be in Sheila's room changing ourselves."

She ran up the stairs without looking back. Eleanor tiptoed down the hallway, trying not to disturb Ned with her footsteps, and she cracked open the door to Sheila's room. On the bed, two sparkling Indian outfits awaited them, a blue and gold brocade sherwani, reminiscent of the one Edmund had worn to the Taj Mahal, although thoughtfully different in detail from that same one that Surpanakha had torn off of him during his birthday torture. For her, Kuveni had laid out the same mint green flowing silk lehenga with ivory accents that she'd worn on that romantic night as they'd trotted through the streets of Agra on the white horse that Ravi Bidkar had arranged for Lord Kalki to look the part.

"Is Kate trying to give my mother a heart attack?" Eleanor asked half-jokingly. "I suppose we'd better not beat around the bush with her. She's going to have to get used to our liberal household, because I'm not changing anything for her curmudgeonly benefit."

"I was surprised by how supportive your mother was earlier, actually. I think perhaps this experience has changed her for the better. She didn't say one word about Stanley and Andrew holding hands in the kitchen."

Eleanor snorted. "That's most certainly because the thought didn't even occur to her that they were an item, darling. People can work hard to change some things about themselves, but I'll eat my hat if my mother can truly accept two men being lovers… and speaking of things that my mother can accept… I know you're not going to be pleased at all by this… but she may… no, she *does*… believe that you're all angels. You, Kate, Percy, Illa, and Mr. Johnson."

"WHAT?!" Edmund exclaimed.

Ned startled and then burst into tears. Eleanor took him into her arms and began bouncing him and whispering into his ear until he calmed down.

"Oh… and the children think so too." She figured she might as well nail the coffin shut. The children had already demonstrated their lax skills at lying. At least this way he would have some explanation for why they were acting so odd.

"Eleanor, I am not prepared to perpetuate another religious farce! It's bad enough the whole town of Margaret River thinks we're both angels. Did you see how disappointed they were when we refused to join them at church? It was like we were cursing them or something! I can't deal with this in my own home! I need a place where I can be my ordinary, boring, slightly foreign self!"

"Darling, she watched our cricket match out the upstairs window of our house. She saw your unusual speed, and she needed an explanation. Mr. Johnson talked her into this one, and it seems to have done its job. You don't see her accusing you of being a demon, do you? Of all the possibilities, this is really a fine outcome."

He sat down on the edge of the bed and humphed. He looked down at the blue sherwani. "A demon is a more likely explanation for what I am."

Eleanor took a seat beside him. "Darling, having dark urges doesn't make you a demon. It makes you human."

"I wanted to kill their wicked fathers today, Eleanor. I spent half the afternoon plotting how I would do it so that the children wouldn't know what had happened."

"So did I, darling." He glanced at her skeptically. "Fly up to Scotland in Percy's plane. Tell no one that we're there. Lure them out to the beach. Drown them. Drop the bodies where the sharks feed off the Shetland Islands. No one will ever find them. Forge one of my sisters' signatures on a few of our cheques in Argentina. It will look like they stole the money and ran. If anyone goes to check up on them, they'll assume that they were on the run with the money. What was your plan?"

"To rip them to shreds."

Eleanor couldn't help but laugh. "That's not a very subtle plan, darling. How were you going to keep the children from noticing?"

"I was going to do it in a back alley as they were leaving the pub. I would have ripped their faces and their fingers right off so they couldn't be identified."

"I see. No wonder you were feeling a bit demonic. It's a rather a gory plan, don't you think?"

"Your plan is much better, but that shouldn't be a surprise. You're much better at planning than I am, and I can't think straight when I'm like this. It's like there's a demon trying to crawl its way to the surface, and I have to put all of my energy into keeping it down in the depths of my soul where it belongs."

"I must admit that I feel like that myself sometimes. But, darling, these dark fancies are natural. Even my mother was plotting their clever murders; it was how she kept her mind occupied during her hunger strike. It doesn't mean we're evil to want revenge on the monsters who hurt the innocent children we love. But we must elevate ourselves to be civilized creatures, and not let our dark fancies rule us. We both have the strength to do that."

"I love you, Eleanor."

She lay Ned down gently in the middle of the bed and held her breath as he stirred, readying to cry, and then he turned onto his side and went back to sleep. Edmund stood up and picked up the sherwani.

"I don't think I love this choice, to be honest. It looks a bit too much like the one the monster dressed me up in on my birthday."

He pulled off his damp, unbuttoned shirt, and put the sherwani on anyway.

"Darling, I'm sure we can find you something else."

"I'll survive," he sighed. "Besides, Oz is definitely too short and stout for me to borrow his shirts."

"Like a little teapot," Eleanor winked.

"At least he isn't like Humpty Dumpty," he winked back, but then he became somber. "Do you think Kate and Percy would have stopped that man from attacking you in Agra? The one whose mad prattling wife said I was like Humpty Dumpty?"

"Didn't they, darling? Sheranee intervened."

"Do you think that she came back for him later that night? Was she the one that the girl thought was the Devil himself?"

"I don't think so, darling… in fact, I know so. Sheranee would never do anything so vindictive. She is purely a loyal, protective, helpful creature."

"You don't think… you don't think that one of them killed him, do you? Percy or Kate? I wanted to so badly, Eleanor. I thought for quite some time that I might have done it in my sleep."

"Darling, I know who killed him. Do you really want me to tell you?"

"I don't know. Do I?"

She realized that she'd just baited him with an idea that would disturb him even more than the truth.

"Darling, the madwoman killed him. She was following us. Leo realized it was her sometime later, after she'd kidnapped us, but all of the evidence supported that it was her. She also killed those men in Paris, and the captain of the steamer."

"Good lord. That's what she meant. She was going on and on about how she was helping me punish my enemies because she loved me… she said…" He paused as he debated whether or not to continue.

"What did she say, darling? You can tell me anything."

"She said that she was my aunt, and that she could make me powerful like her. I didn't want to tell you, because I didn't want you to be afraid. *That's* the kind of monster that I could be if I lost control, Eleanor. And despite whatever Mr. Johnson says to the contrary, I don't believe for one second that we're angels."

"Darling, I think if we've learned one thing in this life, it's that nothing is black and white. Not even angels and demons. There are many powerful creatures in this world who can be good or bad or some of both. Aren't we all some of both? Why else would you and I have spent our afternoons plotting murder on behalf of the innocent. Oversimplified religious dogma cannot capture the complex morality of these real struggles."

"Amen to that."

She kissed him and sighed with relief as he dropped the subject and began pulling on his drawstring pants. She pulled off her damp clothes and wiggled on the blouse and the flowing crepe silk skirt, shivering as Edmund buttoned up the back with his cool fingers. She draped the matching dupatta like an expert without a single pin, remembering momentarily how confounding the large scarf had been the first several times she'd tried to wear it, and then she ran her fingers through her hair, using Uma's most mundane power to smooth the matted mess into soft ringlets, and re-tying the white ribbon she'd been wearing since the night before into a low ponytail.

"You look lovely, dearest."

As Edmund snuck a kiss, Yvie knocked gently on the door.

"Coucou, you three. Are you decent?"

Eleanor opened the door. Yvie, clad in one of Babri's original Indian offerings of a rich turquoise silk lehenga that shimmered to an almost yellow sheen in the gentle light, smiled as she spied them. Her smile widened as she spotted her sleeping son.

"You are a miracle worker, Edmund! I haven't been able to put him down for hours!"

"Well, legends of my divine status have been greatly exaggerated, but I will admit that I have a way with babies."

Yvie threw Eleanor a subtle knowing glance, and then moved the conversation along. "Kate told me that your outfits tonight would have an Indian theme, so I wanted to join in the fun. This lehenga has been gathering dust in my closet for years."

"It still looks lovely," Eleanor said as she re-draped the dupatta for her in a more flattering style.

"You're such an expert now, Ellie! I couldn't make heads or tails of it!" Yvie laughed. "It's a good thing it has a drawstring; otherwise, there's no way I'd be able to wear it after all those pounds it took to bring little Neddie into the world. Shall we? I think Kate is waiting for us, and I'm sure the children are hungry."

"Yes, yes, of course! We shouldn't keep them waiting!" Edmund exclaimed.

Just as Yvie sighed with resignation as she prepared herself to disturb her sleeping son, Illa knocked lightly on the doorframe.

"May I help? I have a lot of practice babysitting."

"My friend, you are a godsend!" Yvie exclaimed. "Are you really offering?"

"It would be my pleasure to serve," Illa said with a polite curtsy. "Someday, if I am good enough, Kate might even let me take over her job."

"Her job?" Edmund asked curiously.

"As a matrika," Illa replied. She cringed as she realized she shouldn't have offered up any new secrets to him.

"A matrika?" he pushed.

"She mothers our people." Illa closed her eyes, and then sighed. "You'd better go, my lord. The children are getting antsy waiting for you." She took a seat in a chair in the corner. "Shall I wait with him until you return?"

"That would be wonderful," Yvie agreed. "If he gets too fussy, please call Kate, and we will come back."

"And what would you like me to do if he disappears?"

"If he disappears?" Yvie asked with equal parts curiosity and concern.

Illa closed her eyes again. "Oh… never mind. Kate tells me that human children don't disappear like ours do. But why do you need to watch him all the time if he can't disappear? Can't you just lock him in the room while he's sleeping and come back for him later?"

"In case something happens to him, Illa," Eleanor explained. "Like if the house burns down, or he falls off the bed. If we were in the same house, we would just leave him for a bit, but we will be down the road, which is too far away to just leave him alone."

"But those things are so unlikely to happen! Our children disappear constantly! It's such a pain to go find them!"

"That is enough, Illa," Kuveni said sharply as she approached from the hallway, wearing a very modern black georgette sari with delicate green vines embroidered into it that looked particularly graceful on her tall, thin form with her black modern bob. "Thank you for watching Ned. You will stay here until one of us returns for him, and let me know immediately if his status changes, understood?"

Illa looked annoyed at herself. "Yes, Auntie."

"Come. Dinner's going to get cold," Kuveni said as she whisked them out of the room and out the front door, swiftly away from Illa's unfiltered mouth.

"Disappear?" Edmund asked.

"Believe me, Edmund, you don't want to know. Your children won't do that." Kuveni threw an apologetic glance at Eleanor at the reference. "You aren't the same as me, remember? Your people's children are much more similar to human children. Now come, before the MacLeod bairns start to worry."

"Similar, but not exactly the same?" he pushed.

"No, my dear boy. Not exactly the same. You know that you are not entirely human? Why would your children be?"

"I suppose I hadn't totally thought it through," he admitted.

"Well, tonight is not the night to start," she said as she guided them swiftly out the door. Eleanor was grateful to have an ally in avoidance.

As they reached the driveway, Sheranee was waiting patiently for them, donning a thick garland of fragrant jasmine and marigolds around her neck.

"Perhaps you should stay here, my love," Eleanor suggested.

Sheranee growled her disagreement.

"I've already warned them that we have a very unusual pet, Eleanor," Kuveni reassured her. "I don't think any of us have the energy to hide Sheranee with all of the other drama unfolding. Don't you think?"

"If you say so." Eleanor would take the excuse, even though she remained concerned that it was tempting fate.

"You are certain that tiger is safe to be around the children?" Edmund asked with fatherly concern.

"My dear boy, she is not a normal tiger. No one of virtue will have anything to fear."

Eleanor laughed. "Sheranee, my love, we must include my mother in that group, whether she earned her position or not."

Kuveni clapped excitedly as a car pulled up the drive, and Oz waved from the driver's seat.

"I reckon someone's gonna need a ride," Oz called. "Hey, where's lil Neddy?"

"We have a babysitter! Quick, let's go before Neddy notices!" Yvie exclaimed as she hopped into the back seat. Kuveni laughed and squeezed in beside her. "What do you think is faster, a tiger or a Ford?"

Oz revved his engine, and Sheranee growled in acceptance of the challenge.

Eleanor let herself be swept up in their good cheer, and she hopped onto Sheranee's back. But instead of hopping on behind her, Edmund slipped into the passenger seat beside Oz.

"I'll give you a fighting chance," he called. "That tiger's going to need a single jockey to compete!"

Sheranee bucked with a louder roar of excitement, and as Oz screeched down the driveway, Sheranee took off through the vineyards, leaping over the vines and into the karri forest beyond. Eleanor squealed and laughed gleefully as she pulled the ribbon out of her hair and let the wind whip through her flowing tendrils as she had done on so many secret midnights as a carefree lass.

Sheranee charged over shrubs and under low-hanging branches, trampling ferns and dodging snorting wombats as she bounded unabashedly through the primal Australian forest, illuminated only by the pale silver moonlight.

As they bounded up Eleanor's driveway, the whole house and garden, and even the massive karri trees, were illuminated by thousands of twinkling electric lights. Strings of marigolds and jasmine were draped across the yard between the house and the trees, creating a dancefloor out of the lawn, and a string quartet was seated on a small stage at the edge of the garden beside Oz and Yvie's Steinway, waiting for their queue to play. A massive rangoli with millions of flower petals covered all of the garden paths, and trickling stone fountains dotted the rest of the yard, brimming with lotuses and flickering floating candles. In the distance, underneath the biggest karri tree, a Yaksha banquet awaited. She laughed as she realized that she'd been thoroughly taken in, and then she and Sheranee trotted up to her impatiently waiting audience.

"Lord Almighty," her mother murmured.

"SURPRISE!"

"SURPRISE!" her cheering entourage shouted again. They all waved sizzling sparklers as they greeted her.

"Do you think it's real?" Charlie whispered.

"It's gotta be! It's moving!" Debbie whispered back.

Eleanor hopped off of Sheranee's back, and Sheranee approached the children and gently nuzzled their free hands in greeting.

"She's a very gentle tiger," Eleanor reassured them as they began petting her. They gasped with awe.

The MacLeod children stood beside Eleanor's mother, who was seated on one of the wicker chairs from the porch, while Shruti stood beside Ravi, Jaap Sahib, Jyoti, and Amit on the other edge of the group. Mae stood in the middle of the pack beside Rohit Patel, Mélusine in the form of Percy, and Vibhishana, who smiled with a hint of guilt. They were all dressed to the nines in sparkling, beaded Indian silks, even the children, who looked adorable in their miniature adult outfits that made them look like the children of a maharaja. Even Eleanor's mother was wearing a tartan sari over a long-sleeved black cashmere sweater that showed no hint of skin, making the whole outfit look surprisingly Scottish. Vibhishana looked especially handsome in his familiar British form of Mr. Johnson, donning a sparkling violet and black sherwani over matching black silk pants. She was at least grateful that he had used a form that Edmund would recognize, so that she wouldn't be forced to keep yet another annoying secret for the evening.

Eleanor glanced over as Oz's car screeched to a halt beside her, and Sheranee offered them a smug humph as she took a seat beside Eleanor's mother.

"How on earth did you beat us here?!" Edmund exclaimed as he hopped out of the front passenger seat and pulled her into his arms. "I thought for sure we'd have time to get in position for your surprise!"

"Sheranee is one clever tiger," she said giddily as she felt her frizzy hair whipping in the cool breeze and decided to keep it in its wild state as a trophy. She let Edmund dip her into a triumphant kiss. "Darling, you did it! You surprised me! How is that possible?!"

"Beats me," Oz said as he jumped out of the drivers' seat to help Yvie out of the back. "He told you what he was planning this morning!"

Eleanor burst into laughter. He wasn't wrong. She'd just assumed that Edmund had immediately given up on the idea after he'd given away the secret, and with all of the other drama unfolding, it had completely slipped her mind.

"Happy birthday, dearest," Edmund whispered into her ear again.

"You all look marvelous!" she exclaimed as she approached her audience. "Mum? I can't believe they got you into a sari!"

"Well, Kate promised that it wunne be so different from a kilt at th'end of it. I told her I'd be the judge after she tied it all up, and here I am, so I suppose it'll do." She leaned in confidingly and held up the edge of the sari, showing Eleanor the muted blue and green plaid contrasted by a bright yellow stripe. "It's me auld tartan, ye know. From when I was a Howard maiden and yer Da had to seduce me right. I always liked it better than that mustardy MacLeod tartan, but I ne'er got my wits up to say so."

Eleanor squeezed her mother's hand. "I like it better too."

Her mother eyed her stomach and then her blouse's copious cleavage under the semi-sheer silk of her dupatta. "Ye'd better hope there isn't a strong breeze, Eleanor Mary MacLeod. It'll make ye the star of the show fer the wrong reasons. Ye don' wann'em talkin' about yer unspeakables when ye rode in here on the back of a magical tiger, I reckon."

"What makes you think she's magical?" Eleanor couldn't help but ask.

"Well, ye rode 'er, dunne ye?"

Eleanor laughed. "I can't argue with that, Mum."

Eleanor returned her attention to the rest of the group. She had to admit, with all the topsy-turvy twists, she found it reassuring that her mother hadn't changed too much.

"*Father* Johnson, I didn't know you'd be here!" Edmund said as he shook Vibhishana's hand and then pulled him into a hug. "What a wonderful surprise!"

"I couldn't let myself miss such a momentous occasion," Vibhishana said as he squeezed Edmund back.

"And Mr. Patel? What brings you all the way down here from Baroda?" Edmund asked cheerfully.

"Mae invited all of us, but Maya was held back with unexpected business, and so the children stayed back with her. I hope I'm not intruding too much? I've always wanted to see Australia."

"No, not at all! Our home is your home! Do you need a place to stay? There's a spare room at Oz and Yvie's down the road."

"Thank you, Colonel. Perhaps I'll discuss the offer later with Dr. Helmsworth."

Edmund blushed as he realized he'd just offered up someone else's hospitality. "That would probably be the most polite course."

"Auntie Ellie, you look like a princess!" Ruthy exclaimed.

"An empress!" Debbie corrected her. "An empress is better than a princess."

"Thank you, my darling girls," Eleanor said as she kneeled down to address them. "You look like princesses yourselves tonight. In India, we call princesses maharanis."

"I don't need to be a maharani. I just want to be a happy lass again," Ruthy sighed. Eleanor's heart ached at the tragic truth of it.

"We'll all do what we can. You have a lot of special helpers now who love you, and we aren't going to let anything happen to you ever again. Alright?" Eleanor glanced up at Kuveni, who nodded her agreement.

"Look at Uncle Edmund's shirt!" Howie whispered. "He looks like Ali Baba!"

"Or Aladdin!" Charlie seconded.

Edmund laughed. "I quite liked reading the *Arabian Nights* as a boy. Abdul Barr and I read it together. Perhaps we should all read it together tonight before bed. I still have my original copy. It's one of the only things I've kept since my boyhood."

"I thought he was just your teacher?" Charlie asked.

"He was the man who raised me. He was the closest thing I had to a father." He glanced at Vibhishana as he said it with some combination of guilt and cheek. "When I felt like I had no family at all in the world, he was there, singing me to sleep, and it didn't matter, in the end, that he wasn't my father. But, that's enough of that for now. We will have plenty of time to talk more about such things. Shall we see what Auntie Kate and Uncle Percy have concocted for our dinner?"

"We already know!" Charlie exclaimed. "We helped taste!"

Edmund chuckled. "Well, I suppose I missed out on quite the delicious afternoon. Would you like to take a little peek with me anyway?"

They followed him across the dancefloor and over to the banquet table, and Eleanor reassessed her audience, deciding who to greet next. But, as Ravi Bidkar dropped into a pious bow, and Jaap Sahib hissed his disapproval and poked him in the ribs with the sheath of his curved sword, a different uninvited distraction intercepted her.

"Eleanor, when you have a minute, I have something I'd like to discuss," Vibhishana whispered into her ear.

She felt Uma stir and sighed with annoyance. "I thought I made my wishes clear earlier, D.H. I don't need any more complications in my life right now."

"I know. But I have a bit of a plan. Uma and I discussed it while you were dozing on the beach earlier."

"Uma? Do you talk with her often while I'm asleep? I don't know what I think about that…"

"We do not talk often without you. Only when absolutely necessary. Please come. Let's discuss it now while Edmund is distracted. Rohit and Mae will join us as well."

He gestured for Rohit and Mae to follow them inside, and she sighed again and followed. He guided them up the stairs straight to her messy bedroom and closed the door behind him, placing his hand over the lock and subtly clicking it into position.

"Really, D.H., you've gotten too presumptuous," Eleanor muttered.

"I'm sorry, Eleanor. This won't take long. Uma and I thought that we might try offering you a special present for your birthday. I brought Rohit and Mae along to spot us in case the plan goes awry. We've never tried anything like it before."

"And what plan is that?" Eleanor asked skeptically.

"Uma is going to hop into me. I will be her vessel for the remainder of the evening. We will connect our energy, and free you of your divine burden."

"I didn't know that was an option!" Eleanor exclaimed. "Why didn't you mention it sooner?! Like, *years* sooner!"

"It is not a permanent solution, Eleanor. I am not meant to be Ardhanarishvara—if I were, I would have been born with Shiva and Shakti equally present within me. You are meant to connect Uma with her next incarnation, and anything we do to stand in the way of that will only create more misery. But, we were hoping, although it is still risky, that perhaps a little reprieve might be something we can get away with."

"What if it's not? We aren't going to get my whole entourage sucked into a tornado or struck by a massive lightning bolt, are we?"

Vibhishana smiled. "You know it doesn't work like that."

"Do I? You and Mélusine have preached to me since *the moment* I learned of your world that destiny is one vengeful fiend when she's thwarted."

"That's why we must not thwart her, Eleanor. We must have no plan to keep you and Uma separated, and we must resist steadfastly any urge to maintain it once the deed is done. But, Uma and I are hoping that if we go into this endeavor with a clear plan to return to how things should be in a timely manner, that perhaps, just this once, we will get away with it."

"Sometimes I think you're the craziest one of us all, D.H.," Eleanor sighed.

"So do I," he agreed.

The proposition was tremendously tempting, even if it was ludicrously unwise.

"And you're prepared to deal with the fall-out when it turns out that the gods were wrong?" she addressed Rohit and Mae. "Do you know how wild things can get for us when they don't go as planned?"

"I have some idea," Rohit agreed nervously.

"I have none," Mae countered. "But when the Lord asks for your help, you don't say no, do you?"

"In for a penny, in for a pound, I suppose," Eleanor sighed.

Uma, you'd better know what you're doing.

We shall see.

That is not reassuring.

Eleanor rolled her shoulders and let Uma come forward into her limbs. She reached her hand out and intertwined her fingers with Vibhishana's. Eleanor felt the waves of intoxicating power working their way up from the depths of her being, and as she connected her energy with Vibhi's, she felt Uma moan with pleasure. But, unlike every other time, instead of the pleasure erupting into a unique form of exceptionally guilty ecstasy, this time, it began to disperse. Eleanor felt her limbs go cold, and the fire of Durga's wrath dissolve. The morbid power that churned deep within her was gone, and suddenly, she was very alone.

Vibhishana fell back onto the bed, and Eleanor almost collapsed as Mae stepped in to catch her.

"Vibhi?" Rohit asked nervously as Vibhishana's form dissolved.

For a split second, he morphed into Uma's Vanara form, and then his divine Shiva form took over. But, as the snake of life coiled across his ashen shoulders and through his matted hair, the left half of his body morphed into someone new, with the exact feminine proportions that Eleanor had come to accept in herself––Shakti's favorites. The right half of his body was still donning the tiger loin cloth of his familiar divine form, but the left was wearing the same sari that Kuveni had made for Eleanor the prior year when she'd gone out on Dasara dressed as the Goddess to bless her many followers. His delicate female features didn't look exactly like his male ones, but they still looked like him, and both sides of him looked divinely beautiful.

He gasped in an awakening Rakshasa breath and looked down at himself. "How odd." He sat up and examined the jeweled bangles that his feminine side had produced.

"Are you alright?" Eleanor asked. She didn't like the empty hole in her gut. The hole where Uma had spent years making herself a nice, warm, soulful nest.

"We're fine." He stood up and went into her closet to stand on the dressing platform and observe his form. "Fascinating."

"What exactly is intriguing you most?" Eleanor asked.

"Uma has manifested as my feminine form. This is the same form I've used from time to time when I've needed to present myself as female. I didn't realize I was emulating Shakti, but I suppose I should have made the connection." He turned around to address her. "Are you alright? You aren't feeling weak, or sick?"

"I'm feeling empty," she admitted. "Although, all longing for you seems to have stopped, so perhaps it is an even exchange after all. I'm glad to have proof that it was just Uma's sentiments."

"So am I."

"How are you feeling?"

"I'm feeling a bit giddy," he admitted. "I am whole in a way I have never been before. There is an energy to it that is utterly intoxicating."

"Then we'd better get back out there and remember why we did this, before you start planning to thwart destiny."

He closed his eyes and scrunched his nose with deep concentration. After much more effort than it usually took for him to change his form, he relegated both of his divine halves and returned to his dashing British form, clad in his glistening violet sherwani, although there was a softness to his features that hadn't been there before. Eleanor recognized them as the feminine qualities that Stanley was often trying to bring out in himself. His cheeks were a bit rosier (making him look even more like Edmund), his eyelashes were darker and longer, the outline of his eyes more defined, as if he were wearing kohl, and then she realized that he'd retained his soulful brown eyes, rather than reverting to the sapphire blue of his European form.

"Your eyes are the wrong color," she pointed out. "I think Shakti has taken a subtle toll on your form." She looked down with a sudden panic, realizing that without Shakti's power brewing within her, her own figure might change back to the skinny, flat body she'd known most of her life. She didn't know what she thought about the idea. There were certainly merits to each set of measurements. Mostly, though, she didn't want the change to be abrupt and public.

He closed his eyes with concentration, but when he opened them, they remained unchanged. "I think this is as good as I can do in my current state. Do you think it's too obvious? I can excuse myself until you are ready to take Uma back, then you won't have to worry."

"Would you notice?" Eleanor asked Mae.

"Maybe not in the dark?" she replied, not adding much confidence.

Eleanor sighed. "You came all this way to give me a thoughtful gift, and I'm already enjoying the novelty of not desiring you. Join us. Edmund probably won't notice. If he does, I have no doubt that you will find a good excuse."

"Please tell me if I'm too conspicuous. I'm feeling a bit tipsy," he said as he descended the dressing platform and leaned on the doorframe of her closet.

"That means that I can be intoxicated too!" Eleanor exclaimed. She'd been lamenting her inability to feel the dull, cozy warmth of a nice nip in her limbs since Uma had taken up residence inside of her. "Let's go! I need some champagne, pronto! And some cognac! And some scotch!"

"Is that wise?" Mae asked politely.

Eleanor laughed giddily. "Certainly not, but that ship has sailed tonight, hasn't it?"

She skipped up to the door and waited for Vibhishana to stumble over and unlock it. With a determined glance, followed by a tipsy wink, he followed her out the door.

"Did you know what we'd signed up for?" Mae asked Rohit nervously.

"Not in the slightest," he admitted. "But I should have realized that if Vibhi thought he needed spotters, it would be a dastardly difficult task."

As they headed down the stairs and out the front door to the wrap-around porch, the string quartet was already playing, and most of the group had taken Edmund's queue and was milling about the banquet table.

"Shruti, my young friend!" Vibhi exclaimed.

Shruti looked up at him from her position sitting between her father and Eleanor's mother, and stood up obediently.

"Yes?" she asked. "Can I help you, my lord?"

"As a matter of fact, you can! May I have this dance? I could use a few tips from an expert in how to modernize my movements." He offered her his hand, and as Ravi struggled to comprehend what was happening, Vibhi winked. "Don't worry, my pious friend, you'll be next. We needn't be so strict in our roles tonight."

Shruti took his hand timidly and followed him to the middle of the dancefloor, where he swept her right into a waltz.

"Good luck keeping that man under control," Eleanor chuckled as Mae and Rohit ran after them.

"Oh, how lovely! Now we won't be the only ones dancing!" Vibhi exclaimed as they reached him.

Rohit smiled politely and then offered Mae his hand as their task at chaperoning their intoxicated lord commenced in earnest.

Eleanor grabbed a glass of champagne from the table beside her mother, and then she spied a bottle of fine scotch. She downed the champagne in one gulp, and then refilled her glass with the scotch, downing it in a hasty second round. She was glad that Ravi was too busy staring at Shruti's position in Vibhishana's arms to notice her intake.

Her mother, on the other hand, eyed her disapprovingly. "The eve's young, Ellie. Ye'd better pace yerself, if ye know whit's good fer ye, or ye'll be stumblin' into the bushes before dessert."

Eleanor poured herself another shot and clinked her mother's more tasteful sipping tumbler as she downed it.

"You're probably right, Mum, but sometimes a girl's just gotta enjoy being wrong."

Edmund smiled and waved at her from the food, and she took the excuse to leave her mother alone with Ravi (a move that she probably wouldn't have considered without the scotch already warming her limbs). She scampered past Vibhishana, who had already started twirling Shruti into complicated moves that he had certainly not learned in a refined European ballroom, hoping that he wouldn't shout something incriminating before she even made it back to Edmund's arms.

"I didn't know he could dance," Edmund said as he glanced over at him. "There is so much about him that I don't know." He sighed with ambivalence. "Come on. You must be hungry. You haven't eaten all day."

He handed her a plate and then began refilling his own. "That one is particularly odd." He pointed at a rich yellow coconut curry filled with unidentifiable lumps of a furry fruit. "Kate said it was Vanara korma, but I'm sure she was just pulling my leg."

"Why, darling?"

"Vanara means 'monkey' in Hindi. Surely she must know how monkeys and I get along."

"I'm sure she does, darling."

Eleanor filled up her plate with a small taste of each item, making sure to note which one was the Vanara korma, a dish that Uma had requested from Kuveni on every possible private occasion, and that Eleanor was quite sure that she herself was going to find repulsive. She was excited to test her theory.

She took a seat at a round table beside the children, who were dutifully eating slowly under Oz's professional purview. She poured herself a generous glassful from a dusty bottle of cognac that was waiting for her. She drank down several gulps, and then she slowed her pace, letting her mother's words and her guilt at not appreciating the rare and fantastic vintage bring her back to her senses.

113

"Ah, ah, ah!" Oz said as he pointed accusingly at Charlie. "Minus one lolly for you, mate. Remember, at least ten seconds between each bite."

Edmund sat down between her and Yvie and began demolishing what was clearly not his first serving.

"Ah, very good!" he said jovially as he noticed all of the children emulating him. "Dearest, I thought that the children should know how to eat Indian food properly. I hope you don't mind that I've taught them how to eat with their hands? Your mother will not be particularly pleased."

"Well, then it's a good thing she's over there tearin' the tartan with Ravi."

She did not, she had to admit, believe it was a very good thing, but she wasn't going to let herself worry about it.

"That sounds like a scandalous thing to do, you know," Oz pointed out. "What happens after the tartan is torn?"

Eleanor snorted with laughter and almost lost her bite of roti. "You know, we said it so often when I was a lass, I didn't really stop to think about what it meant literally. It means 'chatting' in Scots. Come to think of it, I don't know why the tartan would need to be torn at all…"

"Dearest, do you know who that is?"

Edmund paused his meal as he pointed at a tall, broad-shouldered Sikh man in a full Punjabi dress suit with a particularly bulbous turban and a long, curved sword in his belt. He was relatively young in appearance but imposing in stature, and he stood on the edge of the dancefloor beside Jaap Sahib and Jyoti, chatting amicably and cooing at Amit, who was enjoying the attention from his position hoisted against Jaap Sahib's hip.

"I have never seen him before in my life," she admitted truthfully. "Maybe he's Jaap Sahib's friend? Or another of Ravi's guards?"

"Perhaps… but doesn't it seem odd for them to bring a guest all the way from India without even introducing him?"

114

"Yes... it is odd." She didn't like that he was right.

"Captain Singh?" Mae exclaimed as the music stopped and Rohit released her from their dance.

"Captain Singh?!" Vibhishana shouted as he paid no attention at all to releasing Shruti, who twirled away, and then stopped, confused, and then dutifully made her way to the buffet table, as if it weren't an outrageously rude thing for Vibhishana to have done to end their dance without even a 'thank you' or a bow.

Eleanor did not like the genuine panic that she saw in his expression (and, that in his altered state, he wasn't able to hide), and she hopped up to intervene.

"I'll find out who our mystery guest is, darling."

She rushed over to Jaap Sahib, who shifted uncomfortably as the gods surrounded him.

"What are you doing here?" Vibhishana hissed.

"I... I... I... thought I'd come to offer my congratulations."

"To Eleanor Marriner?" he pushed. "On her fortieth birthday?"

"Well... I... er... overheard Rohit and Mae talking about coming down here, and when I heard why... I thought I might come too. You know how much I like a party, Vibhi. I didn't mean to complicate things."

"You didn't mean to complicate things?!" he screeched before he could gather his wits. He returned to a heated whisper. "Believe me, you have no idea what an epic disaster you've just wrought."

Captain Singh straightened his posture. "You don't have the monopoly on offering well wishes to our allies, Vibhi. Quite frankly, I'm surprised by you. Why are you even here? You haven't been spending time with Uma again, have you? You promised me you wouldn't!"

As Eleanor noticed the grimace of jealousy on Captain Singh's face, and Vibhishana stormed away, slamming his hand against his forehead as he muttered to himself with some combination of anger and dismay, Eleanor began to get a strong inkling of who it was that had joined them uninvited. Rohit went after Vibhi, but he shooed him away as he began pacing and whispering his calming mantras.

As she approached, Captain Singh took her hand and squeezed it, staring into her eyes for an extended moment.

"I'm sorry, are you trying to say something?" She was glad that she'd had the scotch as she bluntly addressed him. "If you are, it isn't working."

"I'm sorry, my lady." He glanced at Jaap Sahib and Jyoti. "Perhaps I should introduce myself somewhere else."

"Really, there's no need for that. You and Jaap Sahib have already met. He's the one who was dying of cholera when I summoned you and your talented chum to the rescue."

Captain Singh looked at Jaap Sahib, and then at Jyoti and Amit again with more solemnity.

"You were right to summon us, my lady. I was being overprotective of our mutual friend. But you must understand, he does too many things that put him in needlessly vulnerable positions. The whole world needs me to keep him out of trouble so he can be strong in his fight for the greater good."

"I'm not convinced I was right to summon you, but the outcome was a miracle for these three worthy humans, so it all worked out in the end. I admire that you are such a devoted friend, and I have come to appreciate my devoted friends more and more over the years."

"So you... er... know each other?" Mae interrupted.

Captain Singh threw Eleanor a look of warning, but she refused to demur. "Do you know him, Rohit?"

Rohit glanced around, before he cleared his throat in a stealthy agreement.

Eleanor shrugged. "You know him too, Mae. You've met him before, when his friend healed my burns. This is a rather impressive form, Hanuman. If I didn't know any better, I'd think you were a Rakshasa."

116

He grimaced with offense, and then realized she was attempting a compliment. "Vibhi gave me some pointers," he admitted begrudgingly. "It is much harder for a Vanara to change his forms. It isn't natural to us at all, but I can't just go around in my natural form in the modern world. It attracts too much attention, and my ancient brahmin form doesn't beget the respectful reaction that I want anymore."

"Well, I think it's a worthy endeavor." She glanced over at Vibhishana, who had taken a seat between her mother and Ravi Bidkar, holding his head between his hands as if he were in pain.

Eleanor chose to let him be and returned her attention to Hanuman. "Did you fly all the way from India for my birthday? You must be hungry. Join us. There is an infinite supply at our Yakshini banquet."

He glanced over at Vibhishana, and then accepted her invitation. "I don't mind if I do."

Jaap Sahib and Jyoti gestured for Mae and Rohit to go before them as they followed Eleanor over to the banquet table.

"Vanara korma! What a treat!" Hanuman exclaimed as he piled several of the gravy-covered furry fruits high onto his plate without batting an eye at the miraculously refilling dish. He lowered his voice. "Thank you allowing me to stay, Uma."

Kuveni swooped in. "I daresay, my lord, it is Eleanor's hospitality entirely that you must be complimenting at this juncture."

He eyed her suspiciously. "Which one are you?"

She laughed affectedly, demonstrating that she did not, in fact, find his question or his tone funny. "I'm the one who made that Vanara korma. If by now you can't tell who I am, then you don't deserve to know."

"I don't recognize your form."

"And I don't recognize yours, my lord, but it couldn't be clearer who you are."

Mélusine approached. "We have to have low standards, Kate. We are dealing with a chest-beating primate, after all."

"I do nothing of the sort!" he exclaimed. "And you have not kept your disguise well either, Mélusine. I can always tell who the bad apple is, spoiling the bunch."

"Sshhh." She glanced over at Edmund. "Have you learned nothing about keeping secrets? Why don't we just shout your name from the rooftops while we're at it! I'm sure Ravi Bidkar over there would be pleased to tell every maharaja in India that Lord Hanuman himself has come out of retirement."

"Sshhh!" he hissed as he glanced around.

"Turnabout is fair play," Mélusine said with annoyance.

"My name is far more recognizable than yours is."

"Is it? Why don't you ask Yvie over there who she thinks is more famous? You're not in India anymore, my *lord*." Mélusine rolled her eyes sarcastically as she used his divine moniker.

Jaap Sahib and Jyoti stood behind them quietly pretending not to listen, while Rohit and Mae debated whether or not to intervene. Eleanor, all the while, had no energy for the schoolyard banter, and so she just sighed and gathered up a few flakey, buttery parathas to take back to her spot at the table.

"*Quanto?*"

"*Quanto?*"

"*Il prezzo!*"

Nellie Melba and Andrew began singing on the stage between the Steinway and the string quartet, who had moved off to the side to make room for their dramatic show. Their accompanist took his seat and joined them without missing a beat.

Eleanor realized that she hadn't seen Stanley all evening, and then she spied him watching with a goofy enamored grin from the edge of the stage, dressed in a particularly flamboyant silver sherwani. She wondered in passing who'd helped him put the kohl on his eyes, as it was particularly well-done, and then she scampered to her seat beside Edmund as Andrew's voice boomed villainously.

She poured herself another generous glass of cognac as Hanuman sat down between Debbie and Ruthy and began eating the Vanara korma in an even more ravenous style than Edmund. But, as the children giggled and pointed, he looked down at them, noticing their red hair, and then back at Eleanor, and then at Edmund, working his hardest not to show his jealousy or his despair.

"You didn't tell me you had children."

"Captain Singh, I don't believe you've met my husband, Edmund. He is a retired colonel, and now he is a local magistrate," Eleanor said cheerfully. "Darling, Captain Singh is an old acquaintance of Mr. Johnson, and he also happens to know Rohit and Mae."

"Really? That is a coincidence!" Edmund exclaimed.

Edmund politely wiped his fingers in his finger bowl and then on his napkin to reach his hand over the table in greeting. Hanuman looked at it for an awkwardly long moment, and then did the same. Eleanor watched curiously as they shook hands. Edmund held on for an extra-long moment, feeling Hanuman's unusual warmth.

"Are you another spy who's been following me around for decades, reporting back on my movements to my father?" Edmund asked. "I don't recognize you, if you have. Are you Kate and Percy's long lost brother? I daresay I'm not seeing the family resemblance."

Eleanor found his cheek surprising, although without Uma to damper her spirits, she was glad that Edmund was starting to notice how absurd the farce was around him, and even more glad that he was taking it in stride.

"I'm sorry, I don't know what you're talking about," Hanuman replied truthfully.

Edmund offered him a friendly wink. "Of course you don't."

Hanuman hunkered down and lowered his voice to set him straight. "I overheard Mae and Rohit talking in Baroda about coming down here for your wife's birthday, and I decided to join the party. I somehow managed to convince myself that it was a fine thing to do, although it does occur to me now that your wife is being very generous by letting me stay, given that I wasn't actually invited." As he spoke, Hanuman's voice became lyrical and smooth, dancing in the air almost like music, which produced an odd contrast to the sung argument that was unfolding on stage between Andrew and Nellie Melba.

Edmund was unmoved by the subtle calming effects of Hanuman's voice. "So you flew down to Australia in Sir Percy Blakeney's plane, just so you could crash a birthday party of a woman you didn't know? Why exactly did Percy let you onto his plane in the first place? It seems like you two were already well-acquainted when you were bickering over there at the buffet."

Hanuman looked nervously to Eleanor.

"He means our beautiful blond friend in the white sherwani with the fairy-like locks," Eleanor explained, hoping that Hanuman would understand her reference to Mélusine. "The one you don't like, and for whom, I've gathered, the feeling is mutual."

Edmund laughed. "Do we have an enemy dining with us, dearest? I must say that's a first. Tell me, Captain Singh, how exactly are you acquainted with Sir Percy? Why don't you like him?"

Eleanor took a long swig of her cognac.

"He and I go back a very long time," Hanuman replied. "We haven't always seen eye to eye on things that matter for the greater good. I find him too hard to predict, and so for me, he is not the most desirable ally." He glanced down at the children and censored something in his thought-stream. "And he didn't let me onto his plane. I flew separately."

"That is quite a commitment to crash a birthday party for a woman you don't even know."

120

Eleanor found Edmund's tenacity both thrilling and stressful. She suspected it was a good test of Hanuman's Vanara lying skills, which, from what she had seen, were about as well-developed as his shapeshifting ones.

"I thought that perhaps I could complete some unfinished business with… er… an old friend with whom I'd lost touch. She's here tonight, and so I thought I might catch her ear."

Edmund smiled as a look of recognition dawned in his expression, and then he leaned in confidingly. "Are you after Mae, then? She's quite a catch, I reckon. One of the most open and accepting people I've ever had the pleasure of meeting. I suspect she wouldn't mind braving the uncomfortable social territory of an Anglo-Indian marriage, if that's what you're after."

Hanuman struggled for a response. "That's good to know, Colonel. Thank you for the advice."

"What I still don't understand is what Mr. Johnson has to do with Baroda…"

"It's a small town, darling. People are bound to know each other."

"Are you saying that he lives there, dearest?"

Eleanor took another long sip of the cognac to soften the blow of her sloppy mistake. "I'm not sure, darling. But I believe that the four of them are all acquainted through the Maharaja of Baroda. Am I right, Captain?"

"I'm a guard on the maharaja's staff." Hanuman raised his voice to compete with Andrew's aria. "Mr. Patel made the introduction for me."

Stanley threw them a dirty look as Andrew sang through their conversation.

"Perhaps we can talk more later?" Eleanor suggested. Hanuman realized his faux pas and dutifully obeyed, refocusing on his korma.

"Dearest, is it a surprise?" Edmund whispered into her ear. "Dame Melba came from Melbourne just for your birthday."

"It's a lovely surprise, darling. Thank you."

"You don't need to thank me. All I did was ask, and she was on the next flight over here, and then she was willing to practice all afternoon with Andrew. It was really very kind of her."

"She and I have become very good friends."

"I don't know why I'm surprised, dearest. Everyone who meets you loves you."

Eleanor didn't bother to argue with his effusive compliment. After a lifetime of most of the people she met actively disliking her fiery personality, her recent pile-up of unrequited suitors was still puzzling to her.

Edmund snuck a kiss, and she caught a subtle grimace on Hanuman's face. She refused to let it deter her. She kissed him back, took another sip of cognac, and leaned into his arms.

"This whole evening is lovely, Edmund. It's the best birthday I've ever had, and that is really saying something, given the circumstances."

"I'm glad." He wrapped his arms around her, and she reveled in his cool touch and his subtle pulsating power. She glanced over curiously at Hanuman, who didn't seem to recognize anything familiar about Edmund at all—not that he was a Rakshasa, not that he was the next incarnation of his best friend, and not that he was the son of his ultimate nemesis. As she looked back and forth between the two men, she found herself distracted by the idea of how different Edmund was from how Hanuman would imagine him. That, she realized, at its core, was the reason why so many of the Avatars of Light were drowning in lies. Because none of these men, not even Vibhishana, were ready for a change of such magnitude. And if she'd learned one thing in her time with Uma, it was that they were even less ready for Shakti's role in it all... whatever that would be. She was certain it would be pivotal.

She noticed her mind wandering, and tried to refocus on the thoughtful gift that Nellie Melba and Andrew (and Stanley, by proxy), had pulled together for her.

Andrew's deep baritone voice boomed menacingly as he and Nellie Melba dove deeper into the dramatic scene which Eleanor vaguely recognized as Puccini, but she could not understand a word of it. She tried to appreciate the musical and dramatic elements without being distracted by the plot or the lyrics, but she couldn't ignore a growing longing for Uma that went far deeper than the convenience of her linguistic abilities. She glanced over, and Vibhishana was still seated between Ravi and her mother, shaking his head silently with self-castigation, or, perhaps, a silent argument.

She sipped her cognac and reveled in the simple pleasure of Edmund's quiet support, while glancing at the children's enthralled expressions as the operatic scene evolved, and Nellie Melba began her famous aria.

"*Vissi d'arte... vissi d'amore...*"

Eleanor finally recognized that the scene was from *Tosca*, an Italian opera she'd particularly liked when she and Edmund had accompanied Oz and Yvie to see it at the Royal Opera in Perth several months earlier. As Nellie Melba finished off the climax of her aria, Eleanor hunkered down, readying herself for her favorite moment. But, as Nellie Melba kneeled before Andrew, begging for the life of her lover, Cavaradossi, Stanley joined them on stage, hobbling on in his best impression of a hunchbacked lackey, singing the few lines of Scarpia's servant with a quivering tenor that served the purpose, but was not really his shining glory as a performer. She couldn't help but giggle at the surprise, but as Andrew continued on with his impressively well-acted rendition of the villainous Scarpia, giving his orders to Stanley and then sending him off of the stage, Eleanor controlled her reaction and watched excitedly as Nellie Melba prepared herself to stab him.

"I hope it doesn't frighten the children," Edmund whispered into her ear.

"I'm sure they realize it's fictional, darling." She glanced over at their enraptured faces as Ruthy bit her lip nervously. The whole audience gasped as Nellie Melba pretended to stab Andrew.

"*Questo è il bacio di Tosca!*" she spat.

"*Aiuto... muoio! Soccorso! Muoio!*"

Eleanor worked hard not to cheer while the rest of the audience watched with baited breath as Andrew crawled across the stage, dying from his knife wound, and Nellie Melba gloated at her victory. It didn't matter that Eleanor didn't understand the words, perhaps because she now recognized the scene. The evil villain had tried to use Tosca's love against her, to blackmail her into sleeping with him to save her beloved, and Tosca hadn't let him. She'd killed him in cold blood, delivering a punishment that the justice system would never have enacted against the arrogant, abusive tyrant...

Her mind wandered to the question of which one of them would end up killing Jimmy Buchanan. Would it be Edmund? Vibhi? Herself? Or even her mother? That man had been trouble since the day Martha met him at the pub, and Eleanor, with no input from Uma or Shakti, wanted him dead.

She glanced over at the children. Ruthy was hiding her face in Charlie's shoulder, while Debbie and Howie were holding hands for support. She let the thought go. They couldn't do anything that would make those children's lives worse... now the question was, what would really make their lives better...

As Andrew collapsed, and Nellie Melba made her final ominous declaration, the audience cheered, and Ruthy looked up.

"Is it over?" she asked.

"Marvellous!" Edmund called. "Brava! Bravo!"

"*C'était marveilleux!*" Yvie seconded. "*Encore!*"

At her queue, the pianist immediately began playing an interlude, and Andrew and Nellie Melba both vacated the stage. Stanley rushed on, setting the stage with the chair and the small writing desk from his bedroom. When he was done, he squinted as he looked around the audience, finally spying Vibhishana in his seated position on the porch. He gestured for him to come on up.

Eleanor could feel Edmund tense with excitement at the unexpected turn as Vibhishana refused, and then glanced around at his attentive audience, sighed with resignation, rolled his shoulders, and jogged onto the stage, taking a seat at the writing desk. Eleanor could see him struggling to focus, but as she offered him a reassuring smile, he nodded to the accompanist to begin.

"Let's let Act Three of *Tosca* commence!" Andrew boomed jovially. "*Scrivete,* Cavaradossi!"

The string quartet began, along with the accompanist on the piano, and a clarinet. Eleanor looked around for the mystery musician, and then she clapped with excitement as she spied Mr. Montero (in his stern older form, wearing a full British butler's uniform) standing on the other side of the stage, dutifully playing his somber solo.

"Do you know him, dearest?" Edmund asked.

"He is the Patel's butler in Baroda," she whispered, quite satisfied with the truth of the answer. "He comes across a bit gruff, but he has a good heart."

"He's an excellent musician!"

"Now let's see how good Mr. Johnson is," Eleanor winked.

"*E lucevan le stelle...*" Vibhishana began with a deep, lyrical, unsettlingly powerful tenor voice. "*Ed olezzava la terra...*"

"Good lord," Edmund murmured. "Can he do everything?"

"*La terra stridea l'uscio...*"

"Not *everything*," Hanuman humphed.

Eleanor threw him a disapproving look, and settled back into Edmund's arms. They watched together as Vibhishana finished his aria, but as they cheered and clapped and shouted "bravo," he refused to acknowledge his audience at all. Instead, he rolled his shoulders, refocusing himself on his task, and jumped right into the continuation of the scene as Nellie Melba approached him.

Edmund sighed contentedly and kissed Eleanor's hand as she leaned back into his arms to watch the final scene.

She shouldn't have been surprised that Vibhishana was so excellent at acting, but she still felt a chill go down her spine as he and Tosca made their doomed plans. She appreciated his good sportsmanship in powering through the scene, regardless of his discomfort, and she appreciated even more that her appreciation didn't morph into lust as it always did with Uma at her core. She cuddled deeper into Edmund's arms, and winked as she noticed Debbie and Ruthy watching her.

They all sat silently enthralled as Vibhishana and Nellie Melba sang their love duet, and then Vibhishana marched off to the edge of the stage to his firing squad. The children screamed as Kuveni shot a blank at him and he collapsed. Edmund, fully in control of his faculties despite the loud noise (by the grace of Shakti… or Vishnu), leaned over to comfort them.

"Remember, it's all just pretend. Auntie Kate is helping them make the scene more dramatic. Cavaradossi and Tosca think that they have concocted a clever plan to escape from their evil enemy, but *he* has actually outwitted them."

"But he's dead!" Charlie whispered. "Tosca killed him!"

"That's true," Edmund agreed. "I suppose he got what was coming to him already, and now we have to watch the rest of the cards fall."

Ruthy got down from her chair and walked around the table with her finger in her mouth, and Eleanor smiled and sat up so that Ruthy could sit in her lap. As Debbie noticed her success, she came to sit in Eleanor's lap too, and Eleanor gathered them both up.

As the boys noticed the girls' success, they looked at each other, debating their next move, and then Edmund gestured for them to join him, offering them each a knee.

"Nine is too old to sit in a lap," Howie said as Charlie hopped up.

"Suit yourself," Edmund replied.

As Howie observed the others one more time, he gave in and took Edmund's right knee. Edmund began whispering his translations of the words for them.

"What's going to happen?" Debbie whispered. "Are they going to escape?"

"Do you really want to know?" Eleanor asked.

"I dunno. Not if it's bad, I guess," she admitted.

"Just watch then."

"That means it's bad," Charlie pointed out.

"*Mario! Mario! Morto! Morto!*" Nellie Melba sang desperately.

Stanley and Andrew sang the parts of the villagers from the side of the stage as Tosca leaned over Cavaradossi, realizing he was actually dead.

"Oh no!" Debbie exclaimed. "Poor Tosca!"

"Poor Cavaradossi!" Charlie added. "Is he really dead?"

"*Colla mia! O Scarpia, avanti a Dio!*" Nellie Melba hopped off the back of the stage with a dramatic swoon, and the music stopped.

"Was that the end? What happened to Tosca?!" Ruthy squeaked.

"She died," Howie informed her. "She killed herself."

"That's a terrible ending!" Debbie exclaimed. "I hate it!"

Eleanor laughed. "It's called a tragedy, darlings. We learn different things about humanity when the endings are bad. We see a different side of ourselves than we would if the endings were always happy."

Ruthy burst into tears.

"What's wrong?" Eleanor asked as she kissed her forehead.

"What if our story's a tragedy?!"

Eleanor sighed. "I might cry at the question myself if I think too hard about it. My darlings, your story isn't a tragedy. Look at where you are right now, with the angels by your side protecting you. Usually, if an angel pops in for the rescue, the story isn't a tragedy."

"It is called a *deus ex macchina*," Edmund informed them. "When the writers get themselves so mixed up that only God," he rolled his eyes, "can save their characters. I've always found it to be a cheap ploy myself."

"Darling, we're comforting the children, not teaching them a tutorial on literary criticism," Eleanor admonished him gently.

"You're right, dearest. You all know that we won't let anything happen to you now, don't you?"

"Yes," they agreed, although Eleanor could hear that they weren't entirely convinced.

As Nellie Melba, Andrew, Vibhishana, and Stanley all took their final bows, Eleanor and Edmund returned to cheering, and then the string quartet picked up again, returning to a waltz. Oz offered Yvie his hand and guided her onto the dancefloor, and Eleanor and Edmund cheered them on as Kate and Percy joined them, followed by Jaap Sahib and Jyoti, and Ravi and Shruti.

"How beautiful," Eleanor sighed. "There is so much love here tonight."

"Did you like it?!" Stanley asked as he skipped over to her with Andrew's hand in his. "We've been working on it all afternoon!"

"All of you?" she asked as she eyed Vibhishana, who followed them slowly, almost at a hobble. "Does that mean you were already here earlier when I called you about my mother's plight?"

He cleared his throat. "Er... yes. It does. I hadn't planned to participate, but then I stumbled upon Dame Melba and Andrew here practicing Scarpia's murder scene, and at the time it seemed like a good idea to join them. I didn't realize how complicated the night would be." He threw her a desperate look as he eyed Edmund's close proximity to Hanuman.

"Vibhi, you'll have to tell me later how you became such an accomplished musician," Hanuman humphed.

"V.B.?" Edmund asked astutely. "Are those your real initials?"

Vibhishana looked like he might explode with anger as he threw a furious look at Hanuman, and then he looked like he might collapse from the strain of keeping himself under control. He took a seat beside Eleanor and poured himself a tall glass of cognac, downing it in one Rakshasa gulp.

Eleanor offered Stanley and Andrew her silent congratulations, and then nodded subtly, suggesting that they join the other dancers. Stanley beamed happily as he took his position in the woman's role, and they began their waltz.

"Well, are they?" Edmund pushed.

"You know as well as I do, my boy, it isn't time to discuss my many names."

"Victor Bernard?" Edmund guessed cheekily. "Vincent Benjamin? Vaughn Barnaby? Vladimir Beowolf?"

Vibhishana put his arms on the table and buried his head in his hands. "I can't tell you, my boy. I mustn't. I mustn't. I mustn't…"

"Are you alright?" Edmund asked as he noticed Vibhishana's genuine discomfort.

"I'm feeling rather off, to be honest. Please don't mind me, Edmund. I'm a bit tipsy, and it's causing all sorts of problems that I'd rather not discuss."

"Tipsy? Surely not!" Edmund exclaimed.

"Tipsy?!" Hanuman seconded. "But how?!"

Vibhishana didn't look up as he answered them. "I didn't anticipate the feeling myself. I was very unwise to put myself in this position."

"Do I need to worry about that?" Edmund asked. "I've never reached a point when alcohol impeded my faculties."

Vibhishana finally ripped his head out of his hands to address him. "No, my boy. You don't. You and I are different, remember?"

"If you say so," Edmund replied, unconvinced. "Say… are your eyes brown? I could have sworn they were blue."

Vibhishana replanted his head in his hands. "What can I say? They're brown now."

Hanuman stood up. "Eleanor, I think this is my queue to leave. If you don't mind, though, I'd like a private word before I go?"

Eleanor coaxed the girls off her lap and squeezed Edmund's shoulder as she stood up. "I'll be right back. If you two men can survive without me?"

Vibhishana only grunted, while Edmund reached forward concernedly to rub his shoulder. "Good lord, you're burning up! Perhaps you'd like some water?"

"Yes, Edmund. Please, I need water," Vibhishana agreed. "And some of that Vanara korma while it lasts."

As Edmund got up to find him some, and Rohit took Eleanor's vacated seat, Mae rallied the children to the dessert table. "Now, who wants some cake?"

"I do!" they all shouted in unison.

Eleanor guided Hanuman around the back porch of the house, to a wicker lounging area that was twinkling with hundreds of candles interspersed amongst the flower petals of elaborate rangoli designs that were spread out across all of the surfaces. She poured herself another steep glass of cognac from a dusty bottle that had just appeared on the side table with two glasses. She made a mental note to thank Kuveni for it later.

As she took her first sip, she gestured for Hanuman to sit in the chair across from her. "Don't you want some? It will soften the blow."

"What blow?"

"Whatever it is you wanted to say privately. I assume it must be unpleasant if you couldn't say it in front of the crowd?"

She took another sip, and he eyed the bottle. "I don't need to end up like Vibhi. He's embarrassing himself in front of your entire party."

Eleanor laughed. "I doubt you're at any risk of that."

"Alcohol does affect Vanaras, you know."

"No, I didn't know that. I thought Uma's temperament was what had affected mine."

"Uma is the Goddess. Alcohol has no effect on divinity."

"Huh." Eleanor took another sip, relishing the dull warmth again.

Hanuman gave in and poured himself a modest serving.

"Well, my friend, what did you fly all the way down here to say on my birthday?"

He paused for a long moment, choosing his words carefully. "I was going to say something I shouldn't have. Now I'm stuck here embarrassing myself."

"Well, Uma isn't here now. You've just got Eleanor MacLeod Marriner to spill your guts to. Feel free to say what you were going to say."

"I was going to implore her to find another vessel," he admitted begrudgingly. "A married *firang* is not suitable."

Eleanor laughed. "I promise you, my friend, I am more suitable than many other choices. But what makes you think that you are an appropriate judge of these things?"

"I've been around for a long time. I'm a *chirangivi*. I've guided humans for millennia, and Uma has only had six hundred years of experience."

"Well, my friend, I've only had forty short years of a mostly human life, but I reckon I've had more experience with madness and romance than both of you combined, and I think that you should think about why you're really upset about Uma's choice."

"What do you mean?"

"I was a nurse to the mentally ill for decades. I have an excellent sense for when people are lying to themselves. And you, my friend, are lying to yourself right now."

"She should focus on her divinity! It has nothing to do with me!"

Eleanor raised her eyebrows skeptically. "Really? Nothing? Then why are you so jealous of Vibhishana and my husband?"

131

"I'm not!"

Eleanor stared him down until he conceded.

"Maybe I'm a little jealous. I love Uma, and I always have."

"I know, my friend. And she knows too. But, Hanuman, she's dead, and I'm not her. You couldn't control her choices when she was alive, and you certainly can't control mine now. Why don't you free yourself from this unrequited longing? I can see how sad it's making you."

"I'm not sad!" She stared him down again. "Okay, maybe I'm sad."

Eleanor reached forward and squeezed his hand supportively. "Acknowledging the truth is the first step in recovery."

"Recovery from what?"

"Trauma, my friend. Was it not traumatic when the only female left of your species refused to marry you? It is natural for you to feel a great loss at what could have been."

He contemplated the statement for a long time, and then he took another sip of the cognac. "Seeing your children tonight was hard. Harder than I wanted to admit. It was like they should have been mine."

"They aren't my children. They are my sisters' children. We've rescued them from their abusive parents who were starving them and lashing scars into their backs."

"Good lord," he whispered. He thought about the idea as he took another long sip of the cognac. "But your husband was so kind to them. It was clear that he loves them, and they aren't even his children?"

"He is one of the kindest men I've ever had the pleasure of meeting. His capacity for love is something everyone on Earth should aspire to."

"I suppose that's something," he sighed. "I really am sorry I crashed your party."

"To tell Uma that I wasn't worthy?"

He looked down sheepishly. "It's even worse when you put it like that."

Eleanor smiled. "I forgive you."

"You are too forgiving, my lady. I suppose I will just have to resign myself to being alone. It is something Uma could do for six hundred years, so I suppose I should be able to do it too."

"Why?" Eleanor asked curiously. "This form is quite passable, you know. Your acting could use some improvement, but I wouldn't guess you weren't human just by looking at you."

"Do you really mean it? You don't think my features are too smooth?"

She leaned in to examine him more closely. "Perhaps a few more wrinkles on the edges of your eyes, and some deeper pores. But I'm sure Vibhi will give you more pointers. You've already stooped to asking a Rakshasa for help," she winked. "I didn't think I'd see the day."

"Vibhi isn't a real Rakshasa," he reiterated the incorrect opinion he'd voiced several times before. "He's practically human."

"Are you sure about that? I think he quite likes changing his forms, and I'm certain he enjoys making his clothing."

"That is not what makes someone a Rakshasa," he scoffed. "Vibhi isn't evil. He doesn't use his false beauty to seduce humans so he can tear them to shreds and laugh at their pain for sport."

"It sounds like you're describing a vampire. Or Surpanakha, I suppose. I think she was beautiful once…"

"You haven't seen her, have you? Please, Eleanor, take this!" He reached into his pocket and handed her the figurine she'd given back to him after she'd summoned Rama to save Jaap Sahib. "Surpanakha will kill you!"

Eleanor closed it back into his hand. "She will not."

"She's bloody mad out of her mind, Eleanor." He pushed it back into her hand. "Please, don't let anything happen to you and Uma."

"My friend, do you know who Surpanakha worships?"

"The King of bloody Darkness!"

Eleanor reiterated her return of the talisman as she squeezed it back into his hand. "She worships Durga, my friend. She will do nothing to the Avatar of Durga."

"She does terrible things to those she loves, Eleanor."

"I know, my friend. Oh, do I know. But still, I don't need you to rescue me. I defeated Haranyakashipu last year. I'm not worried about Surpanakha anymore."

"That bastard?! But Lord Vishnu came to Earth as Narasimha and killed him!"

"No, Narasimha banished him to the other side of the earth. Do you know where he ended up? I'll give you one guess."

"In Australia?"

"Excellent powers of deduction, my friend."

Hanuman shrugged at her patronizing comment as he begrudgingly returned the talisman to his pocket.

"You never answered my question before," Eleanor returned to the point as she felt the pull of the rest of her party luring her back. "Why do you have to be alone? You wanted Uma to find a virtuous unmarried brahmin girl to be her vessel. Isn't that so she could marry you as a human?"

"No!" he exclaimed. She stared him down again. "Maybe."

"Is that why you became a guard for the Maharaja of Baroda? So you could woo her in her human form?"

"No!" he exclaimed. She eyed him, unconvinced. "No, I mean it this time. I was feeling too disconnected from the human world. The last time we tried to defeat Ravana, we were too outdated in our techniques. Technology had changed too much, and we were trying to fight a modern war with our ancient weapons. I wanted to brush up on my skills, and Vibhi is the only one I know these days who lives fully in the human world. I told him about my problem, and he suggested I ease my way back into the human world in his presence, so he could help me. He's been doing an adequate job, I suppose."

"What about Rama? He isn't there with you, is he?" Eleanor felt a pang of panic for poor Padma.

He rolled his eyes. "We've parted ways for the moment. He went to Africa to chase a dubious lead on Sita, and I refused to go with him. It is good for us to be apart from time to time; it keeps us grounded."

"I think that is a very mature attitude, my friend. I'm proud of you."

As he smiled with pride at her compliment, producing an expression that looked distinctly ape-like (although she couldn't articulate exactly why), Eleanor contemplated the unexpected twists. She wasn't sure what was more surprising—that Rama and Hanuman had decided to part ways, or that Vibhi had invited Hanuman to live in the city of the Rakshasa Patels. She didn't have the energy to worry about it. Certainly, he was executing a well-thought-out plan, a much better plan than the wild whims that he gave into when she was around.

"Once you've settled in, why don't you seek a human woman for companionship?" Eleanor suggested. "There are plenty to choose from, and you can get some wooing tips from Rama."

He humphed. "We couldn't grow old together. We wouldn't be able to have children. What's the point? I'd be ruining her life."

"Not every woman wants those things, you know. Lots of women have a different vision for their lives, with adventure, and love, and meaning beyond children. Besides, you could always adopt."

"Adopt? A human child?"

"Why not? That may be what we'll end up doing with my sisters' children…" She tried not to let the thought overwhelm her as it fully formed in her mind for the first time. "And Hanu, I promise you, I won't be sad to skip the pain of pregnancy. I'm sure

135

I'm not the only woman who feels that way. You just need to keep an eye out. Let love come to you, and see where it takes you."

"But, Eleanor, you and your husband will age and die like human parents should. How will my future wife and I explain to our aging human children why Papa looks younger than them? Besides, I will find it too distracting from my sacred duties."

"That doesn't stop Rama," Eleanor countered. "I don't know why you should let it stop you."

Hanuman thought through the idea seriously, sipping his cognac until shuffling footsteps approached, and he stood up as he glanced at the culprit.

"This has been an enlightening conversation that I must think about more. Happy birthday, Eleanor."

She followed his gaze as Mae and Rohit escorted Vibhishana around the side of the house towards her. He was leaning heavily on both of them, and he didn't look well.

"Blimey," she whispered as she realized that while he was still donning his sparkling violet sherwani, he was now using his ancient Christian form.

"Vibhi?" Hanuman said questioningly as he shook his head with disapproval. "You'll give us all away, you fool. Shapeshifting at a party like it's a trick for entertainment? I don't know what you ever saw in him, Uma."

"I think it's time for you to go, my friend." She took Hanuman's hands into hers. "Take with you Shakti's blessings."

"Thank you for your hospitality, and I hope that you'll remember who the drunken fool was tonight, even if I am a bit petty to think so."

He pulled her into a hug, and then glanced again at Vibhi. With a smug salute, he jogged into the vineyards, and with a flash of light, he ascended into the starry night sky.

"Eleanor, I can't do it anymore," Vibhishana whispered as Rohit and Mae helped him onto the wicker couch beside her. "Shakti is very unhappy. She's burning me from the inside out. You

136

must take her back. Her power wasn't meant for me; it was meant for you."

"You really do look like hell," she said as she grabbed his hand and intertwined her fingers with his.

She looked into his soulful brown eyes, and as they flashed the green of Shakti's divine power, she felt the heat of Uma's soul rush back into her through their shared connection. She gasped and collapsed onto Mae, fighting back a moment of nausea. The hole in the core of her being was again pulsating with the morbid warmth she'd come to love, and she sighed with relief.

I missed you, Uma.

And I you, my child.

I suppose the greatest gift you really gave me was helping me realize how much I missed you when you were away.

Shakti works in mysterious ways.

As she opened her eyes, Vibhishana was collapsed next to her in Rohit's arms.

"I'm sorry, Eleanor," he whispered. "We should have realized it was a terrible idea and aborted the plan as soon as I lost control of my wits."

"What did you give away? Did you tell Edmund everything? Did you change your form in front of him?"

"I don't know, Eleanor. I started blacking out." He looked at his hands, and then felt his thick beard. "Shiva's wrath, I've made a mess. I don't even know how I got this way. How are you feeling?"

He squeezed her hand, and she felt Uma stir, although she could feel that even Uma was fatigued enough by the experience to settle back in without her typical burst of lust.

"I'm feeling… whole again," she said as she lifted her weight off of Mae's shoulder and rubbed her aching head. "And sober. I suppose that shouldn't be a surprise. Divinity's no fun at all."

He lay down on the couch with his feet on Rohit and his head on Eleanor's lap, covering his eyes with his arm. "I've never felt this weak. Not once in my entire life. It was foolish, Eleanor. If something dangerous happens right now, I won't be able to defend you."

"Then it's a good thing I can defend myself, isn't it?"

"It is." He grunted with pain. "Mae, can I trouble you for some red wine?"

"Really? Are you sure that's wise?" she asked.

"It calms me, Mae. I need something to calm my nerves before I go back out there and manage my mess."

She nodded her agreement and stood up, but as she started walking, Eleanor's heart almost exploded.

"Oh, hello, Mrs. MacLeod. Can I help you?" Mae's sweet tone didn't give away a hint of panic.

Eleanor scrambled up, dropping Vibhishana's head on the cushion.

"Mum?!"

"Yer husband asked me to come get ye. He's puttin' the bairns to bed with a story, and he thought ye'd like te join 'em."

"Yes. I would." She moved to escape, hoping her mother hadn't seen anything incriminating, but her mother grabbed her wrist.

"Ye'rnt dead, are ye, Ellie?"

"I'm sorry, what?"

"Yer one of 'em now, aren't ye? That's how ye called Kate with a prayer?" Eleanor didn't have a response, but as Vibhishana stirred, pulling himself up to try to intervene, Eleanor's mother looked over at him. "It's a dangerous thing lovin' the Lord's son, I reckon. And an even more dangerous thing with the Lord lovin' you. Did He bring ye up to the Pearly Gates before he sent ye back, or did He make ye one of His angels right here on Earth?"

Eleanor stopped for a panicked moment as she decided what to do, and then she grabbed her mother's hand.

I'm not dead, Mum. It's just really, really complicated.

Her mother patted her hand. "Don't waste yer energy comin' up wit another lie fer me, Ellie. I'm just glad yer here. I'll miss ye when I'm down in Hell wit yer Da, waitin' fer yer sisters te join us. Now go on up to the bairns. Yer husband's waitin' fer ye."

Eleanor took the excuse. She tried not to panic as she heard Vibhishana approaching her mother, and she left the explanation to him. She waved and offered her apologies as the remaining party guests meandered about the abandoned dancefloor. The string quartet was almost done packing up, and Nellie Melba was sitting with her accompanist, sipping a glass of fine cognac on the porch swing.

"Happy Birthday, Eleanor daaaarling!" she sang with a flourish.

Eleanor blew her a kiss. "It was the happiest!"

She wished she could join them for a relaxed evening chat before they headed right back to Melbourne, but she knew that she had a much more important audience awaiting her arrival.

Kuveni must have noticed her struggle. "Don't worry, Eleanor dearest," she called from the mostly-cleared banquet table. "Everyone will still be here tomorrow for your birthday brunch."

Shruti stroked Sheranee's tummy and shooed Eleanor inside, while Ravi threw some leftover roti to the dogs, who were too attentive to their snack to even notice her.

Eleanor tried to let go of her many worries as she climbed the stairs and followed the lulling voice of her husband. She peeked in the door of one of the newly-designated children's bedrooms, and all four of them were dressed in new flannel pajamas, cuddled around him on the bed with heavy eyes as he read from a very large illustrated book that looked almost like a medieval manuscript.

"Join us, dearest. I just started *The Arabian Nights*. This is the first book I ever read."

Debbie snuggled closer into Ruthy to make room for her.

He returned to reading, and Eleanor chuckled. "Darling, did you know that you're reading in Arabic?"

He looked down at the children. "Am I really reading in Arabic?"

"It sounds like when Gramma reads in Gaelic," Charlie whispered sleepily.

"Darling, perhaps tonight you can read in Arabic, and when the children are more awake, you can translate it for them? I like just listening to the sound of your voice too."

She snuggled into his nook and gathered Debbie and Ruthy into hers, and she sighed. Somehow, despite the absurd trials of the day, she was feeling more content than she had ever felt in her life. As Uma's subtle pulsating power beat in sync with Edmund's, Eleanor took a deep breath and let herself enjoy the moment.

It was, as it turned out, the perfect way to celebrate her last birthday.

PART TWO
A TASTE

CHAPTER 8 – LIFE GOES ON

Eleanor awoke groggily in the bright midday sunlight, struggling to open her eyes after the intensity of the prior day, but the outlines of four red-headed children staring at her brought her right to attention.

"Auntie Ellie?"

"I told you not to poke her!"

"Uncle Edmund?"

"Please don't be cross!"

"Wake up!"

Eleanor forced herself awake, and gasped with panic as she got her bearings and looked down, hoping desperately, even in her twilight state, that she was properly dressed to be seen by the children. She sighed with relief at her exceptional foresight the night before putting on her silk pajamas after she and Edmund had awoken sometime in early morning and tiptoed back to their room. Now, she just needed to call a locksmith…

"Please don't be cross, Auntie Ellie!" Debbie implored. "It's eleven o'clock, and Father Johnson said he needs to leave soon!"

"Your birthday brunch is getting cold!" Charlie added.

"Kate said we can't have another portion until we get you to join us!" Howie chimed in.

"How many portions have you had already?" Eleanor asked as she rubbed her eyes.

"Three," they answered in unison.

She chuckled. "Then I guess we're late to our own party again, aren't we?"

"Dearest?" Edmund murmured. He sucked in his awakening Rakshasa breath and sat up. He glanced at the children, then at her, and then at his pajamas, and he smiled. "Good morning, mates."

"Good morning, Uncle Edmund," they replied.

"Do you remember where we left off in the story?"

"It was in Arabic," Charlie reminded him.

He laughed. "So it was. Perhaps later today we'll have a little afternoon siesta together in the library, and I'll read it to you in English this time. Would you like that?"

"What's a siesta?" Debbie asked.

"It's an after-lunch nap," Eleanor explained. "They often do it in hot countries, where it's very unpleasant to go outside in the middle of the day."

"Is it hot here?" Ruthy asked.

"It's hot enough!" Eleanor exclaimed as she tickled her. Ruthy exploded into giggles, and Eleanor rallied herself into action. "Now, why don't you all go tell Auntie Kate that we're coming down right now, and that we've agreed that you can have your fourth portion."

"Aye!" they agreed. Charlie, Debbie, and Howie stampeded out of the room, but Ruthy stayed behind with her finger planted nervously in her mouth.

"What's wrong, Ruthy?" Eleanor asked.

"Mammy isn't going to like that we're gone. Da is going to be very cross."

Eleanor glanced at Edmund before responding to her. "Will your father do something to her? Is that why she's been letting him and Uncle Fergus be mean to you? Is she scared of your Da?"

"No!" Ruthy squeaked. She ran out of the room after her siblings, leaving the door wide open.

"Blimey," Eleanor murmured. "It just keeps getting better and better…"

"What do you think we should do? Do you think your sisters are in danger? Are their husbands that beastly?"

Eleanor thought about the question for a long time. "I don't know. Those bludgers were never particularly nice, and some amount of bullying would explain why my sisters let them get away with their shenanigans. But I just don't understand why my sisters wouldn't have skipped out in the night. That's why I was writing the cheques directly to them—so they'd always have a choice."

Edmund's eyes turned black. "I want to kill those evil men, Eleanor."

Eleanor kissed him. "I want to kill them too, darling. But we must focus on what's good for the children. Right now, being stable and loving is the best thing we can do for them. Revenge and punishment can wait."

He closed his eyes and whispered his mantras, and his eyes returned to their human hazel. He kissed her back. "You are a bastion of reason, my dearest thistle."

As Eleanor heard footsteps on the stairs, she hopped out of bed and closed the door. "The world is waiting."

She skipped to her closet and collected a comfortable pair of white linen trousers with a matching white silk shirt along with a half-sleeved grass green brocade jacket that contrasted nicely with the otherwise stark color scheme. She grabbed a gold belt with a jade dragon as the buckle that seemed wonderfully Chinese, and then she tossed Edmund one of his many grey wool suits.

He pulled her into a kiss. "You're even more beautiful today, Eleanor. The acceptance you've given these children is so beautiful to watch."

"Likewise, darling." She kissed him back, and then, as she felt a pang of arousal, she pulled away. "They're waiting for us."

She dressed unceremoniously, hopping into the bathroom for her daily ablutions while Edmund finished up buttoning his vest, and then she did her rudimentary makeup, tied her hair into a loose braid, and rushed back into the closet to gather up one of her many sunhats, this time a matching, wide-brimmed white sunhat with a cute bunch of green leaves and a bird nestled on the brim. She grabbed a pair of sunglasses and green sandals that matched the jacket, and then followed Edmund out.

"Happy birthday!" her audience cheered as she and Edmund squinted in the late morning sun. Kuveni hadn't been exaggerating the night before—everyone from her surprise party was gathered at a long banquet table chatting and eating amicably, including Mr. Montero, Nellie Melba, Stanley, Andrew, and even their accompanist.

"Come sit, lovebirds!" Kuveni exclaimed as she guided them to the center of the table, next to Oz and Yvie, and across from Vibhishana, Mae, and Shruti.

Eleanor's mother watched them silently from the far end of the table, chomping on a carpenter's pie.

As soon as they sat down, Mélusine brought them two full Scottish breakfasts.

"This looks scrumptious!" Edmund exclaimed as he cracked his knuckles and dove right in.

"Thank you," Eleanor said distractedly as she watched Ravi Bidkar stare with a new level of fear and awe at Vibhishana, despite the fact that he had returned to wearing his modest vicar's habit, and was drinking down a cup of coffee at an admirable approximation of human speed.

I guess that cat's out of the bag...

146

Vibhi and I were forced to confide in Sri Bidkar last night. We emphasized the need for discretion.

Like that's ever worked with him!

It was a foolish position we put ourselves in, my child. The fall-out could have been much worse.

Eleanor ended her silent conversation as she noticed Ravi's attention move to her. She smiled politely and then stuffed a large forkful of eggs into her mouth.

Vibhishana ate a few bites of a carpenter's pie in front of him, until he gathered his courage and leaned forward confidingly. "I debated skipping out while you were both still asleep, but I couldn't add another rude offense to my long docket of embarrassments. I'm sorry for my behavior last night. I'm still trying to unravel everything that I did."

Edmund stopped eating to lean forward and gaze at Vibhishana's features, and Eleanor felt Vibhishana cringe with panic.

"I knew it!" Edmund declared triumphantly. "Your eyes *are* blue. Did you change them last night for the performance? The brown with the kohl made you a very convincing Italian opera star."

Vibhishana smiled, not giving away his excessive level of relief. "I must remember that nothing gets past you, my boy."

"It made me wonder, actually..." Edmund hedged.

Vibhishana hid his discomfort. "Tell me, Edmund. What did it make you wonder?"

"It occurred to me on a prior occasion that perhaps you are a Parsi. That would explain the connections we have to India, and our fair skin. You looked more like a Parsi last night with the brown eyes. Were you using lenses to produce the color?"

Vibhishana looked mostly relieved, but Eleanor could see a hint of disappointment in his brow. She couldn't tell whether it was aimed at Edmund's return to his incorrect obsession with the idea that Vibhi was his father, or his perfectly mundane explanation for the phenomenon that took all the effort out of Vibhishana's lies.

"I'm not a Parsi, Edmund, but our family does have quite a long history in India. In fact, I was born there." He took another big bite of the carpenter's pie, and then continued before Edmund could ask him a more difficult follow-up question. "Yes, I was using lenses. I'm glad they had the effect I was going for."

Edmund contemplated his next question carefully. "Do you think the lenses are what drove you batty last night? I had several soldiers over the years go a bit mad when they'd left them in too long. I won't believe you if you tell me it was simply too much tippling. You were the one who told me that alcohol doesn't affect us. Remember? On the boat from Bombay to England that very first time after you collected me from Abdul Barr?"

"I do remember it. That was when I realized what a beautiful person you'd already become, Edmund. It made me so happy." Vibhishana stared nostalgically before him, and then closed his eyes for a moment of silent contemplation, or perhaps conversation.

Edmund reached forward to feel Vibhishana's forehead like a doting father, pausing to feel for the familiar pulsating warmth produced by his copious pots of coffee. "Your fever is gone."

Vibhishana gently took Edmund's hand off of his forehead as he opened his eyes. "I'm fine now, my boy. The fit has passed. I just hope that I didn't do anything too shocking in front of you."

"Like what?" Edmund asked.

Vibhishana chuckled. "If you have to ask, I don't have to worry, my boy. I'm sorry I made a spectacle of myself at your party, Eleanor."

"Well, we got to watch most of an opera between the three of you. That was quite an entertaining spectacle that I never expected to see," Eleanor reassured him.

"It is a privilege that I don't take lightly to perform with musicians of that caliber. I've never done it before, and I probably will not do it again." He nodded down the table and raised his coffee pot to Andrew and Nellie Melba, who both amicably toasted back.

"Why not? I think the Met could use you!" Edmund suggested half-jokingly.

"That is not my fate, Edmund. I have other things to be doing with my time."

"Such as?"

Vibhishana smiled. "I'm glad that you aren't afraid to ask me questions anymore, my boy. But we have reached the point in our conversation when I will be forced to give you unsatisfying answers."

"But surely you can tell me just one thing that you do? Percy is an inventor. Kate is a nanny. They are both excellent chefs…"

Vibhishana threw Kuveni a look of intense disapproval.

"Illa described Kate's position as a matrika last night," Eleanor explained on Kuveni's behalf.

"I see," Vibhishana said as he worked to control his reaction.

"So, isn't there something you can tell me? Or shall you remain a renaissance man of leisure, singing opera with the divas and waltzing the night away in the arms of the most graceful dancer in India?" Edmund threw Shruti a wink. "Or perhaps we shall just pretend you're a simple vicar, puttering around all day and night in some rural rectory of the Church of England?"

Vibhishana debated his response as he ate several more bites of the carpenter's pie.

"I am a leader, Edmund. A silent one. Not one who stands before crowds and riles them up, but one who helps humans find it within themselves to be better and kinder and more accepting than they are without my guidance. These talents I've demonstrated in your presence, these frivolities, are wonderful distractions from the heavy weight of my burden. It is important for people like us to embrace the beauty of life on Earth when we can, so that when we must make difficult choices, and when we must endure excruciating pain, like you did in the trenches, we have something to keep us from drowning."

"You make it sound like enduring excruciating pain is a given," Edmund said nervously.

"My boy, when you have lived as long as I have, you will realize that life consists of cycles. Destruction is necessary for rebirth, no matter how unpleasant it is to endure. It is inevitable in one form or another."

"There was nothing necessary about that wretched war," Edmund countered. "It was purely pointless pain."

Vibhishana reached forward and squeezed Edmund's hand. "Sometimes it takes centuries, or even millennia, to understand the point, my boy."

As Edmund moved to argue, he noticed that the entire table had dissolved into silence to listen in on their conversation, and he blushed with embarrassment. "This topic is too solemn for Eleanor's birthday brunch." He forced himself into cheer. "Shall we play a game of some sort when we've finished digesting? Cricket, perhaps?"

"I wish I could play cricket," Charlie murmured.

"Me too," Debbie seconded.

"Not yet, mates. You need at least a few more days of getting stronger before pushing yourselves that much," Oz reminded them apologetically.

They looked down resignedly at their half-empty plates.

"I bet we can fit in a game of catch later with Uncle Edmund and Auntie Ellie, though," Oz added.

They looked slightly happier at the prospect, but still defeated.

"How about a friendly game of polo? That should be fun for our audience to watch," Eleanor suggested. As soon as the words came out of her mouth, she was excited by the prospect. They'd been caring for the polo ponies Lord Grimby had left there since they'd bought his rental property from its thrilled elderly owner, and the totally uncompetitive matches she and Edmund and Oz had been playing to keep the ponies in shape hadn't been fully satisfying. "Do we have enough people for two teams? We have six ponies who would love to play."

Stanley looked away, and she chuckled. "Don't worry, volunteers only." She glanced around, and each guest demurred. "Really? None of you want to play? Are Edmund and Oz and I really that intimidating? I promise there will be no angry throwing of mallets or yelling of epithets." She finally landed her attention on Vibhi.

"Do you want me to play?" he asked with genuine surprise. "I thought you'd suggest it was time for me to leave."

"Do you know how to play?" Edmund asked with growing excitement.

"Oh yes," Vibhishana agreed. "Did you know that it used to be the game of Indian royalty?"

"Then it's a good thing I'm the emperor, isn't it?" Edmund winked.

Eleanor could feel their cheerful excitement brewing. Somehow, knowing that the longing for Vibhi that had plagued her for years was entirely Uma freed her of most of her guilt, allowing her to relegate the feeling into the depths of her being alongside her Celtic temper and her other mostly controlled unpleasant emotions.

"Alright, we have me, Edmund and Oz on one team, and Father Johnson…"

"Vincent Barnaby," Edmund interjected with a wink. Vibhi did not understand his joke.

"Anyone else?" Eleanor looked around expectantly.

"I can play, my lady," Jaap Sahib volunteered. "I used to play when I was in the Indian Army."

"Excellent! That should balance things a bit…" Eleanor glanced around until Kuveni stood up to volunteer. "Excellent, Kate!"

"Mammy said that only rich people play polo," Debbie whispered.

"Sshhh," Howie hissed.

"Rich people who have nothing better to do," Ruthy added.

"Well then, we'd better prove Mammy wrong!" Eleanor said as she stood up. "We have plenty of better things to do, and we're going to play anyway."

She led the players across the massive lawn to the stables. "Choose your mounts," she said cheerfully.

She hopped up onto Stella, the mare she'd become closest to over the last several months, and without bothering to change her clothes, she rode right out onto the vast lawn that Lord Grimby had had groomed just for the sport. She was glad that the prior day's weather had been warm enough to dry out the mud that had been lingering after their wet autumn.

Edmund rode up beside her and handed her a mallet, and then she glanced over at their audience, who were repositioning themselves onto the back porch to watch. She waved, and they waved back.

"Are they going to ride the horses while they play? I want to play!" Charlie exclaimed.

"Soon, my boy. We will teach you how to ride first," Edmund called.

Oz lined up beside Edmund as Jaap Sahib lined up beside Kuveni and Vibhishana.

"Shruti, who do we root for?" Ravi asked with genuine concern. He lowered his voice. "Lord Shiva and Lord Vishnu should be on the same side. It always ends badly when they're working against each other!"

"You take one, I'll take the other, Father. Then they will balance out."

Mélusine approached with the ball in her right hand. "Let the game begin."

She threw it up in the air, and backed away. Vibhi and Edmund both lunged forward. As they distracted each other, Eleanor swooped in and whacked it up the field, and the game was off to a thrilling start. She leaned in and let her hat fly off her head as she raced to intercept her own pass. Kuveni followed her, and Eleanor giggled as she heard the children cheering both of them on.

"Come on, Auntie Ellie!"

"Auntie Kate, get it!"

Eleanor loved most of all that the girls were watching two women compete alongside the men. When she was a girl, secretly riding her father's thoroughbreds, she'd always envisioned herself as one of the jockeys until a particularly miserly stable-hand had pointed out to her that all of the jockeys were, and would always be, men. She pictured him looming over her with his smug smile as he squelched her dream, and she whacked the ball all the way up the field.

"Nice shot, my dear!" Kuveni exclaimed as she continued to race alongside her.

As they reached the goal, Kuveni swung her mallet backwards and whacked the ball back across the field, over Oz and Edmund's heads, straight to Jaap Sahib's position without even turning her head.

"No Yakshini cheating!" Eleanor exclaimed as she turned around and headed to the other side of the field.

"Who, me?!" Kuveni asked with feigned offense.

They laughed as they raced each other back to the middle of the field.

Edmund reached Jaap Sahib, engaging him in a friendly chase and blocking his attempt to score by riding him off and slamming the ball to Oz, who picked it up and leaned in as he raced away from Vibhishana.

Eleanor relaxed and let herself give into the fun of the mostly mundane match as the ball went back and forth across the field, from player to player, and almost into the goal, until she could feel the horses waning, and Vibhishana went in for a final shot. As he made contact with the ball, the head of his mallet flew off, disappearing into the vineyards beyond, far past where a normal human swing would send it.

Eleanor laughed as all of the players slowed down to a trot.

"I reckon that ends the match, mates!" Oz exclaimed.

"I suppose our equipment wasn't really designed to be used with such force," Edmund conceded as he trotted up beside Vibhishana and offered him a friendly handshake. "It was a pleasure."

"The horses were getting tired anyway," Eleanor said as she trotted back towards the stables. "You did an excellent job, my friend," she whispered into Stella's ear. She walked her around until her heart-rate slowed to normal, and then she hopped off and guided her into the stall.

The other players followed, except Vibhishana. Eleanor focused on treating Stella's legs with poultice, rather than stewing about his absence.

"You were glorious, dearest," Edmund swooned as he joined her. "And, you, Kate! What a pleasure it was to play with you!"

"Oh Edmund darling, you are such a consummate sportsman," Kuveni said as she followed Eleanor's lead, treating her horse's muscles with the muddy mixture.

"Auntie Ellie, you were biordinar!" Debbie exclaimed as the children skipped into the stables to join them.

"Auntie Kate, you almost scored!" Howie exclaimed.

"Uncle Edmund, you hit the ball sooooo far!" Charlie added.

"What are you doing to the horses?" Ruthy asked less enthusiastically.

"We're rubbing their muscles with poultice, to help them recover from their vigorous exercise," Eleanor explained. "Do you want to help us?"

The children gathered around and covered their hands in the muddy clay.

"Do rich people do this?" Debbie asked as she carefully emulated Eleanor's movements. "Mammy said that rich people don't like to get their hands dirty."

"There's a lot that Mammy doesn't know about rich people," Eleanor said diplomatically. Her difficult task of helping the children recover without insulting their worthless parents had just commenced. "It isn't how much money you have that makes you a good or bad person. It is how you treat other people. Uncle Edmund has a lot of money that he earned by doing hard work, and now he shares it with lots of people who need it."

"And I still like to get my hands dirty," he added as he kneeled down beside them to massage his stallion's legs. "It is important to treat your horse like a partner. He has helped us by running his fastest in the game, and now it is our turn to serve him."

The children helped them with every horse, watching curiously as Oz and Jaap Sahib used different styles to complete the task.

"Why do you wear that funny hat?" Charlie finally mustered the courage to ask Jaap Sahib.

"It is a turban," he explained. "I am a Sikh. It is part of my religion not to cut my hair, and so the turban helps me keep all of my hair out of the way."

"All of it?" Howie asked. "Ever?"

Jaap Sahib laughed and kneeled down so they could see him more closely. "I don't cut my beard either. See how it's tied up?"

"You look strange," Ruthy admitted.

Vibhishana finally joined them with his horse and the two pieces of his mallet. But, as he walked past the children with the stick of the broken mallet over his shoulder, Ruthy jumped behind Debbie, who jumped behind Howie, who jumped behind Charlie.

"She didn't mean anything by it," Charlie declared in Ruthy's defense.

Eleanor threw Edmund a knowing glance as they both struggled for a response. She hated the implications of their fear. Vibhishana gently put the stick down on the ground and kneeled down to address them. "I'm not going to hurt you, my children. Did I do something odd last night that would make you think otherwise?"

"That's not it," Charlie whispered. "We're just being silly."

The children relaxed and fell out of their defensive formation.

"Jaap Sahib is from India," Edmund explained, returning cheerfully to their prior topic of conversation. "In India, people look different than they do in Scotland. Most people there find red hair to be very strange."

"That's because it is," Debbie sighed. "People laugh at us for being gingers."

Edmund kneeled down. "We all seem strange to someone. Don't we, Father Johnson?"

"Indeed, we do." Vibhishana hopped up and finished leading his horse into the last stall.

"Kate, can I see you for a minute outside?" Eleanor asked as she gestured for Kuveni to join her.

She led her away from the stables, out across the lawn, and into the vineyards, until she was certain that she was out of earshot.

"I need to know what danger my sisters are in. Those children were afraid that he was going to beat them with that stick."

"Do you want me to pop up to Scotland to spy on them?"

Eleanor thought carefully. "I want to see it for myself. What are my options?"

"Let me see." Kuveni disappeared, and Eleanor's heart raced as she waited for her return. "Hold on tight," Kuveni's disembodied voice whispered. "We're going in."

Eleanor leaned heavily on the doorframe of an empty pantry as she materialized with Kuveni by her side. Kuveni grabbed her hand.

The four of them are just sitting down to an early breakfast.

Breakfast?!

Kuveni snapped her fingers, and two sets of peep holes silently appeared on the door, allowing them to spy.

"Bacon?!" Mary exclaimed. "Where did you get bacon?!"

Martha glanced at Jimmy, who had already taken several pieces onto his plate to pair with a pile of fried eggs. "Ellie's cheques just cleared. I thought we'd celebrate."

"Celebrate?! But the bairns were gone all day and night, and they're still not back!" Mary exclaimed.

"Those spoiled lads threaten to run away all the time," Martha countered. "They're probably waitin' at the ferry right now, realizin' that they need money to get off the isle. The sooner they join us in the real world, the better off they'll be."

"But Mam is gone too! What if she took 'em away somewhere far, and we'll never see them again?! She's been threatening to do it for months!"

"That auld bat couldn't've taken 'em very far, she's at death's door, fer Christ's sake," Jimmy replied, chewing with his mouth open as he gobbled up another greasy chunk of bacon. "Besides, that leaves more fer us."

"I don't understand how ye aren't more worried about the bairns!" Mary exclaimed. "It was freezing last night, and Mam didn't have any money when she skipped out, did she? They could be starving right now!"

"That'll teach 'em, after whinin' day in 'n day out about their soup," Jimmy muttered. "It's better than any soup I ate as a lad."

"Maybe she did have money," Martha addressed Mary. "Maybe she's been holding out on us."

"Well, the cheques cleared, so we know she didn't call up Ellie and her rich sassanack soldier to clipe on us," Fergus chimed in.

"She should've. We're all bloody shameful fools," Mary muttered.

"Haud yer wheesht!" Jimmy screeched. "It takes time to get a business up and runnin'. Everyone knows that."

"Really, Mary. You're very impatient," Martha chastised her. "We only need to hold out for a few more months, and then it'll be deer hunting season. We'll have lots of paying customers coming up here to hunt, and then we'll be able to pay for everything we want and then some. We won't have to depend on Ellie's sassanack money anymore!"

"Where are they going to stay?" Mary exclaimed. "Here? Where there isn't even a bloody boiler? Where we can't even afford good blankets and sheets? What food are we going to feed 'em, eh? Some rotten pea soup? That'll get the lords from the lowlands linin' up! Let's call the *Edinburgh Register* right now to send a critic on up."

"Oh ye of little faith," Martha sighed with annoyance. "Jimmy has a plan."

"Is it as good as the last one?" Mary asked sarcastically.

"Ye'd better watch that mouth, woman," Fergus grumbled as he took a piece of bacon off of Mary's plate and popped it into his mouth.

"He has a plan," Martha reiterated.

"We're gonna tell Ellie and her sassanack soldier that the bairns got into boarding school," Jimmy explained nonchalantly. "One of those highfalutin ones that costs an arm and a leg. They won't bat an eye at the dear tidy price, and we'll get the chunk of change we need to finish this place off before hunting season begins."

"We're all goin' straight to Hell, ye know," Mary muttered.

Jimmy's face turned red. "Those miserly, stealin' sassanacks are goin' te Hell! They made all their money from us breakin' our backs, and now we're just takin' it back!"

"Edmund Marriner's family made their money selling art. What does that have to do with Scotland?" Mary pushed.

"They all have some excuse like that. In the end, they always made their money from rapin' and pillagin'."

"How does one make money from raping?" Mary asked cheekily.

"Woman!" Fergus hissed. "Off wit ye!" He pushed his empty plate towards her.

Mary slammed it against the table before picking it up. "Ye'd better go out and find our bairns if yer gonna use 'em as an excuse to chore more money from Ellie. Ye'd better hope Mam hasn't already called her up."

"That biddy doesn't even know how to use a telephone," Fergus scoffed.

Jimmy shook his head angrily. "I'm gonna skin those bloody nyaffs when I get my hands on 'em." He leaned in threateningly to Mary. "And yer auld mammy'd better watch 'er back."

He gobbled down the rest of the food on his plate and then shuffled out of the dining room, grabbing his hunting rifle from over the door as he went. "Fergy, come on. Let's go get 'em before they flap their mouths."

As soon as the men were gone, Mary grabbed Martha by the wrist. "I will never forgive you if our bairns don't come back safe and sound, ye hear? I've half a mind to call Ellie up and tell her to cut off the funds right now. Maybe then ye'll find yer bloody heids."

"You wouldn't dare," Martha hissed.

"Look at what ye've gotten us into!" Mary exclaimed. "We're bloody starvin', and I'll eat my hat if Jimmy Buchanan gets one bloody lord to come up here to hunt. How is anyone even going to know to come?!"

"Do you think I was born yesterday?" Martha scoffed. "When we're all ready, we'll use some of the money to put ads out in all the papers. We'll be swimming in money, and then Ellie won't be laughin' wit her snide colonel about her poor lil sisters."

"Since when did Ellie laugh at us?! She's never laughed at us! All she's ever done is help!"

"Stop bein' so naive, Mary. Ellie gets off on tellin' us what to do. It makes her feel like the bloody Queen of the World. Can you believe she called the schools to make sure Debbie 'n Ruthy'd applied?"

"She was right!" Mary exclaimed. "Yer a chorin' liar! Ellie was just smart enough to see it!"

Martha slapped her, and Mary stumbled backwards with surprise. "I'm makin' a future fer all of us, and yer just along fer the ride. Don't forget it, Mary MacLeod."

"Get yer bloody heid out of the clouds!" Mary shouted angrily. "Yer just diggin' our graves deeper and deeper, and ye don't even see it! Jimmy's pulled the fleece right o'er yer eyes!"

"Yer just a weak little bampot," Martha snapped. "We've been through worse than this. We starved fer years after Da died. *Years*, Mary. And all ye have to do is go without luxuries for a few months as we get back on our feet, and yer just whinin' and snivelin' like a wee bloody bairn."

"I don't know who you are anymore, Martha MacLeod, but ye'd better get one thing straight, if ye know whit's good fer ye: y'aren't gettin' another penny from me. Got it? I'm keeping my cheques from Ellie, and when school starts in fall, I'm takin' my bairns back to Edinburgh, and with God as my witness, ye'd better do the same before the Good Lord strikes ye down where ye stand. And if I see ye feedin' the men bacon while our bairns eat rotten soup again, I'll take a fryin' pan te yer head till ye don't wake up, got it?"

Martha leaned in threateningly. "You even think of doing any such thing, and I'll tell Fergus yer plan."

"I'm going with or without him."

Martha cackled. "Now whose heid's in the clouds? Remember what Mam did without Da? She'd've been better off dead, that's what."

"Yer a bloody wicked heathen, Martha MacLeod, ye know that?"

"Don't pretend to be an innocent lil lass wit me, Mary MacGregor! Ye're the one who just stood by and watched while he

160

lashed the bairns over that spilled milk. Ye'll never leave Fergus. Don't lie te yerself."

"Yer goin' straight te Hell, Martha Buchanan, and if yer not careful, I'll help ye get there." Mary slammed the dirty plates on the dusty stone floor, and they shattered. "Use yer cheque te pay fer that, ye bloody black-hearted bassa."

Mary slammed the door, leaving Martha alone. She sighed angrily as she began sweeping up the broken dishes. "Those ungrateful bairns are gonna pay fer this," she muttered.

Eleanor squeezed Kuveni's hand. *I've seen enough.*

Kuveni dissolved, and Eleanor went limp as she felt her body go with her.

Eleanor leaned on Kuveni as they rematerialized in the vineyards.

"Good lord," Kuveni murmured. "They're all in a hell of their own making, aren't they?"

Eleanor reeled from the ugly truth, and then she let her mind settle on one resonating thought. "I don't care what it takes. We're keeping the children."

CHAPTER 9 – ABBI AND AMMA

When Eleanor and Kuveni returned to the house, the party was winding down, and Mélusine was coordinating the mundane plans for returning several of their guests back to India in "Percy's plane," which was conveniently parked on the lawn out behind the stables. Her batch of passengers included Ravi, Shruti, Jaap Sahib, Jyoti, Amit, Mr. Montero, Rohit, Vibhishana, and Sheranee, all of whom dutifully offered their goodbyes and well wishes before boarding Percy's plane. Eleanor wondered in passing if the Yakshas would simply convert the plane into a vortex as soon as they were out of Edmund's sight, and then she let the thought go. She didn't care at all how they went about completing their farce, she was just glad that one burden was off of her back.

As soon as the plane sput-sputted into the sky, Oz dropped Yvie and a napping little Neddy at their home down the road, and then drove Nellie Melba, her accompanist, and Andrew (clad in a new wardrobe kindly provided by Kuveni) to the station in Margaret River. Nellie Melba had been so impressed by Andrew's talent that she'd agreed to take him with her back to Melbourne.

Eleanor patted Stanley on the back as he waved them away, and then he carefully wiped his tears without smudging his mascara.

Eleanor pulled him into a hug. "You're a good man, Stanley. You've done a great service for Andrew. You may have just changed his life."

He squeezed her back. "Thank you for helping him, my lady." He sniffled. "I never imagined I'd be caught with a naked man, and anyone would be so forgiving."

"You didn't know we'd be home," Eleanor reminded him.

"Still... Eleanor... ma'am... my lady... It was a nightmare I'd had since I was a boy that the first time I'd get up the courage to be with someone, I'd get caught red-handed. But I was caught... we were caught... and it was still... wonderful."

Eleanor hugged him again. "I'm glad, Stanley. I really am."

"I'm sorry we ruined Edmund's hat."

Eleanor giggled. "Let's just make sure the generals don't get wind of why he needs another one."

Stanley became solemn and lowered his voice. "We must all be more careful now, Eleanor. My father has become a dangerous man. I've never seen my mother so scared of him."

"Really? How so? Dangerous to you, because of Andrew? You know we won't let anything happen to you."

"No, Eleanor. Well, yes... yes and no and yes."

"You lost me."

"He is more dangerous to me, yes, but he is also more dangerous to you and Edmund. He has become very desperate and paranoid. We should fear him, and even if the Yakshinis can help us, he can make things very difficult for us with the amount of power he still has in the government."

"Did your mother tell you all of that yesterday when you were arguing? Do you think she's going to tell him that she caught you with Andrew?"

"Please, Eleanor. Just trust me. It is better for you not to know the details."

"Did Leo teach you that? You know, he thought it was true until the day he died, and then he spilled all his secrets anyway. And I will tell you, greenie, he would have had an easier time of many things if he'd just let me help him."

"It is pivotal that my father finds no evidence that my role at the agency has been compromised. Mac was under orders to execute Leo that night that Surpanakha killed him. My father won't hesitate to do the same to me, especially now. The less you know about the details, the better. It will make it easier for all of us to plead innocence under interrogation."

"Interrogation!" Eleanor exclaimed.

"Let's hope it doesn't come to that." Stanley rolled his shoulders and took a deep breath. "Please let me worry for both of us for now. You have other, more important things to deal with."

"I think, greenie, you might have just earned yourself a more mature nickname."

"Please, ma'am, you really should be calling me Stanley. Or Mr. Abernathy, but I still can't wrap my head around that one. But you should be calling me something that a normal person calls their butler. We both need to be less sloppy from now on."

Eleanor squeezed his hand. "Stanley, I'm proud of you. I knew you'd come into your own someday. It's such a delight to see."

The screen-door into the house slammed with a blustery gust of wind, breaking them out of their conversation.

"We'd better start figuring out how to manage this fuller household," Stanley said as he walked with her up the stairs. "You don't think Kate would stick around to help us, do you? I don't like the idea of bringing new staff in right now."

"I'm sure she'll help out when she can, but she has other responsibilities, and she is far too important to be our cook."

"I suppose you're right. I'll make it work, Eleanor."

Eleanor squeezed his hand with thanks. But, as she moved to go find her burgeoning family, she was startled as Vibhishana materialized right in front of her in his gentle Lankan form. Stanley muffled his own squeal of surprise, and then dutifully left them alone while Vibhishana closed his eyes, thanking his Yaksha escort, and then gestured for her to follow him silently back out the front door.

"I'm sorry, Eleanor. I promise I will leave after this, but I couldn't leave without warning you." He continued on determinedly towards the stables.

"Warn me about what?"

"I'm not entirely sure yet."

The dogs jumped up from their lounging position on the hay as they entered, and the horses began neighing.

"Who rides this mare normally?" he asked as he walked her straight up to the pony he'd been riding earlier.

"I do," she replied as she noticed a grimace on the mare's face that she hadn't seen earlier. "When we exercise them, I take the two smallest mares, Stella, the one I rode earlier, and this one, Luna."

She kneeled down to inspect the poultice, and she noticed the mare's back legs quivering.

"She's injured!" Eleanor exclaimed. "Was she injured when you were riding her earlier?"

"I don't know. Probably. Yes." She didn't like his hedging answers. "She was, but I didn't realize it at the time. I wouldn't have run her like I did if I'd known. I should have noticed her pain sooner, but I was too swept up in the game."

"I'll have to ask Oz to come out later to examine her. It looks like her back tendons are buckling. Do you weigh a lot? More than a human?"

"That's the thing, Eleanor," he lowered his voice, "I made myself hollow earlier as an advantage for the game. I weighed much less than a normal human does."

"You cheated?!" she exclaimed.

"Do you consider that cheating?"

She rolled her eyes. "Next time we'll have to make a set of extra rules for the divine peanut gallery. Kuveni was cheating too."

"I'm sorry, Eleanor. We usually count our special skills as part of our handicaps. Was Uma not helping you? I figured it was two of us plus one human on each side."

Eleanor smiled. "That was all me out there this time. I've been practicing a lot." She returned her attention to Luna. "She was perfectly fine when I rode her three days ago. When did you notice her pain?"

"Only at the end, when I lost the head of my mallet." He reached over to a shelf and collected the two broken pieces to show her. "This is also concerning."

She examined it. "That's a very clean break."

"Exactly. As if someone cut it most of the way, so it would break completely on first impact."

"But you used it for the whole game before it broke?"

"I never made contact with the ball. My game-ending shot was the first time."

"Really? I suppose I wasn't paying close enough attention."

"You all were wonderfully worthy opponents. Some of the best I've ever played."

"Probably we don't deserve our place on that pedestal, D.H., but I'll take the compliment anyway. I was quite happy with how we played." She examined the mallet head with more scrutiny. "You don't think it broke because you hit it too hard?"

"It is possible, Eleanor, but I was working very hard to put on a human show."

"The head went flying into the vineyards. That was not a human shot."

"I suppose I got carried away."

He kneeled down again to examine Luna's back legs. "But seeing the mallet break how it did, and then feeling the mare limping, made me wonder if perhaps someone had sabotaged both of them, the mallet and the horse."

"For what? We've only been playing friendly games amongst the three of us to keep the ponies in shape. You aren't implying that Oz did it, are you?"

"Certainly not. He's one of the worthiest humans I've ever encountered. No... I was thinking more about Grimby. I haven't liked how close he's stayed to your household. I've been following his activities since the incident at the beach last year."

"Is he *here*? In Margaret River?"

"He's arriving in Perth tonight on a flight from Cape Town."

"Cape Town? What was he doing in Africa?"

"I don't know. That's part of my discomfort. He seems to be mobilizing on something, but I'm not sure what. He's been keeping a closer and closer eye on you—on all of your correspondents, on how you're spending your money, and I'm sure he's going to pay very close attention to how the children and your mother got here. He is too interested in us."

"But how do you think he sabotaged our horse and mallet if he's in Africa?"

"What do you know of Norwenn?"

Norwenn. Eleanor had almost completely forgotten her already.

"She's desperate and angry, I suppose. She came all the way down here to try to get Stanley to act how his father wants him to be. But doesn't it seem a bit extreme for her to try to injure me? If Luna had thrown me, I could have died."

"Her son just told her that he never wants to see her again. That, *you*, Eleanor, make him feel more loved than she ever has. I watched her leave in a huff yesterday while you were busy with other things. Grimby may be all she has left, which makes her a very dangerous woman."

"Blimey. What do you think we should do? Do you think she's lurking now?"

"I asked Monty to spot us invisibly to make sure our conversation stays private. I'm going to ask him to keep an extra eye out for you, until we know more. I hope you don't mind the suggestion? He is the most discreet of the Yakshas."

"It's a good suggestion with Kuveni preoccupied with the new Yakshini babies," Eleanor agreed. "As long as you don't need his help in Baroda?"

"With Hanuman around, we will have an extra ally against any of Ravana's minions who come hunting for Maya. It is a good time to shift things around a bit."

"Do you really trust him to be near the Patels? It seems pretty risky, don't you think?"

"It is risky, yes. But it is necessary for him to know personally how virtuous they are. It will help him accept the complex role that the Rakshasa people play on Earth when the time comes."

"You are playing a long game, aren't you?"

"A century or two is not long to me, Eleanor. The Age of Truth is just around the corner… But, that doesn't matter now. I've said what I came to say. Thank you for indulging me. It was a true pleasure to see that you and Edmund are still so in love, and an even greater pleasure to see you with the children. I am so happy to see you both embracing such a beautiful familial life."

"I didn't have a chance to thank you for your gift. It really was nice to remember who I am without Uma."

"It was nothing, Eleanor. I wish I could relieve you of your burden permanently, but Shakti has made it abundantly clear now that she has other plans for you."

He leaned in, and Eleanor felt Uma pull towards him, but she pushed her back with all her might. He caught himself and cleared his throat, stepping away.

"I'm sorry, Eleanor. I'm leaving now. Summon me if you need me."

In a blur, he was gone.

Eleanor looked around and sighed with stress as she mulled over what to do next.

I will ask Oz to come tend to Luna when he's back from the station, Vibhi added. *Go be with your family, Eleanor. Let Monty watch over you for now.*

Eleanor kissed Luna's forehead. *I'm sorry, my friend. Oz will help, and we'll keep you nice and comfortable, even if you can't play anymore.*

Luna neighed as Eleanor stroked her mane, and then Eleanor tore herself away. She glanced at the broken mallet again. She sighed with a combination of stress and resignation, and headed back towards the house.

She wandered through the quiet hallways until she heard the pleasant sound of Edmund's voice reading out loud. She followed it to the library in the back of the house, a former living room that Edmund had filled from floor to ceiling with books and dotted with comfortable chairs and couches for lounging. All four children were curled up around him on the biggest couch. Her mother was dozing in an armchair in the corner, and Mae was lying in a window seat gazing out the window in deep thought.

"Abbi's reading us the *Arabian Nights!*" Charlie exclaimed as he noticed her.

"In English this time!" Debbie added.

"Abbi?" Eleanor asked as they looked around at the packed couch for where they could make room for her. She smiled reassuringly and sat down on a leather couch across from them.

"I hope you don't mind, dearest? I told them they could call me Abbi, because that is what I called Abdul Barr. It was nice to call him something that made me feel like I was special to him, even if he wasn't my real father."

"I think it's a lovely idea, darling. Would you all like a special name for me too?" The children nodded, and as Eleanor thought through her options and remembered the disgusting display she'd witnessed from her sisters, she settled on her choice. "How about Amma?"

"Okay, Amma," Debbie replied.

"Amma!" Ruthy exclaimed.

"I like it too," Edmund winked.

They both knew that the word meant "Mum" in the language of their old home in the mountains near Munnar, and Edmund had admitted on several occasions that he'd called Abdul Barr "Papa" in classical Arabic. And so, with their subtle unspoken agreement, Edmund returned to reading their siesta story, and together, they began their new parental lives as Abbi and Amma.

CHAPTER 10 – THE GREAT PIZZAZ

For two months, the MacLeod-Marriners settled into family life, and while each of their lives was distinctly different than it had ever been before, Eleanor found their new circumstances surprisingly comfortable. She wasn't surprised, however, that Edmund grew more and more contented every day, as he felt more and more like the father he'd always wanted to be, and she loved him more with each story he read and every cricket ball he tossed.

As for the children, every day they learned to trust that Abbi and Amma were never going to lash them or screech at them over minor trivialities, and in addition to fattening up to a healthy weight with the help of Oz and Yvie's cook, and becoming fitter with all of their running and playing outside in the mild winter weather (which was, Eleanor had to admit, generally nicer than a Scottish summer), they became bolder, more curious, and most importantly, happier.

Several days a week, Mae tutored the children while Edmund saw to his minor duties as a rural magistrate, and Eleanor continued helping Oz out in his infrequent duties as the local doctor and veterinarian, for which his primary client was Luna, who was slowly but steadily recovering from the bruises imparted on her back legs by some sort of intentional act of sabotage, which Oz dutifully failed to mention to Edmund, upon Eleanor's request.

Eleanor's mother slowly recovered from her hunger strike, although she had never been a particularly energetic woman, and her self-imposed starvation seemed to have slowed her down even further. She took to sitting by the fireplace in Edmund's library, reading children's storybooks and uncomplicated fictional novels with the help of a pair of reading glasses provided by Kuveni, unless the children were outside playing cricket or learning how to ride the horses with Edmund and Eleanor, in which case she sat bundled up on a wicker rocker on the porch, nursing a glass of tidy scotch and watching them. Eleanor had never seen her mother look more content.

After saying her official goodbyes, Kuveni continued to pop by every so often, out of sight of Edmund, conjuring special snacks and perfectly fitting new clothes for the growing children. However, her distraction by the Yakshini babies was just as thorough as Mélusine had predicted, and despite missing her confidante, Eleanor was glad that Kuveni was occupying herself with something other than being their posh fairy godmother.

The void created by the loss of Kuveni's hovering presence was made up for by Stanley, who had taken his own objective of becoming a better butler straight to heart. If Eleanor hadn't known any better, she would have thought he was a natural at it. He'd even toned down his makeup in the presence of her mother and Oz's staff (who were now graciously tending to both of their households with the help of a hefty raise funded by Edmund), so as to not raise the eyebrows that he had enjoyed raising during his rebellious self-exploration phase. The effort turned out to be a bit late in the case of her mother, as his romantic dancing with Andrew at her birthday party had led her mother to confidingly inform her the following evening that her butler was as queer as a nine-bob note.

174

Eleanor thanked her for her observation, pointing out that none of the angels seemed to mind, and thus ended her mother's commentary on the topic, to Eleanor's extreme relief.

The only thing that had really suffered over the months was Eleanor's marital relations, which, despite Kuveni's helpful addition of a lock on their door, were still dampered by the possibility of children knocking at any hour of the night with their frequent and understandable nightmares, and by the poor sound insulation of their Victorian farmhouse. Fortunately, they had discovered after the first week, when they were both particularly feeling the painful strain of abstinence, that the abandoned beach where they'd spent Eleanor's birthday sunset was nicely unoccupied at all hours of the day, every day, since all of the locals believed it to be haunted by the poor people who hadn't been able to escape from the tsunami the prior year. With that knowledge, they'd taken to secret trysts during their lunch hours, and sometimes on the way home from work, and Eleanor had to admit that the illicit nature of their meetings added a bit of sexy intrigue that she'd never experienced before in Edmund's virtuous husbandly arms.

And so, as the mild winter rolled by and Mae's imminent return to Baroda after the monsoon holidays grew near, the whole family began to worry about losing the lovely little life they'd begun to love. They decided to distract themselves by going to the circus.

"Are you sure you don't want to come?" Edmund asked Mae as the children rushed around preparing themselves for their first overnight outing as a family. "We've rented out the entire Seaside B&B in Bunbury. The whole house is ours for the evening, and the innkeepers are preparing dinner for us after we return from the show."

Mae glanced outside at the pouring rain. "I'd rather curl up by the fire here. Besides, I'd better get used to be being alone again. I used to like the silence."

"Suit yourself," Eleanor said as she pulled Mae into a hug. "We're going to miss you."

"There's still a week until I have to go back," Mae reminded her. "Let's leave the goodbyes for then."

"Don't forget your scarves and gloves!" Stanley's voice echoed from upstairs. "It's going to be cold tonight!"

"It's not cold!" Charlie argued. "It's like home!"

"If this were winter in Edinburgh, our noses would freeze right off!" Ruthy added.

"Ye'd best listen to Stanley if ye know whit's good fer ye," Eleanor's mother informed them.

"Let me carry that for you, Mrs. MacLeod."

Stanley helped her down the stairs and escorted her to the library where Edmund was taking his time choosing the bedtime story to bring along with them.

"Colonel, here's your tea!" Mrs. Jenkins, Oz and Yvie's cheerful cook, exclaimed as she rushed past Stanley and Eleanor's mother with a wooden tray bearing two teapots and one cup. She placed it on an end table and stood back to watch.

"Thank you, Mrs. Jenkins! I'm going to need that for the long drive, I reckon," Edmund said cheerfully as he collected one of the pots and drank down its entire contents in one Rakshasa gulp.

Eleanor caught Stanley watching for Mrs. Jenkins's reaction, but as she seemed to just find Edmund's odd habit amusing, Stanley relaxed and helped Eleanor's mother sit down, placing her small train case on the floor beside her.

"Would you like some tea, Mrs. MacLeod? I can fetch you another cup," Stanley offered.

"No, please, take this cup. I will have my tea after you've all cleared out," Mae suggested. "If you don't leave soon, you're going to miss it. The roads will be slow with the mud."

"Blimey, I hadn't thought of that…" Edmund admitted. "Dearest, do you think we should take the train instead?"

"Darling, there isn't another train today. If we'd wanted to take it, we should have taken it this morning."

"Stanley, can you rally the bairns? Do you have our bag packed?" Edmund asked.

"Colonel, your bag is already by the front door, and I will have the troops lined up beside it, pronto." Stanley saluted jovially. "Mrs. MacLeod, you'd better drink your tea fast. You really should be on the road already."

"Nah, Abbi needs my tea to warm his cold bones, I reckon," Eleanor's mother declined. "I've got a wee nip already packed instead."

"My lady, there is a telephone call for you in the kitchen," Mr. Montero's disembodied voice whispered into Eleanor's ear. "You will want to take it in privacy."

"Darling, I'm going to go check on the children," Eleanor said as she kissed him on the cheek and then rushed out of the room.

"Prepare yourself," Mr. Montero whispered as she picked up the phone.

"Hello?" she said questioningly.

"Ellie!" Martha laughed awkwardly with forced cheer.

"Aye?"

Martha paused for too long. "I have the best news! It's news worth paying for a telephone call all the way across the world!" She burst into more awkward, guilty laughter.

"Really?" Eleanor worked to keep the flames of Durga at bay.

"Yes, the girls got into Eton!"

"Eton? Really? What a feat!"

Eleanor worked harder than she ever had to hide her exploding disdain. Really? *Eton?* The most famous *boys'* school on the planet? The lazy, ignorant, desperate fools hadn't even bothered to find a school that admitted girls for their hoax.

"Well, actually, all four children got in. All that tutoring you've been sponsoring has finally paid off!"

"I bet it has."

Martha paused as she noticed Eleanor's sharp tone, and Eleanor pooled all of her lying reserves into entrapping Martha in her own unskilled web. Martha had no bloody clue that she was trying to con the queen of deception.

"Well, we were just hoping that since you've been so supportive of their schooling that maybe you would help chip in. It's the opportunity of a lifetime, you know, and we can't afford it on our own. We need you, Ellie!"

If Eleanor had been standing across from her in person, she would have smacked her across the face for her unctuous tone.

"That's a pretty penny. I'll have to talk to Edmund about it. You know, he's really tightening the purse strings, just like a miserly old sassanack. I should've expected him to, I suppose. It's his nature, after all. He's been wanting an accounting of all the money I'm spending, like I've been keeping a ledger or something!" She slipped into her thickest Scots intonation as she spoke.

"Oh no! Really? I thought you two were getting along so well!" Eleanor liked the high-pitched panic that she heard in Martha's sickly sweet voice.

Eleanor dropped into a whisper. "Well, he can still tickle my fancy, if you know what I mean, so it's not all bad. A girl's got her priorities, right?" Martha didn't have a response, and Eleanor laughed with feigned frivolity. "Why don't you just send us along the bill from the college, and I'm sure that when he sees it, he won't be able to say no. It is his alma mater, after all. Speaking of which, should he give them a call? I'm sure he can arrange special accommodations for the bairns. He might even be able to help us arrange a scholarship."

"NO!" Martha exclaimed. "No, really, Ellie. It wouldn't be fair to ask for special treatment. That might be what the sassanacks do, but we earn our keep north of the border."

"Aye, I remember. I was busy earning my keep and yours for twenty years. What lovely days those were, weren't they? I have to admit I miss 'em sometimes. It's hard to believe I haven't had to wipe a madman's dirty bum in years. It really keeps ye grounded, ye know?"

Martha paused, once again struggling for words, and Eleanor relished her discomfort.

"Oh well, down here in Oz, I'm sure I can go volunteer my services in the homicide ward at the prison if I really want to. I've just had so many other things to do. Did I tell you that Edmund bought a polo team?"

"No, Ellie. I don't think you mentioned that."

"Oh yeah. He said that we had to have *something* to do with our time, and since he didn't want to get his hands dirty, he thought it was best to pay other people to get their hands dirty for us. I couldn't argue with him, since some of those Argentinian horsemen are just sublime to watch. Their posture is just superb."

"Right…"

"So, if you send us on down the bill, I'm sure I can sneak it in front of him. He trusts me, the poor old miser. Oh dear, I think the telephone line's going to go down. We're having a wicked winter storm raging. Talk to you soon! Send my love to the bairns!"

Eleanor slammed the phone down, and as she turned around, Monty was standing behind her in his preferred stern, elderly butler form.

"I assume that you know that Eton is only a boys' school?"

"Really, Monty, was my sarcasm on the rest of the call not obvious? Why do you think I told her to send us the bill?"

"I assumed you had a clever plan. I just wanted to make sure."

Eleanor smiled. "You don't know what a consummate liar I am yet, I suppose."

"Lying is an important skill for us. Lord Vibhishana considers your prowess exceptional, and he has very high standards."

"Yes, well, he and I both." Eleanor wanted out of that train of thought. "If you hear something else you think I should know, please tell me. I'm not always prideful, especially when I turn out to be wrong."

"I will keep that in mind, my lady."

He disappeared as Stanley peeked into the kitchen. "Is everything alright, Eleanor? Is Kate joining you for the evening? It will be a tight squeeze in the car, unless she tags along through other means."

"Alas, I think she has better things to do. Martha just called. She's initiated her plan to lie to us about the bairns needing more money for school. That means her children have been missing for two months, and she's still marching off the cliff right beside her husband without looking back."

"What did you tell her?"

Eleanor couldn't help but chuckle, even though the whole thing was so infuriating that she could hardly wrap her head around it. "I told her to send me the bill. We'll see how desperate they are. I'm half-expecting to receive a forged bill for Eton in the mail next week."

"Eton?!" he scoffed. "They don't even admit students under the age of thirteen! Thank god, what a nightmare that would've been... bloody hell, four years of it was bad enough..."

"They also don't admit girls."

"It will be good for you if they send you something in the mail, Eleanor. It will be evidence of fraud if they challenge you for the children in court."

Eleanor pushed back a wave of anxiety at the idea. "Let's hope it doesn't come to that, although I will admit the thought did cross my scheming mind."

"It was a good idea, Eleanor. Get them to produce as much of a paper trail as you can. I will help keep it organized in case you need it."

"You are a better and better handmaiden every day, Stanley."

He grabbed her hand and stared into her eyes. *I am a better and better spy, Eleanor.*

He let go. "Come on. You're going to be dreadfully late. The children are almost ready."

180

Eleanor followed Stanley out of the kitchen and back to the library.

"Ah ha!" Edmund declared triumphantly as he spotted the book he'd been looking for and pulled it off the shelf. "Are you sure you don't want this second pot of tea?" he asked Mae.

"Please, take it!"

He drank it down in another long Rakshasa gulp, and then shivered with satisfaction as he felt it push another wave of warmth right through him.

"Are the children ready?" Edmund asked.

"Come on, bairns. The train is leaving the station!" Stanley called as he left Eleanor's side to rush back up the stairs to rally them.

"We're taking the train?!" Howie exclaimed.

"Yes!!!" Charlie seconded.

"Figure of speech, mates. It was just a figure of speech," Stanley corrected himself. "Today Abbi will be driving you in one of Uncle Oz's Fords."

Eleanor laughed. "I suppose we should plan a train trip next. I didn't realize they'd be so excited by the prospect."

"I reckon they'll be excited to do anything wit ye, Ellie." Eleanor's mother leaned heavily on her to stand up. "Ye've been a right tidy mother to 'em, just like ye were te yer sisters… and me. And ye know whit's funny?" She leaned in confidingly. "Ye still're. I've ne'er been to a circus before, mind ye. Tonight's the night."

Eleanor laughed. "I hope it's better than the Bunbury Opera."

Her mother patted her hand. "I wouldn't know the difference."

"The troops are at the ready, Colonel!" Stanley reported as he returned to the library with Eleanor's massive mink coat open, ready to help her put it on over her tasteful winter outfit of an ankle-length plaid skirt (the Howard tartan in honor of her mother), a matching tam o'shanter hat, and a blue cashmere sweater with a wide, buttoning boat neck that Eleanor particularly liked.

"Lord Almighty, they'll think the Queen of England's come for the show!" Eleanor's mother exclaimed.

"Do you think it's too much?" Eleanor asked concernedly, thinking back on her awkward birthday opera excursion.

"If ye have it, flaunt it!" her mother exclaimed.

Eleanor laughed. "The car will be quite cold without a heater to keep us warm. I suppose I'll wear it just in case."

She let Stanley put it on her, and then Edmund twirled her around into a romantic kiss.

"I've missed this coat. I suppose you haven't had much need for it since our honeymoon."

"Tonight seems fitting," Eleanor said as she took his hand and guided him to the front of the house, while Stanley helped her mother follow.

When they reached the front door, the four children were lined up in adorable new winter outfits, complete with jackets with miniature fur collars, wool knickerbockers with argyle socks, tall laced leather rain boots, and matching fur-lined tam o'shanter hats. They looked a bit like the long-lost cousins of the Mountbattens, ready to tromp around in the gardens of Balmoral castle. Stanley left Eleanor's mother to rush to the coat closet and present her with her own tasteful, modern, low-waisted grey wool coat with a lovely white fur collar.

"Is that fer me?" she asked with disbelief.

"It is a gift from Kate," he informed her.

"Lord Almighty," she murmured. "I suppose I'd better be dressed as the Queen Mother to match Ellie here. Lordy, that's warm."

Stanley helped her put on a matching cloche hat, and then he flung open the door. "You'd better get going!"

Edmund and Eleanor both opened wide umbrellas, while Stanley carried the bags designated for Eleanor and Edmund in his right hand and Eleanor's mother's in his left. The children dutifully carried their own knapsacks as they clung to Abbi and Amma. Stanley popped open the boot of the car and helped them toss the bags in, and then he rushed around to open the doors for them.

"Dearest, shall I keep out the story to read in the car? I finally found Kipling's *Jungle Book* on the shelf!"

"I don't like reading in the car, darling. It hurts my eyes."

As Edmund's enthusiasm deflated, Eleanor got a better idea. "I could drive while you read."

He moved to protest, and then he smiled. "Why not?"

God how she loved that man. She scampered around the front of the car to switch places with him. Everyone piled inside, with Edmund taking the middle of the couchy back seat with the three older children, and Ruthy climbing onto Gramma Moira's lap in the front seat beside Eleanor.

"This crowd should keep everyone nice and warm!" Edmund said as Stanley closed them in and waved goodbye.

Eleanor glanced around making sure everything was in place, and then off they went. The tires screeched on the mud of the driveway, but as they reached the freshly paved road, the ride became smooth, and Edmund opened his book.

"*Now Chil the Kite brings home the night That Man the Bat sets free — The herds are shut in byre and hut, For loosed till dawn are we...*"

By the time they arrived in Bunbury, Eleanor's mother was snoring loudly, Ruthy was snoring quietly, and the rest of the children were wide-eyed as they snuggled deeper into Edmund's arms worrying about whether poor Mowgli would escape from the custody of some very bad monkeys (a turn in the tale to which Edmund enthusiastically added his own anti-ape commentary).

The hazy light of day was dissolving into a grey, wet, freezing night. It was definitely the coldest it had been since they'd arrived in Australia, and Eleanor realized it was the coldest it had been since Uma had taken up residence inside of her. She was glad she'd worn the coat, although she was quite certain that Kuveni or

Monty had infused their car with a bit of Yakshini warmth along the way.

She pulled into the muddy, makeshift parking lot, and her mother snorted awake, while the children gasped with excitement as they spotted the tent looming in the light of the uninspiring stormy sunset.

"Look at how big it is! It's like a whole village could fit inside of it!" Charlie exclaimed.

"Are there going to be bears?" Debbie asked.

"Or black panthers?" Howie added.

"Or tigers!" Ruthy squealed.

"Now, now, we don't need to be scared of all tigers, do we?" Eleanor admonished them gently. "Shere Khan was a villain, but Sheranee is a perfectly wonderful mount."

"She was quite patient with us," Edmund admitted. "And I still can't believe she just boarded Percy's plane like a polite passenger!"

"I reckon there's good tigers 'n bad tigers, just like humans," her mother added.

"Exactly," Eleanor said cheerfully. "Now, who's ready for some popcorn?"

"I am!" all four children exclaimed.

"Is the luggage safe being left in the car?" Eleanor's mother worried.

"There's nothing in the bags that can't be replaced," Eleanor reassured her.

Eleanor's mother leaned in and whispered into her ear. "And *that*, Ellie, is whit money's bought ye. That there is freedom from worry. Don't take it lightly, and don't forget that it ain't true for most of the normal human folk on Earth."

Eleanor hugged her. "I'll never forget, Mum. Now, let's get inside before the clouds open up again!"

She grabbed the umbrellas, and then rushed around to hold them up as her mother and Ruthy piled out of the front, and

Edmund and the children piled out of the back. He kissed her as he took one of the umbrellas, and then with happy squeals, they all ran through the mud together towards the entrance.

Music was already playing inside, and Eleanor looked back into the crowded parking lot. "Blimey, it's already started! Do you have the tickets, darling?"

"I thought you had the tickets!" he exclaimed.

"Blimey," she hissed, as she looked down into the expectant faces of the children and reflected on the disappointing consequences of their poor planning.

"Check the pocket of your coat, my lady," Monty's disembodied voice whispered into Eleanor's ear.

"Did you say something, dearest?" Edmund asked.

Eleanor reached into her coat pocket and pulled out seven colorful tickets.

"Yay!" the children exclaimed in unison.

"Amma, you saved the day!" Debbie added.

"Thank you," she whispered.

She handed them each a ticket and urged them toward the bored doorman.

"You're late," he informed them sternly.

"Do I know you?" Eleanor asked. "You were the doorman at the Bunbury Opera!"

He glanced at her with more scrutiny, eyeing her expensive mink coat. "You were with that French Helmsworth dame! You left at intermission!" He leaned in confidingly. "The director was mighty unhappy about that, but if you ask me, if you want people to stay to the end, your tenor'd better know how to sing."

"Amen to that," Eleanor laughed. "Or, least of all, he'd better know how to act."

He softened his demeanor as he glanced down at their tickets. "Front row, eh? Seems like a good spot for a big beautiful family like yours."

Eleanor glanced over at Edmund to catch a look of subtle pride at the compliment. She felt it too, and she pushed back her guilt at the unscrupulous way in which their beautiful family had come together.

"What can I say, mate? We like to support the Bunbury arts. We drove all the way up from Margaret River for this," Eleanor replied.

He scoffed. "These carnies aren't from Bunbury, and they wouldn't know art if it hit 'em in the face."

Eleanor laughed. "Perhaps you and Yvie should talk. I think you might get along swimmingly."

He straightened his posture. "Me and Mrs. Helmsworth, of Helmsworth Ranches, getting along swimmingly?"

"As platonic mates, of course," Eleanor clarified quickly. "She and Dr. Helmsworth are about as in love as one couple can be."

"Well, you send 'em both on up next month when the ballet is in town, and I'll get 'em the best seats in the house. Go on in. You're supposed to wait until a break, but there's nothing in there that needs to go undisturbed, if you know what I mean." He kneeled down to address the children. "And you tell 'em that Jimmy said to give you the biggest popcorns they've got."

All four children cringed as he said his name, and Eleanor thanked Jimmy with a polite handshake and helped Edmund move them along inside.

"And there's good Jimmy's 'n bad Jimmy's..." Eleanor's mother murmured.

"I'm not hungry anymore," Ruthy whispered.

"Me neither," Charlie sighed.

Eleanor squeezed the children's hands. "We'll eat a lovely family dinner later after the show."

As they made their way slowly down the dark aisle, the children watched the stage, mesmerized by the swinging acrobats. Eleanor was grateful that the novelty was enough to distract them from their darker worries.

As soon as they took their seats in the front row, a toddler behind Edmund began to cry, and after some annoyed grumbling by his parents, Edmund politely stretched out his legs and slumped down in his seat so that the boy's view wouldn't be blocked by his excessive height. Eleanor squeezed his hand, and they laid back together to enjoy the show.

Eleanor wondered in passing if Andrew knew any of the performers from his days in the South Australian circus. As a bearded lady walked out to put on a comedy sketch with an animal trainer, the children gasped and pointed at a tiger who joined them on stage, followed by two polar bears.

"Amma, is that Sheranee?" Ruthy asked.

"That's a normal tiger," Eleanor explained. "It's been trained by that man there."

"Abbi, are those bears like Baloo?" Charlie asked.

"Baloo is a wild bear," Edmund explained. "These bears were probably raised by humans."

"Like Mowgli was raised by wolves!" Howie exclaimed.

"Yes, exactly. Sometimes great things can come when people are raised by someone quite different from them."

"Like angels raising humans!" Charlie exclaimed.

Edmund hid his distaste for the explanation. "Yes, exactly like that."

"Amma, that bearded lady looks like Stanley!" Debbie whispered.

"What do you mean?" Eleanor asked, not particularly ready to delve down the path that the question implied.

"He wears dresses too, and they look funny."

"Why do you think that?" Eleanor asked sweetly.

"I saw him drinking milk in the kitchen in a dress in the middle of the night."

"I see. Did he know you saw him?"

"I don't think so. I didn't want him to be embarrassed."

"That was very kind of you, Debbie. Why don't we talk more about it later, okay?"

"Okay." She nestled into cuddling in Eleanor's nook.

The show continued with contortionists and jugglers leaping about the stage, until the ringmaster came out, and the lights went up. The band began playing dramatic finale music as a giant board with a bullseye in the middle was wheeled onto the stage by two creepy clowns.

"And now, for the grand finale, starring the world famous Great Pizzaz! We need a volunteer from the audience! A lovely lady who fears nothing, not even death itself!"

"Amma, that's you!" Debbie squealed. "It should be you!"

"Yeah, Amma!" the boys seconded.

"I don't think so, darlings," Eleanor refused.

"Did I hear a volunteer?" the ringmaster's attention went right to Eleanor, and she squinted as the spotlight blinded her. "You there, the Scottish lass in the front row! Are you a master of fear?"

"Nope, I like my fear. Fear is good. It keeps one from doing foolishly dangerous things," Eleanor replied.

The audience laughed, and the ringmaster pushed harder. "Your ankle-biters seem to think otherwise! Come on up!"

"No thanks," Eleanor refused.

"Aww... you don't want to disappoint the lads and lasses, do you?" he needled her.

Edmund debated whether or not to defend her or egg her on.

"Amma, you should go!" Debbie insisted. "Show them how special you are!"

"Darling, we don't want people to know how special we are, remember?"

"But it's all pretend, isn't it?" Charlie pushed.

Eleanor sighed with resignation. "I suppose."

She stood up, and the audience cheered. She climbed up onto the stage, hoping, among other things, that the bright spotlight wouldn't highlight the outline of her copious cleavage through her cashmere sweater.

"Your ankle-biters sure do think the world of you, don't they? What did they call you, Amma?"

"Yes," Eleanor replied. "It is Gaelic. We're from Scotland."

"Well, Amma, I reckon today's storm feels like a taste of home, then?"

"Indeed. It feels just like a lovely summer day in the Highlands."

The audience laughed again.

"Well, Amma, are you ready to show your youngins your courage?"

"If I have to," she replied unenthusiastically.

"Well, let's give her a little encouragement, shall we?" he addressed the audience. "Let's cheer for our highland lass!"

The audience clapped and cheered, and as Edmund whistled and cat-called from the front row, Eleanor smiled. Surely whatever they had planned, they'd practiced many times before if they were willing to involve someone from the audience who wasn't even a shill... Surely. Still, she didn't like it, and she didn't know exactly why. Perhaps it was her over-active sense of danger lurking around every corner... Although, more often than not, she'd been right...

"Monty, spot me," she whispered.

"I am here, my lady," his disembodied voice whispered back.

The audience cheered louder as a black-bearded man in a sparkling sequined gold costume with an absurdly large wizard hat and long cape moseyed onto the stage.

"Ladies and gentlemen, all the way from Rome, Italy, the Great Pizzaz!" the ringmaster declared.

The Great Pizzaz walked around the stage for a while basking in their applause, and then he offered her his hand. She reluctantly took it, and he kissed it with a gross, wet smacking gesture that reminded her of one of her first boyfriends, who, due to that fact and several others, never made it past first base.

She knew she hadn't hidden her distaste as she took her hand back, and Edmund cheered while the rest of the crowd laughed and jeered.

"These Scottish lasses have to be wooed!" the ringmaster exclaimed.

The Great Pizzaz went down on one knee and bowed before her, but as the massive sapphire in her wedding ring glistened in the stage lights, the ringmaster noticed it, and so did the audience.

"Sorry, mates. I'm already taken," she called.

"What did you say your name was?" the ringmaster asked so the audience could hear him.

"You may call me Her Ladyship, the Countess of Easton." She winked at Edmund as she said it.

"A noble lady!" the ringmaster exclaimed. "Bunbury must be on the up and up!"

The audience exploded into more cheers, and the Great Pizzaz escorted her to the target.

"Let's see if you have the courage of your noble ancestors!" the ringmaster declared.

Eleanor did not like the cold expression on the face of the Great Pizzaz as he strapped her to the human-sized dart board, and as she glanced at Edmund, she noticed that he wasn't particularly fond of the development either.

A female assistant in a skimpy, glittery costume pranced out onto the stage, carrying a tray of knives. The audience cheered louder as the Great Pizzaz took his position across the stage from Eleanor, and the assistant handed him the first.

"Ladies and gentlemen, let's hold our breath for the Countess of Easton," the ringmaster declared.

Before she'd even settled in to worry about what Edmund might do, the Great Pizzaz threw the first knife straight at her, and it transformed into a daisy as it hit her straight in the chest.

The audience, the ringmaster, and the Great Pizzaz all gasped with surprise.

With only one moment of contemplation at the surprising turn, he picked up the next knife and flung it right at her head. It transformed into a tulip as it hit the center of her forehead.

This time, the audience exploded into applause, and Eleanor watched Edmund relax. How he thought they were achieving the magical phenomenon was anyone's guess, but she knew exactly who to thank.

"Monty, keep it up," she whispered.

"He is trying to kill you, my lady. You must be very careful."

"Do you know who he is?"

"Have no doubt that I will find out."

The Great Pizzaz went through each and every one of his knives, and the audience became more and more enthralled as a garden of wildflowers collected on the stage below Eleanor.

Finally, the Great Pizzaz collected a huge curved sword from his own belt, and as the audience held their breath, he threw it right at Eleanor's neck. It burst into a puff of colorful, glittery dust, and the audience went wild.

"Ladies and gentleman, the Courageous Countess of Easton!" the ringmaster exclaimed with bewilderment.

"Monty, get me off of here," she whispered. She felt the bindings dissolve, and without the help of her assassin's hand, she freed herself from the target and smiled as she took a bow.

"Amma!!!!" the children exclaimed.

"Keep an eye on him, Monty," she whispered as she took another bow, and the audience cheered louder. She pulled off her hat and let them see her fiery red tendrils shimmering in the stage lights. "And *that* is the courage you can expect from a bona fide Scottish lass," she declared to the audience. Her mother hollered her approval, and Ruthy and Debbie squealed with excitement.

"You're playing a very dangerous game," she whispered to the ringmaster. "You have no idea who you're dealing with."

The ringmaster smiled to the crowd and took her hand for another bow before whispering back to her. "How'd you pull off that stunt? I'll pay you double whatever he's paying you. No, triple! That was a real crowd-pleaser. We could make the big time with it, and we can replace him in a jiffy. No one likes the Italians after the war anyway."

"You're telling me that you are unaware that your man just tried to murder me eight times in front of this crowd?"

"Murder you!" he exclaimed. He smiled and took another bow before the audience. "I thought you were his shill! He told me to pick you!"

"I've never seen him before in my life. You're lucky he didn't decapitate a mother in front of her children on your stage."

"WHAT?!"

"You should do a better job of checking up on your staff. I could tell he was a homicidal maniac just by looking at him. Now, I have a family to get back to who knows nothing about the tragedy that almost destroyed their lives."

She smiled and took a final bow, and then scampered down off the stage and took a deep breath. "Thank you, Monty."

"I will follow them, my lady."

"Thank you all. Good night!" the ringmaster declared before he ran off the stage after the Great Pizzaz.

"Dearest, you were glorious!" Edmund kissed her, and then the children pummeled her into a group hug.

"Thank you, my darlings. I'm glad you enjoyed it. Now, shall we go eat something before a warm fire? I'm famished."

"How about some popcorn for the road, dearest? I think they still have some. Charlie said he's never had it before."

"Me neither!" Debbie exclaimed.

"Me neither!" Howie and Ruthy added.

"Mate, you were great!" a passerby said as he offered her a high five.

"Are you really a countess?" his wife asked.

"Darling, why don't you take the children before they run out of popcorn, and I'll meet you over there."

"As you wish, my lady," he winked.

Edmund escorted the children through the crowd to the refreshments stand, and Eleanor glanced back at her attentive audience.

"Yes, I really am a countess," Eleanor replied to the woman who was still waiting for her answer. A large group of people behind her were also curiously listening in. "But if you don't mind, I need to sit down."

The woman's husband pulled her along, and Eleanor sat down and rubbed her forehead, trying to disperse her raging adrenalin as the crowds around her thinned.

Eleanor's mother sat back down next to her and waited until all of the other passersby were out of earshot. "I know ye, Eleanor Mary MacLeod, and I know what it looks like when ye're rightly scared. It was something rotten afoot up there, wunne it?"

"That man was trying to kill me. If it weren't for a very skilled angelic helper, the first knife would've struck right where the daisy did."

"Is the Good Lord strikin' him down now?"

Eleanor couldn't help but smile. "It doesn't work like that, Mum. But my angelic helper is keeping an eye on him. We need to know why he was trying to kill me."

"He dunne know he was out fer an angel, did he?" Her mother poked her in the ribs. "He dunne know how hard te kill ye'd be."

Eleanor paused to consider what exactly her mother meant. "I'm still mortal, Mum. You do know that, right?"

Her mother thought for an extended moment about the idea. "But Kate's six thousand, and yer auld colonel's o'er a hundred."

Eleanor lowered her voice. "My power isn't the same as theirs, Mum. I was born human, and I have to be much more careful than they do."

"Well, that's well shan, ain't it?"

"I must admit, sometimes it feels that way to me too," she confessed. "But we can't fight nature."

"What can ye do? Other than talkin' in my heid and callin' yer invisible friends te feed us?"

"I can summon my divine tiger."

"I knew she was yers. She looked up at ye like a pup to its mammy. That isn't a very Christian power, I reckon."

"It is much older than Christianity, Mum."

Her mother paused to consider the implications, and then she let the topic go. "So that dago really could've killed ye?"

"Yes."

"But why'd he wanna do that?"

"I honestly don't know, Mum. We have enemies who are scared of the power we have. It could have been one of them."

"And yer tellin' me that the Good Lord isn't strikin' down the enemies of his soldiers? What's he doin' instead? Lollygaggin' around singin' opera?"

Eleanor suddenly realized that her mother wasn't just referring to the abstract lord, she was referring to Vibhishana.

"No, Mum. He has much better things to do with his time. We can't just go around killing everyone who crosses us."

"But that bassa tried te kill ye, Ellie!"

Eleanor shrugged. "It wouldn't be very Christian to kill him, would it?"

Her mother humphed. "If ye ask me, God's green earth is lackin' a lot of justice, and if the Lord's soldiers imparted more of it, we'd all be better off."

"*Peut-être*," Eleanor murmured.

Debbie and Ruthy raced back to them with popcorn in one hand and candy floss in the other.

"Look, Amma! It was like magic! They made the candy out of thin air!" Debbie exclaimed.

"Just like Auntie Kate!" Ruthy added.

"Sshhh!" Debbie hissed as she glanced back at Edmund. "You know Abbi isn't supposed to know about that!"

"Sorry, Amma," Ruthy said as her posture deflated.

Eleanor smiled reassuringly. "It's too much for me to remember too, darling. Can I try some? I really am famished." Ruthy handed over both of her items, and Eleanor laughed. "No, darling. I just want a taste of each, then you can have the rest."

As Edmund approached with the boys, Eleanor rallied herself up, and then helped her mother.

"Do you think the parking lot's cleared? I'm ready for some dinner," she said cheerfully.

Edmund's stomach growled at the idea, and he and the children laughed together at it. He helped her put her mink coat back on, and then they meandered slowly out of the tent as the children ate their snacks, offering Edmund what they couldn't eat, and laughing as he swallowed down their remaining popcorn in one big Rakshasa gulp (a trick that Eleanor found rather unpleasant to watch, but that the children found delightful).

As they reached the exit, Eleanor peeked outside, noticing that the rain had picked up into a heavy torrent, and she realized that they'd left their umbrellas at their seats.

"Darling, I'll go get the umbrellas. Can you wait here with the children?"

He nodded his agreement with his mouth full of candy floss, and Eleanor scampered back across the empty arena to the front row. As she reached the seats and leaned down to grab the umbrellas that had fallen between them, the Great Pizzaz came running towards her.

Sheranee, come quick!

"I'm sorry!!!" he exclaimed. "I swear I didn't know they were real! I swear it! Your Majesty, you must believe me!"

As he rushed towards her, Sheranee pummeled him from behind like a silent predator, landing both of them between two rows of seats.

Discretion, my love! We mustn't get the trained tigers in trouble! Don't kill him!

Sheranee kept him pinned to the ground, blocked from Edmund's view between the seats. He wet himself. Eleanor glanced over at her family, who hadn't noticed the ruckus as they stood chatting happily, looking out at the rain.

"You are a professional knife thrower, and you didn't notice that your knives were real?" Eleanor asked as she loomed over him.

"They'd been switched! The handles are always heavy so that they look real in the air! But the blades aren't supposed to be real!"

"How did you know they were real after the fact, then?"

"I found my set in my tent! Your Majesty, you have to believe me!!!"

"Why do you keep calling me that?" Eleanor did not like the familiarity of the plea. "If your knives were replaced by a set that turned into flowers upon impact, why aren't you asking me how I did it?"

"Because it's after me!" he exclaimed. "It told me I had to apologize, or it would tear me from limb to limb!"

"Damn it!" Eleanor hissed. She lowered her voice. "Surpanakha, I told you to leave us alone! Durga commands it!"

As tears of terror streamed down his face, she noticed a shadow looming in the light of one of the emergency exit doors. It disappeared in a blur.

Eleanor kneeled down beside him and grabbed his hand.

You will tell me the truth. Shakti commands it! Did you try to kill me or not? Answer me!

I swear. I swear. I swear.

Why did you tell the ringmaster to choose me? Answer me!

We always choose a beautiful woman! It's better for the show! A beautiful woman with children is the best. It makes all the other mothers proud. How are you doing this? Are you in my mind?

This is my interrogation!

Are you a witch? Is that how you changed the knives?

You're a professional magician. Surely you must know that there's no such thing as witches or magic?

Is the monster yours? Is it at your command?

Eleanor didn't like his growing fear, and she liked even less that it was turning towards her.

No one controls the monster. She is a free agent of vengeance, and she always knows when you're lying. And if she is still after you now, you are holding something back. If you don't tell me, I can't help you.

As the shadow returned to the doorway, Eleanor glanced over at Edmund.

Tell me, you fool! Do you want to die?!

I'm a spy!

Whose spy? The Secret Service? Who is your employer?! Tell me now!

Mussolini!!!

Blimey. Eleanor realized at that moment that the entire unspoken conversation had been in Italian. Uma had done such a thorough job of translating that she hadn't even noticed.

What is one of Mussolini's spies doing in bloody Bunbury? ANSWER ME!

It was just one stop! No one questions a carny traveling all around.

What's your job?!

He paused as the shadow loomed.

Tell me!

I'm a recruiter. I recruit spies for the Fascist cause.

Eleanor had known he was a cold-hearted bastard the moment she'd laid eyes on him.

And why did you try to kill me tonight? TELL ME.

I... I... I... was ordered to! By my superior officer!

Eleanor let go.

"Dearest? Is everything alright?" Edmund called.

"Everything's fine, darling!" Eleanor called. "One of the umbrellas was stuck under the seat, but I've got it now!"

She grabbed his hand. *You'd better run, if ye know whit's good fer ye.*

Aren't you going to help me?!

I told you. No one controls the monster. We'll have to leave your fate up to God, and I can tell you with great authority that God doesn't like hate-mongering dictators or their agents.

"Let him go, Sheranee," Eleanor whispered. She lowered her voice until it was almost inaudible. "Monty, find out why he was ordered to kill me. I want to know who his superior officers are and where their orders came from."

"Yes, my lady."

"And do it before Surpanakha finishes the job."

"I cannot stop her, my lady. I must stay away from her or she will try to enslave me."

"Don't worry about it. He deserves to die."

"Yes, my lady."

She stood up to offer the Great Pizzaz her final words of wisdom. "Enjoy purgatory. I'm sure you'll make some friends there."

Sheranee disappeared back to her divine perch, and as the Great Pizzaz struggled to get up, Eleanor grabbed the umbrellas and skipped cheerfully back to her family.

"It's really coming down now, isn't it? Let's go."

She opened the umbrellas and led them outside alongside a few other remaining stragglers from the audience, most of whom were walking towards a series of buses lined up at the far end of the parking lot. Her heart raced with urgency to get her family swiftly away from Surpanakha's vicinity.

"Dearest, are you alright?" Edmund asked concernedly. He leaned in to whisper. "Why are you afraid?"

"Darling, I'm perfectly fine. It's just been a long night, and I'm jumpy from the adrenalin of that knife show."

"It was thoroughly impressive," he said as he accepted her excuse. "I was half-inclined to blur right up there and rescue you before he threw the first one."

"I'm glad you didn't, darling."

"So am I."

As they prepared themselves to run across the parking lot to their lone waiting car, another car screeched around the tent, speeding towards them. But, as she prepared herself to call upon all of her Yaksha helpers to come to their rescue, the sound of broken glass and an ominous thud indicated that someone else had borne the brunt of its impact.

They all looked over, about a hundred feet away, to where a number of people had been walking towards the public bus. A woman began screaming, while several children began crying. The car backed up, drove around its victim, and then screeched its tires as it sped right at Eleanor.

In a blur, Edmund threw himself in front of it. With an excruciating crunch, the car hit him, and the remnants of the broken windshield shattered.

Edmund was thrown back onto the ground. The bairns screamed. The driver shouted a series of epithets that Eleanor couldn't make out as he backed up again and drove around Edmund's body to make his escape out of the parking lot and onto the main road as fast as his broken car could drive.

"Edmund!" Eleanor ran to his side. The bairns followed.

"Abbi!" Charlie exclaimed.

"Abbi, are you alright?!" Debbie whimpered.

Edmund sat up and rubbed his head. He hissed with pain as his plasma worked its way to the surface to heal several gaping wounds on his face and neck. Eleanor held her breath as he glanced down, assessing his own condition.

"Are you alright? It isn't a mortal wound, is it?" she whispered as the bairns arrived by their side, slowing their pace with reticence as they spied the alien sight of his plasma.

He looked down at the surface wounds healing on his hands. "I'll be fine."

"Abbi?" Ruthy squeaked.

He smiled reassuringly, even though Eleanor could feel his anxiety bursting at the seams. "I'm fine, my bairns. I'll be just fine."

Debbie came forward nervously, and then the others followed. He glanced at Eleanor, and then held out his healing hands for them to watch.

"This isn't the first time I've been injured like this, but it is the first time such young bairns have watched. I hope that it doesn't frighten you?"

"A little bit," Debbie confessed.

Edmund smiled. "It frightens me a little bit too. I know it looks a bit alien, but for better and worse, this violet blood has helped me out of a bind more times than I can count."

"Is that angel blood?" Charlie asked.

"I suppose you could call it that," Edmund agreed.

"Lord Almighty," Eleanor's mother murmured as she reached them at her slower pace.

His plasma finished up its work, and a gust of icy wind blew right through their coats. Edmund's eyes turned black. He looked over to the first victim lying in the mud, then to the lights of the escaping car, and then to the wide eyes of his watching family.

"The other victim is dying," he whispered. "And that wanker was aiming right at you, Eleanor."

"That driver's a scoundrel, I reckon," Eleanor's mother muttered. "He deserves to dance with the Devil before supper!"

"Stop him, Abbi!" Charlie exclaimed.

"Yeah, get him!" Howie added.

"He might strike again, darling," Eleanor hated to admit.

Edmund glanced again at his audience and back over to the other victim, debating his options.

"You heard 'em, Abbi! Do yer thing!" Eleanor's mother reiterated.

"Darling, you don't need to kill him," Eleanor whispered. "Do what Percy showed you."

Edmund took one final look at them, and then in a barely visible blur, he went after the culprit's car.

"Lord Almighty," Eleanor's mother repeated.

"I'm going to see if I can help the other victim." Eleanor handed her mother the keys to their car. "Mum, get the bairns into the car and wait there."

Without looking back, Eleanor ran towards the crowd that was gathering around the victim. As she reached the poor girl, she wished that she had Kuveni to lean on. The girl was very pregnant, and Eleanor could feel her life-force fading.

"I was a trauma nurse in the war," she said as she pushed her way through the crowd. "Is there a doctor here?"

No one volunteered. Eleanor leaned over the bloody girl who was struggling to breathe and took her hand, looking straight into her eyes.

I'm an angel, dear girl. Do you know who did this to you?

The girl nodded in the negative.

Are you here with anyone?

The girl nodded in the negative as tears streamed down her face. *I just wanted to see the animals.*

Eleanor's heart almost broke at the tragic simplicity of it. *I'm going to do what I can, dear girl, but I will be honest with you. Your injuries are dire. Please tell me your name. Do you have any family?*

Eliza Humphry, ma'am. I only have my parents. My husband died three months ago in an accident at the docks.

I'm sorry, my darling girl. You will see him soon.

What about my baby?

I don't know, my darling. We will do everything we can to save him—to save both of you. But don't be afraid. No matter what happens now, the cycle will restart, and you will have another life.

Eleanor worked hard to push back her emotions. It had been too long since she'd had practice ignoring the senseless human tragedies that threatened to disarm her completely when she thought too much about them.

Edmund pushed through the crowd and kneeled down beside her. His eyes were still black, and Eleanor hoped that in the dark, their audience wouldn't notice.

"Eleanor, she's dying," he whispered.

"I know, darling. There's nothing I can do."

"Is there anything to be done?"

"Only at a hospital. Darling, why don't you take her? Take her now. She will die here waiting for an ambulance."

He glanced around at their crowd.

"Just do it, Edmund. I will make your excuses! I will take the children to the inn, and you can meet us there. Alright?"

Edmund reached under the girl and gathered her into his arms. "I'm taking you to the hospital. Please don't be afraid."

"Are you an angel too?" she asked meekly.

"Yes."

The crowd gasped as Edmund disappeared in a blur.

"He's an angel," Eleanor explained flatly. She had no energy left to put on a show. "We're both angels. Now take with you our blessings, and go home in safety. Tell your families how much you love them, and hold them tight, celebrating every warm breath that their living bodies produce."

Without letting them get a better look at her, she ran towards the car. "Kuveni, please help him. He can't blur into the hospital with his black eyes, covered in blood."

"I'm already on it," Kuveni's disembodied voice replied. "Be careful, Eleanor. There is darkness in the air tonight."

As she reached the driver's door of their car, the ringmaster came running after her.

"For god's sake, will this night never end?" she exclaimed. "I just want to go home with my family!"

"I'm sorry, countess," he said as he reached her. "You can go in just a minute. After you give me your ring and your coat." He held a petty knife out at her.

Eleanor laughed at the absurdity. "Are you mugging me? After I put on the show of a lifetime with your Italian spy?"

"I just want to retire, lady, and I reckon your ring and your coat will help me do it."

She glanced over at her mother who was holding the children tight as they all watched with dread.

"You picked the wrong night for petty crime, my friend." Eleanor smashed him in the nose with her elbow, grabbed his knife as he reeled backwards with surprise, and then she rushed him and kneed him in the groin. He collapsed into the mud in a fetal position, and she kicked him in the stomach with her heel for good measure. "You'll run as fast as you can, if ye know whit's good fer ye. The angels of vengeance are on the prowl tonight."

Eleanor hopped into the driver's seat.

"Amma?" Ruthy whimpered.

"Everything's perfectly fine, my darlings. Abbi and Amma have everything under control," she said as her mother handed her the keys without a word.

She slammed them into the ignition, and took off with a screech, throwing the children back against the seat with the force of their velocity.

"Now, let's go have a nice family dinner, shall we?"

When they reached the Seaside B&B, the rain had slowed to a gentle sprinkle, and the warm yellow lights of the cute beachfront Victorian were on. The children looked haggard from worry as Eleanor glanced back at them in the light of the streetlamp. Eleanor had hoped to find Edmund there waiting for them, but instead, the elderly innkeepers came rushing out with umbrellas to greet them.

"*Mein Gott*, you are much later than we thought!" the man exclaimed with a thick German accent.

"I'm sorry, Mr. Schindler. We were unexpectedly held back," Eleanor replied as she hopped out and coaxed the children out of the back seat. "What a relief it is to be here now, though."

"Where is the colonel?" Mrs. Schindler asked as she noticed his conspicuous absence.

"He had to help a dying girl get to the hospital. She was hit by a car."

"How horrible!" she exclaimed. "Come! Come inside where it's warm!"

She helped Eleanor herd the children up the stairs and into the foyer. Once they were inside, the couple took their coats and began hanging them in the coat closet.

"Dinner is in the dining room, but it is a bit cold by now. I can refry the schnitzel, if you'd like?" Mrs. Schindler offered.

"We'd better warm the spätzle in the oven too," Mr. Schindler suggested. "Although, you can eat the rottkraut and the pretzels now. You must be hungry."

"Are you... krauts?" Eleanor's mother asked bluntly.

"Mother!" Eleanor hissed. She realized that in her haste, she had forgotten to preempt her mother's predictably embarrassing reaction.

"We are from Germany originally, yes," Mr. Schindler replied politely.

"And Abbi agreed to spend the night with them?" Eleanor's mother addressed her.

"Remember when we talked all about accepting people who are different from us, Mum? Those many, *many* times?"

"But *krauts*, Eleanor! They killed millions of our boys!"

"The war killed millions of our boys."

Eleanor's mother humphed her disagreement.

"Besides, the Schindlers didn't kill anyone, Mum. They've lived in Australia for thirty years."

"Our son fought with the Commonwealth," Mrs. Schindler informed her. "He was decorated with three medals of honor by the king. He lives in London now, working for British Intelligence, using his fluent German to help the Empire."

"Well then, I suppose Abbi knows what he's doing," Eleanor's mother conceded. "But do we have to *eat* like krauts?"

Eleanor laughed. "You'll love it, Mum. All the German food is right up your ally. Fatty and tart and rich and fried with four kinds of potatoes."

206

"Come," Mr. Schindler suggested. "Why don't you wait in the parlor by the fire while we warm your dinner."

All four children clung to Eleanor as she followed him through the old-fashioned hallway, into a warm room with several couches and chairs centered around a deep, roaring fireplace. There was a Christmas tree in the corner, and stockings along the mantle. Eleanor took her seat on the couch, and the children crowded in all around her.

Mrs. Schindler sighed happily at the sight. "You'd almost think it was really Christmas, wouldn't you? How about some hot cocoa while you wait?" She placed a tray with steaming hot cocoa and marshmallows on the low table before them. "We thought you might need something to tide you over, so we kept it brewing all evening. It might be a bit strong."

The children dazedly leaned forward to take the cocoa, and Eleanor smiled and winked as Mr. Schindler handed her a hefty glass of pungent pear brandy.

"I'll have what she's having," Eleanor's mother said as she sat down in a neighboring chair.

"It's German, Mum, are you sure you can handle it?" Eleanor teased.

"I'll manage, if ye'll indulge an auld biddy's whim," she said sheepishly to Mr. Schindler, who offered her a polite smile as she settled in.

Mr. Schindler returned with the brandy for Eleanor's mother and then joined his wife in the kitchen, while they all sat in silence sipping their drinks and staring into the fire. The children began to relax slightly, but Eleanor's nerves were still going a mile a minute as she waited for Edmund to return.

Her brain could hardly process everything that had come to pass on their mundane family outing. How many attempted murders? She'd already lost count. Maybe four? First the Great Pizzaz had tried to murder her, then Surpanakha had tried to murder him, then that driver had tried to murder the poor pregnant girl, and then the ringmaster had tried to murder her… Nope, it was five. She'd already forgotten about the driver *also* trying to murder her, but instead forcing Edmund to demonstrate his most alien trait in front of the bairns and her mother, who so far seemed to be taking it better than she could have dared to hope…

Her mind wandered to wondering what the carnage would be from Surpanakha being there to observe the many nefarious plots afoot. She realized that a large part of her didn't even care; in fact, she rather hoped Surpanakha would finish off their dirty work for them, like she had with Mac. She pushed the thought away. She knew it was a shamefully unvirtuous one, full of petty human vengeance and an unwise failure to respect the unpredictable danger posed by Surpanakha's madness. She squeezed the children, taking the advice she'd given the dying woman's bystanders, appreciating every warm breath that their live human bodies were producing.

"Amma, do you think Abbi killed that man? The one who ran over the girl?" Debbie finally asked. All of the children looked up at her, waiting for an answer.

"I don't know, darling," she replied truthfully. "It depends whether the man tried to hurt Abbi. Sometimes he's too strong, and he can't control himself."

"Do you think he killed the man who tried to rob you?" Charlie asked.

"No. I'm certain that he didn't. Abbi doesn't kill for vengeance. He only kills when he has to, to protect the innocent."

"So that means he won't kill Da?" Debbie asked quietly. "Unless Da is trying to hurt him?"

"Or us?" Ruthy added.

Eleanor was startled by the question. "Yes, that is exactly what it means. Why do you think he might kill your father?"

"He said that he wanted to kill our evil fathers," Ruthy squeaked. "We heard him say so when we were listening to you talking from the hallway on your birthday."

"Ye wee clipe, Ruthy!" Howie hissed as he pinched her.

"Tsk, Howie! Do we express ourselves with violence?" Eleanor captured his hand and squeezed it in a gentle admonishment.

"No, Amma," he sulked.

"One should ne'er regret the truth, the wise women say," she informed him. "Have you all been worrying about this? For months now? That Abbi is going to kill your fathers?"

They nodded, and Ruthy hid her face in Eleanor's sleeve.

"They deserve it," Charlie whispered.

Eleanor pulled them into a tight hug. "We all have dark thoughts sometimes, my darlings. It doesn't mean that we act on them. Sometimes we can wish someone harm, and we must accept that thought so we can let it go and focus on what will make our own lives better. Vengeance never makes our lives better. It only forces us to hold onto the pain of the past. It is a punishment of our own making, alright? Now, we must all let go of our vengeful thoughts, so we can focus on the beauty of being where we are now, together."

She believed her motherly advice was true, even though she knew that it was much easier said than done. She had also strategically omitted promising that Edmund would not kill their fathers, as she knew that it was a strong possibility, given how foolish and desperate they'd already become.

They all looked up as the front door flew open, and a cold draft whooshed through the room.

"Abbi?!"

The children rushed off the couch to go check, and Eleanor pushed past them, hoping to preempt anything that would undo her momentary progress with their nerves.

Kuveni escorted Edmund inside and shut the door behind them. His shirt and his hands were covered in blood, and his eyes were still black. There was no stopping her mother or the children from seeing him in his frightening state, and so she resigned herself to managing the damage.

He looked like he might cry as she approached him. "She died in my arms, Eleanor. I couldn't save her or the baby." He glanced at Kuveni. "Kate intercepted me with her car just outside the emergency room. They sent that poor girl straight down to the morgue."

"Darling, you did all that you could do."

Eleanor guided him into the parlor and glanced down to spy the children staring at him with subtle, unspoken fear.

"*Guten abend*, my friends! Let me help you!" Kuveni rushed to distract the Schindlers until Eleanor could get him out of his demonic state.

"I didn't do everything I could, Eleanor. I should have helped her first. I shouldn't have wasted time going after the culprit. If I'd gotten her to the hospital sooner, she might have survived."

His hands were freezing with Rakshasa frigidity, and she led him to the fire to warm up. She gathered up one of the children's half-empty cocoas and offered it to him, but he put it back down on the table.

"Darling, she was already dying. There was nothing anyone could do for her. You gave her a fighting chance, but in the end, it wasn't her destiny to be saved."

She held his cheek in her hand as she looked straight into his black eyes and reached up onto her tiptoes to kiss him gently on the lips. She knew the children were watching, and she was glad. She wanted them to see that she wasn't the least bit scared of him.

"Now, say your mantras, darling, and get yourself back under control. There is nothing more to be done."

He closed his eyes and grimaced as he forced his demon back into its place. When he opened them back up, she smiled.

"I love you, Edmund. It's been a long night. Why don't I help you change your clothes, and then we can join our family for a nice schnitzel?"

210

"I'm not hungry," he whispered.

"Then perhaps a few pots of tea? Or perhaps some mulled wine? It is almost Christmas in July, after all, and you're frozen through and through."

"I do like mulled wine," he admitted. He glanced over self-consciously at the children and Eleanor's mother. "I'm sorry you had to see that. Sometimes there's nothing anyone can do. Not even us."

As she helped him walk towards the staircase, the children ran after him, pummeling him into a hug. He kneeled down and let himself give into tears. They squeezed him, and he wiped his violet tears into his skin before they could notice. He kissed each of them on the forehead, and they shivered, and then hugged him again.

"I love you all so much," he whispered.

"We love you, Abbi."

Kuveni approached from the hallway behind them. "Dinner is ready, my loves. Edmund, darling, go bathe and change your clothes. I will help the children clean up."

He glanced down self-consciously, noticing the blood that his hugs had accidentally wiped onto their outfits.

"Go, my dear boy. Don't think twice about it," she reiterated.

As Eleanor took his hand to lead him up the stairs, her mother grabbed Edmund's wrist and held him back.

"It was a right mercy of the Good Lord Himself that that poor lass died lookin' into the face of an angel. She dunne die alone, Abbi, and she dunne die scared on an operatin' table, lookin' into the cold face of a doctor who cuddne saved 'er anyway. Don't ye forget it, ye hear?"

She let him go, and he nodded, battling the ball in his throat. Eleanor squeezed her mother's hand in thanks, and escorted Edmund up the stairs.

"Now, you're all clean, and you're all clean..." Kuveni whispered as she tapped each of the children's sweaters, dissolving all of the blood.

As they reached the master bedroom of the inn that they knew well after their months of staying there in transit to and from Perth, Eleanor felt a pleasant breeze rustle her hair, and she knew exactly what it meant.

"Darling, I'll join you in a minute. Why don't you start a bath?"

He trudged into the bathroom and closed the door without another word.

She turned around and guided Mr. Montero silently into the bedroom across from theirs, closing the door behind them.

"I eliminated all of the evidence," he whispered. "All of the blood and gore from the Italian bloke, the ringmaster, and the driver of the rogue vehicle have been cleared. I also dissolved the car completely so it couldn't be traced. I will use Lord Vibhishana's resources to uncover who the driver was and why he was baiting you and Edmund."

"Are you sure he was baiting us?"

Monty handed her two photographs. "Those were in the glove compartment."

The first was a smiling photograph of the dead girl before she was pregnant, posing by a Ferris wheel with her doomed husband at a beach carnival.

"Shiva's wrath." Eleanor gasped as she glanced at the second.

It was a candid photograph of her and Edmund with the children dining in their garden with Oz and Yvie, Mae, and Father O'Donnelly.

"Who could have taken this picture?" she asked as she squinted at it. Stanley was in the background carrying a tray of wine. "Could Norwenn or Grimby have been snooping on the property?"

"No. I have not allowed anyone uninvited onto the property."

"Then who else could it be?"

"My lady, it must be someone who is allowed on your property, but who isn't in the picture. You or the Helmsworths have a mole on your staff."

"Blimey. Did Edmund see these? Did he kill the driver?"

"Your husband left the assassin unconscious after he disabled the vehicle. The photos were in a sealed envelope, with a note left for me. This is not a good development, my lady. As Lord Vibhishana would say, it is very, very bad."

He handed her the envelope. Written in Surpanakha's archaic hand, in an ancient script that took Uma a moment to translate, it read:

We make a good team, Monty. Let's do this again. Victory to the Holy Mother.

"Great." Eleanor sighed. All of her energy for worrying about Surpanakha had been sapped by her many other problems.

"It is not great, my lady."

"That was sarcasm again. The Yaksha people are quite literal, aren't you? Is Kuveni an exception to the rule?"

"Kuveni is an exception to many rules, my lady."

Eleanor felt her patience, and her capacity for bad news waning. "Did you learn anything else about our murderous Italian spy?"

"I was too busy cleaning up Surpanakha's mess, my lady. She left a gory trail, like she always does. If we are not careful, the authorities will start to link the crimes to your presence. We must keep their attention off of you, and their awareness of the severity of the crimes as limited as Yakshaly possible."

Eleanor sighed with stress. "At least it's better than whatever is humanly possible…"

"I will investigate further, my lady. Please summon me if you see any more evidence of Surpanakha's presence. We must keep Lord Vibhishana and Lady Mélusine apprised."

"Aye," Eleanor agreed.

With a pious bow, Mr. Montero disappeared.

Eleanor returned to the master bedroom and locked the door behind her. The fireplace was smoking with Edmund's burning clothes. A fresh, unwrinkled suit was laid out for him on the bed, as was a casual, low-waisted winter wool dress for her.

"Thank you, Kuveni," she whispered.

"Take your time, my darling girl. I will watch over the bairns. Celebrate your triumph of light together."

Eleanor snorted. "It was hardly a triumph of light. It was a gory bloodbath with at least one innocent victim."

"You stopped an evil spy and two greedy, evil men, Eleanor. And after all of it, those children and even your mother saw Edmund's demon, and they chose to love him anyway. Tonight you must focus on that. It is a triumph not to be ignored."

"I love you, Kuveni," Eleanor whispered.

"Go to him, dear girl. He needs you."

She took a deep, calming breath, and found her gentle husband standing naked under the flowing showerhead in the steaming hot bath, watching the blood circle as it went down the drain. Eleanor stripped naked, and then stepped into the bathtub behind him, putting her arms around his waist and holding him for several minutes until he was willing to talk.

"I wanted to kill that man so badly, and then I wanted to save the girl. In the end, what I wanted didn't bloody matter, Eleanor."

"No one is omnipotent, darling."

"It's happening," he whispered ominously as he turned around to face her.

"What is, darling?"

"I'm starting to believe that there's an order to things. It is a dangerous position to be in. God always finds a way to prove me wrong."

"God?" Eleanor asked with genuine surprise.

"Destiny? Fate? The great smiting power?"

"Nature?"

"Whatever you want to call it, an innocent girl and child died tonight, and the so-called angels did bloody nothing to stop it. How are we going to explain it to the children?"

"You tried, darling," Eleanor reiterated. "In the end, that's all we can do. They don't believe you're omnipotent any more than I do. Perhaps it is good for them to see proof of how ordinary you are. You didn't want them to believe you were an angel anyway, did you?"

"I suppose not. But I don't want them to be frightened of me either, Eleanor. I was frightened of myself tonight."

"And yet, there they were, hugging your bloody arms anyway, darling."

He finally smiled. "They were, weren't they?"

"They love you, darling. We all do. And they know you better tonight than they ever have. They know a bit of what your burden really is, and that your life, your responsibility, isn't just about an exceptional prowess at cricket. It is an important thing for children to see, especially these children. I think it is an important thing for my mother to see too, to be quite honest. We can all use a reminder of the limitations of our power."

"I suppose."

"Kate is distracting them downstairs, and the door is locked," she said as she reached around to squeeze his bum. "How about we enjoy the warm bath for a change?"

"Inside the house?" he asked jokingly as he perked up at the idea. "How civilized!"

"I love you, Edmund. I'm proud of you, and I know that the bairns are too."

Edmund pulled her onto him and sighed with relief as he kissed her. "God, how I love you, Eleanor."

And so, the two tired angels pushed back their complicated emotions after an exceptionally difficult night, and allowed themselves to enjoy the novel pleasures of being wonderfully sheltered while making love to each other under the pitter-pattering of a cold winter rain.

CHAPTER 12 – WHAT FALLS IN THE DEAD OF NIGHT

Eleanor awoke to Edmund sitting up beside her in bed, staring out the window. It was still dark, and the room was freezing cold. They were both naked.

"Is that snow?" she asked as she noticed the flurries dancing in the light of the streetlamp just outside the window.

"I reckon it's officially Christmas in July now. Oz promised me before we took the car yesterday that it never snows here. We might be stranded here for days."

"I've been stranded in worse places. We are right across from the beach, you know."

"I suppose."

"What time is it? Should we wake the bairns? They'll be thrilled about the snow. We used to love playing in the snow in the dead of night when I was a lass. It would only snow once or twice a year, and each time it was just as exciting as the last."

"I think it's around three, maybe four." His tone was troubled.

"Are you still thinking about that poor girl? Her death wasn't your fault."

"She is swirling around in my mind, along with many other thoughts."

Eleanor sat up and shivered. She pulled the blankets up to cover her naked chest, and to create a subtle barrier between her bare skin and Edmund's Rakshasa frigidity.

"Do you want to talk about what's troubling you?"

He sat for a long time, struggling with the answer. "I'm not sure if I should."

"Why, darling? Are you contemplating murder again? You know you don't have to hide those dark thoughts from me. It is healthier for us to discuss them."

"That's in there too."

"Jimmy?"

"And Fergus. And that man who was driving the car earlier, and scores of other worthless bastards. Why stop with those three? Why not hunt down and kill all of the abusive wankers and murderers and rapists on Earth? I was good enough at killing those terrified German teenagers in the trenches, surely I'd be excellent at killing those villains who truly deserve to die."

"You're not a dark avenger, darling. It isn't your nature. You're like me. You think about it, and then you do the right thing instead. You bring hope to people who are trapped by the barbarity of others. It is a much worthier calling that allows you to swim in light instead of drown in darkness."

"Then why do all of those worthless bastards get to have bairns of their own, Eleanor? Why do they get to see their own children look up at them, with little hints of themselves at every turn? I've been around for longer than the longest human lifetime, and I still don't know what that feels like."

Eleanor was utterly blindsided. She felt like he'd just walloped her in the face with a cricket bat... or perhaps hit her with a car... no, a bus... no, a train...

He turned to her. "Dearest, I know that you've wanted to take your time, and I've respected that. I really have. But now we have

218

these children, and this beautiful life, and we've figured out how to deal with the responsibility. We've even figured out how to sneak away for marital pleasures! We've changed thousands of Ned's nappies, and we have a house, and a cook, and your mother, and dear friends, and a competent butler... Don't you think it's time that we tried for one of our own?"

It was by far the most assertive he had ever been on the topic. Eleanor was so overwhelmed, she didn't even know where to start.

"So four children aren't enough for you?" It wasn't the most diplomatic point, but it wasn't wrong either.

"I, more than anyone, know how beautiful it can be for children to bond with someone who isn't their father, but they are not my children, Eleanor. They are Jimmy's and Fergus's. And those abusive wankers could be knocking down our door at any moment to take them back."

"I'm not going to let them. They can go to Hell."

Edmund rethought his strategy. "Dearest, the children look so much like you that I understand why you feel like they're yours, but don't you want a child who really is our child? A fiery Scottish thistle just like her mother, or an adventurous little horseman who's just a little bit too shy for his own good just like his father?"

"Darling, it isn't that simple."

"Why not? All you have to do is stop taking that pill, don't you?"

Eleanor felt her fiery Celtic temper burbling dangerously in a cauldron of too many repressed emotions.

"Yes, darling. I just stop taking a pill, and a baby will magically appear in my arms. Didn't your tutors teach you that? Storks are very effective these days."

"You don't need to be sarcastic, Eleanor. I know that it requires more effort than that, but where there's a will there's a way. Look at what we've been able to do with these children in only a couple of months, after their parents have ruined them for years!"

Eleanor's throat hurt as she worked to keep her voice down. "Why aren't these children enough? Why do you have to have more, more, more? Is it really that important that the child be yours? That's a very selfish point of view, you know. I expected more from you."

"Then it is me! You don't want to have *my* child! Why didn't you ever admit it, Eleanor? Why didn't you admit it before we were married?!"

He might as well have shouted, "Ah ha!"

Eleanor's temper was fully ignited.

"Because it didn't matter! Why the hell did it matter?! Would you not have married me? Did you think you were marrying my childbearing womb? Forgive me for thinking that you wanted to marry me for me, and not as an incubator for your future offspring. You're right. We should have talked about it before we got married. If I'd known you cared so much, I would have suggested you avoid disappointment completely and go find a nice vapid lass who could bear your twenty bouncing babies with a smile on her face. Maybe we should get divorced and you can propose to Illa. I bet she's on the prowl for a husband right about now; she did reach the ripe young age of seventy-five. You'll only be cradle-robbing her by half a century instead of almost a whole one."

"I knew it! I knew it was about me. Why didn't you ever admit it, Eleanor?"

"It's not about you."

"Kate is downstairs right now. Why don't we go ask her how my people's children are different? Even Mr. Johnson said they are almost the same as human children. We can't just keep limiting ourselves out of fear, Eleanor! We don't even know what we're afraid of!"

"Speak for yourself," Eleanor scoffed.

"So you *are* afraid!"

"OF COURSE, I'M AFRAID!" she shouted. "Why wouldn't I be? Any woman with half a brain *should* be afraid. Being pregnant and giving birth is *dangerous*, Edmund, and it is even more dangerous for a forty-year-old hag!"

"It wasn't dangerous when we were newlyweds, was it? Why did you have to wait, Eleanor? Why couldn't we have talked about this three years ago?!"

"IT *WAS* DANGEROUS! HAVING BABIES IS DANGEROUS!" She stood up and began pacing, trying to keep the flames of Durga at bay. "Did Kate ever tell you how old your mother was when she died?"

"No." He looked at her imploringly. "She's told me nothing about how or when she died."

Eleanor's reserves were gone, and she rolled her eyes at his ignorance. "She died in childbirth, Edmund. How could you not understand their thousands of references to it? They weren't even good at beating around the bush. You should pay better bloody attention."

He was finally speechless.

"She was twenty-seven, Edmund. Twenty-bloody-seven. And Yvie's mother died in childbirth when she was thirty-five. She'd already had six children, Edmund. *Six*. Why couldn't she stop at five? Why in the bloody hell was *five* not enough? And Yvie almost died herself! She was thirty, Edmund, and we were *this* close to losing her!"

"What do you mean?"

Eleanor sighed a long sigh of annoyance. "Why do you think we were all so attentive to her for weeks after she had Ned? She hemorrhaged the day after he was born, and she was bedridden for almost a month! If it weren't for Kate's exceptional skills at midwifery, Yvie would be dead right now, and she still can't run or ride the horses! Why did you think she wasn't playing polo with us?! She used to be an excellent equestrian, and now she has to watch from the sidelines!"

"Why didn't any of you tell me?!" he exclaimed.

"She didn't want you to know! She didn't want everyone knowing her private tragedy, Edmund, and it was her right to decide who would and wouldn't treat her like an invalid. Now I've given up her confidence, all to make a point that I'm not sure you're even understanding. GIVING BIRTH IS DANGEROUS!"

"But your mother had three! And Martha had two, and Mary had two... and the human species continues to march along! Queen Victoria had nine children, didn't she? And she was the most powerful queen in history!"

"Well, *George Ridgeway*, why don't I just bear it like Queen Victoria?"

"That's not a fair comparison, Eleanor. I'm nothing like George Ridgeway, and you know it. All I meant to say is that it must be safe normally, or else there wouldn't be so many mothers around. Can't you see that you'd have the finest resources in the world? Martha and Mary didn't have Kate's help, and you would!"

"No, Edmund. They had mine. And let me tell you, it was as gory as the bloody trenches. I will never forgive your tutors for keeping you in ignorance about the bloody mess that is human reproduction. It is disgusting and awful and painful, and I didn't want to do it before I met you, and I don't want to do it now! How four beautiful children who adore you isn't enough for you is something I will never understand, and I honestly don't know if I can forgive you!"

"I was just saying how I felt, Eleanor."

"And I'm saying how I feel. It isn't about *you*, Edmund. It's about me not wanting to put myself through the risk and the pain of pregnancy and childbirth when I have everything I've ever wanted right here in front of me. Now, if I'm not enough for you, then I'd rather know now. I have many better things to do with my time than to nurse a pining soldier who's too busy longing for something I'll never bloody give him to see the perfect life he's letting pass right by. Do you know what kind of fortune it is to have four beautiful, brilliant, respectful children just fall right into your lap? It NEVER happens! Now open your bloody eyes!"

The conclusion was far harsher than anything she'd ever considered, let alone anything she'd dared to utter out loud, but her Celtic temper was raging, and she was focused not on back-peddling, but on keeping other, even more dangerous thoughts from bursting out of her mouth in her uncontrolled rage.

"I don't see why the two things are related, Eleanor. I'm being a wonderful father to the bairns, and I thought that you would see me doing it, and realize what a wonderful father I'd be to our child."

"How many times do I have to bloody tell you that *it isn't about you?* The fact that you don't seem to care about my welfare in this makes me question how much you really love me, Edmund. I have never, ever questioned it like I am right now."

"That's not fair, Eleanor! You know how much I care!"

"Then why do I have to produce your bloody child, Edmund? WHY?!"

"I didn't say that you did, Eleanor. I just said that I wanted it, and for three years, I thought that you did too."

"Would you have married me if I'd told you outright the first time we met that I was barren?"

"Are you?"

Eleanor rolled her eyes with such vigor that they hurt. "It was a theoretical question, Edmund. What if I'd told you I was barren? Would you have moved on and sought greener pastures? When we met were you really just in the market for an incubator for your offspring?"

"You know that I wasn't, Eleanor."

"So why can't you just drop it? Why can't you be happy with the great fortune of what you already have right in front of you? Why does the fact that I'm choosing not to risk the dangers of pregnancy and childbirth have to be any different than if I were barren?"

He thought for a long time about his answer. "It just is. If there is possibility, there is hope, Eleanor. And I will wait as long as you need me to."

"Then you will wait until I'm so bloody old that I'm barren."

"But, why, Eleanor?! We would make such good parents!"

"WE *ARE* PARENTS!!!!!! We have four children who call us 'Mummy' and 'Daddy' for Christ's sake. *You* are an orphan, Edmund. Do you realize how hypocritical you're being? How can they possibly not be enough for you?!"

"It just isn't the same, Eleanor. There is something special about having your own children. In all my life, I'd never met a woman I'd *wanted* to have children with, and then I met you. Your children would be the most beautiful children in the world! Don't you wonder what they would be like?"

"OF COURSE I DO!!!! But I wouldn't be around to enjoy them! I'D BE DEAD!!!!"

"But why???!!! Did they tell you something? Did Kate tell you that you would die in childbirth? Tell me, Eleanor. I deserve to know."

Eleanor paused. She had been trying to crawl her way out of their abyss without giving away the true source of her valid fear, and she couldn't do it anymore.

"Your mother died in childbirth, Edmund. Kate said that it is very common for human women to die having hybrid babies with your people."

"Why didn't any of them tell me that?"

"Because you don't accept truths that you don't want to hear, Edmund. When you stop acting like a child, they will stop treating you like one."

"Did she say that it was a given? Is it a given that women die in childbirth having our children, or is it just more common?"

Eleanor wanted to slap him as she heard the hint of hope in his voice. She'd been holding onto the truth for so long, guarding it with her aching soul, protecting him from the dark, ugly, tragic possibility that she would die in childbirth, and now she'd let the cat out of the bag, and it didn't even matter!

In that moment, she hated him. She hated him for the lies she'd been forced to tell, she hated him for the truths he refused to see, and she hated him for making her feel like it was her bloody fault for not wanting to dive blindly into a painful and dangerous endeavor that *she* would have to bear, all for an objective that she didn't even care about.

"The fact that you just asked me that question makes you more of a villain than when you ripped those men to shreds."

"Which men?"

"All of them."

"I was just trying to get all of the information, Eleanor."

"Hogwash! Don't you dare lie to me, Edmund. It's bad enough you're lying to yourself. You were looking for a loophole! A detail that would still make it possible for your dream to come true! Well, there isn't one, for Christ's sake. There isn't *always* a magical solution to solve your bloody problems! You're in the real world now, where you have to live imperfectly like us mere mortals."

"I wasn't lying, Eleanor. I don't understand why I'm the villain here."

She leaned in and stared him straight in the eye. "You tell me honestly, Edmund George Marriner, if I threw chance to the wind and told you right now that I would gladly get pregnant and bear your child, even though every other woman *on the planet* who's ever tried it has died, would you say yes or no? HONESTLY."

He hesitated, and she began hyperventilating as she tried to hold in her raging sobs.

"NO! I'd say no, Eleanor!" he lied to himself and to her.

She gathered up the dress that she'd worn to dinner many hours earlier out of its crumpled pile on the floor and slipped it on without any undergarments.

225

"Eleanor, wait." Edmund hissed as he put his feet down on the freezing floor. "I was just saying what I was feeling. You always talk about how we should be open about these things, don't you?"

"Darling, if I told you that you were a worthless, bloodthirsty demon, would you forgive me? Just because it was what I was feeling?"

"Is that what you think?"

"No, Edmund. You're much worse. You're a selfish, thoughtless, insatiable human man. You care only about yourself, making me feel like there's something wrong with me just because I don't want to die so that you can have what Jimmy and Fergus and Oz have. You're just like the rest of the greedy, egotistical buggers I never had any interest in marrying. You've shown your true colors now. I hope you're happy."

"Eleanor, wait."

"I'm going out. Perhaps a night in your cold bed alone will give you a taste of your wonderful future life with our child. I hope she's enough for you, because you'll be raising her alone while I'm rotting in the ground… But at least she'll have your smile."

She slammed the door and ran down the stairs. She grabbed a pair of snow boots that were waiting for her by the door and threw on her mink coat, barely holding in her sobs before she ran out into the snow and slammed the front door behind her.

It was the fight that would haunt him for the rest of his life.

Eleanor sat alone on the white sand beach across from the Seaside B&B as the fluffy snow flurried listlessly around her. It was hardly a snowstorm at all, and certainly not a blizzard. Even with Uma's unaccustomed temperament, the mink coat was perfectly sufficient in the still night. It was as if the clouds were squeezing themselves dry to produce a few measly clumps of crystalline ice, just to prove that they could do it.

She sat for a long time as the fight and its implications somersaulted over and over again in her mind. She was still angry and hurt, but most of all, she was mourning the loss of blissful ignorance... of the youthful innocence and fleeting perfection of their relationship that had preceded the fight. Some part of her would have done anything to get it back.

Eventually, as she began to shiver and the horizon became a barely visible ray of grey, Kuveni materialized beside her. She was wearing a matching mink coat and fur snow boots and offered Eleanor a fluffy fur blanket to lay over both of their bare legs.

Eleanor leaned into the warm nook of Kuveni's arm, and laid her head on her chest.

"All this Yakshini fur doesn't come from dead fluffy animals, does it?"

"We didn't kill any animals to get it, if that's what you mean? We sometimes harvest it from particularly beautiful animals who have died naturally. We keep it in the basement by the Sacred Well, along with all sorts of other things we store in stasis for when we need them. It seems like a waste to let it decompose naturally when the animal went to such effort to create it in the first place, don't you think? The scavengers eat the meat, of course. We don't stand in the way of nature."

"Huh."

"Is that really what's on your mind?"

Eleanor shrugged. Her mind had been numb almost as long as her fingers had.

"I wonder who's warmer right now, me or Edmund."

"He has been stewing alone for hours, but I didn't come out to parley with you on his behalf."

"I didn't think I'd be seeking comfort in my mother-in-law's arms after a fight like that."

Kuveni kissed her forehead. "We both know I'm much better than a mother-in-law."

"Truer words have never been spoken."

"Tell me, my dear girl. Tell me everything that's been on your mind as you've frozen alone out here."

"I don't know if I should." Eleanor sighed. "That's what Edmund said right before our fight. Turns out he was right. He shouldn't have said anything."

"Now, now. One should ne'er regret the truth, or so the wise women say."

"I don't really believe the adage," Eleanor admitted. "I regret plenty of truths. I wish they weren't true. And, I've regretted telling the truth on so many occasions I can't even count them, so when exactly should I ne'er regret it? When it isn't coming back to bite me? That's a small percentage of the time."

"It sounds good, though. Doesn't it?"

"Very wise," Eleanor agreed. "I suppose most good sayings are easier said than done."

"They're for simpler people than us."

"They're for postcards and knitted doilies."

Kuveni snapped her fingers and handed Eleanor a handkerchief with the phrase embroidered into it in delicate, archaic cursive.

"No one appreciates how funny you are, do they?"

"It is my curse." Kuveni winked, but then she became more serious at the thought. "Everyone underestimates me. It goes with being a matrika, I think. You put your heart and soul into raising up these innocent creatures who depend on you for absolutely everything, and as soon as they can keep their particles together and hold their heads up straight, they have to prove that they aren't so innocent anymore by rebelling against the one who cared for them most."

"Way to sell motherhood."

"I'm not here to sell motherhood to you, Eleanor. I haven't raised my own children in six thousand years. I wouldn't produce more of my own for anything, *anything* on God's green earth."

"I'm not against the concept of having my own children. I'm against everything else that goes with it."

"You were right to blame us for avoiding the topic of childbirth with him. We have done you a great disservice. He does not understand how bad it is."

"I can't stop thinking about whether he's right," Eleanor admitted. "Humans wouldn't exist if enough mothers didn't survive. Maybe I'm just not brave enough, or strong enough, or maybe I just don't love him enough."

"Posh, Eleanor. You know what the risks are for carrying a Rakshasa child, and even if Edmund weren't a Rakshasa, it is reasonable for human women to avoid pregnancy and childbirth. I am surprised that so many women are willing to endure it now that there are means to prevent it. It is like going to war for men, and you know as well as I do that the suggestion to those young men to buck up and bear it was absurd. Almost all of them would have run away in a heartbeat if they'd had a choice, and you, my dear girl, have a choice."

"I don't think most women feel like they have a choice, and even if they do, they don't know how bad it is, either. All they see in their mind's eye is their beautiful bouncing baby and their proud husband, without any concept of how awful it's going to be for them to get to that point... if they make it at all. Sometimes I feel like it's a societal conspiracy to hide the true nature of childbirth so that women will be willing to do it."

"It wasn't hidden from you," Kuveni pointed out.

"I was already a nurse when my sisters gave birth. I served as their midwife to keep the local witch from doing it with her herbs and all sorts of other superstitious nonsense."

"I'm surprised your mother let them even consider it with her preachy commentary at your wedding against all things pagan."

"My mother had had four children. She was as scared as I was for them, and she would have entertained anything to keep us safe––I realize that now. She really did love us, and that love scared her. She was afraid it was going to curse us, like it had cursed her, and so she hid it. Who knows, if I'd been in her position, maybe I would have done the same."

"Four children?"

Eleanor dug back into her deepest childhood memories. "I hardly remember it, but between Martha and Mary, there was a boy who was stillborn. My father disappeared for weeks after that. I should have realized how weak he was then to leave my mother alone in her state with two children and her grief. I had to walk down to the church myself to get the minister to help us with the burial, because my mother couldn't get out of bed. He brought a lady doctor along with him, who probably saved my mother's life. I remember seeing how relieved my mother was when they arrived, and that was, perhaps, the first time the idea of medicine crossed my mind."

"You would have been a wonderful doctor, Eleanor."

She shrugged. "Woulda-coulda-shoulda. I was singularly focused on making enough money to pay for their livelihood. That's how I ended up in the insane asylum. It was the only place that would employ a seventeen-year-old nurse."

"You could still become a doctor. Oz's medical programme in Perth is specially designed for people who already have medical experience. At first it was meant to help medics from the war finish off their training, but now it has several openings available to women."

"Did you look it up on my behalf?"

"Oz did. He brought it up months ago after you saved that farmer's arm in Boranup without him. He asked me if he should suggest it to you, and I told him he didn't need to ask me. I'm surprised he didn't bring it up."

"I probably said something too cheeky at some point and it scared him off." Eleanor thought about the completely novel prospect for a long time. "But I'm forty, Kuveni. I'm too old to go back to school."

"Hogwash. The real question is, would you want to?"

"I don't know. I'd still end up in women's medicine, and I don't really want to be doing that. It was a great fortune for Mary that I was there when she was giving birth to Howie—you should have seen the bloodbath—but the whole thing still haunts me."

"Did she hemorrhage?"

"Yes, but the more dangerous turn was that the placenta broke into pieces, and I had to use every medical technique in the book to get the last piece out. I thought I might have to adopt that baby boy if she died, since it was clear even then that Fergus was going to be a worthless father. He was like a meaner, dumber version of my father, who constantly reminded Mary how lucky she was that he'd stooped to marry a lass with such a jaded pedigree, as if a stocky, grumpy, hooligan bricklayer had a line of lasses beating down his door for the privilege of making him dinner and cleaning his soiled breeches."

"Do you think she could have found someone more suitable?"

"I don't know. Could someone in her position? Yes. Could she? Maybe not. She was always very dependent. I think that's why she can't leave him, even now. She'd rather watch him beat her children than risk being alone. I have no bloody respect for her anymore, although I suppose she's less of an active villain than Martha. You know, I think Surpanakha might have more redeeming qualities than Martha at this point."

"Don't joke about such things, Eleanor. Monty told me that Surpanakha was there last night. You must be very careful. Her presence puts all of us in danger, the Yakshas most of all. I have sent Illa away with orders not to come back, even when summoned."

"Why? What can Surpanakha do to her? Surely she isn't at risk of bodily harm? I've never seen a Yakshini injured."

"She is not clever enough to keep herself from being enslaved, and we don't need to lose another generation of offspring to the evil Rakshasas' whims."

"I don't understand," Eleanor admitted.

Kuveni lowered her voice so that it was barely audible over the splashing of the gentle waves. "Surpanakha and Ravana capture Yakshas, Eleanor, and try to use our power as their own. When they succeed, it is bad for all of us. The more powerful the Yaksha, the more our shared power is depleted when he's yanked out of our network. They use all sorts of ancient tricks to trap us in objects, and when the objects are destroyed, so are the Yakshas inside. It is one of very few ways of killing a Yaksha, but it is the most common, and the most effective. It is how both of my children were eventually killed."

"Blimey, I'm sorry."

"My worthless human husband was the one who did it."

Kuveni looked down and slowly transformed into her ancient Lankan form.

Eleanor felt the smooth silk of her jeweled crimson sari. "So that's the great pain that you endured in this form."

Kuveni sighed as she stared out over the grey water to the growing horizon. "I loved that conniving son-of-a-bitch when I married him. I should have realized then how doomed the whole thing was. Love marriages were extremely rare, and unheard of for royalty, but I was entranced by his foreign human qualities, and it was my choice. The surviving stories, of course, got most of the details wrong. They painted me as some desperate love-struck demon who gave all of Lanka over to humans, who then massacred the Yaksha people while I stood by and watched. In reality, there were only a handful of us there to begin with, just like the Rakshasas, and we ruled as gods, because our power and our intelligence were so much greater than the childlike human primates. My mother warned me that Vijaya would turn on us and use his position as my husband for a human coup, but I didn't believe her. I was so young and headstrong and foolish."

"I don't think any hormonal adolescent should be making decisions on behalf of the state."

"Well, we don't have hormones, per se, and I was about eighty at the time, a fresh young Yakshini adult. The truth is that the world was changing, and I didn't realize the extent of it until it was too late. Humans had never thought themselves equal enough to us to even contemplate marriage before that. It turned out they were developing a certain type of avarice that you know well in the modern world, but that was utterly unheard of so long ago. Six thousand years ago, the world was so different you can't even imagine it, Eleanor."

"I have no doubt."

"So, I happily married that greedy fool who'd wooed me with false declarations of his love, and after thirty-six whole hours of Yakshini gestation, I gave birth to twins, a boy and a girl."

"Only thirty-six hours?!"

"Thirty-six hours was quite long for Yakshini gestation. It can be less than an hour if the child is entirely Yakshini."

"Maybe I should've been born a Yakshini... I told Edmund that he should have married Illa if he wanted a troop of bouncing babies."

"There's a reason our species is on the brink of extinction, Eleanor. It took me almost a month of more excruciating childbirth than you can comprehend to actually bring them into the world."

"A month?!" Eleanor exclaimed.

"Time is stopped by the Sacred Well, so it didn't feel like a month to the outside world. To me it felt like eternity. Yakshini children must take their energy from their mother, so as they became more and more corporeal, my life-force faded. It took me three more weeks alone in the Sacred Well with my children floating in the air around me before I was strong enough to rally them into human form and emerge."

"It sounds like a more poetic version of what happens to human women."

"I suppose in some ways that's true. There's never any blood, of course, but the pain is unlike anything else on Earth. That's why Lady Mélusine began a policy many centuries ago to wipe the mother's memory of the experience before sending her back out of the Sacred Well. She hoped that not remembering would encourage more Yakshinis to procreate, but the Peruvians are the only ones who are willing to endure it."

"Why do you always call them the Peruvians? Surely they have names?"

Kuveni smiled. "They don't, actually. Not in a human sense. They have chosen not to take names so that humans cannot have power over them. They have identities, of course, in a way that transcends language and that comes very naturally to our people, but they believe language is too human of a trait to value. It is a very traditional way of life for Yakshas. They live entirely non-corporeally, and when their children reach an age to decide whether they want to engage with the human world, I name the ones who choose to stay, while the others return to the Andes to live communally with their tribe. They are the only community of Yakshas left who live this way, although it was quite common when I was a girl. I was a scandalous exception when I chose to engage with humans as I did, and I learned my lesson when I was trapped alone in childbirth, and no one knew how the twins' humanity would manifest. I was terrified that I'd end up with bloody human babies, or, even worse, a placenta or two." She shivered at the thought.

"Why does being a woman have to be so bloody painful? And don't give me some Adam and Eve nonsense. I don't believe for one second that it's God's punishment for one instance of ancient poor judgment."

"You want to know the truth?"

"Yes, I do."

"It's entirely scientific, Eleanor. Humans evolved to walk upright, and it made the whole process a damned painful one. There's nothing else to it."

"But what about Yakshini women suffering?"

Kuveni leaned in confidingly. "Yakshas could do it if they had the nerves. Lady Mélusine was born male, and she produced Puck. If Monty or Tawhiri or Thomas, or any of the other male Yakshas, truly had the nerves to do it, they could. Yaksha gender is purely a construct, as you might expect, from a species that is by its nature non-corporeal. We don't even need a vagina to push out a baby. That isn't how Yakshas come into this world."

"Huh."

"Your husband is stirring. Now that it's light outside, he's contemplating coming to find you."

"How do you know?"

"I know him, Eleanor. I was his matrika."

"How do we get over this, Kuveni? I've never felt disconnected from him like I do right now. I'm still livid. Why can't he just bloody give up on the idea of me producing his child? I really thought that having these bairns was a godsend that had given both of us what we really wanted, and now I feel like I don't even know him anymore. How can he want me to risk my life? He's the one who's always going on and on about how worried he is that something might happen to me, and now, it's like he's so driven by greed, he doesn't even care. I told him that human women die when they have Rakshasa children, and a selfish part of him still wanted me to do it!"

"Give him time. He is intelligent and sensitive and reasonable. He is one of the best men I've ever known. You have given him some very unpleasant truths to think about, and we both know that it takes him time to accept truths that he doesn't want to know."

"I wish you hadn't let him bask in denial for a century."

"Take it up with D.H. If it were up to me, we would never, ever have initiated a single farce with him. He would have been raised in our world like the prince that he is, and he would already be the strong leader that we need to eliminate the scourge of his evil father. But, I must have faith that Lord Shiva has another plan that will eventually get us where we need to go with as little unnecessary suffering as possible. I don't always agree with Vibhi, but I do believe that his wisdom transcends mine… at least some of the time."

"When I'm not around, you mean?"

"That is one example of when his judgment is impaired," Kuveni winked.

"Eleanor? Dearest?" Edmund called from the open front door of the inn. "Is that you out there? Please come back inside. You must be freezing!"

Kuveni closed her eyes and returned to the form of Kate.

"Thank you, Kuveni. You really are much better than a mother-in-law."

"It is my pleasure, Eleanor dearest."

Eleanor sighed with resignation. "I suppose I'll have to go coddle the bairns. They must be shaking in their boots after that midnight shouting match. I'd thought they'd never have to hear anything like that again now that they're in our perfectly angelic household. So much for that."

"Sometimes it is necessary to have a row, Eleanor, to discuss things that otherwise can't be discussed with the appropriate level of severity. Besides, I cut off the sound from your room as soon as I heard where the conversation was going. The bairns slept soundly through the whole thing."

Eleanor hugged her. "Much, much, *much* better than a mother-in-law, even if you do listen in on *everything*."

"Not *everything*..." Kuveni corrected her guiltily.

"Wait a second... Does that mean that you can cut off the sound to our room when we are in the heat of passion?"

"All you have to do is ask," Kuveni winked. "Although, best if you ask me instead of Monty. He's always been a bit of a prude."

Eleanor hopped up with fresh enthusiasm. "I love you, Kuveni."

As Kuveni hugged her again, a boy on a bicycle tossed a newspaper at Edmund, hitting him in the chest.

"Sorry!" he called as he continued along.

"You'd better be careful on the ice!" Edmund called back.

Kuveni and Eleanor walked hand in hand back across the snowy sand. Edmund looked down nervously as they approached. He was wearing the wrinkled suit that he'd worn to dinner the night before. He hadn't bothered to tie the tie or button the vest. He stood on the icy porch waiting for them, even though he was only wearing socks on his feet.

"I'm sorry, Eleanor. I've thought about what you said. You were right. I shouldn't ignore the beauty of the life we have together now. It is not like me to seek greener pastures. I suppose I just got ahead of myself."

It wasn't the full concession that she was hoping for. He was regretful of voicing his desires, but she could tell that his desires hadn't changed, nor had his acceptance of the true dangers facing her. Eleanor sighed. It was something, *anything*, that would allow them to move on, and she would have to take it.

"I'm sorry I ran out like that," she replied. "Come on. Let's warm up before the bairns wake up. They might be able to play in the snow before it turns back into rain with the heat of day."

"Hello, what's this?" he said as he glanced at the paper in his hand. "*'ANGELS OR DEMONS? Three missing and one dead as the Bunbury Circus becomes a real-life horror show.'*"

"This is very, very bad," Eleanor and Kuveni murmured in unison.

"'Who is the mysterious Countess of Easton, who thrilled audiences from near and far last night with her magical disappearing knife act, and what is the connection between her and the four apparent victims of foul play?'" he read. "Four?! But you had nothing to do with any of them, dearest! And I only helped that girl! I swear to you, Eleanor, I didn't kill anyone, not even that man who ran her over. I only stunned him, like Percy taught me, and left him in the car for the authorities."

"I believe you, darling." Eleanor took the newspaper out of his hand and guided him to the parlor. "What time is it anyway? How can they say people are missing when it's only been ten hours since we got home? How did they even get an article into the paper this fast?"

Eleanor's mother shuffled into the room and took a position warming her hands in front of the fireplace. She was wearing a thick evergreen-colored winter wool dress with a brown fur-lined collar, and she'd already put on her new coat and her matching cloche hat, her stockings, and her shoes, as if she were ready to go out for a stroll.

"Don't mind me. I was shakin' like a leaf in me bed. It was so cold, I thought I was back in Skye. I decided it was time to warm up properly." As she noticed their nerves, she lowered her voice. "Whit's amiss?"

"The press noticed us last night," Eleanor said as Edmund began pacing and rubbing his eyes.

She looked more carefully at the article. A picture of all seven of them sitting bright-eyed with wide smiles, illuminated by the reflection of the stage lights, was prominently placed in the center, and a close-up of her strapped onto the bulls-eye graced the bottom right corner. Eleanor sighed with stress. The development was already bad enough, but the clear outline of her modern bra was visible through her sweater even in the grainy black-and-white printing of the picture. She sighed again, this time with annoyance, as she accepted that her concerns about her modesty had, apparently, been warranted.

"What is it, dearest?" Edmund asked nervously.

"There are two photos of us on the front page. They took them while we were watching the show. This is very, very bad."

She sat down on the cushy couch as she continued reading out loud:

"'*The Earl and Countess of Easton (identities yet to be confirmed) and their four children enjoyed the family-friendly performance from the front row of the Bunbury Circus before a hit-and-run in the parking lot brought the life of a young widow (Mrs. Eliza Humphry, 19, originally of Busselton) and her unborn child to an untimely and tragic end. Numerous witnesses reported that not only did the Earl miraculously escape unscathed after the culprit's car hit him head-on in a second collision during the driver's hasty escape from the scene, the Earl and Countess of Easton then displayed additional powers beyond the ordinary in their attempts to save the girl. Too fantastic to be true? Not according to several witnesses who insisted that the Countess of Easton declared herself and her husband to be 'angels of the Lord' before leaving the scene with her mother and children, while her husband escorted Mrs. Humphry to the hospital in his arms. Hospital officials confirmed that a man matching his*" *description arrived with the girl but waited outside while a woman 'of similar build and character, likely a blood relation,' brought the body of Mrs. Humphry inside, after she had expired on the journey. Officials continue to question how the Earl reached the hospital with Mrs. Humphry only minutes after he is said to have left the scene on foot.*

"Further mystery was provoked after numerous witnesses reported hearing 'screams of terror' from several grown men echoing in the night. The car and driver of the hit-and-run (yet to be found), the ringmaster of the circus (a Mr. Ronald Gleeson, originally of Kalgoorlie), and 'the Great Pizzaz' (a Mr. Antonio Rinaldi, originally of Rome, Italy), were reported missing by the personal secretary of Mr. Gleeson (a Miss Elda Masterson, originally of Nannup), who told reporters and the local constables that Mr. Gleeson had sought to compensate the Countess of Easton for her exceptional performance that evening, but did not return. Several witnesses described Miss Masterson as 'intensely frightened' and 'hysterical' when making her report to the police, and reported that she claimed to be running from 'a demon dark enough to swallow the Earth.' Authorities took her in for further questioning, and 'for her own protection,' and are seeking witnesses and information that will shed light on this bizarre and tragic mystery as it continues to unfold."

"I didn't kill anyone," Edmund reiterated.

"Darling, we all believe you," Eleanor reassured him again.

"Pah, even if ye did, they'd've deserved it, Abbi," Eleanor's mother scoffed.

"But I *didn't*," he reiterated. "I man up when I've killed a man, Moira, let alone *four*. It's been years since I've killed so many at once, and there'd better be another war before I do it again."

Eleanor's mother was startled by his unusually sharp tone. "I dunne mean t'say otherwise, Abbi."

"I'm sorry, Moira. It's been a long night," he said as he returned to pacing. "Eleanor, what did these other men have to do with anything? What did any of them have to do with us?"

"Nothing, darling. It was just bad luck. Last night was a bad night, and we happened to be there. We did what we could, which wasn't enough, and now we all have to move on."

He stopped his pacing. "You don't think the whole thing was another wicked trap, do you?" He glanced at Kuveni. "Like it was on the steamer?"

Eleanor was equally impressed by his reasoning, and concerned by the potential accuracy of his suggestion. She couldn't ignore the photographs Surpanakha had left for Monty to show her, photographs that made both of them—their beautiful family, and poor, tragic Eliza Humphry—targets of assassins. Her mind began racing as she debated whether or not to share the information, and if so, how was she going to explain acquiring it?

"In Bunbury? At the edge of the world?" Kuveni countered.

"If the trap was set for us, then it would have been wherever we were."

"Did you give your names when you bought the tickets for the circus?" Kuveni asked.

"No, I bought them at the train station last week when I was up in Bunbury with Oz fetching supplies for the clinic," Eleanor replied. "They didn't ask a single question about who I was."

"Abbi?" Charlie called as he stumbled sleepily down the stairs in his flannel pajamas. "Amma? Is it snowing?"

"Snow, snow, snow!" Debbie exclaimed as she rushed past him with Ruthy's hand in hers.

"Amma, can we go play in the snow?" Ruthy asked.

Eleanor picked her up and twirled her around. "I think that's a wonderful idea."

She guided them to the coat closet and began helping them dress, while Edmund looked on nervously.

As her mother and Kuveni began helping her dress the bairns, Edmund couldn't contain his concern any longer, and he switched into Gaelic to address her without the children understanding. "Do you think it's wise, dearest? To go out in public if there's someone after us?"

"Darling, if we stayed inside because someone might be after us, we'd never go anywhere. We have a lot of resources at our disposal, and we are both very clever. We can't stop our lives just because something might be afoot."

"But you *do* think that someone might be after us?"

She was not happy that he'd noticed her subtle acceptance of the premise. "I think it is always a possibility, darling. There were a lot of parties involved in the steamer incident, and all of them are quite covetous of power. If there's been a shift in the power dynamics of any of the groups involved, we shouldn't be surprised if they come sniffing around to see if the rumors about us are true."

As she thought back to the steamer incident, suddenly the presence of the Italians in the new context of the Great Pizzaz's confession piqued her interest. They hadn't seemed particularly well-organized on the steamer, but perhaps news of the magical MacLeod-Marriners' role in the British triumph had gotten back to Mussolini after all. Could Il Duce have been so upset that he sent assassins after them? But surely, that would be too personal of a vendetta over their defeat of some drunken mercenaries? Once again, the Italians' involvement was as confounding as it had been the night before...

"But I thought that we averted the disaster on the steamer? They didn't see anything unusual, did they? What rumors would they be checking up on, dearest?"

"I don't know, darling. Maybe someone saw more than what we realized at the time."

Maybe that was it... could there have been some other Italians lurking, who reported back to Mussolini about their unusual power? Perhaps the photograph of them in the driver's car wasn't a hit list, maybe it was instructions for making contact...

"Edmund, dear boy, you've got me and Percy and many others to look out for you. Please don't worry too much about it," Kuveni chimed in.

"Really? Others? Which others?" he asked astutely.

243

Kuveni looked equally annoyed at herself and at him. "Shall we call Sheranee? I don't think she likes snow very much. Only the Siberian tigers really have a taste for cold paws."

"But Sheranee is only one other. Who else is watching us? Do I know him? Is it Doctor Carpenter? Or that Captain Singh bloke? He seemed familiar, but I couldn't place from where. You know, it would be much more civilized all around if your allies would just join us openly. I don't like this feeling of spies lurking everywhere."

"Abbi, are you coming?" Debbie forced them to snap out of it. "You need your shoes, or your toes'll freeze."

Edmund looked down at his socks and smiled, letting her pull him out of his worry, at least temporarily. He slipped on his shoes and his overcoat.

"I reckon I'm about as dressed for the snow as Amma is now." He winked at Eleanor, who looked down at her bare legs under her mink coat.

"I'm dressed for it!" Howie said as he ran down the stairs fully clothed in his outfit from the night before. "Charlie, yer gonna freeze yer bum off!" Howie grabbed his coat and hat and gloves from the closet, and then ran outside without looking back. "Catch me if ye can!"

Charlie ran after him, and then Debbie and Ruthy followed, and so Edmund and Eleanor rushed after them, chasing them out onto the snowy sand of the beach. They threw snowballs at each other and ran around playing tag, until Ruthy and Debbie decided to make a snowman (albeit a very tiny one in the wet, thin layer of snow), and the whole group gathered around to help them. Eleanor loved how the bairns' energy could distract her and Edmund from even the most stressful of disputes.

"I reckon we have ourselves more of a snow dwarf," Edmund said as he stood up to look at their creation.

"It's a snow fairy!" Ruthy exclaimed.

"No, a snow gnome!" Debbie argued.

"It needs a face," Charlie pointed out. "Right now it's a snow blob."

"Well, what shall we collect for his features?" Edmund asked. "Perhaps I can go sneak a bite of sausage from the kitchen while I gather him up a face."

"It's a her!" Ruthy exclaimed. "She's a fairy!"

"Yer a fairy," Howie teased.

"Hello? What's this?" Edmund skipped across the sand towards the road, where a carrot, a pipe, and two perfectly round bits of coal were placed neatly on a small boulder marking the normal pathway to the beach.

Eleanor spotted a subtle mischievous twinkle in Edmund's eye as he glanced over at the warm yellow lights of the B&B, where the Schindlers were now clanking pots and pans, and the rich scents of frying bacon and baking stollen were wafting up out of the chimney.

"Come on out, if you dare, our lurking friend! I, the Honorable Edmund Marriner with all the powers vested in me, demand to see the spy our midst!"

Charlie hit him with a snowball, and Edmund growled jokingly and swooped down to counter with two more lightly packed snowballs.

But, as Eleanor noticed Kuveni panic, she followed her attention to the porch of the house, where Mr. Montero had just materialized with an even more concerned grimace. His body language indicated that his abrupt appearance was not voluntary. He glanced around ensuring that there was no one looking, and morphed into the beautiful, youthful blond form of Mr. Marlowe (or, as you would know him, Ellie, Oberon), rather than the stern butler form that Edmund already associated with the Patels. He closed his eyes and morphed his butler's uniform into a plain modern winter suit. Next to him, Illa stood sheepishly, dressed in a traditional Incan outfit covered in colorful woven embroidery that she quickly morphed into the Scottish one she'd used months earlier when she'd first arrived to offer her help with the children.

"Illa, I told you not to come back here!" Kuveni hissed. "It's dangerous! Do you want to be enslaved?"

Edmund noticed Eleanor's attention and looked over to see what she was looking at.

"Hello, there?" He skipped up off the beach and across the road to greet them. "Illa? Where did you come from?"

"You summoned me, my lord." She looked down nervously.

He squinted as he tried to place Monty's form. "Have we met? I'm quite certain that we have, but I don't remember where." He reached out his hand, and as Monty shook it, Edmund held on, feeling his Yaksha warmth. None of them liked seeing the wheels turning in Edmund's head.

"I drove the car that collected you and Mr. Valov from the hospital in Bombay," Monty informed him. Eleanor was impressed by his ability to hide his discomfort. "Moments ago you demanded to see the spies in your midst, and here we are. It was Illa who produced the accessories for the snowman. She thought she was helping, but now I believe she understands the mess that her move has made for us. Doesn't she?" He eyed her disapprovingly.

"Yes, Uncle," she whispered.

Edmund scratched his head as he worked to fit all of the pieces together. "So you were staying in the house with us all night? Did Kate bring you along?" Kuveni rushed over to join them. "Why didn't you just tell us they were around, Kate? Surely you didn't need to lurk about unseen. It would be much more civilized of all of us to get to know each other as equals. What exactly do you do, Mr.?"

"Marlowe," Monty replied. "You may call me Mr. Marlowe."

"Then you may call me Colonel Marriner," Edmund winked. "If we're going to be so formal."

"It is my preferred state."

Edmund laughed. "And did you write some plays at some point, perhaps during the Renaissance?" Monty hesitated, and Edmund winked. He seemed to be enjoying his little triumph more than Eleanor expected. "Are you a chauffeur by trade, then? Surely Kate doesn't need a chauffeur. She is wonderfully competent at the wheel all by herself."

"I am a guard," Monty replied.

"A guard?" Edmund paused as he became more serious. He glanced at Kuveni. "Do you think we need a guard? Is this about what happened last night?"

"It was just a precaution, dear boy." Kuveni couldn't hide her fatigue at Edmund's questioning tenacity.

"But why didn't you just tell us you were here, Mr. Marlowe?" He pushed. "Why didn't you and Illa join us for dinner? You needn't be hiding away from us out of sight, even if you are a guard."

Mr. Montero gestured subtly for Kuveni to step in on his behalf. "Edmund, dear boy, they didn't want to be seen. They have many commitments that they must attend to at the drop of a hat, and if they are ensnared into your jovial social clutches, they will not have the flexibility that they need to move quickly when the occasion arises."

Edmund laughed. "Well, you aren't going anywhere fast today! These roads are going to be a nightmare for hours!"

Mr. Montero threw Kuveni a subtle look of annoyance. Eleanor glanced up and down at the completely deserted, icy street and decided to give him his out.

Sheranee, please come. Your mistress commands you.

Eleanor guided the children off the beach to join them on the porch. "Darling, they don't need a car." She pointed as Sheranee slinked unhappily up the icy road.

He stared at her with momentary disbelief, and then shrugged as he accepted the outrageous explanation. "I suppose you've proven that she's faster than a Ford."

"Sheranee!" Debbie exclaimed as she slipped and slid across the ice to greet her with some ear scratches. The other children followed.

"Now, if you don't mind, we'd best be getting to the station," Mr. Montero said as he guided Illa onto the road and mounted Sheranee.

Eleanor scratched Sheranee's ears. *Thank you, my love. Now get them out of sight so they can return to their duties in peace.*

Without her normal enthusiasm, Sheranee slinked carefully away, turning down an alleyway between the two closest houses.

"Breakfast is served!" Mrs. Schindler called from inside the house.

Kuveni rallied the children into the house and began helping them remove their wet, snowy clothing, and Edmund took one last look where Sheranee had turned, and then sighed with resignation and joined them in the foyer without another question.

"Who's ready for some bacon?" Kuveni asked cheerfully.

"I am!" the bairns declared in unison.

"I reckon you'd better beat me in there then, because my stomach is growling like a tiger!" Edmund growled.

The children squealed and then burst into laughter as he chased them into the dining room.

As Kuveni followed them at a more adult pace, Eleanor unenthusiastically pulled off her snow boots, hissing as her bare feet hit the cold, wet floor. But as she rolled her shoulders, preparing to ignore her discomfort just like she usually did over such minor trivialities, her mother grabbed her wrist and whispered into her ear.

"Eleanor Mary MacLeod, ne'er forget who yer in it wit, or so the wise women say."

"What do you mean?"

"You 'n Abbi're in it together, Ellie. And whatever's between ye'll work itself out. He's a good man, and a good partner fer ye, even if he does have the Devil in his eyes. I reckon it's better to see him outright when he's there than to keep on guessin' like ye do with normal folk. If I'd seen him in yer Da's eyes, at least I'da known what I was in fer." She chuckled at the memory. "Oh, Ellie, yer Da and I could have it out like two champions at a right braw boxin' match. The bloodier the fight, though, the better the reward was when it was o'er." She leaned in confidingly. "That's how the Good Lord made ye, ye know."

Eleanor snorted at the idea she'd tried hard never to think about, and she chose to address one of her mother's other points. "Did you hear our row last night? I thought Kate helped us keep it private. I hope the bairns weren't too upset."

"I dunne need t'hear it, Ellie. I could see it in yer eyes and feel it in yer bones. It's makin' ye sad, and I'm sorry fer 't. But he'll come round. He's smart enough to know what a catch ye're, and if he's not, ye've shown 'im again that he's got the best ride in town." She poked Eleanor in the ribs and winked at her double entendre. "Ye know, on the back of a tiger, that is."

"That's not the only position he gets to enjoy," Eleanor winked back.

"I reckon ye learned a thing or two down in France. I hear those trollops can tickle fancies that the Scots don' even know about."

"And that, Mum, is where our conversation on the topic must end."

Her mother pulled her into a hug. "I know I ne'er said it, Ellie, but the Good Lord's been keepin' it steady on the edge of my tongue. I love ye." As Eleanor reeled from the shock of hearing the words she'd never expected to hear her mother say, her mother spanked her playfully and nudged her along towards the dining room. "Now go on in to yer husband and the bairns. I'll take off me coat and join ye."

Eleanor skipped down the hallway, but stopped short of the dining room as she heard her mother muttering.

"I hope ye know whit yer doin', Moira MacLeod. If yer not careful, the Good Lord'll strike both of ye down."

And, there it was. The sword was pointed right back at her.

Eleanor slammed her hand against her forehead in self-castigation for believing for one second that her mother could change as much as she had. Not even Jesus Christ himself could achieve such a feat, and some part of her had always known it.

She was livid at her mother for whatever foolish shenanigans were afoot, but she was much angrier at herself. For one beautiful moment, she'd let her guard down. She'd taken off her well-fitted armor and let herself be who the innocent ten-year-old lass should have been if her parents hadn't been so rotten. But that wasn't the real world. That was a fantasy, and not even genies or fairies or angels or gods could make the cruel world kind.

Eleanor took in a deep breath as her mind began racing at the possible outlets for her mother's misguided treachery, but before the flames of Durga could ignite the entire house with her rage at whatever wicked game had enticed her mother into saying the three little words that she didn't mean, she slapped a fake smile on her face and rushed into the dining room. She needed the hopeful energy of the bairns and the gentle pulsating power of her husband to rip her out of it.

She took a seat next to Edmund and squeezed his hand. "I'm in it with you, Edmund," she whispered.

"What?"

"Life."

After a cheerful, warm German-Aussie breakfast with the Schindlers, the slushy snow turned back into rain. They all sat around in the parlor by the Christmas tree sipping hot cocoa by the fire, waiting for the ice to thaw, and listening to Edmund's lulling British baritone read all about Mowgli's daring escape from the incorrigible, thoughtless, trouble-making monkeys.

After Eleanor's short night of sleep, she eventually gave into her heavy eyelids, even though she'd vowed to keep at least one eye open to watch her deceitful mother.

By the time she woke up, the sky had cleared, and bright sunlight filtered in through the frosty windowpane. Everyone was dozing, even Edmund. As she stirred, Ruthy and Debbie, who were both lying with their heads on her lap, awoke and yawned, and Mrs. Schindler tiptoed into the room with a fresh tray of tea and biscuits.

"You'd better wake the colonel, my lady. If you don't leave soon, it will be dark before you get to Margaret River."

"My lady?" Eleanor asked groggily.

"You never told us you were a countess, but I suppose down here in the bush, it doesn't matter so much. Mr. Schindler's aunt was a lady's maid to the Duchess of Saxe-Coberg and Gotha, although I can't say we understand much about how all the dukes and duchesses really live."

"I can't say that we do either. Did you read the paper this morning then?"

Mrs. Schindler handed Eleanor the afternoon edition, where the same picture of their bright faces watching the circus was prominently positioned in the middle of the front page.

"*EARL AND COUNTESS OF EASTON IDENTIFIED. The mysterious heroes of the Bunbury Circus Affair have been confirmed by the Secretary of State for Constitutional Affairs and Peerage as The Honorable Colonel Edmund Marriner, formerly of Basingstoke, England, and Eleanor MacLeod Marriner, formerly of Elphinstone, Scotland, who currently reside in Prevelly, a coastal settlement in the Margaret River region of Western Australia. Further mystery abounds as the couple's four children are not registered with the Peerage and records of their identities could not be found. Lord Marriner, a war hero and commander in the trenches who received (among other awards) the Victoria Cross for valor, serves as the judicial magistrate for the Augusta-Margaret River Road District. Lady Marriner, despite her familial obligations, serves as the nurse in the medical practice of Doctor Jack Helmsworth (a former lieutenant of the Royal Army Medical Corps and Chairman of the Board of Helmsworth Ranches, the largest producer of dairy cows in Australia). Why have our local angelic aristocrats kept mum about their peerage? To avoid a scandal, sources close to the Marriners report, as Eleanor MacLeod Marriner is the bastard daughter of Robby MacLeod, notorious thoroughbred trainer from the Musselburgh racetrack in Scotland, who made news thirty years ago as a bigamist who committed suicide upon the public revelation of his crime to his second wife (a Moira Howard MacLeod, formerly of Elphinstone, Scotland, reported to be currently residing with Lord Marriner and family). Did Lord and Lady Marriner escape to Oz for a love marriage that conservative English society would have shunned, or is there more to the story? What should we make of the continued claims from witnesses that*

252

Lord and Lady Marriner demonstrated godly powers beyond the ordinary? Did Mrs. Eliza Humphry, tragic victim of the hit-and-run last night, benefit from the presence of two heavenly visitors? And what should we make of the mysterious stabbing death of the local reporter (a Mr. Elias Mumble of The Bunbury Register's competing newspaper, The Bunbury Post) this morning, with a confessional note outlining his involvement with the Fascist Italian cause? Are the mysteries related? Where are the three missing persons and the missing car that ran over Mrs. Eliza Humphry in cold blood? Read The Bunbury Register tomorrow for the next installment of this actively unfolding saga.'"

Eleanor reeled from the intensity of the exposé.

"I'm sorry about your father, my lady," Mrs. Schindler said quietly. "But it is wonderfully romantic that you and Lord Marriner chose to marry out of love anyway. It's like a storybook."

"Or an absurd melodrama..." Eleanor muttered. "This is very, very bad... Edmund is not going to be happy to see this..."

She was so overwhelmed with what the revelation was going to mean for their ability to get around unbothered in public that she didn't even have time to worry about the implications of the dead murdered spy tacked on at the end. The confessional note certainly made the culprit clear, and at least Surpanakha was busying herself with a trail of bodies away from their immediate vicinity... Her standards had never been so low...

"Amma, are we in trouble?" Debbie asked nervously.

"No, my darlings. No one is in trouble. Abbi and I just like to be very private, and with a newspaper telling everyone about us, it's going to make it harder for us to go about our business unnoticed."

"We don't have to go back to Scotland, do we?" Ruthy asked with even more anxiety.

"No, my darlings. You don't."

Kuveni tiptoed into the room and took a seat beside Eleanor on the couch, gathering Ruthy onto her lap.

"You've got the angels to watch over you, remember my little loves? You have nothing to fear."

As Eleanor reached forward and poured herself a cup of tea, Edmund gasped in his awakening Rakshasa breath. She handed the newspaper back to Mrs. Schindler, gesturing for her to hide it.

"What time is it?" he asked as he reached into his vest pocket to pull out his pocket watch. "Good Lord! It's half past two! We should hit the road!"

At his exclamation, the boys woke up and rubbed their sleepy eyes.

Edmund reached for the tea, but then stopped himself. "Would you like to feel me melt?" he asked the children.

All of the children gathered around and picked a spot on his left hand to poke. He waited for an extra dramatic pause with the tea pot in his hand, and then slurped it down loudly. They squealed with excitement as his Rakshasa frigidity morphed straight into the pulsating warmth of his body matching the temperature of the steaming tea.

"There we go. No more abominable snowmen in sight." He stood up and stretched as he glanced out the window at the bright winter sun working its way towards the hazy horizon. "I reckon we only have a couple hours of daylight left. We should get going. I don't want to be driving in the dark if it's icy."

The children unenthusiastically obeyed, and Kuveni tapped Eleanor's mother awake in her chair in the corner. She snorted, looked around tiredly, and then sighed and leaned on Kuveni to stand up. "I reckon it's time to go on home."

Eleanor led Debbie and Ruthy into the hallway, ignoring her mother. They all dressed for the cold weather in a sleepy daze, and then Mr. Schindler joined Mrs. Schindler from the kitchen to help them carry their small bags out to the car.

"Dearest, shall I drive, or do you want to?" Edmund asked.

"You're better at driving on the ice," Eleanor suggested, letting her responsibility for the children overwhelm her desire to enjoy her time behind the wheel.

The children piled into the back, along with Moira, and Eleanor looked at them, and then took her seat up front. She could feel the children sigh with disappointment that she hadn't joined them in the back, but she was still fuming at her mother, and so she did what she had always done. She pushed it down, deeper and deeper, and pretended that it wasn't true.

"My dearests, this is where I will take my leave." Kuveni hugged Edmund and then Eleanor, reaching into the back to offer each child a kiss on the forehead. "I'm sure we will see each other again soon." She hopped into the sleek silver Rolls Royce that she'd used to intercept Edmund the night before, a very similar model and make to the car she'd popped into existence for similar circumstances many times before. "Toodaloo!"

She sped off with a screech.

"My lord, it has been a pleasure as always," Mr. Schindler said as Edmund handed him a thick wad of cash for their bill and shook his hand.

"My lord?" Edmund asked.

"Aw, don't worry about us. We're very discreet." Mr. Schindler tapped his nose and winked.

"Right then." Edmund sat down in the driver's seat and shut his door. "I don't think I want to know what he meant."

He carefully started off down the beach road, which was wet but completely free of ice, and they were finally on their way.

"Shall we play 'I spy'?" Edmund suggested.

"I spy with my little eye something starting with an A!" Ruthy exclaimed.

"Ye always start with angel, Ruthy. Ye have to pick something different if ye want to play!" Charlie informed her.

"Angel wasn't it!" Ruthy argued. "It was Amma!"

"Same difference," Howie muttered. "I spy with my little eye, something starting with a B…"

The children began their game in earnest, and Eleanor took Edmund's left hand, and sat back to just listen.

She had to protect the bairns. She had to keep the bairns. She had to make all the promises they'd made to them true. Her brain circled and circled with all of their many complications, but it kept settling on those three simple facts.

The drive was mercifully uneventful and surprisingly short, since most people had stayed in on a Sunday to begin with, and the weather had scared off the few regular Sunday travelers. By the time they pulled up their long driveway through the vineyards, the sky was erupting into a striking winter sunset of blazing orange and magenta with unusual high-atmospheric angular streaks intermingling amongst the broken-up cumulus remnants of the storm.

"I wish I hadn't napped so long," Edmund sighed. "This would have been a wonderful sunset to paint."

"Can't ye just paint it later?" Moira asked.

"Oh no. Never. I can never remember the full beauty of it afterwards. It's quite a shame really. I suppose it's a shame about everything ephemeral in life. That's why it's important to keep your eyes open to appreciate what's right in front of you. It might never be quite the same again." He glanced at Eleanor. "Thank you for reminding me of that, dearest."

"All in a day's work, darling." She was grateful that their argument seemed to be sinking in in the right direction.

As they pulled up to the house, the lights were on, and smoke was billowing from the chimney. One of Oz's cars was parked in front, and people were moving about inside.

"I reckon we won't be alone for dinner tonight," Edmund said cheerfully. "The more the merrier!"

"Welcome back!" Stanley looked tired with dark bags under his eyes as he called to them with forced cheer. He was dressed quite properly in his full butler's uniform except that he was conspicuously missing his gloves. He rushed down the stairs to greet them, and as soon as Eleanor was out of the car, he took her hand. *Eleanor, find an excuse to escape from the crowd. We need to talk.*

He let go, shook Edmund's hand, and skipped around to the boot to gather their bags.

"Bairns, Uncle Oz and Auntie Mae are waiting for you inside," Stanley informed the children with a hint of intrigue. "They'd like you to know there's no time to waste."

"Aye!" They charged up the stairs and disappeared into the house.

"I almost forgot!" Howie whispered.

"Sshhh," Charlie hissed. "It's a surprise!"

"Darling, I'm going to make sure Stanley knows which bags are which," Eleanor said. "We don't need the children's bags ending up on our bed."

Without even glancing at her mother, who was slowly making her way from the car, she skipped into the house and followed Stanley up the stairs. She hardly noticed that the entire house had been cheerfully decorated with holly and pine and twinkling electric Christmas lights.

He'd already placed the bags in the correct rooms, but gestured for her to follow him into his bedroom. He quietly closed the door and guided her to a small loveseat, squishing down next to her and taking her hand.

We shouldn't even be whispering in this house right now, Eleanor. The walls have ears.

What do you know? Have you identified our mole?

What do you know of it?

"Monty, the pictures," Eleanor whispered. The envelope Surpanakha had left them in the glove compartment of the culprit's car materialized in her lap.

Do you know who took this picture?

257

Stanley squinted as he examined it. *That* must *have been about a month ago. Father O'Donnelly was here for lunch, and we're eating outside, so it must have been that warm Sunday a few weeks back. Where did this come from?*

Surpanakha found it and left it for us in the car of the man who ran over that poor pregnant girl in cold blood last night. Have you heard what happened?

Surpanakha?!

Yes, but I don't think she's our biggest problem. Stanley, I need you to help me understand what this means. What do you know about what happened? Did you read the newspaper today?

DID I?! Eleanor, this is a disaster!

Well, Edmund hasn't read it yet. He doesn't know what the damage is.

I don't think you do either, Eleanor. I got a call at about midnight last night from Jules Martin, the editor of The Bunbury Register. *He and I have… er… gotten to know each other over the past month or so, since Andrew moved to Melbourne…*

Are you sure that's wise?

I trust him, Eleanor. And we are breaking the law equally. He knows nothing of my real position. He thinks that I'm just a very loyal butler, and he has a cottage out in the bush where we can be private. But the point is that he warned me, Eleanor. He recognized you immediately when he saw the picture from the circus, and he called to ask what he should allow them to write.

Well, you could have told him that the story read perfectly well before the mention of my father's suicide.

I know. That's what we need to talk about. It turned out that a different story with a different telling of the facts that slandered you and Edmund had been mailed to them anonymously that morning.

That morning?!

Yes. BEFORE the accident.

Blimey, I knew it. It's just like the bloody steamer all over again.

It isn't. It's worse.

How can it be worse?!

258

The steamer incident, however unwisely, was sanctioned and overseen by numerous members of our secret services. The fall-out and humiliation that Colonel Snell suffered was sufficient to discourage any further incidents. General Kettering got involved after that, personally overseeing all cases of extraordinary interest.

All? There's more than one?

Yes, Eleanor. And as far as I can tell, they are all related to you... your world, that is—Surpanakha, Edmund's evil father, Mr. Johnson, Mélusine, and others—they've all tipped off various raised eyebrows, but no one in the government realizes how related they are. I can see it very clearly with what I know of your power. But, that is beside the point. General Kettering's position usurped my father's, adding an extra level of command between my father and the Crown, and my father did not respond well.

Is that what your mother meant when she said that his reputation was in shambles?

My father has never done well with his temper, Eleanor. You saw him degenerate when Edmund started challenging him. He's like a raging bull at the slightest provocation. When General Kettering got involved, my father revealed his true colors, and they didn't look good. He tried to blame me, by telling himself and my mother that it was my deviance reflecting poorly on him that had caused General Kettering's involvement in the first place, but it wasn't. When I was up in Perth last month on leave, I was actually meeting with General Kettering. I, being the horrible spy that I am, confessed to my deviance right then and there, assuming that he was there to arrest me or sack me or shoot me—one of the three outcomes my father had been threatening my whole life. He told me that not being swayed by the wiles of women was a highly coveted trait amongst the Secret Service, and that he trusted that the skills I'd learned at the agency would prevent me from making a public spectacle of myself, and that if I did, I could expect no help or acknowledgment from them. I chose not to think about our little incident with Andrew, and I agreed with him.

Eleanor squeezed his hand. *I'm happy for you, Stanley. Do you feel free now?*

He shrugged. *Free of one problem, burdened by another, but I suppose that's adulthood, isn't it?*

259

Amen. But what does this have to do with the hit-and-run, and The Bunbury Register, *and the mole in our midst? Do you know how it fits together?*

My father is the key, Eleanor. They have been suspicious of his loyalties for over a year. General Kettering tasked me with finding out as much as I can about what he's really up to, and I agreed to do everything in my power to help, including baiting him if I have to.

Don't tell me that you knew anything about what happened last night?!

NO. Eleanor, I didn't. I swear. He looked her straight in the eye. *My lady, as your chief handmaiden, I swear that I knew nothing of his plans. If I had, I would have kept you and the bairns back here in safety. I owe everything that is beautiful in my life to you. Every moment I feel like I'm not the greatest failure on the planet, I pray to you in thanks. My loyalty is to you, first and foremost, and it always will be.*

Eleanor let his heartfelt declaration quell her burbling rage. *Tell me everything you know.*

When General Kettering was brought in, my father began tapping his allies amongst the generals in an effort to reposition himself and ruin General Kettering. He found no support, whatsoever. I think the truth is that none of them trusted him to begin with, and the many scandals he'd used his power to squelch, including the murder of his wife, as well as his failed attempts to slander Edmund, a decorated war hero whom many of them knew and liked, bred a distaste for him that the generals could finally admit once he was falling out of favor. So, he barely held onto his position, even in title, and he stepped back, avoiding all but the most mandatory interactions with his colleagues. He then tried to tap into his old Eton chums in the House of Lords, perhaps in some effort to gain new power legislatively, rather than through the military. But he couldn't tell them anything about what his real position was in the military! On paper, he is as unimportant as a general can be, just like General Kettering is. My father's official position is overseeing the documentation of the Empire's flora and fauna! And so, most of the lords who'd respected him before the war assumed that he'd fallen out of power after some weak, shell-shocked episode. They told him so, which only made him madder. The only one who gave him the time of day was Lord Montagu, who has always been a slimy bastard. Ever since I was a child, Lord Montagu has scared me. When he was visiting the cottage in Bretagne, he used to grab my mother and corner her to get a feel under her dress. He would hit me with his walking stick, and tell my mother that if she'd had his bastard, I'd be a real man. It got so bad that my mother would take me away when he was coming. We'd stay with her brother until he was gone. No matter how much it enraged my father for her to skip out, she never let him win. It was the strongest I've ever seen her fight for herself, or for me.

Where is she in all this?

I don't know, to be honest. I shouldn't have sent her away like I did, and I haven't been able to find her, even with the resources of the Secret Service. They are also interested in her whereabouts, since they've started keeping a hawk's eye on my father's contacts. It makes me sick when I think about it, and the fear often awakens me in the middle of the night. General Kettering told me that there is no record of my father marrying her, so whatever she considers their relationship, my father did not do the paperwork for it to be legal in Britain.

The bastard.

It gets worse, Eleanor. Lord Montagu and my father have been spending too much time together. They're up to something, and last night's shenanigans are a part of it. After the incident, when my editor friend called me up, I gave him the information that I thought would put you in the best light.

You could have told him to just leave it alone.

That was my first suggestion, Eleanor. I went on and on about how private you are, but he reiterated that it was not an option for them to avoid printing altogether. There were witnesses left and right, and the same slanderous article had been sent in the morning to <u>The Bunbury Post</u>, and they printed it! He knew they would. He told me they would just print whatever landed on their desks! Did you see it?

Blimey. No.

He reached under the couch and pulled out a stack of newspapers, handing her the one on the top. The same photograph of them sitting in the front row of the circus was even bigger than it was on *The Bunbury Register's* front page.

"COWARDS OR DEMONS? BUNBURY CIRCUS PLAGUED BY MISCREANTS AND MURDERERS. Scores of local residents were enjoying a peaceful evening out at the circus, when an out-of-control vehicle sped through the muddy parking lot after the ending of the show, bringing the life of a young widow (Mrs. Eliza Humphry, 19, originally of Busselton) and her unborn child to an untimely and tragic end. Witnesses report that as Mrs. Humphry's life faded, Mr. Edmund Marriner, a retired soldier known to the military to suffer from debilitating psychological damage from shell-shock, and his wife, Mrs. Eleanor Marriner, the daughter of the late notorious polygamist, Robby MacLeod, interrupted valiant attempts to save the young mother's life, distracting emergency workers and passersby with soapbox talk of angels and demons until it was too late to escort her to the hospital, and Mrs. Humphry and her unborn child passed on. Following their failed attempt to insert their evangelical agenda into the scene of an unfolding human tragedy, numerous witnesses reported that Mr. Marriner threatened the life of the driver, chasing after him at an unnatural speed with 'the Devil in his eyes.' Their four children (identities yet to be confirmed), watched the incident, cheering for their father to 'get him good, like all the others.' Too fantastic to be true? Not according to several witnesses who reported that Mr. Marriner caught up with the car on foot, and rather than helping the driver regain control, he ripped him out of the car, and murdered him with his bare hands. While the second victim's body has yet to be found, Mr. and Mrs. Marriner remain on the loose, and local authorities warn that they are dangerous and should not be approached."

Blimey. How is it not a crime to publish something so fraudulent?

You can sue them for liable, Eleanor, but Jules pointed out that it will only backfire. It will keep the story in the news longer, and show that you are threatened by their assertions.

What a bloody mess.

We needed to control the message, and Jules agreed to buy you time by pretending that you hadn't been identified yet in the morning edition. I was up all night helping him write the articles about you, but at four in the morning, when he submitted them to the printer, he was told that the owner of the newspaper demanded that the 'truth' from the anonymous source be included. I

262

had him tack on that paragraph about your father so that he was technically in compliance with the order, or else he would have been sacked before we could use his influence on your behalf. He still might lose his position, but we need him, Eleanor. We need an ally.

Blimey.

It's still worse, though! Of course, I couldn't leave that alone. How would the owner of The Bunbury Register *have even known about an anonymous letter? Owners of newspapers aren't that involved, Eleanor, and Jules confirmed my suspicion. He said he'd never once heard from the owner of the paper until he got a livid letter in late morning today, threatening him that he must publish 'the real truth' about you in the afternoon edition. Well, that stoked his fire, since he's very passionate about truth and justice, so he went right ahead and added some even more glowing flourishes about you, just to spite them. He was sick with worry about getting sacked, and I was livid myself over it, so I used my contacts, and I discovered that the owner of* The Bunbury Register *is my bloody father!!!!*

WHAT?! Doesn't he have anything better to do?!

And the owner of The Bunbury Post *is Lord bloody Montagu!*

Oh, for Christ's sake.

There is something rotten afoot, Eleanor. He's been simmering in the distance for months, and he's finally making his move, but I don't believe for one second that the plot is limited to sadistically undermining your beautiful, uneventful, divine life down here at the edge of the world. You must be a piece of a bigger puzzle. He must *think that by doing this, he will become more powerful himself somehow. That is the only thing that really motivates him.*

What else do you know?

Both papers were bought at the same time about six weeks ago. But here's the kicker, Eleanor: No money was transferred out of my father's accounts. None. The money to buy the paper must have come from a secret account that is undocumented in the UK. Do you know who uses secret accounts?

Criminals. Spies. Traitors. Rakshasas...

Stanley paused to consider Eleanor's flippant, if accurate, suggestion that Rakshasas also used similar means of hiding their money.

263

Don't let me distract you, Stanley. It was just an offhand remark.

It wasn't wrong, Eleanor. I've never seen anything like the kind of web that surrounds Edmund's accounts.

Blimey. You've seen it?! You know how his money is organized? Does your father know? He could ruin us!

You will be fine, Eleanor. Leo wisely kept as much from him as he could, as have I. He knows nothing about Jack Johnson & Sons, which holds millions upon millions of pounds across many untraceable foreign accounts. I wouldn't be surprised if Mr. Johnson owns half the property on Earth at this point... although, I suppose it's his right as the King of Kings...

We're getting distracted, but I have to ask how you found them if they are so untraceable.

The Crown is aware that the holding company is special. General Kettering showed me a map they'd made for a different case relating to the Patels' business dealings, and asked me if I recognized anything about it. I told him I didn't. It is all getting very messy, Eleanor. I am helping General Kettering spy on my father, but he will not be pleased at all if he discovers that you and I have connections to the Patels that I haven't revealed. It's a miracle that he didn't find out that Rohit Patel was here for your birthday. I know why Leo died young...

Eleanor put her arm over his shoulder and squeezed him into a hug. *You're doing a wonderful job, greenie. I'm sure that Leo would be proud.*

Well, it's going to get worse before it gets better. I will hold out on my pride until we're out of this. Jules fought back with the afternoon edition, but I don't know how much longer he will remain employed there. I wouldn't be surprised if he's been sacked already.

We will help him find another job. I hear Nellie Melba has some good connections in Melbourne with the papers there. It will be a step up for him to work in a real city paper.

Thank you, my lady. But my primary concern is about what that means for the next several articles, until the public tires of this story.

Eleanor sighed. *We will weather it. Neither of us are strangers to hiding who we are, and I'm no stranger to being attacked by the press.*

264

It might not be that simple. They could cause real problems for you. What if the MacLeods get wind of it, and they see that you've kidnapped their children? What if the slander in <u>The Bunbury Post</u> *causes problems for Edmund's position in the judiciary?*

I doubt <u>The Bunbury Post</u> *has any sway at all now after Surpanakha unmasked their Fascist spy of a reporter.*

She did what? Eleanor, how is she involved in this?

She's an angel of vengeance, and we need her, greenie. Just like we needed her to dispose of Mac. It is a dark truth to admit, but sometimes it is helpful to have our enemies killed before they can set their evil plots in motion. Surpanakha is going to do it whether we ask her to or not. I think I have just accepted her role in this.

What did she do, Eleanor? I don't know if I have the sway to cover her tracks like Leo did.

I'm quite sure she murdered the three missing men, but we have Yaksha help in covering her tracks. You don't have to do it alone.

But how are they related, Eleanor? Even my contacts couldn't find any connection between the driver of the car and the other two missing men.

The ringmaster may have just had bad luck. He tried to mug me last night in front of the children, and I fought him off. Surpanakha probably just punished him for good measure. But the Great Pizzaz, the knife-thrower at the circus, was trying to kill me on stage. Without Yaksha intervention, I would have been executed in cold blood in front of everyone.

The bastard! I'm glad she killed him.

So am I. It's not a very godly thought, so we will keep it between us.

But I thought that he went out and killed that Fascist reporter last night?

The reporter was certainly killed by Surpanakha. Writing a confessional note on behalf of her guilty victims is her calling card. Impersonating the Great Pizzaz as she did it must have been part of a bigger plan, since she mostly prefers to dismember her victims.

Gast ahas.

We should keep that in mind as we move forward.

But what does a random Italian carny have to do with anything?

265

That bastard was a recruiter for the Fascist Italian cause. He admitted his treachery to me last night under extreme duress, and he admitted that he'd targeted me under orders from his superiors—it wasn't random. He is also undoubtedly the one who'd recruited the reporter from The Bunbury Post. *Surpanakha taking the effort to kill that boy is significant. He must have been an important pawn for someone. She's really very helpful sometimes…*

As the thought occurred to her, Eleanor squinted to read the bi-line of the slanderous article from *The Bunbury Post*, and she grinned and pointed.

That, greenie. That's what we needed. The little worm who published the false article about us was the Fascist spy. It completely discredits everything slanderous about us in The Bunbury Post, *and it makes them look like a mouthpiece for Il Duce. You must call Jules now and tell him to put this exposé on the front page: FASCIST SPY PUBLISHES SLANDEROUS ARTICLE ABOUT BRITISH WAR HERO. It will tank that paper completely and discredit everything negative they said about us! Jules can then argue as the Register's readership soars that he saw the whole thing for what it was, and he was the greatest editor in the world to not fall into the Fascist trap! It will scare off your father, because if he sacks Jules, it will make him look like a Fascist.*

Eleanor, I don't think I will ever be half as shrewd as you are. You're bloody brilliant, you know. But then how does the hit-and-run driver fit into it all? Was he a Fascist Italian spy too?

Eleanor looked down at the photographs that were still in her lap. *I'm certain he was a hitman. He was targeting that poor girl intentionally, and he was doing it in front of us for a reason. Someone was baiting us, and given everything else we've just discussed, I think we can both assume that it was your father. But I still don't see what he would have had to gain from staging something so risky. If he'd wanted to slander us in the newspapers, he could have just done it. It wouldn't have required a public incident. There must be more to it… What would help him crawl back up into his powerful position? Repeating a Colonel Snell wouldn't help him gain any clout, would it?*

No. The incident is now being used as a cautionary tale amongst the agencies about what not to do. The only thing that would help him now would be to have someone exceptionally important pull him straight up to the top. No one in our government would dare to do that now. He's a loose cannon, and they all know it.

Stanley... what do you think the chances are that your father is a Fascist?

Stanley snorted. *He certainly has the temperament... and the views... If he were born Italian, I have no doubt he'd be kissing Il Duce's hand right now, but for all his faults, he has lived his entire life devoted to Britain. Treason would be the ultimate betrayal.*

But think about it. If he was desperate enough to defect, last night's incidents make perfect sense. Maybe the knives were meant to show someone in that audience that our power was real, and there was no better way to do that than to have an Italian spy executing the plan. If an Italian agent was watching, perhaps the Great Pizzaz's superior officer, then your father's claims about our power would have been proven true. They would have no reason to question it, because they partook in the testing. Your father could be trying to offer us as pawns to solidify his position with the Italians. He will need to bring something important to the table to go straight to the top, and we are a powerful token of his loyalty.

Stanley paused to consider the implications for a long time. *It is possible. It was a concern General Kettering brought up as well when I met with him last month. I didn't want to believe it, but I have never seen my mother so scared of him. Maybe she knew... blimey, Eleanor! Maybe she knew!!! Maybe that's why she came all the way down here to warn me! And I sent her away! How could I have been so blind?!*

We are all blind when it comes to our mothers, Stanley. Speaking of which... I must ask you to think very carefully about this. Do you think your father might have enlisted my mother to help him with his scheming?

Your mother? But she's been doing so well?

I know. Too well, I should have realized. I overheard her muttering to herself last night about being smited. She said that the Good Lord might smite 'us both.' Do you know who the other person in 'us' might have been?

I have no idea, Eleanor.

Do you think she could have taken this picture?

She pointed to the photograph taken by their mole.

He squinted as he stared at it. *She isn't in the picture. But, Eleanor, do you believe your mother could figure out how to clandestinely use a camera? Mae's autochrome is extremely complicated. Even I have trouble using it. And there were four other people who also aren't in the picture—all of Oz and Yvie's staff, and Sheila.*

Blimey! Sheila was there, wasn't she?

She was, Eleanor. Her demanding presence is impossible to forget. But that is beside the point. You must forgive me if I seem a bit wary of jumping to conclusions about our treacherous mothers at the moment.

Eleanor sighed. *I suppose you're right. We will just need to take that much extra care. Someone in this household took this photo, and a few weeks later it ended up in the car of a Fascist assassin. That is not a coincidence.*

I will be vigilant, Eleanor. You should also know that I found a hole poked into the pantry wall, just like the one Sheila made in Oz and Yvie's kitchen. Kuveni helped me patch it up, and she placed a sound barrier around the room until further notice. It was a concern that I haven't had time to bring up with you, but that all happened last week. That's why I didn't even want to whisper.

Eleanor sighed with annoyance at the continuously snowballing stress. *I suppose that means we should be extra wary of Mrs. Jenkins, as well. Speaking of which, it's going to be best for you to stay only in your room while you're dressing up. Debbie caught you in the kitchen a few weeks back in the middle of the night. She brought it up in passing, but she may not be the only one lurking.*

It was Stanley's turn to sigh with annoyance. *I suppose for now I'll need to be more vigilant than ever. When we use Jules to corner my father on his newspaper scheme, he might come gunning for us more overtly. We don't need to give my father or the papers any more fodder if he manages to get the police to invade our household. I will put all of my dresses in your closet for now, if you don't mind, Eleanor?*

It is a sensible precaution. Does your father still believe that he can control you? And that by controlling you, he can manipulate us?

Stanley smiled. *As much as he ever did. He knows I'm still going to fall back into deviance, but otherwise he seems to be satisfied with the uninspiring reports I've been sending. He has always underestimated me. It is a powerful ace in our hand. He will be shocked when Jules punches him right back in the face on this newspaper battle, and I've already started composing my wide-eyed, whiny report on the inconvenience of the press's meddling that will only enrage him more.*

I wish I could be there to see him break the telephone receiver.

Or throw a type-writer out the window. He's done it twice right in front of me. But we'd better get back to the bairns. They've been working on a little surprise for you and Edmund for weeks now.

Stanley stood up and offered her his left hand. She smiled as she took it and let him help her up out of the cavernous couch. *I'm glad to see you've given up on fighting that battle.*

General Kettering told me that some of their best agents are left-handed. It turns out that deviance creates an element of surprise which is good for a spy. Who knew? Apparently not my father.

Your father knew nothing of consequence, Stanley. Absolutely nothing.

Stanley pulled her into a hug. *I love you, Eleanor... but not like Leo did.*

She winked. *At least my wiles still know some bounds.*

We will triumph, Eleanor. My father doesn't have any idea who he's really dealing with.

Neither does Il Duce.

Thank God for that!

And, I hate to admit that we must also thank Surpanakha.

How should we proceed with her, Eleanor?

How we always have. We must let her do what she wants to do. I will tell her to control herself, and she will try unsuccessfully. Perhaps in trying, she will manage to contain the goriest of her instincts. But whatever you do, do not stand in her way. She doesn't see you as a threat, and you must keep it that way. If ever she catches you spying, make sure she knows that you are still our ally. She especially loves torturing traitors.

I'll try not to think about it.

Me too.

"Amma?! Amma, come quickly!" Debbie called up the stairs.

"We have a surprise for you!" Ruthy added.

She followed Stanley out of the room, and Debbie and Ruthy squealed and ran down the stairs away from them. They were wearing elaborate Shakespearean costumes, undoubtedly produced by Kuveni, and their hair was all braided up in a distinctly Roman style.

Eleanor let the impending cuteness of the bairns' surprise pull her away from the simmering stress that their conversation had only made worse. As they reached the library, which was filled from top to bottom with elaborate Christmas decorations, complete with a twelve-foot tall real pine tree in the corner covered in twinkling electric lights and ornaments, and a roaring fire in the fireplace with brimming stockings for each of the MacLeods, plus Oz, Yvie, Neddy, and Auntie Kate and Uncle Percy, and even Gramma Moira.

"Merry Christmas!" they shouted.

"Merry Christmas, dearest!" Edmund said giddily as he pulled her into a romantic dip. "It has been too long since we've had a Christmas that felt like Christmas. In fact, I'm not sure we've ever really had one. It was rather anti-climactic in India, and it wasn't much better when we were all simmering at the beach last summer, but now it really feels how I dreamed it could be. Doesn't it?"

"It does," Eleanor admitted, working to bury her raging stress.

"The bairns have a surprise for us!" Edmund added.

"This isn't surprise enough?" Eleanor asked.

"We had help decorating," Debbie admitted. "But we made something for you, Amma!"

She and Ruthy guided Eleanor and Edmund to the center couch. The couches had been rearranged so that there was a makeshift stage in front of the roaring fire. Eleanor's mother was already seated beside Yvie, who was holding Ned sleeping in her arms, and Mae, who was wearing her own elaborate costume, complete with a black beard made out of yarn. She winked.

As Eleanor and Edmund sat in the seats of honor, Stanley took his butling position by the door, and Oz came up onto the stage, wearing a costume that could only be described as a wizard with a long sparkling cape made of a beautiful silky material that shimmered and changed color in the light, and a matching pointy hat. His own yarn beard made all the children giggle, but then they got themselves under control as he held up a massive wooden staff that was simpler but not completely unlike Mélusine's divine staff, and declared: *"Now does my project gather to a head. My charms crack not, my spirits obey, and time goes upright with his carriage. How's the day?"*

As Edmund laughed and clapped his enthusiastic approval, Debbie hopped up onto the stage, dancing around with a wand that matched her sparkling green fairy dress. *"On the sixth hour, at which time, my lord, you said our work should cease."*

The players continued on with their adorable rendition of the last act of Shakespeare's *Tempest,* and Eleanor tried to focus on anything other than her conversation with Stanley. She tried to focus on how cute the bairns were as they earnestly went about acting the advanced material, and how kind Oz and Mae were to have helped them with their little plan. She tried to embrace the truth of Edmund's statement, that it really did feel how she'd always imagined Christmas could be, and she tried to wonder with childlike enthusiasm about what adorable gifts might be waiting in her stocking.

But she just couldn't shake a dark sense of foreboding, and she wasn't sure if her mother's presence was compounding the problem. Of all the conclusions that had been made clear by her conversation with Stanley, her mother's role in the whole thing remained unrevealed, and it was driving her nuts. If her mother hadn't said those three little words, the words that she'd longed her whole life to hear and that had the power to shoot right through her armor, then she wouldn't have cared so much. But to hear them said in treachery... she simply couldn't get over it...

The sound of the phone ringing in the kitchen pulled her out of her thought-stream, and Stanley rushed away to answer it. Oz continued delivering Prospero's monologue like a champion, and Edmund squeezed Eleanor's hand.

When Stanley returned, his face was pale, and he nodded subtly for Eleanor to join him, but a wave of his genuine fear aroused Edmund's senses, and as his eyes turned black, Oz stopped, and the children stopped, and all eyes landed on Stanley.

"What is it?" Edmund said as he stood up in a blur and pulled Eleanor up beside him. "Why are you scared, Stanley, my boy? Are we in some sort of trouble?"

Stanley cleared his throat, but he couldn't hide a quiver in his voice. "Eleanor, Mary MacLeod MacGregor wants to talk to you about her missing children."

Edmund followed Eleanor into the kitchen, while Oz, Yvie, and Mae comforted the whimpering children. They all knew what the call meant. Their beautiful lives were about to change, and chances were, they were about to get worse. The unburdened time they'd bought with their hasty Yakshini exit had just ended, and now the cruel world had caught up with them. Eleanor couldn't think about them. She couldn't think about Edmund. She could only think about herself and all that she had to lose as she picked up the receiver.

"Do you want me to stay or go?" Stanley asked.

"Stay. Please stay."

Edmund paced back and forth whispering his mantras, and Stanley leaned in to listen beside her.

"Mary?" she asked.

Mary was breathing heavily and sniffling. "Ellie?" she asked meekly. "Ellie, is that you?"

"Aye, it's me."

The connection was crackling. "I'm sorry I made the call collect, Ellie. I know it must be expensive."

Eleanor and Stanley threw each other a shared look of disbelief at the odd opening. At the very least, she didn't sound angry. "Don't worry about it."

"Ellie, please tell me ye have 'em. Tell me they're there and they're safe? Please say so!!! I have to hear ye say so!!!"

Eleanor felt like her heart might explode. Could she still get away with lying? Could she just say no, she hadn't seen the bairns? Was it all a trap? Was Scotland Yard listening in for a confession? Eleanor refused to answer. She just stood silently, waiting for Mary to make the next move.

"Ellie, I saw the picture in the paper. With you and Mam and the colonel and the bairns. It was in the newspaper all the way up here in Edinburgh."

Eleanor rolled her eyes so intensely that they hurt. "Really? In Edinburgh? How's the commuter traffic these days? It must be awful getting the bairns back and forth to school. It's a good thing they got into Eton to spare you the trouble. You know, I was thinking, maybe we should talk to the *Edinburgh Register* about writing an article. It's quite newsworthy that the first two girls ever admitted to the school were Scottish lasses, don't you think? I think it would be quite an inspirational story."

Mary paused for a long moment as she tried to collect herself. "That wasn't my idea, Ellie. I swear it. It was Martha's idea. All of it, the whole bloody mess was Jimmy's idea, and then Martha and Fergus went marching along off the cliff beside him."

"You had a choice," Eleanor hissed. "Don't you dare pretend that you didn't. I told you the first time I sent you a king's ransom from Edmund's accounts that the cheque was in your name for a reason. With a tenth of one cheque you could have walked away with your children in tow to a better life than the one you had, so don't you dare make excuses. You defrauded us for years. You abused your children, and you practically starved our mother to death. Are you going to deny any of those indisputable facts?"

Mary cried longer and louder, and Eleanor waited silently for her response.

"I didn't realize it would get that bad!"

"Well it did. And you stood by and watched."

"But, Ellie, I'm scared!" Mary wailed. "I'm bloody terrified! Ye don't understand!"

"Then make me understand, because right now I don't even know who you are anymore, Mary MacLeod."

Mary cried some more. "Ye know I'm not strong enough to say no, Ellie. I never have been. I needed ye to tell Martha what was right, and when ye left, I didn't have any allies to help me be a right braw lass! She's rotten to the bloody core! She's so much worse than I ever realized. You kept her good, Ellie, but then she went off her heid, and now…" She dissolved into sobs.

"So you're saying that it's my fault that you defrauded me and my husband out of tens of thousands of pounds, you starved and lashed your children, and you almost killed our mother. Those crimes that you committed are my fault because I didn't stop you? Is that what you're saying?!"

Mary sobbed. "No, Ellie. That's not what I meant to say. I'm just all mixed up these days. I'm so bloody scared, Ellie. After you got off the telephone with Martha yesterday morning, she knew she'd made a mistake. She could tell ye dunne believe her, but when she went flappin' her mouth about it to Jimmy and she told him that ye'd asked fer the bill from Eton, he bloody lost his heid! I've never seen him so furious. He told her that she'd blown their whole scheme by being stupid enough to name a school in the first place, and *Eton*! Even Jimmy bloody Buchanan knew it was only for lads!"

"I'm sorry. Are you calling me to complain that our sister failed at bamboozling me properly? I'm hearing nothing here that deserves any sympathy."

"He chased her out of the house, Ellie! He chased after her with his hunting rifle! She ran away screaming, and I haven't seen either of them since! They've disappeared! I think..." She dissolved into uncontrollable sobs. "I think he killed her, Ellie."

Eleanor handed the receiver to Stanley and stepped away to catch her breath. Of all the ways she thought the call that she'd been dreading for months would go, this particular outcome had not even crossed her mind. Did she believe Jimmy was capable of murdering his wife in a fit of rage? She had no doubt about it. It was a wonder to her that Martha hadn't shown up with bruises more often over the years. A pang of guilt echoed deep within her that she hadn't properly respected how violent her sisters' husbands could be, and that for whatever reasons, they were not willing to save themselves. Should she have tried harder to save them? She returned to her position, bracing herself.

"So you haven't seen Martha or Jimmy since yesterday morning? What about Fergus? Where was he in all this?"

"He was out!" Mary exclaimed. "He had nothing to do with it!"

"Really? Was he busy working hard for your shared business endeavor? Perhaps purchasing some advertisements in the Edinburgh newspapers to attract some patrons up to Skye for a hunting weekend? Or perhaps out shooting a deer to hang triumphantly over your door?"

"He was at the pub," she whispered shamefully. "He dunne believe anything I said about it. He thinks it's just a ploy to manipulate him into going back to Edinburgh because I've been needlin' him about it fer months. But that's not the end of it, Ellie. It got worse. Yesterday afternoon, while I was stewing at home, terrified for my life that Jimmy was going to come back and kill me too, a solicitor showed up. He told us that Lord Grimby had sent him to help us get our bairns back."

"Lord Grimby?!" Eleanor exclaimed. "You will tell me everything that you know about Lord Grimby, Mary. *Now.*"

"I dunne know anything!"

"I don't believe you. You are very close to me hanging up the phone, Mary, and if I hang up, every penny is going to dry up, ye hear? Every bloody penny, and you can expect to see a lawsuit for the thirty-thousand pounds you stole along with a policeman at your door to arrest you for embezzlement."

Mary began sobbing again, and Eleanor waited until she got herself under control. "Please don't hang up, Ellie! Please! Ye're the only one I have in the world!"

"Then stop lying to me!" Eleanor shouted.

"He came up to the castle about three weeks ago!" Mary confessed through her sobs. "He and some other lord, Lord Montagu, both showed up at our door just out of the blue. Fergus thought it was a godsend, but there was something wrong with them, Ellie. That Lord Montagu wunne right in the heid! They had a wild look about 'em, like they were up to something devilish, but Martha invited them right on in! They asked a few questions about us like they were fishin' fer something, and then they said they were lookin' fer a place to let fer the season to invite some other lords up to hunt—some counts or dukes or some such nonsense that had foreign-sounding names that impressed Martha, the swooning bassa—and that all we had to do was get it ready for them! But we dunne bloody have the money, Ellie! We dunne have a bloody shilling left! That's what got Martha to call ye. We argued about it fer weeks, and I told her that I'd clipe on her if she tried to chore the money from ye, but then she did it anyway!" She trailed off into uncontrollable sobs, and Eleanor grabbed Stanley's hand.

Are you taking mental notes? Can you corroborate what she's saying with your sources?

I will do everything I can, Eleanor. We should assume she isn't lying. How else would she know their names?

"Ellie, I swear, I just wanted out. I just want out now! When the solicitor showed up yesterday, he said that we could get gobs of money from ye for stealing our bairns, and ye should've seen Fergus's face! He was salivatin' at the idea. The man was talking about our *children*, Ellie. They're my only reason for being! But fer Fergus it was all about the bloody money! I slapped him and ran right out the door, and I used a bit of money from yer last cheque that I'd kept aside for an emergency to get off the isle. I'm in Edinburgh, Ellie, I swear to ye. I escaped yesterday, and I spent the night at an inn, and I'm not going back."

Eleanor paused as she considered her options.

"Ellie, please believe me. I know that we've been lying to ye something awful, but I'm not lying now. I need yer help, and I need to know that the bairns are okay. The article in the newspaper, the one I saw this morning… it said that the colonel murdered a man in cold blood in front of the bairns?"

"He didn't murder anyone. You will see in the news tomorrow that the vicious author of that rubbish article committed suicide and confessed to being a Fascist spy. He was out to create strife in the British Empire by slandering noble war heroes, and Edmund was his victim."

Stanley, please make sure that Jules's follow-up goes out on the wires. We have international damage control to deal with.

It will be done, Eleanor. You have other things to worry about.

"That's at least something," Mary said as she sniffled. "But, Ellie, I'm scared. I don't know what Fergus'll do when he finds me, and…" She trailed off into tears. "I'm pregnant, Ellie. The doctor confirmed it last month, and I'm so bloody scared. I canne do this alone, and I dunne wanna do it with Fergus. Please, Ellie. Help me. Please. Please. Please."

Eleanor worked hard to keep the flames of Durga at bay, and she let the first thing that entered her mind slip out. "Well, I'm glad to hear that the disappearance of your children didn't hurt your performance in the sack."

Mary sobbed some more. "It wunne my choice, Ellie. I was doing the wifely duty. He made me do it!"

"You could've left him years ago!" Eleanor shouted. "Why in the bloody hell didn't you just leave?!"

"We canne all be married to auld sassanacks who tickle our fancy while paying endless sums of money fer our whims, Ellie!"

"Are you chastising us for sending you money? Because you're the only bloody whim Edmund has ever paid for."

"Why cunne ye've just married that auld crotchety doctor, Ellie? That Teddy fellow who cunne tell his arm from his leg? Yer colonel's money ruined us! It ruined Martha and Jimmy and Fergus and *me*! It let the Devil right in the door!"

Eleanor lowered her voice into a furious hiss. "You let your husband slash scars into your children's backs over spilled milk. You need to look in the mirror to find someone to blame, Mary MacLeod, and in the meantime, you'd better think long and hard about the pain that you've inflicted on your own children. That wasn't the Devil starving them to death, it was *you*. Now grow a bloody spine, ye spineless bassa! I'm hanging up now."

"Wait! No! Please don't hang up! I dunne leave because I wunne strong enough, Ellie!"

"I think that might be the first true thing you've said in years, Mary MacLeod."

"Ellie, please. Ye canne keep my bairns from me. They're all I've got. They're all I live for. I need to see 'em. I don't care about the money; I just want to see 'em, and hug 'em, and tell 'em how much I love 'em. I miss my lads so much it's killing me. The only thing that got me out the door, away from Fergus, was the idea of seeing 'em again, and it's good fer 'em to know how much I love 'em, isn't it? Please, Ellie, lemme tell 'em so. Dunne let 'em believe that I never even bothered to find 'em."

It could be a trap, Stanley warned her.

I don't know what to do. God, why couldn't she just leave on her own years ago?! It would have been so simple! I would have been so happy to help! I wouldn't have had to rescue her children from her, and no one would've had to coax them out of shells of pain and fear that they could've avoided in the first place!

You should not just give them back. You promised them that you would keep them safe, Eleanor. Even if everything she's saying is true, she has proven that she isn't a good mother.

But they ARE her children! If they were my children, I'd go to the ends of the earth to get them back! What if I say no, and the solicitor comes after us?! Mae said that she'd testified in a case where the children were handed right back to their abusive father who was so bad that he'd broken their arms! There was no contention about whether he'd broken their arms! The judges just believed that their natural father had the right to do ANYTHING to them. I've been fighting off dread about this scenario since day one, and your bloody father swooped right in to make it happen.

He is excellent at finding weaknesses to exploit, Eleanor, and love is the greatest weakness. You can't let him win.

I kept telling myself that the reason I was keeping them was because she refused to leave Fergus. If she's really left him, I don't have a morally superior argument.

Maybe you don't need one, Eleanor. You're the Holy Mother. It's better for them to have you as their mother. Maybe it's just that simple. God, how much better my life would have been if you'd been my mother...

Eleanor thought about Norwenn, and how Stanley's rejection of her had ended.

You know that your mother loves you, Stanley. She came down here to hassle you about your lifestyle because she loves you. You know deep down that she cared enough about you to do it.

Eleanor regretted bringing up the sore subject, but she knew the point was true, and she needed confirmation as it boiled in the cauldron of her many other irrational thoughts.

You're right, Eleanor. She did it because she loved me. She told me many times how sad she was that I was going to Hell because she loved me. Alongside everything else she made me feel, I had no doubt that all the pain she inflicted was because she loved me. It wasn't enough.

Maybe so, but these bairns don't even have that. All they know is that their mother stood by and watched while they were starving to death. They may very well think that it was because she didn't love them, but that is wrong. She does love them. She just wasn't bloody strong enough to fight for them.

Mary took her long pause to get herself under control. "Ellie… I dunne tell Fergus about the baby. If ye come back, if ye help me, I'll give it to ye. You can say that it's yers. All I want is to know my brood. Ye're a better mother than I ever was, I can see that now. I could see joy in their faces in that newspaper photo that I dunne ever see before, not once. Even Mam looks happy! I dunne deserve yer sympathy, or yer pity, or yer help, Ellie. I deserve nothing after everything I've done. But I will give you this baby if ye let me see my bairns again, and I will tell that solicitor to leave us all alone."

Eleanor sighed a long sigh of stress. It felt like a trap, but if Mary was indeed telling the truth about everything, if Lord Grimby was involving them in his Fascist scheming, and Jimmy had *murdered* Martha, and Mary had finally found it within herself to leave her worthless bastard of a husband, then it would certainly be her fault for leaving Mary to be devoured by wolves in her moment of greatest need.

She tried not to think about the alluring prospect of adopting the baby as her own, of giving Edmund *almost* what he wanted so badly. It was as close as they could possibly get to raising their own child together, and perhaps, if Mary wasn't lying, she could let Mary move in with them, and they could somehow become a bigger, happier family… It *would* be better for the bairns if their real mother was there without the corrupting influence of the villains who'd abused them, but what if she were some sort of spy? The likelihood was extremely high, given the mess that was still actively unfolding and Lord Grimby's involvement… And what if Mary's presence was going to lead Fergus and Jimmy right to their door? Eleanor couldn't let those bassas ruin the beautiful life they'd created at the edge of the world. But, as she listened to her sister sob, she also couldn't ignore the simmering unpleasant truth that it was, by many reasonable definitions, wrong to have kidnapped her children, and if she wasn't lying, it was wrong to leave her all alone, pregnant, without any help. She would certainly go running back to Fergus, because Eleanor would have given her no other choice…

Desperation is the mother of tragedy, Uma murmured. *Don't let her get too desperate, my child.*

Do you think she's lying?

You and I both know that she isn't, Eleanor. We both have the talent to judge such things. This must be the next step in Shakti's plan. We mustn't fight it.

"Ellie? Ellie, please say something. I need somewhere to go."

"Fine. Go to Basingstoke. Go to Edmund's house there. Wait for us to contact you, and *do not* contact Fergus or that damn solicitor. When our agents have confirmed that every detail that you have told me is true, we will talk more. I trust you have enough money for a train fare and a taxi?"

"Yes," Mary whispered.

"Then do it. And, Mary, the consequences for treachery are severe. If you're lying, you should run away and disappear and never, ever come back. There are entities that punish those who cross us, and we don't have control over them. Don't move forward with another lie. Got it?"

She fell back into sobs. "Thank you, Ellie. Thank you. Please, just tell me they're alright."

"We'll talk more later."

Eleanor hung up the phone.

"You did not admit that you had them," Stanley pointed out. "That was very wise."

"It took all my self-control. It's still a strong possibility that the whole thing is a trap. If Grimby's solicitor was sitting in listening, they may have been fishing for a confession."

"Do you believe it's all really about the money?"

"No. I don't. I believe that most of what she said was true, but I am not going to take it at face value. Stanley, if you can call

Mr. Marlowe, please let him know that we need his help checking up on everything that Mary said as soon as he can manage it. He may want to call upon Titania's help in ascertaining the status of a certain personal detail that my sister asserted. We shouldn't make any decisions until we know what we're actually dealing with."

"Yes, Eleanor, I'll call him right away." Stanley did an impeccable job of hiding the fact that he had no idea who Mr. Marlowe was.

They both glanced over at Edmund, who was still whispering his mantras as he leaned up against the far wall, breathing in and out soothingly.

"Darling, I'm not sure how much of that conversation you could hear from just our side?" Eleanor approached him.

"Why did you send her to Basingstoke?" She could feel him working to keep his rage under control. "She deserves nothing after what she did to the bairns!"

"Darling, we must think carefully about how we proceed here. She is their mother. She wants to see them. She has a solicitor, and she has the right to take them back. It will be a bloody boxing match to try to keep them away from her, and it won't be good for them or for us. She believes that Jimmy murdered Martha..."

"Murdered her?! Surely she must be exaggerating?"

"I believe he's capable of it, darling, and they've gotten exceptionally desperate over their money issues. Martha called just yesterday, claiming that all four of the bairns had gotten into Eton."

"Eton?! But that's a boys' school! Those conniving bastards..." He whispered his mantras more heatedly. "Why didn't you tell me, Eleanor?"

"I didn't have time, darling. She called when we were packing up to leave for the circus. Given your reaction now, I think it was a good idea to keep it from you until we could discuss it in private."

"And you think that she's telling the truth now, that your sister was *murdered*?"

"It was Martha who called yesterday, darling. Mary has always been more reliable. I believe that she believes she's in danger, and that was enough to give her a refuge for the moment. If she is right, then she's in grave danger. Jimmy may come after her. She claims that she's left Fergus and that she's on the run, and... that she's pregnant."

"Good lord."

"She offered to give us the baby to raise as our own if we help her."

"*Good lord.*"

"I don't want to think too much about the prospect until we know more about the truth of her assertions. The whole thing is a wicked mess full of imperfect options, and I don't want to get too attached to any ideas yet."

"How are we going to check up on what she said, Eleanor? I can't live in limbo for very long. I'm already going mad at the idea of losing the bairns. I don't know how I can get myself under control."

A light tap at the kitchen door startled her. Without waiting for a response, Mr. Montero entered the room, clad in his full butler's uniform, but using his younger, more attractive form that Edmund now knew.

"My lord, I will help," he said simply. "I will use my network of spies to have answers for you by morning."

"You mean Mr. Johnson's network?" Edmund asked.

"Does it matter?" Monty countered.

"Nothing matters right now except the bairns," Edmund conceded. "Please, do whatever you can. I won't ask any questions about your methods, including what you're doing here right now."

"As you wish, my lord."

Mr. Montero offered a respectful bow, and exited back into the hallway through the kitchen door.

"What are we going to tell the bairns, Eleanor? We promised to be there for them forever and always."

"And we will be. Darling, I meant it when I said that I'd fight to keep them. But maybe we don't have to fight so much. Maybe we can find a way to bring Mary in, and if we can, it will be better for everyone."

"And what do we tell them about Martha? Surely we can't walk in there on Christmas and tell the lasses that we think their father murdered their mother?"

"Nothing. We tell them absolutely nothing for now. We will figure out what to say when we know more about what happened. We are in this together, Edmund. We will find a way to keep our family together."

She stood on her tiptoes and kissed him gently on the lips. As she pulled away, his eyes returned to their human hazel. He took Stanley's hand and squeezed it. "Thank you, my boy, for being the man that I can't always be. I should've been standing there with you by the phone, Eleanor. Instead, I was focused on keeping myself from destroying everything in this kitchen."

"Darling, we do what we can. Now, let's go relieve the bairns of some of their worry. Whatever happens, we will face it together, and they need to know that."

She took his hand, and took a deep breath. After a lifetime of battling madmen and demons, she'd never been more terrified in her life than she was at the thought of facing those bairns.

Fate had finally come to collect.

CHAPTER 17 – JOURNEY HOME

Eleanor awoke to a familiar pleasant breeze. The embers were crackling in the library's fireplace, and the children were all snuggled up in blankets on the floor beside her and Edmund.

Earlier in the evening, after Mary's call had sent each one of them into an uncontrollable panic, the bairns gave up on their Shakespearean performance. Eleanor told them that they were all going to wait for Auntie Kate's friend to check up on some details back in Scotland, and that they would only be able to decide what to do next after they had all of the information.

"You promised we wouldn't go back to Scotland!" Debbie wailed.

"You aren't going back to Scotland," Eleanor reiterated. "But Mary loves you, and she misses you. We want to find a way for her to be with you, without the others. We will not let anything happen to you, and we will always be your Abbi and Amma, okay?"

They took their dinner as a picnic in the library, since the children couldn't bring themselves to move more than a few feet in their anxious malaise, and then Oz and Yvie took Neddy home, and Mae and Moira went to bed in their rooms. Edmund read them more of the *Arabian Nights*, but as he kept distractedly slipping into Arabic, no one noticed or cared. None of them were listening to the story, including him. Their minds were all focused solely on the uncertain future.

Eventually, they'd fallen asleep in the comfort of each other's arms, and Eleanor had allowed herself to doze, although she'd required herself to keep one eye open for the dreaded news. She wasn't sure what she even wanted to hear. Did she want to hear that Mary had been lying the whole time so that they could go back to their daily lives unburdened? Or did she want Mary to be telling the truth? She had wanted Mary to find the strength to leave Fergus for so many years, although the truth would also mean that Martha had been murdered by her worthless husband. She felt completely torn about Martha. Certainly she hadn't wanted her to die, but the woman she'd observed with Kuveni's help had so thoroughly descended down a path of darkness that she didn't have much confidence in her ability to crawl out of it. Her vindictive side that cared only about the pain inflicted on the bairns wanted Martha to suffer, while the part of her who'd mothered Martha for years of their shared childhood knew that she'd been dealt a wretched hand.

And so, as Mr. Montero appeared beside the Christmas tree, Eleanor scrambled up trying not to wake the bairns, to ambivalently receive the news of their shared fate.

She glanced down at Edmund who remained solidly asleep with the children nestled into the nooks of his arms, and then led Monty out of the library and into the kitchen.

She grabbed his hand. *Please secure this room.*

He closed his eyes and whispered a quiet mantra, but as she let go, a subtle tap at the door distracted them.

"It is your spying butler," Mr. Montero whispered.

"Let him in."

Mr. Montero raised his eyebrows in disapproval but obeyed her command anyway, reaching over and pulling the door open for Stanley, and then closing it and locking it as soon as he was inside.

Stanley looked him up and down first with suspicion, and then with appreciation for his muscular, fairy-king form that looked especially handsome in his formal butler's uniform. He snapped himself out of it and returned to business.

"Do I know you?" he asked Mr. Montero bluntly.

"Stanley, this is Mr. Montero. He is a loyal Yaksha ally."

Stanley grabbed her hand. *This room isn't secure. You shouldn't say anything of consequence.*

"Mr. Montero has secured it," she replied out loud. "Haven't you, Monty?"

"Nothing comes in or out without my approval, including soundwaves," he reiterated. "Now, my lady, there is much work to be done. You have a very complicated mess unfolding, and I have good news and bad news to share. What do you want to hear first?"

"The most important news, Monty. How much of what Mary said was true?"

"Most of it, my lady. Lady Mélusine confirmed that she is four months pregnant."

"Blimey," Eleanor murmured.

"She is making her way to Basingstoke now. She changed trains in York and Reading. Fergus is not with her, and I have not yet been able to locate him. However, I did locate Jimmy Buchanan. He is making his way to Glasgow now where he intends to use the few shillings he has left to gamble his way into more funds."

"For Christ's sake," Eleanor muttered.

Mr. Montero braced himself to deliver the worst of the news. "I do not believe he will get very far, my lady. The dirt and blood on his clothing and hands from burying Martha's body will certainly tip off the authorities when combined with his guilty demeanor and short temper."

289

Eleanor leaned on Stanley, who helped her to a chair at a small table in the corner. Even after the idea had circled in her mind all night, she still wasn't prepared for the harsh reality of what it really meant.

"Do you wish for me to continue?" Mr. Montero asked.

"Just tell it to me straight," Eleanor said as she buried her face in her arms. "I'm listening."

"He shot her in the back with his hunting rifle, my lady. The body was already cold when I found Jimmy burying it in a glen not too far from the castle. He buried the rifle a few miles farther, in the bed of a babbling brook. I have left traces on both locations so that we can report the crime to the authorities when you see fit to involve them."

Eleanor reeled as the imagery of Martha running and running until she was shot in the back bombarded her.

It is a great loss, my child. It is natural for you to feel it.

"Are you alright, Eleanor?" Stanley asked as he rubbed her back.

"It was my bloody fault," she whispered. "I should have rescued her years ago. I shouldn't have let her dig her own grave. I should have seen how far she'd fallen, and tried to pull her out of it!"

"Do you want me to argue with you?" Stanley asked.

Eleanor finally looked up at him. "Maybe a little."

"She was an adult, Eleanor. You gave her every resource in the world to save herself. God knows you couldn't *make* her do anything."

"Edmund is stirring," Mr. Montero informed them.

"Is there anything else that I should know before we bring Edmund in? Either of you?"

"Lord Montagu has moved in with my father at his estate in Shropshire," Stanley replied. "It is very likely that Mary's story of them arriving together in Skye was true, although I do not have hard evidence to support it yet. It is very odd for them to move in together, for so many reasons, we don't have time to discuss them."

"You don't think...?"

"No, Eleanor. There is absolutely no way they are lovers. No bloody way. There must be something else going on. Something sinister. But what is most important is that it means that my father no longer cares about his reputation, because if he did, he would never have done anything so scandalous. He must be aiming for some prize that doesn't require British society's approval."

"What about Fascist Italian society's?"

"If their cohabitation is a means to an end, such as setting up a base for the Fascist Italian infiltration of Britain, then Il Duce will not bat an eye. I have already reported the involvement of the Italian spies at the Bunbury Circus to General Kettering, and he agrees that their involvement in that incident combined with my father's is highly suspicious. He is putting another detail in place to observe my father's movements night and day. He has also already found evidence of connections between Lord Montagu and the Italians. It is possible that Lord Montagu has been leading my father in this direction for quite some time."

Stanley shifted uncomfortably as he prepared himself for a request that he wasn't completely behind.

"Eleanor... General Kettering has asked if it is possible for me to sway you and Edmund to return to England for a bit. He thinks that my father's obsession with you may bait him into giving away the full extent of the Italians' meddling in our politics, especially now that we have thwarted him in his efforts to slander you in the press... which we have, Eleanor. We won. I worked with Jules for hours on the morning edition, and he has already sent it out on all of the international wires. By morning, *The Bunbury Post* will be a poster child for Fascist Italian meddling, and you and Edmund will be the British heroes who stood up to Il Duce himself."

"That sounds a bit melodramatic, doesn't it?"

"A heavy envelope of incriminating papers was delivered to *The Bunbury Register* this afternoon. It included a list of Fascist spies who'd already been recruited across the Empire, clear evidence that the Great Pizzaz was an Italian agent and that the driver of the car that hit Mrs. Humphry was an assassin, and the text of several unpublished articles slandering you, all with the dead spy's bi-line. Unless it came from you..." He glanced at Monty who nodded his disagreement, "then I think that we must have Surpanakha to thank for this boon?"

"She is not an ally you should count on," Monty warned. "She will lure you into a false sense of security and turn on you when you are at your most vulnerable."

"Well, I will take the help for now. The information she provided was enough to incriminate many and exonerate the illustrious Marriners many times over. And..." he smiled. "My father made a mistake. A big one, Eleanor. It is why General Kettering suggested that we enlist your help in entrapping him. One of the slanderous articles in the stack mentioned the steamer incident. It went on and on about you putting innocent British lives at risk, and it even mentioned George Ridgeway losing his life under your purview."

"Under *our* purview?!" she exclaimed indignantly.

"My father has always been very good at twisting facts to meet his own ends. But that incident was highly classified, Eleanor. Almost no one knew the details, and he was one of only a few generals who knew George Ridgeway's name. Its inclusion in the proposed articles for *The Bunbury Post* clearly implicates him, given all of the other evidence."

"It's too much," Eleanor said as she slammed her face back into her arms. "It's all too much."

A gentle tap at the door distracted them.

"It is your husband, my lady," Mr. Montero whispered.

"Stanley, please let him in," she mumbled into her arms.

"Eleanor?" Edmund said tentatively. "What's the news?" He glanced at Monty and Stanley.

Suddenly, his emotions enflamed hers, and she lost control. She stood up, buried her face in his chest, and cried.

"My lord, I have confirmed that Eleanor's sister has been murdered," Monty whispered.

Edmund tightened his grip on her as she wailed at the tragic simplicity of the statement.

"Jimmy Buchanan is on the run, and Mary MacGregor is making her way to Basingstoke," Monty added.

Edmund held her while she cried. "I'm sorry, Eleanor. I'm so sorry."

Finally, her sorrow turned to anger. "This is all Lord Grimby's fault! *He's* the one who was pushing them to find the money to finish up their doomed project! That's what led Martha to call me with that absurd story about Eton! *He's* the one who sent the solicitor to their door and put the idea in Mary's head that she could sue us for custody of the children! *He's* the one who's responsible for Eliza Humphry's death! All so he could offer us to the Fascists as a prize?!"

"Dearest, what are you talking about?" Edmund asked nervously.

"You'll see it in the paper tomorrow! The driver of that car that killed Eliza Humphry was an assassin, Edmund! He was trying to get you to use your special talents so the Italian spies could see! The whole thing was cooked up by Lord Grimby to ruin our lives!"

"Why on earth does that man care so much? Because we treated his son with the same dignity as any other human being? Surely that is not an offense worthy of such an attack. Is he upset that Stanley sent Norwenn away? Wouldn't a conversation on the topic be warranted before stooping to murder and treason?"

"Colonel, my father's gone mad," Stanley stepped in. "Some of the other generals have contacted me with their concerns. There is mounting evidence that my father may be defecting to the

Fascists, and he somehow believes that attacking you will help him do it."

"Blimey, it was that goddamned steamer!" he exclaimed. "Good lord, those Italians hold a grudge, don't they? Years after we disabled their mercenaries, they're still coming after us? No wonder the Brits are mobilizing for another war!"

At the thought, and all the others, he began hyperventilating, and Eleanor led him to the other chair at the small table in the corner. They sat across from each other, battling their overwhelming emotions.

"I knew it was too good to be true," he muttered. "All of it. This life was too beautiful for a bloodthirsty demon like me. I just had to kill those men on the Orient Express, and now it's come back to hurt all of us. This is my fault, Eleanor!"

"Darling, that is patently absurd," Eleanor said sharply. She used her passion to pull herself out of her paralyzing malaise. "Now, before we wallow in pity at the many unfortunate events that led us down this road, we must decide what to do. Martha is dead. Jimmy's on the run. Mary's pregnant and alone. She's left Fergus and is reaching our home in Basingstoke any minute."

"She really is pregnant?" he asked Monty.

"An expert confirmed it," he replied. "She's due in January."

"Good lord."

Eleanor continued undeterred. "Lord Grimby has gone off the deep-end and has started sending assassins after innocent people in Western Australia, just to entrap us. We must do something to stop this now."

"You don't think Yvie and Oz are at risk?" he asked with another burst of anxiety.

"I don't know, darling. I don't think we can make any assumptions right now." Her mind began flying a mile a minute as she contemplated their options. "Darling, I think we should go to Basingstoke until this blows over. We must help Mary. We must lead Lord Grimby away from Oz and Yvie. We must keep the

294

bairns safe, and help the lads believe that their mother loves them. I should have helped Martha, and now it's too late, but it isn't too late for Mary. I love my sisters, Edmund. For most of my childhood, I was their mother. I can't just leave Mary out in the cold."

"Why don't we just buy her a ticket down here?"

Eleanor thought carefully about the idea. Certainly, they couldn't use Yakshini magic to pop her down in the blink of an eye. Whatever amount of truth Mary had thrown in with her desperation, the chances that she was a spy were still quite significant. In any circumstance, they would all need to be extra careful not to do anything extraordinary in front of her, and Eleanor decided not to think about what the restriction would mean for their happy, mostly honest household. But, as she thought about using human means to bring Mary down to the edge of the world, she couldn't ignore the impracticality of it.

"I don't think it makes sense to bring her here. The journey by air will be taxing on her and the baby, and a steamer journey will take weeks. We can fly in Percy's plane and be in England by the end of the week."

"I do not want to give up the beautiful life that we have here," he sighed. "It is more beautiful than I imagined life could be."

"I know, darling. I know. But we can come back down to Oz when all of this is sorted, and maybe then we will have a healthier family in tow. We might even have a baby that we can raise as our own, if that really is what Mary wants. Perhaps we can take everything in baby steps, and our problems will work themselves out along the way. Stanley's friend who works for the Bunbury paper has helped clear our names over the hit-and-run nonsense, so now we can focus on doing what is best for the bairns, and I believe, darling, as much as I don't want to admit it, that having Mary in their lives is good for them."

Edmund glanced up at Mr. Montero. "Can you tell Percy that we need to borrow his plane?"

"As you wish, my lord."

"What are we going to tell the bairns about Martha?" he asked Eleanor.

She thought carefully about their many unpleasant options. "I don't think we should tell them anything yet."

"But surely it is going to be all over the news?"

"The body has not yet been discovered," Mr. Montero informed them. "I can take measures to keep it from being discovered, if you prefer."

"I don't know," Eleanor admitted. "Then the bairns might think that she abandoned them, which may be worse in the long run…"

Edmund lowered his voice. "Certainly it can't be worse than them knowing that their father killed their mother? I don't know how I would get over it if I learned that my father had done anything so horrific."

Stanley threw Eleanor a subtle knowing glance.

"I don't know…" she murmured. "There is no good solution. It was a horrible tragedy. It's going to be painful no matter what we do."

"Perhaps we can let things unfold naturally," Mr. Montero suggested. "We have means to influence the situation if need be."

"Thank you, Mr. Marlowe," Edmund said as he finally collected himself and shook Mr. Montero's hand. "Thank you for all of your help. I will tell my father how much I appreciate it the next time he graces me with his presence."

Monty raised his eyebrow at the idea. "Your father?"

Edmund rolled his eyes. "The illustrious Mr. Johnson."

"Ah." He glanced at Eleanor. "I see. Yes, feel free to sing my praises to Mr. Johnson for what good they'll do. I prefer to prove my worth through action, and on that note, I'd best get going. Percy's plane will be here soon."

"But you haven't even called him?" Edmund asked.

"I believe, my lord, you promised not to ask too many questions when you sought my help in these delicate matters last night."

"You're right, I did," Edmund conceded. "I'm a man of my word."

"There are too few of us in this world," Mr. Montero replied. With a pious bow, he made his way to the door and left them alone.

"I will help the bairns pack," Stanley said as he moved to follow.

Edmund pulled him into a teary hug. "Thank you, my boy. It is reassuring to know that you are sticking with us, even in your father's wake."

"As long as I live, you will be able to count on me, Colonel." Stanley squeezed him back.

As Stanley left them, Eleanor squeezed Edmund's hand. "We will get through this, darling."

"Perhaps…" Edmund said distractedly. "But I can't shake this feeling of dread. It's been rattling me since our fight, dearest. It is like I tempted fate by not appreciating all that I had, and now, just hours later, I'm watching our beautiful life slip through my fingertips."

"I don't believe that fate is such a conscious entity, darling. Let's just accept these misfortunes as an unhappy coincidence. There are plenty of those to go around. And our fortune, at the end of the day, is much better than Martha's or Mary's."

Edmund kissed her on the forehead. "I'm so sorry, Eleanor. I can't imagine losing a sibling."

"I can't think too much about it now. We have things to do and bairns to coddle. They're going to need us to be stronger than ever."

She took his hand and led him into the hallway, where Kuveni was standing behind all four children, who were waiting for them, wide-eyed with fear.

Eleanor slapped on a wide, fake smile. "How would you like to live with us in Abbi's English castle for a while?"

"We want to stay here," Ruthy squeaked.

"We will come back here when things are sorted, my loves. But right now, there are many things happening, and we want to protect you and Mary. We can do that best at Abbi's English castle. Mary will be there, but Martha and Jimmy and Fergus won't. It will be just us, and we will make sure the others stay away. Alright?"

"I will be with you the whole time," Kuveni reminded them. "All will be well with the angels by your side."

Mélusine in the form of Percy came right in through the front door. "Come, mes chéris. It is time to take a little trip. The dogs and Moira are already boarded, and Stanley has already loaded your luggage."

"That was fast," Edmund pointed out.

"We were promised no questions, mon chéri. Now come."

Edmund wrapped his arms around the boys' shoulders, while Eleanor pulled Ruthy and Debbie into her arms.

"We are staying together, my loves, I promise. But right now, Mary needs us, and we must help her."

"Abbi, are you going to kill Da?" Charlie asked.

"Not if I can help it," Edmund replied truthfully. "But I sometimes kill to protect the innocent. If he comes after you, I will do what's necessary."

Charlie squeezed him. "I love you, Abbi."

Edmund kneeled down and pulled all of the children into a hug. "We love you so much. Now, let's take a little flight, shall we? I've always dreamed of flying with my own wings, but I suppose a plane will have to suffice."

Debbie slammed her hand onto Ruthy's mouth as Ruthy moved to comment, and the children clung to Abbi and Amma as they walked out to the plane parked on the edge of the crisp, frosty polo field that had served as their makeshift runway many times already.

"This is happening so fast," Eleanor murmured as she leaned on Edmund for support.

"We can return as fast as we depart," Kuveni reminded her. "Faster even, in the right winds." She winked.

"What about Mae, and Oz, and Yvie, and the horses?!" Eleanor panicked.

"Our spies will settle everything," Kuveni reassured her. "And Mr. Marlowe will remain on guard to make sure that Lord Grimby does nothing to harm our beloved allies."

As they boarded the plane, Ovid and Pliny barked and jumped up to greet them, and Stanley rushed to corral them out of the way. The family took seats on two comfortable leather couches, each up against the windows along the edges of the fuselage. Eleanor glanced down a narrow aisle to spy a small WC and two sets of bunks at the back of the plane. Two stacks of books from Edmund's library were strapped to the floor beside the couches, and several bottles of water and red wine were strapped into purposeful nooks on the outer wall of the WC.

"I wondered what it would be like to fly in this thing... It's like a yacht in the sky!" Edmund exclaimed. "What genius, Percy. It looks so much more comfortable than any other plane."

"Settle in and enjoy it, mon chéri. It's going to take us at least five days to fly all the way to Basingstoke. Our first rest stop will be in Malé."

Kuveni closed them inside and took a seat beside Mélusine at the controls. Without any time wasted, they took off into the clear morning sky, and Eleanor stared intently at the cerulean blue waters of the Indian Ocean, where she'd spent so many pleasurable hours in the arms of her loving husband. She knew in that moment that she would never see it again.

The beginning of the end had silently commenced.

PART THREE
BASINGSTOKE AT LAST

CHAPTER 18 – A PUNCH IN THE GUT

The journey felt interminable.

The soul-crushing uncertainty was compounded by the endless hours of flying. While it was much more pleasant than the low-altitude, open-aired flight Eleanor had taken with Edmund on their honeymoon (in Lord Grimby's plane, an irony that struck her often throughout their journey), even with all of the Yakshini magic that was keeping the plane afloat and the air inside pleasant, hour upon hour of flying in a metal capsule became increasingly maddening, not just for her, but for all of them.

At their first stop in the Maldives, she was not ready to take a few hours to stretch her legs and embrace the powdery white sand and crystalline waters. By their second stop, in Ceylon, she couldn't get off the plane fast enough. She began appreciating the breaks from monotony more and more, and eventually the nervous bairns and her distracted husband joined her in her subdued cheer.

Like the impeccable butler he'd become, at each stop, Stanley saw to the dogs and fluttered about helping Kuveni and Mélusine with a wide range of unusual tasks required to maintain their high effort farce. Eleanor's mother, in contrast, refused to get off the plane. For five long days, she said nothing of consequence, and as far as Eleanor cared to observe, she ate nothing. Eleanor didn't say a word about it.

By the time they reached Baghdad, they'd become experts at hopping off the plane in the peaceful outskirts of a bustling city, finding the closest mode of transportation that could carry all of them (usually a donkey cart with a cheerful driver that Eleanor was quite sure was Illa), and then speeding around town with the help of Edmund's linguistic talents to find the most delicious local delicacy on offer. They had to try many, as Edmund reminded them, just to make sure that they were giving each town's cuisine a proper go.

Hers, so far, had been a persian lamb kebab in Esfahan that was so tender she barely even needed to chew it, while Edmund was quite devoted to a pocket of fried dough full of spiced, ground mutton that they'd collected just outside of Lahore, upon Kuveni's suggestion. Debbie preferred a baklava soaked in honey from Constantinople, while Ruthy, Howie, and Charlie all agreed that the rich chocolate cake that they'd found in a twee little café in a back-alley of Vienna was unbeatable, especially when paired with the thick hot chocolate covered in whipping cream and sprinkles on offer. Edmund had managed to drink five before the café closed up for the evening.

And so, Eleanor was completely overwhelmed by bittersweet emotions as they approached the familiar emerald green of the Hampshire hills, and the shadows of the fluffy clouds all around them danced silently across the landscape. She would be quite happy to never fly in a plane again, and yet, she didn't want their beautiful time together as a family to end. Every time they'd given into the laughter and cheer of their adventurous rest stops, she'd felt the clock ticking, closer and closer to some sort of amorphous doom, and now, here it was, covered in a thick layer of soft green grass and late summer wildflowers.

Most of all, she dreaded seeing Mary and dealing with the stinking heap of social refuse that they'd managed to temporarily escape in their haste. She hadn't dared pick up a paper on any of their stops, but she knew that she couldn't revel in avoidance for much longer.

She squeezed Debbie and Ruthy into her arms. "We will always be Abbi and Amma," she reiterated. "Having Mary around isn't going to change that, alright? She is here on our terms, and if she does anything hurtful, we will send her away. We will never, ever send you back to that hell on Skye, alright?"

"Yes, Amma," they mumbled.

She held them tighter as the plane veered in for a landing. She'd forgotten how lush the English summer foliage was, or perhaps she'd never really known it, at least not in the way that Edmund's unique Yakshini-gardened property could show it. They'd left on their honeymoon in March over three years earlier, and had never looked back. She was glad. Their lives had been so much more interesting than she'd ever imagined, and if she was going to be honest with herself, she liked having Uma nestled deep within her soul. She was warm and loving and powerful. A perfect partner with whom to share a body (if one was going to do such an odd thing), and she wouldn't have met her at all if they'd just hopped over the pond for a simple honeymoon in Paris, as she'd originally imagined on the rare occasions when she'd let her spinster mind fantasize about such things.

The ancient lindens rustled with the wind of the plane's draft, and as they hit the ground and slowed to a crawl, the wild roses that lined the babbling brook that Edmund had painted so many times during his lonely decades there swayed gracefully in the warm summer breeze. Eleanor was grateful that the English weather had allowed some sun to break through for their arrival.

She held her breath as Kuveni opened the hatch and dropped the ladder onto a bed of violets. She spied Mary standing on the stone veranda watching them, and as she climbed down the ladder and held her arms up to help Ruthy and Debbie come down, Mary came running.

The girls looked down at their feet, refusing to acknowledge her, while the boys climbed down the ladder unenthusiastically and gazed at their mother with unabashed disdain. As Edmund hopped down beside them, Mary pulled them into her arms, sobbing and kissing them. They stood stiff as boards, refusing to hug her back.

"Mammy missed you, dearies!" she sobbed. "I missed you sooooo much!"

"Ye should've missed us longer," Howie muttered as he kicked his toe into the dirt angrily. "Forever!"

"Is this why we had to come back? Fer another lil ankle-biter?" Charlie said as he noticed his mother's pregnant belly bulging through her simple cotton dress. "Why cunne ye just leave us alone? We were happy with Abbi and Amma, ye know? An' ye ruined it! Ye ruined everything!"

He ran off towards the woods.

"I hate ye, Mam!" Howie shouted as he ran after Charlie.

"Did ye turn 'em against me?" Mary asked meekly.

"You did a fine job of that yourself," Eleanor replied, working to keep her temper under control. Mary's denial of her own role in their family's tragedy was irking her more and more.

Mary sobbed as she watched them go. Eleanor wasn't sure what to do. She wasn't particularly interested in consoling her. Kuveni hopped down out of the plane and helped Eleanor's mother carefully make her way down the ladder. Stanley hopped down after her, and braced her on his arm.

Moira took one look at Mary and shook her head. "Ye were a selfish lass all along, Mary Fiona MacLeod, an' yer an even more selfish woman. Yer greed dragged yer bairns down from Heaven itself, and ye dragged the angels down wit 'em." She pointed at her accusingly. "You oughtta be ashamed of yerself, ye hear?"

"That's it?!" Mary exclaimed. "That's how ye greet yer pregnant daughter, Mam? Do ye know how awful all of it is?"

Moira looked down at the girls and over to the boys who were picking up rocks and smashing them down into the brook with loud glugs and splashes. "Do *you*? The Good Lord gave ye a pair of eyes and a brain fer a reason, Mary MacLeod, an' it's about time ye start usin' 'em!"

"Yer other daughter was *murdered*, and that's all ye have to say to me?" Mary whined.

Moira looked like the statement had punched her right in the gut, and Eleanor threw Mary a furious look of disapproval as she kneeled down to gather Debbie and Ruthy into her arms.

"This is not the time nor the place," Eleanor hissed angrily.

"What do ye mean she was murdered?" Moira whispered.

"It's been all over the paper!" Mary wailed. "I thought ye'd already know! I dunne think I'd be the one to break the news! They found her body yesterday, and now Jimmy's on the run!"

Debbie and Ruthy were stunned into silence, and Eleanor hugged them tighter. "You're safe here, my loves. Nothing can harm you with the angels by your side."

As Mary dissolved into more sobs, and Eleanor's mother looked like she might collapse from the strain, Eleanor whispered to Stanley. "There are a few guest rooms on the first floor. Feel free to give her any of them."

He nodded dutifully and escorted Moira into the house.

Kuveni kneeled down to help Eleanor console the shocked girls so that Eleanor could address Mary face to face.

"Think before you open your mouth again, or you'll be out on the street without a penny to your name, got it? We're done playing games. You're in the presence of civilized folk now, and you will be *civilized*."

"I'll go talk to the lads," Edmund said. He didn't even look at Mary as he headed towards the brook.

Mélusine hopped down from the plane and urged the dogs to hop down into her arms. They licked her thankfully as she caught them, and then they ran right off to explore their new kingdom. She pushed the ladder back into its storage position as she closed the door hatch.

"Mary, you've met Lord Blakeney. You can call him Percy," Eleanor said flatly. "He is Kate Marriner's husband. Kate, if you'll remember, is Edmund's cousin from Somerset. Come inside. We need to talk."

Eleanor picked up Ruthy, who clung to her like she would never let go, and Kuveni picked up Debbie, even though Debbie was quite a big girl to be carried. Neither of them minded as Debbie buried her face in Kuveni's shoulder, letting her burgeoning sobs finally erupt.

They left Mary alone in the field by the plane, watching Edmund as he explained to her children with more kindness than her husband had ever demonstrated in his life what had happened to Auntie Martha. She took a long moment to look up at the unusual technology of the plane, and then she rubbed her pained lower back and trudged up the stone stairs behind Eleanor into the house, closing the door behind her.

Eleanor and Kuveni took the girls into the front parlor and sat down next to each other on an extra-long, cavernous velvet couch. The girls snuggled into their arms and refused to move, and they each kissed their foreheads. It felt like centuries had passed since she and Edmund had spent their steamy winter weekend there making love on the persian carpet. So much had happened... so many adventures and so much pain... She had been a completely different person... literally, in many ways. And while she felt so much older it was hard to quantify (certainly more than three years older), the room hadn't aged at all. It was as if it had been frozen in time after they took off on their honeymoon, and given the impeccable condition of Lord Vibhishana's ancient Roman palace in Smyrna, Eleanor wondered if perhaps it *had* been frozen in time.

"It'll all be alright, my loves," Eleanor whispered soothingly. It was all she could say, and she hoped deep down to the core of her being that she wasn't lying.

"Mes chéris, I'll go check the kitchen's supplies. We'll be sure to have a warm supper as soon as I can humanly manage it."

As Mélusine made her way down the hall, Mrs. Murray rushed up to her, followed by Stanley.

"Is he here?" she asked excitedly. "Where's the colonel?! I've got three years of wages to make up for!"

"Mrs. Murray," Eleanor murmured. "I'd almost forgotten about her."

It felt like a lifetime ago that Edmund had hastily employed her to cook for their new married life in Basingstoke after her unjust sacking by the household of the Baron of Heathfield. Somehow, Mrs. Murray's presence made their move feel final, as if they'd returned from a three-year-long honeymoon, and it was now time to settle into the domestic life they'd envisioned in their very first months together.

"I called her down from her sister's house in York when we left Australia," Kuveni whispered to Eleanor. "She was ecstatic about it, the lovely dear, and I didn't think you'd want your sister here alone poking around Edmund's kitchen... or anywhere else in his house, for that matter. I thought a reliable person on staff might deter her."

"Thank you, Kuveni, it was a very good idea." She fought back tears. "I don't know where we'd be without you. You aren't shirking your other duties too much to be with us, are you?"

"Oh posh," Kuveni scoffed. "I told the Peruvians that if they had expected me to drop everything to raise their brood for six or seven decades, they should have asked me about my availability.

They'll be fine. They've been parents for thousands of years. Just because they don't love doing it, it doesn't mean that they can't."

"Thank you for being here all the same," Eleanor whispered.

Kuveni squeezed her hand. "It is my pleasure as always, Mistress Eleanor."

"The colonel is occupied at the moment," Stanley reiterated as he chased Mrs. Murray down the hall past the open french doors. "Perhaps the lady of the house can advise you on supper?"

"Yes, yes, of course!" Mrs. Murray exclaimed. She curtseyed as she entered the parlor, but her enthusiasm waned as she noticed their somber demeanor. "My lady, has something dire happened?"

"I see my sister saved her flapping mouth for those who would be hurt the most by it," Eleanor muttered. She collected herself and kissed Ruthy's forehead again. "Yes, Mrs. Murray. My sister Martha passed away earlier this week. Ruthy and Debbie are her children, so they've lost their mother."

As the girls hid their faces and sobbed quietly at the reminder, Mrs. Murray's eyes teared up. "I'm sorry, my lady. How horrible. Is there anything I can do? I made a cake this morning in preparation for your arrival. Perhaps the lasses want some now?"

"I'm not hungry," Debbie squeaked.

"Me neither," Ruthy said with a sniffle before reburying her face in Eleanor's wide silk collar.

Eleanor smiled sadly. "Thank you for the offer, but I think they just need some time. Please have Percy help you design the menus for now. He knows our taste well."

Mrs. Murray curtseyed again and followed Stanley and Mélusine out of the parlor and back to the kitchen. Mary stood in the doorway watching them.

"Ye don' have any idea whit our life was like, Ellie. There were no cooks or butlers or lords or airplanes. It was just grinding an' grinding, day after day."

"No, Mary, the twenty years I spent wiping madmen's bums so that I could pay for your life and Fergus's was just a fun little picnic. I know nothing about what a grind real work is. Remind me again, how many days in your life have you worked?"

"You know raising up bairns is work, Ellie."

"It is for good parents, you're right. I don't know what was keeping you busy, though. It wasn't taking your children to school, or keeping them fed and clothed, or standing up to your wanker of a husband when he was lashing them for sport."

"I dunne come down here fer a lecture from Mam," Mary whispered. "I thought ye'd help me, Ellie. I thought ye'd understand."

"Do you know what I understand? I understand what starvation is, and so do you. We endured it because we had to. We didn't have a choice after Da died. But you did that to your children *willingly* while I was sending you enough money to buy everything you could ever want and more. You could've even bought a big, beautiful house if you'd bothered to look around! But no, your husband's bloody ego had to have a bloody castle way off in the middle of nowhere where none of you could have a job, and where your children would wither on the vine. And for that, for his bloody ego, you *starved* your children. You taught them how it felt when our stomachs were so empty we thought we'd collapse in on ourselves, when we were so starving that Mum prostituted herself for a Christmas goose. What about that am I supposed to understand?"

"It wasn't my fault!" she exclaimed. "Why can't ye understand that! It was Jimmy bloody Buchanan and our evil bloody sister behind all of it! They stole my cheques, Ellie! They told me that if I dunne give it to 'em, they'd shoot me in the back, and look what happened! They weren't bloody lying! That money corrupted 'em, Ellie. It turned 'em rotten from the inside out, like the Devil himself was talkin' through their mouths!"

Eleanor worked hard to keep her temper under control as Ruthy sobbed and clasped her tighter. "Ye'd best tame that mouth of yers, if ye know whit's good fer ye, Mary MacLeod." Eleanor didn't care that she sounded exactly like her mother. "I will say this once, and only once: You're not in Martha's house anymore. You're not on Skye. You're not at a pub chuggin' down a pint with Fergus while your bairns are eating rotten soup back at home." Mary began sobbing. "You're in my house, on my terms. If you hurt the bairns again in any way, you will be out on the street. Do you understand?" Mary paused to make an argument, and Eleanor threw daggers at her with her eyes. "Do. You. Understand?"

"Aye, Ellie," Mary whispered. "I'm goin' to take a wee cat nap."

She slinked away without another word.

"I knew that the Devil'd taken Mam," Debbie whispered. "I could see him in her eyes. He took both of 'em the day the first cheque came. They said it was Christmas in July." She trailed off into sobs. "But I like Christmas in July!"

"The Devil only takes those who aren't strong enough to fight him, my loves, and you are stronger than anyone, ye hear?" Eleanor said. "You can stand up to him and tell him to go stalk someone else, because you've got the power of all the love in the world—of all the love the angels can give—protecting you and keeping you always on the path of light. Alright?" She squeezed both of their hands. *Take with you the Holy Mother's blessings, my children.*

"Are you an angel too, Amma?" Ruthy asked. "Gramma Moira said so, but Charlie and Howie didn't believe her."

"I am," Eleanor confirmed. "I'm a different kind of angel than Kate or Abbi. There are many different kinds of angels who can do many different things. Sheranee is my mount, you know. She helps me fight evil." Eleanor listened carefully as Mary's shuffling steps dissolved into a guest bedroom upstairs, and then she smiled and winked as she called forth her divine crown.

Both girls gasped and reached out to touch it.

"I knew you were a princess," Ruthy said as she fingered one of the sparkling red sapphires.

"She's an empress. That's better than a princess," Debbie corrected her as she ran her hand along the smooth gold of the crown.

"She's a goddess," Kuveni corrected them. "That's better than everything else in the world."

"Can a goddess beat the Devil?" Ruthy asked.

"I already have," Eleanor informed her. "I slayed him through the belly with my divine trident."

"Then how did he take Mammy?" Ruthy asked.

"He takes many forms," Kuveni explained. "We slay him over and over again, and still he returns. He grows strong from hatred and greed, and sometimes he destroys people who aren't strong enough, just like he destroyed your parents. But he won't destroy you. You are too strong for him. Your love and kindness and intelligence will keep him at bay, and you will do wonderful things to help humanity. I'm sure of it."

"I want to be a doctor," Debbie sighed. "Like Uncle Oz."

"Then that is what you will be," Kuveni declared. "There will be nothing to stand in your way now. It will take a lot of hard work, but I have no doubt in my mind that you will triumph. It will be easier than so many things you've already endured, and if you ever see him again, you'll tell the Devil to run away with his tail between his legs."

Debbie finally giggled, and then she remembered her sorrow and collapsed back into Kuveni's arms.

As Ruthy sighed and snuggled back into Eleanor's arms, Eleanor kissed her forehead again and rocked her. "It's a good thing you've got the angels by your side, isn't it?"

"Mm hmm," she squeaked as she gave into tears again.

Eleanor dissolved her divine crown and sat back, rubbing the palm of Ruthy's tiny hand with her thumb until Ruthy's eyes became heavy, and she finally fell asleep.

"Everything has changed, hasn't it?" Eleanor murmured. "Our beautiful peace is lost."

"It has only transformed, Eleanor dearest. You, of all people, know that transformation is required for growth. It can be painful, yes, but it can also be wonderful and surprising and invigorating. It can sometimes be the reason for living."

"Maybe I'll embrace the idea when I've had six thousand years of experience."

"I will embrace it for both of us, my dearest girl."

And with that, Eleanor gave into her fatigue from her many days of travel and worry, and in the warm arms of her most beloved girls, she slept.

After many hours outside tromping through the woods with the boys and talking about all sorts of things that had been building up in their young minds over the months, Edmund returned and showed all four bairns around his house, proudly pointing out the many hidden doors into secret passages and the modern WCs that Percy had added during his renovation three years earlier.

Eleanor was grateful that they were calming down enough to gasp with wonder as they spied the over-sized canopied master bed (that still looked like Mélusine had stolen it right out of a Roman emperor's palace) and the mosaicked Rakshasa bed in the master bathroom that Edmund and Eleanor had only used once, on their wedding night. After some serious begging, Abbi and Amma promised that the bairns could swim around in it during their baths, although only with permission and supervision, since it was rather deep for children so small.

They then let the bairns choose their bedrooms, with the boys choosing to stay together in the neighboring room on one side, and the girls choosing to stay together in the neighboring room on the other, creating a compact family quarters, to which Mary and Eleanor's mother were conspicuously not invited.

After taking a look at Edmund's extensive library, which was even more impressive than the one he'd made in Australia, with taller walls of books and many more deep, cushy couches around a massive old fireplace that looked like something Henry VIII would have used, the family settled down to an awkwardly silent dinner in a formal dining room that Edmund admitted later he had never once used in his life.

The children refused to look at Mary, who, Eleanor had to admit upon further examination, was dreadfully thin herself for her condition, and Kuveni attempted to relieve the tension by discussing Roman history with Edmund, who only offered her distracted yeses and nos. With each curried course, produced thoughtfully by Mrs. Murray using input from Mélusine alongside the Punjabi recipes she'd learned for the Baron of Heathfield (minus the turmeric, of course), Mary looked increasingly bewildered, while the children began settling in and following Edmund's lead, eating course after course with their impeccable Indian table manners. Even Moira was eating the food without a peep of protest, focusing her attention on one of the sweeter coconut curries that Mélusine had invented to accommodate her bland palate many months earlier with the help of some beautifully flakey Malabar parathas, which Eleanor liked to think of as mostly a flattened buttery croissant.

By the end of the meal, Mary's silence had allowed the children to peek out of their well-fitted shells, and the boys began discussing their plans for a fort in the linden grove, while Mélusine and Edmund bantered jovially with minor disagreements over the proper engineering direction for such an endeavor.

As the children began yawing, and Mary looked like she might collapse from fatigue, Abbi and Amma guided the children up to bed, but the children did not want to go.

"We want to stay with you!" Ruthy exclaimed.

316

"I suppose it wouldn't hurt for us to read together for a while," Edmund gave in.

The children followed him into the master bedroom and climbed onto the bed, snuggling into the green silk pillows, and rolling around on the smooth sheets.

Edmund winked at Eleanor. "I've had half a mind to do that myself. The shining silk looks so marvelously cool and soft."

"Is it real silk?" Debbie asked.

"It is," Eleanor confirmed.

"That means that it came out of a worm's bum!" Howie exclaimed.

"No, it doesn't!" Ruthy argued.

"Yes it does. Auntie Mae said so in science tutorial!" he shot back.

"Amma, did this silk come from worms' bums, or did Auntie Kate make it?" Debbie asked. She glanced nervously at Edmund, unsure if her comment was giving too much away.

"I think that you should ask Uncle Percy where it came from tomorrow," Eleanor suggested as she climbed onto the bed amongst them. "It was actually a wedding gift from him."

Edmund glanced around the room, and then smiled as he spotted a heavy old book on the writing desk in the corner.

"What a perfect volume to welcome us back to Basingstoke."

The children made room for him to climb up into the middle of their bunch. Eleanor took her position in the nook of his arm, and Ruthy and Debbie lay down with their heads on Eleanor's lap, while the boys cuddled in on the other side of Edmund.

"It's not in English," Charlie said disappointedly.

"No, my bairns, it is in Latin," Edmund said excitedly. "And it really is much better in the Latin. The meter and rhyme are like music. I will read each verse in Latin, and then I will translate it for you, if you'd like? These are the works of Ovid. He was a very wise chap whose advice brought me and Amma together."

"Ovid?!" Debbie exclaimed. "Like the dog?!"

"Just like him. This Roman poet is his namesake."

Edmund glanced over at the door, and they all braced for impact as they heard the heavy paw-treads of the dogs barreling up the stairs. They jumped right onto the bed, and the children squealed. Both dogs' paws were covered in mud from their long day of adventuring in the creek outside, and their long golden fur was littered with sticks and dried leaves.

"Aren't they in trouble?" Charlie asked. "They're ruining your silk!"

"A little mud never hurt anyone." Edmund ruffled the dogs' muddy coats, spreading the chunks of semi-dried dirt all over the bairns and the bed. They squealed, and Edmund laughed. "I quite like getting my hands dirty; it makes me feel accomplished. Remember when we were putting the poultice on the horses' legs? That was downright pleasurable for us and for them. It's quite nice when everyone wins, isn't it?"

"Abbi, are the horses going to be alright without us to take care of them?"

"They're going to be perfectly fine," Eleanor chimed in. "Auntie Kate told me just yesterday that Uncle Oz is taking care of them, and no one is better at caring for horses than Uncle Oz is."

"Abbi is," Charlie countered. "He cared for the king's horses, didn't you, Abbi?"

"That's right, I did. And you know, the chap who took over my position when we moved to India is quite a nice young bloke. I suspect we might be able to visit the king's horses, now that we're back in England."

"Yes!" the children all exclaimed in unison.

"I want to care for the king's horses!" Howie exclaimed.

Edmund laughed, but then he became serious. "You can do whatever you set your mind to, my boy, but there are many ways to care for horses that don't require you to join the military. Uncle Oz grew up on a ranch in the outback riding horses all day long."

318

"I want to do that!" Howie and Charlie exclaimed in unison. Eleanor was exceptionally grateful that they were feeling secure enough to think about their futures.

Edmund laughed again. "I'm sure that if you both work hard, we can arrange an apprenticeship for you out on the ranches when you're old enough. In the meantime, though, how about a bedtime story? For all you know, you'll change your minds and become Roman philosophers."

"Ew!" Charlie exclaimed.

Edmund chuckled. "I thought it sounded like a fine occupation when I was your age, apart from being exiled and executed for crossing the emperor, that is."

As Debbie cringed at the thought, Eleanor hugged her tighter, and Edmund realized his error.

"Well now, that's enough of that. Let's get these dogs squared away, shall we?"

He picked off the most obvious of the sticks and leaves from the dogs' coats and dropped them onto the floor, and the children followed his lead while the dogs panted with joy at the attention. When they were done, the dogs curled up together at the foot of the bed, and Edmund brushed the last of the dirt off his hands and onto the floor.

"Well, now that we have both Ovids in tow, we can begin," Edmund said cheerfully.

"You'd better choose your passages carefully, darling. Not everything Ovid says is for children's ears," Eleanor reminded him, feeling rather motherly at the thought.

He flipped through the heavy book, landing on a page with an elaborate illustration of a calendar.

"This one should do nicely. *Fasti*... The festivals," he began.

They all cuddled in to listen as Edmund's lyrical baritone read all about the Roman months, and the gods and goddesses, and about all sorts of odd ancient rituals. The children interrupted every so often to ask a question, and Edmund did his best to dance around with his answers in a way that didn't entirely give away the innovative debauchery of the Romans. Eleanor was quite sure that they were each relieved that the relaxed hominess they'd come to love in Australia had indeed made its way to England with them, even though Edmund's love for the literary material of the evening seemed to far outweigh everyone else's.

As the children began snoring, Eleanor attempted to wiggle her way out from under them. She had too much to do. Too many newspapers to read. Too many unpleasant facts to learn. She needed to talk to Stanley, and Kuveni, and Monty… She needed to get her bearings. They were settling in, and she needed to be prepared for all of the battles that were brewing.

"Amma, are you coming back?" Debbie whispered.

"Yes, my love. I am always coming back. I just have some things I need to do before I fall asleep."

She slipped out of bed and looked back at the brood. Edmund was sound asleep with the book still open on his chest, and the dogs eyed her, and then settled back into sleep. She loved the sight of them, all of them. That, right there, was her home.

As she left them alone, she almost fell over as she stumbled upon Mary sitting in the hallway right outside the open door. She was sitting up against the wall with her head against her folded knees, crying silently. She looked up at Eleanor, and Eleanor gestured for her to remain silent. She helped her up, and led her out of the master suite and down the stairs to Edmund's library.

Eleanor sat her down on one of the couches and took a seat across from her. She offered Mary a handkerchief from her pocket, and then poured herself a tall glass of cognac from a dusty bottle on the table before her, focusing on the rich caramel aroma as she waited for Mary to calm herself.

"I dunne mean it when I said it on the telephone, Ellie. I said ye could have the new bairn to getcha up here. But I mean it now. He's yers, ye hear? I'll sign whatever I have to sign."

Eleanor just gazed at her, contemplating her response.

"I dunne know, alright? I dunne know how good ye were! I dunne know how good the colonel was!"

Eleanor wasn't particularly comfortable with where Mary's thoughts were going. She hoped that her mother hadn't spilled all of their secrets.

"I thought… Martha kept saying… and Fergus kept saying… and I convinced myself… that the money was something else! It was control or judgment or meddling or *something* sinister. It wasn't what it was… it wasn't just… kind!"

"I only ever wanted you to be happy, Mary." The simple truth of it hurt as Eleanor said the words. "I wanted you to have an easier life than I did, and I worked *so hard* to give it to you. But the harder I worked, the worse your life got. It was wretched to watch, and I convinced myself that I just needed to work harder, that some magical amount of money would make your problems go away. It is a great tragedy of my life that I was wrong, for you and for Martha. If I could take back every penny that ruined you, I'd do it, but you can't blame me for everything. You made many choices that I couldn't make for you, and you can't move forward and earn your bairns' forgiveness until you admit it to yourself and to them."

Eleanor sipped her cognac while Mary cried quietly. The rich flavor reminded her of one of the most disturbing details of the whole affair, the detail that had prompted her hasty kidnapping of the children in the first place.

"Mum brought a flask that Charlie nicked from Jimmy. It was filled to the brim with Nectar D'Or. I knew it the moment I tasted it. Do you know how much Nectar D'Or costs?" Mary nodded in the negative as she continued to cry. "One bottle costs enough for six months of groceries." She took another sip of her cognac. "When the bairns arrived at my door, they'd starved for so long that their hair was falling out. They were so weak they couldn't even climb onto the counter for their examination. The local doctor said they'd been starving for at least six months. *Six months,*

321

Mary, while Jimmy and Fergus were drinking dear tidy scotch. Now answer me truthfully: Did you know?"

Mary took many sniffles to be able to speak. "I caught him with the bottle right after he'd bought it. I told him if I ever caught him again I'd leave. He laughed at me, Ellie! He just laughed in my face and took a long swig..." She dissolved into tears. "He deserved to laugh. He knew I wunne do it."

Eleanor sighed with resignation. It wasn't any different from how she'd assumed the whole episode had unfolded.

"I shuddne married Fergus," Mary finally admitted. "You were right, and I dunne wanna admit it. Ye knew he was a bampot the moment ye met him, but I thought ye just dunne want me to be married. I thought ye wanted me to be a spinster like you were."

"Mary, you were eighteen!" Eleanor exclaimed.

"Eighteen was auld back then, Ellie! Times were different! There weren't auld, rich sassanack soldiers left and right on the prowl fer auld spinster brides!"

"Is that what you think happened? Edmund ensnared me into some sort of auld sassanack soldier spell?"

"Dunne he?"

"I suppose in some way he did. I was quite happy as a spinster. I was happy with my salary from the veteran's hospital. I was happy with my life, Mary. I didn't need your pity. But then I met this man who was kind, and strong, and beautiful inside and out, and I really thought that all of our prayers had been answered. I thought you'd be happy that I'd finally joined your club as a married woman, and when it turned out that he had gobs of money that he was happy to send along to help you and the bairns, it seemed like it could only be good. I just keep asking myself, how could that not have been good?"

Mary thought for a long time before answering. "We were all blown away when we showed up fer yer weddin', ye know. All the way down here from Elphinstone, Martha'd blethered on and on about how desperate ye were to marry an auld broken soldier who was so poor that ye had to have the wedding in the garden. And then we arrived at the station, and the beautiful black car was waitin' fer us, like we were the bonny Queen of England, and the chauffeur carried our bags like we were important, and then we drove on up the lovely drive with the cherry blossoms snowing all along the way to the fairy tale castle, and then yer auld sassanack colonel wasn't even that auld! And he was so dashing in his uniform, like Prince Charming himself! And then there were all those fancy folk, and the lords and ladies, and even the Hindus and the Mohammedans in their foreign clothes, and it was like ye'd been sucked right up into a different world with no place fer us in it. And then ye flew away, Ellie, right off into the sky, and we never saw ye again! It was like we'd lost ye! Ye might as well have been dead! And then when the cheques started coming… I thought… I thought that maybe we could use them to become the folk that ye needed us to be, so we could see ye… That was why I didn't walk right out the door the moment Fergus came up with the idea fer the castle hunting lodge. I imagined ye comin' wit yer sassanack colonel up to Skye, and the men out huntin' with the lads, while we sisters were warming by the fire inside. I got lost in the dream, Ellie, and before I knew it, I was trapped in a nightmare, and I dunne know how to get out of it, and I blamed ye fer it. I know it wunne right, but I blamed ye anyway."

"That isn't an excuse," Eleanor rebutted.

"It isn't, Ellie. I'm not tellin' ye it was right. I'm tellin' ye it was."

Eleanor conceded and took another sip of her cognac.

"So I kept tellin' myself more and more as things got worse and worse that ye wunne understand. Ye wunne help. Yer rich auld sassanack colonel wunne let ye listen to my side of things, because it was him who'd taken ye away because he dunne like our kind! I made up all sorts of stories in my head about him, and about you, and about all the things ye were sayin' and doin' behind my back, and oh, Ellie, the things Martha said! The ideas she planted in my head, I cunne ignore 'em! It's like she planted the seed of the Devil in me and kept watering and watering and watering until he'd strangled all that I was! And he started whispering in my mind all sorts of evil thoughts, but he was wrong! He was whispering and whispering, even today he was whispering! He was saying that ye'd taken the bairns and turned 'em against me because I wasn't fancy enough! And then I came up the stairs to make a scene if ye'd made me, all to see my bairns to bed like their proper mam, and there ye were, on yer fancy silk with yer dirty clothes and shoes on, cuddlin' on up like a tidy wolf mam and her pups! And then the Devil held his wheesht, Ellie! He was finally quiet! I sat there and listened as yer fancy sassanack colonel answered the bairns' silly questions about the fancy Roman book that wunne even in English, fer Christ's sake! Do ye know how many times Fergus read to the lads? Never, Ellie! Not once since they were born! He always said readin' was for pansies who were too weak to work with their hands! And there was yer colonel thrilled to be readin' to 'em like they were his own bairns! And I suddenly realized that he wunne puttin' on airs like Martha always said. He just *was* fancy, Ellie! He cunne help it! That was him, and that was you, and that was who the bairns could be too! He wunne who the Devil said he was, Ellie. Yer fancy colonel told my lads to be ranchers in the outback, and then he dunne pay it any mind at all when those filthy dogs slobbered all over ye and climbed all o'er with their muddy paws. Do ye know what Fergus wudda done if a dirty dog'd jumped on our bed? He'd have shot it, Ellie! Or beat it, or kicked it, or lashed it, and then he wudda done the same to me and the bairns fer lettin' it in in the first place. But yer auld sassanack just let the filthy buggers lie with ye all over yer royal bed like a big happy family!"

Eleanor sighed. At least Mary had started telling the truth. She tried to use the boon to pull herself out of the simmering rage that she still couldn't quell. "We *are* a big happy family. We love the bairns like they're our own brood. When you called up threatening to take them, it was like you'd shot me in the back." Eleanor cringed at the mental imagery of Martha running from Jimmy. "But you're my sister, Mary. I still love you. I want you to know your children, and that's why we're here. But I won't let you or Fergus hurt them anymore. We're here to help you crawl out of your abyss, but you have to let us. And in the meantime, you don't need to bribe us with a baby."

"I want ye to have him, Ellie. I want him to only know what I saw tonight. Can you imagine a whole life like that? Only ever knowing safety and love and comfort?"

"I remember it vaguely from before Da died. I don't think you do, though."

"No. I don't remember anything from before that night. It's like it was someone else's life."

"I know how that feels," Eleanor commiserated. She drank down the rest of her cognac. "We can't solve a problem that took years to pile up in one night, Mary. But it's good for the bairns to know that you love them. You need to give them time."

"What if Fergus finds us?" she asked nervously. "He's gonna be furious when he realizes I actually left."

"We'll do what we have to do to keep everyone safe. No option is off the table, and if you're going to stay here, we'll need your cooperation. Do you understand? *All* options. Our sister was murdered in cold blood."

Mary nodded and sniffled.

"You're looking unhealthy. You should go ask Mrs. Murray to make you something. You should be eating whatever you can stomach from now on, and if you don't want the curries, you can ask her to make you whatever sounds good. I'm sure she's an expert at Scottish breakfasts."

"Y'aren't goin' to be angry wit me if I break yer fancy dinner rules?"

Eleanor snorted. "When you know us better you will realize how funny that question was. Eat what you want, how you want, when you want, okay? No one here stands on ceremony, especially Edmund."

Eleanor helped Mary up off of the couch, and Mary pulled her into a hug.

"The Devil's devious, isn't he? He twists our own thoughts against us."

Eleanor hugged her back. "It is time to let the angels pull you out of his arms, Mary. We will help you, if you let us."

And with that, the next chapter of the MacLeod-Marriner's complicated lives commenced.

CHAPTER 20 – WHO CAME TO CALL

The next few months passed by with mercifully (and somewhat surprisingly) little to challenge their precarious peace. Stanley's influence with Jules and the Associated Press had managed to quell the public's interest in their role in the circus incident, which remained unsolved along with a string of mysterious stabbing suicides of Fascist spies all across the Empire. General Kettering himself had stepped in to quiet the chatter surrounding Martha's murder after Mary's descriptions of Lord Grimby and Lord Montagu's visit revealed the distinct likelihood that they had been scoping out the castle to create a base for the Fascist cause in Britain. The entire affair got swept up into the highest echelons of the Secret Service's leadership, and with it, General Kettering revealed to Edmund that he was not just an ordinary general. He enlisted Edmund's help as a loyal colonel of the British Army in stopping the Fascist traitors (if ever the occasion arose), while stealthily avoiding any mention of the close eye and helping hand the Secret Service had kept focused on him for decades.

In the meantime, Jimmy's status as a fugitive after murdering Martha made transferring custody of Debbie and Ruthy to Edmund and Eleanor a brief and painless affair with only a few papers initialed before a local magistrate; although, everyone avoided discussing the future of Mary's lads, as the whole family worked hard to make a place for her in their bruised hearts.

Kuveni and Mélusine took up residence in the house in Basingstoke, both for familial moral support and Yakshini protection, as Jimmy Buchanan was still on the run, and Fergus MacGregor had disappeared silently along with him. Mr. Montero continued his silent guarding with a particularly sharp eye out for any evidence that Surpanakha had caught up with them, but so far, she too had generously kept her distance.

Mélusine and Kuveni took turns tutoring the children, as they all agreed that their temporary situation and the many lurking dangers were not conducive to their attendance at traditional school, and every so often Edmund would stop into the library to join them. He'd engage them in lively debates that the bairns found highly entertaining, even though Mélusine and Kuveni were both unnerved by the prospect of Edmund recognizing how similar the whole set-up was to the tutorials Mélusine had given him in Bath for the years of his extended adolescence.

With every day that passed, the children began to believe that Abbi and Amma were going to keep them, and with that, they slowly returned to their happier, bolder, more curious selves. Debbie and Ruthy remained clingier with Eleanor and Kuveni than they ever had been before, a development that didn't surprise anyone given the circumstances, and Eleanor and Kuveni took their presence in stride, reiterating as often as they needed to how safe and loved the lasses were. Mary, all the while, calmed her overt fervor in demanding her sons' immediate forgiveness, and with her resigned silence, they began to slowly accept her presence, even hugging her back when she tucked them in at night after they'd finished listening to Abbi and Amma's storytime, which continued to happen every night, no matter what else they had on their schedules, which wasn't much, since the move had abruptly dragged both Edmund and Eleanor into retirement from their formerly fulfilling posts.

On weekdays, they all worked to keep their minds occupied and their nerves at bay by breaking the bairns' tutorials with family cricket matches and visiting the neighboring farmers' horses, while Edmund and Eleanor steadfastly resisted the urge to fill their empty stables with a new equine family of their own. Whenever the idea came up, they ended up falling back into the reality of their uncertainty and their longing to return to the peaceful life with Oz and Yvie that they'd left behind down under. They held onto the idea of moving back as soon as their problems disappeared, but as the days passed, then the weeks, and then the months, the prospect of returning to Australia seemed less and less likely. Eleanor and Yvie commiserated on nightly telephone calls (secured against uninvited listeners by Monty's Yaksha magic); although, as time passed, even the phone calls began to fall by the wayside.

On weekends, they entertained themselves by taking long drives in another beautiful silver Rolls Royce that Kuveni had popped into existence on their second day in England, before they even remembered that they didn't have Oz's Fords to drive around at their whim. They'd drive all around the rolling green hills of Hampshire, down to the beaches at Eastbourne and Brighton, stopping to visit every cute old castle and ancient stone ruin they stumbled upon (a privilege that Edmund particularly enjoyed, compared to the limitations of the train travel he'd primarily used during his many decades in Basingstoke in the 19th century). They even drove over to visit the countryside of the Cotswalds near Bath where Edmund had spent his happy teenaged years with the kind old farmer, Mrs. Hopper, or, as everyone knew but him, Kuveni. Eleanor could see Kuveni bursting at the seams to reveal her identity as Edmund gushed about how nice and helpful and loving she was, almost like a mother to him. But, Kuveni dutifully held

329

her tongue and accepted Edmund's praise silently like the long-suffering matrika that she was.

Mary, who was growing bigger and healthier every day, and Moira, who had eventually regained her appetite as the family settled in, always stayed back at the house, subtly monitored by Mélusine. Mostly they sat on the veranda reading when the weather was fine, or in the library when it wasn't, although as far as Eleanor could tell, they hadn't said a word to each other since Moira's harsh chastisement upon their initial arrival.

And so, one chilly day in early December, as Edmund was out with the bairns feeding Mr. Wilson's horses at the farm down the road, and Eleanor was frantically digging through her closet to choose a dress to wear to a military banquet in London that evening (their first night away from the bairns), it came as an unpleasant and rather shocking surprise when the front door opened and slammed, and the sound of a single person's footsteps shuffling back and forth in the foyer distracted Eleanor from her task.

"Darling, are you back already?"

No response.

"Mary?" she called. "Did you go out?"

No response.

"Stanley?"

No response.

"Mum?"

Eleanor stopped completely still. She'd become so used to the hovering presence of the Yakshas offering her immediate reports on anything out of the ordinary that the silence sent her heart racing.

"Kuveni?"

Silence.

"Monty?"

Silence.

"Mélusine?"

The pacing in the foyer stopped, and the uninvited guest began muttering.

This is bad. Very, very bad, Uma murmured.

What is?! Who is it? Is it Surpanakha?

The footsteps did not sound like Surpanakha's. They were heavier, more human, and definitely male.

Uma didn't answer. Instead, Eleanor could feel her debating what to say.

Just tell me who it is!

Reveal nothing about who we are, Eleanor. Do you understand? Nothing! NO MATTER WHAT!

Eleanor felt Uma burying herself deeper into the core of her being, like a frightened pig burying itself in mud.

"Oh, for god's sake," Eleanor muttered.

She threw on the closest dress, a skin-tight, floor-length beaded black number that she'd already rejected for being far too revealing of her copious cleavage for polite company. She sighed with annoyance and grabbed a mink stole to cover her chest, and then she paused, contemplating the unnerving intrusion, and then grabbed her silver pistol from its locked box in the top of the closet and strapped it to her leg with the straps Leo had procured for her shortly after her honeymoon. It had been years since she'd seriously considered carrying it, but in that moment, she was grateful that it was there.

"What are *you* doing here? How did you get inside?" Stanley spoke with his unnatural deeper voice that he'd used when they'd first met, back when he was forced to conform to his father's rigid ideals of manhood. She could hear his concern because she knew him so well, but he did an excellent job of hiding it.

"Blimey," Eleanor muttered. "Lord Grimby sure has some nerve coming here."

"I've come to see the lady of the house," the man responded. His voice was not Lord Grimby's. Eleanor had never heard it in her life. He spoke with a posh accent, not entirely dissimilar to

Edmund's, although perhaps more affected, and it had a harsh ring to it that vibrated strangely inside of her. It was familiar yet foreign.

She pulled her dress down and made sure the bulge of the pistol wasn't visible in the mirror, and then she slipped on her heels and braced herself to face their mysterious visitor.

He glanced up at her as she descended the grand staircase. She hated how he licked his lips with a subtle smirk of appreciation for her curves as she approached. He was an older man, similar in age to Lord Grimby, perhaps in his late sixties or early seventies, with a head of thick silver hair that was relatively long and groomed into a greasy curl in the front that she would usually have expected to see on a much younger man. He wore a black pin-striped formal suit, although not a tuxedo, and he held a black trench coat with a matching fedora in his left hand while he carried a walking stick topped by an elaborately carved ivory lion's head in his right.

"I am the Countess of Easton. Now you will explain to me before my butler sees you right out the door why you saw fit to invade my home uninvited," Eleanor came out swinging.

A flash of sinister delight crossed his expression at her aggressive introduction. He handed his coat, his hat, and his walking stick to Stanley without even looking at him, as if Stanley was a hat rack, and then bowed an absurdly formal bow, not dissimilar to the one Edmund had presented to Queen Victoria. When he was finished, he grabbed her hand gruffly and kissed it. His flesh was hard and cold. She knew the feeling too well, not from Edmund, whose frigidity was tempered by his mother's humanity, but from... Vibhishana. It was the flesh of a full Rakshasa who hadn't bothered to warm himself at all.

"My lady, please forgive my intrusion," he began. "I am Lord Montagu. I have come to know you by reputation, and I would like to discuss an opportunity with you, *privately*."

Eleanor glanced at Stanley. Fear and bewilderment were battling in his expression.

"And to set the stage for your proposition, you didn't bother knocking on my front door before entering?"

Lord Montagu laughed a toothy, awkward laugh. "My dear, I follow my own rules of decorum. I've found that the element of surprise is often a useful tool to unnerve my opponents."

"Your opponents?"

"Everyone is my opponent, my dear, until they earn their place in my inner circle. Now, tell me, where can we discuss our opportunity privately?"

Eleanor considered pushing him right out the door, but without any of her Yaksha allies to help, and with Uma buried deep inside of her, she decided that navigating her way out of the danger stealthily was her safest option.

"Our front parlor should be perfectly sufficient." She gestured for him to go through the french doors, but as she followed, Stanley grabbed her wrist.

Be careful, Eleanor. He's a vicious bastard.

Stanley followed them in, closing the french doors behind them.

"I said private," Lord Montagu said as he eyed Stanley.

"Stanley is the most loyal man's man in the world," Eleanor countered. "Anything you can say to me, you can say to him."

Lord Montagu laughed. "Ah, loyalty. It is something I value very much myself. Still, I have asked for privacy," he narrowed his eyes threateningly at Stanley. "And that is what I shall have."

"I'm not leaving," Stanley countered. "You may have scared my mother, but you don't scare me."

Lord Montagu relegated a moment of panic. "Ah yes, your mother, you say? How is she doing? Remind me of her name? My memory isn't what it used to be."

Stanley glanced at Eleanor with a more intense look of warning. They both knew that the real Lord Montagu should have recognized Stanley from his many interactions with Norwenn and Lord Grimby over the years.

"Don't you remember her? Louisa Abernathy?" Stanley fished.

"Ah, yes. Louisa. What a fine steer of a woman she was. Do send her my best."

"She's dead," Stanley shot back.

"How sad. I'm sure she's playing the harp in the clouds, or some other Christian heavenly nonsense."

Lord Montagu paused to consider his next move carefully, but then found himself distracted as Eleanor took a seat on the divan across from him. He stared lustfully at her leg revealed by the slit in her dress, and then his eyes moved upward to the flesh of her cleavage that was peeking out from the open front of the mink stole. She sighed with annoyance and buttoned the stole, but there was nothing she could do about her dress's revealing slit.

"My husband is going to be home any minute. You'd better get to the point."

He glanced at Stanley one more time and gave up on that battle. "I like you, Eleanor. I like a hot little firecracker, so sizzling to the touch."

Eleanor stood up and joined Stanley by the door.

"If that's all you have to say to me, you can say it on the stoop outside."

He hissed with feigned disappointment. "Is it just business with you? Whatever happened to taking one's time to revel in pleasantries? The modern world is in such a hurry to get things done. Hurry, hurry, scurry, scurry, like ants running about, so determined in their drudgery. But do you know what happens to ants, my lady, when something bigger than them comes along?" He leaned in confidingly. "They get squashed by something so large, they couldn't even see it coming from their teeny-weeny world in the dirt. Come sit, Eleanor."

He patted the seat beside him, and she returned to her seat across from him, crossing her legs in the other direction to avoid the revealing slit. He sighed with disappointment and poured himself a tall glass of cognac from a tray on the low table between them, and then glugged it down in one Rakshasa gulp. He paused for a moment of surprise, appreciating its quality, and then poured himself another tall glass without offering a hint of apology for his uncouth move, or offering a pour to Eleanor.

"I'll get straight to the point, since you're a busy little bee. We have a shared acquaintance, my lady. A Lord Chester Grimby."

"Lord who? It's quite difficult to keep track of all these so-called lords when they all look the same and prattle on endlessly about the glory of the Empire." Eleanor caught an approving twinkle in his eye at her insult. "Perhaps you can jog my memory."

"He's a weasely, conniving chap, without enough of a spine to meet his full potential."

"You'll have to be more specific."

He smiled indulgently. "I've become very disappointed in him, but that is beside the point now. What matters is that your husband worked for him in the military some years back, and that your husband demonstrated, shall we say, unusual aptitudes."

"I wouldn't know. We've only been married for three years," Eleanor replied.

"Yes, yes, of course, how little the innocent wifey usually knows... but, you see, after Chester insisted upon it, we orchestrated a little test for you, for both of you... if you'll remember that unseemly affair at the circus in Australia... and I was impressed by what I saw."

"You were there?" Eleanor worked hard to relegate her fear at the idea before he could smell it.

"Oh, no, no, no. No. I have much better things to do with my time than to gallivant across the globe to a bumpkin country town to take in the sights and sounds suggested to me by a desperate, foolish human who knows nothing of what powers really make the world go round. No. I did, however, watch the reel sent back to England for me by my Italian colleagues. They were very interested in what they saw, and so was I."

Eleanor could not believe her ears. This man, this Rakshasa, had come to her house because he was interested in Edmund's minor showing of a common (and not particularly interesting) Rakshasa trait? And now, with whatever skills the Rakshasa had himself, he'd come to recruit Edmund for the Fascist cause? It didn't make any sense. The pieces that had seemed like they were coming together were quickly being ripped apart.

"And you, my lady, were not surprised at all by what you saw him do that night."

She contemplated her answer. To play dumb, or to toe the line and extract more information? He seemed surprisingly willing to reveal certain details that had alluded Stanley's spies for months.

"There are many powers in this world about which ordinary people know nothing."

"Truer words have never been spoken. Like I said, Eleanor, I like you."

He drank down his entire glass of cognac and poured himself another. This time, he poured a glass for her, but as she reached forward to take it, he stroked her fingers, shivering with excitement as he pulled away. There was something particularly disgusting about how he expressed his lascivious pleasure, as if taunting her with it was just as enjoyable as his lecherous appreciation itself.

He watched her take a slow sip, and as she held it in her mouth, appreciating the rich caramel notes, and using the physical sensation to distract herself from her raging nerves, he grinned.

"God, you're an attractive woman, Eleanor. That frumpy coat you were wearing at the circus didn't do you justice. Those curves, and that fiery hair, and that mouth of yours... Mmmm... you are driving me wild. I just want to eat you up!"

She swallowed. "You have one minute before I throw you out."

He chuckled indulgently. "I like you, Eleanor. God, how I like you."

"So you've said."

336

"So I'm going to be straight with you. I have friends in high places. I am a much more powerful man than I seem. I am a much more powerful man than Lord Montagu ever was. Now, my interest in your husband is quite straightforward. Chester shared with me how the British military gave your husband his unique abilities during the war, and I simply wish to recreate the gift that he was given for others. Can you imagine a world where humans can transcend mortality itself? And soldiers... oh, soldiers... if soldiers could transcend mortality, there would never be war ever again."

Eleanor scoffed. "You mean there would be war all the time, as immortal soldiers blow each other's brains out over and over and over again."

"Mmm... what a poetic idea, don't you think? Humans endlessly destroying each other over trivialities like *religion*..."

He rolled his eyes in a gesture that distinctly mirrored Edmund, and Eleanor suddenly realized who exactly it was that had come to call. *Blimey, what were the chances?* He did not notice her epiphany.

"... and territory. While apes beat each other to death with sticks, the rest of the world will be open for the select few of us who are worthy of our God-given superiority, and, of course, our pets."

"I didn't take you as a religious man. That eye-roll certainly implied a distaste for the divine, and yet here you are talking about God's will. Or did I misread you?"

Lord Montagu grinned. "You are a singularly unique woman, Eleanor. Do you know how many decades it has been since I've met a woman worth talking to?"

Eleanor looked him up and down. "I'm going to guess... hmm... shall we say... ten-ish? A century, I reckon, maybe even with some change."

"Do I really look that old?"

"Does my husband?"

His grin grew wider. "I'm half inclined to throw you over my shoulder and carry you out the door as a prize right now."

"That would be a very bad plan. He would be very cross."

He chuckled again. "Believe me, my lady, I have never let possessive husbands deter me from taking what I deserve. But first things first. While we're on the topic, I am very interested in your husband, but I understand that with special people, extraordinary people, the best things come from willing partnerships. I've come to offer you an opportunity to come with me. Il Duce has already offered you and Edmund a palace of your own overlooking the sea in Naples. All Edmund will have to do is cooperate with some harmless tests to help the world's foremost scientists recreate what the British military was able to achieve, and then you both will be free to go, unless you fall in love with the sunshine."

"Why don't you just ask the British military how they did it?"

Eleanor, of course, found it fascinating, and worth further inquiry, that Lord Grimby had felt the need to lie to his ally about the origin of Edmund's power. He certainly hadn't realized that he was lying to the Devil himself.

"Those involved in the initial experiment seem to have already met untimely and unfortunate deaths," he replied. "But I'm sure your husband knows nothing about that."

"I'm sure he doesn't," Eleanor agreed truthfully.

He leaned in. "You will never be offered a better opportunity, Eleanor. Il Duce is rising, and he will only rise faster with my help."

Eleanor was suddenly enflamed with curiosity. This man before her lacked the finesse that she'd expected in a creature who had silently corrupted the world's greatest leaders for millennia.

"So you've given up on Britain? I thought you were quite fond of our foggy isles? Haven't you found a place in our royal court many times over?"

Uma was buried too deeply to chastise Eleanor for her risky baiting.

He did not understand her reference for what it was. "Lord Grimby has helped me realize that the British are not ready to rule the world. They're so preoccupied with bureaucracy and arrogant self-righteousness that they can't even hold their own empire together. It is only a matter of time until another force will come to claim it, and those who choose the right side will flourish while the rest of the world burns."

"So, you're saying that it will be like Hell on Earth? That's a bit clichéd, don't you think?" Eleanor hoped that her cheek wouldn't push him too far.

"It is not a laughing matter, Eleanor. You really are the most curious woman. I sense no fear from you at all at the prospect. That must be because you are incredibly brave or incredibly foolish."

"Or I don't believe your dire proposition." She took another sip. "What makes you think that Il Duce won't turn on you the moment you show up with your trunks to move on into his palace? Has it occurred to you that he might just be using you to destabilize the British lordships with your meddling? And that you aren't even doing a good job of it? Lord Grimby's been ousted from his social circles and his military position, hasn't he? You've got one down, and about seven hundred peers in the House of Lords to go."

He snorted at her insult and spit out his drink all over the table.

"Do you have any idea who you're talking to with that mouth?" She could feel his temper and his hedonistic urges becoming aroused by the confrontation.

"Lord Montagu?" she asked innocently. "I don't believe you told me your first name. Do you know it, or did that elude your memory too?"

She could hear Stanley shifting uncomfortably from his position by the door.

Lord Montagu leaned in to hiss threateningly. "I've had emperors begging at my feet. I've strangled gods and murdered angels. Empires move by my hand, and only my hand, and I have very little patience for the impudence of spoiled countesses."

"Well, in that case, you'd better be going. I'll tell Edmund you stopped by, and if we find ourselves in need of an Italian holiday, we'll be sure to call you up. Should we just ask the operators for Il Duce himself, or will you have your own title in his new world order? I hear *Il Principe* is available, or perhaps you would prefer *Il Diavolo?*"

"You will not be laughing when Fergus MacGregor takes his children back."

Eleanor was stunned by the abrupt transition.

"Did you think I'd come here without any leverage, Eleanor?"

She was suddenly speechless, and he made no effort to hide his thrill at his triumph.

"Imagine how trying it will be for those adorable little lads to sit there in court while their mother explains why she starved them. Poor Fergus begged her and begged her to feed them better, but she just couldn't kick her expensive drinking habit. It was really a tragic tale, but it can have a happy ending when they're back in their loving father's arms."

"No judge on Earth would hand them back to that bastard. We have all the proof of his abuse that we need."

"Are you sure of that? Are you ready to submit them to month after month of testimony? Are you ready for the press to revel in the rich tales of Edmund's bloody killing sprees when they compare his qualifications for fatherhood to Fergus's? Can you imagine, *eight* men killed with his bare hands on the Orient Express. *Eight*... It's almost superhuman."

He threw his crystal glass into the fireplace and laughed as it shattered. Then he stood up and loomed over her.

"Don't play games with me, my little firecracker, or I will burn you. You have twenty-four hours to convince Edmund to come on a little Christmas holiday to Italy. Bring the brats or not, but if you fail to comply, you'll wish that the only thing you have to worry about is a day in court." He leaned in. "I will crush you, Eleanor, and I learned a long time ago that the fastest way to crush a woman's heart is to crush her children, preferably slowly while she watches."

As he spied a bigger peek of her cleavage, his expression turned primal. In a blur, he jerked her up and threw her against the wall by the fireplace.

Stanley ripped open the french doors and ran across the foyer, whispering the names of all of their allies in a row as he begged for help.

"Does your husband know how to use his special speed in bed? If he doesn't, I'll show you a thing or two you can teach him, or perhaps I will show both of you together while I use you to demonstrate the techniques for him. You will both thank me later."

She leaned down to reach for her gun, but he grabbed her wrists and slammed them up against the wall. He ripped off her stole and took a long, lecherous look at her body in the skin-tight, low-cut dress.

His eyes turned black with desire. "Mmmm. God, you arouse me, Eleanor. You are like a siren and a queen and a goddess all wrapped up into one sensuous, sassy package. I must have you!"

Sheranee, please come!

Sheranee didn't dare to stir.

D.H.? Vibhi? He's here! Come now!!!

She closed her eyes and called forth her trident, but it too would not come.

As she noticed his eyes light up with arousal at her spicy puff of fear, she kneed him in the groin.

He let go of her, reeling with surprise at her aggressive move. He took a moment to collect himself, and then grinned ghoulishly.

"Oh, how I love a challenge!"

As her mind raced with what to do next, she glanced down and spied a fireplace poker. Without hesitating, she ripped it off its holder, cutting her hand on the tip in the process, and thrust it right through his belly.

He looked down at it with shock and stumbled backwards across the room with it still lodged in his hard Rakshasa flesh.

As he took in a deep whiff of her fresh blood, he burst into his demonic form. Ten ghoulish spiked heads erupted from his neck, each far uglier than anything she'd seen from any of the other Rakshasas, even Vibhishana, and twenty extra arms erupted from his shoulders. He no longer wore his dark pinstriped suit. Instead, he was only wearing a golden, jeweled loincloth of undoubtedly ancient design, highlighting his bright patches of blue, green, and yellow flesh studded from head to toe with the same black spikes she'd seen Edmund produce on the unfortunate night that Surpanakha had taken it upon herself to force him into his demonic form. Despite all that she'd seen in her bizarre divine life, it was, without a doubt, the most bizarre of them all.

Boom.

A bullet ricocheted off of the fireplace mantle.

Boom.

Another blew a hole into the velvet divan.

Boom.

He stumbled towards Eleanor with a hole in his spiked chest, oozing red metallic plasma.

In the doorway, her mother stood holding the smoking pistol.

Boom.

Boom.

Boom.

Her mother emptied the pistol into his back. He looked down at the injuries with unbridled ferocity, and then he burst into booming, disharmonious laughter.

"You think these measly human weapons can stop the King of Darkness?!"

He blurred towards Eleanor, and she stepped out of the way.

As he hit the wall with the force of his own speed, the house shook, and he turned around with an even darker look on his ten faces.

Vibhi, come now!

He loomed over her, licking all ten of his lips. "Sweetest is the flesh of the pig that squeals the loudest."

BOOM.

He looked down with shock and then grimaced as a gaping bullet hole opened up in his demonic chest.

Stanley stood behind him, hyperventilating as he held the smoking gun.

The red metallic plasma oozing into the fresh wound turned black and crumbled into ashes. Before he could say another word, he dissolved into a puddle. In a blur, the puddle disappeared right out the front door, leaving a sparkling red sapphire bullet in the middle of the persian carpet.

"Eleanor, who was that?" Stanley whispered as he reached down to collect the bullet and place it in his breast pocket for safe keeping. He kept his smoking pistol still poised in his left hand.

She almost collapsed as she tried to catch her breath. "That, I'm quite sure, was my father-in-law."

"Eleanor?" Vibhishana, in his gentle Lankan form clad in a tasteful western suit, rushed in from the foyer to steady her. "Thank god you're alright!"

As Eleanor looked up at him, she spied Mary leaning up against the staircase bannister, shaking. She didn't have the energy to deal with her yet.

"It took you long enough." She leaned on him. "You know I'm the last one in the world to admit to being a damsel in distress, but your brother is one vicious wanker. I shouldn't have baited him like that. I just didn't expect to be left without any weapons at my disposal."

Sheranee slinked in shamefully and bowed before her in apology.

"It wouldn't have mattered, Eleanor. He would have found your divine energy seductive no matter what. At least this way you learned more about his plans."

"How did you get here?" Eleanor stumbled over to the closest divan and sat down, and Sheranee laid down at her feet, humphing with self-castigation. "Our Yaksha allies seem to be MIA."

"I'm glad that they realized who they were dealing with. If he'd felt their presence, he easily could have enslaved them. That would have been a game-ending blow for the Avatars of Light." He kneeled down and stroked Sheranee's ears supportively. "It was wise for Sheranee to stay away as well. It is absolutely pivotal that he doesn't learn who you are, Eleanor. If he knew, he would become singularly obsessed with harnessing your power for himself."

She sighed. "I suppose Shakti realized that herself. She wouldn't let me summon my trident. I'm surprised she didn't cut off my connection to you while she was at it."

"I knew to come through the fire in the library. It took all of my energy not to come straight to you, but he couldn't know that I'm connected to either of you. It would have given away our entire hand."

Eleanor laughed. "You mean to the British engineered super-soldier? How could that man possibly be so ignorant about his own kind? It should be clear as day that Edmund is a Rakshasa!"

"Hybrid children are extremely rare, Eleanor, and as the King of the Rakshasas, he considers himself apprised on where *all* of our people are. That is why Maya is in such constant danger. It is extremely unusual for anyone to escape from him."

"Like Edmund's mother…" Eleanor murmured.

"Exactly. She couldn't have been luckier that she got out of the palace before he knew she was carrying his child, and it is a miracle today that Lord Grimby lied to him about Edmund's origins. Whatever his foolish, self-interested motivations were, it is a boon that we should not take for granted."

"Well, it's clear *Lord Montagu*," she rolled her eyes, "doesn't know Edmund is his son. That's something."

"It is a turn of exceptional fortune for all of us, especially Edmund." He sat down beside her, but took a deep calming breath as he noticed her enticing cleavage and then her bleeding hand. "You should bandage up that wound before Edmund gets home. We don't need him demonstrating any of his darker traits before the bairns."

"They've already seen his black eyes," Eleanor shrugged. "And for that matter, so has Mum. They decided to love him anyway, just like I did."

She glanced at her mother, who was leaning against the opposite divan with the bullet hole in it, still clasping the empty pistol. Stanley coaxed it out of her hand and helped her sit down, and then he noticed Mary. He glanced at Eleanor for instructions.

"Bring her on in," she whispered. "It's a good thing I've got the Good Lord by my side for this one."

He escorted Mary to the spot beside Eleanor's mother, but as she sat down, she was still shaking.

"I'll go get some tea and the first aid kit," Stanley offered.

"You did well, my boy," Vibhishana said with a supportive nod. "You made your one shot count."

"Thank you, my lord." Stanley rushed away.

Vibhishana leaned in to whisper in Eleanor's ear. "I thought that he could use a red sapphire bullet after our encounter with Haranyakashipu, but there isn't much of the substance left to work with. Rama's used up most of it over the centuries trying to defeat my brother once and for all."

"I assume the King of Darkness isn't going to die from this wound?"

"No. There are many other factors that will have to align for that to happen. But he won't be back any time soon. That wound will take him months to recover from, possibly years."

"A blow to the Fascist cause?" Eleanor asked half-jokingly.

"They align perfectly with his agenda. I have no doubt that he will be back on their side in no time, and he will be harder to stop than ever. But at least now we know where to look for him, and we have you to thank for that."

Eleanor sighed with resignation. "All in a day's work, I suppose."

As she noticed Mary staring at Sheranee with a look of utter bewilderment, she hunkered down for the extremely unpleasant chat that she'd hoped quite avidly never to have.

"What would you like to ask us?" Vibhishana asked her.

It was not where Eleanor expected him to start, but she had to admit that he had several thousand more years of experience than she did with managing the awkward conversation.

Mary looked back and forth between Eleanor, Vibhishana, Sheranee, and Moira, observing for an extra-long moment that her mother did not seem the least bit surprised.

"Ye popped down the chimney like Santa Claus!" she finally blurted.

He smiled. "I actually came through the fire itself, but I can see why you made that conclusion. Eleanor asked for my help, and it was the fastest way to answer her call." He closed his eyes and transformed into Mr. Johnson, clad in his vicar's habit. He reached out his hand in friendly greeting. "We've actually already met. You can call me Father Johnson if you'd like, although, I think the cat's out of the bag that I'm not an ordinary vicar."

"Lord Almighty," Mary murmured. "That's what the bairns meant. I thought they just meant that ye were nice fer playin' cricket wit 'em!"

She reached forward timidly and shook his hand.

"Yer freezing," she whispered. "Although, I half-expected not to feel ye at all."

"I can assure you, I'm quite real. Some of us, like me and Edmund, are naturally cold, while others, like Kate and Percy, are warmer than humans. It is all quite natural, how God intended it to be."

"Kate," Mary murmured. "I knew there was something strange about her, always pullin' steamin' snacks from the strangest wee cupboards."

"Yes, Kate does often let her desire to help overwhelm her need for discretion." Vibhishana did not look amused by the description of Kuveni's poorly disguised magic, but he smiled graciously as he focused on his explanation. "We are each divine in our own way. Edmund and Kate and Percy and myself... and Eleanor."

"Eleanor?" Mary whispered. "Ye dunne die, did ye?"

"That's what I asked too," Moira confided as she poked her. Mary smacked her hand away.

"I'm still human," Eleanor explained. She summoned her divine crown. "But I have a few special talents, and a special companion." Sheranee stretched out her neck so that Eleanor could scratch her ears. "It all came to pass after I married Edmund, although, it seems to have happened in its own right, not just because I married an angel."

"Eleanor is exceptional in her own right," Vibhishana reiterated. "She has become one of the most powerful humans on Earth, and it has not corrupted her at all. It is a feat so unusual that I have never once seen it before in my very long life."

Blimey, D.H., you never told me that! I'd have been on the lookout for my own disintegrating morality! She offered the statement jokingly, even though she meant it.

I knew that you were exceptional the moment I met you, Eleanor, but that is a conversation for another time.

"Lord Almighty," Mary murmured as she stared at Eleanor's green eyes glowing with their unspoken exchange.

"Edmund doesn't know that I have this power, and he is still very young compared to the others like him. He hasn't fully accepted his fate. He wants to think of himself as mostly ordinary, and we are all knee-deep in supporting him until he's ready to... er... become fully divine," Eleanor added. "Even Mum is in on it."

"Lord Almighty," Mary repeated.

"Poor Abbi," Moira murmured. "I knew he was fightin' something dark, but if his father's that creature…" She trailed off. "He's the spawn of the Devil himself, ain't he?"

"Evil takes many forms, including the form of Edmund's father," Vibhishana confirmed. "But you must never forget that Edmund is unquestionably an Avatar of Light. The angels delivered him from evil before he was even born, and he has chosen to use his many talents for the cause of peace, just like the other angels do. You already knew that the Devil was a fallen angel, and I suspect that you understand what that really means now. The only real difference between angels and demons is the choices we make."

"I'm startin' to…"

Eleanor's mother twiddled her thumbs as she worked hard to process the information, and Eleanor held her breath. It was, without a doubt, a far more unpleasant truth than she ever thought her mother could handle, although there were still the unidentified nefarious ends to which her mother had apparently committed.

"But what does the Devil need all those heads and arms fer? Is he gonna take twenty bassas down to Hell wit him at once?"

"I've asked myself that question many times," Vibhishana admitted. "He's always enjoyed putting on a show."

"Can you look like that?" Mary asked.

Moira smacked her in the arm. "Ye'd best watch that tongue if ye know whit's good fer ye, Mary MacLeod. He's not a circus act."

Vibhishana smiled. "I can, but I choose not to. I can take whatever form I need to take to meet my ends, just as he does. I only take a monstrous form when I must be equally matched with him to protect the innocent. Although, I have always found that brains are better than brawn, even when both are called for."

"Can we see it?" Mary pushed. Moira smacked her again more vehemently as Eleanor threw her a disapproving look. "How else will we know it's you if we see some monstrous creature?!" Mary defended herself.

He switched into his demonic form, still wearing his vicar's habit. He held out his clawed, spiked hands for them to touch.

Mary gasped, and Eleanor sighed with resignation.

"Lord Almighty," Moira murmured. "I dunne really wanna see that."

"If you see a creature like this and it isn't trying to kill you, you will know that it is one of us, and you'd better make yourself scarce, because evil won't be far behind." He morphed back into Father Johnson, but before relaxing back into their talk, he startled Mary as he grabbed her hand and looked straight into her eyes. "You will not have an opportunity to report this back to Lord Grimby, my child. He is certainly dead in a closet somewhere for crossing my brother, and now you understand the kind of protection you have under your own roof against your brutish husband. You have no reason left for treachery."

"I... I... I..." she stuttered as he let go of her.

"Mary?!" Moira hissed with shock. "What's he sayin'?"

Eleanor worked hard to keep her temper at bay. The news wasn't particularly surprising, although it was still intensely disappointing. "For god's sake, can't any of you just be trustworthy?" she muttered. "It's like we're bloody Romans or something."

Sheranee growled her agreement.

"Lord Grimby promised to keep Fergus away!" Mary exclaimed. "He swore it! A week after ye came from Australia, Lord Grimby called while ye were out! He told me that I only had to tell him if I saw anything extraordinary, and he'd keep Fergus and Jimmy away fer good!"

"You didn't have to make a deal with the Devil," Vibhishana informed her.

"I dunne know! I dunne care! I only wanted to keep those beasts away from the bairns! I thought I was helping!"

351

"Did you tell him anything?" Eleanor kept focused on the less painful point.

"I dunne have anything to tell! He was so furious at me, but I dunne know what he wanted me to see!"

Moira snorted. "Now ye know, don't ye?"

"Now I know," Mary whispered. "I'm sorry, Ellie. I dunne have any idea what it was all about. I just wanted to do something to help."

"And it really seemed like spying was your best option?" Eleanor pressed her, at least so that Mary could understand the flaw in her own logic.

"Aye," she whispered. "I thought it was. I dunne realize he was in league wit the Devil himself, but I shudda. When Lord Montagu came to Skye, he wunne right in the heid. He was a scary, monstrous bloke wit fire in his eyes."

An idea suddenly occurred to Eleanor. "Did you touch him when he came to Skye?"

"I wunne that desperate, Ellie!"

"I didn't mean like that. Did you shake his hand?"

"I suppose."

Vibhishana reached his hand out to her again. "Was it like mine? Frigid and slightly too hard to be human?"

She shook his hand. "I dunne reckon it was. I'da noticed it, like I did when ye shook my hand a few minutes ago. It was so obvious, I cunne keep my mouth shut, even to *you*."

He leaned in to address Eleanor. "That means that my brother must have killed and replaced Lord Montagu very recently. He was either feeling very confident in his future success, or he was desperate enough to make a final move before seeking greener pastures. I suppose with his attempt to recruit you on behalf of Il Duce, we know which one it was. I will put my spies on the lookout for him in Italy as soon as I'm done here."

"Always undoing yer brother's evil schemes? I suppose Ellie knows a thing or two about that," Moira snickered.

"My brother and Mary have almost nothing in common," Vibhishana said sharply. As Moira looked down at her hands like a scolded child, he softened his tone. "You must work on understanding degrees of sin, Moira. Spying on your sister to protect your children, however misguided, and murdering millions of innocent humans for sport should not be compared."

"I reckon they shunne," Moira murmured.

He thought for a long moment about his next move. "My brother and I were born of the same womb, in the same home, with the same unique talents that our ancient race conferred. But he chose the path of darkness, and I chose the path of light. Over time, our paths diverged into what you've seen today. This is an important lesson for you, Mary, to keep in mind."

"Me?" she asked nervously.

"You were quite confident in the rectitude of your deeds when you were following Eleanor's advice all those years, but when she left, you followed Martha straight off a cliff. Now you are wondering if you're doomed to follow in her footsteps... if perhaps, that is just who you really are."

"Aye," she whispered. "I reckon I am. Can you read my mind?"

He smiled. "Not exactly. But I know humanity, my child. I have spent five thousand years getting to know humans, and you are not the first to feel this struggle. But the truth is, you always have a choice. After the many unpleasant experiences of the last few months, you will know yourself better from now on, and you will know how to catch yourself wavering from the path of light."

"Five thousand years," Mary murmured. "But Jesus was only born two thousand years ago?"

"Darkness and light have been struggling for balance since long before the Christian era," he explained. "The coming of Jesus was only one battle for the hearts and minds of humanity, a battle that we continue to fight as my brother uses the pulpits of evil humans to corrupt my simple messages of love and acceptance with hate and fear. Your mother was almost taken in, but I think we saved her."

"Did we?" Eleanor spoke the words before she realized she was saying them out loud.

"What do ye mean?" her mother asked with shock and a burst of rich, spicy fear.

Eleanor was committed. "Did we save you? The Good Lord's right here." She leaned forward and gazed into her mother's eyes. "Now you can tell both of us what you did that made you afraid that he'd smite you."

"I... I... I..." she stuttered. "I don't know what yer talkin' about!"

"'I hope ye know whit yer doin', Moira MacLeod. If yer not careful, the Good Lord'll smite ye both,'" Eleanor did an impression of her mother's thick Scots intonation as she repeated the phrase that had carved itself permanently into her mind.

Vibhishana leaned forward and took Moira's hands into his. "Tell us, my child. Tell us what you meant."

"I... I... I dunne think ye heard me!"

"Well, I did," Eleanor said sharply. "And now your time's up. You're lucky I didn't burn the bloody house down with my temper enflamed after you used the three little words you knew I longed to hear just to manipulate me."

"But I dunne! I dunne do anything of the sort!" she exclaimed.

"Then tell me what you meant!" Eleanor felt her fiery temper working its way to the surface, but instead of supporting her with another growl, Sheranee reached up and began licking her hands soothingly.

"I gave in!" she exclaimed. "I let myself fall in love wit ye, Ellie! Wit ye, and Abbi, and the bairns, and our life down at the edge of the world with the kind doctor n' the French tart n' baby Neddy n' the poufy butler! I let myself feel how I felt when yer Da came home that night and told me that he was gonna tell that lord who wanted him to throw the race to go piss somewhere else! God,

354

how I loved him that night. Don't ye remember, Ellie?" Her voice quivered with emotion. "He brought home a pheasant, even though it was nothin' but a cold February eve, an' he sat wit ye an' yer wee sisters in his lap, tellin' ye tales of fairies and ogres while I roasted it n' dressed it like it was a merry Christmas Eve! I thought my life cunne get any better! And then wham, wallop, kabaam! It was gone! It was like I'd dared to take more than I deserved, and the Good Lord whipped me tidy fer it. I swore I'd ne'er be so foolish again. I *swore* it!" She gave into her tears. "But then I gone and done it again! I told ye, Ellie! I said the three wee words, an' the next bloody day that life was gone!" She turned her attention on Vibhishana. "Ye don' have to tell me why, 'cause I know I wunne worthy o' that bliss, not wit the rotten Devil dancin' on my tongue, but I reckon ye'd better tell Ellie here why ye decided to punish her an' Abbi an' the bairns alongside me. It seems like a mighty unjust hand, if ye ask me, an' I'm too auld n' desperate n' foolish to keep the thought to myself anymore."

Eleanor was too overwhelmed to respond. She channeled all of her energy into combatting the ball in her throat.

Do you believe her, Uma? Please tell me you believe her.

You and I both know that she is telling the truth, my child.

But what if she isn't?! I can't give in only to be hurt again! Another blow will be too much!

Then, I believe, my child, you understand exactly how she feels.

Blimey.

Moira closed her eyes and took a deep breath through her snorting sniffles, as if she was waiting for Vibhishana to smite her, but he only gazed at her with a look of intense pity.

"My child, I do not have control over these things. I am not omnipotent, and if I were, I would not spend my time smiting suffering humans for celebrating their joy. It is a great miracle when any creature transcends the cruelty that is innate to our ever-changing universe. The tragedies that have befallen you were not caused by a lightning bolt aimed by some angry god watching you for a hint of indiscretion."

"They weren't?" she asked meekly.

"I promise you, Moira, they weren't. Tragedy is an unfortunate reality of our universe. It is a natural manifestation of the constant change that is required for life to exist. Without death, there cannot be rebirth, and without endings there cannot be new beginnings. I am here to help humans navigate these crooked, painful paths, but even I cannot change them."

"Well, that's a right shame, ain't it?"

"Sometimes it is excruciating," he agreed. "You cannot imagine the tragedies I've endured. Some were enough to make the angels and the demons weep in each other's arms."

She pulled her hands away self-consciously so that she could wipe her eyes and her snot with a handkerchief from her pocket. When she was finished, Eleanor let herself reach over Sheranee to take her hands, and Moira patted them and squeezed them, like she had the night that Eleanor had come to her deathbed in Skye. Eleanor couldn't stop a few tears from escaping.

"So ye've been thinkin' that I was up to no good all this time? Since that mornin' it snowed, and we ate bacon with the krauts? Is that why ye wunne talk to me, Ellie? I thought it was because I asked about yer unspeakables! I dunne even wanna know, really!"

Eleanor couldn't help but laugh as she wiped her eyes. "I didn't think you did, Mum."

Stanley returned with a silver tray with three teapots and three tea cups, and Eleanor's first aid kit propped up on the edge. He put it all down on the table between them, poured the three cups, and handed one of the full pots to Vibhishana.

"You know us well, my boy." He winked, and drank it down in one long Rakshasa gulp.

Eleanor hissed as she cleaned off her minor flesh wound with some rubbing alcohol and then wrapped it in a bandage.

"Eleanor, what should we do with these?" Stanley asked as he carried in Lord Montagu's coat, hat, and walking stick. "I'm assuming he won't be back for them?"

"My brother was carrying that?" Vibhishana blurred out of his seat and startled Stanley as he grabbed the walking stick. "Yes, yes, of course! That's how he got across the threshold!" He closed his eyes and took in a deep, long breath as the black sparkling eyes of the ivory lion lit up.

"My lord?!" Mélusine appeared right beside him in her most natural female form, clad in her favorite white medieval dress. "How did you get here? I don't even care! Is that it?!"

"There is life in it," he whispered.

"Eleanor! Eleanor, please come! Please!" Mélusine begged. Eleanor had never seen her look so desperate. "Please, you must release the Yakshas who are trapped in the cane! It can only be done with divine power of the highest order!"

Sheranee got out of her way as she stood up and joined them by the french doors. "What do I need to do?"

"I don't know! Ask Uma! Please!" Mélusine squeaked.

I will do it, my child. Just hold the lion in the palm of your right hand.

Eleanor felt the warmth of Shakti's power erupting from the core of her being as Uma worked her way into her limbs. She was barely conscious as the green flames oozed out of her fingertips, melting the lion and dissolving it into ashes in her hand.

"*Viens!*" Mélusine called. "Hear the sound of my voice, *mon fils*! Come to me now, Puck, my dearest boy! Use *Maman* as an anchor!"

A pleasant breeze ruffled Eleanor's hair as Uma retreated back into her secondary position. Two beautiful bronze-skinned naked Polynesian girls who looked like they were both about twenty bowed before Mélusine.

"My lady?" one of them asked dazedly. "Where are we?"

"Hina?" Mélusine asked as she frantically glanced around the room. "Haumea? Was Puck with you?!"

357

"No, my lady. We were alone," Haumea replied.

Mélusine wailed with such blood-curdling anguish that Eleanor shivered, and Sheranee whimpered. With a gust of wind slamming shut the front door and setting all of the curtains aflutter, she disappeared.

"My brother's been holding her son captive for three hundred years," Vibhishana explained solemnly. Eleanor could see the devastation in his eyes. "He must have left him trapped in another object somewhere else for safe keeping."

The two Yakshinis bowed before Eleanor and Vibhishana, and as Eleanor glanced at Vibhishana for a cue about what to do next, Kuveni appeared and pulled both girls into a tight hug.

"Kuveni?" Hina whispered. "Is that you?"

"Oh, my darling, darling girls, how I've missed you!" Kuveni exclaimed. "It has been two hundred years!"

"It felt like eternity," Haumea admitted.

"Come with me. You must rest by the Sacred Well and recover before we discuss how much the world has changed. Eleanor, dearest, thank you for your divine gift. My lord, we will talk later. Stanley, my boy, you are more of a hero than you know. Now, you'd all best get into position. Edmund and the bairns are making their way up the drive now."

Kuveni gathered the Yakshinis into her arms, and all three of them disappeared.

Vibhishana paced into the parlor debating his options, while Eleanor dissolved her crown, but as she glanced over at Sheranee who had settled back down to enjoy her corporeal visit on the floor before the fireplace, she heard the bairns chasing each other up the stairs.

"Last one inside is a rotten egg!" Howie exclaimed.

"No fair, you were already ahead!" Charlie whined.

"I'm too little to compete!" Ruthy added.

"Ha!" Debbie pulled Howie back out the door and ran past him, and Edmund skipped happily up the steps behind them, wiping the droplets of cool mist from his coat into his skin and taking off his hat and scarf to place them politely on the hat rack by the door without troubling Stanley.

"Good lord, dearest, you look stunning in that gown!" He leaned in to kiss her gently on the cheek, and then he whispered, "You're so sensuous, I could throw you over my shoulder and carry you upstairs to bed right now."

Eleanor pulled away, working hard not to hear the very similar words his evil father had spoken resonating in her head. She knew rationally that they couldn't have been more different, and yet, suddenly, she couldn't ignore the family resemblance. She wished dearly in that moment that she'd never seen the Devil himself for comparison. It wasn't, of course, their physicality that was so similar, but there was something about their mannerisms that Eleanor found downright unnerving. She hated that she felt that way.

"I'm sorry, dearest." Edmund looked concerned. "Should I not have said anything so scandalous in front of the bairns? I didn't mean to make you uncomfortable." She let his genuine softness pull her out of the infuriating torment in her mind.

"No, darling, it's perfectly alright. I'm just a bit distracted."

"Oh no, what happened?!" he asked as he spotted her bandaged hand. "You're hurt!"

As one of the floorboards in the parlor creaked with Vibhishana's weight shifting uncomfortably, Edmund glanced around the corner, spying first him, then Sheranee, and then the bullet hole blown into the couch.

"Good lord! Something did happen! Is everyone alright?!"

"Everyone's perfectly fine now, darling," Eleanor said calmly.

Edmund glanced around the parlor as he approached Vibhishana in greeting, and as his attention landed on the bullet damage on the mantle, Vibhishana stepped in front of it to distract him.

"Eleanor took care of herself, as always, my boy," Vibhishana reassured him. "I didn't even get here in time to rescue her."

"It was actually Stanley who saved the day," Eleanor said as she hugged each of the bairns, helping them take off their coats, as if there was nothing wrong at all. "Lord Montagu paid us a visit, but we let him know that he should not be calling here again."

Edmund's eyes turned black at the thought. "He didn't threaten the bairns, did he?"

"Darling, we took care of it," she evaded a direct answer to his question.

He pulled Vibhishana into a familial hug, as he leaned in to whisper. "Did you kill him?"

"Believe me, Edmund. He will not be back."

Edmund sighed with relief.

"Now, say your mantras, darling. We have a banquet to get to in London, and I need to change my dress."

"Really, dearest? Why? I really do like it."

"So did Lord Montagu."

At the thought, he leaned over Sheranee, holding himself up against the mantle and returned to his mantras. As soon as he got himself back under control, he glanced around at the many wide eyes watching him.

"Are you sure you still want to go to London after your ordeal, dearest? I might rather have a nice evening at home with our family."

"Come to think of it, darling, that sounds like a fine plan," Eleanor agreed. "Now, if you'll excuse me, I have a thick frumpy sweater and some trousers to put on."

"Will you stay for dinner, Father?" he asked Vibhishana.

Vibhi moved to decline, and then as he glanced at Mary and Moira, noticing just as Eleanor did that they had an extra curious eye on Edmund now that they knew too much about him, he gave in.

"It would be a pleasure as always, my boy. But, perhaps we should move ourselves to the library while we wait. This room has seen enough action for the day, I reckon."

Vibhishana guided Edmund down the hall, and the bairns followed them. Stanley helped Mary up, and as Eleanor reached over to help her mother, her mother grabbed her hand.

"I know I dunne deserve yer trust after the rotten Mam I was to ye, but I mean it, Ellie. I love ye, wit an' witout yer tiger, and I love Abbi, wit and witout the Devil in his eyes..." Eleanor let a few more tears escape as she hugged her. "...But I'm too auld n' foolish not to tell ye, that that dress ye've got on is trouble. It's no wonder ye had the angels n' demons boxin' it out fer a glimpse."

Eleanor found the prudish insult intensely reassuring. "Mum, I'm not even going to argue with you."

"Yer a good tidy lass, Ellie."

Moira took Mary's arm from Stanley and led her into the hallway. "Let's go prove to the Good Lord that ye have a decent bone in yer body, Mary."

As soon as they were gone, Stanley grabbed Eleanor's hand.

We're bloody lucky that Mrs. Murray was out at the market.

We're bloody lucky that you weren't. You saved the day, greenie. I think you officially get a new nickname.

Stanley will do just fine, Eleanor. Now, I need to check up on the tip that Mr. Johnson slipped in.

Which tip was that?

I'm surprised you didn't catch it. I'm sure he said it for our benefit. It's my father, Eleanor. Mr. Johnson thinks he's dead. If he's right, we need to know.

Were you listening to our entire conversation?

I was spying from the foyer while the tea was steeping. I'm certain that Mr. Johnson knew I was there. He even winked at me.

You're really coming into your own, aren't you?

It's about time.

The phone rang in the kitchen. *Speak of the Devil.*

Eleanor followed Stanley as they rushed to answer it before anyone else did.

"Colonel and Lady Marriner's residence," Stanley said cheerfully.

"Stanley?" Norwenn's voice whispered meekly.

"Maman?!"

CHAPTER 22 – THE UNWORTHY

"*Maman?!*"

"Stanley?" She dissolved into sobs. "Stanley, please save me. Please. Please. Please."

"Maman, where are you?! I'll come!"

Eleanor was startled as Mélusine appeared beside them in her preferred female form.

She grabbed Eleanor's hand. *It could be a trap. It could be Ravana himself baiting you! Don't let him win! That bastard is still enslaving my Puck!*

But we just defeated him?

He is the King of Darkness, Eleanor. Never, ever underestimate him!

But he didn't recognize Stanley. He didn't know Stanley was related to Norwenn. How could he be behind this now?

"I'm at your father's estate in Shropshire! They locked me in the cellar for weeks, Stanley! Weeks! They only fed me bread and water once a day! Your father's gone raving mad, and Lord Montagu…" She trailed off into a whimper. "He's a monster, Stanley! Please, I beg you, please help me."

"I'm coming, Maman. Leave if you can! Go to the village, and I will find you!"

"Stanley, you don't understand! Your father's hunting me like I'm an animal! Please come. *Gast*, that's him. Please, Stanley!"

She hung up the phone.

"It is a trap, mon chéri. It is classic Ravana. He probably had a knife to her throat, or he's already killed her, and he was impersonating her voice. He is trying to lure you there so he can take you hostage as leverage to make Edmund do what he wants."

Stanley straightened his posture. "I don't care if I have to steal that Rolls Royce and drive myself to Shropshire, I'm going to help my mother."

"I will go with you," Eleanor decided.

"What? *Non! Ma chérie*, did you hear what I just said?!"

"Vibhi thinks that we defeated Ravana for months, maybe years. Stanley shot him with a red sapphire bullet. I think there's something else going on, and I am going to help Stanley save his mother."

"Shiva's wrath!" Mélusine hissed. "You can't go alone!"

"Then I guess that means you're taking us," Eleanor tried to temper her cheek.

Mélusine shook her head in avid disagreement and whispered under her breath.

"In case you will listen to some other voice of reason, Kuveni also thinks it's a horrible idea."

Eleanor grabbed the car keys from beside the kitchen door, and Mélusine sighed with extreme annoyance. "You won't need those, ma chérie, obviously I'm going to escort you. Kuveni will keep Lord Vibhishana apprised, in case we need his intervention."

Eleanor looked down at her copious cleavage bulging out of her dress. "Can I trouble you to change this thing into something more modest before we go?"

Mélusine rolled her eyes and tapped Eleanor's arm, transforming her dress into an exact copy of the same white medieval dress that she was wearing, which wasn't, for the record, that much more modest.

Eleanor sighed bemusedly as she looked down. "That wasn't exactly the practical choice I was hoping for."

"I've always been wretched at making human clothing. You'll have to take what you can get, unless you want to stay here, which is what both of you should be doing right now."

"I'm going to save my mother," Stanley reiterated.

"Fine. It's your funeral. My only priority is to keep Eleanor safe on this outrageously unwise endeavor, *tu comprends?*"

"*D'accord*," Stanley agreed.

"Do you know where she is?" Mélusine asked.

"I know it well. My father's owned that old rock of a castle since long before I was born."

She grabbed his hand. "Picture it in your mind. Picture everything about it. Picture the village and how it looks from the sky, and where the roads are, and anything else you can remember about where exactly it is. It's in Shropshire, you said? There aren't so many castles there."

"*C'est vrai.*" Stanley closed his eyes and followed her instructions.

After almost a minute, Mélusine pulled away. "I have it. *Allons-y*. Let's get this over with."

Mélusine grabbed them forcefully into her arms, and with a dizzying breeze, they were gone.

They materialized on a stone stoop before an imposing metal door guarded by weeping angels and screaming gargoyles. The sky was gray, and it was already dark enough that Eleanor could barely see the woods beyond the open fields surrounding the ancient castle. Stanley had been correct in his description of it as an old rock of a castle, as most of it was clearly medieval and built directly into a bed of natural smooth sandstone, with only one boxy modern stone quarters slapped onto what was otherwise a Norman tower. It looked somewhat akin to how she had pictured

365

Rapunzel's hideaway, although the tower itself was quite wide and short, like a citadel that had been intended as a great Roman fortress until they ran out of stone, tidying up a roof where they'd otherwise planned to add several more floors.

Mélusine closed her eyes and took in a deep breath, feeling for something in the air. "This must be it. I can feel the remnants of the Yaksha power that he was using to guard it. The barrier was broken when you dissolved the lion's head of his cane, Eleanor. But we must be vigilant. If he felt the need to fortify it, he must have been doing something especially sinister."

As Stanley pulled out his pistol and held it poised, Eleanor reached down and pulled hers from the straps on her leg. Mélusine conjured Percy Blakeney's walking stick, and then whispered a quiet mantra. "I've made it so your bullets will endlessly replenish, mes chéris. I suggest using the surprise of it wisely. *On y va.*"

Mélusine ripped open the front door.

"Stanley, you go where you think she might be, and do not give away our presence until you must," Eleanor whispered. "Surprise is always our greatest weapon."

He nodded.

The massive stone foyer was hauntingly silent. Eleanor followed Stanley into the hallway, and Mélusine guarded their rear. At each door, Stanley pointed his gun into the empty space, looked around, glanced at Mélusine to nod her agreement that there weren't any humans present, and then moved on. They passed the parlor, then the living room, then the library, and then the formal dining room… all empty.

As they were about to move on, Eleanor grabbed Stanley's arm and gestured for him to listen. Through the swinging servants' doors to the kitchen, they could hear someone clanking around.

With one glance between them, Stanley and Eleanor readied their guns. Together, they kicked the doors in.

A man who looked relatively young other than his mostly grey hair was wearing a disheveled half-unbuttoned dress shirt that was tied up at the elbow of the left arm, hiding the evidence of whatever ugly injury had resulted in the rest of his arm and hand being entirely absent. Unbuttoned, ripped, soiled dress trousers that were barely staying propped up around his thin hips made him look unsettlingly similar to the madmen that Eleanor had nursed for too many years at the insane asylum. He was standing at the counter in front of the knife block, holding a knife in his teeth. Several days of stubble on his chin and dark yellow stains in the armpits of his formerly white shirt indicated that he hadn't been able to keep up with basic hygiene, which was no wonder, given that his right arm was tied behind his waist with a rope that was twisted around him several times, serving as a makeshift alternative to handcuffs.

"Reggie?!" Stanley exclaimed.

He rushed over to him and took the knife out of his mouth. He used it to cut the rope, and then Reggie sighed with momentary relief, letting his right arm stretch out and wiggling his fingers. They were bloody, as was his arm, with scratches and bruises, as if he'd been trying to beat his way out of a locked room.

"Stanley? What are you doing here? I thought you'd gone off to Canada to be an actor?"

"I live in Hampshire now on permanent assignment for the Secret Service," Stanley revealed without hesitation as he re-poised his gun, aiming it towards the door.

"Blimey, I wouldn't have guessed that. I suppose that means you're doing a bang-up job."

"That remains to be seen."

Reggie glanced at Eleanor and Mélusine, and then returned his attention to Stanley without a peep about them. "Well, thank god you're here! My father's gone stark raving mad. He's making the mad hatter seem like a bloody fine fellow!"

"Tell me everything now," Stanley whispered. "Is he still here?"

367

"I don't know! He called me over from Oxford last week saying that he had some important news. When I got here, that awful Lord Montagu chap was here, and together they gave me some outlandish spiel about moving to Italy with them! My father claimed that Mussolini had found some Italian princess for me to marry, and I thought it was all some bizarre practical joke! I laughed, and they laughed, but then they stopped laughing, Stanley! I tried to be polite, telling him that shell-shock had made me too worthless of a man to be anyone's husband or father, and then he went off accusing me of being a pouf just like you! The whole thing was utterly ludicrous!"

"I am a pouf."

"Well, everyone knows that, Stanley, that's not what I meant. My father, General Lord Grimby, Master of the Isles, Obsessive Devotee of the Crown and All That It Stands For began badgering me about defecting to the Fascists! He was as serious as serious could be, and when I told him how mad he was being, he went positively wild! That awful Lord Montagu told him I couldn't be trusted, and then he tied me up and locked me in my old bedroom! It took me six days to get out, and I was banging and screaming, but no matter what I did, I couldn't get the doors or windows to open! And the whole time he was pacing around like some sort of guard dog, just listening! He'd come to my door once a day, asking if I'd seen the light yet, and today, I told him I had, but he didn't bloody believe me! He was *wild*, Stanley, like the Devil himself had possessed him."

"He had."

"I'd believe it! I just managed to break my way out of my room about an hour ago, when I heard him go running off down into the wine cellar, hollering for Norwenn."

"Where is she? Did you see her?"

"I haven't seen anyone, her or that Montagu chap. But I heard my father run out towards the stables, so I came down here to call

368

for help, but I couldn't get the blasted phone off the hook with my arm tied up."

"We have to find my mother," Stanley muttered.

"Your mother? But I thought she was in Brighton at the health retreat with old drunken Uncle Arthur? No offense intended, of course. He's the nicest drunk I've ever met."

"I'm not offended. He isn't my father. Norwenn is my real mother, and Chester bloody Grimby's my real father. Congratulations, Reggie, you have a pouf of a brother."

"Blimey... It all makes sense now."

"What does?"

"When I rejected his offer to marry Mussolini's princess, he chattered on and on about how he can't trust anyone anymore, how everyone had betrayed him, even his sons. That awful Montagu chap was just fanning the flames, and I thought he'd just lost his bloody mind."

"He did. And now we need to save my mother before he hunts her down like a fox. Are the hunting rifles still stored in the stables?"

"I reckon they are, but, Stanley, I need some water or something. I've been hallucinating for days, and the doctors have told me many times that I shouldn't go anywhere near a gun with my mind in this state."

"I meant that we need to keep the rifles away from *him*."

"Blimey, I reckon we do! But, Stanley, I'm not right in the head!"

Stanley grabbed a glass and filled it with water from the sink. Reggie chugged it down, and then squinted and blinked at Eleanor and Mélusine.

"Oh, Reggie, these are my... er... colleagues. Eleanor and Mélusine, this is my brother, Reggie. He was in Edmund's regiment for three years of the war, and that's where he lost his arm."

"You're real?" Reggie asked as he reached forward and poked Eleanor's forehead. "Bloody hell! I thought you were just in my head!" He blushed with embarrassment and offered her his hand to shake. "I reckon that wasn't the most polite greeting I've ever offered."

Eleanor shook his hand and smiled. "I've had worse."

"Why are you dressed like angels?" He asked as he shook Mélusine's hand.

As she held on for an extra-long moment, his clothing mended itself, and his stains (and his stench) disappeared. He looked down, blinking several more times.

"Because we are angels, mon chéri, and we have a job to do. Now, you're sure that you didn't hear anyone or anything that could lead us to Norwenn?"

Reggie looked confused and poured himself another glass of water. "I suppose I heard someone clomping around down here while I was still trying to beat my way out of the room. There were several doors slamming, and then I saw my father running across the lawn to the stables."

"But you didn't see Norwenn?" Eleanor pushed.

"I reckon she must still be in the house. I heard someone running up the stairs."

"*Maman*?!" Stanley called. "Maman, it's me! Stanley! I found Reggie, and Chester's out of the house. Come out now, and we'll all escape before he comes back!"

He kicked open the door to the hallway, and Reggie grabbed the largest knife from the butcher's block, following Eleanor and Mélusine out.

Stanley climbed up the stairs, walking down the first-floor hallway and kicking open each of the doors. "Maman?! Maman?!"

When they reached the servants' staircase at the end of the hall, Stanley rushed up to the second floor, repeating the exercise.

"Maman?!" he became more desperate as he switched into Breton. "Maman, please come out! You called for me to save you, and I'm here! Now please come out!"

They climbed up to the third-floor attic, where rows of old, disintegrating cots served as an eerie reminder of the large staff that used to be employed by the illustrious Grimbys.

Mélusine grabbed Stanley's arm. "She's here, mon chéri. I can taste her fear."

"*Maman*?! It's me, Stanley!"

The room looked empty, and Eleanor and Stanley kneeled down to look under the beds. In the corner, shivering and praying silently with a rosary in her hand, Norwenn was crouched under the farthest cot.

Stanley ran to her. "Maman?! Please come out! We need to leave now!"

She shoved the cross of her rosary into his face. "Be gone with you, Devil!"

"Oh, for god's sake, Maman, I hoped you were over that! It's not the bloody Devil making me queer. I was just born this way, and now that I've stopped hating myself for it, I'm happy with who I am!"

"Stanley?" she whimpered. "Is that really you?!"

"Of course it's me!" He coaxed her out from under the cot.

"But I just called you! You can't be here! It can't be you!" She pulled away from him. "The Devil is devious!"

He grabbed her hand. "Maman, it's me. Feel my human warmth. You know that the Devil feels different, don't you? He's cold and hard, but I'm warm and alive and as human as they come."

"Stanley?!" She burst into tears as she grabbed him and held him tighter than she ever had before. She was waifish and weak, with dark bags under her eyes, and her fingernails were still dirty and bleeding. "But how did you get here?"

"The angels brought me, Maman. I'll explain it all later." Norwenn eyed Mélusine and Eleanor, and then gave in. "Stanley, Lord Montagu, he's the Devil! He's taken your father's soul and replaced it with madness! He is a savage beast now!"

371

"I know, Maman. The Devil came to threaten us too. He wanted the angels to go with him to Italy to become pawns for the Fascists."

"Those bloody Fascists!" Norwenn exclaimed. "They saw the desperate greed in your father's eyes, Stanley! They exploited it, and the Devil helped them do it!"

"I know, Maman. We can talk all about it later, but right now, we need to leave. Mélusine, can you take all of us?"

Boom.

Mélusine blurred in front of Eleanor and Reggie as they ducked, while Stanley sheltered Norwenn. The bullet blasted a whole in the stone wall behind them.

"Another one, eh? Let's see how bullet-proof you really are! Are you a demon lackey or another self-righteous half-breed?" Lord Grimby hissed.

His hair was completely white and wild, and he hadn't shaved in weeks, giving the grotesque impression that there were roots growing out of the scars that had settled permanently into his face from Surpanakha's maiming of him back on the beach in Australia. He was wearing only a sweaty dress shirt from a tuxedo that had been half-removed quite some time earlier, with the vest open, revealing spots of dried blood on his chest. His trousers were stained with mud, and his right leg was ripped at the knee, as if he'd been running from a beast himself.

"Blimey," Eleanor whispered. "So that's what it looks like when you've been dancing with the Devil."

"He is an unworthy, ma chérie," Mélusine whispered. "That is what it looks like when someone with too much avarice and too little virtue encounters us. It always ruins them. Ravana only hastened his downfall."

Boom.

Mélusine absorbed his second bullet straight into her form.

Lord Grimby reeled with surprise at her completely unaffected state. "You're one of them. You're one of the guardians! But he said you couldn't enter with the spells he put on the house! He swore it!"

"The Devil isn't here to help you anymore," Mélusine spat.

He backed away, looking around frantically at his limited options, and then he aimed his hunting rifle at Norwenn. "So it's a rally of traitors, is it?" He gazed at Eleanor with fiery hatred in his eyes. "Welcome to my humble abode, Jezabel. Were my life's work and my younger son's future not enough for you? You had to take my only love and my firstborn too? Be gone, you she-devil! I know what you really are!"

"I can assure you, you do not," Eleanor replied.

"SILENCE!" he shouted. "Keep that twisting tongue in your mouth, or I'll kill everyone!"

"You most certainly will not," Mélusine said with an annoyed eye roll. Eleanor could see her debating whether or not to simply overpower him, or to let him reveal more details of Ravana's plans with his mad ranting.

"Dad, calm down," Reggie said as he slowly stood up, dropping the butcher's knife on the floor and holding his arm up in surrender. "I know how it feels to have your mind fail you."

"SILENCE!" Lord Grimby screamed. "YOU KNOW NOTHING! You know nothing about being betrayed by everyone you ever loved! All I ever wanted was to make your lives better! All of you! And how to you repay me?! TREACHERY!!!"

"Let's talk about it like civilized men, Dad," Reggie said calmly.

"Do you know what it took to keep Mac by your side for that whole bloody war?! And to get you assigned to the most powerful commander in the whole bloody empire?! The only man on Earth who could keep you alive?! No! You have no bloody clue! All I hear now is whining about your arm and your lungs and your shell-shock! Do you have any idea how much I've done for you? And how did you repay me? By puttering around Oxford dabbling and wabbling, diddling and widdling, and doing every bloody thing you could think of to avoid producing an heir. You're just a weakling, Reggie! A puny weakling who betrayed me and brought humiliation to my title! Do you want it to go to *Stanley*? That queer bloody pouf who dances around in tutus and spends his sinful nights lusting for sodomy?"

"Dad, I didn't realize you were so unhappy with your sons. Why don't you put the gun down, and we can talk about it?" Reggie suggested.

"DON'T PATRONIZE ME, YOU UNGRATEFUL LITTLE BRAT! And *you*!" He gazed at Norwenn scornfully. "Don't get me started on you, you thankless wench. You were nothing, *nothing*! NOTHING BUT A SCULLERY MAID WHORE! And still nothing I did was ever good enough for you! I killed my wife to prove my devotion, and still it wasn't enough!"

"You killed Mum?!" Reggie exclaimed.

"With God as my witness, I never, ever told you to kill anyone!" Norwenn hissed. "You swore she killed herself. You *swore* it, Chester!"

"SHE DESERVED IT! That philandering slut!" Lord Grimby screeched. "And then I forged all the papers so your bastard son would be second in line to inherit my title, and still it wasn't enough!"

"I stayed with you until you sold your soul to the Devil himself," Norwenn whispered. "I told you to send him away, and you invited him right on in."

"Don't you dare bring Lord Montagu into this, woman! If you hadn't insulted him, he wouldn't have taken the measures he did!"

"You let him lock me in the cellar! You let him…" She trailed off squeezing Stanley harder as she gazed into Lord Grimby's wild eyes and the barrel of his gun.

"He let him *what*, Maman?" Stanley whispered.

"Nothing," she whispered. "Nothing for you to worry about, *mon fils*."

"You stood by and let the Devil rape her?!" Stanley exclaimed.

"A whore can't be raped," he spat.

Boom.

Lord Grimby fired right at Norwenn, and in a blur, Mélusine blocked the bullet, absorbing it right into her form.

Boom.

Before she could rip the gun right out of Lord Grimby's hands, he looked down with shock at a gaping bullet wound in his chest.

"And a dead man can't be killed," Stanley rebuked as he looked down at his own smoking gun. "You're dead, *Father.* Now go back to Hell where you belong and wait for the Devil to join you."

"I'll meet you there," Lord Grimby whispered.

He collapsed dead onto the floor.

Norwenn wailed and collapsed into Stanley's arms, while Reggie rushed over to check his father's body.

"He's dead, mon chéri. Leave him to the wolves. It's more than he deserves."

"Are you going to be in trouble?" Reggie asked Stanley nervously. "You know, for patricide?"

"I will call in the troops as soon as we're gone," Stanley said as he held his sobbing mother firmly in his arms. "I've had permission to execute the final option for months now."

"The troops?" Reggie asked dazedly as he stared at Mélusine, still blinking as his mind struggled to comprehend her supernatural speed.

"There's a Secret Service detail that's been watching him for months. They'll want to go through all his papers now. This will be an important breakthrough in fighting the Fascists."

"Why didn't they rescue us days ago?!" Reggie exclaimed.

"I'll ask them later. But for now, let's get the hell out of here. Mélusine, can you indulge us?"

"I will need some help." She closed her eyes and whispered a mantra.

Reggie stumbled backwards as Kuveni appeared beside him. She took one look at Lord Grimby's carcass.

"Good riddance," she muttered. "Stanley, dear boy, your shots are improving by the hour. Now come, come."

She coaxed Reggie over towards Eleanor and Stanley, and without any ceremony, she and Mélusine engulfed all of them into a Yakshini vortex, leaving Lord Grimby's empty shell behind.

They rematerialized in the kitchen in Basingstoke. Edmund and Vibhishana's booming laughter echoed in from the dining room while the children jeered and squealed.

"Bloody hell, that was a trip, wasn't it?" Reggie murmured as he leaned on Kuveni.

Stanley guided Norwenn, who was still crying, to a chair at the table in the corner, and Kuveni led Reggie to sit across from her.

Kuveni snapped her fingers, producing two steaming carpenter's pies and two tall glasses of water. "You both need to eat and drink. Once you've taken care of that, I'll show you to your rooms. You can bathe and rest, and then we will introduce you to the rest of the family."

"The rest of the family?" Norwenn murmured.

"Our beloved Stanley has proven himself to be quite the apt ally for the Avatars of Light. We love him like a son, and so we shall extend that love to you. Do not take it for granted. It is exceptional for us to extend the gifts of our special household to humans. You have seen now what knowing about our world does to the unworthy."

"Is this real?" Reggie asked with disbelief. "I didn't die of starvation in my old bedroom, did I? That would be a crying shame, to make it through the war just to be murdered by my mad father in my childhood bed."

"It is all perfectly real," Kuveni reassured both of them. "Now, Eleanor dearest, your husband and the bairns await you. Vibhi has been keeping them occupied so they don't worry about your absence. I told them that you went over with Percy and Stanley to help Mr. Wilson's cow give birth."

"Don't you think they're going to notice when there's no calf in the barn tomorrow?"

Kuveni smiled. "My dearest girl, do you think I'm an amateur? Mr. Wilson will be thrilled when he wakes up to an adorable surprise in the morning. There are so many dairy cows, the little orphan will be able to choose her own mother. Now come. They are thrilling each other by discussing the most disgusting things they've ever seen (violence excluded, of course). You won't want to miss it."

Stanley grabbed Eleanor's hand and pulled her into a hug. *Thank you, my lady. I can't thank you enough.*

"All in a day's work, Stanley," she whispered. "I couldn't be prouder of you."

"Maman, I'm going to check on the colonel. A butler's duties never cease."

Norwenn nodded, unable to speak through her tears.

Reggie stood up and pulled Stanley into a hug with his good arm. "You know, I have to admit that I never expected you to be the manlier of the two of us, but you were just a bona fide hero, squirt."

Stanley shrugged. "I might be a good shot, but I'm still as queer as a nine-bob note."

Reggie squeezed Stanley's hand. "It doesn't matter, Stanley. You were braver than a frontline private back there. I hope that we can get to know each other now, as we really are? As brothers?"

Stanley hugged him. "Brothers."

"Amma?! Is that you? Are you home?!" Debbie called.

Mélusine tapped Eleanor's arm, morphing her dress back into the scandalous evening gown she'd been hoping to escape all night, and then she sighed with resignation and morphed herself back into the form of Percy.

"Good lord," Reggie murmured. He reached out and touched Mélusine's flamboyant purple jacket. "Is the whole world bloody bonkers now? It isn't just me?"

Stanley guided him back to the table beside Norwenn. "Get some food into your stomach. We have a lot to talk about, *mon frère.*"

And so, with the Devil and his lackey defeated, and two more enemies off of their list of worries, Eleanor and her allies rolled their shoulders, slapped on a smile, and, like the expert liars that they were, they pretended wholeheartedly that the whole world wasn't bloody bonkers.

CHAPTER 23 – FATHER CHRISTMAS?

The day after their defeat of Lord Grimby, General Kettering arrived at noon to join the Marriners for lunch (orchestrated, of course, by Stanley), and then he promptly recruited Reggie and Norwenn into a special taskforce designed to untangle the complicated mess of Lord Grimby's treacherous plans with the Fascists, which Chester had, through some combination of arrogance and madness, documented quite well both in his official papers and in his personal journals, several of which were unstealthily disguised in Breton. In a move that Leo would have admired, Stanley slipped in casually as he offered them the papers to sign that their engagement with the Secret Service also included a perpetual vow of silence regarding any and all unusual happenings relating to Edmund, the Devil himself, and any other powerful beings they happened to encounter.

With the immediate Fascist threat at bay, General Kettering then offered Edmund a new position as the editor of his written histories of the Great War, a role offering a full colonel's salary and military privileges, which Edmund was welcome to perform from the comfort of his own home, with only an occasional visit to London to discuss his progress. Eleanor was certain that the offer was intended to entice Edmund into a pattern of direct meetings with General Kettering, and Stanley confirmed her suspicions, adding that the generals had decided to take the most obvious path towards preventing further defection of important military leaders, mainly by providing them, within reason, with the money and privilege that Il Duce had used to lure Lord Grimby to his doom.

With nowhere left to go, Norwenn took refuge in their household, choosing a room as far away from Stanley's as possible, a choice supported by both of them. She didn't say one more word about her opinion of Stanley's private lifestyle, and instead, she just hugged him and whispered how much she loved him every time they happened to pass each other in the hallway. She took to sitting by the fire in the parlor, translating Lord Grimby's journals, and drinking a constant flow of chouchen (the sweet Breton mead that Eleanor had first tasted on her honeymoon the day she first met Norwenn) provided by Kuveni, who sat with her often, consoling her as she stumbled upon example after ugly example of exactly how evil the man she'd loved for decades really was. Mélusine had been right that Ravana's entrance had not been the beginning of Chester Grimby's downfall, it had only hastened the end.

After a few days of food, rest and recovery, Reggie (now the new Lord Grimby) returned to his doctoral program in linguistics at Oxford, where he had a mountain of final tutorial papers to grade after missing the last two weeks of the term. He was reluctant to leave the haven by the angels' side as Kuveni drove him to the station, as he now had his father's hectares of property to manage, a funeral to plan, and a hereditary seat in the House of Lords to occupy, all while battling the phantom pains in his missing arm and the tormenting war memories that still haunted him day and night. She hugged him tightly and reassured him that all he needed to do was whisper her name, and she'd be there in the blink of an eye to help, whether or not his enemy was visible.

Almost three weeks passed by, and the days became insufferably short and dark and cold. Uma was languishing, and Eleanor tried her hardest to remember her former love of the Scottish climate in the vain hope that somehow her own temperament might extend to the tropical goddess inside of her. It wasn't working. More disturbingly, her efforts to forget Lord Montagu's visit weren't working, and the harder she tried to ignore Edmund's clear relationship to the Devil, the more she noticed nuanced similarities between them. As she pulled away from him night after night and began wearing thick flannel pajamas, he began asking more questions about what exactly had happened with Lord Montagu, to which she couldn't offer anything but lies. He could tell.

"Dearest, please tell me what happened. He's dead now, but it's like he's still haunting you... haunting us. Please let me help?"

"There's nothing you can do, Edmund." It was the only response she could offer that was true. "Please, darling, just be your loving, kind, gentle self, and at some point, I'll get over it."

He'd sigh and turn over. "I'm always here, Eleanor. When you're ready to talk, I will be here."

And so, it was an extremely pleasant relief when, on a very cold, crisp Christmas Eve, Edmund enthusiastically suggested that they take the bairns out to the church's soup kitchen in the village to help distribute Christmas meals to the less fortunate. The suggestion was so saintly (and rather surprising to hear coming from his atheist mouth), that she let herself be drawn in.

"Amma, are you coming?!" Debbie exclaimed as she ran up to Eleanor in the foyer and handed her a wool winter coat in a beautiful sky blue with a thick white fur lining (a more appropriate choice for the soup kitchen than the ostentatious mink, albeit still conspicuously lavish compared to what she knew the villagers would be wearing) and a matching white fur-lined hat that looked a bit too Russian for her taste, although, it was unquestionably warm. Eleanor was quite happy with how smart the combination looked over her long Howard tartan skirt with the blue cashmere sweater with big buttons on the boat neck that she'd worn on their fateful trip to the circus, along with her favorite tall leather boots. "Auntie Kate and Uncle Percy are already there. They've been *cooking* all day!" she winked.

"I see. Darling, which church was it that you said we were visiting?"

"I don't know. I assume it's the big one in the center of town? Kate said we couldn't miss it. There are going to be carolers and wassail and a little carnival too!"

"Yay!" the bairns exclaimed in unison.

"Mum, do you want to come?" Eleanor called towards the library.

"I reckon I'll stay here with Mary in case she bursts at the seams," Moira called back.

Mary was only three weeks from her due date, a fact that had subtly contributed to Eleanor's anxiety for weeks. Mary had continuously insisted that she wanted the child to be theirs, even after the Devil had come to call, but Eleanor hadn't let herself give into the fantasy. After all the lies Mary had told over the months, Eleanor simply didn't have the emotional strength to deal with the disappointment, and so she'd avoided the topic altogether, reiterating every time that Mary brought it up that they could always decide later. She didn't want to admit that 'later' was approaching full steam ahead.

"Mum isn't going to burst, is she?" Charlie asked nervously.

"Not literally. Gramma Moira was just being metaphorical," Eleanor reassured him.

"Let's go, let's go, let's go!" Ruthy exclaimed as she slid down the bannister, landing right in Edmund's arms. She giggled as he twirled her around.

"What's that?" Eleanor asked as she noticed Ruthy holding several dolls in her right arm.

"I'm going to give them away!" Ruthy exclaimed. "Abbi said that lots of other wee lasses don't have any dolls at all, just like I didn't, and I have five now, so I thought they should have them instead. This way I can be like Santa Claus!" She looked down guiltily. "I'm not giving away Netty, though. She's my favorite."

Eleanor hugged her. "I think you're a very thoughtful lass, my little love." She stood up and kissed Edmund gently on the lips. She'd missed the rich flavors of fresh snow and rosemary over the weeks of her malaise-induced abstinence. "And I think you're a very thoughtful man, darling."

He kissed her gently back, and then pulled away, careful not to take advantage of her invitation with a more aggressive move. He offered her his arm, and she took it, allowing him to escort her down the icy steps to the Rolls Royce parked right in front of their door.

They stopped to watch as a sporty little racecar zipped right up the driveway, screeching to a halt behind their sensible family car.

"Whoa!" Charlie and Howie exclaimed in unison as they ran over to examine it. "Is that a Napier?!"

Reggie stepped out of the driver's seat and straightened his suit, followed by a younger man who stepped out of the passenger seat. Reggie looked much healthier than he had after his ordeal, and the young man who looked closer to Stanley's age was exceptionally handsome, with a chiseled jawline that somehow looked especially masculine, bright brown eyes, black hair, and olive-colored skin that was striking in contrast to the crisp white collar of his well-fitted suit. Eleanor wondered if he was a new form of Mr. Montero, but his cheerful, slightly nervous demeanor didn't seem familiar.

"I'm so glad I caught you, Colonel!" Reggie said as he shook Edmund's hand. "I hope you don't mind the intrusion? I have a little Christmas surprise I cooked up for Stanley. Is he around?"

"I reckon I saw him going about his business about an hour ago," Edmund agreed. "Why don't you ring the doorbell? He's sure to be the one who answers."

Reggie winked at the mysterious visitor and gestured for him to hide behind one of the stone pillars, and then he followed Edmund's suggestion, while Eleanor coaxed the girls back out of the way to watch as the surprise unfolded. Reggie bounced up and down excitedly while he waited.

"May I help you?" Stanley's subtle annoyance at the uninvited intrusion morphed into cheer as he realized it was Reggie. "Fancy seeing you here, *mon frère*. Couldn't stay away, eh?"

He pulled him into a hug, and Reggie hugged him back, but then pulled away.

"I was going to get you a wickedly expensive bottle of Scotch, and then I was going to get you a Napier, and then I realized that probably you wouldn't care about either of those things, so I kept them for myself." Reggie winked. "So I asked myself, what would my little brother want if he could have anything in the world, and, well, I think I got it!"

The mysterious stranger stepped up next to him.

"Jules?!" Stanley exclaimed.

He pulled the stranger into a hug, and they both held on for an intimately long moment. Then Stanley cleared his throat and glanced at Reggie, pulling away.

"I didn't realize you were in England?" he said nonchalantly.

"I have a new job, mate. You're looking at the newest junior editor at *The Guardian!*"

Jules spoke with a thick Aussie accent, and Eleanor suddenly put together that this was the man who had helped them so much by refusing to let Lord Grimby slander their names in *The Bunbury Register*. She'd somehow pictured him older... and perhaps less attractive...

Stanley squealed with excitement before he got himself under control. "Congratulations. You earned it, mate."

"Stanley, is everything alright?" Norwenn asked as she approached from the parlor. "Were you screaming just now? Oh, hello, Reggie. What a pleasant surprise." She looked down awkwardly, and Eleanor didn't blame her for not having any idea how to act around either of them after the scale of the changes to their familial circumstances that had unfolded so quickly.

"I was expressing joy, Maman. Reggie brought an old friend over to see me. Maman, this is Jules. We met when I was still living in Australia."

Norwenn politely shook Jules's hand.

"Can we ride in the Napier?!" Charlie interrupted.

Reggie laughed. "If it isn't too much of an imposition, Colonel, do you mind if Jules and I stay over for Christmas? Jules just arrived from Australia, and I have no one to keep me company back at Oxford."

"The more the merrier!" Edmund agreed.

"Then yes, squirt. I'll drive each of you around in the Napier tomorrow," Reggie agreed.

"Yay!" the boys cheered in unison.

Norwenn cleared her throat awkwardly. "Colonel, I believe you only have one spare room left. I will stay at the inn tonight to make room, if it suits you."

"No need, Maman. Jules can stay with me." Stanley glanced at the bairns as his mother cringed at the idea. "The couch in my reading room is really quite comfortable. I'm sure we can set it up as a guest bed."

"Yes, that sounds just fine," Jules agreed.

Norwenn relaxed slightly at the semblance of propriety that Stanley had thoughtfully offered her, and while she was not particularly happy with the blatant reminder of her discomfort, she sighed with resignation and straightened her posture.

"I have never met one of Stanley's friends before. I look forward to getting to know you better. Perhaps I will learn more about Stanley. I must admit that he has finally grown up, and I feel like I hardly know him anymore."

"Maman, perhaps you and Jules can talk about France. Jules's parents moved to Australia from Marseille when he was a boy, and he still speaks fluent French."

"*C'est vrai?* Perhaps you would like some chouchen. It is from my hometown in Bretagne, and I still have half a bottle in the parlor."

"That sounds lovely," Jules agreed.

As Norwenn guided him into the house, Stanley pulled Reggie into a tighter hug. "Thank you. He's much better than a Napier," he whispered. "I wasn't convinced you were okay with this aspect of my life. You were always such a... er... bloke's bloke."

"I was a bit of a bully, wasn't I? I've felt awful about it for years, you know. There I was harassing you left and right like I was the king of the bloody world, and then I came back crippled and madder than a hatter from that wretched war, and all you ever did was help me out. You were the only one who seemed to accept how awful it must have been. Lord knows our father didn't. I'd like to see him get shot at for three bloody years while rats bit through his boots. He was so bloody out of touch with what was happening, Mac must have been telling him all sorts of lies about it."

"Mac," Stanley muttered. "He's dead, you know. He died betraying the angels to our father."

"Well, I'm sure they're getting on like great chums in Hell right now." He glanced at Edmund. "I just finished my father's journals from the war, Colonel. Our wicked father told Mac to stay out by the frontlines so that I would go after him, and you would go after me. We were both just pawns to satiate my father's obsession with testing your limits."

Edmund grimaced. "Then I suppose we were all victims of the misguided whims of a monster." He shook his head. "I will never understand how any man could willingly hurt his own sons so much."

"I never thought he was the nicest man, but I wasn't prepared to learn what a spiteful wanker he really was," Reggie admitted. "It does worry me a bit about who I might become."

As Jules and Norwenn both laughed jovially from inside the parlor, Edmund glanced inside at them, and then put his hand on Reggie's shoulder reassuringly. "No one is doomed to follow in his father's footsteps, my boy, and I have no doubt that you're on the right path. That was a very thoughtful gift you just gave your brother, and your father would have abhorred everything about it."

Stanley and Reggie laughed together. "You've got that right," Reggie said as he relaxed.

As Norwenn and Jules began talking louder and more avidly in French, Stanley smiled with relief. "How did you find him anyway? I didn't even tell you his last name, did I?"

"Our father was going on and on in his journal about his plans for squashing Jules like a bug after he refused to publish those rubbish articles, and I remembered that you'd mentioned how much he'd helped you and how much you were missing him. I thought I'd use my new contacts to look him up, and lo and behold, there he was on a steamer headed straight for Southampton. He was rather surprised when I greeted him at the port, but I managed to barely convince him that it wasn't all a trap set up by our mad father. I'm not sure he totally believed me until you came on out, but he was perfectly obliging anyway."

Stanley lowered his voice. "You can't tell anyone about us, you know. He'll be sacked in a second if anyone finds out."

"Don't worry, squirt. I'm an expert at knowing what not to say. If the chaps at Oxford knew how mad I really was, there's no way they'd be giving me a doctorate with their name on it."

"Abbi, can we go to the Christmas festival now?" Ruthy interrupted.

Edmund whisked her up and twirled her around until she giggled. "Isn't this fun enough? Chatting with grown-ups on the stoop in the cold?"

"No!" she squealed.

"No?!" he exclaimed. "Then we'd better get going!"

Eleanor winked as Stanley waved goodbye and escorted Reggie into the house.

"Stanley, we need more chouchen!" Norwenn called.

"Then, by all means, the no-good butler'd better fetch it!" Stanley declared as he closed the door.

The bairns piled into the back of the Rolls Royce, and Eleanor sat down next to Edmund, putting her hand on his as he shifted into gear. He smiled with intense relief at her showing of affection, and they sped off down the muddy drive towards town.

When they arrived, the whole village was buzzing with excitement. Holly and ivy and wreaths with big red bows were complemented by glittering white electric lights that lit up all of the buildings around the town square. Right in the middle, a massive Christmas tree decorated with the biggest ornaments Eleanor had ever seen towered over several tiny fairy tale cottages that had been set up to serve not just wassail, but swiss raclette, steaming chestnuts, and frosted cookies of all different shapes and sizes with the aroma of sweet ginger and cinnamon uniting them.

"Oh, Johnny, that isn't for you," a woman in a drab wool coat with a baby in her arms and a toddler by her side tsked as she handed a cookie back to Mélusine, who, in the form of Percy, was dressed in a particularly flamboyant red velvet jacket to go with her pointed Santa hat. The whole get-up seemed surprisingly festive for Mélusine's otherwise gruff attitude towards the exploitation of the holiday for commercial ends. "I'm sorry, we don't have money for frivolities," the woman explained shortly.

"Then you are in luck, ma chérie, because everything you see before you is free. Merry Christmas."

"Free?" the woman asked suspiciously. "You aren't going to come round for donations to pay for it next week, are you?"

"Do you think Jesus would have done that?" Mélusine asked curiously.

"I think the vicar would!"

Mélusine smiled as she addressed a growing crowd of people listening in on their exchange. "It's entirely free, my friends. If the vicar comes around asking for money, send him on up to Colonel Marriner's place, and we'll set him straight."

With her believable declaration, the villagers swarmed the stations, and Mélusine threw Monty, who was graciously manning the raclette station in the form of Mr. Marlowe, a look of apology. She glanced over to the opposite station, where Illa was dutifully concentrating on pouring each steaming mug of wassail without spilling.

"You're doing nicely, Illa," she called.

Illa didn't respond, she only stayed focused on her task.

"Merry Christmas!" Kuveni exclaimed as she rushed over to greet the bairns. They were the only car there, so Edmund just parked it right on the edge of the festivities, and the bairns piled out onto the damp cobblestone street. "You're just in time. The soup kitchen is beginning its serving of Christmas dinner inside the church over there, and, my lovely lads, I believe Uncle Percy could use your help serving chestnuts in that little cottage over there."

"Yes!" Charlie and Howie exclaimed as they raced each other to the only remaining empty stand.

Eleanor laughed as they stood up on a stool and began pouring heaps of chestnuts into little paper bags.

"Come one, come all to the amazing Christmas chestnut stand!" Charlie called.

"Now, my darling lasses, you can either help your cousins, or you can help Illa with the wassail, or you can help Abbi and Amma with the dinner inside," Kuveni suggested.

"I want to stay with Amma," Ruthy declared.

"Me too," Debbie seconded.

"I thought as much," Kuveni agreed. "It's warmer in there too. Rumor has it, it's cold enough that it might snow tonight."

"Yay!" they cheered.

"I hope the car does okay," Edmund fretted. "I think horses are a much better bet in the snow. If I'd known, I would have borrowed a couple of Mr. Wilson's mares and dusted off the old buggy."

"Don't worry, Edmund dearest. All will be well with the angels by your side." She winked. "Now come, my little loves, or the vicar will go positively mad. I don't think he's ever dealt with a charity event of this magnitude. I think perhaps we're too much for him."

Edmund chuckled. "I can't imagine why!"

"Why, whatever do you mean?!" Kuveni exclaimed with feigned offense.

Eleanor could see that both of them were reveling in the honesty of the exchange. Whether Edmund fully understood the scope of the magic around him or not, he had certainly spent enough time in the presence of Kate and Percy to recognize that they were simply incapable of hiding all of their unique talents, especially when it came to food and charity.

They followed her inside the church, where a long line had already formed at the end of a massive buffet of silver platters. The elderly vicar was standing at the front of the line, sweating and shaking as he attempted to hold off the crowd.

"We aren't ready yet!" he exclaimed. "Please, just wait one more minute!"

"But, Father Clarke, we've been standing here an hour!" a curmudgeonly old man complained from his position third in line. "That goose is going to be as cold and wet as a fish outta water!"

"Don't let it go to waste!" an elderly woman behind him implored with a hungry look in her eye that didn't help her disguise the self-interest of her selfless declaration.

"Can we help you, Father?" Edmund asked amicably. "Are there some garrisons that need to be fed?"

"Thank god you're here, Colonel! I don't know how your cousin talked me into this!" he exclaimed.

"Kate can be very persuasive," Edmund agreed.

The vicar was unmoved by his cheer as he shook his head gravely. "You don't even come to church, and here you are serving up a Christmas dinner in my parish? You aren't Catholic, are you? Blimey, I forgot to even ask!"

"Father, it's going to be alright," Eleanor chimed in. "We worship in our own way, and today, we're here to help our neighbors celebrate with their stomachs. It is one of the many ways we appreciate the beauty of God's bounty on Earth."

"But we're going to run out of goose with this many people to feed!" he panicked. "I thought we'd only have a handful who heard the announcement at services last Sunday, and then the whole village showed up!"

The people at the back of the line began chattering and jeering at the news.

"My dearest vicar, calm yourself," Kuveni chimed in. "How many times have I told you that we will have enough goose? It will be as if Jesus himself were handing out loaves and fishes… except with more flavor… and with some very rich tasty gravy on the side."

"What shall we do?" Edmund asked as he took off his overcoat, scarf, gloves, and hat and placed them on the closest pew.

Eleanor opted to keep her warm coat on in the cold church, and unbuttoned it while putting her gloves in her pocket. She spotted a pile of aprons and put one on, and Edmund and the lasses did the same.

"Why don't you carve the goose, Edmund, and Eleanor, dearest, why don't you distribute the mashed potatoes. And

Debbie, my dear, you can serve the Yorkshire pudding, and Ruthy, you can serve the Christmas pudding."

"Aww," Debbie whined.

"I will do the Yorkshire pudding and the mashed potatoes," Eleanor offered. "Then you can do the Christmas pudding with Ruthy. Is there a prize in each one?" Eleanor asked Kuveni as she eyed the eight puddings that were lined up to be served.

"It wouldn't be Christmas without a sovereign in the pudding, would it?" Kuveni replied cheerfully.

Eleanor laughed. "You put a whole sovereign in each pudding?"

"Well, I very well couldn't have put half of one, could I?"

The line became even more impatient at the news.

"Why don't you and Ruthy help each other manage the puddings, darling. I think it's a two-woman job," Eleanor suggested.

"Yes!" Debbie exclaimed triumphantly.

"And I will be in charge of refilling our bounty!" Kuveni clapped her hands. "Bon appetite, everyone, and Merry Christmas!"

Edmund began carving the goose with a somewhat ogre-like style that indicated that he had never carved a goose before, although he did get the job done, and Eleanor appreciated his good-natured perseverance as he made it through the entire bird, which was, not so surprisingly, wondrously hot and fresh. As the long line of unfed villagers held their breath, Kuveni ran into the rectory and returned with another whole steaming goose dressed just as beautifully as the first with cranberry sauce, gravy, and roasted root vegetables all around it.

"Where did that come from?" Father Clarke exclaimed. "I don't even have an oven!"

"Did I not say that we would be feeding the multitudes today, my dear vicar?" Kuveni asked nonchalantly.

"Yes... yes, you did say that..." he murmured with fresh humility, as the miraculous nature of their presence fully dawned on him.

As Edmund placed a quarter of the goose on a young girl's plate, Father Clarke glanced at the long line and stepped in.

"Colonel, perhaps I can do that?" he suggested.

"If you'd like. I'm making a mess of it, aren't I?" Edmund agreed affably.

"You were doing just fine, Colonel, just fine..." Father Clarke said as he took the carving knife. "But perhaps you'd like to help your wife."

"Dearest, can I relieve you of those mashed potatoes?"

"Please do, darling."

Eleanor handed him the spoon, and then focused on her Yorkshire pudding, smiling and chatting with the villagers as they came through the line.

After almost an hour, and another eight gooses, Edmund stopped abruptly.

"Ralph?"

"Ralph?" Eleanor repeated.

Ralph Crowden, the man whose foolishness was responsible for their fateful first meeting looked around, pretending he didn't hear them.

"Oh, yeah, hi," he said sheepishly. "I heard there was a Christmas dinner, and I couldn't resist. You know how tragic it is to be an impoverished baron." He laughed awkwardly. "It's a good thing Basingstoke has the Earl and Countess of Easton to keep it on the up and up now. At least one of the local aristocrats can afford to host a dinner instead of just eating one with the rest of the paupers in town."

The people all around him threw him furious looks of offense.

"Did the Barons of Heathfield ever host a Christmas dinner for the town? I don't remember any from my boyhood? I would have found it delightful to come on out in the snow to say hello to everyone over a lovely meal," Edmund replied, quelling some of the brewing outrage.

Ralph scoffed. "Those old misers made Scrooge look like a saint."

"Well, then I suppose it's a good thing for everyone that they're not around anymore squelching Christmas cheer. Perhaps you should be careful not to carry their cantankerous torch."

As Edmund noticed the line behind Ralph getting antsy, he slapped a spoonful of mashed potatoes onto his plate. "Merry Christmas, Ralph."

Ralph shrugged and moved on to Eleanor, noticing Ruthy and Debbie for the first time.

"Good lord, has it been that long? It couldn't have been, could it? Are those children... er... yours?"

Ruthy and Debbie both looked at Eleanor for an answer. "They are," Eleanor replied. "They are as much our children as if I'd birthed them myself. But, your powers of observation are unmatched, Ralph. Ruthy and Debbie were born to my sister Martha who passed away unexpectedly some months back. We've adopted them, and it couldn't be a greater miracle that Debbie and Ruthy came into our lives."

Both girls dropped their pudding duties to hug Eleanor. When she was finished, and she noticed the impatient line stewing behind Ralph, she placed a pudding onto his plate, and then she grabbed his wrist. "Take with you our blessings, my friend. Let them guide you to where you need to be."

She let go, and he stepped back dazedly. Without another word, he took a slice of Christmas pudding from Debbie, and took a seat in a pew in the corner by himself to eat his Christmas dinner.

Eleanor sighed with resignation as she watched him. "Some people just can't save themselves from themselves, can they?"

"He's a scrooge, isn't he?" Debbie asked. "I don't want to be like him."

"Me neither," Ruthy agreed. "Wait, Amma, I forgot to bring my dolls to give away! Can I go get them from the car?"

"I will go with you," Kuveni offered.

Kuveni escorted her outside, while Edmund and Eleanor cheerfully filled plates and wished a Merry Christmas to everyone in line until finally it began to dwindle, which, without Kuveni to refill the food, was good fortune for everyone except the vicar, who looked rather dejected as he served the last bites of goose to a young boy. As a cold draft and a flurry of fresh snow blasted in with the opening of the church's front door, Ruthy ran back inside in tears, followed by Kuveni, who had magically acquired an armful of warm winter coats, mittens, and hats from the boot of their car.

"Amma, someone stole my dolls!" Ruthy cried as she buried her face in the skirt of Eleanor's wool coat.

"Weren't you going to give them away?" Debbie asked.

"But now I can't be like Santa Claus!"

Eleanor kneeled down and coaxed Ruthy onto her knee, wiping away her tears. "My little love, think about how sad this is for the thief. Someone felt the need to steal those dolls because they didn't have any themselves, and now every time they look at them, they will be thinking about what a rotten thief they were."

"My dearest vicar, you're looking quite forlorn," Kuveni pointed out as Father Clarke served himself up some potatoes. "But I daresay you offered up a fine example of selfless Christian charity on this Christmas Eve." She reached under the table and handed him a steaming plate already assembled with a heaping pile of fresh roasted goose in the middle. "Merry Christmas."

He took it gratefully. "Merry Christmas, Kate. I hope we'll see you for services on Sunday?"

"*Peut-être,*" she refused politely. Eleanor reminded herself to call Yvie later.

"Ho, ho, ho!" A familiar voice boomed from the front door of the church. Another blast of swirling snow blew in behind him.

"Santa!" Ruthy exclaimed as her eyes lit up.

A jolly man with familiar sparkling blue eyes who didn't look particularly old other than his long white beard, clad in a rather old-fashioned floor-length red velvet robe lined with soft white fur crossed the threshold into the church.

"Is he with you?" Father Clarke asked Eleanor.

"I reckon he is," Eleanor agreed as she tried to decide whether he was Mr. Montero or Mélusine.

"But it isn't even dark yet!" Ruthy exclaimed. "Santa, you're early!"

She raced around Debbie to reach him as a troop of children followed him inside from the street. He kneeled down as she approached.

"Are you Ruthy MacLeod Marriner?"

She nodded with wide eyes. "How'd you know?"

He winked. "Kate told me all about your generous idea, and she thought that you might enjoy helping me out with my duties. You see, I have this heavy bag of presents here, and it would be much easier if I had an assistant or two to help me give them away."

"Aye!" Ruthy exclaimed.

Debbie demurred. "I don't deserve to help you, father."

Santa glanced over at Eleanor for guidance, and Uma stirred. *Ah. I should have guessed, D.H. It is your holiday, after all.*

Debbie looked down guiltily at Ruthy and then at the other attentive children. "I'm sorry. I shouldn't have said that, father." She smacked her forehead again. "I mean Santa. I mean, Father Christmas. Yes, that's what I meant."

He reached his white gloved hand out to her. "Join us, Debbie. And when we're done, you can tell me all about what's troubling you, aye?"

"Aye," she agreed.

He turned his attention onto the other children, eyeing the ones who were pushing the others for a spot closest to him, and the ones who were putting their younger siblings before themselves, and then he made his choice. He whispered to Ruthy and opened his bag, letting her pick out a beautifully wrapped box to hand to a girl about Debbie's age who was standing politely behind her little brother, who was watching them nervously with his finger in his mouth. Several pushing boys jeered as she passed them up.

"Merry Christmas," Ruthy squealed as she handed the girl the present.

"For me?" the girl asked.

"For you!" Ruthy exclaimed.

Santa whispered into Debbie's ear, and Debbie picked out a box for the girl's brother. They both whispered a wide-eyed 'thank you' and then carried their presents to the pews to sit politely while they watched the other children.

Eleanor leaned into Edmund's arms as they watched Debbie and Ruthy help Santa with his rounds until every child in the church had a present, ending with the pushing boys who became more and more concerned, and then repentant, and then polite as Santa repeatedly passed them up. In the meantime, several different families gasped and jumped with joy as they stumbled upon the sovereigns hidden in the pudding. Kuveni only winked at Father Clarke and held up a mug of steaming wassail in a toast.

As Ralph approached with a stack of dirty dishes he'd collected from the pews, Santa joined them. Kuveni took the dishes, and as Ralph saluted listlessly to Edmund, Santa reached into his bag and handed him a box. With his other hand, he grabbed Ralph's hand.

"Merry Christmas, Ralph. May you find the peace that's been eluding you."

Ralph looked like he might cry, and he took the box, then took a deep breath that dissolved into coughs, and ran right out of the church.

As Santa shook Edmund's hand, Edmund held on for an extra-long moment and looked into his eyes questioningly. His amiable smile grew into a grin as he recognized their visitor.

"I should have guessed. What a nice surprise to see you for a happy occasion. Will you stay for dinner? Mrs. Murray's been working all day."

"I can't, my boy. It's my busiest night of the year!"

Edmund glanced down at Debbie and Ruthy, and his grin grew wider. "How silly of me. Of course! I reckon the reindeer are all ready to go?"

He winked. "They're waiting right outside, my boy, but before I introduce you, I've got a few more tasks here."

He kneeled down and offered presents to Ruthy and Debbie, who hadn't said a peep about themselves the entire time they'd helped him. Ruthy took hers and hugged him, while Debbie looked down at her feet, refusing to take her present.

"You feel like Abbi," Ruthy said. "Are you an angel too?"

"I am," he agreed. "Now, maybe you can open your present with Kate while I talk with your sister."

"Okay," Ruthy agreed as she took a seat beside the polite children who'd gotten their presents first. "My name's Ruthy. What's yours?"

"Come," he whispered as he took Debbie's hand. "Maybe Amma wants to come too?"

Eleanor pulled off her apron and squeezed Edmund's hand. She followed Vibhishana as he guided Debbie into the rectory and shut the door behind them. He put down his bag of presents and took a seat in a simple wooden chair, gesturing for them to sit across from him on an old beat-up loveseat that was patched with several mismatching rags.

As Vibhishana leaned forward confidingly, Debbie hid her face in Eleanor's shoulder.

"Darling, what's wrong?" Eleanor asked. "You can tell us anything, you know. Absolutely anything. Did something happen?"

"I haven't been a good lass," Debbie cried. "I shouldn't get any presents."

"My darling, I promise you that no matter what you've done, we love you, and we'll forgive you," Eleanor whispered into her ear.

Debbie finally looked up at Santa. "Are you really Father Johnson?"

He dissolved his Santa features and sat before her in his vicar's habit.

"I'm sorry I told the other children that you weren't actually Santa Claus," she said miserably.

"Did you? They didn't seem to notice. Sometimes, my child, we are harsher on ourselves than we need to be. In fact, many of the best people are the most critical of themselves. You notice how strict Abbi is on himself? Perhaps even stricter than you think he should be?"

"Aye," she agreed. "But I'm really a rotten lass." She trailed off into more tears. Eleanor kissed her forehead as Vibhishana considered his next move.

"I was impressed that you recognized me. It is quite unusual for humans to be able to see past our disguises. And, because you are so perceptive and kind and trustworthy, I will tell you a little secret that almost no one knows." He leaned in. "I *am* Santa Claus."

Debbie wiped her tears as she calmed down, deciding whether or not she believed him. "But I thought you were an angel."

"Many truths can exist at once, my child. I am Father Johnson, and I am Santa Claus, and I have many other names too. I take different names and different forms depending on my task at hand, and every Christmas, I make a point of helping a few villages embrace the spirit of giving. I don't fly all across the world to every house, but I've found that visiting just a few villages each year is enough to guide humans to do the same. It's actually one of my most successful endeavors in leading by example, although, to be honest, I could do without the long red robes. They used to be more practical before the artists started improvising for dramatic effect." He leaned forward. "Right now, I am just a simple vicar, and in some ways, I'm a bit like your grandfather, because I love Abbi like he's my son. So, you must believe me when I tell you that you can tell us *anything*, and we will still love you."

Debbie hid her face in Eleanor's shoulder again. "I'm glad Mam's dead," she whispered. "I wish she'd died sooner. I wish she'd died before we ever went to Skye, and I hope Da dies too. I dream about killing him sometimes, and it feels so good. He runs and he runs, and I chase him down in the blink of an eye like Abbi, and I shoot him in the back like he shot Mam. I wish you were my real Mam so badly, Amma. I wish they'd never even been born!"

Debbie refused to look at them, she only cried.

Vibhishana threw Eleanor a knowing glance. "My dearest darling, it is perfectly normal for you to feel this way." Eleanor coaxed Debbie into looking up at her. "Your Mam hurt you and Ruthy, and then Abbi and I saved you. It is perfectly natural for you to wish that you'd never suffered, and it is natural for you to want revenge on your father for the evil things that he did. Having these feelings doesn't make you a rotten lass. They make you human." She kissed her on the forehead. "I love you, my darling Debbie. There is nothing rotten about you."

Debbie sobbed. "Are you sure?"

"I'm positive," Eleanor reiterated.

Vibhishana leaned in. "It takes an exceptional conscience to be so moved by your own thoughts, my child. Everyone has dark thoughts from time to time, and those of us who have endured too much struggle more than others. Even I struggle."

"You do? But you're Santa Claus, and an angel... and the Good Lord." He raised an eyebrow. "That's what Gramma Moira calls you. She said not to tell." She suddenly grimaced. "Was I not supposed to tell you either?!"

He smiled reassuringly and took both of her hands. "My child, we have burdened you too much with our secrets. It was not fair of us to tell you so many things that you were not allowed to share, and yet, you have done such a wonderful job of keeping our confidence. I don't think we've told you enough how exceptional you are, and how grateful we are for your help. You are a very special lass, Debbie, a lass worthy of all the love the angels have to give."

Her eyes teared up. "I still have evil thoughts."

"It is what you do with those thoughts that matters. You have taken to punishing yourself for a crime you haven't even committed. Do you know who I see doing the same?" Debbie nodded in the negative. "The most loving, kind, gentle people I know, my child. Just like Abbi and Amma, and even Kate and Percy. It is good to recognize when you aren't proud of your own thoughts, but they do not define your moral character. It is the struggle you are feeling now that defines you, and you, my child, are a good tidy lass."

He whispered a mantra, and then reached into his bag of presents and pulled out a smaller box, wrapped simply in red paper without any bows.

"This is a very special present, my child. It is a present that only a handful of humans have ever received. Amma has one, and now I would like you to have one too."

Debbie carefully unfolded the paper without ripping it, and then gasped as she opened the little black box. On top of a soft white silk pillow, a gold bangle with one sparkling green sapphire on the inside was engraved with beautiful ancient handwriting.

She glanced at Eleanor, and Eleanor smiled. "Would you like Father Johnson to read it to you?"

"It is in Latin, my child. It says, 'the truest heart aches the most but loves the deepest.' I want you to always remember that the pain you feel is the other half of a kind of joy that not everyone can feel. Only very special people are lucky enough to feel so deeply, and you, my child, are one of those people." He slipped it onto her wrist, and it shrunk until it fit perfectly. "It will grow as you grow. And if you or the other bairns ever need me, all you need to do is pray with it, and I will hear you."

Debbie stared at it and then compared it to the one Eleanor always wore. "It's beautiful." She wiped her tears away and sniffled. "I still don't think I deserve it, though."

"Perhaps, my child, you can try to earn it, then. Keep it on to remind you to do the deeds that you believe will make you worthy of it."

"Aye," she agreed.

He glanced at the door. "Father Clarke is coming." With one subtle wiggle, he was back in the form of Santa Claus. He reached down and offered them each a hand.

"You're colder than Abbi now," Debbie pointed out. "I'm sorry, was that rude? I like that Abbi's cold. He feels like home."

Vibhishana smiled. "To tell you the truth, I like being cold too. It is my nature, and it is very useful for flying about on crisp Christmas nights delivering presents."

He glanced past them to the old, beat-up couch, and whispered another mantra. Suddenly, a new, modern red velvet couch was in the same spot, making the rest of the spartan room look particularly shabby. Vibhishana whispered again, and the couch transformed into a comfortable but less showy soft grey wool.

"How'd you do that?" Debbie asked with wonder.

"Do you really want to know? Some people prefer to keep a little magic in their lives."

Debbie thought carefully about her answer, and then she nodded. "I like knowing."

He winked. "So do I."

He whispered another mantra. With a pleasant breeze, Thomas, the Yaksha priest who'd come to counsel Edmund after his massacre on the Orient Express, was standing beside Vibhishana, although instead of being clad in the ostentatious priestly robes from Bulgaria, he was wearing simple orange holy robes in a much more ancient style.

"Thomas is my elf," Vibhishana winked.

"I thought Santa has lots of elves at the North Pole," Debbie said shyly as she reached out her hand to shake Thomas's.

"I only need one when he is such a skilled and generous Yaksha," Vibhishana explained.

"You feel like Kate and Percy," Debbie pointed out. "But they're not elves... are they? I suppose it makes sense with all the gifts they make out of thin air..."

"Yakshas are *not* elves," Thomas reiterated. "And in three thousand years on Earth, I have never once encountered a magical elf, so we'd best not perpetuate the misinformation, my lord."

"It was not meant as a literal statement, my friend, but I see your point." He refocused on Debbie. "Saint Thomas has been helping me with my Christmas offerings since we came up with the idea many hundreds of years ago. It was quite simple at first, but over time, it has required a bit more showmanship than either of us originally intended. It is a common problem for us when we set off on these seemingly simple endeavors."

Thomas snapped his fingers, and another pile of warm winter clothes appeared in his arms. "Kuveni has almost run out of her offerings for the villagers. They'll need them with the storm raging like this. It's much more of a blizzard than I intended, although there is a nice base for the sleigh now. It should be a smooth ride out of town."

"You're going to ride in a real sleigh?" Debbie asked.

"Perhaps someday you and the other bairns will come with me," he smiled. "But not this year. This year, you will have all the Christmas cheer in the world with Abbi and Amma at home."

Thomas stuffed the winter clothing into Santa's bag and then whispered a mantra as he closed it up. "It will produce as many coats as you need."

"Thank you, my friend."

"It is my pleasure as always, my lord. Now, you'd best hurry up if you want to make it through Prague and Bethlehem by morning." He nodded piously to Eleanor. "My lady."

As Father Clarke flung open the door, Thomas dissolved.

"Er... Santa?" he asked Vibhishana questioningly. "I believe your... er... sleigh is waiting out front. You've got quite a crowd waiting to watch your departure."

Vibhishana reached into the bag and handed Father Clarke a festive, bright red cashmere scarf and some matching mittens. "Then I'd better not keep them waiting. I've got a long journey ahead of me."

"Yes... yes, of course..." Father Clarke watched Vibhishana re-enter the church. As he began handing out the coats, Edmund rushed to help him.

"Thank you for hosting our little festival, Father Clarke," Eleanor said. "We'd better be going soon, or we won't be able to make it home in the snow."

As Eleanor led Debbie back into the church, Father Clarke noticed his new couch. "Good lord," he murmured. "Maybe the papers were right..."

"Merry Christmas!" Vibhishana boomed as he and Edmund pulled a conspicuously magical number of winter clothes out of his cheerful red bag. The grateful audience didn't even notice. He finished his rounds with festive red cashmere hats and mittens and scarves for Debbie and Ruthy.

"Thank you, Santa!" Ruthy exclaimed.

He reached into his bag and handed a set to Edmund and Eleanor. Their hats weren't cute little berets like the girls', instead they were long, pointed Santa hats in red velvet lined with soft white fur.

Edmund chuckled good-naturedly as he put his on and adjusted Eleanor's. "You look marvelous, dearest!"

"I think you might be the tallest elf of them all, darling." Edmund did a little jig, and the children pointed and laughed.

"Now, Edmund, my boy, I'd really better be going," Vibhishana said reluctantly. "But you'll want to join me for my favorite exit of the year."

Edmund put on his overcoat and gathered his other winter accessories, while Eleanor kneeled down to help Ruthy and Debbie button up their winter coats before buttoning her own and putting on her delicate white, cashmere-lined gloves from her pocket.

"Now, my children, share your Christmas joy with everyone you meet," Vibhishana declared.

He threw his bag over his shoulder and pushed open the doors into the storm. Darkness was fast approaching, but waiting right in front of the church under the warm yellow lights of several street lamps were not one, but two sleighs. The front sleigh was just big enough for Vibhishana and his magical bag of presents, and was pulled by two majestic reindeer with bells, holly, and red bows braided up the reins. The second sleigh was a traditional Victorian sleigh with two rows of seats and reins attached to two beautiful white stallions, each wearing a big red bow.

"Merry Christmas, Edmund," Vibhishana whispered. "They're yours now. I know you've been missing the polo ponies, but perhaps it's time to settle in a bit here."

Edmund hugged him. "Thank you, Father. Please feel free to come by any time, perhaps tomorrow after you've finished up your sacred duties."

Vibhishana was startled by Edmund's use of the term that was thrown around so commonly by everyone in their divine club but him, but as Edmund winked jovially, Vibhishana relaxed and accepted that the term had been meant in jest.

"Amma, can we go now?!" Ruthy exclaimed. "My ears are freezing!"

Eleanor pulled the beret down over Ruthy's ears and wrapped her arms around her.

"Merry Christmas to all, and to all a good night!" Vibhishana declared one last time for the enamored crowd. As he hopped onto his sleigh, he saluted to Edmund, winked at Eleanor and Debbie, and then used his operatic tenor voice to sing, "Ho ho ho," as he set off on the fresh layer of snow straight out of town.

Charlie and Howie were already bundled up in the back seat of the remaining sleigh under a pile of fur blankets, wearing their own matching red hats and scarves. Eleanor helped Debbie and Ruthy squeeze in beside them, and then Kuveni jumped onto the back of the sleigh.

"Let's get home, Edmund dear, before it's too dark!"

Eleanor scrambled onto the sleigh beside Edmund, and he took the reins.

"Merry Christmas!" he called to the crowd. "Hya!"

The bairns squealed with the thrill as the sleigh took off at a surprising speed, but even as they drove through the wind and the heavy snowflakes, Eleanor felt surprisingly warm. "Thanks, Kuveni," she whispered.

"Merry Christmas, Mistress Eleanor. The night has just begun."

By the time they pulled up the drive, the snowfall had slowed to a gentle flurry of fluffy flakes, and twilight was setting. Several feet of fresh snow covered everything in a thick layer of white frosting, and blobs of snow attached to every leaf and branch made the forest look magical, like gumdrops and powdered sugar adorning a gingerbread wood. The remnants of daylight illuminated the sparkling white snow, giving everything an unusual glow against the pink, cloudy sky, and the house was warm and cheerful with a yellow glow inside and thousands of electric lights illuminating its renaissance architecture on the outside. Sweet-scented smoke puffed out of each of its many chimneys, and movement and laughter emanated from the front parlor.

As Edmund slowed the sleigh to a stop at the front steps, Eleanor finally pulled down her scarf and took a deep breath of the fresh, crisp air.

"I love fresh snow," she sighed. "It makes it really feel like Christmas."

"It really does feel festive, doesn't it?" Edmund said cheerfully as he hopped out of the driver's seat and into the snow. "It hasn't snowed this much here since the great blizzard of 1881. Hello, what's this?" He sunk into the drift, and wiggled his foot around. Eleanor and the children leaned over to see what he'd kicked, and then Eleanor burst into laughter.

"Darling, I don't think Reggie's Napier has a very bright future."

"Oh no!" He dug out a little more snow with his foot, revealing that the sleigh had just parked on top of the low-lying sports car that had been completely covered by the drift. "I'll have to buy him another one!"

"It might not be hopeless," Kuveni said as she hopped off the back of the sleigh and joined him. "There could always be a Christmas miracle."

"Hop out of the way, darling. Let's get the sleigh off of it. It's possible that there's enough snow that our weight didn't crush it. I didn't feel it sink, did you?"

"I suppose not." He helped Kuveni up the snowy, crunchy stairs to the front door, and Eleanor took the reins, clicked her tongue, and coaxed the horses several feet forward.

"How's that?" she called.

"I think it has a fighting chance," Kuveni winked. "Now come inside and warm up before you freeze right through! I'll ask Mr. Marlowe to tend to the horses."

Eleanor helped the bairns out of the back and held Ruthy and Debbie's hands as they carefully climbed up the slippery stone stairs.

The door swung open, and Stanley, looking quite a bit rosier than normal, stumbled out to greet them. "Merry Christmas, my dearest Marriners!" he declared. "Come inside! Mrs. Murray has been fretting for hours that you wouldn't be home in time to enjoy her Christmas goose in all its glory!" He leaned on Edmund. "I strongly recommend the chouchen, Colonel. It tastes much better than I remember it tasting when I was a lad."

Edmund chuckled. "I daresay you've tasted quite a bit of it since we last saw you, my boy."

"Have I? I lost track!"

Edmund guided him into the house and seated him in the parlor on the couch beside Jules and across from Norwenn and Reggie, all of whom were glowing and giggling.

"*Mon dieu*, it is a family of saints!" Norwenn exclaimed when she saw their matching hats. The four of them laughed heartily at her joke, while even the children giggled at their tipsy state.

"Amma, can we drink chouchen?" Charlie asked.

Eleanor laughed. "Perhaps you can have a sip with dinner. You will have to be a grown-up, though, before you can drink enough of it to be so silly."

"Aww," he whined.

"It might make you a wanker, ye know," Howie whispered. "Like Da."

As all of Charlie's cheer dissolved, Illa rushed out of the kitchen to greet them. She was wearing the same Scottish outfit she'd copied from Kuveni when they'd rescued the bairns, although she looked much more comfortable, as if her months of practice interacting with humans was finally paying off.

"Welcome home, my lord." She bowed and then immediately started helping them remove their snowy coats, subtly dissolving all of the moisture as she hung them in the closet. "If you will follow me, Mrs. Murray is ready to serve your meal in the dining room."

Edmund took Eleanor's hand and led the way, and as they reached the dining room where the rich aromas of spices and roasted goose filled the air, he pulled her into a romantic twirl. He kissed her gently on the lips, but then glanced down apologetically. "I'm sorry, dearest, I didn't mean to push you."

"Don't be, darling." She kissed him again. "I'm sorry I've been so distant. I've missed being in your arms."

He pulled her closer to him, but as his excitement erupted and she felt a pang of arousal, she pulled away, and he cleared his throat, blushing intensely with embarrassment as he took several breaths to get himself back under control as he noticed that Moira and Mary were already seated at the center of the table watching them.

"Where did the bairns go?" he asked as he noticed that they hadn't followed.

On cue, the bairns, along with Kuveni, Mr. Montero, and Mélusine, helped Stanley, Norwenn, Reggie, and Jules stumble into the dining room.

"Blimey, I'd better go help Mrs. Murray!" Stanley exclaimed as he almost fell over.

"No need," Mrs. Murray said as she joined them. "Illa has volunteered to take your place for the evening. Now sit down and get some food into you, Stanley, before you remember this Christmas for the wrong reasons."

"*If* you remember it at all, *petit frère!*" Reggie teased.

He helped Stanley stumble to the table and tipsily maneuvered Jules next to him. Once all four of the drunken diners were seated at one end of the table, Edmund took his place at the head, and Eleanor and the bairns gathered around him, leaving room for Kuveni, Mr. Montero, and Mélusine in the middle by Moira and Mary.

When they were all seated, Illa came in carrying a huge silver platter. "Oh dear, Illa! You're going to burn your hands without any gloves on!" Mrs. Murray exclaimed.

Illa placed the platter right in front of Edmund. "I'm fine, Mrs. Murray. Look." She showed Mrs. Murray her perfectly unscathed hands. Mrs. Murray looked confused, and then reached forward to lift the lid of the platter, but she pulled her hand away as she touched it and yelped, putting her finger in her mouth to cool it.

Illa lifted the lid with her bare hand, bowed, and then returned with it to the kitchen.

"This looks scrumptious!" Edmund exclaimed as he took in a deep, satisfied whiff of the roasted goose. "I daresay it looks even better than the gooses we were serving earlier today, and I didn't think that was possible!"

"Neither did I," Kuveni laughed. "Mrs. Murray, I'll have to get your recipe."

"Yes… yes, of course…" Mrs. Murray murmured distractedly. "They must have stronger skin down in South America, I reckon…" Edmund's stomach grumbled loudly. "I'll go help Illa fetch the rest of the meal… with gloves."

"Tell us about your afternoon, Colonel!" Reggie said cheerfully. "Did you see Saint Nick down at the church?"

"We did!" Ruthy squealed. "Santa came, and he gave all the children presents, and I got to help!"

"He wasn't really Santa. He was Father Johnson," Howie clarified.

"He was too!" Ruthy argued. "We saw him! Didn't we, Debbie?"

"Many truths can exist at once," Debbie replied.

"What does that mean?" Charlie asked.

"He was Santa," Debbie shrugged. "Ruthy's right."

"Told you so!"

"So you helped feed the poor?" Mary asked.

"We fed everyone!" Ruthy exclaimed. "Everyone from the village came! It was like Jesus with the fishes, but with gooses and pudding!"

"Howie and I gave out chestnuts just like the Christmas market in Edinburgh, but they were free! People didn't even believe us at first!" Charlie added.

The bairns jumped right into a proud description of their roles in the village festivities as Illa and Mrs. Murray served up the rest of the dishes, and the grown-ups listened with genuine interest as the bairns talked all about the many things people had told them about the colonel's grandfather, old man Marriner, the kind old painter who'd employed quite a few of them for odd jobs around his estate way back in the 1880s. The conversation morphed into stories of Christmases long past, then of Christmas traditions in Marseille and Australia and Bretagne and even India, until all the food was gone, and Edmund was rubbing his stomach with satisfaction.

"Amma, do you think Santa will come tonight?" Charlie asked.

"He doesn't need to come!" Ruthy argued. "We already saw him!"

"I meant the real Santa," Charlie said haughtily.

"I reckon he will," Edmund moderated their sibling spat. "But only if you're all asleep in bed. Shall we go get ready for bed and read a story so he can come?"

"I don't need anything else," Debbie sighed. "I already have everything I need."

Eleanor reached over to hug and kiss her. "I feel exactly the same way."

"I hope he comes soon!" Ruthy exclaimed. "We made cookies for him this morning with Mrs. Murray. Do you think he'll eat them, Amma?"

"I have absolutely no doubt," Eleanor agreed with a wink at Edmund.

"It's pretty early to go to bed," Charlie sulked.

"You can keep reading on your own, if you'd like. Santa might not notice as long as you're quiet as mice," Eleanor suggested.

"Aye," Charlie agreed.

He got up and raced Howie to the door, and then Ruthy and Debbie followed.

"Get ready for bed, and we'll meet you upstairs in a minute!" Eleanor called. "Abbi needs to choose a book!"

"It'll be ten minutes then, I reckon," Edmund laughed.

"More like twenty," Moira scoffed good-naturedly.

"Darling, do you have *The Night Before Christmas* on your shelf?"

"I reckon I do!" he said happily as he got up. "Now, let me think what section would I have put it in?"

"Wait!" Mary exclaimed. "Please wait a minute," she said more calmly. "Before you follow them upstairs, I have something for you. Stanley, can you get it?"

Stanley leaned back in his chair and opened the closest silverware drawer behind him. He pulled out a stack of documents and worked his hardest to soberly hand them over.

"*Venez*," Norwenn whispered to Stanley and Jules as she leaned heavily on Reggie to stand up. "Let's let them be."

"I will help Mrs. Murray in the kitchen," Mr. Montero said as he took their cue to leave.

As Kuveni and Mélusine stood up, Mary gestured for them to stay. "Please stay, this concerns you too."

As soon as the room had cleared out, Mary handed the stack of papers to Eleanor. "I know ye dunne believe me, and I know why, but I meant it, Ellie. It's all there. Charlie and Howie and the new bairn are all yers. I only ask that they keep our name so they dunne forget who they are... MacLeods. I changed mine back too, now that I'm divorced."

"You did this all on your own?" Eleanor asked as the reality of what it meant barely hit her.

"I asked Stanley fer help, and he called up a solicitor and a magistrate that General Kettering recommended. They helped me do it up all proper. They said that because treason is a capital crime, and Fergus is off wit Jimmy and the Italian Fascists now, that he's a dead man walking, and he doesn't have any legal claims left to the bairns, so they only needed my signature. I got the divorce fer unreasonable behavior. It didn't take much convincin' after what happened to Martha."

"You don't have to do this," Eleanor said as she thumbed through the papers. Edmund stood behind her, reading them over her shoulder. She could feel him tense with some combination of nerves and excitement.

"That's why I did it without ye, Ellie. I wanted all of ye—you two, the bairns, the judge, and Mam—to know that it wunne coerced. And that's why I'm also leavin'. I already accepted a position as a secretary at a girls' school up in the outskirts of Edinburgh, not too far from Elphinstone. I'll start as soon as the new bairn is weened. They said they'd wait fer me to take my time."

"But you don't have to do that!" Eleanor exclaimed. "Mary, we don't want to run you out of town! It's good for Charlie and Howie to know you!"

"I know. And I'm not runnin' away, Ellie. But they can only have one Mam, and it's better fer them if yer her. I'll come down and visit fer all the holidays, and maybe ye can come on up once in a while before they talk entirely like sassanacks." Eleanor's eyes teared up at the unexpected selflessness of the plan. "I want this, Ellie. I thought about what ye said, about how I'd never worked a day in my life, and yer right. I dunne. I dunne know what it feels like to make my own way, and I wanna know. I was in secretarial school when I met Fergus, ye know. I sometimes wondered how my life wudda been different if I'd done it. Now I'll know. All ye have to do is sign on the dotted lines."

Eleanor put the papers down and rushed around the table to carefully hug her. "I love you, Mary."

"Ye've given us all a life that we dunne imagine, Ellie," Mary whispered back. "I'm gonna earn it now."

Eleanor hugged her again. "We'll keep your room for you. You should come down whenever you can."

"Aye," Mary agreed. She grimaced and rubbed her belly. "She agrees. She's gettin' ready to make her appearance, I reckon."

"You think it's a girl now?" Eleanor asked curiously.

414

"Percy and Kate swear it," Mary replied. "And I reckon they know a thing or two more than I do about these things."

Mary put Eleanor's hand on her stomach to feel her kicking. "Blimey, she is strong, isn't she?"

Mary smiled. "Just like her Amma, Ellie."

Eleanor squeezed Mary as tears ran down her face. "Thank you."

"I hope yer ready fer another daughter, Abbi. I hear they're a handful." She gestured for him to come around the table to join them, and then she placed his hand on her belly.

"Good lord," he murmured as the baby kicked. He smiled as his eyes teared up. "That's our daughter."

"Amma, are you coming? We're ready for bed!" Ruthy called.

"Go," Mary said as she wiped away her own tears. "I'll be in the library like always, waitin' to burst."

Kuveni handed Edmund an illustrated copy of *The Night Before Christmas*. "Go on up, my darlings. Read to the bairns. I'll help Mr. Marlowe clean up down here and get us ready for morning."

"Yer a good lass, Mary MacLeod," Moira whispered as she patted Mary on the shoulder and then pulled her into a hug. "I'm glad to finally see ye in yer full glory."

Eleanor led Edmund up the stairs. She could feel his heart pumping. "I can't believe it's real," he whispered. "It is a true Christmas miracle. I don't think I'm going to ever be able to be a scrooge again."

"As if you ever were!" Eleanor laughed giddily.

"You saw that picture of me from 1895," he pointed out.

"Everyone looks like that at some point, darling. I'm sure you were as thoughtful and generous as a man could be. It sounds like the villagers spoke very highly of you earlier today."

"To be honest, I was shocked that so many of them remembered me."

"I think you make a bigger impression than you realize, darling."

"Ditto." He snuck a kiss and then squeezed her bum as she kissed him back. "Come on, we've still got a long night ahead of us."

"Is that a proposition?" Eleanor teased.

"It's a surprise," he winked.

She followed him into their bedroom where all four bairns were in their pajamas, snuggled up under the covers of their royal canopy bed with the dogs sprawled across their feet.

"Yay!" the bairns exclaimed as they saw what book he had. They made room for Abbi and Amma to snuggle into the middle of their huddle.

"Did you know, my bairns, that this is the first time I've ever read this poem out loud? I can't think of a better night to do it than right now with all of you." Edmund kissed each of them on the forehead.

"I love you, Abbi," Debbie whispered.

"Me too," Charlie seconded.

"Me three," Howie agreed.

"Me four!" Ruthy squealed.

"*A Visit From Saint Nicolas*, by Clement Clarke Moore." As the bairns nestled into his arms, Edmund sighed contentedly. "*'Twas the night before Christmas, and all through the house, not a creature was stirring, not even a mouse...*'"

The children engaged enthusiastically as Edmund read them the whole poem, and when he was finished and he maneuvered to get up, they jeered.

"But, my bairns, I've got work to do!"

"Are you Santa too?" Debbie asked seriously.

"There is only one Santa," he replied. "But perhaps the angels help him out just a bit from time to time."

Eleanor was genuinely curious about what he meant, since in the three years of their marriage, he had never once expressed an interest in doing anything particularly festive for Christmas.

As Edmund helped Eleanor out of the pile of bairns, Charlie pulled a book out from under the covers. "Can we stay here and read together, Abbi?" he asked.

Edmund grinned as he noticed which book he had. "I think that's a wonderful idea."

"*A Christmas Carol* by Charles Dickens," Charlie began, imitating the way Edmund always started their storytimes. "*Marley was dead, to begin with. There is no doubt whatever about that. The register of his burial was signed by the clergyman, the clerk, the undertaker, and the chief mourner…*"

Eleanor closed the door gently, and Edmund took her hand. He guided her down the staircase, glancing in at the parlor to spy all four of their drunken revelers dozing on the couches by the fire. As they reached the kitchen, all of the food and dishes were put away, and Mrs. Murray and the Yakshas were nowhere to be found.

Eleanor's heart raced with excitement as she spied a twinkle of mischief in his eye. He lifted up his heavy old iron stove and placed it to the side, and then pushed open the door to the secret passage down into his lair that he'd shown her for the first time the day after their engagement. He took a kerosene lamp off a hook on the wall and lit it, and then pulled the door closed behind them as he guided her down into the old stone cellar.

"You *have* been busy!" she exclaimed.

It was spotless. From wall to wall, the stone floor had been covered by a soft persian carpet. All of his old clothing and junk had been put away in a series of dressers and wardrobes along the far wall blocking his secret compartments that were built into the wall, while the other walls were covered in his neatly hung paintings. A deep green velvet couch with soft white furs draped over the back was pushed against the wardrobes to make room for a heaping pile of toys in the middle. In the closest corner, their Victrola from their house in Australia was neatly tucked alongside their stack of records.

Edmund placed the pin on the record and turned on the gramophone to one of their favorite ragtime albums. "Kate and Percy helped a bit. Kate's Christmas gift to us was bringing the Victrola on up, as long as we don't ask how she did it."

"It's all marvelous, darling! Have you been collecting Christmas presents for weeks? I'm sorry I've been so preoccupied. I completely forgot to shop."

He poured her a glass of cognac from a bottle beside the Victrola and then poured one for himself. He clinked her glass, and then enticed her into a silly little dance as they both sipped it.

"Blimey, where'd you get this?"

"It's rather atrocious, isn't it?" He blushed. "It was a free gift thrown in by Harrods as a consolation for my terrible negotiation skills."

"I didn't think you needed to negotiate at Harrods?"

"Neither did I."

He twirled her around, and she laughed with the thrill. God, how she'd missed the simple pleasures of being silly with him, as if they didn't have a care in the world.

"You remember last week when I was late coming home from my meeting with General Kettering?"

"Aye."

"I may have stopped for some Christmas shopping in London… and it may have gotten a bit out of hand."

Eleanor laughed. "Were there any toys left for the other children of England?"

"Maybe one or two."

He released her from their dance and dug into the pile. He pulled out a cute little box wrapped in gold foil paper.

"This is for you, Eleanor."

"Shouldn't I wait until morning?"

"You can do as you'd like. I thought it might be more romantic if you opened it now… I thought… I thought perhaps it

418

could be a new tradition for you to open your present while we wrap the other presents for our children."

Eleanor kissed him. "I think it's a wonderful idea, darling."

She carefully unwrapped the box and gasped as she opened it. A pair of earrings with enormous blue sapphires surrounded by diamonds and a matching necklace with a blue sapphire that rivaled the one on her wedding ring sparkled in the light of the kerosene lamp.

"In case you ever want to wear a color other than green."

"Good lord, Edmund. These must have cost a fortune!"

"It doesn't matter, Eleanor. I'm ashamed that I haven't given you more jewelry over the years. You're still mostly wearing that paste that Shruti gave you."

"I don't need to go about town adorned in royal jewels, darling, but I love them all the same." She kissed him again.

"Good, because I think if the Earl of Easton comes back to Harrods to return his wife's rejected gift, it might end up in the tabloids." He chuckled and shook his head. "Someday, Ravi will have to tell us how he managed to perpetuate that title so thoroughly. It is the joke that just won't end."

He put the necklace on her, carefully placing it underneath her green pendant from Mélusine. She took off the pendant and put it in her pocket, and then she shivered as he kissed her neck. She put on the earrings, and then looked over at herself in the mirror of one of the wardrobes.

"They're lovely, darling. Thank you. I suppose this means we'll have to go out on the town sometime so I can wear them, although they will probably look best down here in your lair as a complement to my naked breasts."

She kissed him again, but he pulled away. "I don't want to push you, Eleanor. I didn't give you a gift so you'd feel pressure to be with me if you're not ready. I gave it to you because I love you."

God, how she loved that man.

She kissed him again. "I love you, darling. Sometimes it's hard for me to fathom how much I love you, and then you prove to me over and over again how much you deserve to be loved. Now, before we distract ourselves, what do we need to get done before morning?"

He sat down on the floor in the middle of the room next to the presents using the Hyderabadi style that always looked so strangely natural to him. He gathered up some wrapping paper and scissors and tape, and then motioned for her to sit beside him while he began wrapping a beautiful porcelain doll with flaming red curly hair wearing a kilt.

"Ruthy is going to love that, darling. What a wonderful choice," Eleanor said as she collected a matching set of cricket bats and balls to start wrapping for the lads.

They wrapped to the beat of the ragtime band for a very long time, stopping often to turn over and then switch the records, working their way through Edmund's excessive generosity, until Eleanor's back and legs were aching. As the pile dwindled, Eleanor gathered her wits, until finally Edmund tied the last bow and the record ended, and she forced herself to bring up the topic that they'd been agonizingly dancing around for weeks.

"Darling, I need you to know that Lord Montagu didn't rape me."

Edmund stopped and put his supplies down on the floor to focus on her, but he didn't say anything.

"I know why you think he did, because I've been so distant lately, but the truth is that he tried, and he almost succeeded. I stabbed him through the belly with a fireplace poker, and then my mother shot him, and then Stanley shot him. Mr. Johnson helped us clean up the mess before you got home with the bairns."

Edmund thought for a long time before responding. "It took that many tries to kill him? You don't think... you don't think he's like me, do you?"

Eleanor thought carefully about her answer, and as she contemplated how painful the prior weeks had been as she'd silently stewed in her own misery, she decided that she wasn't going to do it anymore.

"Yes, darling. I'm certain that he was. After I stabbed him, he popped right back up. It was the first time I haven't been able to fight off a man on my own."

"How many times have you had to fight off a man?"

She took a moment to quantify her many unpleasant experiences. "About twelve, give or take, depending on your definition. That doesn't include the maniacs at the asylum, of course. Those men go on a separate list because I knew what I was getting into by bathing them."

"Twelve?!"

Eleanor shrugged. "Living in France during the war was a dangerous thing to do, darling. I was constantly surrounded by horny men who knew they were going to die. I was lucky it wasn't more."

"No wonder you wanted to carry a gun. Leo was right."

"Leo was right, but a gun wasn't enough for Lord Montagu. When I heard someone come inside the house uninvited, I thought I might be in trouble, so I took it out of the box in our closet and strapped it to my leg, but I couldn't get to it in time. He had me cornered, and he was too strong for me to fight off."

"I wish I'd been there. I would have stopped him, Eleanor."

"I have no doubt, darling. But if you'd been there, it would've been even uglier than it was. Too ugly for the bairns to witness. It was already like a scene out of a penny dreadful. It was as if all the things that are different about you that I love were twisted into something dark and violent. I'd never thought of them as quite so sinister before, and I haven't been able to shake it off."

"Is that it, then? Is that why you've been scared of me?"

"I hoped I was hiding it," she admitted.

"I can taste fear, Eleanor. You've never been afraid of me, not even after you saw me kill all those men on the Orient Express. I've been worried that whatever it was was never going away. I thought perhaps... perhaps Mr. Johnson told you something about me that you couldn't forgive."

Eleanor stood up and stretched her legs before kneeling down right before him and kissing him gently on the lips. "Darling, I love you. I love all that you are. There is nothing Mr. Johnson could tell me that would make me love you any less. The truth is that I have never felt more powerless than I did in those moments, and my memory has been tormenting me for weeks with flashes, almost like shell shock, as if I'm reliving the whole thing again and again. All I can think about is how bloody terrified I was that he'd win, and you and the bairns would get home and find me raped and dead on the parlor floor. I have never, ever been that scared in my life, and I think that's why I haven't been able to get over it." She was grateful as she said the words that she finally believed that they were true.

Edmund's eyes turned black at the idea, and he whispered his mantras. "Do you think he's dead now, or do you think he might come back? If you'd stabbed and shot me, I would have come back stronger."

Eleanor resigned herself to delving a step deeper into the truth. "I don't think he'll be back, darling. Stanley shot him with a special bullet that Mr. Johnson gave him. It is designed to stop otherwise unstoppable people."

Edmund took several minutes to think about the implications. "That means that Mr. Johnson knew that one of my people might come after you. Why wouldn't he have warned me? Unless... unless it was to protect you from me."

"Darling, he trusts Stanley, and it is good to have human allies who can help us do things we can't do ourselves. The bullet is made of a substance that would be quite dangerous to you. Mr. Johnson told me that even he can't touch it."

"I suppose I'd better not cross Stanley then." He meant the statement facetiously, but then he considered the idea seriously. "Did he get the bullet back?"

"He did. The whole thing was quite gory, but Stanley still has it, in case someone else uninvited shows up."

"So your mother and Mary saw the whole thing unfold?"

"They saw enough."

"That explains why they were scared of me that night... but then after our dinner with Mr. Johnson, they seemed to forgive me, but you were still scared."

"I'm sorry, darling. If it's any consolation, I love you even more now. You've been so patient and kind and supportive. I have seen a side of you that I'd never seen before. It makes me so impatient to see you with... our daughter. You are such a wonderful father, Edmund. Watching you coddle the bairns as I've been struggling has been a beautiful reminder of the depths of your kindness... of why I fell in love with you in the first place."

He leaned forward and kissed her. "I love you, Eleanor. You are such a wonderful mother. The bairns could not be luckier to have you, and neither could I. I must admit, though, that it feels a bit wrong to be so happy about our good fortune being bred from such misery. If your sister and the bairns hadn't endured so much pain, they never would have come into our lives. Our new daughter wouldn't even exist. Can you imagine that that tiny foot kicking out of Mary's belly is a person?"

"It really is hard to believe. But we shouldn't get ahead of ourselves. It will be a painful and dangerous process for Mary to bring that person into the world. There is a lot that could still go wrong."

"Yes... yes, of course. I know I shouldn't be so excited about it, not yet, especially after everything that's happened this year, but I'm getting a bit giddy when I think about it. Her hands are going to be so tiny!"

"I'm sure Mr. Johnson would tell us to embrace the miracle of it all." She pulled off her cashmere sweater. "Like the miracle that it took for us to meet in the first place."

He pulled off his jacket and vest, and then she reached forward and helped him unbutton his shirt. "And for me to get up the nerve to talk to a woman so beautiful."

He unsnapped her bra, and as she tossed it onto the floor beside them, he ran his fingers gently across the supple flesh of her breasts. She shivered with pleasure, and then pulled off his undershirt so that she could return the favor. As his nipples hardened, they hastily ripped off their bottoms, and Eleanor straddled him. Her loins ached with desire. She hadn't felt such painfully urgent arousal in months, since their weeks of reticence after the bairns had first arrived in Australia.

"You can't taste my fear at all anymore, can you?" She leaned down to lick his lips, and he licked her back.

"God how I've missed your taste," he whispered. "You taste like my beloved, Eleanor. Like the woman who gave me a life I didn't even know was possible."

They both sighed with satisfaction as he entered her. She lay her head down on his cool chest, listening to his human heartbeat, and then she licked his nipples and worked her way back to his mouth.

"Make love to me, Edmund. Love me like a husband should love his wife on Christmas Eve while their children are sleeping peacefully upstairs dreaming of sugar plums."

She moaned as he thrust, and their divine energy intertwined, but instead of giving into the magnetism of their otherworldly connection, she focused on all that was human about her beautiful, kind, gentle English soldier. She felt the life emanating off of him and felt for the blood pumping through his veins. She felt the heat of him inside of her as every bit of his warmth channeled into her, and she held his hands pulsing along with the rhythm of their hearts beating in sync. She rode him and kissed him and felt the softness of his skin against hers until she couldn't hold off any longer, and together they gave into a wonderfully human orgasm.

Eleanor collapsed and then leaned into the nook of his arm, cuddling up and putting her head on his chest.

"I missed you, Edmund, but I think I needed that time away. It helped me appreciate how much I love you."

He kissed her forehead. "I love you, Eleanor. All the poetry in the world cannot begin to express how whole I feel when we are together."

As she finally let the stress of the last several weeks dissolve, her fatigue hit her. "I suppose we shouldn't sleep too long."

"Do you think we should go upstairs now?"

"I want to lie naked in your arms, and the bairns are asleep in our bed. I'm sure Kate will fetch us when the time comes."

He yawned. "Then I suppose we shall leave our punctuality to fate and the angels' meddling."

"Kate, wake us when it's time," Eleanor called.

Edmund looked around, momentarily waiting for an answer, but Kuveni knew well enough not to answer either of them with a disembodied whisper.

"Goodnight, darling."

"Goodnight, dearest."

And in each other's naked arms, the two lovebirds slept.

PART FOUR
INEVITABLE

CHAPTER 25 – LOOPHOLE

Eleanor was shivering violently when she jolted awake. It was pitch dark. The kerosene lamp had gone out. Edmund's arms were frigid. But, that wasn't the source of her problem.

She sat up and gasped as a fierce pain cut through her abdomen like a butcher's knife cutting straight through a slab of fresh meat. The pain was throbbing and piercing at once, burning her from the inside out, but it wasn't hot... in fact, it was wickedly cold. It was as if a block of ice was carving a nest amidst her hottest organs, and they were cowering and withering against an acute case of ice burn. She muffled a whimper, and as Edmund stirred and rolled over back into sleep, she stood up and almost fell over as a ferocious spasm unlike anything she had ever felt before stabbed her again.

"Kuveni," she whispered. "Help!"

A wave of nausea rolled over her as she felt herself dissolve. She leaned on Kuveni as they materialized in the room that Kuveni and Mélusine had taken as theirs in the attic of the house, but unlike every other time when Eleanor had been able to let the lightheadedness of her Yakshini transportation pass, the hot nausea overwhelmed her, and Eleanor vomited the contents of her mostly empty stomach onto the floor. She and Kuveni noticed at the same time that it had an unquestionably violet hue to it.

"Kuveni?" she whimpered.

She already knew what it meant. She'd known it the moment she'd felt the knife slicing into her organs, readying her body to incubate a fetus that would be distinctly more frigid and less human than she was.

Kuveni only stared at it with horror, and then she whispered a quiet mantra, and Mélusine appeared beside them.

"*Mon dieu*," Mélusine murmured.

She placed her hand on Eleanor's bare belly, closed her eyes, and took in a long, deep, questioning breath.

As she reopened her eyes, they were watering. She didn't have it within herself to deliver the death sentence, and so she just glanced at Kuveni and shook her head.

Kuveni wailed with the anguish of a mother who'd just lost her child in a senseless tragedy and dissolved, and another penetrating pang of pain knocked Eleanor right off her feet. Mélusine caught her.

"How did this happen?" Eleanor didn't have the strength to curb her sharp tone. "Tell me, Mélusine! *How did it happen*? I had no desire whatsoever to have my own child!"

"I don't know!" Mélusine exclaimed. "You must have! It is the only explanation! In my two thousand years on Earth, it has only ever happened when both parties consented! It is one of the most sacred truths of our people!"

"You're telling me that Edmund's mother *consented* to having the Devil's child?"

"She loved him, ma chérie. Elizabeth Marriner loved her mad king. She softened him in a way no one else could."

"I don't believe for one second that all it took was a little love from a woman to tame that beast. This isn't a bloody fairy tale."

430

"He was still a beast, ma chérie, but she loved him anyway. She was the most loving woman I have ever met in my life. She was too loving for her own good."

"So am I." The truth of the words stung as Eleanor said them.

"You must both have been thinking longingly about parenthood, Eleanor. It is the only explanation."

"Of course we were thinking about it! But not with *our* child! With Mary's bairn! That child was supposed to be our daughter, not this... thing." She looked down and noticed a grotesque web of violet veins darkening the skin around her belly button, branching out from the hard nest that had already carved itself a place in her human uterus. It looked unquestionably alien as it pulsated in sync with her heartbeat.

"Destiny takes what's hers, Eleanor. She will take any wicked loophole she can find to do her bidding."

Eleanor finally gave into tears. "But I don't want to do this! I have a life. I have the bairns! What about the poor, tragic bairns! I have four children who've suffered enough already and another on the way! And what about *Edmund*?! I can't leave them like this, Mélusine. I CAN'T!"

Mélusine let her cry into her arms.

Eleanor called upon the last stoic strength that she had left. "Can it be undone?"

"No, ma chérie. There is absolutely nothing we can do to stop it now. Every time intervention has been attempted, it has killed the mother and the child."

Mélusine escorted her to a roman chaise in the corner, and Eleanor fought back another wave of nausea. She couldn't process what it really meant. She wouldn't. Suddenly, she had to escape. She felt like she was going to crawl out of her skin, and then a more wretched idea crossed her mind.

Uma, did you know?! Answer me! Did you know?!

Great misery stalks those who thwart destiny, my child. If it hadn't happened like this, some other, greater tragedy would have unfolded.

But what about my so-called glorious destiny connecting you with your next incarnation?!

It will happen, my child, just not how you envisioned it.

You let me believe a lie?

Should I have told you the truth and ruined the unburdened beauty of what you had? There is a reason the Oracle's visions are damning, Eleanor. Knowing too much only leads to misery.

What about this misery?! Is this not miserable enough for you?!

Tragedy is unavoidable, Eleanor. It is how the universe works. You of all humans should understand that.

I understand that there are four children and a gentle, loving, fragile god who are going to wake up on Christmas morning to a nightmare. Eleanor's fear morphed into rage. *Did Vibhi know?!!!*

I don't know, my child. But you mustn't blame him, even if he did.

Don't you dare tell me what I mustn't do!

We are the gods, Eleanor. We cannot let our selfish desires overwhelm our sacred duties, and it is our sacred duty to prepare the worlds for the greatest transformation they have ever known. One human's life, no matter how precious, is not worth the lives of billions.

"I have to get out of here." With another excruciating spasm, Eleanor began to panic. "I have to get out of here! Please! Mélusine, take me somewhere! Take me where no one will hear me! Take me to India! Take me to Munnar, to our empty house where my screams will only dissolve into the jungle mist!"

Mélusine moved to protest, and then sighed with sadness. "As you wish, ma chérie."

She gathered her into her arms, and they dissolved.

The afternoon fog was thick as they materialized in the garden of the home Eleanor had left too abruptly after her fateful revelatory Dasara, after Shakti had solved the little problem of her public display of divinity by cruelly eliminating all that they'd come to love about their married life. It suddenly occurred to Eleanor how cold and cruel the power that brewed within her truly was. It was the power of the ever-changing universe, that created beauty and love and wonder only to brutally destroy them.

"It hasn't changed at all," Eleanor murmured.

A blustery breeze nipped at her naked limbs as a wave of fog swirled into the garden from the jungle's lush canopy. The moisture infused her skin, and she took in a deep, satisfied breath. She could feel her body absorbing the moisture, almost as if she was drinking in the fog, and for a moment she felt more alive than she ever had. It was as if all the life in the jungle just beyond the garden gate was singing to her, and with her, and in her, infusing her with a frenetic energy that her human sensibilities had never been able to perceive before.

"We've been preserving it," Mélusine admitted. "In case you two ever wanted to come back. If we'd left it to nature, the jungle would have reclaimed it."

"You should have just let it rot. Wasn't it Shakti's will you were thwarting by preserving it? The same natural cycle that has decided to claim my life as a morbid lesson to the gods about the limitations of their power?"

Mélusine didn't argue. She didn't even offer a *peut-être*. As Eleanor's uncontrollable shivering worsened, Kuveni appeared beside her. She tapped her arm, and a soft red cashmere dress covered her from head to toe while Kuveni wrapped her up in her heavy mink coat.

"I'm sorry, Mistress Eleanor. I couldn't hold myself together." She took Eleanor's hand and pushed a wave of Yakshini warmth right into her. Eleanor gasped as the heat traveled from her limbs into the core of her being, warming not only her struggling body, but the block of ice in her uterus. It was the first moment of relief she'd felt since her rude awakening.

"Did it help?" Kuveni asked.

"Thank you," Eleanor whispered. She hugged her and let another round of tears escape. "I love you, Kuveni."

"I have never loved a human like I've loved you, Mistress Eleanor. Not once in six thousand years."

Eleanor held her until another piercing cramp cut through her gut, and she pulled away.

"I think I need to lie down."

Kuveni and Mélusine flanked her as they ascended the whitewashed stairs to her colonial plantation house. The door was unlocked and swinging open in the wind. Mélusine stopped to stare at it.

"Mes chéris, be on guard. I didn't leave the door open." She pushed in front of Eleanor and Kuveni and materialized her walking stick.

Kuveni squeezed Eleanor's hand. "I will protect you, my dear girl."

Mélusine walked ahead of them with her stick out in front of her, but she stopped and glanced back at them with a confused look. Then Eleanor heard it too. From her old bedroom at the far end of the house, a girl was crying.

"Hello?" Eleanor called.

"Eleanor?" the girl called back.

They followed Mélusine as swiftly as Kuveni could escort Eleanor while she limped with the constant throbbing pain that was becoming harder to ignore.

The girl peeked her head out from under the covers of Eleanor's messy bed.

"Anya?" Eleanor asked confusedly.

"Eleanor?!"

Anya jumped out of bed, ran past Mélusine, and tried to hug Eleanor, but Kuveni intercepted her. "My dearest little princess, you mustn't hug Eleanor right now. She isn't feeling well."

Anya was wearing one of Eleanor's abandoned mysore silk saris draped in the Northern style of Gwalior, but she was much taller and skinnier than she had been the last time Eleanor had seen her, on the night of the fateful Dasara when Vibhishana had accidentally summoned his divine wife to Baroda through the flames of the sacred fire. Anya was a woman now instead of a girl, but Eleanor's blouse was markedly too big on her adolescent chest, and she'd used several awkwardly placed sari pins to try to improve its fit.

"Eleanor?" she asked meekly. "Oh, Eleanor, I'm so ashamed! Did you come for me? Please tell me you came for me!"

Mélusine dissolved her walking stick and took another scrutinizing look at the girl. "*Viens*, ma chérie. Come to the kitchen, and we will make you something to eat. You are malnourished."

"No!" Anya squeaked with a burst of rich, spicy fear.

"Why not?" Mélusine pushed. "Come, we don't have time for these human trivialities right now."

She took Anya's hand and dragged her towards the kitchen. When they entered, it was a mess. Pots of chickpeas had boiled over and stuck steadfastly to the stove, spice powders were spilled all over the floor, and the sink was full of crusty old dishes.

"I'm sorry!" Anya squeaked. "I didn't know how to cook or clean! The servants always did it for us!"

Kuveni helped Eleanor to a seat at the small table in the corner, and with a tap of her finger, all of the dirty dishes disappeared. She snapped her fingers again, materializing a bowl of creamy yellow northern curry on top of a delicate basmati rice with a side of roti.

"Eat, my little princess," she suggested. "Then we will get you all squared away."

Anya's eyes widened as the scent reached her nose, and despite all of her other reservations, she sat down and hungrily ate the entire bowl in silence. Eleanor worked hard to keep her nausea under control, as she found the idea of eating any food overwhelmingly grotesque.

"Try this, my dearest girl," Kuveni whispered as she snapped her fingers again. A porcelain cup of steaming, sweet-scented milk appeared. "Every Rakshasa I know can stomach hot honeyed milk."

Eleanor sniffed it skeptically and took a small sip. It worked its way begrudgingly down her esophagus and landed in her stomach. Her whole body tingled as the warmth spread through her struggling veins and began to pulsate.

"Is this what it feels like when Edmund drinks hot liquid?" she asked.

"It is possible, ma chérie. It is a very pleasurable feeling for all of us, even for me," Mélusine replied. "Edmund's mother began to feel many things through him that humans cannot normally feel as the weeks passed. That is one unique benefit to the otherwise wretched condition."

As it stayed down, she drank another few swallows, noticing in passing that the cup refilled itself automatically.

"Eleanor?" Anya asked meekly. "What's wrong with you?"

"I'm pregnant." It was the first time she said the words out loud. They were the words she'd hoped her whole life never to say, even before she'd met Edmund. "And it's killing me."

"But you're the Avatar of Shakti?"

"I am still human, darling. She'll have to pick a stronger avatar if she wants to be immortal." Eleanor was numb as she said the words. "Now tell me what you're doing here."

Anya looked nervously between the three of them.

"*Viens*," Mélusine said impatiently. "We don't have time for this!"

"I ran away!" Anya blurted. "Mummy wanted me to marry a fat old maharaja, and I ran away! I took all my jewelry and some of the gold candlesticks from the palace, and I came here because I thought you would help me! But I got robbed in the train station in Kochi, and then I spent the last of my money making it up here, and then I got lost, and I had to go around and around asking for where the Goddess lived, and when I got here, you were gone!" She burst into tears. "I thought it was Shakti's punishment for

436

disobeying my parents, but I didn't have anywhere else to go! So I stayed here alone and used all the old food you had in your pantry, but I didn't know how to cook it! It was so awful! I don't know how the cooks make all our food taste so good!" She looked down shamefully. "I've been eating you out of house and home for almost three weeks, my lady."

Eleanor sighed with resignation. "Anya, I don't have the strength to help you anymore."

Anya cried quietly. "I'm sorry, my lady."

"You must go home, ma chérie. We will take you."

"No!" Anya exclaimed. "I won't marry a fat old maharaja! I won't do it! I want to be a thoroughbred trainer!"

"Sometimes we don't get what we want, *Princess!*" Eleanor snapped. "You're not going to be a bloody thoroughbred trainer, so just bloody drop it! Women can't be thoroughbred trainers, and even if they could, *you* are going to be a bloody maharani! You can't even clean a bloody kitchen! Do you really think you'd be happy shoveling manure twice a day while selfish lords who don't give one lick about their fine horses yell at you to make them run faster? Your mother's bloody right! Just marry the bloody fat old maharaja, and let your servants do all the back-breaking work! That's how life works, Anya. You can't bloody be anything you want. I was born to die birthing the grandchild of the bloody Devil himself, your poor servants were born to shovel manure, and you were born to produce the ungrateful progeny of a fat old maharaja! The world isn't bloody fair, Anya, and we have no bloody choice in our fates!"

"But... but... but..." Anya stuttered. "But I thought you would help me! I thought you'd do something, my lady. I thought it was Shakti's will for me to do something that matters!"

"Take us." Eleanor felt her Celtic temper rising, mixing dangerously with the fiery power of Durga and her rage at the senselessness of her own unfolding tragedy. "Take us back to Gwalior now!"

"Ma chérie, you'd best leave it. You aren't in a state to manage such mundane matters right now."

"TAKE US!" Eleanor shouted. "Shakti commands it!"

Eleanor felt another wave of nausea as her body dissolved.

Kuveni held her up as they materialized by the massive swimming pool of the Maharaja of Gwalior's palace. With a roar, Sheranee pounced right out of the forest beyond, across the manicured lawns, and straight to Eleanor's side. She licked Eleanor's hands soothingly, but Eleanor pulled away. She'd had it. She'd had it with being nice. She'd had it with the mundane rubbish of flawed human society. She'd had it with humanity.

"Where is the maharani?" Eleanor shouted at a passing servant. He took one look at them and ran away.

"Eleanor, what are you going to do?" Anya asked nervously. "If you really want me to marry a fat old maharaja, I'll do it, my lady. I promise!"

"What is it?" Rane's sharp voice echoed. "What are you rambling on about? I told you to have these towels folded and ready for our guests an hour ago!"

As Rane entered the pool area from one of the many cavernous open-aired hallways, she stopped in her tracks as she spied them.

"Anya?! Madho Rao, come now!" she screamed. "Anya's back!"

Rane ignored everyone and everything as she rushed to Anya and engulfed her into her arms.

"I'm going to kill you for this!" she cried with a combination of joy and rage. "Do you have any idea how worried we were?!"

Anya hugged her back. "I'm sorry, Mummy. I'm sorry, I'm sorry, I'm sorry."

Rane stepped back and looked at her. "You look affright! You're just skin and bones! Please tell me that nothing happened to you!"

"I'm alright, Mummy," she whispered.

Rane glanced at her again. "You didn't lose it, did you? Tell me honestly, Anya. It is pivotal."

Anya blushed. "Don't worry, Mum. You can still sell off your prize of a virgin to a fat old maharaja. I'm sure to fetch a good price after I stuff myself for the next few weeks to fatten back up."

Rane was horrified by Anya's blunt response as she glanced at Eleanor, and then Kuveni and Mélusine. Mélusine had been right. The entire encounter was too mundane for the boiling cauldron of emotions that were mixing dangerously with Eleanor's shooting pains.

"Why... why... why, my lady, that isn't what I meant!" Rane stuttered fearfully to Eleanor.

"Wasn't it?" Anya pushed her. "What did you mean, Mum?"

"Well, I... I... I... just meant that it would have been a horrible thing for you to lose such a valuable prize! It is valuable for *you*, Anya! It gives you power! With your prize intact, you can marry any eligible maharaja in India! It doesn't have to be the one I suggested, I swear! You don't want to be a spinster, do you?!"

"Anya?!" Madho Rao rushed to join them, pulling her into a tight hug. "Thank god you're alright! Where on earth did you run away to?!"

"Munnar," Anya replied. "I ran away to Munnar. I thought Lady Eleanor would help me."

Madho Rao looked up at Eleanor and gulped fearfully. "My lady, we didn't realize that Anya cared so much. We would never have made her marry a man she didn't want to marry!"

As Eleanor spied the dishonest quiver of his eyebrow and a nervous sweat on both of their foreheads, her anger at their lies exploded.

"I don't care about your bloody domestic spat, but don't you dare insult me by lying to the Goddess."

Without conscious thought, her flaming trident appeared in her hand.

"My lady, please forgive us!" Rane wailed as she kneeled, dragging Madho Rao and Anya down into a position of prostration with her.

Eleanor pointed her trident at Anya. "You: Find a bloody maharaja that you *do* want to marry, or be a spinster, or use your endless wealth to go to school and become the first female doctor in India. You have more choices than any other girl on the bloody planet, Anya! But stop fantasizing about being a bloody servant like it's some sort of glorious calling. It's a bloody thankless job that you won't last one minute in!" She moved her attention to Rane and Madho Rao. "And you: Stop pretending that you don't know Shakti's will! I bloody blessed you already! God can't bloody intervene every time you don't like reality, got it?! I'm going to be dead soon enough, and you'll *have* to figure it out! Start now!"

Eleanor felt the flames of Durga consuming her as they worked their way into her fingertips, battling fiercely with the block of ice that pounded with throbbing, burning pain in her gut. Sheranee began pacing back and forth anxiously between Eleanor and the royal family.

"Eleanor?" Anya whimpered.

"I can't control it!" Eleanor squeaked. "Please run! I don't know what's happening! RUN!"

They scrambled away as green fire erupted from her hands. Another pang of agony shot straight through her, cutting its way from her gut into her chest, knocking the wind out of her.

"Eleanor?!"

She heard his voice before she felt his familiar frigidity. Vibhishana wrapped his arms around her, placing his hands gently on her belly.

"Focus on me," he whispered soothingly into her ear. "Let me take it, Eleanor. Let me take all of the pain. You must release yourself before the flames consume you."

She turned around. She felt paralyzed as she took one look at the divine sorrow in his eyes. Her rage and fear and misery and

440

pain combined and then dissolved, and then Uma grabbed his hands.

She collapsed into a dark, dreamless sleep.

CHAPTER 26 – BLACK

When Eleanor awoke, she wasn't shivering. The pain had mostly subsided, but as she took in a deep breath, it returned, more as an echo of its former intensity. She was still wearing the soft red cashmere dress Kuveni had made for her, although the mink coat was nowhere in sight. She was lying in the middle of a cushy bed, much larger than even her oversized bed in her royal master bedroom, and the air was warm and comfortably humid, like it had been on her favorite summer days by the ocean in Margaret River.

On one side of her, Vibhishana, in his gentle Lankan form, lay gripping her hand in his, biting his lip as he stared up at the black sapphire that surrounded them in Mélusine's crystal cave. On the other side, Kuveni lay beside her, holding her other hand as a stream of Yakshini warmth flowed between them. Above her, Mélusine lounged sideways on the mattress like a Roman, stroking Eleanor's hair like a doting mother, and at her feet, Sheranee lay curled up listlessly.

"Are they alright?" Eleanor rasped. "I didn't set Gwalior on fire, did I?"

Sheranee stirred at the movement, and began licking and nuzzling Eleanor's bare feet.

"They're perfectly fine. Don't worry for one second about them," Kuveni said as she squeezed Eleanor's hand. Vibhishana and Mélusine moved in closer. "How are you feeling?"

"I've been worse." Eleanor found it hard to muster the strength to speak, and her lips were painfully cracked and dry. "The pain and the cold aren't so bad at the moment, but I don't think I've ever been this weak."

"That is expected, ma chérie. She's taking her life-force from yours," Mélusine explained. "You will only get weaker from now on."

Kuveni let go of Eleanor's hand to materialize a carafe of hot honeyed milk. She helped Eleanor lift up her head to drink a few sips. "You must stay hydrated and warm, Eleanor. Drink as much as you can stomach. It will keep you stronger longer."

"How long do I have?" Eleanor was too drained to dread the answer.

"It's hard to say, ma chérie. Your daughter is developing quickly. Full Rakshasas are usually born in six to eight weeks, but as a hybrid, she could take nine months."

"I won't last nine months like this."

"I know, ma chérie. It will be sooner. We must make arrangements."

Tears streamed down Mélusine's face, but she continued massaging Eleanor's hair and working her way down to Eleanor's forehead chakra, rubbing her in soothing, gentle circles. As Eleanor coughed and gagged, trying to keep the milk down, Kuveni put the carafe down beside them and returned to stroking her hand.

Eleanor looked to Vibhishana. "Did you know? Is that why you gave Debbie your talisman?"

444

"I didn't think it would happen so soon." Violet tears streamed down his face. "I wouldn't have gallivanted around as Santa Claus filling the bairns with hope if I'd known they'd all wake up to Amma dying."

"I'm dying," Eleanor murmured, trying to wrap her head around it.

Vibhishana kissed her hand. "I hoped with every fiber of my being that you'd have at least a few more years of bliss before your inevitable demise, but even I couldn't stop it."

"My inevitable demise... It feels too bloody mundane to be so poetic."

"There is nothing poetic about it."

He hissed as she felt another echo of pain course through her.

"That's my pain you're feeling, isn't it?" Eleanor squeezed his hand.

"I will bear it, Eleanor. I will spare you as long as Shakti lets me."

"But it's only going to get worse?"

"It will only get worse, ma chérie. It is a great boon for you to have this much relief. I've never seen anything like it before." She glanced at Vibhishana, who only stared up at the ceiling. "Perhaps I should have summoned you to my other suffering mothers, my lord. Have you always been able to do this?"

"It is a unique situation that we will discuss when the time is right, Melysium." He gasped as another shooting cramp erupted. "Shiva's wrath, I didn't know such pain was possible."

"Welcome to humanity," Eleanor quipped.

"That can't be the point," he murmured. "No. It can't be that simple. Your life is worth far more than a lesson in empathy for a bloodthirsty demon."

"I'm going to ruin all of them, aren't I?" Eleanor let her mind go to the place she'd been avoiding since the fateful weekend she met Edmund and she'd reluctantly let herself love her fragile, shell-shocked soldier. "All the love and joy was just a cruel joke. It was a taste of Heaven that none of them, not Edmund, not the bairns, and not even my mother, were allowed to keep. It was just a means to an end. A glimpse to send them straight to Hell after it's ruthlessly snatched away from them."

"Nothing about it is so conscious, Eleanor." He stopped and squeezed her hand again as he endured another wave of pain. "Horrific tragedies happen every day to the purest of souls, and after five thousand years, it is still just as excruciating to watch as it was when I was a boy."

"It sounds pretty conscious when you go on and on about destiny coming after us, you know."

"It is hard to explain. There is a balance that must be maintained on a path towards a greater emergence that transcends individuals. I think I understand it until it snatches someone I love, and then I suffer endlessly, just like any mortal would."

"So it turns out that time doesn't heal all wounds? Don't tell Edmund that."

"Time helps us survive through the black abyss of grief, but we are scarred by losing the ones we love, Eleanor, and the more we love, the deeper the scars. Even after five thousand years, I sometimes dream of being back in Lanka with my Rakshasa wife and my daughter, frolicking about in the palace gardens as if we didn't have a care in the world. I had them with me for five hundred years, and yet, when I wake up, it's like I've just lost them again for the first time. No amount of time is ever enough."

"I didn't need immortality. Just a decade or two of familial bliss would have been plenty."

He kissed her hand. "I'm so sorry."

"I know why Edmund is an atheist now. Because if he weren't, he'd have to believe in a wickedly cruel god."

"It is a wickedly cruel universe, Eleanor. Even the gods can't change that."

"Can't they?" A dangerous thought suddenly occurred to her. "Some can."

"He can't," he said steadfastly. "Rama can't heal Rakshasas, and he never could."

"I'm not a Rakshasa."

Mélusine shook her head. "Forget about it, ma chérie. He's already tried. Several times now we've convinced him to help a suffering human mother, and each time it's failed."

"Did he try to heal Edmund's mother?"

Mélusine glanced at Vibhishana guiltily. "He did."

"He *what*?!" Vibhishana exclaimed. He gasped with pain as Eleanor felt a stirring inside of her. He took several deep, calming breaths, but he still spoke sharply with disapproval. "Melysium, how many times have I warned you not to involve him in our affairs?"

She shrugged. "We told him she was suffering from a disease that only afflicts pregnant women. He was in England anyway to go after Ravana in Brighton, and he did not know that she was related to our world. He tried to heal her just days before Edmund was born, and it didn't work. It did nothing whatsoever as far as we could tell."

"Except planting the seed of divinity for Lord Vishnu's final avatar." Eleanor didn't mean to speak her thought out loud, and Vibhishana became pensive at the idea.

"All's well that ends well, my lord." Mélusine returned to rubbing Eleanor's forehead.

He shook his head. "You shouldn't lie to me about such important things, Melysium."

"My lord, you are the last person on Earth who should be lecturing about lies. If we'd been honest with Edmund from the beginning, he wouldn't have endured any of these tragedies. Eleanor wouldn't be dying right now."

She spoke the words with more anger than sorrow, but tears still streamed down her face.

"He wouldn't have known the beauty of human familial life either," he shot back. "Would you take from him the beauty of his life with Eleanor simply to spare him the pain of losing her?"

"*Peut-être*," she said pensively. "I honestly don't know. Eleanor isn't wrong. This is going to ruin him. He isn't strong enough. None of them are."

"They are all stronger than they realize," he countered.

Mélusine stared listlessly before her as she ran through thoughts that she didn't share in her head.

Kuveni placed her hand gently on Eleanor's pregnant belly, which was already round and protruding as if she were several months in. As Eleanor glanced down at it, she noticed that the violet web of veins had now extended through her arms and onto her hands. She looked down, past the edge of her cashmere dress, at her toes where Sheranee was still licking with her soft tongue. They were just as ghastly.

"Does this always happen?"

"It only happens to human women. Rakshasa women do not manifest their suffering in such a visual way," Vibhishana whispered.

"It looks distinctly alien, you know. Like if Jules Verne had written a penny dreadful about outer space." She held up her hands and watched as the veins pulsated. "Rakshasas aren't from Earth, are they? You haven't wanted to say it, but you know as well as I do that it's true. Nothing natural on Earth looks like this."

Vibhishana hissed again with pain. "I honestly don't know, Eleanor. When I was a boy, there was Rakshasa folklore about other worlds, but the stories were already ancient. The prophecies refer to multiple worlds, but I still don't know which worlds they mean. We could be from a neighboring planet or somewhere else in the universe entirely, or the term could be purely metaphorical. I just don't know. I wish that I had an answer for you."

"Don't worry about it, D.H. I have a much more important list of wishes than that." She felt him cringe as he glanced at

Mélusine, who dutifully held her tongue about the unfamiliar nickname.

"We must make arrangements in case my beautiful boy mourns like a Rakshasa," Kuveni said as she infused Eleanor with another wave of Yakshini warmth.

"What do we need to plan for? What are you worried that Edmund might do? Do we need to get the bairns away from him?"

She tried not to let her imagination wander with visions of the potential catastrophes that were brewing beyond the silence of their peaceful refuge.

Kuveni returned to massaging her hand, working her soft, warm fingers gently up Eleanor's arm. "My beautiful boy will not be violent, but he might frighten them in other ways."

"Will he become as ugly as I am?"

"No, ma chérie, he won't."

"Rakshasas freeze with grief," Vibhishana explained. "It is like turmeric poisoning but much, much worse. When Miriam died, I sat as still as a statue for twenty-seven years. I didn't break myself out of it until my wicked sister showed up to offer me a slave she'd captured."

"I was the slave," Mélusine confided. "He was so horrified by the whole affair that it finally got him to move."

"Blimey."

"Please don't worry about it, Eleanor. We will be there every step of the way. We will make sure they are all okay," Kuveni said soothingly. "You must focus on yourself."

"If I do that, I will wallow in misery."

"We must all keep ourselves moving," Mélusine replied. "None of us can give into our grief. It isn't just about Edmund anymore. We have six children now who are all going to suffer mightily."

"While the Good Lord stands by and watches," Eleanor murmured as she let a tear escape. "I knew we should never have told them we were angels. Edmund was right."

449

"*Peut-être,*" Mélusine murmured.

"What are your dying wishes, Eleanor?" Vibhishana asked.

The question plowed right over her. She'd managed to pretend momentarily that they weren't talking about her. It was all theoretical, far off in some distant future, or perhaps just an extension of a particularly troubling nightmare. But as she mulled over the question, her mind stuck like mud.

"I don't know. I need to think about it." She suddenly panicked and tried to stand up. "Blimey, we need to get back! They're all going to panic when I'm gone on Christmas morning!"

As soon as she let go of Vibhishana's hand, the full brunt of the agony that he had been bearing on her behalf hit her. She gasped and collapsed as another ferocious cramp shot through her. Mélusine held her hands on Eleanor's chest and belly as she pushed a hefty dose of euphoria right into her. Eleanor sighed with temporary relief, but the throbbing, burning pain still pulsated with every beat of her heart.

"Time is stopped here, ma chérie. It isn't even dawn yet in Basingstoke. But you'd best get back soon. You're only going to deteriorate."

"How am I going to do this?" The full reality of it hit her, and she couldn't fight back a flood of tears. "How am I going to face them?! I can't! I can't go tell them that our beautiful life is over, and it's my bloody fault!"

Kuveni leaned over and coaxed her into her arms.

"It is not your fault," Kuveni whispered. "It is a senseless tragedy."

"It's my bloody fault," Eleanor argued. "I was too bloody reckless. I should have been using a diaphragm the whole bloody time. How could I be so stupid?"

"It's my fault," Mélusine interjected. "I'm the one who told you that consent was required for Rakshasa conception. If I hadn't told you that, you would have treated Edmund like a human man."

"If you hadn't told me Rakshasa pregnancy was a death sentence, I would have stopped using contraception on our wedding night. I wanted to have his children. I just didn't want to die from it!" Eleanor cried.

"It is my fault," Vibhishana joined in. "I should have told him a century ago what the risks were. I didn't want him to be afraid of falling in love with a human woman, but it was selfish. It was too idealistic, and now you're paying the price."

"Edmund is going to blame himself," Eleanor said as she wiped away her tears. "There is nothing we can say that is going to convince him otherwise. We must remind him steadfastly that he isn't alone in his guilt or his grief."

She glanced down and noticed that her tears were now laced with violet, although they were not metallic in the way that Edmund's plasma was. It was more as if his plasma had infused her own bodily fluids, converting them into something else, some poisonous mixture of alien and human life. If she was going to be totally honest with herself, she had seen something similar many times before while toweling off after making love, when she'd thought in passing like an utter fool how lucky she was that she didn't have to be worrying about her diaphragm.

"It won't be enough," Mélusine said darkly. "Nothing will be."

"We will all do what we can," Kuveni said more optimistically. "But, Eleanor, my dearest, most beloved girl, before we return to the worst Christmas morning in history, we must prepare ourselves for the immediate unpleasantries."

She conjured a looking glass and held it up for Eleanor to look at herself, and Vibhishana and Mélusine braced themselves to support her.

"Shiva's wrath," Eleanor murmured.

The violet veins had reached up into her face. Her hair now had a violet hue to it, as did her eyes and her lips. She looked like the carrier of a very alien disease, or perhaps a zombie, an ice queen, or even a swamp monster stuck in some unflattering middle stage of evolution. The worst part were her eyes which looked unquestionably ghoulish as the violet of the veins popped from her dilated violet retinas.

"I suppose lying about it just isn't going to work, is it?"

She worked her hardest not to give into her horror. Her life as she knew it was already over. She'd wrapped some presents, made love to her husband, and then the powerful, beautiful goddess bursting with life died in the night. Some part of her wished she'd just been hit by a bus so she wouldn't have to watch her own tragedy unfold in excruciating slow motion.

"What do we do? I'm going to scare them all to death! The bairns, my mother, Mary, Edmund and everyone else in the household! I'm a bloody monster!"

"Now, now, Mistress Eleanor, you are right to be scared, but they have all proven exceptional acceptance already. Your mother and Mary and Stanley have all seen Lord Vibhishana's demonic form, and they did not go looking for their pitchforks. You have taught them extraordinary kindness, and now it is their turn to show you how much they've learned."

Eleanor looked away as more violet tears broke through. "I'm scared. I'm really bloody terrified." She hid her face in Kuveni's shoulder and cried.

"I know, my beloved girl. I know," Kuveni whispered. "But all will be well with the angels by your side."

"I wish I believed that," Eleanor sobbed. "It's all just a beautiful lie! Why does it have to be a bloody lie?!"

Eleanor cried, and the gods cried with her, until another jolt of pain, even more acute than the last cut through her, and she gasped.

"We can't wait. I have to face them while I still have the strength."

"I will scope out our options," Kuveni offered as she transferred Eleanor into Mélusine's arms. Without any ceremony, she disappeared.

452

"They're going to be so bloody terrified," Eleanor repeated as she cried into Mélusine's shoulder. "I'm scarier than bloody Frankenstein."

Vibhishana took her hand. *You will not be alone, Eleanor. You will never be alone again. We will be with you however you need us, through the end of this life and into the next.*

Look me in the eye and swear to me honestly that there is nothing that can be done. You tell me that Lord Shiva and Shakti cannot do anything to save one human life. You tell me!

His violet tears flowed freely. *I would do any foolish thing on Earth to save you right now, Eleanor. Do you understand what that means? ANYTHING. I would gladly give my life for yours. I would give millions of innocent lives… billions. I would give up suns and planets and moons and entire species if it would keep you alive and well just for a human lifetime.*

That's very selfish for the Good Lord, you know.

I want it for you, Eleanor, and for me, and for Edmund, and Kuveni and Mélusine, and your poor suffering mother, and the bairns, and the beautiful little girl inside of you who's going to long so desperately to know her mother. I want it so badly that it hurts almost as much as the pangs of agony that are tormenting you.

I know what you mean. I don't care about me, you know. Not really. But I can't watch them suffer, Vibhi. That's going to be a crueler punishment than any physical torture I could endure. I would do anything to spare them.

He squeezed her hand. *This is a very perilous position for me to be in, Eleanor, not just for you, but for the world. I am a dangerous, desperate fool of a god right now, and still there is nothing, NOTHING, to be done.*

Eleanor wiped away her tears. *I love you, D.H. In the next life, you can return the sentiment.*

He kissed her forehead and took several deep, calming breaths in a row as he attempted to relegate his tears.

Kuveni reappeared. "My beautiful boy is setting up the presents under the tree. The bairns are stirring but they are still upstairs. We should go now before the bairns come down.

Eleanor, my beloved, Mary and your mother are in the library with Edmund. Shall I send them away?"

Eleanor wiped her tears into her skin. "I don't know! I don't bloody know! Is there anything we can do to make this better? There's nothing! It's a catastrophe for everyone no matter what we do!"

"What will make you feel better, my darling girl? That is all that matters now."

Eleanor leaned on Vibhishana as she thought through her options. "I don't want to have the conversation more than once. I just want it over with."

"I will go in before you," Vibhishana suggested. "I will prepare him as best I can."

He squeezed her hand, tempering her pain as Kuveni and Mélusine helped her up. Sheranee nuzzled her.

"Go, my love. I will call you when I'm ready for you again."

Sheranee humphed disappointedly, and then leapt straight into the black sapphire wall of the Crystal Cave.

Eleanor leaned heavily on Mélusine and looked down. Her belly was even bigger than it had been before, and her fingertips were now solidly violet, like gangrene after a nasty case of frostbite.

"Kuveni, can you get me out of this red dress? I don't need to draw more attention to how grotesque I am."

"I will make you anything you want, Eleanor. Just say the word."

As another cramp cut through her, the thought of wearing any modern clothing felt dreadful, and she liked the feel on her skin of the soft knitted cashmere of the dress she was wearing. In fact, she realized as she thought about it that she felt the fabric more than she usually did, almost as if the nerves on her skin were electric and alive.

"Maybe you can just make it grey? Perhaps with a wide, layered turtleneck that will cover more of my skin? And perhaps a long black cashmere vest to help cover the bump and my breasts.

They're a bit scandalous as it is without a bra, although I suppose I won't ever have to care about being too alluring again." She beat back a wave of melancholy at the thought.

Kuveni tapped her arm, and the dress transformed.

"Thank you," Eleanor whispered.

Kuveni kissed her forehead. "My wish is your command, Eleanor. Whatever you need, please just ask."

"I'm really bloody scared," Eleanor whispered as she cringed at the thought of facing Edmund.

"No matter what happens, we will be here, ma chérie," Mélusine reiterated. "No human has ever been more loved."

"Are you ready?" Kuveni asked gently.

Eleanor nodded.

With a pleasant breeze, all four of them dissolved.

CHAPTER 27 – WORDS

The hallway leading into the library was illuminated only by old-fashioned gently flickering gas lights. Edmund had loved them so much more than modern electric ones that Mélusine had kept them during her modernization of the house for their wedding, and Eleanor had gotten so used to them that she hadn't noticed them in months. But now she could hear the subtle sizzling as the gas burned, and it seemed like the shadows were dancing vivaciously all around her. She suddenly understood why he'd cared so much about keeping them.

She leaned heavily against Kuveni and Mélusine, fighting off another wave of nausea with all her might. The pain was so distracting that she hardly noticed Mélusine wiggle back into the form of Percy. Vibhishana squeezed her hand and let go to make his entrance before them. He breathed in several calming breaths in a row and whispered his mantras, transforming back into Father Johnson as an afterthought as he noticed his Lankan hands.

She startled as she caught a glimpse of herself in one of the many mirrors lining the hallway. For one fleeting moment, she thought she'd seen Surpanakha.

"Kuveni, can you cover the mirrors, please? I don't want to know how bad I look."

Kuveni snapped her fingers, and black cloths covered every mirror. "As you wish, my beloved girl."

"Dearest?" Edmund called as he heard Vibhishana push open the door to the library with a creak.

Eleanor hid behind the door and watched Edmund flit about, reorganizing the presents under the tree so that the ones with the biggest red bows were prominently displayed in front. He was wearing the wrinkled wool trousers from his prior days' suit, paired with a bright red cashmere sweater over a striped white dress shirt and green silk tie, making him look equal parts festive and silly.

"Dearest, is that you? I asked Stanley to keep the bairns occupied until you were ready to join us. I hope you don't mind that I set it all up without you?" He trailed off as he saw Father Johnson. "Well, well, it looks like Santa Claus finished his task with plenty of time to spare! Are you joining us for breakfast?"

Edmund smiled and rushed to greet him, but he stopped in his tracks, and his eyes turned black as he took in a deep whiff.

"Why are you scared, Father?"

Eleanor could hear the panic exploding in Edmund's voice.

"Is he here? Is it Lord Montagu? Tell me quickly what we need to do to kill him. Eleanor said that you gave Stanley a special bullet?"

"It isn't Lord Montagu," Vibhishana said as he began pacing, looking around and up to the ceiling as he struggled with what to say.

"What is it then? Has something happened? I've never tasted your fear before." He glanced down at Moira, who threw a nervous look to Mary. "The bairns aren't in danger, are they?"

"No." Vibhishana paced more frantically. As a stabbing pain shot through Eleanor's abdomen, Vibhishana cringed and grabbed his abdomen at the echo. "I don't have the words, Edmund. I'm doing an appalling job of it. You'd think after all this time, being who I am, I'd know how to do this, but I don't. I don't have the words."

Edmund grabbed his shoulders and looked him in the eye. "Just tell it to me straight, Father."

Vibhishana teared up. "I'm so sorry, my beautiful boy. I'm so, so, so sorry."

As Vibhishana pulled him into his arms and hugged him, Eleanor caught a subtle taste of Edmund's rich, spicy Rakshasa fear intermingling with Vibhishana's. "So that's what it tastes like," she murmured. She finally understood why he was always so tormented by it. It tasted singularly delicious, like a fine cognac with notes of spiced wassail and vanilla.

"You're scaring me," Edmund said as he pulled way. "Please just tell me what you want to say."

"It's Eleanor," Vibhishana whispered.

"What about her? What's wrong?" Edmund asked as another burst of spicy fear attacked her.

This time human fear from her mother and Mary joined the bouquet, adding an even more enticing layer to the aroma.

As Vibhishana stuttered, Eleanor couldn't stand it any longer. She grabbed Kuveni and Mélusine, and stepped into the library. The sweet smoke of pine burning in the fireplace and the bright electric lights of the Christmas tree assaulted her senses, and she held up her hand to block the burning aura from her sensitive eyes.

Kuveni pulled the door closed behind them and whispered a quiet mantra, locking it with her Yakshini magic.

"Lord Almighty," her mother murmured.

"Ellie?" Mary gasped.

In a blur, Edmund was by her side. "Eleanor?" He glanced at Kuveni and Mélusine. "What's happened? What is this?"

Another burst of pain shot through her, and she whimpered. "Edmund, I'm pregnant."

He glanced back at Father Johnson questioningly. "What do you mean? You look like you have some sort of alien disease!"

Eleanor pulled back the black cashmere vest to show him her pregnant belly through the grey cashmere dress.

A primal look darkened his expression. "Is it Lord Montagu's? Did that monster do this to you? I'll kill him!"

Eleanor's heart raced, and she gasped with an acute explosion of cutting cramps. "Darling, I told you he didn't rape me, and I meant it. Do you think I was lying to you last night?"

"Were you? I don't know what to believe anymore!"

"Believe *me*!" Eleanor exclaimed. "Of all the things that you must believe, *that* is it! There is nothing else! This is your child, Edmund! She is ours—yours and mine!"

"But you were perfectly fine a few hours ago when we were making love in the cellar without a care in the world!" He was too distressed to blush at the declaration in front of their familial audience.

"What can I say, darling? This is how it works for your people. Gestation is much faster than it is for humans. I find it just as alien as you do."

"I don't believe it! I can't! None of it makes any sense!"

"*Arrêtez*! Stop it this instant!" Mélusine admonished him sharply as she stepped in. She grabbed Edmund's wrist, and as he tried to use his Rakshasa strength to pull away, she held him steadfast. "Edmund, meet your daughter." She placed his hand on Eleanor's belly, and Eleanor lost her breath as she felt the subtle vibration of the icy blob inside of her interacting with him. "Your people always know. She is yours. Don't pretend that you can't feel the connection."

"Good lord," he murmured. "What in god's name is this?"

Eleanor fought back another wave of nausea as he pulled away. "I need to sit down."

Edmund took her arm and escorted her to the closest couch, taking a seat beside her. He inspected her ghoulish hands, and Eleanor cringed as he moved his scrutiny to her monstrous face. He felt a strand of her hair between his fingers, but it fell out right into his hand. He stared at it as another burst of rich, spicy fear erupted from everyone in the room.

"What in god's name is this?" he repeated the question to Vibhishana.

As violet tears streamed down Vibhishana's face, Mélusine answered on his behalf. "Mon chéri, this is what it looks like when a human woman carries a child of your people. It is an ugly truth that we kept from you. We thought we were helping relieve you of your burden, but I think we can all agree that it was the wrong decision."

"This can't be real," he whispered. "Eleanor, please tell me it isn't real. Please tell me that it's some awful Christmas prank? I don't care how you did it, I will forgive you, dearest! You've all gotten me good, and I will forgive you entirely for scaring the living daylights out of me, but please end it before I go mad!"

"It isn't a horrible joke, Edmund. Our daughter is already growing inside of me, and I need you to understand what this means before the bairns come downstairs." Her eyes teared up. "I'm dying, darling. Take in a good whiff, and smell the death on me."

Moira gasped with horror and whispered a quiet prayer, but she didn't dare interrupt them.

Edmund looked away, glancing desperately between Vibhishana, Kuveni, and Mélusine.

"Smell it!" Eleanor cried as she grabbed his head and pulled his nose towards her neck. "I need you to be as terrified as I am, Edmund! I need you to accept that it's real! I can't be alone in this!"

He blurred up away from her and grabbed Vibhishana by the shoulders. "You knew this would happen?"

Vibhishana looked down, refusing to answer.

"Good god, man, answer me!"

The house shook, and Eleanor shivered as a burst of divine power wafted off of him.

"I hoped she wouldn't conceive," Vibhishana whispered woefully. "It is very rare for human women to bear our children, Edmund. Most of the time it can't happen at all."

"Did this happen to my mother?"

Vibhishana nodded as more tears flowed.

"You watched this happen to my mother, and you didn't warn me? Not one word as you married us, preaching on and on about celebrating our human love? What kind of monster are you?!"

"A horrifically foolish one," Vibhishana whispered.

Edmund let go and began pacing, whispering his mantras more and more frantically as he processed what was happening.

"WHAT WERE YOU THINKING?!" Edmund boomed.

"I didn't want to deprive you of love!" Vibhishana cried. "I wanted you to know the beauty of human life! Would you give up these three blissful years you've had with Eleanor? Please tell me honestly, my dearest boy, for I will punish myself forever whatever your answer, would you have done it differently?"

"I WOULD HAVE USED A CONDOM, YOU LYING BASTARD! THIS ISN'T THE BLOODY DARK AGES!" Edmund shouted.

Vibhishana leaned up against the fireplace mantle, staring into the roaring fire as he processed Edmund's tragically reasonable point. "It is my fault, Edmund. It is entirely my fault. I will burn in a living hell for eternity repeating that fact to myself every moment, and it will do nothing to save her. I've doomed all of you with my hubris."

Eleanor struggled to stand up, and she relegated her piercing cramps with all of her might as Edmund rushed forward in a blur to help her.

She reached up and cupped his cheeks in her hands. "Darling, I knew what the risks were. Kate and Percy warned me even before we were married, and I decided marry you anyway."

"Why didn't you tell me?" he asked meekly, unable to channel his anger towards her.

Eleanor didn't have the strength to drown him in lies any longer. "Darling, I did tell you. Don't you remember our row after the circus in Australia? I told you as clear as day that carrying your child would be a death sentence, and you chose not to believe me. We both charged on without protection, and here we are. It is a senseless tragedy that together we brought upon ourselves."

"But you were on that pill?"

"I lied about that, Edmund. There is no such thing as a magic pill to keep women from getting pregnant. I thought that the reproductive constraints of your foreign race would protect me, but I was wrong. It was my fault entirely for not being more careful."

"It wasn't your fault, Eleanor. It was HIS!" He threw daggers with his eyes at Vibhishana, and the house shook again with his anger.

She stroked his furrowed brow, mustering all of the calm confidence she had left. "It was my fault, Edmund. I could have used a diaphragm the entire time we were together, like I did with every other man I loved before we met, but I chose not to. If you are going to blame someone, it must be me."

"But this." He ran his cold fingers gently along the violet veins on her hand, and then her neck, and then her cheeks. "It is like I've infected you, Eleanor. I've made you into whatever it is that we are… I've made you into a demon." He returned his attention to Vibhishana. "You look me in the eye and swear to me that we aren't demons, Father. Only a demon would do this."

Vibhishana turned around to face him. "It's complicated, Edmund. There isn't one simple answer to that question."

"I see a simple answer. It's killing my wife right now."

463

"That is one answer," Vibhishana conceded. "But many truths can exist at once. Someday you will understand."

"I will understand *now*!"

Eleanor felt an echo of anguish from Vibhishana's core. "It is not time for you to know, my boy. God, how desperately I long to be honest, but I can't, Edmund! There is too much at stake!"

Edmund narrowed his gaze, and Eleanor shivered as he spoke with concentrated divine fury. "You name one thing in the whole bloody universe that is more important than Eleanor's life. *One*!"

"I can't!" Vibhishana wailed.

"Get out," Edmund whispered.

"Darling, it's alright."

"No, it isn't." Edmund positioned himself between Vibhishana and Eleanor. "I said get out. Your wicked lies killed my mother, and now they're killing my wife, and I want you *gone*! Do you hear me? Get out! Go, before I chase you out of here with Stanley's gun!"

Vibhishana nodded stoically. "I love you, my boy. I will always be here when you need me. Today, tomorrow, and in a hundred years."

"GET OUT!" Edmund roared as he rushed towards Vibhishana in a blur.

The house shook as he hit the fireplace, but as he looked around with seething rage burning in his eyes, Vibhishana was gone. He turned his attention onto Kuveni and Mélusine.

"Darling, we need them," Eleanor stepped in. "I need them. I can't do this alone."

A knock on the library door distracted them. "Colonel?" Stanley called. "Is everything alright?"

"Wait there!" Edmund called back.

"But…"

"I SAID WAIT!" Edmund boomed. He gazed at Kuveni and Mélusine with his black demonic eyes. "Are you demons too? You

464

will tell me the truth for once in your lives! The demon fool commands it!"

Kuveni approached him and took his hand, pushing a hefty dose of Yakshini warmth right into him. "My dearest, most beloved boy, we have told you from the beginning that we are not the same as you. Our people are the sacred guardians of Earth."

"But, mon chéri, it isn't what we are that makes us an angel or a demon. Father Johnson is just as much of an angel as we are, and so are you."

"A wolf in sheep's clothing is still a wolf. In the end, nature will win, and innocents will die," he countered.

"My darling boy, Father Johnson has lived for five thousand years, and he is still an angel. We are not so different from each other."

"Have you ever made a human look like that?" He pointed at Eleanor, and she worked hard to ignore the desperate fear in his eyes.

"No, mon chéri. Neither of us have. Our people reproduce differently than yours do."

Eleanor hobbled over to the fireplace to intervene. "Edmund, darling, you didn't know that this could happen. Even I didn't realize it would be so grotesque, and it's scary! I'm more terrified than you are! But we don't need to descend into a medieval debate about angels and demons. You know that the world is not so black and white."

"All I see is what I've done to you, Eleanor. It's as demonic as anything on Earth."

"Darling, what if your people are Martians? For all you know, your people were the sacred guardians of Mars, and at some point, they found themselves here, living on Earth alongside similarly talented beings like Kate and Percy. Doesn't that seem like a more realistic explanation than something out of a penny dreadful?"

"Is that what he told you? Did my father tell you we were Martians?"

"He doesn't know, mon chéri. No one does," Mélusine interjected.

"He swore to me he didn't know, and I believed him, darling. But doesn't it make sense that carrying an alien child would kill a human woman? Our tragedy doesn't need to be based in some religious commentary about virtue or morality, Edmund. Nature is the cruelest god of them all."

"Then why did my father agree with me?"

"Edmund, darling, he didn't. He said it was complicated, and I shouldn't have to remind you that oversimplifying complicated realities is a very easy path to overlooking the greater truth. It is the technique that you detest evil charlatans using to manipulate the masses with lies that seem to be based in fact."

"Colonel?" Stanley called again through the door. "Colonel? I'm sorry to interrupt, but I can't find the bairns. It's like they just disappeared!"

As another bouquet of rich, spicy fear engulfed Eleanor from all directions, she collapsed into Edmund's arms with the worst shooting cramp yet.

"Eleanor, what's happening to you?" he asked in a panic.

"I don't think our daughter likes the taste of fear, darling. I, however, am finding it grotesquely pleasant."

"Good lord," he murmured.

"I understand you better now, darling. Please don't fret about the odd side effects."

"What could have happened to the bairns?!" he shouted at Kuveni. "No more lies!"

Kuveni closed her eyes, communing with her Yaksha brethren. Then she sighed with resignation and glanced up towards the bookshelves on the second level of the library and pointed to one of the many disguised secret passage doors that Edmund had lovingly shown the bairns upon their arrival in England.

All four bairns were crouching with their faces between the balusters of the balcony's railing. Ruthy whimpered, and Debbie stood up, coaxing her to stand beside her, ready to face the music. She grabbed Charlie's arm, pulling him up, and he did the same to Howie, until all four bairns were standing on the balcony, watching them with dread.

"I will fetch them," Kuveni whispered.

She pushed open the library door and whispered something to Stanley as she passed him, saying nothing to the hungover crew who was gathered behind him.

He entered the library hesitantly, and gasped as he saw Eleanor.

"*Gast ahas*," he murmured. He cleared his throat and straightened his posture as he turned around to address the others, blocking Eleanor from their view. "Maman, go to the kitchen and keep Mrs. Murray there. Reggie and Jules, you'd better start digging out the Napier. Christmas is over."

"That little buzzer isn't going anywhere on the snowy roads," Reggie pointed out.

"I don't care what you do! Take the sleigh if you have to, but both of you need to leave *now*, alright? This is a private family matter, and you're not invited."

"Got it, mate," Jules agreed. "Don't be a stranger." He kissed Stanley on the cheeks in a gesture that was slightly too personal even for the French, and they dutifully followed Norwenn away.

Kuveni escorted the bairns past them, but the children slowed and grabbed onto her skirt as they got a closer look at Eleanor.

"Amma?" Ruthy whimpered.

Charlie and Howie ran past Eleanor, straight to Mary. They squeezed onto the couch on both sides of her, holding on for dear life. She kissed their foreheads, but said nothing.

Moira stood up and rubbed her back with a subtle sigh of pain before limping over to the lasses, stroking Eleanor's arm lovingly as she passed her. She hugged each of the girls, but as she stood back up, her face was drenched with tears. "It's gonna be alright, my bairns. All will be well with the angels by yer side."

"Are you really dying, Amma?" Debbie squeaked.

Moira coaxed the girls over to Eleanor and pulled her into a careful hug. "Don't ye worry about a thing, ye hear? We've learned how to be oxen from ye, an' now the Good Lord is makin' us prove it."

As Moira urged the girls to hug Eleanor, Ruthy hid her face in Moira's skirt. Debbie took in a deep breath, working hard but unsuccessfully to swallow her fear.

Eleanor hugged her gently, keeping her a steady distance away from her sensitive belly. "I'm scared too," she whispered. "But no matter how bad I look or feel, I will always be your Amma, alright? I will always be watching over you, in this life and the next."

Debbie coaxed Ruthy out of Moira's skirt and held her shoulders as Ruthy hugged Eleanor. Ruthy didn't say anything, she only cried and squeezed Eleanor's legs.

As another shot of pain attacked her, Eleanor gasped and rubbed her belly. "I need to sit down."

Edmund, Moira, and Debbie helped her to the couch. Edmund sat down next to her, taking her hand into his and kissing it, and Debbie climbed up next to her, hissing authoritatively at Ruthy to join them.

Moira sat down next to them. "Yer good, tidy lasses," she whispered as she patted their hands.

"Eleanor?" Stanley asked with bewilderment. "What should we do?"

Eleanor looked around at the overwhelmed group and mustered all of the strength that she had left to smile.

"I'm not dead yet, and those stockings have been taunting me since Christmas in July. I think it's only fair to see what's in them, don't you?"

Stanley brought each person's stocking to them, saying nothing about her grotesque state or Edmund's demonic eyes. Mélusine and Kuveni whispered to each other, and then Mélusine headed for the kitchen.

468

The group stared listlessly at the stockings, so Eleanor dug right into hers. Six handmade picture frames, carved out of beautiful karri wood, housed a series of color photographs that Mae had taken with her autochrome. Each bairn had posed with a silly face, and then there was one with Edmund and Eleanor sticking their tongues out mischievously, and then there was an impromptu extended family photograph with all four bairns, Edmund, Eleanor, and Moira that Oz had suggested one cold, sunny day in June when they were sitting on the porch playing checkers and drinking tea.

The simple beauty of the life she was losing hit her.

"They're beautiful," she sobbed. "It was all so beautiful while it lasted."

As she lost her battle with tears and buried her face in Edmund's chest, everyone else did too, and they each sat silently sniffling in their misery. He held her so tightly she couldn't move, while Debbie squeezed her arm, and Ruthy squeezed Debbie. Stanley paced back and forth in front of the door, wiping his eyes, and trying to get himself under control.

After a long period of catharsis, another kick of pain pulled Eleanor out of it. She wiped her tears into her skin, squeezing Edmund's hand as she saw him notice the familiar phenomenon, and then she smiled with feigned cheer.

"This is going to be a long day if we cry after each present."

"You are with us, Eleanor. If we could make the day last forever, we'd do it," Edmund sniffled.

"Aye," Moira agreed.

Mélusine rushed in with a silver tray carrying a full supply of tea cups and several steaming carafes of hot honeyed milk. She placed it right on the small table before Eleanor and handed her a steaming mug. Eleanor took a small sip, and then sighed with satisfaction as it filled her freezing gut with warmth. Mélusine offered a cup to each person, but as Mary refused, and then Charlie and Howie did too, Eleanor sighed with resignation. She knew it was the first inkling of a much bigger problem, and she didn't blame them. The consequences of her unexpected transformation were terrifying. If she'd seen it happen to someone else, she would have done everything in her power to avoid it, and now here they were, being offered magical alien snacks from creatures who no longer seemed nearly as angelic as they had minutes before.

Moira took a big sip of hers. "Aye, that hits the spot," she said with an exaggerated sigh.

Ruthy and Debbie took reluctant little sips, while Edmund drank his down in one Rakshasa gulp. Mélusine refilled his, and then offered one to Stanley, who sniffed it, and then drank it, despite still being woozy from his hangover.

"What did you get in your stocking, darling?" Eleanor asked cheerfully.

He pulled out a stack of watercolor and oil paintings that the bairns had made with him in the vineyards of Margaret River. He smiled through his tears. "Masterpieces in the making, I reckon."

Eleanor smiled, but she was the only one. The rest of them only stared pensively into the fire.

"I don't want any presents," Ruthy finally squealed. "I just want things to be how they were before!"

"So do I, my little love. So do I," Eleanor sighed tearfully.

"Our life *is* a tragedy!" Ruthy squeaked. "You promised it wasn't. You promised!"

They all cried, until the wallowing became too overwhelming, and the hot honeyed milk was gone.

Norwenn came to the door, but before Stanley could chastise her disobedience, she spotted Eleanor and gasped. "*Gast ahas.*"

"Maman, I told you to keep Mrs. Murray occupied in the kitchen!"

"She asked me to tell you that breakfast was ready!"

"When I tell you to do something, I mean it!" Stanley hissed in Breton. "Now go keep her away, got it? No one is to see Eleanor in this state, and you'd better keep your mouth shut and your eyes down if you know what's good for you."

"Aye," she agreed. She glanced once at Kuveni, and then rushed away.

"I'm not hungry," Eleanor said as another cramp exploded. "I'd like to go take a wee cat nap." She glanced at the fearful faces of her audience as she struggled to get up, and Kuveni rushed over to help her. As she noticed Edmund's black eyes, she sighed with resignation. "Darling, will you join me? I think I'll find it relaxing for you to read to me. I think our daughter deserves to hear her first story."

"I'm not hungry anyway," he agreed.

"Amma, can I come?" Debbie asked.

"Aye, my little love," Eleanor agreed. "I'd like nothing better."

As Debbie tried to coax Ruthy, Ruthy pulled away. "No! I don't want to go!"

Moira coaxed Ruthy into her lap. "It's alright. Ye can stay down here wit Gramma. I've got a roarin' hunger for one of Mrs. Murray's Scottish breakfasts."

As Edmund and Debbie helped Eleanor slowly hobble across the room, she looked back at the devastation in her wake. She couldn't hold back a surge of mourning.

Their beautiful life was officially over.

Eleanor lay in Edmund's nook for hours focusing on the lulling baritone of his voice as he read *A Christmas Carol,* which was still sitting open on the bedside from Charlie's reading the night before. That life already seemed like it was miles behind them, almost as if it had just been a fleeting dream, a momentary escape from her wickedly hard life of bathing madmen and worrying about her sisters' beastly husbands, who'd turned out to be far worse than her imagination had dared to dwell.

While he was reading, even though every ounce of his human warmth dispersed, her shooting pain mercifully subsided, leaving only the throbbing and burning sensations of her daughter's freezing Rakshasa nest. After he finished the first chapter, and a shooting cramp attacked her at his silence, she decided that their daughter was listening. "Just one more chapter, Daddy!" The words echoed in her mind—a phrase he was sure to hear too many times, and that she would never get to hear even once. A burst of anger at the injustice of it all morphed into a cramp, punishing her for her painful emotion. She had to let it go.

"Please keep going, darling," was all that she could say.

Debbie lay beside her, carefully cuddled against her arm, sobbing quietly until Eleanor would kiss her forehead, and she'd try to get her emotions under control.

"Cry all you want, my little love," Eleanor whispered each time. "You're the kindest, bravest lass in the world."

By mid-afternoon, Edmund's eyes had finally returned to their human hazel, and his stomach was growling. Eleanor was ready for a break from their huddle, although the idea of getting up and walking around was decidedly unappealing.

"Darling, why don't you go eat something?"

She gasped with pain as he moved away from her.

He stopped moving away and returned to his spot, quelling her cramps with his presence. "Dearest, I don't want to leave you."

Even with the reprieve, Eleanor was feeling antsy. There was too much to do, and she could see a haggardness in him that she knew she needed to mitigate. There was a long road ahead of them that they both needed the strength to endure.

"I'll still be here when you're done, darling. You need to eat, and I need some time alone. Why don't you go find Stanley and have him set you up, and when you're done, send him on up with some hot honeyed milk for me."

"Hot honeyed milk?"

"It is what we were drinking earlier, darling. I've developed a taste for it today. It warms her, and relieves some of the burning of her frigidity inside of me."

In a blur, he left her in bed to ring the servants' bell by the door that she had never once seen him use before. "I will just call for it, dearest. Why didn't you say something earlier? Stanley should be sending us a continuous supply!"

"Darling, I'm sure he will, but you still need to eat and rest your eyes. You aren't a young man anymore, you know. If you aren't careful, you'll make yourself blind again."

474

At the thought, Edmund glanced across the room to the writing desk, and Eleanor sighed with annoyance as she caught him eyeing the letter opener.

"Darling, don't do anything rash. Not now and not later." He eyed her guiltily. "That's an order, Colonel. With or without me, you have a life here now. You have a new job with General Kettering that will give you all the time at home you need to spend with our children, you have friends, you have a place in the town, and you have the respect that your age and title wield."

"I'm not the bloody Earl of Easton," he muttered.

"I meant your military title, darling. You are a decorated colonel in the British Army, and like it or not, you are not ready to start over as a spring chicken yet. You must promise me not to make this harder on yourself."

He sat back down on the bed beside her and buried his head in his hands. "I'm not going to survive without you, Eleanor. You know me better than I know myself. How can I possibly live without you?"

"You will find a way, darling. Now, go find Stanley and let me have some time to myself." Debbie hid her face in Eleanor's sleeve. "Go with him, my little love. You need a break too."

Debbie wiggled off the bed and glanced up at Edmund. He moved one more time to protest, but as Eleanor waved him along, he offered Debbie his hand and pushed open the door. A subtle puff of fear wafted off of her, and then she swallowed it and took his hand.

"You're too cold, Abbi. You should drink something to warm yourself up."

"Yer a good, tidy lass, Debbie MacLeod," Moira said as she greeted them in the hallway. Eleanor had heard someone pacing slowly outside the door for hours, although she'd assumed without much thought that it must have been Stanley. Moira squinted to scrutinize Edmund's eyes, and then she squeezed his hand. "Mrs. Murray's got two Scottish breakfasts waitin' fer ye down in the kitchen. I reckon ye'd better go claim 'em before someone else does." As his eyes teared up at her kindness, she squeezed his hand again. "Go, Abbi. We've got plenty of time to blether on later about the cruelty of it all."

Eleanor shooed him away, and he guided Debbie into the dark hallway. Moira shut the door behind her and took a seat in a chair by the bed. She ran her fingers along the violet veins on Eleanor's face with a look of intense, helpless sorrow that only a mother facing her doomed child could produce. Eleanor took her hand and moved it onto her belly. She stifled a pained whimper as the fetus moved.

"Lord Almighty," Moira murmured.

They sat, listening and feeling as she settled back into position, and Eleanor began to shiver. Moira pulled the silk duvet up and tucked her in, but Eleanor pulled out her hand to feel her mother's warmth. Her mother climbed onto the bed beside her, coaxing her into her arms, and Eleanor couldn't fight back another wave of tears. Her childhood self had longed so desperately for that affection, and here they were again full cycle, watching the world around them crumble.

"I'm gonna ask ye once and only once, Ellie, and I promise ne'er to say one more word about it… Is it Abbi's, or was he right? Did the Devil get ye?"

"It's Edmund's, Mum. I wasn't lying. For once in our lives, none of us were lying."

"I hoped so," she sighed. "At least that's somethin'."

"What is?"

"She'll be a child born of love, Ellie. She'll have something that none of the other bairns have. It'll have to be something, I reckon, because it's gonna be a dark road without ye to light the way."

"I don't want to go," Eleanor sobbed.

Her mother stroked her hair gently until a strand fell out. Eleanor only sobbed louder, and Moira stroked her forehead instead, snorting as she sobbed herself. They sat for many minutes, and then Moira stopped and wiped away her tears as she contemplated an idea.

"Tell me this, Ellie: Do ye think there's anything the Good Lord can do to save ye? There's the stories in the Bible, ye know, of him healing the sick. Maybe ye just need to beg him."

"Those stories weren't about him, Mum. There is someone else who can heal, but he's human, and his power doesn't work on Edmund's people or the women carrying their children. He tried to heal Edmund's mother, and it didn't work."

"I reckon the Martians must have their own gods fer these matters."

"Maybe we should send up a beacon to ask them." Eleanor couldn't help but laugh through her tears at the silly idea. "We wouldn't need to. If the Good Lord can't do it, none of them can."

She refused to think about the wicked irony that if anyone on Earth could do it, it was Edmund. But she knew what that divine power was. She'd felt it when Rama had healed her burns, and she'd watched it when he'd healed Jaap Sahib, and as she thought back to watching Edmund try his damnedest to heal Ravi Bidkar, she knew that he didn't have it in him yet.

Not until he ascends, my child, Uma murmured. *And for that, Rama must die once and for all. His cycle of torment must finally come to an end.*

I assume that isn't going to happen in the next few weeks?

It will not happen for a century, my child. No Preserver can save you.

"Maybe the Good Lord can't do it because the Martians don't need to be healed," Moira posited, bringing Eleanor's attention back into the room. "They've all got that violet blood to heal 'em, don't they? It's just the humans who love 'em who get the short end of the stick."

"I knew what I was getting into, Mum. Percy warned me the day I met Edmund. He wanted me to break it off kindly and swiftly if I wasn't okay with the risks. I'm the fool who didn't use a diaphragm while sleeping with a Martian. It's all my fault."

477

"Do ye really think Abbi's a Martian?"

"It's as good an explanation as any. They don't like to think of themselves like that since they were all born on Earth, but I think that the heavens and the stars are one and the same for a reason. Whether I'm right or not, I like the explanation better than most. It takes the Devil out of it."

"The Devil's real, Ellie. Ye've seen him, and so have I."

"And so are the gods."

Eleanor closed her eyes and concentrated as her trident materialized in her hand, but it was too heavy, and she had to lay it down beside her. Sheranee crawled out from under the bed and climbed up next to her, licking her hands and then nuzzling Moira's until she started scratching her ears.

"Yer one hell of a house cat, ain't ye?" Moira said as Sheranee began to purr.

Eleanor sighed. "I'm one of the most powerful humans on Earth, and I can't even save myself, so I'd rather not think of any of it in terms of gods and monsters."

Her mother sat pensively, rubbing Eleanor's belly gently and massaging her hands. "They're scared, Ellie. Mary and the lads. I dunne know how to help 'em. I taught 'em to hate while they were still babes in arms, and now it's comin' back to bite me... and you an' Abbi. They're all linin' up behind Judas as we speak."

"I don't blame them, Mum. I look like a monster. If I weren't the victim of my own idiocy, I'd be bloody terrified of myself too. It's a wonder to me that you're taking it so well."

"I'm done runnin' away, Ellie. It's my turn to be the mam I should've been while ye were slavin' away, making our end's meat all those years. The Good Lord saved me from myself, and I'm gonna pay him back. I'm gonna pay all of ye back fer wrestling me outta my own Hell."

"I love you, Mum."

Moira sniffled through her tears but pushed on. "They're talkin' about leavin' ye, Ellie. Mary wanted to go right back up to

Scotland on the afternoon train. She sent the lads out to help Reggie and Jules dig out the Rolls Royce to take 'em to the station."

"Why? Kuveni can just pop them wherever they want to go?"

"They're scared, Ellie. They dunne want anything to do with the angels anymore."

"Blimey. Is it just Mary, or do the lads really mean it?"

Moira sighed with resignation. "The lads were so scared, they were willin' to run back up to Skye, Ellie, to the Hell ye saved 'em from. Howie suggested it, and Charlie dunne say one word of protest."

"Well, they'd better find somewhere else to go, because that castle was confiscated weeks ago by the Crown as evidence of Fergus and Jimmy's involvement with Lord Grimby and the Fascists."

"Good riddance," Moira muttered. "I dunne even care that the sassanack king dunne need to steal another Scottish castle."

Eleanor chuckled and then hissed with pain. As the throbbing picked up again, Eleanor forced herself to face the ugly facts. "What about Ruthy?"

"She's scared too, Ellie. She's feelin' rotten about it, but she's feelin' it all the same. She followed Norwenn around until Norwenn picked her up, and now she hasn't let her put her down. I'm right sorry to say it, but I think she needs someone human to make her feel safe."

"Blimey. I've ruined everything," Eleanor muttered. "But they can't go back to Skye. Even if they could squat in the castle, there isn't even a school there, and there isn't a hospital for Mary and the new bairn."

"They aren't thinking straight, Ellie. So ye've gotta tell me what to do. Ye're the one with the sense in ye, and ye've gotta sort 'em all out before it's too late."

Eleanor pushed back a wave of despair as she thought about their options pragmatically. "Kuveni?" she called.

Kuveni appeared by her side. As she noticed the shivering that Eleanor had already stopped noticing herself, she grabbed her hand and pushed a hefty dose of Yakshini warmth into her. Eleanor sighed with relief as she realized how cold she'd been.

"Mum, go with Kate to Elphinstone. Find a pair of townhouses near the school. Not too flashy, but comfortable. There should be one for Mary and the lads, and one for you to share with the lasses that has an extra room for Kate and Percy when they stop by, and for Edmund and our daughter to use when they visit. Buy it with Kate's help, and keep both deeds in your name. Have Kate fill it with whatever furnishings you want. Make it feel safe and warm and comfortable, like a home they can live in until they grow up. Mary can take the lads there now, and if Debbie and Ruthy don't want to stay here either, they will have a place to go."

"I'm gonna stay," Moira informed her. "I'm stayin' till last call, Ellie. I dunne care what anyone says, not Abbi, not Mary, and not the bairns. I'm not leavin' ya, and if the lasses want to stay here wit Abbi when all is said and done, I'm stayin' here with 'em."

"Surely Debbie and Ruthy will stay?" Kuveni reiterated.

"If Edmund is consumed by his grief, keeping himself alive may be all he can handle at first. It might be better for everyone for the lasses to let him be for a while. We must prepare for the worst."

"I dunne think Mary'll wanna host the angels and the demons fer Sunday tea," Moira said resignedly. "And if the lads had a lick of sense in 'em, they wouldn't be high tailin' it outta town before Christmas dinner."

"I want my daughter to know who we are, Mum. I want her to be a MacLeod, and I have faith that in time the bairns will forgive Edmund and my lass for taking me away. They love their Abbi, and in the end, when I'm long gone, they'll let themselves remember the beauty of the life he gave to them."

"But, Ellie, that could take years!"

"It'll be your money and your house, Mum. Wield it like the weapon it is."

"I dunne think that's wise, Ellie. I shunne be trusted."

"Why not? You'll have an army of angels to keep you in line if the Devil starts whispering in your ear. I'll ask Father Johnson to set up a modest salary for you and Mary, and trusts for the bairns' educations. We'll do it right this time, with a divinely scrutinous eye on the details."

"What if she keeps that new job at the school? She won't need yer money."

"Then I will be happy for her, Mum. There's only so much we can do. And if the lads refuse to accept their cousin, then my lass will still know you and Debbie and Ruthy. It will have to be enough."

Moira squeezed her hand. "It'll be enough, Ellie. We'll make it enough." She leaned on Kuveni to stand up. "Kate, I reckon we have some real estate to peruse before my other daughter gives birth on tomorrow's island ferry."

"As you wish, my fierce firecracker. And you may, at some point, if you'd like, start calling me Kuveni. It is my real name, after all, and I'm quite sure you've heard it plenty of times now."

"Sounds foreign," Moira said gruffly like she had the very first time Kuveni had introduced herself before Eleanor's wedding and Moira's reaction had sent her down the complicated path to where her farce as Edmund's cousin had landed. Moira smiled and poked Kuveni in the ribs. "At least yer from Earth!"

"Indeed I am," Kuveni agreed.

A light knock at the door interrupted them.

Kuveni closed her eyes. "It's Stanley and Norwenn," she reported. "Come," she whispered to Moira. "Let's let our beloved girl continue on with her audiences."

Kuveni put her arm around Moira's shoulders, and together, they dissolved.

"Eleanor?" Stanley called.

"Come in," she called back.

She hissed and repositioned herself, and Sheranee snuggled up next to her, emanating warmth. Without the calming presence of Edmund or her mother or Kuveni, the pain in her abdomen was overpowering.

Eleanor, how are you doing? Vibhishana's voice echoed in her head. *I felt the pain just get worse. What would you like me to do? My only priority is you. I will respect Edmund's wishes and stay away, or I will come to your side in another form. Tell me what you want me to do.*

Please come, D.H.

I will be there.

Stanley peeked his head in. "Eleanor, my mother would like to speak with you. Is that alright? I can send her away."

"Bring her in, as long as she doesn't have a rosary and a cross to exorcise me."

A rich puff of spicy fear wafted off of Norwenn as she eyed Eleanor and then Sheranee, but she looked Eleanor in the eye and relegated it.

"My lady, I have come to offer you my services."

Eleanor was at an utter loss as to which services Norwenn might possibly be able to offer.

"And those are?"

She glanced questioningly at Stanley. "I am a housekeeper, my lady. I've been a housekeeper for thirty years."

"Thirty years?" Eleanor had always thought that Norwenn looked too young to be Stanley's mother, but she hadn't thought too much about it. "How old are you?"

Norwenn cleared her throat and glanced at Stanley. "I'm forty, my lady. Just like you are."

"Good lord," Eleanor murmured.

"I began working in Chester's household when I was ten, and I had Stanley when I was sixteen. After that, Chester kept me in service. It's all I've ever known."

"Then don't you want to do something else with your life? Kate just suggested a few months ago that *I* go to medical school. Surely you can find something more fulfilling than service now that you're not enslaved to a selfish fiend?"

Norwenn cringed but did not disagree with Eleanor's insulting point. Then she glanced at Stanley again.

"Ah. I see. General Kettering wants another spy in our midst. It's really not my decision anymore. I'll have to trust Stanley's judgment on these matters."

"It actually isn't what you think, Eleanor. General Kettering doesn't even know yet that I suggested it. Edmund told Percy that when you don't need him and Kate anymore, they are to leave and never come back," Stanley explained.

"But that's absurd!" Eleanor exclaimed. "He needs them! Our daughter will need them!"

"He blames them, Eleanor. He said that they made him believe that too many things were possible, that it lured him into a false sense of security believing that your magical life was finally real, and that he won't let himself be such a fool ever again."

"Blimey."

"I thought that if he meant it... and it seems like he did... we will need more human help, and my mother really is an excellent housekeeper."

"Lord knows I have too much practice with discretion," Norwenn added.

"And you really want to do this?" Eleanor asked Norwenn. "You want to keep the house of the demon Earl of Easton and his demon daughter?"

"I want to keep the house of the angels who saved me, my lady. If it weren't for you, I would have been hunted down in cold blood by a soulless monster."

"And you think you will get over your fear? Edmund can taste fear, you know. It could compound his condition when he doesn't have me around to help him out of it."

"He will have me, Eleanor," Stanley interjected. "He will always have me."

Eleanor offered him a sad smile. "Well, at least that's something."

Norwenn took a deep breath, and the scent of her fear dispersed. "I've endured every torture that the Devil himself could dream up, my lady. He forced me to learn the difference between good and evil, and there is nothing evil about this household. Only tragic, just like me. I have no fear of tragedy. It's all I've ever known."

Eleanor sighed with resignation. Making arrangements felt so torturously mundane.

"If it's alright with you, Eleanor, I'll suggest it to Edmund," Stanley offered.

Eleanor gasped with another wave of pain. "Please do."

Norwenn nodded her agreement. "You can call me Mrs. Walsh from now on, my lady. Ring the bell, and I'll be here."

"Mrs. Walsh?"

"It's my name," Norwenn shrugged. "It is proper to call your housekeeper and your butler by their formal names. The 'Mrs.' denotes respect for marrying myself to your household instead of to a husband. I've given up on needling Stanley about his manners, but Chester always called me Norwenn to remind me I was his pet on a tight leash. I'd rather be respectable now, for once in my life."

"Isn't it an Irish name?" Eleanor asked distractedly.

"Aye. The Bretons found it dastardly hard to pronounce. My father was an Irish priest who met my mother on pilgrimage in Bretagne. He left the church to marry her when the Good Lord sent me along to unite them in their sin. I'd always hoped to shed it for Grimby, but God went to quite the effort to rid me of that foolish notion."

"It's nice to meet you, Mrs. Walsh," Eleanor smiled. "Would you like to meet your next mistress?"

Norwenn looked nervously to Stanley, who urged her on. Eleanor took Norwenn's hand, ignoring another delicious puff of fear, and placed it gently on her belly. She gasped with another burst of pain as the child moved at the stimulation.

"*Gast*," Norwenn murmured as she pulled away. "I think she just said hello. Is it possible?"

"I have no boundaries now for what I think is possible."

Stanley looked like he wanted to try it, but he dutifully kept his mouth shut.

"Come and say hello, Stanley. There's an excellent chance that you will know her much longer than you've known me."

She took his hand and positioned it where Norwenn's had been. He laughed and pulled away. "I think we're going to be great friends!"

"Did she say something?" Eleanor asked curiously.

"Not precisely. It was just a feeling."

"I know exactly what you mean," Eleanor agreed. "I've been feeling it all day. It is not specific enough for language, but it's perfectly clear somehow anyway... who she is, I mean. It is like I know her already. Timid like her father, with a fiery Celtic temper from her mother. She's longing for real connections that will fill her life with love and vivacity, but she's dreading everything else."

"I know how she feels," Stanley admitted.

"So do I," Eleanor agreed. "Edmund and I both do. I suppose she was doomed to it."

"Or blessed with it," Stanley countered amicably.

"I like the way you think, my friend," Eleanor said with a burst of cheer. Somehow having him there, and even having Norwenn, filled her with a glimmer of optimism that had otherwise been abruptly demolished upon her death sentence. She grabbed his hand and looked into his eyes. "Love her, my child, like the daughter you'll never have. It is Shakti's gift to you." He reeled as they both pulled away. "That must have been Uma, but I agree with her, greenie. My daughter deserves all the love she can get, and I won't be able to give it to her." Eleanor trailed off into tears at the tragic thought.

"I promise, Eleanor," he said solemnly. "I will love her as the daughter of the woman who saved my life. You saved it so many times, I lost count, and I'm really still a young man to have been saved so much. I'm reminded every day how young I really am."

"If you weren't surrounded by ancient demons, you'd feel perfectly adult at twenty-four, you know."

"If I weren't surrounded by compassionate angels, I'd feel like a doomed deviant, Eleanor. Do you really understand what it means for me to not constantly feel like I'm a wretched, vile imposter of a man?"

Eleanor squeezed his hand and looked down at her violet veins. "I'm starting to."

"You're still beautiful, you know. Even like this."

"I'm glad you learned the importance of flattery, greenie," she winked.

Stanley's eyes teared up. *I love you, Eleanor. You've made my life worth living.*

I love you, Stanley. I'm so proud of the man you've become. I couldn't love you more if you were my own son.

Norwenn patted his back as he and Eleanor both dissolved into silent sobs.

Another knock at the door interrupted them. Without waiting for a response, a beautiful young Indian woman dressed in a nurse's uniform that looked several decades out of date (since long before the Great War), pushed her way in. Sheranee looked up and then humphed and returned to cuddling Eleanor. Eleanor recognized the visitor's form from the unwise experiment on her birthday, even though she had never seen a full human version of it.

"Excuse me?!" Stanley wiped his eyes and stepped in front of her. "Were you invited?"

486

"I was." She morphed into the form of Father Johnson. "You are a worthy ally, my boy. Now let us be. Eleanor and I must speak alone before Edmund returns." He morphed back into his female form.

Stanley looked to Eleanor for confirmation, and she smiled at the gesture, as if there was anything Stanley could really do to stop him. "I invited him, greenie. It goes without saying that you are not to tell Edmund who she is."

"You should call me Parvati," Vibhishana suggested. "I am here to relieve Eleanor's pain."

Stanley nodded. "Eleanor, please ring us if you need anything. I'll bring up some hot honeyed milk as soon as Mrs. Murray has it ready. Percy was just showing her how to make it."

Eleanor squeezed his hand. "You're doing a bang-up job, Stanley. I couldn't have asked for a better handmaiden."

He nodded stoically as his eyes watered. "Let's go, Maman. We have work to do."

He led Norwenn out of the room and closed the door behind them.

Vibhishana took the seat beside the bed and took Eleanor's hand. She gasped as a wave of relief washed over her, and they sat for many minutes in silence as he cried, enduring her pain and his anguish in equal measures.

He finally smiled through his tears. "She will be a lovely person. Thoughtful and kind, just like her parents."

"You were as worried as I was that she'd take after her grandfather, weren't you?"

"The thought did cross my mind."

"It'll be tragic enough dying to bring that wanker's progeny into the world. The least we can do is make sure she's as good as her father."

"And her mother. It is a tall order, Eleanor, but if anyone can do it, she can. She will know more love than any other child on Earth."

"Edmund told Kuveni and Mélusine that they are to leave as soon as I'm dead and never come back."

"I know. He's pulling away, and we must let him. We should never have been this involved in the first place. I will blame myself for eternity for dooming you, Eleanor."

"I'd rather have had these three years as they were than thirty more years bathing madmen and eating stale shortbread to quell my boredom. I didn't know what love really was until I met Edmund, and I don't regret anything about our life together. I'm going to make sure he knows it. The only thing I regret is not using a goddamned diaphragm."

"We were all ancient fools," he murmured. "But you must understand, Eleanor, in five thousand years, only three human women have been able to conceive a Rakshasa child. Rakshasas must give up using all of our abilities for years, sometimes decades, before it can happen. I should have realized with Edmund being so sluggish in his use of our powers that he was at a higher risk... I should have bloody realized it... I will never forgive myself for not realizing it."

"I should have realized with Edmund's desperate longing for a baby that I needed to be more steadfast in my own mind. Destiny used Mary's baby against us, that heartless shrew. We had the adoption papers in our hands. We had bloody everything."

He shook his head. "It shouldn't have mattered, Eleanor. I don't understand how it didn't matter. Every woman who conceived, even Edmund's mother, knew full well what she was doing. They wanted to conceive, and they didn't care what the risks were. None of us believed that you could get pregnant against your will. It has never, ever happened before."

"Edmund's mother knew this would happen?"

"She didn't realize it would look so ghoulish, but she knew, Eleanor. She knew exactly what my brother was. She lied to Mélusine and Kuveni about it because she was ashamed, but she couldn't hide it from me. She'd married the Devil in secret, and she believed that having his child would save him. She believed it would save the world."

"She wasn't wrong," Eleanor sighed. "Edmund will save the world."

"Someday. God, how I wish you could be there to see it. I don't know exactly how it will happen, but it will be glorious."

"Edmund and my lass will both need to know the whole ugly truth, you know. You won't be able to avoid it forever, and when Edmund realizes who his father really is, he will only feel guiltier about my death."

"I know. But we must let him take control of his own destiny. He has never distanced himself from us like this before. Even in the trenches, he was longing so desperately for our help. I should have realized that it would take a blow like this to force him to take the reins of his own life."

"Glad to be of service."

"I'm so sorry, Eleanor." He let more tears escape. "I don't have the proper words still. I have this powerful being inside of me that is cold and ruthless. He must be, to be the Destroyer, and the universe needs destruction, but then I feel the life fleeting from you, from the most precious human in the universe, the woman worth a billion lives, and I hate myself. I hate what I am. I hate the cruelty of my divine calling. I hate that as my soul is breaking, the natural cycles must continue unabated. The contradiction is crushing me… and now I'm complaining to the dying victim of my foolishness about how sad it makes me. I'm a worthless, flawed fiend, Eleanor. Please ignore me."

Eleanor squeezed his hand forgivingly and glanced down at her trident that was still lying next to her. "I understand you completely, D.H. I have learned a thing or two from hosting Uma. Please don't despair. Someday, you will have your divine wife by your side to share your burden." She squeezed the trident, and then closed her eyes and dissolved it. "I thought I was going to have the chance to anoint her and send her in your direction, but I suppose I'll miss that too."

"I don't have any idea what the prophecies mean now," he admitted. "Sometimes it is better not to overthink them. More often than not when they become clear, I realize that there was no possible way I could have solved the riddle on my own."

He glanced at the door. "Edmund is coming. Just tell me when you'd like me to leave, Eleanor. I will keep myself scarce in Kuveni's room while I wait. I am at your service from now on."

Edmund gently pushed open the door. He was carrying a silver tray with two carafes of hot honeyed milk and a full Scottish breakfast. He focused on not dropping it as he took it to the writing desk, but when it was out of his hands, he glanced at Sheranee lying in his spot on the bed, and then at Vibhishana, and his eyes turned black.

"Darling, this is Parvati. She is a friend of Kate's and Percy's. She specializes in managing pain, and I have asked her to stay."

"You're one of them?" Edmund asked bluntly with a twinge of hatred.

"I am one of your people, Edmund."

"You're not welcome here."

"Colonel, snap out of it," Eleanor said sharply. "You should be the last person on Earth hating strangers just because of their race. You are not evil, and neither is Parvati. Now come be the man that I married. Your daughter has been missing you." Eleanor nudged Sheranee out of Edmund's spot, and she humphed her discontent and lay down on the floor.

Edmund glanced again at Vibhishana. "I was hoping that we could be alone, Eleanor. Privately. We haven't had a moment alone together since... since all of this unfolded."

Eleanor squeezed Vibhishana's hand. "Go. Help Kate and Percy make their arrangements. I'll call you when I need you again."

He nodded his agreement and took his hand away. She gasped as a burst of her full pain exploded.

Edmund watched as she took in several deep, calming breaths, trying to get herself under control.

"Please stay, Parvati, you said your name was?" he changed his mind. "Dearest, I didn't realize how much she was helping."

"No, you're right, darling. I'd like some time alone with you too. Parvati, please leave us."

"As you wish, Mistress Eleanor." Vibhishana didn't glance at Edmund again as he left them alone, closing the door behind him.

Eleanor covered her nose as a whiff of fried eggs assaulted her senses. "Darling, I thought I asked you to eat downstairs. The scent of the food is nauseating me."

"I brought it for you, Eleanor. You need to eat something."

"Maybe I'll have more of an appetite later," she declined.

He stared at her, debating his next move, and then he sat down on the edge of the bed beside her and buried his head in his hands.

Their daughter stirred, and Eleanor ignored the pain as she moved towards him, but he only sobbed silently refusing to face her. "I can't even beg you to forgive me, Eleanor. I don't deserve to be forgiven."

"I forgive you anyway, darling."

She rubbed his back as his sobs evolved into wails, but he'd lost control of himself, and she didn't blame him. She turned her attention on her throbbing belly. Somehow, in a way she couldn't describe at all in words, she felt their daughter crying with him.

He choked on his sobs, and Eleanor reached over and took his hand. She pulled up the cloth of her dress so he could feel her skin directly, and she placed his hand where she could now distinctly feel a tiny foot.

"She loves us, Edmund. When you can't remember anything else, remember that."

He sobbed as Eleanor kept his hand in hers against her belly, holding their family together.

"My life is over, Eleanor," he finally mustered enough wherewithal to speak. "I keep waiting to wake up on Christmas morning with you and the bairns, to the beautiful life we had yesterday, and it's like I'm trapped in my worst nightmare."

"I know, darling. I know."

He snorted in a deep breath, but his tears wouldn't stop. "The lads are leaving with Mary on the evening train. She asked Stanley to ask me to give her back the adoption papers. She was too bloody terrified to ask me herself."

"They've been through a lot, darling. This is all very sudden. When they've had a chance to adjust, they won't be scared anymore."

"They *should* be scared, Eleanor! I did this to you! I'm a monster! Who knows what horrific thing I could do to them that my father and the others were hiding from me!"

"Darling, this is a unique situation that blindsided all of us. It doesn't mean that you're a monster, and it doesn't mean that you should be scared of yourself."

"I'm a demon, Eleanor. There's no other explanation. The bloodthirst, the intoxicating taste of fear, *this*. You should never have let me in. You should never have loved me. Alice was right. I don't deserve to be loved."

Eleanor brought his hand to her mouth and kissed it. "Alice couldn't have been more wrong, Edmund. I loved you the moment I met you, I love you now, and I will always love you, and no one on this planet has better judgment of character than I do."

He dissolved into tears again, and she coaxed him into her nook so he could cry on her shoulder. He curled up into a fetal position and let his sobs flow free.

"I can't live without you, Eleanor."

"You will have to. If you can't do it for yourself, do it for our daughter."

"But how?!" he exclaimed. "How can I possibly love her, when every time I see her, I see what she did to you, what *I* did to you?! I will see your suffering in her eyes, Eleanor!"

Eleanor stifled a moan as their daughter somersaulted violently at the idea, and she hunkered down. "Do you remember what you made me promise you the first night we ever made love?" He only sniffled. "You made me promise to remind you never to punish an innocent child for the tragic death of her mother. You made me promise, and now I'm going to make you promise. You must love her. You must love her enough for both of us. You must make her life so beautiful that it was worth every moment of agony I'm enduring to bring her into this world. Promise me. Promise us, Edmund. Now."

He put his hand back on her belly. "I promise."

"Good. Now I can rest in peace."

Eleanor lay back and pulled the covers up over herself.

He returned to sobbing, and they lay in silent despair, holding each other as the last grey light of day dissolved into darkness. Eventually, another light knock at the door disturbed them.

"It's me," Stanley called.

"Come in," Eleanor called back.

Stanley carried a tray with two more carafes of steaming hot honeyed milk. He put them down on the bedside table, and then shifted uncomfortably as he prepared himself to deliver more bad news.

"Ruthy has asked to go with Mary and the lads. You're her legal guardians, so Mary can't take her without your permission."

Edmund buried his face in Eleanor's shoulder as he tried to get himself under control.

"How does Mary plan to take care of three bairns while she's giving birth? My mother made it very clear that she's planning on staying here with me."

"Reggie has offered to escort them up to Elphinstone and stay with them for now, just until they get things sorted." He glanced guiltily at Edmund's dire state. "He's just trying to help. I'm sorry if he's helping in the wrong way."

"That's very kind of him." Eleanor was somewhat surprised by the generosity of the offer.

"I think the lads remind him of himself when he was their age," Stanley explained. "I didn't think you'd mind the offer, now that Kate and your mother have squared away the townhouses."

Eleanor smiled. "I should have realized that when those two firecrackers are on a mission, they get things done. I'll have to ask my mother later how they managed to buy two adjoining townhouses on Christmas Day."

"I reckon they did it with a great deal of money," Stanley shrugged.

"What are you talking about, dearest?" Edmund asked meekly as he wiped away his tears.

"My mother warned me that Mary was planning on leaving with the lads. I asked Kate to get her sorted with a house in our hometown that you and our daughter can visit when the time comes. I thought it was better than having her take the bairns up to Skye."

"But why?!" he exclaimed. "They're leaving us, Eleanor! Our bairns are leaving us! Why are you helping them?!"

Neither of them had any emotional reserves left to sugarcoat.

"Because I love them, Edmund! I love all of you, and while I still have the strength, I need to make sure that everyone is prepared to survive without me. Mary and the lads aren't handling this well, but they're still good people, and I want our daughter to know them. Right now, they need to feel safe and secure, and most importantly, they need to be able to forgive you for taking me away from them! I think we can both agree that the less they see of my horrific condition from this point on, the better. So if that means that I have to buy them a house and send my mother on up to manage the family diplomacy after I'm dead and buried, then that's what I'll do." She kissed his head as he sobbed into her shoulder.

494

"To be honest, I didn't think Ruthy would want to go. I hoped Debbie would talk some sense into her."

"She should go!" Edmund wailed. "We aren't monsters, holding young girls prisoner in our castle. If she wants to go, she should go! If I were her, I'd run away from me too!"

Eleanor nodded to Stanley. "Let her go. Can you ask Reggie to give you regular updates?"

"I will see to it, Eleanor. There is one more thing," Stanley cringed.

Eleanor sighed as she braced herself. "Just tell it to us straight."

"Debbie asked if I could call the vicar to come collect the unopened presents. She suggested we give them to some of the needy children you fed at the church yesterday."

"She's a good, tidy lass, darling, and she's staying right here," Eleanor whispered into Edmund's ear as he wailed into the pillow at the thought. "Please do whatever you think is best, Stanley. I think that's very thoughtful of her. But please make sure none of the personal presents get lost in the shuffle. In fact, I'd like to have the photographs from my stocking and their paintings by my bedside."

"Aye," Stanley agreed. He eyed Edmund's wretched state, and then the uneaten food. "Is there anything else, Eleanor? Is there anything you will eat? I can ask Kate to make you something if the human food isn't sitting well." He cringed at his unintentional reminder of her foreign plight, but she smiled reassuringly.

She closed her eyes and thought carefully about whether there was anything she could stomach.

"Could you bring me a bowl of baked beans? The brown sugared ones from the Scottish breakfast, but nothing else."

"I will see to it at once," Stanley agreed.

He closed the door gently behind him as he left them alone.

Eleanor rubbed Edmund's back as he sobbed into the pillow, and then she gave up on holding back her emotions, and she cuddled up next to him and sobbed into his back. Their daughter sobbed with them, and Sheranee cried quietly from her position on the floor. All they could bring themselves to do was wallow.

Another light tap at the door finally ripped them out of it. Without waiting for an answer, Debbie peeked her head in. As Eleanor looked over, Debbie was dragging Charlie inside. He looked down at his feet.

"We're leaving for the station," Charlie whispered. "Mum's worried we're going to miss the six o'clock up to Kings Cross."

Debbie kicked him.

"I'm sorry I'm leaving, Amma." He glanced at Edmund, who refused to dig himself out of his pillow to look at him. "Mum and Howie and Ruthy need me, and they're not brave enough to stay, so I'm going with 'em."

Debbie dragged him towards the bed, but he kept his eyes locked on the floor.

"You don't have to look at me, Charlie. I know I look dreadful. But I'm still your Amma, and I still love you. Abbi and I both love you, and when this is all over, I'll need your help getting the others to forgive him. *You* must forgive him, for my sake. It is my dying wish."

Charlie finally looked up at her with tears in his eyes, and she invited him to come closer. She carefully maneuvered out from under the covers, making sure her dress was decently covering her, and then she kissed his forehead and hugged him. "I love you my beautiful, brave bairn. I'll always love you." He nervously let her place his hand on her belly, and as Debbie watched, she invited Debbie to join him. "Say hello, my bairns. She can't wait to meet you."

They both looked up at her with wonder as she felt the vibrations of her daughter interacting with them.

"What's her name?" Debbie asked.

Eleanor glanced down at Edmund, and then closed her eyes and listened for her daughter's opinion.

"Her name is Eleanor, but you should call her Ellie. Every time you say her name, I want you to remember how much I love her, how much I love you, and how much I love Abbi." Eleanor tugged on Edmund's sweater, and he finally emerged from his pillow, puffy-eyed and miserable, to look at them. "Do you like it, darling?"

"It is the loveliest name in the world." He glanced at Charlie. "It will always remind her who you were. The kindest, most loving mother in the history of the world."

"I'm sorry!" Charlie squeaked. "I dunne wanna be so scared! I just am!"

He took one last look at Eleanor, and ran out of the room. Debbie shook her head. "I'm sorry, Amma."

"You have nothing to be sorry about," Eleanor reassured her.

"I'm gonna go say goodbye to them, and then I'm gonna help Gramma pack up the presents to take to church in the morning."

"There is a new bicycle for you hidden in the pantry." Edmund could barely get the words out through his sniffles. "I bought it in London last week. Please keep it, if you want it. I had some fanciful idea that you'd learn to ride on it and give it to your daughter someday to do the same." He swallowed hard. "Keep anything you want from under the tree. There are two cricket bats for the lads, some dolls for Ruthy, some books for each of you, and some other toys. I don't remember what they are now. I'm having trouble thinking straight."

Debbie came around the bed to hug him. "Thank you, Abbi. It would've been the best Christmas ever."

They all teared up, and Debbie sniffled and wiped her eyes. "I'll be back later. Mrs. Murray's working on your beans. It takes her a lot longer than it takes Kate." She hugged Edmund again.

"I love you, my little lass," he whispered.

"I love you, Abbi."

She hugged Eleanor. "I love you, Amma."

"I love you so much, Debbie," Eleanor whispered.

As Debbie opened the door, Norwenn was standing there with another silver tray. Debbie helped her take it to the writing desk, and they placed it next to the untouched Scottish breakfast.

"I'll get this out of your way," Norwenn said as she picked it up without another word and carried it swiftly out of the room.

Debbie followed her out and closed the door.

The scent of the beans finally aroused some appetite.

"Darling, can you bring those over for me? I should eat them while they're hot."

In a blur, Edmund collected the beans and two carafes of hot honeyed milk, placing them on the bedside table. He built up the pillows so she could sit up, and then he offered to feed the beans to her.

"Save that practice for our daughter, darling. I can still feed myself."

She took the bowl, and her stomach growled. "It's funny, I've never really liked baked beans. I suppose we know Ellie's first favorite food."

She took a bite and shivered as the warmth exploded in her gut, traveling swiftly to her fingertips. A voracious hunger exploded, and she scarfed it down until every last bean was gone. He took the empty bowl and offered her a carafe of milk. She chugged the whole thing down as if it was contest night at the Elphinstone Arms. Her stomach gurgled in protest, but then settled as the heat infused her and her daughter. Edmund watched with some combination of relief and concern.

"You're eating like I do."

He took her empty carafe and placed it on the bedside table.

"It tastes so good! It's like every nerve on my tongue is alive. Is this how it feels when you eat?"

"Only things that I like, but yes, I suppose often it does."

"I have never tasted food like this, Edmund. Not once. It must be another one of your foreign traits that our daughter has invited me to experience."

"I'm sorry, dearest," he said miserably.

"Why? Don't be sorry for that! It's exciting to learn how these things really feel for you. I had no idea how beautiful the gas lights in the hallway were until this morning. It's like they're dancing!"

He sniffled deeply and smiled sadly. "I've always thought so too."

"It's no wonder you're a wonderful artist, darling. You see things that humans can't see. You *actually* see more beauty. What a lovely gift you give humanity to share what that looks like."

She smiled wistfully as a selfish thought occurred to her.

"What is it, dearest?"

"If I'd known that that lighter fluid from Harrods would be my last sip of cognac, I would have chosen something better. I can only imagine what good cognac tastes like for you. But our daughter has absolutely no interest in it at all. Even the idea of it nauseates me now."

He kissed her forehead, and then her cheek, and then her lips. "I love you, Eleanor. If I could trade my life for yours, I'd do it in a heartbeat."

Eleanor sighed. "There's no point in tormenting yourself with the idea, darling. Now, before we succumb to our grief again, our daughter and I would both like to find out how Jacob Marley's ghost is doing."

He collected the open copy of *A Christmas Carol* from the bedside table.

Edmund stared at it pensively.

"A penny for your thoughts?" Eleanor asked as she nestled into the nook of his arm.

Their daughter calmed down, and the sharp, cutting pain settled back to just throbbing and burning. Her limbs pulsated with warmth, and Edmund noticed her other untouched carafe on the bedside table. He offered it to her, and she refused, and so he drank it down in one Rakshasa gulp until his body was pulsating with the same temperature.

"I would choose to be haunted by you for eternity if it meant that I'd have you with me, dearest. That's the silly thought I was contemplating."

"It would be a rather unpleasant ending for me, don't you think? Wandering the earth for eternity as a ghost?"

"I'm sorry, Eleanor. It was an entirely selfish thought."

"Don't be sorry, darling. We're all allowed to have selfish thoughts. Speaking of which, I shouldn't have picked a name for our daughter on my own, and naming her after myself was a bit egotistical, now that I think about it. She will be her own person, and I don't want her to cower in my shadow."

"It is your right, Eleanor, and it was a perfect choice. Besides, you never liked being called Ellie anyway."

"You're right. I didn't." She kissed him gently on the lips. "What do you think her middle name should be?"

"Something clever and beautiful. Something better than Mary or George."

"Is there something Roman you like? Ovid did bring us together, after all."

"It would be hard to name her after a Roman and not have a doomed or debauched namesake." Edmund finally let himself smile. "Although, I did always like Ariadne. Ovid wrote of her quite a bit, and not always nicely, but she was actually a Greek heroine, a goddess, in fact, in her own right."

Eleanor kissed him again. "It sounds like a perfect choice, darling, and she likes it too. Now, where were we?"

He opened the book and sniffled in a deep breath. "I believe we're about to meet the ghost of Christmas Yet To Come." Another few tears escaped. "How am I possibly going to smile on Christmas for our little Ellie, dearest?"

"You will find a way, darling. I promise."

And so, to the lulling baritone voice of her despairing husband, with the life-force of her daughter subtly growing with every beat of her waning heart, Eleanor closed her eyes and said goodbye to her last living Christmas.

CHAPTER 29 – THE WAIT

Eleanor awoke the next morning shivering. The sharp winter sun was streaming into the window, and she was cuddled up under the covers next to Edmund, who was lying on top of them, with Debbie spooning her from behind. She carefully turned over and snuggled Debbie's warmth, and Debbie yawned and stretched. As soon as she was fully awake, Eleanor caught the look of dismay in her eye, and she kissed her gently on the forehead.

"I'm so sorry that it wasn't all just a nightmare, my little love," she whispered.

She settled back in, and they both fell back asleep.

She awoke again alone. The sun was gone. The sky was grey, and the light was fading. As she tried to move and a sharp pain cut through her, she realized that not having the servants' bell next to the bed was an oversight that would need to be rectified immediately.

"Kuveni?" she whispered.

Kuveni appeared beside her. She grabbed Eleanor's hand and pushed a hefty dose of Yakshini warmth into her.

As Eleanor gasped with relief, Kuveni snapped her fingers and produced a bowl of baked beans in one hand and a carafe of hot honeyed milk in the other. She climbed up onto the bed beside her and held the carafe while Eleanor gobbled down the entire bowl of beans. Then, she switched the empty bowl for the carafe, watching without comment as Eleanor drank down the entire carafe in one Rakshasa gulp. She dissolved the dishes and coaxed Eleanor into her arms.

"Wait a bit before you eat anything else," she advised. "It will only do you good if you can keep it down."

"I've heard that one before."

She kissed her forehead. "I'm sorry that you have. The callous tragedies of this wicked universe are enough to make the angels weep," Kuveni sighed. "My beautiful boy went with Debbie to take the presents to Father Clarke. I will love her forever for keeping the bicycle."

"So will I. I assume the others are long gone by now?"

"They had to spend the night in London and change trains in Durham and Edinburgh, but they'll be reaching Elphinstone any minute. Reggie's been keeping me updated. It was very wise to help them at this juncture, by the way. The more angelic we can all be in these tough times the better. It will reiterate for all of them as their human fear subsides how foolish they were to run away. If you'd forced them to stay, you would have reiterated their fears."

"That was generally my plan. Some selfish part of me hopes that they regret it. When I'm dead they won't have a chance to apologize to me, so they'll have to apologize to Edmund. I'm hoping that is the crack in the door he needs to re-enter their lives when he's ready."

"I don't want to think about you being dead, my beloved girl. I am wholly focused on your life right now."

Eleanor nestled into Kuveni's arms. "I love you, Kuveni."

Kuveni sniffled, letting a few of her own tears escape. "You are my most beloved girl, Eleanor. I love you more than I loved my own daughter, and I've been ashamed to say it. She turned out to be a rather opportunistic miser, but you, my dear girl… I have never known anyone who was more compassionate and forgiving and kind. You almost make me want to endure the torment of a Yakshini pregnancy, just in case my daughter could be like you."

Eleanor laughed and then held in her grimace of pain from the movement. "You're one ox of a woman to think about enduring pregnancy while watching me languish."

"I suppose it's been on my mind watching you. Even through this, you've been an exceptional being, Eleanor, by every standard, not just human ones."

Eleanor gave into a pang of guilt that had been tormenting her in the back of her mind. "I would have ended it if I could."

Kuveni took a moment to consider her response. "I would have encouraged you. You had five bairns depending on you, and a fragile husband, and half of your life ahead of you. It would have been selfish of you not to think of saving yourself. Think of the things you could have accomplished. You could have saved endless lives as a doctor, or saved just as many languishing men as a counselor for struggling veterans."

"I can't think about it. It will make me too depressed."

Kuveni kissed her again. "I'm sorry, my dear girl, I shouldn't have said anything about it."

"I'm glad you reminded me what I was worth, Kuveni. Lots and lots of lives. Not just the bairns, but so many others too."

"You were worth a billion lives, my dearest girl. You could have been a goddess so great that the gods would have prostrated themselves at your feet."

"That would have been unnecessary. They'd have been better off doing something that mattered themselves."

"God, how I love you, Eleanor." Kuveni squeezed her gently, and then she placed her hand on her belly. "It doesn't mean that I love you any less, my little bairn. Soon enough, you will have an invisible fairy godmother to make up for the cruel joke that has wrenched your mother away from all of us."

"Do you think Edmund really plans on keeping you away?"

"He does, my darling girl, and Lord Vibhishana is right. We must let him. Lady Mélusine and I are working tirelessly now to educate your human staff to take over in our absence."

"What about poor Debbie? She can't lose you too."

"Don't worry, my beloved. We will be there for the bairns however they need us, and that includes your little Ellie. We'll just be more clever about hiding our presence from Edmund, and perhaps Mary and the lads if they don't come around. Debbie already has Vibhi's talisman, and Mélusine gave her hers this morning while Edmund was away in the cellar reorganizing his lair. My poor boy was re-hiding all of the precious objects from his past in preparation for lying to your daughter about his age and demonic status."

"Is he really planning on doing the same thing to her that Vibhishana did to him?"

Kuveni sighed with resignation. "The bairns leaving with such haste has hit him hard, Eleanor. He loved them like they were his own, and he thought they loved him just as much. Perhaps they did, it is hard to know. He's terrified now that your daughter will leave him too."

"But she won't!"

"I know, my darling girl. But we must let him do what he feels he needs. If we try to direct him otherwise, he will only push back harder."

"Is Debbie still holding steadfast?"

"I don't need to tell you how exceptional she is. That lass is going places, Eleanor. I can't wait to see. She is so curious and rational, and yet, after everything, she still has that beautiful imagination." Kuveni laughed at the memory. "She was pleasantly surprised when Lady Mélusine revealed her preferred feminine form earlier, although she was confused about how the two of us were married. We had to explain that it was all just a mischievous farce, which I admitted I never should have perpetuated. Debbie thought the idea was hilarious. It was the first time I've seen her smile since the news."

Eleanor laughed and then grunted with pain. "Of all the bairns, she was always my favorite. I suppose I can admit it now that they aren't my children anymore." Eleanor fought back a wave of despair at the thought.

As she noticed Eleanor's mood change, Kuveni changed the subject. "Your mother's downstairs in the library. You may want to join her while you are strong enough to move from room to room. Once you can't move from the bed, it will be almost unbearable."

"Let's go."

Kuveni helped her up, and she gasped with another piercing attack of pain, much worse than anything she'd felt yet. She leaned heavily on Kuveni, who could only whisper sweet assurances in her ear, and then with another pleasant breeze, Mélusine was standing before her with Vibhishana in his female nurse form.

"That uniform looks more modern. Did Mélusine advise you?" Eleanor asked.

"She is more up to date with current female disguises than I am," he admitted. "I wasn't surprised that Edmund didn't notice how out of date I was, but it will be better for everyone if we do the best job we can at the farce. I do not want him to endure anything that will make this harder than it already is."

He took her hand, and they gasped together as he took her pain into his body.

"Shiva's wrath, Eleanor. I don't know how you're even standing up," he said as he leaned on Mélusine.

"I will take it back as we go down the stairs," Eleanor suggested as she let go and he sighed with relief. "Then you can let me know when you can't stand it anymore. Perhaps together we can last longer with a livable life."

"I will do whatever you need me to do, Eleanor. When this is over, I will have an eternity to recover as I contemplate my many arrogant mistakes that got us here."

"As you like; although, with my blessing, you should certainly be doing more useful things than that. At some point, you should even be reveling in the arms of your other half." Eleanor winked mischievously, and she took in a deep breath of relief that her daughter let her have her moment of good humor.

As a trio, they escorted her down the stairs. The kitchen door was closed, and the trio escorted her swiftly past it.

"We agreed that Mrs. Murray is not educated enough to find your condition acceptable, Eleanor, but she really is a very good cook. Stanley has agreed to help us keep her in the dark," Kuveni explained.

As they arrived in the library, Moira practically jumped out of her seat to greet them.

"Are ye feelin' up to it?" she asked Eleanor hopefully.

Stanley and Norwenn were swiftly but carefully dismantling all of the Christmas decorations.

"To sitting in the library?" Eleanor asked.

"That's where ye're, ain't it?"

Eleanor couldn't help but laugh, and as Ellie stirred unhappily at the movement, Eleanor took Moira's hand and placed it gently on her belly.

"Lord Almighty," she whispered. "She's got much more to say than she did yesterday."

"Is it in words?" Eleanor asked curiously.

"Naye, just a feelin'. She's a MacLeod, that's fer sure! But there's a bit of Abbi in there too, I reckon. She's afraid of all she's got to say, like it's too much fer the rest of us." Moira guided Eleanor to the couch in the middle of the room directly across from the fireplace and helped her sit down before sitting down beside her. "I reckon the Good Lord should sit on the other side of ye, nice 'n cozy. Maybe he'll think of a miraculous cure that's just slipped his mind." She eyed Vibhishana tauntingly.

"You recognize him?" Eleanor asked with surprise.

"Aye, I've seen him like this before, on yer birthday down under. Got a glimpse of his ladylike unspeakables while I was at it."

"Good lord," he murmured. "I don't remember using this form at all that night. Did anyone else see me like that?"

"I reckon ye'd of heard of it by now if they did. Ye've got quite a stubborn memory fer a Martian god, and I'm too auld 'n foolish not to say so."

"I can assure you, Mrs. MacLeod, that if there was anything in my power I could do to save your daughter, I would do it. *Anything.* It is a very frightening proposition for the rest of the world with the power that I have, and still I can't save her."

"I figured as much," she shrugged. "Yer in love wit 'er, so I dunne see why ye'd be holdin' back."

"I love her more than I ever loved my human wife," Vibhishana confessed. "And not just because my divine partner dwells within her. Eleanor is a singularly unique woman. She has set a bar that I will find hard to surpass."

"Glad to be of service," Eleanor winked. She patted the seat beside her, and he glanced guiltily at Kuveni and Mélusine as he sat down.

"Ahh!" Stanley squealed. A rich puff of spicy fear bombarded Eleanor, but then Stanley laughed. "I thought we got rid of you this morning, you little bugger!" He reached under the tree, which was now almost stripped bare, and picked up a mouse by the tail. It squirmed unhappily, and he carried it right out to the front door and tossed it outside. "And don't come back!" He brushed off his gloves as he rejoined them. "I don't blame the little bugger, really. It's wickedly cold outside still, but we don't need an infestation to deal with now that we're losing the angels' help."

"I will return to educating Mrs. Murray on my recipes," Mélusine said. "Kuveni, you'd better help Stanley and Norwenn find a place for those decorations. You shouldn't keep storing Edmund's unused things in the basement of Avalon."

"We will use the carriage house." Kuveni snapped her fingers. "I just shoveled a path to it through the snow." Mélusine threw her a disapproving look. "My beautiful boy is still at the church with Debbie. It will look perfectly man-made when he comes back. We must do what we can to make things easier, my lady, whether he wants us to or not." She glanced at Vibhishana, waiting for him to disagree with her, but he only sighed and took Eleanor's hand, gasping again as he took over her pain.

"Well now, what'll we do to keep us occupied?" Moira asked. "I'd read ye my story, but it ain't good 'n tidy."

"You aren't reading Edmund's Roman literature, are you? I thought it was all in Latin," Eleanor asked.

"Worse," she winked. "It's French. Translated, though, by someone who must've been flushed fer weeks comin' up wit the English words." She eyed Stanley and Norwenn. "I reckon they know a thing or two over the pond that even the sassanacks haven't dreamt up yet."

"*C'est vrai*," Norwenn agreed. "More than two."

Moira picked up her book from the side table and showed it to Eleanor, glancing with minor guilt at Vibhishana.

"I thought it was gonna be about knights 'n damsels 'n chivalry 'n such, but it turned out to be more modern than I reckoned."

Eleanor laughed. "Can you go back to the beginning?"

Moira put on her reading glasses. "I ne'er thought I'd be readin' such filth to the Good Lord himself, but I reckon I ne'er thought I'd be livin' a life anything like this at all. *Madame Bovary* by Gustave Flaubert..."

As Eleanor began shivering again, Kuveni took Eleanor's free hand into her left and Vibhishana's free hand into her right, and pushed her Yakshini warmth into both of them. She materialized two carafes of hot honeyed milk on the table in front of them, and after Eleanor gulped down the whole thing, she nestled in and listened for hours as her mother read with her familiar lyrical lilting brogue that made Eleanor feel like she was a lass again, long before she knew what a tragedy even was.

When Edmund and Debbie returned, they shuffled around seeing to various household tasks and spending some time in the kitchen, and then they both joined the group in the library to listen. Debbie sat in Edmund's lap in the chair by the fire with her head nestled against his shoulder. He held her small hand as he stared pensively at nothing.

When Eleanor began shivering, Kuveni brought her a new batch of hot honeyed milk and baked beans, and when her back began aching, her entourage escorted her upstairs. She lay with Edmund and Debbie, while Sheranee lay on the floor cuddling their listless dogs, and thus began the pattern of the next many weeks of increasingly unbearable torment.

CHAPTER 30 – FREEDOM FROM WONDER

In the first week of January, Mary gave birth to a baby girl up in Scotland. Moira didn't even call to ask how she was doing, and Eleanor sighed with ambivalence, appreciating her mother's staunch support, while despite everything, feeling a bit guilty about Mary's plight. Mary had, after all, found an admirable selflessness within her before destiny had promptly sent her running right back to her ordinary human ways. Mary named the girl Rose Eleanor MacLeod as a gesture of repentance, but when Eleanor rang her up a few weeks after the fact, Reggie reluctantly admitted that Mary was still too afraid to talk to her.

He reported that the bairns were doing well. They'd even gone back to public school in Elphinstone with comments from their teachers about their advanced knowledge for their ages, no doubt a result of Auntie Mae and the angels' exceptional tutelage. Eleanor was glad to hear it, even though it set off a wave of melancholy in her. They weren't, she was certain now, ever coming back. Edmund had lost them for good, and it was, in the end, because of what he was. No amount of love and security and kindness in the world had been able to rid them of their primitive human fear, and as the weeks passed, and she tasted his fear increasing by the day, intermixing grotesquely with the scent of her own impending death, she didn't really blame him for his steadfast plan to keep their daughter in ignorance as long as he possibly could. Still, she tried to throw in a bit of reason to his brewing internal battle.

"Darling, she's developing like one of your people. You will not be able to keep what she is from her forever. You may not be able to keep it from her at all. Don't you think it will be less traumatic for her if she always knows that she's special? If she knows that her loving, gentle, kind father is the same?"

"I will not tell an innocent baby that she's a demon," he protested each time.

"I'm not suggesting that you do, darling. I don't know how many times I have to tell you that you aren't a demon."

He refused to argue with her. He'd only refocus on massaging the violet veins that had, over time, developed a metallic lustre to them.

By the beginning of February, Eleanor couldn't move from the bed. All of her hair was long gone, and Kuveni had made her a white suede hat lined with soft, warm fur to match a robe of the same material that was easy to open and close. She was shivering constantly, even after infusions of Kuveni and Mélusine's Yakshini warmth, and while her daughter continued to insist upon her rigid diet, she herself never wanted to see a baked bean again, in this life or the next.

"Ellie-bean, don't you want to try something else?" she'd ask hopefully every morning. "The world is full of delicious foods to try. How about a jelly bean? That will be sugary and delicious. Or a garbanzo bean stewed in Indian spices? Your father loves those. Or a string bean! Mmm, string beans in butter would be such a treat!" Painful cramps and a wave of nausea always reiterated the answer, and back to another bowl of baked beans it was.

In the meantime, Vibhishana could barely walk as he wavered back and forth between borrowing her pain and feeling the echoes of it rumbling deep within him, and Edmund lay beside her, reading and crying and sleeping and communing with their daughter as she grew and grew, with only brief breaks insisted upon by Eleanor to encourage his continued sanity, or when he'd catch another mouse squeaking in the corner, grab it by the tail, and fling it out the window into the snow, which had remained hard and icy since the Christmas storm. The gesture was quite unnatural for the man who'd once gently gathered up an Australian tarantula and released it onto the bark of a tree, but Eleanor was grateful that he was at least letting his anger out on a pestilent creature that would otherwise be snapped up in a trap in the kitchen.

Every day, Moira and Debbie joined them for storytime as Edmund dutifully read through all of Jane Austin's works, and then switched to Charles Dickens until Eleanor and Ellie agreed that his subject-matter was markedly too dreary for their already melancholy mood, and so Edmund switched to Alexandre Dumas. As the three musketeers swashbuckled about, Eleanor's mind often wandered, thinking about Yvie and the beautiful life they'd had together that none of them would ever know again. She debated often whether or not to ask Kuveni to escort Oz and Yvie to her bedside, but as the weeks passed by, and Mary and the bairns stayed steadfastly away, she decided against it. Edmund would need them, and for their support to be guaranteed, Eleanor knew that they mustn't see how grotesque she'd become.

Time passed. Her life-force depleted. They cried themselves to sleep. Repeat. She tried hard to embrace the mundanity of the wait as a manifestation of her fleeting humanity.

And so, it came as a jarring surprise one dark, snowy evening while Eleanor was enjoying a moment of silence as the rest of her entourage ate dinner in the dining room downstairs, when the frame to her window, and then its glass, broke right off, falling into the snow below without a sound. In a blur, Rama came tumbling inside. Behind him, red metallic plasma oozed into the form of Surpanakha. She chose her natural form that Eleanor had seen twice before that gave away the beauty she'd once had, clad in a flowing lehenga made up of shimmering black dragon scales. Sheranee leapt up from her position guarding Eleanor on the floor and cornered Surpanakha up against the gaping hole in the wall that had been her window. Sheranee growled, refusing to let Surpanakha move.

"Do it!" Surpanakha hissed at Rama. "Or I'll kill you where you stand!"

Rama glanced around the room with equal parts confusion and panic. As his eyes finally landed on Eleanor's grotesque state, illuminated only by the dancing light of the old-fashioned gaslights Edmund had brought in for her at the beginning of her bedrest, he gasped.

"Uma?"

"Eleanor," she corrected him. "But Uma is here too, just as she was before. I'm the one who's dying this time."

"*You know her?!*" Surpanakha exclaimed. "You know she is the Avatar of Durga, and you didn't come to heal her yourself, you scum! You're even more of a coward than I thought!"

Rama collected himself up off the floor and took a seat in the chair beside the bed. He was dressed only in the thin orange robes of an Indian holy man, and he shivered in the cold winter air streaming in through the gaping hole in the wall. He stared at her, racking his brain. "I've seen this before."

"I'm pregnant," she rasped. As her throat went dry, she reached over to the nightstand and drank down an entire carafe of lukewarm honeyed milk. "There's nothing you can do."

"TRY!" Surpanakha screeched.

"It won't work," he told her. "I've tried twice to heal this ailment before. I don't know why it doesn't work."

"Because there is nothing for you to heal, Rama. It isn't a disease."

"Isn't it? Mélusine said it was an infection that could only afflict pregnant women."

"I suppose that isn't wrong," Eleanor said as she glanced at Surpanakha and her tired mind rushed as fast as it could to figure out what she could say that would not cause a mess of trouble for Vibhishana and the others to deal with after she was gone.

"Melysium," Surpanakha murmured. "Melysium asked you to heal this ailment before?" Her eyes turned black as her impatience morphed into mad rage. "ANSWER ME!"

"Twice," he replied with feigned calm. "Once during the middle ages in France, and the last time perhaps about a century ago in England. Neither time it worked. The poor women were suffering mightily."

"And you tried to heal them?" Surpanakha asked. "WHY?! What was in it for you?!"

"Diplomatic relations," he shrugged. "She almost never asks for favors, and she has helped us often enough that I thought we ought to pay her back. Besides, once I see such suffering, I can't just leave it alone. It is a weakness that you have exploited too many times already."

He rubbed his hands together until the silver light erupted, but before Eleanor could shoo him away, in a flash of light, Hanuman blasted into the open window, trampling down Surpanakha.

"Rama?!" he exclaimed in a panic.

"Get off of me, you ape, before I rip your head right off!" Surpanakha screeched as she threw him off of her, slamming him against the stone wall.

As they stood back up, Sheranee growled at both of them, cornering them together.

"How dare you kidnap Rama!" Hanuman exclaimed. "He will heal no one for a monster like you, *ever!*"

Surpanakha cackled with mad glee at her triumph. "Won't he?"

"Uma?!" Hanuman exclaimed as he realized who Eleanor was. "Uma, what happened?!" He grabbed Surpanakha by the shoulders and slammed her up against the wall. "WHAT DID YOU DO TO HER?!"

Surpanakha cackled louder. "I brought a god across the world to save her life. You can thank me later."

Sheranee growled at him with a stern warning but let him pass as she focused on keeping Surpanakha cornered. He took Eleanor's hand, and she appreciated his Vanara warmth.

"She didn't do this," Eleanor said calmly. "It was no one's fault except my own, but it's too late now. Please don't waste your strength."

Hanuman threw a desperate look to Rama, and Rama rubbed his hands together, bringing forth the divine silver light of his healing power. Eleanor sighed with resignation. Some part of her hoped desperately that it would work, but she knew deep down to the core of her being that the gesture was futile. Still, she realized as she looked into their woeful expressions that all of them, even Surpanakha, needed to know for sure, and someday, even Edmund would need to know. He would need to know that there was absolutely nothing between all of the avatars on Earth that could have saved her.

Rama laid his hands on her, one on her belly, and one on her chest. He closed his eyes and took in several deep, calming breaths, moving his hands around gently as he whispered his healing mantras. But, as the seconds passed by and then the minutes, Hanuman's grimace of grief grew, and she eventually placed her hands on Rama's and nudged him away.

"Not even you can combat Shakti's will, my lord, but I will never forget that you tried. None of us will." She glanced at Surpanakha, whose mangled face was drenched with red metallic tears. "It was an act of selfless divinity that even your greatest enemies must respect."

Hanuman began sobbing, and Eleanor squeezed his fluffy hand. "My friend, I am mortal. My demise was inevitable. Now the cycle must continue for me, just as it does for the rest of the universe. Please don't let it torment you too much."

"But, Uma?!" he wailed.

"I'm already dead, old friend," Uma reminded him. "Think of the last two years you've had with me and Eleanor as a special gift."

They all glanced at the door as the sound of footsteps coming up the stairs distracted them.

Eleanor grabbed Rama's hand in her right and kept Hanuman's in her left. "Take with you Shakti's blessings, my lords. Release yourselves from all that is holding you back, and be the great gods you were destined to be. It is my will."

She let go, and with a burst of divine strength, she conjured her trident and pointed it right at Surpanakha.

"You will let them pass unharmed. It is Durga's will."

"Yes, my lady." Surpanakha bowed her head.

"GO!" she urged them. "Take with you all my love and my blessings. We will meet again in the next life!"

As soon as she said the words, she knew that they were true. She wondered how it would come to pass, although she didn't have the energy to think too much about it.

With a flash of light, Hanuman scooped Rama into his arms and flew him out the window, into the grey winter sky.

As the footsteps went past the door and continued on, Eleanor took a moment to consider her options.

"How did you get past the Yaksha threshold?"

"I followed my brother inside," Surpanakha confessed. "I came to report on my efforts to please you, my lady. I killed all of the Fascists on the list of spies, every single one of them. When I saw what wicked blasphemy my brother was up to, I stayed to make sure that he didn't return."

It was only with the last sentence that Eleanor realized which brother she was talking about.

"You've been hiding in my house since the beginning of December?"

She was horrified by the idea, but somewhat impressed that Surpanakha had managed to contain her madness thoroughly enough to go undetected by her divine entourage.

"Yes, my lady. Once I was in, I decided to stay. I almost killed the traitors on their way out the door, but I knew that it would displease you in your weakened state."

"You will not harm them," Eleanor commanded. "You will harm no one on our behalf ever again, no matter what they do. Do you understand? Promise me. Promise the Goddess."

"I promise," she whispered.

"Mean it!" Eleanor reiterated as strongly as she could muster.

"I mean it, my lady," she agreed.

"Come."

Be careful, Eleanor, Uma warned.

Now you're telling me to be careful? How about a warning to use a condom, huh?

Uma settled back into silence.

Sheranee growled her disapproval, but let Surpanakha pass at Eleanor's command, following her and making herself a barrier between them.

Eleanor pointed at the chair. "Sit."

Surpanakha was confused, but she took a seat. Eleanor looked right into her dark brown eyes and the gaping hole that was once her nose, and she smiled.

"We were both beautiful once. And yet, here we are, the victims of time and wicked circumstance. I suppose we're supposed to learn a lesson from the transition, but I have yet to decide what it is."

"I do not understand, my lady. I do not understand how you have no fear of me at all. Everyone fears me."

"I am the Holy Mother, my child. Don't you remember what I told you back in Australia? The Holy Mother loves all of her children, even the lost ones."

As a red metallic tear escaped from Surpanakha's eye, Eleanor sensed a wave of madness coming on. "Let it pass, my child. We have better things to do right now than to wither in darkness."

Surpanakha closed her eyes and said her own mantras in the hissing tones of the ancient Rakshasa language that Eleanor had only heard a few times when Edmund had been particularly addled.

Sheranee growled, but Eleanor stroked her ears reassuringly, and then she reached forward to take Surpanakha's hand. Surpanakha watched her with puzzlement, but let her make the personal gesture. Her hand was frigid, even colder than Ravana's had been, and while she didn't have the complete claws of her demonic form, her fingernails were long and pointed, like a storybook witch's. Eleanor felt Ellie stir with anxiety, but she opened her robe and held Surpanakha's hand against her bare belly.

"Meet your niece. Feel her life-force, my child. It is the same as mine. You must love her as much as you love me. You must love her enough to protect her, even from yourself. I know you have it in you."

Surpanakha held on as more tears oozed down her face.

"Let her live the beautiful, innocent life that you never had," Eleanor continued.

Surpanakha wept. "She is… perfect. She is a worthy heir for both of you."

Eleanor smiled. "I'm glad my suffering is not in vain."

Surpanakha's eyes turned black. "Love ruined you, Your Eminence. Just as I warned you it would."

"I do look ruined, don't I?" Eleanor leaned in confidingly. "But, my child, someday I will be reborn, and my grotesque human physicality won't matter anymore. It is my mind that matters most, and that is stronger than ever."

Surpanakha sat silently with her eyes closed, communing with Ellie. "But what of me, then, Your Eminence? My body and my mind are both empty shells, and yet I'm trapped here, a slave to the wicked immortality that I should never have coveted in the first place."

"Someday, when you let go of all the pain that has ruined you, you will be reborn too, my child. Start preparing for it now by releasing yourself from the darkness. It is Durga's will."

She pulled away. "I can't! It is my nature! It is my only power, Your Eminence. It is what makes me who I am. Am I to be someone else?"

Eleanor squeezed her hand. "You are more than a vengeful villain, my child. So much more. Take with you my blessings. Let them guide you." Eleanor narrowed her eyes and became more stern. "And do not, under any circumstance, hurt my beloveds. Do you understand? I will crawl out of the grave to smite you myself. That is a promise."

Surpanakha let go and wiped her tears into her skin. "Yes, my lady."

As more footsteps approached, Eleanor glanced towards the window. "Go. Take with you my blessings, my child, and let me and Edmund spend the rest of our time together in peace."

Surpanakha stood up, took one last look at Eleanor, bowed piously, and then dissolved into the form of a mouse. In a blur, she disappeared out the window.

"Ellie, I think our pest problem was just solved."

Ellie stirred, and then settled back in. Eleanor could feel her relief as the danger passed.

"Kuveni, she's gone. Can you fix the window?" Eleanor whispered.

"You are too courageous, my beloved girl. Too frighteningly courageous sometimes," Kuveni's disembodied voice murmured.

The window rematerialized as good as new just as Vibhishana, in his female form, pushed open the bedroom door and sat right down in his chair. He glanced around suspiciously as Sheranee licked his hands.

"Are you sure she's gone?"

"Aye, as sure as a great goddess can be. Was that you spying in the hallway?"

"Shiva's wrath, Eleanor, I was going out of my mind! What were you thinking letting her get that close?"

"You are not going to be able to guard them constantly. The only way they will be safe from Surpanakha is if she is protecting them from herself."

"Still, Eleanor. Still! She's a raving mad monster! She could have killed you in an instant!"

"And yet she chose not to. Instead, she chose to kidnap her greatest enemy and fly him halfway across the world to save my life. She loves us. All of us. And she needed to be rewarded for letting herself feel it."

He shook his head. "You are a greater god than I've ever been."

"Look at all the good it's doing me." Eleanor sighed. "If you were so worried, why didn't you burst your way in to rescue me?"

He took her hand and gasped as he took on her pain.

"I was running through all of my forms in my mind trying to remember which one all three of them have never seen, but I can't think straight anymore. I'm far too weak. I couldn't risk revealing my presence."

"My friend, your sister has been hopping about the house for months disguised as the mice we keep ejecting. Do you really believe for one second that she didn't realize you were here?"

"Shiva's wrath," he muttered. "At least the other two didn't know it. For god's sake, think of the catastrophe that would have unfolded if Rama and Edmund had met, or worse, if Hanuman had realized you were carrying a Rakshasa child! It could have started another war!"

"Well, they've managed to escape in blissful ignorance again. At least we know now that it wouldn't have mattered. Surpanakha did you a favor, you know."

"How?" he asked skeptically.

"She freed you from wondering, D.H. I don't believe for one second that you didn't contemplate bringing Rama here yourself just in case his power would work."

"I have been fighting the urge with all my might," he admitted. "I am ashamed that she turned out to love you more than I did."

"She didn't. She just loved the rest of the world less. You have divine responsibilities, D.H. Don't ever forget that I forgive you entirely for fulfilling them against my better interest."

He kissed her hand. "Thank you."

As he gasped with another wave of pain, she pulled her hand away. "You shouldn't let yourself become so weak. I can bear the agony myself. You need to stay strong."

He retook her hand. "It doesn't matter, Eleanor. I am weak because my life-force is dying. Whether I helped you bear the pain directly or not, your weakened state would be hurting me."

"Surely you must be used to it? What did you do before Uma was born?"

"I was weaker. I've gotten used to the energy that we have together, Eleanor. It will take me time to readjust."

"Well, there's no time like the present."

He glanced at the door. "Edmund is coming."

Edmund pushed open the door, carrying another silver tray with baked beans and hot honeyed milk. He said nothing to Vibhishana as he followed their daily routine, setting up her pillows and sitting beside her to hold her food as she ate. He shivered at the cold air that had come in while the window was missing, and after looking around the room with scrutiny, eyeing the moderate fire in the fireplace, he rang the servants' bell and waited for Norwenn to arrive.

"Please bring up some more wood for the fire and turn up the thermostat for the modern heater."

She nodded her agreement and left them alone. As Edmund retook his position, he glanced around again questioningly.

"Was someone here?"

"Why do you ask, darling?"

"I don't know. It feels… odd. Like there is a familiar energy in the air." His eyes turned black. "Was my father here?"

Eleanor took his hand and placed it on her belly. "He wanted to meet our daughter, Edmund, and I let him. Someday, she will want to know him too."

"He isn't welcome here," Edmund hissed. "He did this to you just as much as I did."

"And yet, I've forgiven you both." She glanced at Vibhishana. "It is my forgiveness to give, darling, and you must let me do what I want." She kissed him gently on the lips. "Now, Ellie-bean wants some more of these wretched beans, and we both want to hear how D'Artagnan is faring. You mustn't keep your lovely ladies waiting."

Edmund handed her the bowl and dutifully picked up the open book from the nightstand. The last hopeless chapter of their vigil had finally commenced.

CHAPTER 31 – LABOR

On February 12, 1926, Eleanor awoke with a start. A jolt of pain far worse than anything she'd ever endured stabbed through her loins. She was so weak, she could hardly whimper, but she knew exactly what it meant. She struggled to lift up the covers. The bed was soaked in a thin, metallic, violet-hued liquid.

"Dearest?" Edmund asked meekly as he noticed her fear. His eyes were already black. "Dearest?!"

"It's time," she whispered. "Darling, she's coming. Please go get Kate and Percy. I will need their help."

A rich burst of his fear bombarded her. "Eleanor, I can't lose you! I can't do this without you!"

"Darling, you don't have a choice. It's happening. Please don't make it worse than it is."

As tears streamed down his face, he gathered up his wrinkled trousers from the floor and dutifully followed her orders.

"Darling, I know it's been too painful to talk about, but we can't avoid it any longer. I want to be buried in Scotland, next to my father in Elphinstone. I don't want to be buried here, haunting you for eternity. I want this house to be a place of love and light, where you and Ellie can celebrate the beautiful life we shared. Please do that for me, okay? Promise me."

He choked on his sobs as he nodded his agreement, pulling a black cashmere sweater on over his bare chest.

"Darling, come."

She patted the bed beside her. His despondent frown was almost too much for her to bear, but she grabbed his collar and pulled him towards her anyway. She kissed him on the lips. "I love you, Edmund. I don't regret a thing, and neither should you. Our life together was more beautiful than anything I ever imagined, and I wouldn't give it up for anything, alright? I'd rather have three beautiful years with you than thirty without knowing the depths of kindness and courage that we've witnessed together in each other's arms."

"Eleanor, my Eleanor!" he wailed. He couldn't get any other words out.

She kissed him again. "Now I need you to promise me, *promise me*, that you will be here for our daughter. No matter how you feel, you must be the loving father that she deserves. You must be alive for her, Edmund, do you understand? You can't let your grief consume you. Promise me! It is my dying wish!"

"I promise," he sobbed.

She kissed him again, and he kissed her back, but another stinging pain shot through her, and she lost her breath and pulled away.

"Darling, please go get them."

In a blur, he was gone. He didn't even remember to shut the door behind him.

"Kuveni, please initiate our plan," she whispered.

"Aye," was all Kuveni could murmur through her own sobs.

Edmund returned in a blur, followed by Kate, Percy, and Vibhishana in his female form.

"Please wait out here," Kuveni suggested, barely holding herself together.

528

"WHAT?! NO!" Edmund roared.

"Darling, please do as I ask. For now, I need you to wait outside." He looked like he'd just been kicked in the stomach.

"DO IT!" Eleanor shouted.

He grabbed his head in his hands and began pacing in the hallway. Vibhishana tried to console him, but he pushed him away.

"Don't you dare touch me."

Vibhishana leaned up against the wall in the hallway bracing himself against Eleanor's increasingly excruciating waves of pain, and Kuveni closed them out.

With a snap of her fingers, Kuveni prepared the birthing room. She warmed the air to a balmy, humid temperature, and Mélusine morphed into her preferred female form. They gathered towels and blankets and a water basin, and a bucket of medieval looking tools that Eleanor couldn't bear to look at.

"Eleanor!" Edmund called desperately. "Please don't shut me out! PLEASE!"

"How long do I have?" Eleanor asked as another burst of agony shot through her. This time Kuveni placed a cloth in her mouth to bite.

"I don't know, ma chérie. It could be hours, or it could be days."

"Days?!" Eleanor exclaimed. Her panic morphed into a moan.

"She is not positioned properly," Mélusine said as soon as she placed her hand on Eleanor's belly.

Kuveni closed her eyes, whispering something that Eleanor could not make out to the other Yakshas.

"Edward Rutherford is here," Kuveni reported. "Stanley is leading him upstairs now. Monty is fetching Oz and Yvie as we speak."

"WHAT?!" Eleanor exclaimed. "I told you they weren't invited until I'm dead and buried! Edmund can't lose them too!"

"He needs them, Eleanor, and so do you," Kuveni argued. "You can blame me for eternity if it turns out to be the wrong decision, but I have faith in them. You should say goodbye to them, and they have earned the right to say goodbye to you."

Eleanor screamed as Mélusine tried coaxing Ellie into position.

"*Mon dieu*, she's as stubborn as they come!" Mélusine exclaimed.

"Just like a MacLeod," Eleanor rasped. "Where's my mother?"

"Monty will check as soon as he's back. Now focus on me, Eleanor." Kuveni pushed another dose of Yakshini warmth into her, and then placed her warm hand under the covers between Eleanor's thighs. "Let's see if we can convince her to get ready on her own."

Eleanor screamed as wave after wave of shooting pains sliced through her, but even after so many spasms she lost count, she could feel that Ellie was still turned around.

"I can't do this," Eleanor cried. "We're both going to die!"

"You're not," Kuveni said calmly. "Ellie will be safe and sound in your arms in no time, Eleanor. Now take a deep breath while you can, have a little rest, and we will try again."

Eleanor lay silently sobbing as she heard Edmund's voice speaking in low, desperate tones with Edward Rutherford and Oz.

"Eleanor, my beloved girl, we should invite Yvie to join us," Kuveni said as she let go of her hand to approach the door.

"In for a penny, in for a pound," Eleanor muttered.

Despite everything else weighing on her tired, struggling mind, anxious butterflies still fluttered in her stomach at the prospect of facing Yvie in her monstrous state.

She took the deepest breath she could muster, and nodded to Kuveni, who readied herself to open the door as Mélusine covered Eleanor's legs with the blankets. Eleanor held her breath as Kuveni attempted to let Yvie in, but Edmund pushed past her and threw himself onto the floor by Eleanor's side. He was too focused on her to notice Mélusine's female form; he only grabbed Eleanor's hand and kissed it, looking imploringly at her through his blurry, violet tear-soaked eyes.

"Please, dearest, I beg you. Please let me stay. Please." He kissed her hand again. "Please, please, please, please, please."

His heartbroken entreaty was killing her, but as another puff of his rich, spicy fear bombarded her, and another agonizing spasm cut through her, she knew that Kuveni's wisdom had been correct when they'd planned the wretched endeavor weeks earlier.

"Darling, your fear is making it worse. Ellie hates the taste of fear, yours most of all. Kate will give you updates, and if we reach a stage when your fear does not make it worse, I will invite you in. Please help me, Edmund. Help me do this as painlessly as possible."

He kissed her hand again and let go. "I will be right outside."

"I love you, Edmund," Eleanor squeaked through her sobs. "You're the finest man I've ever met."

She caught a glimpse of Edward Rutherford and Oz, who were both pale with stress as they consoled Edmund, and then she closed her eyes, waiting for the puff of Yvie's fear to engulf her as Yvie entered the room, closing the door behind her.

"*Mon dieu,*" Yvie whispered. "Ellie, why didn't you call us sooner?!" She rushed to Eleanor's side and took her hand. The puff of spicy fear didn't come, only a grimace of sorrow.

"I didn't want you two to be afraid of the angels," Eleanor admitted. "Three of the bairns left us when they saw how grotesque I was, even after everything we did for them. Edmund can't lose you too."

"He won't!" Yvie exclaimed. "Ellie, he won't! Never! Saint Mélusine was in her beastly form the night I delivered our Neddy, remember? We know how to tell the difference between good and evil, no matter what it looks like!"

Eleanor squeezed her hand. "I love you, Yvie."

Yvie kissed Eleanor's hand. "Tell me what you need, Ellie. Anything."

"I need you to help my midwives for now. When I'm gone, I need you and Oz to keep Edmund alive. He must know how much he and our daughter are loved."

Yvie leaned forward and kissed Eleanor's forehead. "They could not be more loved. They are our family, Ellie, and so are you." As she pulled away, a sad smile crept onto her face. "How is he going to feed her without you?"

"We will provide all that she needs," Kuveni replied. "We've been perfecting the recipe for centuries."

"There will be no need. I'll feed her. I'm still nursing Neddy, and I will nurse her too. She should know what a warm, loving mother feels like."

Eleanor felt another round of tears surging. "You would do that? Knowing all that you know about us? Seeing me looking like a shriveled-up swamp monster?"

Yvie intertwined her fingers with Eleanor's. "It would be a privilege."

Eleanor devolved into sobs, and Ellie and Yvie sobbed with her.

Eleanor finally broke herself out of her emotions enough to speak. "I don't know why I'm so surprised. You're the best friend I've ever had."

"*C'est vrai,*" Yvie cried. "*Et toi, aussi, Ellie.*"

"But it isn't just that. Yvie… Did Leo ever tell you that you actually *are* our family?"

"I don't have any relatives in Scotland," she replied. "But it is a lovely thought. We don't need to be related by blood, Ellie. You are the sister I always longed to have."

Eleanor felt a wave of determination wash over her. "I feel that way too, but that isn't what I meant. You are related to Edmund. His mother was the rightful Comtesse de Saint-Cyr. She died giving birth to him in 1818, after her younger sister had already moved back to France. You are his cousin, Yvie, through his human mother, whose exceptional capacity for love I think you must have inherited."

"*Mon dieu,*" Yvie whispered.

"You can't tell Edmund, though," Eleanor sighed with annoyance. "Have Father Johnson explain to you exactly why. My mind is too addled now to remember all of his many obsessive lies."

Yvie squeezed her hand. "Don't worry about it, Ellie. Don't worry about anything. We will take care of Edmund and your daughter, just as you have taken care of us."

Eleanor gave into another round of tears. "Thank you."

She took Yvie's hand and placed it on her belly. "Ellie, meet Yvie. She is the kindest, most loving human in the world."

"It takes one to know one," Yvie smiled sadly. "*Mon dieu,* how extraordinary. Is it from you, this ability to communicate without words, or is it from Edmund?"

"I suppose I've assumed that it was from Edmund. Do all Rakshasa children do this?"

"She is uniquely talented," Kuveni replied. "It could very well be from you, Eleanor. Her life is your life. She is a new being evolved from your uniquely powerful life-force."

"Blimey, that's what the prophecy meant," Eleanor murmured. "That's how it's going to happen! Kuveni, take the talismans." She stifled another moan of pain as Kuveni helped her take off Mélusine's pendant and Vibhishana's bangle. "Keep these. Give them to Ellie as soon as she is old enough to keep them safe. Tell her to wear them. They are a gift from me. If Edmund objects, tell him that it was my dying wish."

"It will be done, Eleanor."

"Good. Now, remember the box of my favorite things I asked you to give to her on her eighteenth birthday?"

"Of course, Eleanor. I don't forget such important things."

"Add to it. Add some bottles of my favorite cognacs and some bottles of Margaux."

"If you'd like."

"I would!"

"Ma chérie, what are you thinking?" Mélusine asked reservedly.

"I think that I will know my daughter after all! It is Shakti's will! If you ever get a call from me, please try to answer? I will only do it if the situation is dire. She is already her own person, and she must stay that way. It's dastardly difficult to manage voices chattering on and on in your head... No, we will remain silent and dormant unless we must, absolutely *must*, step in."

Won't we, Uma?

It will be much more difficult than you imagine, my child.

Do you think I can do it?

I know you can. That is why I chose you.

"Ma chérie, it isn't possible. Even if your soul somehow ends up inside of her, you won't be able to work your way to the surface. Humans can't do it. It will be torture to be conscious and not be able to do anything about what you're witnessing."

"I know how to fight my way to the surface!" Eleanor said with a burst of renewed energy. "I've had years of practice with Uma!"

"You must be careful, ma chérie, these types of endeavors have unintended consequences. Her life should be her life, and you must respect that."

"Of course I will!" Eleanor exclaimed. "Oh, it will be so wonderful to watch her grow up! My wistful dying wish will come true after all!"

"*Peut-être*, ma chérie. You will have to watch her pain as well as her joy."

"Isn't that what being a parent is all about?!"

"It is, my dearest, most beloved girl," Kuveni cut off Mélusine before she could add any more pessimism.

"Take this." Eleanor slipped off her wedding ring and closed it into Kuveni's hand. "Give it to Ellie when she's met a worthy partner. Tell her it was Edmund's mother's gift to me, and it's my gift to her. Can you make me a copy to be buried with? We mustn't make Edmund think about it at all."

Kuveni snapped her fingers, and a new ring appeared on Eleanor's wedding finger. Eleanor placed her hand on her belly.

"My little love, you must listen to Auntie Mélusine. We must get you out in one piece so I can say hello in person before we are rejoined."

A feeling of overwhelming peace washed over her, and she moaned as she felt Ellie slowly obey.

Kuveni closed her eyes, whispering heatedly with an angry grimace. She was arguing with a Yaksha.

After a light knock on the door, Stanley cracked it open, slipped inside, and locked it behind him, closing his eyes as the raging jeers of Edmund, who was being held back by Vibhishana, Oz, and Edward, echoed through the wood.

"Eleanor, we have a problem!"

As Kuveni growled with disagreement, Mr. Montero materialized beside her.

"Oberon?!" Mélusine exclaimed. "Leave here this instant! You know men are not allowed to witness the sacred undertaking of birth! That goes for you too, Stanley. OUT!"

"I beg your forgiveness, my lady." Monty averted his eyes. "But you must be informed. Jimmy Buchanan and Fergus MacGregor are in the linden grove. They have taken Mary and the bairns hostage, and are planning to demand a king's ransom from you that they plan to use to escape to Italy. They've been trying to get up the driveway for over an hour, but the Yaksha threshold has kept them at bay. They are getting very angry, and they are waving their guns around, threatening the bairns if they can't come up with a way to get inside."

"Blimey," Eleanor whispered.

She screamed as Ellie turned over.

"Report, greenie!" she hissed.

"They shot Reggie."

"*Mon dieu,*" Yvie whispered.

"Is he alive?" Eleanor asked.

"He's in the hospital in Edinburgh. The doctors expect him to live, but he was unconscious long enough that he couldn't call to warn us. They've been gone for hours, Eleanor... I suppose long enough to get here. What do we do?"

Eleanor screamed again as she felt Ellie turn too far, returning to her breech position.

She looked around the room. "Where is my mother?" she repeated the question that hadn't received an adequate answer. "Where is Debbie?!"

Mr. Montero closed his eyes, grimaced, and reopened them. "They are headed for the linden grove. Debbie has your pistol, and your mother has her own... Charlie has stolen Stanley's pistol, and he is running with them. He appears to have used a ruse of diplomacy to leave the hostage party and come get help."

"Why didn't you just dissolve their guns and have it bloody over with?!" Kuveni exclaimed.

"Surpanakha is lurking. She just captured Illa."

"WHAT?!" Kuveni exclaimed.

"WHAT?!" Eleanor seconded. "I'm going to *kill* that disobedient fiend."

She screamed with another explosion of pain shooting up from her loins, across her abdomen, through her uterus, and into her chest.

"Shiva's wrath," Eleanor murmured. "They're all going to die. Bring Vibhi in here now."

"Eleanor," Mélusine moved to protest. "You must focus on your sacred task. Let us handle this."

"BRING HIM IN!"

Kuveni blurred to the door. "Parvati, we need you. *Now.*"

Vibhishana blurred past Edmund and slammed the door behind him.

"Let me save them, D.H. Let me hop into you like Uma did on my birthday."

"Ma chérie, you must focus on your one and only task," Mélusine reiterated.

Uma, will you do this for me?

It is your dying wish, my child.

"Uma will stay! Ellie is letting me do this, D.H. She's returned to her holding position. It is Shakti's will."

"Eleanor, this is a horrifically dangerous thing to do," he protested. "If your body dies while you're away, I don't know what will happen to your soul. Nothing like it has ever been done before!"

Uma, will you summon me? Summon me when I must return.

It will be done, my child.

"We've got it covered. Trust me, D.H., let me do this."

Vibhishana kneeled beside her and took her hand. *My body is yours, Eleanor. Use it well.*

As she felt Ellie settle in for the wait, she looked into his eyes and called upon all of the divine power within her to force her essence into his fingertips, up his arm, and into his hollow gut. She shivered as she felt the cold power coursing through him, and she felt his body transform.

"*Mon dieu*," Mélusine and Yvie murmured at once.

Uma wailed with pain in Eleanor's body, as Eleanor looked down at her perfectly formed hands. They were hers, as she had known them before her human shell had withered. She was wearing Durga's bejeweled crimson sari, the same one Vibhishana had produced himself on the night of her fateful birthday party, and she could see the rich red tendrils of her healthy, beautiful hair flowing down her shoulders.

Let's do this, D.H.

She felt a burst of vigor at the miraculous gift the gods had given her.

"You must go now," Mr. Montero reiterated. He snapped his fingers, and the window dissolved. "Go!"

She felt the utterly odd sensation of a slippery fish swimming up her back, until a massive pair of golden falcon wings burst forth. As the sound of gunshots echoed across the linden grove, she soared right out the window.

It was time for her last battle.

CHAPTER 32 – GLORIOUS

She landed in the woods just beyond the druidic ruins in the clearing where her wedding ceremony had taken place. She absorbed her wings and took in a deep, calming breath. The fluffy white snow made the surroundings ominously quiet, leaving only the sounds of human brutality in their midst.

A baby was screeching. Ruthy was crying, and Howie was grasping onto his mother in stunned silence as terrified tears streamed down her face. Their fear tasted even more delicious than it had in her own body, intoxicatingly delicious.

"Is that clear enough?!" Jimmy growled as he pointed his rifle straight up into the air. "One more minute, and it's gonna be aimed at yer head, Mary MacGregor!"

"He's coming!" Mary cried. "I'm sure Charlie's coming right now! You know it takes time to negotiate with these sassanacks, and Edmund Marriner is the most miserly of 'em all! He doesn't care one lick about any of us!"

"Shut yer lyin' mouth, woman," Fergus spat.

Jimmy aimed his gun at Mary.

Where are the others? Do you know, D.H.? Debbie, and Charlie, and my mother?

I know just as little as you do, Eleanor.

As Eleanor heard a crunch in the woods across from her, Debbie raised her pistol. Before Eleanor could think through her options, Debbie closed one eye, aimed, and pulled the trigger.

BOOM.

Mary screamed.

Ruthy screamed.

The baby screamed.

Howie threw himself on the ground behind one of the druidic megaliths, covering his ears and closing his eyes.

Fergus looked around with wild eyes for the perpetrator.

Jimmy collapsed dead onto the ground, and blood soaked into the snow all around him.

She'd shot him in the back.

Debbie gasped and dropped the gun as if it had burned her hand. Moira stepped in front of her, aiming her pistol at Fergus.

Fergus lifted his rifle and pointed it at Mary.

"Ye were always a lying, connivin' bitch, Mary MacLeod. I'll see ye in Hell."

As Fergus pulled the trigger, Eleanor blurred in front of Mary. She startled as the bullet hit her, blowing a grotesque hole into her gut.

Everyone screamed.

The injury didn't hurt one bit. She felt Vibhishana coaxing his plasma to fill in the wound, and within seconds, it was completely filled in, and her sari was perfectly reformed.

As she looked around, readying herself to explain what exactly they'd just seen, she realized that Fergus was gone.

"Ellie?" Mary whimpered.

"Amma?!" Debbie exclaimed.

"Lord Almighty," Moira murmured.

The baby in Mary's arms screeched louder.

Moira guided Charlie and Debbie into the center of the clearing, keeping her pistol poised.

"I didn't touch him!" Eleanor exclaimed. "Did any of you see where he went?!"

Howie rolled around on the ground screaming. Ruthy ran to Eleanor and hid her face in her sari.

Debbie gasped and pointed past Eleanor to the top of the tallest linden.

Fergus MacGregor's corpse was hanging lifeless in one of the tallest branches, his arms dripping with blood from freshly carved wounds. Vibhishana's eyes could see that they were engraved with Rakshasa script, but even he could not make out what they said.

Surpanakha.

The one and only. So much for Shakti's blessings.

"Everyone gather around me," Eleanor ordered them. "Now!"

Debbie ran over to Howie, dragging him kicking and screaming to Eleanor's feet. She gathered Ruthy into her arms and held her tight.

Sheranee come now. Your mistress commands you. Wait on the sidelines for my cue.

Eleanor called forth her divine trident, and she felt her crown materialize on her head. A burst of rich, spicy Rakshasa fear erupted from the far end of the clearing, and Eleanor blurred in front of her wards, creating a barrier between them and her mad enemy.

"Show yourself, Surpanakha!" she boomed. "Durga commands it!"

Surpanakha's red metallic plasma oozed up out of the snow into her human form. Eleanor aimed her trident at her, and it burst into the green flames of Shakti's power.

"My lady?!" Surpanakha exclaimed breathlessly as she kneeled in prostration. "How can it be true?! You were dying!"

"I told you I would smite you from the grave, and I meant it!" Eleanor shouted. "You have disobeyed me, and now you will be punished!"

"But he was going to kill your sister!" Surpanakha exclaimed. "A mother with a babe in arms! He was evil!"

Eleanor walked towards her slowly, pointing her trident at Surpanakha's head, stopping only when her trident was touching the gaping hole in Surpanakha's face.

"You enslaved a Yakshini!" Eleanor boomed. "You will release her now!"

"But... but... I need her, my lady! I need her power to combat my evil brother! He already has too many Yakshas. He is unstoppable! But with enough power, I will be able to equal him. I will be free!"

"You will not free yourself on the backs of others! She is not a prize to be collected. She is a sacred immortal being!" Eleanor boomed. "You will free her now! DURGA COMMANDS IT!"

"But I can't! I don't know how! No Yaksha has ever been freed! It can't be done!"

Eleanor took in a deep breath, using her divine power and Vibhishana's to feel for the energy of Illa's stolen life.

Eleanor reached forward and ripped a gaudy necklace from Surpanakha's neck. She closed her eyes and reveled in a wave of intoxicating power as it worked its way through her fingertips. The charm dissolved into ashes.

Illa appeared by her side.

"My lady?!" she squeaked.

"GO!" Eleanor shouted. "Go back to the Crystal Cave now and wait for a Yaksha to help you."

Illa dissolved.

"My lady, how is this possible?" Surpanakha asked with wonder. "Such power has never existed on Earth. Not in five thousand years! You will be our savior! You will be the one to free all of us!"

Eleanor stumbled backwards as an echo of her birthing pain shot through her.

My child, the time is near.

"What is this?" Surpanakha hissed.

Eleanor looked down. Her body was no longer hers. In her moment of weakness, she had dissolved back into Vibhishana's Lankan form.

"WHAT IS THIS?!" Surpanakha screeched. "LIES! IT IS ALL LIES!"

She threw herself at Eleanor, and in a blur, they were engaged in a battle of titans. Surpanakha slammed her against one of the druidic ruins, and Eleanor kicked her off, throwing her against another. Surpanakha burst into her full demonic form, and with a surge of cold, invigorating power, Eleanor shivered as the spikes exploded from Vibhishana's body. She drank in a delicious gulp of fear, and then launched herself straight at her enemy.

Surpanakha grabbed onto Eleanor's shoulders and pulled her into the sky. Eleanor burst forth her wings and chased after her, aiming her trident for the gaping hole in Surpanakha's face, but suddenly Surpanakha dove straight down.

"You are slow today, brother!"

As Eleanor approached her, Surpanakha whipped out her arm, morphing it into a tentacle. She grabbed Eleanor's trident right out of her hand and cracked it over her knee, breaking it in two and throwing it into the woods below.

"LIES! Do you think I was born yesterday, brother?! Does your blasphemy know no bounds! How dare you impersonate the Holy Mother!"

Eleanor rushed Surpanakha and kneed her in the groin. Surpanakha was so surprised by the bizarre human tactic that she tumbled downwards, crashing into the branches of the ancient linden below. Fergus MacGregor's corpse came tumbling down with a thud, and Eleanor followed it, blasting a puff of dirty snow into the air as she landed back in the clearing.

She glanced around, assessing her options, but another burst of pain knocked her right off her feet. She moaned and grabbed the place where her human abdomen would be.

Mary and the bairns screamed as Surpanakha landed beside them. She honed her attention in on Mary.

"Traitor," she hissed. "I will punish all of you! For the glory of the Mother!"

Now! Eleanor called to Sheranee as she lay on the ground, trying to muster the strength to push through the pain.

Sheranee roared as she leapt into the clearing, pummeling Surpanakha. Surpanakha screeched as she kicked her off, but Sheranee dug her fangs into her thighs, refusing to let go.

Surpanakha ripped at Sheranee's fur, and as Surpanakha slashed ugly wounds into Sheranee with her demonic claws, Eleanor forced herself up off the ground. She glanced around frantically looking for a weapon, and then she spied it.

In his shaking hand, Charlie was bravely trying to point Stanley's gun, waiting and moving and repositioning as he tried to get a clear shot that wouldn't hit Sheranee.

"Yer a tidy, brave lad," Eleanor whispered. Charlie looked up at her demonic form, and as another puff of rich spicy fear invigorated her, she took his gun and aimed it right at Surpanakha's head.

Sheranee roared as Surpanakha broke her back legs with one excruciating crunch.

BOOM.

Surpanakha splattered into a million droplets of red metallic liquid, and Eleanor held her breath.

Everyone watched as the droplets wriggled and oozed, pulling themselves together into a conscious puddle, but as the final droplets came together, Surpanakha disappeared in a blur. The bullet was gone. All that was left was a smattering of blue powder sinking into the glistening snow.

Eleanor collapsed. With the last bit of strength she had left, she dissolved Vibhishana's spikes, forcing his weak body back into her form.

"Amma?" Debbie whimpered. She looked back and forth between her father's dead body and Eleanor.

"Yer a good, tidy lass, Debbie MacLeod," Eleanor said as she pulled her into her arms. "The best I've ever met."

Debbie buried her face in Eleanor's chest. "I killed my Da! The nightmare came true!"

"I know, my little love." Eleanor kissed her forehead. "You saved them. You saved all of them. And did you like the feeling of killing him?"

"No!" Debbie cried. "It was awful! It's haunting me!"

"That's because you're your Amma's daughter, my love. Don't ever forget that. I am with you now and always." Eleanor kissed her again.

Debbie buried her face in Eleanor's sari. "I keep seeing it, Amma, like its happening again and again. It's stuck in my mind, and it won't go away! It's like I'm going mad!"

Eleanor hugged her. "This is perfectly natural, my little love. In time, it won't be so bad." She glanced over to her mother. "You should go back with Gramma to Scotland for now. Start rebuilding your life away from here, and when you are ready, come visit Ellie and Abbi. They will be missing you."

Moira leaned on one of the megaliths. "Are you my Eleanor, or are ye the Good Lord? Just tell it to me straight."

"I am both," Eleanor said as she hugged Debbie again. "He let me borrow his body to save you, but I can't stay. My time is up, my loves."

She let Debbie go and pulled Ruthy and Charlie into her arms. "Amma will always love you."

She glanced at Howie, who covered his face with his arms, hiding his eyes, and she sighed with resignation, keeping her distance. "Amma will always love you, Howie. And you, Mary, and even you, Rose, my little love. You must all love me through Ellie now, and when you are ready, you must love Abbi again too."

She kneeled down to inspect Sheranee's wounds. *Are you going to be alright, my love?*

Sheranee nodded in the affirmative and nuzzled her hands. Eleanor kissed the top of her head, rubbed her ears, and giggled as Sheranee licked her face for the last time.

Wait for my call, my love. Our work is not done.

Sheranee bowed her head and dutifully disappeared.

Eleanor looked around at the ugly carnage and the wide-eyed bairns, and then she pulled her mother into her arms. "I love you, Mum." She leaned in to whisper in her ear. "Please make sure that Edmund knows what happened. That he knows that Debbie isn't leaving because of him."

"Aye, don't ye worry about a thing, Ellie. We'll take care of him and yer lil Ellie-bean." Her mother squeezed her until her aged arms gave out. "I love you, Eleanor Mary MacLeod. Ye made my life worth livin', and I'm too auld 'n desperate 'n foolish not to say it. I'm gonna make ye proud. Ye'll see."

Eleanor almost collapsed in her arms as the worst wave of agony yet bombarded her.

Come, my child. You cannot wait any longer.

"Monty," she whispered. "Come clean things up, will you? I've got a daughter to meet."

She burst forth her golden falcon wings and blew them a kiss. It was time for her last glorious triumph.

CHAPTER 33 – TRANSITION

Eleanor could barely fly as she veered towards the open window. She collapsed onto the floor, and Kuveni snapped her fingers and reformed the glass.

The bed was soaked with blood and milky violet metallic liquid. She couldn't bear to see Uma writhing in her grotesque impending corpse. She refused to look at it, fighting every instinct to grip onto Vibhishana's immortal body and refuse to let go.

"Did you save them?" Yvie asked.

"Aye, all five bairns are intact, and all the human villains are dead. Now it's time to face the music."

You must go now, or we will all pay the price, Vibhi warned her.

He grabbed the hand of her dying human body and ejected her soul back into it, dissolving back into his gentle Lankan form as she went. He collapsed into the chair beside her.

Eleanor screamed as the most excruciating pain yet ripped through her.

"You must tell Ellie to get into position, ma chérie. She cannot wait much longer. It will be dangerous for her."

Eleanor grabbed her belly. *Come on, Ellie-bean. It's time. Neither of us can stall any longer.*

She screamed again as Ellie reluctantly agreed, and she tried to focus her mind on something, anything, other than the pain. She landed on listening to Edmund sobbing as he paced frantically outside the door.

Come on, Ellie-bean. You can do it!

"It is working, ma chérie!" Mélusine said as she grabbed her hand. "There! She's ready!"

"Go send Edmund in," Eleanor said to Vibhishana.

"It isn't a good idea, ma chérie."

"If there's going to be a man in here, it's going to be my husband!" Eleanor shouted. "Send him in!"

"Vibhi," Mélusine said as he moved to open the door. "Your form."

"And yours," he replied.

She returned to the form of Percy, adding a white doctor's lab coat for propriety. Vibhishana morphed back into Parvati, took a deep breath, and pulled Edmund inside, glancing back mournfully at Eleanor one last time before closing the door behind him.

It's been nice knowing you, D.H.

He couldn't hear her. She'd already given his talisman to Kuveni for safekeeping.

"Eleanor?" Edmund sobbed as he kneeled beside her and took her hand. He kissed it, and then looked searchingly at Kuveni and then Mélusine.

"She must come now," Mélusine reiterated. "Ma chérie, you must encourage her."

Eleanor smiled. "Everything's going to be alright, darling. Absolutely everything. You'll see." She placed his hand on her belly. "Ellie-bean, your Daddy wants to meet you."

She braced herself as a ferocious explosion shot through her loins.

"Push!" Mélusine shouted. "Push!"

Eleanor squeezed Edmund's hand and screamed as she pushed. Her scream dissolved as the pain consumed her, shooting up into her chest, down her arms and legs, to the edges of her fingertips and toes, and out.

With all the power left in her withered shell, she held onto her consciousness, listening to her daughter's screams.

Her eyes blurred, and the room dimmed.

Eleanor, we must go.

Not yet.

Kuveni wrapped the baby in a blanket and placed her in Eleanor's arms.

The darkness was pulling her under.

Eleanor, now.

"Hello, my little love," Eleanor whispered as she fought to keep her eyes open. She looked up into Edmund's tear-drenched face and smiled. She urged him to take their daughter into his arms. "Love her, Edmund. Love her enough for both of us."

Now!

She closed her eyes and relaxed. As her consciousness dispersed into the ether, Uma dragged her away from the peaceful silence, into a place that was warm and safe and alive. Into a place that wasn't hers, but was familiar all the same. She nestled in and curled up.

Ellie Ariadne MacLeod Marriner's life had just begun.

PART FIVE
WHILE SHE WAITS

CHAPTER 34 – PICKING UP

He wept as he held her. She sobbed as his sorrow infused her, but all he could do was cradle her as the angels wept around him, silently going about the orders Eleanor had left them with.

"She needs to eat," Kuveni reluctantly interrupted.

She felt his panic explode. "But how?!"

"I will feed her. I'm still nursing Neddy, and now I will nurse Ellie as long as she needs me to," Yvie whispered. "Come. Let's leave this room and go somewhere comfortable. You may stay beside me the whole time, and when she's done, you can have her back."

He carried her. No one said a word as they passed by, but she could feel their despair swirling in the air. Yvie's warm, loving arms were comfortable. Her calm human heartbeat pulsed in sync with Ellie's as the hot milk filled her tiny body with warmth. She didn't want to let go.

When she was finished with her first meal, she returned to her father's arms. They pulsated with warmth, just like hers did. He held her until she needed to eat again.

For her first six months, Ellie was held. Night or day, her father refused to sleep unless she was safely in someone's warm arms. From Auntie Yvie to Uncle Oz to Stanley to Mrs. Walsh she was passed. When Gramma Moira was visiting with Debbie and Charlie from Scotland, they held her too.

Slowly but steadily at a perfectly human pace, Ellie sat and then stood and then walked on her own. Edmund followed her. Wherever she went, he went too, from room to room in the house, from bush to bush in the garden, and from tree to tree in the linden grove. She wanted to catch up with Neddy, but he was too fast. He was so big that she couldn't imagine the day when she could run as fast as he could. It happened just before she turned four.

Uncle Oz and Auntie Yvie were reluctantly packing up to return to Australia as she chased Neddy into the library. The stock crash had hit the family business hard, and Oz and Yvie tried to hide their panic, but Ellie could taste it.

"We'll be back after I sort things out," Oz kept telling them. "The world will always need milk. My brothers just need a steady hand to whip them back into shape."

They didn't return to England for seven more years. By then, Ellie hardly remembered them at all.

While Ellie grew up, Edmund grew older, and with his aged decline, he slowly gave her the space that she refused to admit she needed. She loved him so dearly, her kind, gentle, clever father, and she knew that someday soon she would lose him. He was, after all, a good forty years older than any of the other fathers of her peers. He was almost as old as Gramma Moira.

Every year, they trekked up to Scotland for Christmas to sit before Gramma Moira's roaring fire in her comfortable parlor by the Christmas tree, reading stories and decorating gingerbread houses, and keeping her father's spirits up. She didn't know why he was so melancholy on Christmas, but she knew that it was her daughterly duty to combat it. Debbie and Charlie helped her, while Howie and Ruthy and Rose and Auntie Mary only stopped by for a brief hello, delivering a box of shortbreads and a fruitcake from the grocer down the lane. Ellie always thought it was strange that they lived next door and were always too busy to stay, she figured it was because of Auntie Mary's important secretarial work at the school, but in the evenings, when Auntie Mary was listening to the radio, Rose would sneak through the secret passage to Ellie's room, and they'd play.

And so, life moved on in a precarious peace until the bairns were no longer bairns, when Hitler invaded Poland, and they all went to war. Her father was terrified, and so was she. She'd always detested the taste of his fear most of all.

One night after dinner a month into the war, Stanley paced uncomfortably in the hallway just outside the dining room. He waited for them to finish, and for Ellie to head to the library to study for her fall exams, and then he made his move. Ellie waited in the hallway to listen.

"Colonel, General Kettering called."

"General Kettering?" Edmund asked. "Is he still alive? He must be more ancient than I am by now."

"He's eighty-five, sir. He's been retired a long time, but he's been called back to advise on special cases for the Cause. He's asked... he's asked if there's anything you can do to help. If perhaps... you might be willing to... er... regain your strength."

Edmund stewed about his answer for a long time, and then he sighed a long sigh of resignation. "Stanley, the stories of my heroism from the Great War did not include all the facts. My shell shock made me a danger to everyone, not just our enemies. I have the capacity to become a beastly fiend in the wrong circumstances, and the blood of a battlefield is something I must avoid, for myself, and for Britain."

"I will tell him."

As Stanley moved to leave, Edmund stopped him. "What else do they need? What can I do from the sidelines that will save more lives than one man charging into battle? Let's think for a minute about all the special things an old crotchety man like me can still do."

Stanley took a seat beside him. "Whatever you want to do, I will help you, Colonel. Between Lord Reginald Grimby and myself, we know all the military leaders in Britain."

"They aren't trying to send you off to the frontlines?"

"I'm a pouf, Colonel, and they all know it. They've decided not to shoot me for it, but they don't want me... er... causing trouble amongst the ranks."

"It's a saving grace for you, my friend."

"I know, Colonel. But I can't just sit back and watch."

"Neither can I. Let's think."

Mrs. Walsh popped her head in from the kitchen. "Do you need anything else tonight, Colonel?" she asked in Breton. "I'm almost done cleaning up."

"Thank you for another wonderful meal, Mrs. Walsh," he replied in the same.

"That's it!" they exclaimed at once.

"Colonel, I will ring General Kettering now. We will get a covert communications station set up here by lunchtime tomorrow. Translating, transmitting, and code-breaking. That's how we're going to do it. I'll do the French, and you'll do everything else. Maybe even Reggie can help! Think of the lives we'll save! We'll be Britain's secret weapon! The war will be over by Christmas!"

"We'll do what we can," Edmund said reservedly. "But it's going to be a long, ugly war, Stanley. Uglier than the world has ever seen."

"How do you know?"

"I can feel it."

Ellie tiptoed to the library. She was proud of both of them. She hoped, secretly, that she might be able to help, although the only languages she spoke fluently were the Hindi and Latin her father had used with her when she was a lass, neither of which, she had to admit, were particularly relevant to the Cause.

By lunchtime the next day, the library was off-limits. Reggie arrived by dinnertime, and for the next six years, the three of them worked around the clock, only stopping when their bodies forced them to eat or sleep. Ellie saw to every detail in the management of the house while Mrs. Walsh cooked and cleaned, but it wasn't enough. She wanted to do more, like Debbie was doing. She wished she was old enough to matter.

By the Christmas of 1944, Edmund's back had curved from his endless hours crouched over the telegraph, and his vision had faded to near-blindness, even with the help of some very unflattering heavy glasses. He continued on. Stanley and Reggie both had heads of entirely white hair from their years of tireless work, and all of them forgot it was Christmas until the doorbell rang, and Ellie rushed to get it.

"Keep working!" she called to Stanley. "I've got it!"

"Ho, ho, ho!" Debbie declared as she held Charlie steadily on her arm.

"Good lord," Ellie murmured as he limped with her over the threshold. "Are you really walking?"

He'd lost both of his legs in combat nine months earlier.

She rushed to flank him. "If you can call this walking," he replied. "Merry Christmas, Ellie."

"Merry Christmas!" she exclaimed. "We completely forgot!"

"That's why we're here!" Debbie said cheerfully. "Gramma told us that Abbi was too weak to come up to Scotland again, so we decided to bring Christmas to you."

"How kind," Ellie murmured. "How is Gramma?"

"Still kickin'!" Moira exclaimed as she hobbled up the stairs.

"Gramma!" Ellie exclaimed.

She rushed down to help her, and Moira pulled her into a hug. "Yer a good, tidy lass, Ellie Marriner."

"Who is it, Ellie?" Mrs. Walsh asked as she approached from the kitchen. "Why, it's a band of carolers, indeed! Come in, come in!"

"I hope it's not an imposition?" Debbie asked. "If you need more food to feed us, I can order some to be sent along from the grocer."

"On Christmas Eve?" Ellie asked.

"Naye. I had a feeling we'd be having guests." Mrs. Walsh winked. "Come on. I've got a Christmas goose all ready to serve that will almost be as good as Mrs. Murray's were."

They pulled off their wet coats and piled into the dining room.

"Would you like some chouchen?" Mrs. Walsh asked.

"I wouldn't mind a wee nip," Moira said cheerfully.

"I'll go tell Dad that you're here," Ellie said as she left them alone. She tapped on the library door. "Dad? We have guests! It's Christmas Eve!"

Stanley cracked the door open. "He can't come right now. We just received encoded plans straight from Hitler's desk in Bayreuth. Seven spies died to get them to us."

"Aye. I understand. I'll keep them occupied."

"Merry Christmas, Ellie. If we work hard enough, this might be what we need to end the war."

She squeezed his hand. "That'll make it the merriest Christmas of all."

By the time she returned to the dining room, the whole meal was beautifully spread out across the table, and Mrs. Walsh had taken a seat to join them.

"This looks lovely!" Ellie exclaimed. "I'm glad someone here remembered it was Christmas!"

"Where's Abbi?" Debbie asked.

"He's sleeping in the library," Ellie lied. "He wasn't feeling up to it."

"Did you tell him it was us?" Charlie asked with a hint of annoyance.

"Aye. He's spending all the time he can get in there these days."

"Well, we should go keep him company! It's Christmas!" Moira exclaimed. "Abbi isn't allowed to be alone on Christmas, it's a rule!"

"He's fine!" Ellie protested a bit too strongly.

"Is it Howie?" Debbie asked confidingly. "He died bravely."

Charlie scoffed. "Is that the lie you're telling everyone these days?"

"It is the lie I'm telling myself," Debbie shrugged.

She took a hefty chunk of goose onto her plate and began serving it to the others. Ellie followed her lead and passed the mashed potatoes.

Mrs. Walsh poured them each a generous serving of chouchen and raised her glass. "To next Christmas, when the angels shall have defeated the forces of darkness once and for all!"

"Here, here!" Debbie toasted.

They all drank down big gulps.

"That'll be over six years of war," Charlie muttered. "*Six* years. It could've been over millions of lives ago if *someone* had found more courage."

Debbie kicked him under the table.

"Ow!" he exclaimed.

Debbie was startled by his reaction.

He grinned mischievously and winked. "Don't start thinking your genius idea is magic, Debs. I was just taking the piss out of ye. Kick that wooden stick all you want."

"Did you invent them? The prostheses?" Ellie asked, working to ignore her subtle anxiety at the tone of their conversation. She could always tell when they were leaving her out of something, but they would never, ever give away the secret.

"I've been working on them in my spare time."

Moira laughed. "Yer spare time?! I dunne know when ye e'en sleep, Debbie!"

"They won't let me work double shifts at the hospital." She rolled her eyes. "They think it's too much for my delicate female disposition. It's given me time to set up a lab to work on my ideas. Before the war is over, I'm gonna have ye walking fer good, Charlie MacLeod, ye'll see."

"If anyone can do it, you can, Debs." He held up his glass in another toast.

"At least they're lettin' ye be a doctor," Moira pointed out.

"The MD has something to do with it, Gram."

"They dunne let ye out on the frontlines, did they? Yer lucky they dunne make ye wear a nurse's uniform just so ye don't scare the public too much wit yer unladylike doctorin'."

Debbie laughed. "I suppose you're right, Gram. Before the war, they never would've let me be a chief of medicine at a hospital in London. When it's all over, I'm sure they'll boot me right out the door again, but I have a plan." She grinned. "I'm gonna get my doctorate. I'm gonna get a real proper lab, and I'm gonna make my prostheses for everyone. Reggie's solicitor already helped me submit my paperwork for the patents."

"How wonderful!" Ellie exclaimed. "Congratulations! I wish I could do something like that."

"Why don't you, Ells?" Debbie asked. "You should apply to Oxford while they're still letting women in the door! After the war, you'll be at the back of the line!"

Ellie shrugged. "I don't know what I would study. I've been so distracted by the war for so long, I haven't let myself think about it."

Charlie snorted. "I don't know how. It's like the war isn't even happening here. Why don't ye go take a snooze with Abbi while ye think about it."

Debbie kicked him again.

Ellie felt her Celtic temper brewing. She had trouble controlling it when anyone made a snide comment about the aged decline of her father.

"My father is a great man," Ellie declared.

"Yer father is a coward," Charlie muttered. "If he weren't, he'd have taught the Nazis a thing or two about honor years ago."

"Leave Abbi alone," Debbie warned him as she threw a glance at Ellie. "He knows his limits, and so should you."

"Abbi has his reasons," Moira seconded.

"He's old!" Ellie exclaimed. "What did you want him to do, hobble onto the beach of Normandy and beat them to death with his cane?"

"Naye, that isn't what he should've done," Charlie replied. "He should've done what he could, and he didn't, and that's why yer Da is a coward."

"You take that back, Charlie MacLeod!" Ellie shouted as she stood up to loom over him.

"Enough," Debbie hissed at him. "Why'd you even come down if you're so cross at Abbi?"

"It was better than sitting around with Mum sobbing over her tragic Howie and my missing legs. I wanted a break. It was a bad idea, though. I shouldn't have come." He glanced angrily at Ellie. "Abbi didn't even care enough to wake up and see us."

Moira stroked Ellie's hand. "Now, now, Ellie-bean, it's been a long war, and a long journey down here from Scotland. Charlie's just in a mood. Sit down an' eat yer supper."

"I'm not hungry," Ellie said as she threw her napkin onto her plate. "I'll eat in my room later."

She stomped away, but stopped in the hallway to listen as Debbie kicked Charlie again.

"What'd ye go an' rile her up for!" Debbie hissed.

"I'm not taking it back. It's true. Abbi could've hopped down over the pond and ripped Hitler's head clean off before supper was cold, and instead he's been napping in the library for the whole goddamned war."

"If the angels could've ended it that quick 'n clean, they would've," Moira argued. "They've been workin' tirelessly fer years now, and it's still not enough."

"Even Father Johnson hasn't been able to stop them," Debbie added. "If he can't do it, Abbi can't either."

"He should've tried!" Charlie shot back. "He should've been there! He should've done something other than sittin' around whinin' about Amma before my goddamned legs got blown off!"

"It's not his fault," Debbie whispered. "It's not fair for you to blame him."

"I'll blame him if I wanna blame him," Charlie huffed. He drank down the rest of his chouchen. "Now, if you'll excuse me, I've lost my appetite too."

He stumbled against the chair leg, almost falling over, and then hobbled into the hallway with his two canes. He glanced at Ellie.

"I'm not sorry for saying it. One should ne'er regret the truth."

He glanced at the staircase, growled with anger at his inability to climb it, and hobbled into the parlor muttering.

"Why don't you think Abbi's done anything?" Debbie whispered to Moira. "Surely he can't be so consumed by his fear to just sit by and watch."

Moira sighed. "He's a broken man, Debbie. We can't understand how bad the first war was fer 'im."

"I wish he weren't so broken. We all could've used his help."

Ellie ran up the stairs to her bedroom and hid her face in her pillow. She cried herself to sleep.

Eleanor waited. She waited until the clock struck midnight, and Ellie was in one of her deepest sleeps. She'd held off so many times for so many years, waiting for the perfect moment, the moment when it would be most worth the risk to make her presence known.

She'd watched with perfect discipline as Ellie had struggled with her broken arm after she'd fallen out of the same linden where

Fergus MacGregor had met his doom, and as Ellie had wondered fearfully for years, without saying a peep about it to her father, what the healing violet metallic plasma meant for her. She'd watched as the bairns had grown, and Howie had been shot for desertion. She'd watched as Edmund had let himself go far too long into aged frailty without re-setting himself, dreading with more and more urgency the impending day when he wouldn't be able to lie to his Ellie-bean any longer, and she'd pick up and leave, just like the bairns did.

And so, as she took in an awakening Rakshasa breath, feeling the air in her lungs for the first time in almost twenty years, she knew that every minute was precious. She wiggled her toes and hissed as her feet hit the cold stone floor. She looked at herself in the mirror, wondering if Ellie's plasma would have enough instinct to present her as she remembered herself, or if she would have to do something else, something awkward, to convince them of who she was. As she caught a glimpse of her sharp nose in the mirror, she smiled. *Excellent.* She couldn't wait for the day when Ellie would take hold of her many Rakshasa talents herself.

She wrapped Ellie's robe tighter and tiptoed into the hallway, straight to Debbie's room. It was the same room Debbie had chosen upon their arrival in Basingstoke so many years before. Edmund had kept it, and Debbie had used it every time she frequently visited. Eleanor smiled as she cracked open the door and spied the bicycle in the corner, gathering dust without the Yakshinis keeping the house miraculously clean.

She stopped for a moment, solidifying her plan. She'd dreamed of this moment for so long, but now she was scared. Mostly, she didn't want to scare Debbie as a spectre haunting her in the dark night. Debbie glanced up from her book and put it down on the nightstand. She wasn't asleep.

"Ellie? Come on in. You know Charlie didn't mean it. He's been having a hard time."

Eleanor closed the door behind her, but stood in the shadows, too nervous to come forward.

Debbie patted the bed beside her. "Come. Let's talk, just us girls."

Eleanor walked slowly into the light of the lamp. Debbie squinted and blinked, and Eleanor put her finger on her lips, gesturing for her not to make a ruckus.

"Amma? Am I dreaming?"

Eleanor sat down beside her on the bed and pulled her into a tight hug. "Yer a good, tidy lass, Debbie MacLeod. The best I've ever met."

Debbie teared up as she hugged her back. "I hope I don't wake up too soon. I've missed you so much, Amma."

Eleanor wiped Debbie's tears into her skin, and Debbie watched. She looked at her again, noticing Ellie's robe.

"You're not asleep, my little love. I've used Ellie's body to come to you."

"Are you the Ghost of Christmas Past?" Debbie asked half-jokingly.

Eleanor smiled. "No, my love, I am the Ghost of Christmas Present. Come. I want to show you something. Ellie was too disciplined to give away the secret, but you need to know. You're young enough still that I don't want you to live the rest of your life wondering."

"Wondering what?"

"Why Abbi didn't hop over the pond to show the Nazis a thing or two about honor. Come. Let's get Gramma and Charlie."

Eleanor took Debbie's hand, but Debbie stopped at the door. She pulled her into another hug. "Are you always watching?"

"Aye," Eleanor smiled. "I reside in Ellie now. I know what she knows. She doesn't know I'm there, though, and I trust you won't tell her."

"You know you can trust me with anything, Amma."

"Yes, my darling Debbie, I certainly do."

"I don't want to agree with Charlie about Abbi," she confessed. "But I don't know what else to think. It isn't like him to stand by and watch while innocent people suffer."

"Then it's a good thing the Ghost of Christmas Present is here, isn't it?"

Eleanor squeezed her hand as she guided her down the stairs to Moira's room. She pushed open the door, and took a seat by her mother's bed. She kissed her on the forehead, and Moira woke up groggily.

"Ellie?"

Eleanor handed her her glasses from the nightstand.

"Lord Almighty," she murmured.

Eleanor kissed her again. "Hello, Mum."

"Ye ain't the Good Lord, are ye? Ye've got better things to do than take the piss outta an auld lady!"

"Mum, do you really think he would joke like that?"

She sighed. "I reckon he wouldn't."

"I'm using Ellie's body," Eleanor explained. "I shouldn't dilly dally. I want to get this over with before she tries to wake up."

"Get what over with?"

"Come." Eleanor helped her up, and Debbie took her arm. "Let's go collect Charlie."

Eleanor led the way. Now she was a woman on a mission. As she entered the parlor, the fire was still crackling, and Charlie was staring at the ceiling, awake. He glanced over at her.

"I'm still not sorry, Ellie."

"Aye, ye were always a stubborn lad, Charlie MacLeod," Eleanor replied as she came closer. "Just like every other MacLeod."

He pulled himself up with his strong arms to look at her, and then he glanced at Debbie and Moira, who nodded their heads, smiling with excitement.

"Biordinar," he whispered as he realized who she was. "Amma?"

565

"I'm the Ghost of Christmas Present tonight, my brave little love. Now come, I have something to show you."

She helped him put his prostheses on and handed him his canes, pulling him up in one tug with Ellie's Rakshasa strength.

"Follow me."

She pushed open the camouflaged door to one of the many secret passages in the house and guided them through the dark tunnel to the secret door built into the back of one of the ground floor bookshelves. She gestured for them to stay quiet as she cracked it open.

Edmund was crouched over, whispering heatedly into one of many telephones, while his other hand was tapping on the telegraph so fast that they couldn't make out his movements. Stanley and Reggie were on either side of him, doing their own similar work, although their human speed served as a useful comparison for the feat Edmund was able to accomplish in his otherwise decrepit state.

Eleanor stepped back and made room for each of them to take a good, long look. As Charlie sighed with some combination of relief and self-castigation, she closed up the door and led them back to the parlor.

Charlie sat down and buried his head in his hands. "I'm such a fool."

"And so, my loves, you must all remember that just because he isn't tearing men apart with his bare hands, it doesn't mean he isn't a hero. He's saved thousands of lives these last six years, possibly millions, all from the comfort of his library."

"If the Nazis knew what he was doing here, this would've been the ripest target south of London!" Debbie exclaimed.

"And that, my little loves, is why Ellie cried herself to sleep after dutifully letting you go on and on about her coward of a father."

"She must've been goin' mad!" Charlie exclaimed. "I'm such a brute! I should've known he wouldn't just be lyin' around! I've been mad at him for months! Years, really. I thought he was just bein' a coward while the humans were dyin' left 'n right!"

Eleanor sat down next to him. "I know, my bairn, I know."

"I'm not a bairn anymore," he said. "I should've known better."

"We're all bairns compared to Abbi," Eleanor reminded them. She squeezed his hand. "I have to go. Ellie is stirring. I love you all so much. You've made me so proud with the vast depths of your courage and kindness. Do me a favor, though?"

"Anything!" Debbie exclaimed.

"When the time comes for him to start over, don't let Abbi pull away from you. He might try, and you mustn't let him. Ask Kate to help you find him if you must. And for god's sake, don't let him pull away from Ellie!"

"Do you think it will be soon?" Debbie asked.

"I bloody hope so," Eleanor admitted. "He's gone too long as it is." Eleanor stood up and pulled her mother into a hug.

"Sure as day, it'll be done," Moira whispered.

"I love you, Mum. You've been so good to all of them. It has made watching everyone grow up a gift instead of a punishment."

"I'll see ye in Heaven soon enough, ye hear?"

Eleanor kissed her on the forehead. "I have no doubt."

She pulled Debbie into a hug. "Take with you Shakti's blessings, my little love. You're already knocking their socks off. I can't wait to see what you do next."

"I love you, Amma," Debbie whispered as she hugged her back.

Eleanor finally pulled away and blew them a kiss. She ran up the stairs and returned to Ellie's bed. Ellie turned over, grumbled, and went back to sleep.

In the morning, her father emerged from his library, stretching his crippled back and smiling. "I'd say we got more done than Santa Claus last night."

"I reckon we did," Stanley agreed as he escorted him to the parlor.

"Why, Charlie MacLeod, fancy seeing you here!" Edmund exclaimed. "It's been too long."

As he noticed Charlie's prostheses, a grimace of grief darkened his expression, but Reggie rushed around him to intervene.

"Welcome to the club, Chuck," Reggie said as he used his one arm to help him up. "We're a crippled bunch, but we take nothing in life for granted. That's gotta be worth something, or so I'm told."

As soon as he was standing, Charlie hugged Edmund. "I've been better, Abbi. But I reckon it would be a more proper Christmas if we sing songs of our woe over some chouchen?"

"Sounds lovely," Edmund agreed as he patted him on the back. "Is Debbie here?"

"Aye, I reckon she'll be down any minute."

"Dad, how are you?" Ellie asked as she came down the stairs, throwing Charlie a disapproving look.

"Never better," Edmund said cheerfully. "You know, for a wartime Christmas, that is."

Eleanor settled back into her nest. Her first apparition had done its job.

CHAPTER 35 – THE ONE?

She watched and she waited as the fateful fire at their house in Basingstoke in 1945 finally forced Edmund to re-set. She was glad Ellie watched. She was glad Vibhi was there. She was glad that after it was all over and they were settling into a temporary apartment in Kensington, Edmund pulled Vibhishana into his arms and thanked him. She was glad when Vibhishana hugged him back like the forgiving father of a prodigal son and told him how much he loved him.

"I told you I would always be here, my boy, and I meant it."

Ellie found him unsettling. Every time he was around, she had an odd feeling about him that she couldn't quite articulate. A stirring of something dark deep inside of her. Something powerful and scary. Something that found him alluring but dangerous. That something was Uma. She buried herself deeper until he left them alone.

Eleanor couldn't have been gladder as Ellie settled into art school, and she watched Edmund finally make his entrance at Oxford, a place they both knew he would feel at home, spending his days and nights arguing about esoteric topics over pints with similarly brilliant people. His willingness to join the Oxford cricket team surprised her, but she was glad to see that the decades he'd spent practicing the art of hiding his talents from Ellie had finally done him some good. He even made friends with Ned Helmsworth, a fresh young Aussie student just down the road at Magdalen College who'd turned out to be a rather bookish chap, and who was just as kind as his parents; although he was, perhaps, a tad less sensible. But what he lacked in street smarts, he made up for in joviality, and all the while, Edmund spent many a weekend sneaking off to spend time with Oz and Yvie, who'd bought a home in the beautiful countryside just outside of Gloucester for their retirement. Sometimes, Debbie even took a weekend away from her medical research lab to join them.

And so, it came as a total surprise when, one day in the summer of 1958, she felt the subtle vibration of the talisman bangle she'd left to her daughter calling her up for a chat. Ellie rubbed her wrist, unsettled by the feeling, but continued on with her photographic portrait session anyway. After all, she had a long line of paying customers to finish up before the day was over.

She waited until Ellie fell asleep to answer him.

D.H.?

He waited so long to answer that she almost returned to her slumber.

Eleanor? Is it really you?

At the moment. Ellie felt your summons. I didn't expect the talisman to be used this direction. She didn't know what it was.

Shiva's wrath, I didn't think it was possible. How did you achieve this miracle?

Shakti works in mysterious ways.

Another long pause.

My friend, I don't have endless time. I must nestle back in before Ellie wakes up.

Can I come?

To London?

Is it possible? Is it possible to see you in person?

Aye, if you hurry. Have Kuveni bring you. I'm in Edmund's townhouse.

She wrapped herself up tighter in Ellie's robe and hopped out of bed to put the kettle on. Ellie's hands were frigid, as they often were in the middle of the night, although she hoped that the burst of warmth from the tea wouldn't wake her.

With a pleasant breeze, they appeared right beside her. Kuveni was back to the buxom, jolly, middle-aged English form she'd used the very first time they'd officially met, and Vibhishana was in a stylish modern suit in his dashing British form. Without the vicar's habit, he looked a bit, she had to admit, like a cad.

"Shiva's wrath," Vibhishana murmured. "What a great goddess you are."

Kuveni pulled her into a tight hug. "It has been too long, my dearest, most beloved girl."

Vibhishana only stared at her with some combination of confusion and stress. She'd hoped to see relief, but instead, she could feel his unease.

"Do you want some tea?" Eleanor asked.

"No, thank you," he said. He reached forward to touch her arm.

"I'm real, D.H. It's Ellie's body. Now, tell me what you need to commune with the dead about."

He sat down on an old velveteen couch, and Eleanor took a seat across from him, squeezing Kuveni's hand affectionately as Kuveni sat down beside her.

"I know what we need…" Kuveni snapped her fingers and conjured a dusty bottle of cognac and three crystal glasses. "Drink up, my lord. It will distract you."

Eleanor poured herself a taste and sat back to sniff its nose with satisfaction. "Mmm… how lovely. Ellie never had the taste for it. I hoped perhaps her eighteenth birthday stash would convince her, but she still had no interest." She took a long, savoring sip and waited for Vibhishana to do the same. "Tell me, Vibhi. I don't have all night."

"I'm so confused!" he confessed. "I didn't think summoning you would work! I'd hoped... I'd hoped it wouldn't!"

Eleanor laughed. "Because you'd hoped I'd taken up harp playing in Heaven?"

He did not find her quip amusing. "This isn't how it works, Eleanor. You shouldn't be here like this. You should have gone through the natural karmic cycle and been reborn. Something is wrong."

"Have you come to rip my dead soul out of my daughter's body, Lord Shiva? Uma will have something to say about that. This is all part of some plan that she thinks is going swimmingly."

"I didn't come here for you... I came here... because I needed to know."

"Know what?"

"If she was the one."

"Ah." It suddenly all made sense. "It's about a woman."

"I'm such a desperate fool, and now I know even less than I thought I did."

"Tell me, D.H. Let's see if I can help you sort it out." She took another long, languid sip.

He glanced guiltily at Kuveni.

"Well, spit it out!" Eleanor encouraged him.

"She's the Rakshasa heir of the Patels of Baroda. She is Rohit Patel's granddaughter, and she is special. She has more power than any Rakshasa I've ever encountered, other than my siblings, whose circumstances were unusual... Although, I don't know... She may be just as powerful as they are... in some ways she is already more powerful, and yet she's so humble and curious and kind..."

"Sounds like a decent match so far. You have a little smile as you're describing her, you know. I've never known you to be so cute."

He blushed in a gesture that reminded her lovingly of Edmund.

"She is truly exceptional for a hybrid, and there is something else about her. It feels… it feels how you felt… but different. It is hard to explain. It is magnetic and terrifying, and I know she feels it too, but she is so bloody young, Eleanor. It's shameful."

"How old is she?"

"Nineteen."

Eleanor laughed. "At some point when you're both adults it doesn't matter, Vibhi. It's not like you have a line of five-thousand-year-old brides to choose from." He looked down at his glass, unconvinced. "How old was Miriam?"

He smiled wistfully. "Shanti asked that same question when I told her I was too old for her."

"I see. She's a firecracker too, is she?"

He nodded and finally took a sip. "In some ways, wonderful ways, she reminds me of you, but in other ways she's so mysterious. There is a depth to her that I don't fully understand yet, and it keeps surprising me in such delightful ways."

"I have yet to hear a problem with her. Is it just the age difference?"

"Eleanor, it is very dangerous for me to fall in love. You saw how dangerous I was when I was in love with you. I would have sacrificed Earth to save you, and I need to be even more careful now. The final battle is brewing." He debated momentarily whether or not he should continue. "The demon of the apocalypse is rising, and he has taken refuge… inside of her. He has been tormenting her since she was a child, and she doesn't even know it."

"That sounds like a problem," Eleanor admitted.

"It is catastrophic, Eleanor. I have to be so bloody careful. While she is luring me in, I know I must pull away, but I can't! It is so much harder to keep myself away now! Infinitely harder than it was to keep myself away from you and Uma. It's like all of my discipline from centuries of asceticism has slipped right through my fingers, but I can't just walk away. I've already fallen in love with her."

"You, my friend, have a demon in you, and so does Edmund. Both of you have managed to turn it into a strength for the greater good. What makes you think she can't do the same?"

"The problem is that some part of me doesn't care whether she can or not, Eleanor. I've become dangerously irrational, and it's scaring me."

"Then why are you here? It sounds like you've already made your decision?"

He stared at his glass. "I've already made the wrong decision, you mean."

"If anyone can manage the complexity of such a wicked conundrum, it's you, Vibhi. Follow your instincts."

"I thought that I was, Eleanor. I'd convinced myself that somehow it would all be alright because she was you, and I knew that you had the strength to stay on the path of light, even with the demon of the apocalypse whispering in your ear. Now I don't know what to believe. Maybe I've doomed all of us, and it's only a matter of time until the world is burning."

"But you knew the apocalypse was inevitable, didn't you? The prophecies were going on and on about it. Maybe this is all meant to be. You are not destined to stop destruction, Lord Shiva, you are destined to manage it as painlessly as possible as you guide the worlds into the Age of Truth. Maybe she's meant to stand by your side."

"*Upon the return of the blind changeling child to the land of her destiny, the gods will weep, the world will bathe in blood, and the darkness of men shall know no bounds.*" He quoted the prophecy that the Vanara Oracle inside of Eleanor had delivered so long ago, and then stared pensively into his glass. "Shanti's mother came to Baroda from England on a teaching position posted by Mae. She married Rahul

Patel, and the war started shortly after that. Rahul died a couple years later, in combat by Rama's side."

"Blimey, that must have been a dire wound to kill a half Rakshasa?"

"I wasn't there. I was surprised by it too. But the gods did weep, the world did bathe in blood, and the darkness of men truly did know no bounds, Eleanor. I've never, in five thousand years, seen a war as brutal as that one. It makes sense that the prophecy was about Shanti, but there is still something pivotal missing. I'm afraid I'm letting my love lead me astray."

"Was her mother blind?" Eleanor asked curiously.

"Not at all. I still have no idea what that part of the riddle meant, but I don't think it was literal. Her mother survived Rakshasa childbirth. She didn't manifest any of the gruesome traits of a human carrying a Rakshasa child, but as far as any of us can tell, she isn't a Rakshasa. In fact, she is Edward Rutherford's daughter. I think the term must be referring to that, but I don't have the faintest idea how."

"Edward Rutherford's daughter?! I think I've met her! Was she one of his adorable little blonde girls?"

"She was."

"Blimey, and now she has a grown-up daughter of her own. Time flies, doesn't it? That little girl might end up being your mother-in-law." She winked, but he didn't find it funny.

"Now do you understand my hesitation about Shanti's age? I've known her Patel ancestors since they were babes in arms for more generations than I can count, and I was there, waiting outside with Rohit, when Shanti was born."

"Does it bother her that she's known you her whole life?"

"I wish it bothered her more, to be honest."

"Does it bother you?"

"I don't know! In some ways it does, but I've been waiting so long for my divine wife to be born in a form I can be with, Eleanor! I've been waiting thousands of years! I wanted so dearly to overcome my reservations, but here you are! She can't be my divine wife if you're here!"

"Are you sure?"

"What do you mean?"

"Edmund and Rama are both alive on Earth right now, aren't they? What makes you think that Shakti couldn't have done the same? Chosen two overlapping avatars for two different tasks?"

He thought carefully about her assertion. "The idea did not cross my mind."

Eleanor took in another long, satisfied sip, and then she smiled. "Here's an idea for you: Here you are, asking for my permission to be with her. Here I am giving it to you. Is it possible that as we speak, I am somehow connecting Uma with her next incarnation?"

"But what would happen to you? Are you going to be stuck riding around consciously in Ellie until the end of her natural Rakshasa life? Human souls are not meant to retain their memories as they transition. You are meant to be freed when you're reborn to live again uninhibited by your past lives, and you are meant to be in control while you're conscious, Eleanor. It is a wonder to me that you aren't finding the entire experience to be a form of torture."

Eleanor shrugged. "I'm a singularly unique woman."

Vibhishana drank down the rest of his cognac and put the glass on the table.

"Have you been with her yet?" Eleanor asked as he stood up.

"She's wanted to for quite some time, but so far I've refused."

Eleanor smiled. "Make it special, D.H., for both of you. It is not every day that two halves of a perfect divine whole join together. I'm sure Kuveni can help you out with the romantic details."

She stood up and drank down the rest of her cognac. "I'd better go. Ellie usually stirs in the middle of the night. I don't want her to wake up."

576

She hugged him, and Uma held on slightly too long. "That is what it feels like to connect your divine energy with your other half. Trust yourself. If she's the one, you'll know."

Vibhishana kissed her on the forehead. "I love you, Eleanor."

"I'm dead," she reminded him. "Now go give your love to the living."

She hugged Kuveni one last time, and then blew them a kiss.

They disappeared. She drank a glass of water to flush the cognac from Ellie's taste buds, and then she went back to bed.

Two years later, he summoned her again.

Ellie was out at lunch with some old friends from art school, and this time she noticed it. It buzzed and buzzed. She showed it to the gals, and they all looked under the table for a magnet, some sort of little boys' prank from a neighboring table, but then it stopped and no little boys laughed, and she continued on with her bangers and mash.

Ellie was awake late that night processing photos in her dark room. The wait was interminable. Eleanor worked her hardest not to infect Ellie with her nerves, after all, it was exceptionally rare that the Good Lord put in a request for a commune with the dead.

Ellie finally retired to bed at about three am, and she was restless. Eleanor had to wait until five for her to finally go to sleep.

I'm ready, D.H.

She waited another ten minutes.

With a pleasant breeze, Vibhishana appeared in his Lankan form with Mr. Montero beside him. In Vibhi's arms, he held a beautiful little girl with light brown skin, silky black hair, and sparkling blue eyes. She looked familiar, although Eleanor couldn't place from where, and she seemed to be about two, maybe three years old, although Eleanor had never been particularly good at telling children's ages, and she knew that with Rakshasas, there really was no point in even guessing.

"Wee!" the girl squealed. "Daddy, that was fun! Can we do it again? Please, oh, please, can we do it again!"

Vibhishana glanced at Eleanor, and her grin couldn't have been wider. "Vibhi, I believe there is someone you'd like me to meet!"

"Neha, say hello to Eleanor," Vibhi instructed her. "Eleanor is a very special human. The most special."

"A HUMAN?!" Neha squealed.

She wriggled aggressively out of his arms, and he put her down, throwing Mr. Montero a look of warning to be on guard, for what, Eleanor didn't dare to guess.

Neha walked right up to Eleanor, but as Eleanor kneeled down to greet her, instead of offering her little hand to shake, she engulfed Eleanor into a tight hug and kissed her on both cheeks.

Eleanor giggled and kissed her back. "It's nice to meet you, Neha!"

"You feel cold. Are you really human?"

"Actually, I'm a hybrid," Eleanor explained. "I'm always cold at night when I haven't been drinking tea or hot honeyed milk."

"Like you, Neha. She's a hybrid like you," Vibhi reiterated.

Neha's jaw dropped with delighted surprise, and then she took Eleanor's hand and led her to the couch. She crawled up onto it, gestured for Eleanor to join her, and Eleanor threw Vibhi a happy wink at her exceptional adorability as she sat down and Neha crawled into her lap. Neha fingered one of Ellie's loose red ringlets.

"Is it real?"

Neha closed her eyes and scrunched her nose, and with a wiggle, her black hair turned red and burst into a wild mat of ringlets. Eleanor laughed heartily. "I see she takes after her father!"

Vibhi took a seat beside Eleanor, and Mr. Montero stood behind the couch with his arms crossed, watching them in his guarding position.

"Why is your hair red?" Neha asked as she inspected her own work.

"Because I'm from Scotland. Lots of people in Scotland have red hair like this."

"But why?" Neha asked.

"Well, I suppose because it's very cold there, and somehow fair skin and red hair were good for people in that climate," Eleanor explained.

"But why?" Neha asked. "Why not blue?" With a wiggle, she turned her hair blue. "Or violet?" She turned her hair violet. She nodded with satisfaction at her violet ringlets. "These look better. I don't understand why everyone doesn't have beautiful hair like this. Daddy, wouldn't violet hair be good in the cold?"

"Yes, my darling, I'm sure it would."

"Then why isn't it? Why did God make Eleanor's hair red and not violet?"

Vibhishana sighed with fatigue. Eleanor could tell that this was not his first or even his hundredth conversation about why things were the way that they were.

"Such details are not so conscious, my darling. God lets the planets evolve naturally, and beautiful, strange, wonderful things emerge."

Neha was intrigued by the idea. "How?"

"We can talk about it later, darling. Right now, I'd like to talk to Eleanor. Why don't you drink some hot honeyed milk with Monty in the kitchen?"

"Why not here?" she asked as she snuggled deeper into Eleanor's arms and sighed. "Eleanor feels nice."

"Because the milk is in the kitchen," Mr. Montero replied.

Eleanor kissed Neha's forehead, and Neha kissed hers back. She then climbed onto her father's lap and kissed his forehead, shook her head until her violet hair dissolved back into its natural silky black, and walked over to Monty, taking his hand, and leading him right into the kitchen.

"How does she know the kitchen is over there?" Eleanor asked.

"Because it smells like hot honeyed milk!" Neha squealed back.

Mr. Montero shut the door behind them, and Eleanor's grin returned, but Vibhishana only took a deep, calming breath. He took Eleanor's hand and kissed it, feeling for Uma's energy. He took in one long swig of it, and then let go.

Eleanor suddenly saw his sorrow. "Oh no. Please don't tell me Shanti died? I thought Rakshasa women could survive Rakshasa childbirth?"

"By the grace of every god, she's still alive. But she's recused herself from our lives for now to protect Neha from the demon within her. It was a singularly selfless decision that is torture for all of us. I'm sure it's my punishment for the profligacy of it all."

"The profligacy? Do you mean that you were reveling in the joys of being with your other half?"

"Yes, that is a tactful and overly generous way of looking at it. She intoxicated me, Eleanor. All reason went right out the window... the dormitory window... of the dormitory we stayed in together at her medical school, while I pretended for a whole year to be her sister so I could be with her."

Eleanor laughed heartily again. "It is very hard for me to picture you letting go like that. It must have felt marvelous!"

"It was like I was nineteen again, for better and worse. And now we are both paying the price. I'll never forgive myself for bringing such misery upon her, and my greatest punishment is to watch Neha long for her mother."

"A wise man once told my mother that there isn't an angry god with a lightning bolt pointed at her, waiting for an indiscretion to strike. Do you really think there's one pointed at you?"

He teared up and then hugged Eleanor. "You are a bastion of reason, as always."

"It looks like your punishment has quite an upside to me," Eleanor pointed out. "She makes it impossible to fully regret your tragedy, just like Ellie does."

"I never knew it was possible to love as deeply as I love Neha. She exudes so much vivacity that everyone must forgive her for her incessant questioning."

"She is her father's daughter."

"She is her mother's daughter. She is much more curious than I ever was, and much more brilliant. She systematically tests her boundaries in a way I've never seen anyone do before. I've never met anyone who made me feel like I know less about how the world actually works than she does."

Eleanor winked. "Isn't that what children are for? To keep their parents humble?"

He smiled. "She succeeds every moment at that."

Eleanor felt Ellie stir, and she sighed regretfully. "Ellie wasn't sleeping well tonight. You'd better go."

They stood up, and Neha whooshed into the room, laughing mischievously. Mr. Montero chased after her. She threw her arms around Eleanor's legs.

"Will I see you again, Eleanor?" she asked.

"I don't know, darling. Perhaps someday."

"Why not sooner?" She looked to her father as her lip began quivering.

Eleanor threw Vibhishana a questioningly look, unsure of what he wanted her to say.

"Because Eleanor is dead, Neha. We must wait for her to be reborn for you to see her again."

"But she's here now!" Neha protested.

"That is only because I'm a great goddess, my little love. And now, I must go back to my peaceful slumber, and you must go back home with Daddy. You have a whole life of exploring ahead of you."

Eleanor kissed her one more time, and Neha kissed her back.

"Take with you Shakti's blessings, my little love."

Neha sniffled and wiped her tears into her skin, but dutifully climbed up into her father's arms, and with another pleasant breeze, they were gone.

Eleanor watched and waited as, on one sunny day in 1966, Ellie and Edmund suffered through their first mortal blow together. It happed just before noon, on a country road in Devonshire, when the drunk driver of a lorry packed with squawking chickens slammed into their car head on while they were cheerfully singing along to the Beatles. She didn't need to step in, since Surpanakha swiftly executed the driver for his crime and slipped away before Kuveni popped Vibhishana to the scene.

It was only as Edmund helped Ellie climb out of the car, and he spied the violet metallic plasma healing the wounds on her freshly youthful face, that he fully believed the beautiful truth that she had inherited enough of his Rakshasa heartiness to survive. That night, freshly youthful again and feeling unusually vivacious, together they tried to cook Mr. Johnson a dinner to thank him for his help after he escorted them home. But, as the drapes in the kitchen went alight with the oil fire they set accidentally, they vowed with guilty giggles to keep themselves realistic about the limitations of their power.

By the end of the week, they were in Morocco touring the bazaar in Fez, and by the end of the month, with Edmund fully confident in Ellie's safety for the first time in her life, they embarked on a mission as a freelance journalistic duo that was so absurdly heartwarming, Eleanor could hardly believe it was real. She wished she could jump for joy.

They toured around Africa, Europe, and South America, even making their way to the very edge of the Brazilian rainforest, all while Edmund served as their writer and Ellie as their precociously talented photographer. By the end of the year, their work was offered on a continuous contract to the BBC, and by the end of the decade, Ellie's photographs had graced the cover of every major English newspaper and photojournalistic magazine. Edmund kept a scrapbook with all of his favorites in the cellar in Basingstoke, and while Ellie protested half-heartedly, she secretly loved that after forty years of their lives together, he still cared so much.

And so, it was bittersweet, when, on her particularly warm birthday in February of 1967, after they'd just returned from shooting a fluff piece on safari in Africa, she came upon Stanley sitting in the dining room of their house in Basingstoke, twiddling his thumbs nervously. It was a very unusual position to see him in.

"Is Edmund around?" he asked.

"I don't know where he is. Why? What's wrong?"

"I was hoping I could talk to both of you."

Ellie sat down across from him. "You can tell me whatever's on your mind."

He smiled. "I know, Ellie-bean. You've been like a daughter to me. It's a funny thing to say, given how much of a father you have already, but I hope you know it's been lovely watching you grow up. Your mother would have been so proud."

"What is it?" she asked. "Why are you so melancholy? You aren't dying, are you? You're not that old!"

He laughed. "I'm sixty-five, Ellie. It's old enough for a mere mortal, but no, I'm not dying."

Edmund came in the back door whistling a merry tune. It was the most cheerful he'd ever been on her birthday.

"Ellie-bean, what do you say we play a game of catch before dinner?"

"Catch!" Ellie exclaimed. "I'm not ten, Dad!"

"No, you're forty-one! Can you believe it?" He became pensive, and then sad, and Ellie knew what was coming.

She sighed. "I've officially lived longer than Mum did."

He slapped on a fake smile. "And a wonderful forty-one years it's been. Oh, hello, Stanley. Would you like to join us? With three we can use a bat!"

"I'm too old to play cricket with you, Colonel," Stanley refused.

Edmund's fake cheer dissolved. "I reckon you are, my boy. I reckon you are. Maybe we should drink some cognac instead. Ellie-bean, I think there's some chouchen in the cellar if you want to join us for a tipple."

"Colonel, I need to tell you something." Stanley took a deep breath. "I'm retiring. You don't need a butler anymore. You haven't really needed me for years now, and it's, well, to be honest, rather maddening to sit at home here alone waiting for you to hop on in for a sandwich every few months. Jules just retired, and we've decided to move together to France. We can be together legally there, and my mother left me the house in Bretagne that Reggie gave her for her retirement."

Edmund stopped to contemplate what he was saying, and then he smiled with genuine support. "I'm happy for you, Stanley."

"Are you sure?"

Edmund pulled him out of his seat and into a hug. "I couldn't be happier for you. What a wonderful way to retire. We'll be here for the next two weeks before we hop up to the North Pole to ride

585

some reindeer under the Northern Lights. Why don't you invite Jules on over to visit in the meantime?"

Stanley smiled with intense relief. "I'll ask him to bring some fresh fish to make his bouillabaisse."

"Is there a spare room in that house in Bretagne?" Edmund asked. "We can't cook you dinner, but I'm sure we can make ourselves useful some other way in exchange for a Breton holiday from time to time."

"You're welcome anytime, Colonel. Anytime!" Stanley exclaimed. He rushed around the table to Ellie and pulled her into a hug. "You too, Ellie-bean! Just wait until you taste Jules's *fruits de mer bretonaises*! I didn't think it was possible to top my mother's, but he figured out a way to do it!" He rushed through the servants' door into the kitchen and then popped his head back into the dining room. "I'll call him right now!"

Ellie pulled her father into a gentle hug. "I love you, Dad."

He kissed her forehead. "I love you so much, Ellie-bean."

"You're going to miss him, aren't you?"

"I've known that boy since before he became a man. I can't believe he's so old he can't play cricket anymore. The cruel clock just keeps ticking along, claiming every mortal in its wake." He hugged her and kissed her again. "I will give thanks to the universe every night for the rest of my life that you'll stay with me for a Martian lifetime, Ellie. You are my saving grace."

"Should we play cricket?" she asked. "I'll bat, if you bowl and catch."

"I can't think of anything I'd rather do," he said as he put his arm over her shoulders, and together they walked out to the garden to celebrate her forty-first birthday.

That night, long after Edmund had gone to bed, Eleanor awoke. She'd been waiting all evening, watching the three of them eat and drink merrily. She tightened Ellie's robe over her oversized flannel pajamas and headed for the liquor cabinet. *Excellent*, she thought. She knew it would be there. Several of the bottles from

586

her eighteenth birthday collection for Ellie decades earlier were still waiting for her. Ellie hadn't wanted to admit that she deviated from her mother's taste, and so she'd kept them safe in the cellar, sparing them from the flames when the rest of the house burned. Edmund had found them when they'd returned to the house after their last re-set, and in a move that Eleanor found to be a reassuring sign of his ongoing recovery, he'd decided to take them out, ready to be drunk on special occasions. He'd opened the first with Ellie's permission on the night they'd set the kitchen on fire hosting Vibhishana for dinner, and ever since, they'd remained ready for someone special. She knew Ellie would agree that Stanley's retirement qualified.

She scurried up the stairs, carefully tiptoeing past Edmund's room. She knocked politely, and then cracked open the door to the suite Stanley had lived in throughout his forty years of service there.

"Are you decent?" she asked.

"Ellie? Is something wrong?" He threw his feet over the side of the bed and pulled on a robe over his pajamas before he even turned on the lights.

"Guess again, greenie," Eleanor said as she sat right down next to him.

"*Gast*," he murmured. "I knew I should've held back on the chouchen. It gets me every time."

Eleanor smiled. She used Ellie's fingernail to cut open the foil, and then popped the cork out of the cognac. "Mmm… Hine, 1848. Nothing beats it." She held it up for him to sniff, and he scratched his head confusedly. "I heard you're heading over the pond for retirement, greenie, and I had to offer you my congratulations."

She poured them each a glass and then put the bottle on the floor. She sniffed it lovingly and then took a long sip. "God, I wish Ellie liked this stuff."

Stanley poked her in the arm, and she laughed. "I'm real, greenie. I've been riding around inside of Ellie for forty-one years now. I only make myself known in exceptional circumstances, and I couldn't let you leave without saying thank you. You've been so good to them. It's been such a pleasure to watch."

Stanley stared at his glass, and then he squinted as he looked at her in the dim light. "Is it really you, Eleanor?"

"As plain as the hole on Surpanakha's face, greenie."

"*Gast*," he murmured again. "Why didn't you tell me sooner? God, Eleanor, how many times I've needed your advice!"

"That's why, greenie. That's exactly why. You've done just fine without me, and so has everyone else. If you'd had my ghost following you around, you wouldn't have grown so much." She held up her glass for a toast. "To the wonderful man you've become."

He clinked her glass, and they both took a long sip.

"I still have quite the sequined wardrobe in my private closet," he admitted.

"I expected nothing less," she smiled. "Did Kuveni keep it up for you, or did you shop for it on your own?"

"A bit of both. She hasn't been around so much these last few years. I'm sure she has better things to do than to check up on your old poufy butler."

"Let's see," Eleanor said with a mischievous wink. "Kuveni?"

With a pleasant breeze, Kuveni stood before them in the form of Kate. She glanced down at her arms. "My, my, it's been a long time since I've used this form. It's been decades now."

She hugged Eleanor and then turned her attention on Stanley. "What's this I hear about retirement, my dear boy? Weren't we interesting enough for you?"

Stanley looked down guiltily.

"That was a joke, my boy. Live your life. We couldn't have asked for a better human ally, and now it is time for you to revel in your reward."

Stanley took another sip as he debated something in his head.

"Out with it!" Kuveni encouraged him. "Eleanor doesn't have all night!"

"I was debating the wisdom of a rash fancy," he admitted.

"My, my, that sounds exciting!" Kuveni egged him on.

"Shall I introduce you to my replacement at the agency?"

"You tell us," Eleanor replied. "Do you think that's wise? What do they know about us?"

Stanley smiled proudly. "Far less than they knew when Leo passed the torch. What matters most is Edmund's exceptional service during the war. We have a whole generation now who won't dare to question his virtue. They've decided to take a more hands-off approach now that I'm retiring."

He drank down the rest of his cognac. "Yes. I think it's a good idea. He needs to know the gravity of his assignment. Lord knows it took far too long for me to grasp it."

"I trust your judgment, Stanley." Eleanor drank down the rest of her cognac.

"He's in London at the moment, finishing up his training. Shall I just tell you his address?" he asked Kuveni. "I don't remember how this works."

"Still in training!" Eleanor exclaimed. "I suppose it worked out once before."

"He's good. I chose him myself, and I had the pick of the litter."

"Close your eyes and picture where he is, my boy." Kuveni took his hand. "I have it."

With a moment of lightheadedness, all three of them dissolved.

The room was dark. A young man who looked about twenty, the same age as Edmund and Ellie currently did, lay in a single bed in the corner of a spartan room. It looked like a dormitory.

"Blimey, greenie! You didn't say we'd be popping into the Secret Service dormitory!" Eleanor whispered.

"Trust me, Eleanor. I know what I'm doing."

The man stirred, and Stanley switched on the electric lights.

"Attention, Cadet!" he boomed. Eleanor had missed seeing the twinkle of mischief in Stanley's eye that was glistening as the man hopped out of bed and saluted.

"Sir, yes, sir! General Abernathy?" the man asked nervously as he realized who Stanley was.

"At ease," Stanley released him. Eleanor and Kuveni threw each other a look of impressed surprise at Stanley's title. "Hamish, I'd like you to meet Eleanor and Kuveni. Eleanor is Colonel Marriner's dead wife, and Kuveni is his six-thousand-year-old foster mother. They wanted to meet you before you take the reins."

Hamish smiled at the joke, but Stanley straightened his posture and deepened his voice. "That's an order, Cadet."

Hamish rushed to shake their hands, pausing for a long moment with each of them as he felt their unusual energy.

"Pleased to meet you?" Hamish said questioningly.

"Yer a Scot? I like ye already," Eleanor said with her mother's intense brogue. "Now, I've known good Scots and bad Scots in my time, and I trust that yer the former. General Abernathy has excellent judgment."

"Aye, I reckon he does," Hamish said with bewilderment. "Ye're Colonel Marriner's *dead* wife, ye said?"

"Aye. I died in 1926 bringing our beautiful daughter into the world. I'm borrowing her body at the moment to say hello to you." She closed her eyes and scrunched her nose, coaxing Ellie's plasma back into her skin, revealing Ellie's natural human form that looked about twenty years younger than Eleanor's had. "This is what Ellie looks like, so you know her when you see her." She let the plasma flow back into her own form, finding the task surprisingly easy.

"Biordinar," Hamish whispered with wonder. "This is so much better than I thought it would be! I thought I'd be following around some crotchety lord on his hunting trips, making sure his gun didn't run out!"

"What do you think your assignment is?" Eleanor asked.

Hamish glanced at Stanley.

"Answer her, Cadet."

"To secretly support a sacred protector of the realm by any means necessary?"

"I'll need you to sound more sure about that before I can leave," Eleanor teased him.

"Why are you devoting your life to this cause?" Kuveni grilled him.

"Because I can?" he replied. "It seems like the right thing to do?"

"Why?!" Kuveni pushed him.

"Because I was too young to fight in the war, ma'am. This way I can do something that matters like my father did."

"Did he tell you to sign up for this?" Eleanor asked.

"No, ma'am. He told me to be a dentist."

"What about for king, for country?" Kuveni asked him skeptically.

He looked like he was in pain as he searched for the right answer. "We have a queen, ma'am."

"What rank in your class were you?" Eleanor asked.

"Fourth from the bottom, ma'am."

"Out of how many?"

"Fifty-five, ma'am."

"What did you fail?"

He glanced at Stanley again.

"Answer her, Cadet."

"Manipulation and assassinations, ma'am. Both of them made me feel too down."

"How good at lying are you?" Eleanor asked him.

"Mediocre at best," Hamish admitted. "General Abernathy has already started tutoring me."

Eleanor smiled. "I know why you picked him, Stanley."

"He reminds you of me, doesn't he? But I don't think it will surprise you that I was actually last in my class. Hamish landed

591

three whole spots above my record." Stanley smiled. "Cadet, if ever you come across anything out of the ordinary that you can't handle, call for Kuveni, and she'll answer you."

"Can I have her number, sir?"

"You don't need one, greenie," Kuveni informed him. "Just say my name, and I will come."

"But how, ma'am?"

"Like this." Kuveni dissolved and reappeared behind him. He startled as he turned around to look at her. "I assume I don't need to remind you about the story of the boy who cried wolf."

"He was gruesomely devoured, ma'am."

Eleanor laughed. "Exactly."

"That's all for now, Cadet. I'll be in touch with you next week with your detailed orders. Not a word about this to anyone, not even the other cadets. Do you understand? Your mission has already started."

"Sir, yes, sir!" Hamish saluted.

Kuveni walked around him to join Stanley and Eleanor, and Eleanor smiled as she waved goodbye. "Take care of them, Hamish. They'll be worth it. I promise."

Stanley saluted with exaggerated authority, and she loved Hamish's shocked gasp as he watched them dissolve.

When they landed back in Stanley's bedroom, Eleanor felt Ellie stir.

"Thank you for everything, Stanley. You've been the best handmaiden in the world. I meant it forty years ago, and I've only been more and more proud of you at every turn."

He hugged her. "I love you, Eleanor. You made me who I am."

"That's right, *General* Abernathy! Good on ya! I have renewed faith in the Crown for that."

"It was a long road, Eleanor. Believe me."

"I have no doubt. Enjoy your retirement, and remember to hold back on the chouchen. You don't want a ghost waking you up in the middle of the night too often."

"Wake me up whenever you want, Eleanor. I can think of nothing I would like better."

"Really, nothing?"

He blushed. "Perhaps a few things. All in respectable moderation, of course."

She kissed him on the forehead. "Take with you Shakti's blessings, my child, and share them with Jules."

"Thank you, my lady."

She hugged Kuveni one last time, and then calmly returned Ellie's body to her bed so the cruel clock could keep marching on.

CHAPTER 37 – THE FINAL SPRINT

Eleanor waited as Edmund re-set yet again in 1975 when an IRA assassin stabbed him in the back in a dark alley of Belfast over an unflattering investigative story he was writing about the Sinn Fein. He and Ellie were both grateful that his heartiness had allowed him to chase the man down and teach him a lesson, and Eleanor was particularly glad that Ellie never asked what exactly her father meant by that. She was quite sure that Ellie's innocent mind had not, in fact, understood that her father meant he had killed the man, and she was grateful. For her fragile, shell-shocked soldier to have made it fifty years without his daughter having any inkling of his dark struggles was a triumph that she knew he himself did not appreciate, but that she knew full well was one of his greatest.

Most importantly for the lives of Eleanor's beloveds, the unpleasant encounter created the awkward situation of Edmund looking distinctly younger than Ellie. They adopted the story that he was her kid brother, a story that both of them regretted immediately, but stuck to all the same as he re-entered university,

Cambridge this time, on a mission that Eleanor considered entirely a distraction from his discontent at abruptly losing his career as a journalist. He looked just a tad too young to come up with some farce involving grey hair dye and makeup, a farce that would have been impossible for him to pull off, and he knew it. He'd always been dreadful at farces.

And so, Ellie continued on with her photographic career while Edmund marched through his second doctorate and settled down in Cambridge, buying a modest house, and setting himself up for a quieter life, so as to not hold Ellie back as she stretched her proverbial wings entirely on her own for the first time. Eleanor cheered silently as Ellie hopped about the planet on her own, digging her way through the underbrush of jungles, riding camels across vast deserts, and diving deep into the sea, until one fateful, rainy evening at a pub in the old town of Edinburgh, when the Devil walked right in the door.

He wasn't Edmund's father. His simmering greed wasn't so apparent. He wasn't a Rakshasa or a Yaksha or a demon. He was as human as they come, in the worst way possible. His name was Craig.

Ten minutes later, ten hours later, ten months later, and ten years later, Eleanor regretted that she hadn't forced her way to the surface and kicked him in the groin as he walked right up to the bar and lied with a smile, reveling in Ellie's swoon.

But, like the exceptionally disciplined goddess that she was, Eleanor waited, cringing and wailing in silence as she watched her daughter march right down into an abyss for the love of two little boys who called her Mummy. The tragedy of it broke Eleanor's heart. Ellie had been so afraid of dying like her mother that she'd never let herself admit her secret desire for children, and so when Craig brought her home to meet his young lads who'd lost their mother, lads about the age that Ruthy was when Eleanor had fallen in love with the bairns, Eleanor knew that Ellie was a goner.

Ellie married him by the end of the year. He'd beaten her twice before she even said her vows. She said them anyway.

Eleanor buried herself deeper, wrapping her soul around Uma's as deep as she could go, but still she had to watch. She finally understood what Mélusine's warning had meant. For the first time since her death, Eleanor was in Hell.

And so, it was a guilty mixed blessing for Eleanor when her stint in Hell finally ended, and she watched Ellie suffer through the horrific night of her tenth anniversary. After a long night of selfish blethering, Craig drunkenly crashed their car right into a tree. Ellie only had minor wounds, but as the violet metallic plasma came to the surface to do its work, Craig saw, and the Devil made his move. Before Eleanor or Ellie even knew what was happening, he'd taken a piece of the broken windshield and done his best to finish the job. When it didn't work, he told her he'd kill her if she ever tried to see his sons again. With her throat still bleeding, she believed him.

Eleanor had never wished more for Surpanakha to be there, but as Ellie crawled out of the car and limped away sobbing, Craig sat alone and unpunished, contemplating his next move without a hint of guilt, only cunning. He called his lawyer before he even got out of the car.

Kuveni pulled up, into the empty field, and coaxed Ellie into her car. Ellie looked down with horror at her Rakshasa plasma. "Please don't hurt me," was all she would whimper.

"Sshhh." Kuveni whispered sweet assurances as she hugged her. "All will be well with the angels by your side."

"Where are you going?" Ellie asked meekly from the back seat as Kuveni sped off into the darkness.

"I'm going to Cambridge, my darling. Now close your eyes and sleep. We will be home by morning."

Ellie didn't have the strength to contemplate what she meant.

They arrived just before dawn. Edmund was grumpy as he begrudgingly answered Kuveni's incessant knocks. His eyes turned black as the scent of Ellie's dried human blood bombarded him. Kuveni helped them into the house.

"It is over, my loves. It is all over," Kuveni reassured them. She went into the kitchen and brought out two carafes of hot honeyed milk.

As Ellie stared pensively before her, still shivering under a heavy blanket in the parlor, Kuveni took Edmund aside in the foyer.

"I would have killed him myself right then and there, if not for those two innocent boys waiting back at home. Think of them and only them as you try to control yourself. Ellie needs you to be her father now, not her avenger."

"Kate?" he said meekly.

Kuveni pulled him into a hug.

"You don't need to thank me, my dear boy. I love her as much as I love you. Now go comfort her in your arms. It's going to be a long road."

Kuveni let herself out, closing the door behind her.

Eleanor was ready for the torture to end, but the cruel universe had other plans.

By noon, Ellie's Rakshasa plasma had eliminated all physical evidence of her trauma, but her bruises on the inside were just starting to set.

Slowly but steadily, with Edmund by her side, Ellie began to recover. Their life became quiet and mercifully uneventful as she began a new career as a kindergarten teacher, in an attempt to fill the gaping hole in her heart left by losing her stepsons. It didn't work.

Edmund landed on another, even more doomed tactic for dealing with the loss of yet more beloved bairns. Her name turned out to be Grace.

Eleanor watched and waited as Edmund headed straight into the ludicrously foolish marriage, even as Ellie warned him time after time that he was making a mistake. It was the first time in her life that her father didn't listen to her, and she hated him for it. She almost left him to wallow in his own misfortune, in the misfortune he had thoughtlessly brought down upon both of them in his obsessive quest to adopt a child, but as she thought back on how desperately she wished her father had rescued her from Craig, she hunkered down and readied herself for battle on his behalf.

Throughout years of grinding paperwork, Edmund held steady, focused entirely on the prize, while Grace held steady in her own way. At church. Twice a day. Every day. Ellie could only shake her head. What a desperate fool her father was.

And then they went off for a week to Ukraine, and when they returned, Edmund was beaming. Charles Edward Marriner had entered their lives. For the first several weeks, Edmund accidentally spoke Russian to the boy. The boy spoke Russian back. Grace hissed disapprovingly each time, and Edmund spoke it more just to spite her. They were off to a running start.

Ellie maturely warned her father as the row escalated that Charlie would need to speak English to get on well in England, and so Edmund begrudgingly fell in line with Grace's wishes, making his mark secretly by speaking Hindi when Grace wasn't around, which was often, because she was at church. Three times a day, then four. By the time Charlie turned three and he'd been in Cambridge for a year, Grace was hardly at home at all.

And so, Ellie joined her father in raising his son, until one fateful April evening when the apocalypse began. A series of events too preposterous to be real unfolded one on top of the other, as the bizarre, alien world they had always been a part of yanked them into the limelight kicking and screaming.

By the end of the week, Edmund's evil father had set them on fire. Before their healing plasma had finished its work, her father flew her with his own devilish batwings all the way to Lanka to take refuge in the ancient palace of their one and only Mr. Johnson. As it turned out, his real name was Vibhishana. Ellie still felt the odd resonance of Uma stirring as she said his name.

Eleanor watched with relief as Edmund finally set about his inevitable struggle to accept the full ugly truth of who he was, and she didn't blame him one bit as he took off his silver wedding ring from her that he'd kept safe for more than eighty years. It was about time. But then, she noticed it. There was a certain twinkle in his eye on the first evening when they arrived at the ancient estate of the Rakshasa Patels of Baroda, and a troop of freshly self-aware Rakshasas were being swiftly rounded up to their divine callings as Avatars of Light.

Mr. Montero made the whole thing worse as he asked Ellie and Edmund awkwardly if they were married before assigning them a room, and Edmund's passion to dispel the idea burst out of him with alarming haste. It was more than his normal discomfort with their well-practiced farce of being siblings. He was making room, room in his life for the girl who'd put the twinkle in his eye. Her name wasn't Padma.

That night, after the house had settled down and Ellie's nerves had finally dispersed enough to let her go to sleep, Eleanor blurred through the hallway, straight to the door Vibhishana had retired to early. He was already communing with the Yakshas as she took a seat at the table.

Kuveni put her arm around her shoulders in welcome.

"Is it all going to plan?" Eleanor asked as Kuveni materialized a hefty glass of cognac for her.

Vibhishana drank down a carafe of hot honeyed milk. "As much as it possibly can. No matter how much preparation I think I have, things never turn out as I think they will. This time it's worse. The wicked Oracle is meddling, and the Avatars of Light aren't ready. As we speak, Shanti is in the arms of my evil brother, executing a farce more dangerous than any I've ever attempted myself. I can only pray that she's strong enough to resist the demon inside of her. She could be the destroyer of two worlds."

"Why don't you send a Yaksha along to report back?" Eleanor asked as she took a savoring sip.

As Kuveni moved to answer, Mr. Montero threw her a frown of disagreement. She answered anyway.

"The Yakshas must stay away from her. If the demon Kali enslaves any of us, it would be the end. We don't have any Yaksha power to spare with our ranks so depleted."

"She's gone all this time without encountering a Yaksha? That must have taken exceptional self-control!" Eleanor exclaimed. "I didn't think you had it in you!"

"I served her for years in Baroda, and she never figured out I was a Yaksha," Mr. Montero said with a hint of pride.

"Oh, Oberon, that was because you were foolish, not brave."

"Still, it was an exceptional performance for a Yaksha. You know as well as I do that it is not our nature to endure such elaborate farces. I've now endured enough for a lifetime."

Vibhishana moved to interject, and then thought the better of it. All three of his allies stared him down, not letting him get away with his silence.

"As part of her preparation for her hoax, I informed her of the existence of Yakshas."

"You did *what?!*" Kuveni exclaimed.

"My lord, what were you thinking?" Mr. Montero asked more calmly, although still more assertively than Eleanor expected. That was when she realized how much the world really was changing.

"The prophecies led me to believe that her full integration into our world was a necessary step in defeating Kali. Yakshas are pivotal players in our world. We will all just have to trust that she will be able to control herself when it matters most."

"Do you really think she can do that?" Mr. Montero pushed.

"I wouldn't have sent her into the arms of my brother if I didn't have faith in her."

Eleanor could see in his expression that he was not fully convinced himself.

Kuveni hunkered down for an unpleasant confrontation. "My lord, you didn't send her. She concocted the plan all on her own.

601

You were very unhappy about it, in fact." He didn't argue. "Don't you think it's possible that Kali was simply using you? Even taunting you by using her to collect secrets that he could use to defeat all of us?"

"I've kept the idea top of mind for decades. There hasn't been one moment when it hasn't been tormenting me." He lowered his voice. "But she *is* my divine wife. She *is* the Avatar of Parvati. When she was dying on the floor of her living room after that brute stabbed her with a stake, I had to transit between the worlds to save her because her fading life-force was depleting mine. It weakened me so much more than your death did, Eleanor. I thought I might have reached the end of my immortality altogether until I was able to save her with my Rakshasa plasma. I must trust that Shakti chose a vessel who was strong enough to triumph, and that, in the end, Shanti's connection to me as her divine husband will yank her out of any dark abyss in which she happens to find herself."

"A stake?" Eleanor couldn't help but ask.

"He mistook her for a vampire."

"Blimey."

"It is a story for another time. We must focus on the delicate matters at hand. I knew that Edmund learning of his father's dark nature would be difficult, but I did not expect him to suffer so mightily at his hands. It has made this transitional period much harder for all of them, but we don't have time for them to acclimate for much longer. What can you tell us, Eleanor?"

"Well, Ellie is still dreadfully overwhelmed by all of it. It goes without saying that Edmund is too... which wasn't helped by your mistake earlier, Monty. What was that about, anyway? 'Are you two married?' Surely you knew I was dead?"

Mr. Montero glanced at Vibhishana, who nodded for him to respond.

"My lady, the prophecies spoke of him uniting with his other half. It is a necessary step for the Avatars of Light to ascend. I thought…" He blushed with embarrassment. "I thought he simply had an affinity for redheads."

Eleanor sighed with resignation. "I knew this day would come, and I'd hoped not to have to watch. I love him, of course, and I want him to be happy, but still… it stings being replaced." Kuveni patted her back supportively. "But I thought Padma was supposed to be his other half? Where's she in all this?"

"She resides in Supriya," Vibhishana replied. "My wicked sister murdered her decades ago, and she was reborn."

"Blimey. Even the Holy Mother couldn't save that lost soul. Where is Surpanakha now?"

"She's dead. Supriya finally killed her."

"Good on her!" Eleanor exclaimed. "That means Sita finally saved herself!"

"I was relieved by it, as well. Now we have one less villain to worry about," Vibhishana agreed. "But Supriya and Sita are so different from each other, I don't know what it means. Supriya has a much darker tinge to her power, and it's stronger than Sita's ever was. I think perhaps she got it from Shanti."

"Shanti?! Blimey, Supriya isn't your daughter, is she? First cousins really shouldn't be married, no matter what Victoria and Albert had."

He offered her a reserved smile. "She was Shanti's child with another man. A human man who was enough of a villain himself for Supriya to understand Edmund's struggle now." He sighed apologetically. "She is a good match for Edmund. They are good for each other, and they will need to be. They will need their full strength as the united Preserver of the Universe to save Earth. I'm not convinced now that it can even be done."

Eleanor scoffed. "Surely, they'll succeed? What about the Age of Truth?"

"The prophecies are dire, Eleanor. Two planets will be destroyed. Venus and Earth are the two inhabited planets in our solar system. They are the most likely victims. One way for the worlds to be peaceful is for all mortal life to end."

"Venus, you say?" she asked as Ellie's lifelong mystery came to a head.

"It is our home planet, as it turns out. We don't have time to go into the painful journey it took for Neha to make that discovery. There are still billions of Rakshasas there, inhabiting the burning skies as vapor. Neha wanted to be around for the big reveal to our reluctant relatives, but she's off at the moment, checking up on her mother."

"I see. So, you didn't need a Yaksha for the task," Eleanor winked.

"No. It is time for the Yakshas to take their place openly by our side. It is the moment that Kuveni has been impatiently awaiting."

Eleanor squeezed her supportively, but then she sighed, refusing to selfishly ignore her thought. "You shouldn't tell Edmund you're Kate right now. He's falling in love with Supriya, I can see it in his eyes, and you and Mélusine should not remind him of his life with me. It will drag his buried guilt right up to the surface again."

Kuveni kissed her forehead. "You're a dear, selfless girl, Eleanor. We will wait until the time is right."

Eleanor drank down the rest of her cognac and stood up. "I should go. Ellie needs her rest."

She walked around the table and hugged Vibhishana's shoulders from behind.

"Take with you Shakti's blessings, and give me a call if you need me. In the meantime, have faith in all of them. They're all stronger than you think."

She kissed him on the cheek, and then, in a blur, she left them alone.

She watched and she waited as Edmund fell in love and initiated his own silly wedding ceremony naked in an ice cave while intoxicated by the karmic power of a Venusian Rakshasa god. She watched as he and Supriya came back to their senses and realized that their hasty decision hadn't been a catastrophe, but a miracle, and she watched as they flew off to rescue Charlie from some alien-hunting human brutes on the way to their beautiful divine honeymoon. She was happy for him, but she was ready. Ready to go. She was tired of watching and waiting. She was tired of being dead.

Months later, she stood with the other wards of the Avatars of Light in Mélusine's refuge by the Sacred Well as Edmund finally ascended on live international television. She watched as the worlds descended into chaos, and billions of lives were lost. And finally, as the worlds settled into the Age of Truth and the Preservers of the Universe stepped up to their divine thrones, guiding the species of Earth to rebuild for a lasting peace, she made herself known. The time she'd been waiting for was almost at hand. She was ready.

It was Ellie's ninetieth birthday, and after all he'd been through, Edmund was still scared. He was scared of what his long dead wife would think of his choice to move on. He was still, after everything, scared of losing her.

And so, on one snowy February evening ten months earlier, Eleanor had awoken him in the parlor of a cheerful house in Elphinstone, and she'd released him from his misery.

But still, it wasn't time yet.

Uma, how much longer? She'd begged afterwards. *Please tell me it will be soon!*

Soon, my child. Soon.

PART SIX
THE END OF MIDNIGHT

CHAPTER 38 – LIMBO

Neha paced around frantically, holding her head in her hands as she dodged the Sacred Well and Mélusine's Roman chaise. She'd been doing it for so long, she'd memorized the route.

"Melly, I can't do this anymore!" she exclaimed.

"*You* can't do this anymore?!" Mélusine shouted. "I'm the one who's in labor!"

"I thought I could handle it! I really did! But it's been five months! FIVE MONTHS! I'm losing my mind!"

"We're in the Crystal Cave, Neha. Time doesn't exist."

"But my watch keeps ticking!"

"Then smash it!"

"I can't! I need to know! It's like we've been down here for an ETERNITY!"

"Imagine how it feels for me."

"I can't! I can't fathom it! Why didn't you tell me it would be this bad?!"

"Would you have done it?"

"NO! OF COURSE NOT!"

"You've answered your own question."

Neha blurred to Mélusine's side and took her hand, kissing it and rubbing it against her cheek. "I never would have suggested it in a million years if I'd known how bad it would be. Never, Melly. Never!"

"I know. That's why I wipe the memories of Yakshini mothers. If anyone knew how bad it really was, they'd never bloody do it. Our species would have gone extinct long ago."

"But why didn't you tell *me*? I'm your Nazza! I'm your wife! I'm the other mother of your child! Why didn't you let me make an informed decision?!"

"Because I wanted this, Neha. I wanted us to have a child, and I didn't want fear or rationality to stand in the way."

"But I'm not ready!" Neha exclaimed. "I thought I was ready, but I was wrong! I'm not even sixty yet! We could have waited thousands of years!"

"We're in this, Neha. There's no way out of it. Now I need you to keep it together for me and for her."

Mélusine laid her hand on her belly, where there was no evidence of a bump.

"But I don't understand! How is she even in there! There's no baby!"

"We're a non-corporeal species, Neha. Why would you think our procreation would look anything like a human pregnancy?"

"Sabrina! When Sabrina had Maya, she looked like a normal human pregnant woman!"

"Because that's what she *thought* it should look like! We manifest our thoughts into form all the time. That is *what we are*!"

"I don't even really want a baby!" Neha exclaimed. "God, Melly, what if she takes a whole century to grow up? That's like the prime of my life out the window! What about all my projects?! Earth's scientific research is going to come to a grinding halt!"

"You should have thought of that *before* we decided to procreate, Neha. If you didn't want a baby, what were you even

610

thinking about when we were doing the deed? You must have wanted it. Consent is required for conception, and don't you dare claim that this was the product of a wicked loophole!"

"I wanted to have *had* a baby!"

"How is that different?!"

"I don't know! I wanted a child that was ours who we could hang out with! I guess... I guess I didn't really want to go through the process of rearing her. I wanted to bask in the glory *after* she'd been reared. I was a terror of a child, you know."

"I *know*, Neha. You are legendary as the worst child any Yaksha has ever had to deal with."

"That was just Monty being mean!"

"Everyone agreed. You were really bloody hard."

"But she'll have both of her parents! She won't need to be bad like I was when I was trying to get my mum's attention! She'll have a whole family with grandparents and aunties and uncles, and the two best mothers on the planet! It will be as wholesome as *Leave It To Beaver* but with the zany quirks of *The Munsters*."

"I have no idea what those references mean."

"I guess we'll use my last name for her, since you don't have one... *The Vishravans*, a touching tale of shapeshifting and shenanigans from Venus to Mars... Maybe I should pitch it to a TV producer."

"Focus, Neha!"

"I'm trying! I've been going nuts for months, Melly! I need to give my mind a break!"

Mélusine grabbed Neha's hands. "Here comes another one."

Neha braced her and held on as Mélusine screamed. The cave shook as the sound bounced back and forth between the black sapphire walls and then dissolved into the Sacred Well.

"This isn't right," Mélusine said as soon as she could speak again. "I'm not making any progress. Each time, she should be taking my life-force into her, using it to become more whole. She hasn't been doing that for the last twenty contractions. It's like she's stuck."

Neha gulped. "You don't think it's me, do you? God, Melly, what if it's all me! My selfish fear is keeping her from coming alive! My will isn't strong enough!"

"That isn't how it works."

"Are you sure?! We're the only two Rakshini goddesses who've ever had a baby! How do you have any idea how it works?!"

"Touché, ma chérie."

Neha stood up and began pacing again. "How long were you in here when you had Puck? How far off are we?"

"He was fast. He had a Rakshasa gestation and came out in a few minutes when he was ready."

"So for you, this is especially unusual, right?"

"One example does not constitute a sample size, my beloved scientist."

"But, Melly, we both have Rakshasa in us. I'm *mostly* Rakshasa, and we've been in here for *five months*. What's the longest you've ever had a Yakshini birth last?"

"I don't know. I didn't keep track."

"Think, Melly! You have a Rakshasa memory! Remember how long it lasted in comparison to now! Has it *ever* taken this long?"

Mélusine spent several minutes running through her memories in her head.

"No. The longest was about half this amount of time."

Neha paced some more as she forced her fatigued mind to function.

"Melly, I think we should leave."

"We can't. She needs the black sapphire of the walls to keep her essence intact. If we leave, she won't be able to come together. She'll just dissolve into the air, and all of this will have been for nothing."

"How do you know? Has it ever happened?"

"Yes, ma chérie. It was very unpleasant."

"But did it happen with two Rakshinis? Rakshasas have babies outside of the Sacred Well all the time! What if she's taking after that side of us?"

"Neha, Puck was born like a Rakshasa. I still needed to be in the Crystal Cave."

"Are you sure?!"

"Here comes another one."

Neha braced her again as she screamed.

"Anything?"

Mélusine nodded in the negative.

"Melly, I beg you, we can't be down here suffering like this for eternity. Please let us try to have a Rakshasa birth? I promise that if it doesn't work out, we'll have another child when we're ready, and I'll be the carrier. It will be my turn to bear the torment, and I will do it with a smile."

Mélusine raised her eyebrows skeptically.

"Okay, fine, I won't be smiling. But I'll do it, Melly. I swear! I can't watch you suffer like this anymore!"

"Kuveni, please come," Mélusine called.

Kuveni materialized beside them. "Good lord!" She kneeled down beside Mélusine and placed her hand on her belly. "You both look affright! How long have you been down here?!"

"FIVE MONTHS!" Neha exclaimed. She pulled Kuveni into a desperate hug. "Something's wrong! It isn't working! Our daughter is stuck in limbo!"

"Now, now, Mistress Neha, we mustn't panic."

"DON'T TELL ME NOT TO PANIC!" Neha shouted. "We've been down here *forever!*"

"Something is wrong," Mélusine reiterated.

"How many contractions has it been?"

"Sixty."

"Oh my. Yes, that does sound wrong."

"How many did you have when you had your twins?" Neha asked.

"Five."

"Neha wants us to try leaving the Crystal Cave for a Rakshasa birth."

"But that could make her fall apart!"

"We know."

Kuveni considered the idea carefully, looking back and forth between them.

"If it doesn't work out, perhaps it was not meant to be. You can always try again."

Mélusine let a tear escape. "I don't want this to have been for nothing."

"Then why don't we wait," Neha suggested dutifully, fighting every impatient cell in her body. "Now we know we have the option. We can give it another year and see."

Mélusine threw her an annoyed look at her subtle cheek, but she couldn't deny that there was truth in it.

"Where is it most likely to work without the Crystal Cave?" Neha asked both of them.

"She will need familiar energy to latch onto if she's going to have any chance," Mélusine replied.

"Everyone is gathered at Edmund's house in Basingstoke for Christmas. Perhaps the energy of your divine family will help?" Kuveni suggested. "There is a Rakshasa bed in Edmund's storage room. It's the room where Eleanor died having Ellie, and he refused to ever go in there again. I can clean it up in a jiffy."

Kuveni disappeared.

"Do you really want to give birth in the room where Eleanor died?" Neha asked.

"I just want this over with," Mélusine admitted. "We're both immortal goddesses. *Que sera sera.*"

Neha squeezed her hand and kissed her. "I love you, Melly. Whatever happens, we're going to get through this."

Mélusine smiled and brushed a strand of loose hair out of her face. "There's my reasonable Nazza again. I knew you were in there somewhere."

Kuveni returned. "It's ready."

Neha lay down on the chaise next to Mélusine and engulfed her into her arms.

"*On y va.*"

Ellie collapsed onto the floor, and Supriya rushed to her side. Edmund gently nudged Charlie out of his arms to join them.

"Ellie? Ellie-bean? Are you alright?" he asked as he took her head into his lap and stroked her hair.

Ellie gasped in an awakening Rakshasa breath and looked around. Vibhishana and Shanti were standing above her. The MacLeods and Grace were watching with wide eyes. Sheranee licked her face supportively.

Ellie grasped her gut. "I'm cold." Tears erupted. "And *alone!*" She struggled to sit up, and she grabbed Shanti's hand.

Mum? Mum, are you there?! Please come back, I need you!

I'm sorry, my child. She has moved on. Her destiny was fulfilled, and now it is time for her to have a new destiny.

Ellie fell back into Edmund's arms. She buried her face in his shoulder and sobbed.

"It'll be alright, Ellie-bean," Edmund whispered into her ear as he helped her up and guided her to the chaise. They sat down together, and she kept crying.

"I hate Christmas!" she exclaimed.

"No one will argue with you there, Ells," Debbie said as she glanced around the room. "I reckon even Father Johnson will agree."

"I do," he said helplessly. "It makes every tragedy of the day more painful to be couched in the illusion of cheer."

They all looked up as a primal scream resonated from upstairs.

"I hope Amma didn't just become the Ghost of Christmas Past!" Debbie exclaimed.

Edmund's face turned white at the horrific reminder of the most traumatic moments of his life. His eyes turned black.

"I swear if this is a prank by Neha, I will *kill* her. I don't care if she's immortal!"

Supriya put her hand on his. "There is no need to jump straight to violence, my love. I'll go see what it is."

"I'll go with you," Shanti suggested. "Someone may need help."

Another scream, even more ferocious, shook the house.

With one momentary glance of agreement, every Rakshasa in the room whooshed upstairs.

Edmund pushed open the door to his former marital suite with Eleanor, and Mélusine was in a frenzy as she splashed out of the Rakshasa bed completely naked.

"Come to me, *ma fille*! Listen to the sound of Maman's voice! Use it as an anchor!"

"What in god's name is going on?" Edmund demanded of Neha, who was too panicked to answer him as she followed Mélusine around the room, looking under the bed and inside the cupboards.

"Come, my child! Come to Mum! I'll be the coolest mum of them all, you'll see!" she called into the air.

"Come to Maman!" Mélusine repeated more desperately. "I'm here waiting for you! Feel the moisture in the air! Feel my energy. It is the same as yours! Latch onto it!"

618

Mélusine collapsed.

A gust of wind sent everything loose in the room aflutter.

Next to Mélusine, a young adult woman lay peacefully. She had beautiful brown skin, the same color as Neha's, and silky tendrils of black hair that extended all the way down to her waist. She was naked, with proportions that each of the goddesses in the room found strikingly familiar. Shakti's favorites.

Neha threw herself onto the floor between them. She grabbed Mélusine's hand. "Melly?! Melly, are you okay?!"

Mélusine opened her eyes and looked over. She sat up woozily and smiled, gathering the head of the woman into her lap and stroking her hair.

Neha gently touched her sleeping eyes. "Shiva's wrath, Melly." She teared up. "She looks like Maya!"

"She looks like you, ma chérie."

Neha ran her fingers along the girl's jawline. "She looks like you too!"

"She is our daughter, Neha."

"Are you going to… breastfeed her?"

Mélusine smiled indulgently at Neha's silly question, as she saw the concern in her expression.

"No, ma chérie, that is not how Yakshinis feed their young."

"Good, because that would have been really awkward with everyone watching."

Mélusine laughed, and wiped the tears from Neha's eyes. She glanced up at her overwhelmed audience.

"Mes chéris, say hello to the first Christmas miracle of the night."

They tiptoed into the room, and Supriya braced Edmund who braced Ellie as they struggled to comprehend what they were seeing against the exceptionally painful backdrop.

"Wake up, ma fille, it is time to meet your family."

The woman opened her eyes. They were green and sparkling, not dissimilar to Shanti's. Vibhishana and Shanti kneeled down beside Neha.

"Dad, I hate to break it to you, but you're a grandpa. That makes you officially old."

He put his arm around her. "It's about time."

"Is this normal?" Shanti asked. "Are Yakshini children born as adults?"

"I have never seen it before in my life," Vibhishana replied.

"I am a singularly unique woman," the woman whispered back to him, as if she was remembering the phrase from a dream.

"Shiva's wrath," Vibhishana murmured.

The woman sat up. She held up her arms and inspected them, looking at her fingers curiously. She felt her face, and then a tendril of her black, silky hair. She stared at her large, round breasts, cupping them with her hands and pushing them together into copious cleavage, and then she let go to run her finger up her leg and around her perfectly formed belly button, feeling her smooth skin with satisfaction. She looked around to each member of her audience, drinking each of them in. Then she closed her eyes, scrunched her nose, and a sari materialized to cover her. They had all seen it before. It was made of crimson silk and draped in an ancient style, held together by a golden, bejeweled sari belt. It matched the one that Shanti was still wearing.

She smiled as she kissed Mélusine on the forehead.

"Hello, Maman."

She smiled as she kissed Neha on the forehead.

"Hello, Mum. Do you have a name for me?"

"Do you have a name already?" Mélusine asked.

She looked down at herself. "In my last life, my name was Eleanor."

"Wicked," Neha whispered with wonder.

"I hope it isn't too disappointing?" she asked Mélusine as she looked down at herself again. "I didn't mean to rob you of raising an infant after you endured the torment of a Yakshini birth."

Mélusine hugged her and kissed her as tears of joy streamed down her face. "I would endure it a million times over to give you new life, ma chérie. A million times."

"I don't think I should be called Eleanor anymore. I have been reborn. I think my mothers should choose my name."

Neha looked to Mélusine, who nodded her agreement. "We discussed... Gauri. Gauri Padma Brahmani Vishravan."

She smiled. "It is a perfect name, Mum." She hugged Neha again.

"Hello, Grandma. Or should I call you Gran?"

She addressed Shanti, who was still bewildered. Gauri hugged her anyway.

"Would it be too strange for you to call me Shanti? I don't want you to think I don't love you, it's just... I don't know... it seems like we're equals. In fact..." She took Gauri's hand and held on as she connected her energy. "We are the same... but not exactly... I can't explain it."

Gauri smiled knowingly, but turned her attention onto Vibhishana. "May I call you Grandpa?"

He hugged her. "Please do, Gauri. Welcome to our family." He glanced at Neha and then leaned in with a mischievous twinkle in his eye. "When I am back from my sacred duties later tonight, I will give you a list of every naughty thing Neha did as a child."

"Dad?!" Neha exclaimed.

He winked. "I'm sure Monty already has his ready."

Gauri placed Neha's hand in Vibhishana's and smiled.

She stood up and pulled Kuveni into a hug. "I've missed you." Kuveni hugged her back, sniffling with tears of joy. "Maybe while my mothers are busy at work, you can babysit me." She winked, and then left Kuveni, took a deep, calming breath, and approached Edmund.

He backed up against the wall. An aggressive puff of his rich, spicy Rakshasa fear aroused everyone in the room. Ellie hid her face in his shoulder, while Supriya squeezed his hand. Eleanor closed her eyes, scrunched her nose, and returned to the form she had known for so long.

"My darlings, please do not fear me. You have all seen stranger things. If I were a babe in arms, you wouldn't find this so strange, but there was no time for that. Earth needs another goddess now that the Holy Mother's avatar is residing on Mars."

She hugged Supriya, and then took her hand, connecting their energy.

"What is that?" Supriya asked. The tingling sensation was strange but pleasant.

"It is our power," Gauri smiled. "I am the Holy Mother. I carry the power of all of Shakti's forms, the Creator, the Preserver, and the Transformer. You and I are sisters, Supriya. We are two parts of one whole. Together we are the Goddess."

Edmund looked like he might collapse from the strain.

"Please forgive me for this. I promise I will only ever do it once. It is for the greater good."

She leaned forward and kissed Edmund on the lips, even as he tried to pull away. She held on for an extra-long moment until she was sure that he'd had enough.

"How did that feel, darling?"

He wiped his mouth on his sleeve. "Inappropriate."

She smiled. "That's true, I hated it too. But it was a necessary evil, darling. It didn't feel how it feels when you are kissing your other half, did it? You know what it feels like now to be joined with someone who truly makes you whole, and I am not that woman. Now neither of you will be worried about it."

She turned her attention onto Ellie. "I am your mother, Ellie, but I am more than that too. I don't know exactly what that means yet, but I'm hoping that we can come to know each other again as equals."

Ellie nodded, wiping the tears from her eyes. Gauri kissed her on the forehead, and then returned to her most natural form.

"Now, come. All of you. You have a long night ahead of you, and if you don't mind, I would like to inaugurate the first Christmas Eve of the Age of Truth with the evening's first miracle."

"We've already had that," Neha corrected her. "It was you."

She took Neha's hand in her left and Mélusine's in her right, and Mélusine pushed a hefty dose of Yakshini warmth into her.

She laughed giddily. "So that's what that is! Blimey, *that's* the Yakshini equivalent of breastfeeding? You have all been far too generous with the Rakshasas over the years, feeding them your energy like they're your babes in arms!"

As she noticed the discomfort of the others, Neha squeezed her hand. "Keeping us honest from day one, that's my girl!"

Gauri skipped happily between her mothers as she led them all down the stairs to the library. Charlie was sitting in Grace's lap, while the MacLeods were chatting politely as they waited for their divine hosts to return.

"Hello, my bairns!" Gauri exclaimed. She rushed right up to Debbie to shake her hand. "My name is Gauri. I'm Neha and Mélusine's new daughter, but if you'd like, you can call me Amma." She relished the revelation as she switched back into the form that the MacLeods recognized.

"Lord Almighty," Debbie murmured.

"Exactly," Gauri said excitedly. She rubbed her hands together until the divine silver light of the Preserver of the Universe emerged. "Now, I know that Abbi was planning on making himself into a decrepit old man later tonight to give you a second chance in this life, Debbie, but if it is something that you would like, I'm going to do it instead."

"What do you mean?" Debbie asked.

"Would you like to be young again? To re-set like Abbi and Ellie did? It's really a selfish request on our part. Otherwise you'll go through your natural lifecycle and be reborn after your transitional period. It really is up to you. There are benefits to either option for a soul as virtuous as yours."

"Would I still be human?"

"Aye, we can't change what you are, my little love. Even our power still has its limits."

"Alright," she agreed with disbelief.

Gauri kneeled. She rubbed her hands together again, whipping up her divine energy. She placed her hands on Debbie's chest and forehead, and then took in one long, calm, powerful breath. She felt her life-force ooze out of her fingertips and infuse Debbie, and when she could feel that Debbie was full, she pulled away. Neha and Mélusine stepped in to catch her, but as she felt a moment of weakness, Mélusine pushed another dose of Yakshini warmth into her, and she felt her whole body rejuvenate, stronger than it had been before.

"Good lord," Edmund murmured.

"Praise the Holy Mother," Grace whispered.

Gauri looked down at her perfectly vigorous form that didn't show a hint of the painful sacrifice that manifested in Supriya and Edmund every time they used their life-force to heal. She looked at Debbie, who was just as beautiful as she remembered her from 1944, and she smiled. "Merry Christmas, Debbie."

Debbie pulled her into a tight hug. "I love you, Amma. I'll keep making you proud!"

"Merry Christmas to all!" Gauri exclaimed. "Now, if I'm not mistaken, Santa Claus himself was planning on making an appearance tonight in as many villages as he could manage! Could you use some help, Grandpa?"

"Ma fille, are you sure you're up to it?" Mélusine asked with motherly concern. "You have been through an epically difficult ordeal. Perhaps you should rest before pushing yourself too hard."

"Maman, I've been itching to be alive for almost a century! It's like I just woke up from the most invigorating cat nap of my life. Can we please get at it?!"

"That's my girl!" Neha exclaimed giddily again as she squeezed Gauri's hand.

"So, Gramps? Shall our family of saints band together to make up for a century of rotten Christmases?" Gauri asked, taking in the cheerful décor with fresh eyes.

"I can think of nothing I would love more," Vibhishana agreed.

"Can I come?" Debbie asked as she stood up and almost fell over with surprise at the dexterity of her youthful limbs.

"It is long overdue," Vibhishana agreed as he pulled her into a grandfatherly hug. "What a gift it is to have you with us for another lifetime."

"Thank you, father," she whispered as she hugged him back. "Thank you for everything."

"You're a good, tidy lass, Debbie MacLeod," he replied with one more squeeze.

Gauri noticed Charlie, who looked almost as bewildered as his struggling father. She approached him and offered him her hand in greeting. "Hello, Charlie. I know you better than you know me, but I'm sure we'll be great friends. You can call me Auntie Eleanor when I look like this, so that we don't confuse your father too much." She returned to her most natural form, morphing Durga's sari into a thick red velvet Christmas robe lined with white fur. "And when I look like this, you can call me Gauri!"

"Okay," Charlie squeaked.

Gauri approached Edmund and Supriya. "I don't blame you for how you're feeling about all this, but I promise, it will all be okay. I'm going to leave you alone after Christmas is over tomorrow, and I'll stay away for a while so you both can adjust."

"You don't have to go," Supriya argued. "I want to know you! You're my niece!"

"Really, please don't go," Edmund seconded. "I will not run you out with a pitchfork in the night just because I find the new circumstances uncomfortable. I promise I will sort myself out. It is a wonderful gift to have you in my life like this, and, to be perfectly honest, it's less frightening than having you show up in Ellie's body for a tidy nip."

She pulled them both into a hug. "I want to spend time with my mothers anyway, and, if she would like to join us, Ellie." She addressed Ellie, who nodded her agreement. "It is time for all of us to figure out who I am. I will see you soon enough. Our world is very small."

Gauri looked around at the group and clapped with excitement. "Mums, are you coming?! If we time it right, we can still hit every time zone! Mum, do you think you can conjure a sleigh with some reindeer? I think I can make myself into Santa Claus, and with Grandpa's help, we can hit twice the houses!"

"I think she got this enthusiasm from you," Mélusine whispered to Neha.

Neha snapped her fingers, and two teams of reindeer mooed in the hallway. With a roar, Sheranee took her lead position at the front of the first of two enormous sleighs.

"Can she really fly?" Charlie asked, finally mustering the courage to join them.

"I reckon we're about to find out!" Gauri replied.

"Let's go. I've been plotting how to make this work since I was a kid!" Neha agreed.

Kuveni snapped her fingers, and everyone's clothing transformed into the festive red velvet and white fur outfits of Santa's helpers.

Grace looked down, startled by her own transformation. "Oh, no thank you. Someone has to hold down the fort. I have a feeling there are going to be a lot of hungry angels to feed by morning."

Gauri took her mothers' hands, and Ellie took Charlie's, and as all five of them were climbing into Sheranee's sleigh, Edmund and Supriya approached.

"May we join you?" he asked. "I have a problem with hating Christmas that I think I might just be getting over."

626

Gauri pulled them in, and they all squealed as Neha took the reins and Sheranee guided the sleigh right out the open front door and into the sky.

"Come on, slow pokes!" Gauri called.

In a blur, Vibhishana and Shanti, along with the illustrious MacLeods, caught up with them, and as Vibhishana tipped his red pointed hat in playful competition, the race was on.

"Catch us if you can, Amma!" Debbie called.

And so, as the snow gently flurried, and the fire crackled alone in the library that had seen too many dark Christmases, the Avatars of Light joyfully embarked upon their first of many magical Christmases in the Age of Truth.

Eleanor MacLeod's last glorious triumph was finally complete, but Gauri Padma Brahmani Vishravan's first chapter had just begun.

~THE END~

SNEAK PEEK: THE RIDDLE
or Edmund's 200th Birthday Surprise
A Novella by Ashley Mayers

CHAPTER ONE: APRIL 26, 2018

Edmund's heart raced with anticipation as he followed his loving Rakshasa wife through the wispy clouds of an unusually warm April afternoon sky. His golden falcon wings flapped in sync with his increasingly impatient temperament, and he reveled in a moment of childlike excitement that he had only ever felt a handful of times throughout his two hundred years on Earth. His giddiness only grew as he caught a glimpse of their angelic shadows gracefully flitting across the rolling green hills of the Cotswalds below.

"My love, won't you tell me anything about my birthday surprise?" he implored. "I know Neha has been up to all sorts of shenanigans for weeks now!"

"And what would be the point of spoiling all of her hard work? A man only turns two hundred once, you know."

Supriya sped up playfully and enticed him into a chase.

As he caught up with her, she paused in mid-air with her wings poised, gliding up several meters on a gust of wind.

"Just one clue, my love? What would be the harm in *one* clue? Surely one clever clue would make the game more fun, don't you think? Perhaps even a riddle?"

Supriya returned to their course, flying faster than they had in several hours as she contemplated her response to his challenge, and then she smiled and waited for him to catch up. "The wise men argue about whether man came first or god came first, but who came before both?"

He grinned as his mind raced for a response. "Is this about a person? A person from my past? Is she here? Is she coming to my surprise party?"

Supriya engaged her tried and true poker face and veered in for a landing, watching her shadow enlarge as she aimed for a cobblestone street surrounded by cute thatched-roof houses dotted amongst blooming spring gardens.

As soon as they landed, they absorbed their wings and looked around. A crowd of people dressed in regency-era clothing right out of a Jane Austen novel cheered. Several men on horses stopped their trotting to wave hello, and a young girl in a high-waisted yellow dress with a huge matching bonnet that made her look distinctly like Little Bo Peep rushed up and handed him a colorful bouquet of tulips.

Edmund took the flowers and watched with puzzlement as the girl skipped away down the cobblestone street. "Good lord, Neha didn't discover some Rakshasa ability to time travel, did she? Or perhaps a Yakshini one? Mélusine does meddle with time by the Sacred Well... But surely she realizes we will create all sorts of problems for our future selves by meddling in the past..."

Supriya only laughed with satisfaction and wiggled herself into her own rendition of an empire-waisted Jane Austen gown made of delicate ivory silk with a mint green overcoat. With one expert gesture, she gathered up her long, silky black hair into an elaborate old-fashioned up-do, and then closed her eyes and concentrated, subtly enhancing her features, just as if she'd spent hours expertly making herself up.

Edmund looked around their enamored crowd as they watched her complete her transformation. "My love, are you sure it's wise to be so... er... public about your talents?"

Supriya giggled with delight at his perfect reaction to the beginning of her plan. "Don't you want to fit in, my love? Your linen pants are a bit futuristic."

Edmund glanced around the crowd again, assessing their reactions, but they didn't seem the least bit concerned. In fact, they seemed downright entertained.

He closed his eyes and dug into his less-than-Rakshasa-perfect memory, back to the clothing Vibhishana was wearing when they traveled together from India to England in 1830. He wiggled himself into the dark, high-collared suit, and then looked down to judge his success.

"I suppose this style is from a bit later. I wasn't really paying enough attention to notice fashion when I was an infant."

Supriya enticed him into a kiss, wrapping her arms around his neck and licking his tongue. "Well, I think you look perfectly dashing, Colonel."

He melted into her arms for a delicious, passionate embrace until Supriya caught herself and refocused on the more important matter at hand. She took his hand and guided him through the streets of the village, waving back amicably at everyone who stopped their anachronistic business to offer them a "good afternoon."

When they finally reached the edge of town, a carriage was waiting, and Edmund smiled and laughed as he recognized the driver. "I should have realized this was all just part of Neha's elaborate Rakshasa birthday hoax. Did she costume everyone in this entire village? And get rid of all the cars? And warn them that we were coming? But then how did she possibly bring back the thatched roofs? I haven't seen those in over a hundred years in this part of England…"

"Think not of the how, my love," Supriya winked. "Just enjoy it. We will have her explain all of her brilliant tactics tomorrow."

"Good afternoon, Master Edmund," Mr. Montero called from his chauffeur's perch as he held the reins to two noble white horses with glistening golden tails. "You are looking quite dapper on this fine spring day."

"As are you, Monty!" Edmund called. He sighed nostalgically as he gazed at Mr. Montero's outfit. "You were wearing that when you took me from Bath to India, weren't you?"

Mr. Montero relegated a look of regret. "Indeed, I was. I am glad to wear it on a happy occasion for once. It is a privilege to see you fully ascended to your rightful position, my lord."

"It took me long enough, didn't it?" Edmund winked.

"Two hundred years is hardly a blink to us," Mr. Montero reminded him. "I remember when you were just a babe as if it were yesterday. You were the calmest child any of us had ever encountered. We knew then that you were special, but we didn't realize how lucky we were that you had joined us in this world until much later."

Edmund shook Monty's hand with both of his. "I was lucky to have you, Monty. I was so concerned about finding my real family that I didn't realize you were my real family. You and Kuveni and the others."

"Be sure to tell her that this evening, my lord. I have no doubt she will be thrilled to hear it."

They both looked around, waiting for Kuveni to materialize beside them, admit to her invisible eavesdropping, and pull Edmund into a motherly hug. Edmund laughed as the moment passed. "Neha must have her busy!"

"Lady Neha has kept all of the Yakshas busy for weeks." Mr. Montero rolled his eyes with his typical annoyance, but then he caught himself. "Although, this time it was for a most worthy cause, my lord. Two hundred is indeed a birthday worth celebrating."

Edmund approached the horses and stroked their ears affectionately. "Hello, my friends..." He glanced back at Monty. "Did you bring Grani and Sleipnir all the way from Himinbjörg for this?"

"The Vikings brought them," Mr. Montero replied. "They were just as excited as the rest of us were to celebrate your happy day. But I'd best not give away any more details of Lady Neha's plot. Your carriage awaits, my lord… and my lady."

Supriya winked at Monty as Edmund pulled open the door and like a perfect gentleman, offered her his hand to help her into the carriage. As soon as she was seated, she offered him her hand, and she pulled him inside with a powerful tug, laughing as he landed in her lap. She snuck a sly kiss as the carriage began moving, and then directed his attention to two beautiful redheads, both in similarly elaborate period costumes, and a beaming boy whose costume included an oversized top hat that made him look a bit more like the Mad Hatter than Mr. Darcy.

Charlie giggled as a puppy in his lap, and a puppy in Ellie's lap beside him, both clad in matching knitted cashmere dog sweaters, squeaked their excitement.

"Happy birthday, Dad!" Charlie jumped straight into a flood of the thoughts that had been rushing through his mind for hours of anticipation. "These puppies are for you!!! I picked them myself! I mean, Kuveni and Supriya helped, but I found the nicest street puppies in all of Sri Lanka for you! That way, they won't mind the heat when you're back home at the palace! Although, they did start shivering as soon as we got here, that's why Kuveni made them these sweaters. I don't think they like England very much, but that's okay, because Dharmapala said he'd take care of them when you're traveling, and Mélusine said they are always welcome at Avalon, and Vi…" Ellie smacked his arm and he trailed off, berating himself for almost giving away one of Neha's many surprises. "Never mind. I hope you like them?"

He hopped over from his spot and squeezed onto the bench beside Edmund, bringing the sandy-colored, floppy-eared puppy from his lap with him.

"Thank you, Charlie. I've missed having dogs around. It has been too long." Edmund laughed as the puppy crawled into his lap, and he pulled Charlie into a hug. "Now, what should we name the new members of our family?"

"I was thinking…" Charlie trailed off as he glanced at Supriya.

"Yes?" Edmund encouraged him.

"Garuda and Uluka… you know… because they are the mounts of the Preservers of the Universe."

Edmund smiled. "I think those are wonderful names for our new companions. Perhaps someday they will even meet their namesakes."

"You think?" Charlie asked excitedly. "Are they still around, just like Sheranee?"

"Yes… yes, I'm quite sure they are still around. Perhaps we should summon them sometime to say hello. Sheranee has been a valuable ally to… to all of us."

He threw a self-conscious glance at the beautiful redhead seated beside Ellie. She smiled reassuringly, and her green eyes flashed. She squeezed his hand, and then she reached forward and kissed his forehead.

"Happy grump day, darling."

He smiled as joy and melancholy battled fiercely in his expression. "Thank you for coming."

"I wouldn't have missed your two-hundredth grump day for anything in the world, darling, not even death."

He nodded and took in a deep breath, working to keep his emotions under control.

"Was that it then? Was that the answer to the riddle?" he asked Supriya.

"Do you think it was?" she asked playfully. She glanced to the others and repeated it. "The wise men argue about whether man came first or god came first, but who came before both?"

"Do you think I came before man and god, darling? I suppose in some ways I did, but I am not the answer to Supriya's riddle." The beautiful redhead threw Supriya a knowing glance.

Edmund repeated the riddle several times, observing them each with more scrutiny, and then he shrugged. "I suppose I will have to wait for the plot to unfold."

"Happy birthday, Dad," Ellie said as Charlie's puppy wandered onto Supriya's lap. She nudged her puppy onto his lap, and he pulled her into a hug.

"I love you, Ellie."

They both laughed as the puppy gnawed at his cravat. Edmund coaxed his finger into its mouth instead, and it began suckling. "I can see someone will have to have a bit of training when we get home."

"Firm but supportive, just like an army cadet?" Ellie asked.

"Just like an army cadet," Edmund agreed.

He sighed with contentment as the carriage picked up speed. He looked around at his loving family and swallowed hard, working to keep tears of joy at bay.

"I never imagined in my wildest dreams having all of you together... and on my birthday, no less? It is nothing short of a miracle."

"It will never be called grump day again," Ellie winked.

"No... no it won't..." he murmured.

Supriya took his hand and kissed him on the cheek. "My love, the miracles are just beginning."

They sat in contented silence while the puppies crawled around from lap to lap, and Edmund held Supriya's and Charlie's hands tightly in his. From time to time, Edmund glanced out the window, observing with utter puzzlement that the modern roads seemed to be gone completely, replaced by the cobblestone and mud that he remembered from his adolescence in Bath. Every so often they came upon a farmer or a shepherd wandering about in the fields beyond, and they waved at the carriage until he waved back.

"Extraordinary," he murmured as they reached a village he finally recognized, and a horde of costumed schoolchildren ran alongside the carriage throwing fresh flowers at them and cheering. "Are we really in Priston?"

"What do you think?" Supriya asked slyly.

636

"It looks just like it did when I lived at the farm with Kuveni just outside of town... back in the 1830s... But surely Neha couldn't have made such a thorough change? They demolished that schoolhouse over there in the 1950s! And a fire burned down that mill there at the edge of town back in the 1890s! It was a Tesco just last year! And the cobblestone has been paved over since the 1970s... How on Earth did she change it so thoroughly? Surely the residents would have had something to say about that. It must have been dastardly inconvenient for them to give up their local supermarket for Neha's whim."

"Ask not how," Supriya winked again.

As the carriage picked up speed again, Charlie began bouncing up and down with excitement, working his hardest not to give away any of the surprises he'd helped plan for weeks. They all smiled as the tell-tale Yakshini fog that kept Vibhishana's ancient Anglo-Roman estate hidden from the wider world engulfed them, and the wind whipped up their hair from the open windows.

Supriya took in a deep breath of moist air. "Oh how I love the fog," she sighed.

"You should visit us in Kerala next week," Ellie suggested. "The mountain fog rolls in every afternoon, and we can revel in it for hours outside in the garden."

"Can I come, Dad?!" Charlie exclaimed. "It's spring holidays from school! Mum wouldn't dare say no!"

"Yes... yes, I would like that very much," Edmund agreed as he glanced at the other beautiful redhead for reassurance.

"Yes!" Charlie exclaimed triumphantly.

"Join us, darling," she reiterated. "It is your house too, and we had such good times there. We can tell Ellie and Charlie all of the stories Supriya hasn't told them yet."

"There are stories you didn't include in your manuscripts?" Ellie asked Supriya.

"A few," she smiled. "But I won't spoil them. I think it's a wonderful idea to visit. I haven't seen the house in person, only in Eleanor's memories."

As the carriage slowed to a trot, the fog cleared, and the warm afternoon sun shone down on the verdant gardens of the ancient estate. The hustle and bustle of an active garden party echoed in the distance, and Edmund leaned over Charlie to spy the large crowd gathered amongst beautifully set tables and trickling fountains on the wide lawn.

"Good lord, there are more humans here than there have ever been in Shambhala. I hope our Yaksha security is tight enough…"

"Do not worry for one moment about our security," Mr. Montero said as he opened the carriage door and offered Ellie his hand. "I am an expert with five thousand years of experience. If a ruffian made his way inside, I will eat my hat… literally… as a penitence to Neha for breaking my solemn vow."

As Supriya helped Edmund out of the carriage, two very familiar people rushed to greet them. Edmund grinned happily as he pulled them both into a hug.

"I didn't expect to see you today. Did you come all the way from Mars just for my birthday?"

"My boy, I wouldn't have missed this for anything in the vast universe," Vibhishana declared.

"Hi, sweety," Shanti whispered as she hugged Supriya. "You look lovely in that gown."

"Thanks. Kuveni gave me her memories from the era, and Padma helped me recreate my favorite. This was the dress some duchess wore to a party in Bath in 1815."

"Kuveni had to make my costume for me," Shanti admitted. "I haven't had enough practice with Rakshasa clothing yet. Our non-corporeal state on Mars isn't particularly conducive to practicing our Rakshasa talents, but the joke is on me. This corset is wickedly uncomfortable."

"Well, practice makes perfect," Supriya shrugged.

Shanti wouldn't let her brush off her praise. "I'm so proud of you, sweety, for everything. You are doing such a wonderful job of leading the people of Earth. You should be very proud of yourself for everything you've accomplished."

"Thanks." Supriya blushed self-consciously. "It's taken a lot of effort... many of our divine choices are still excruciating."

"I know exactly what you mean," Shanti commiserated. "But we shouldn't think about anything so unhappy right now. Today we celebrate!"

Shanti greeted Ellie affectionately, and then pulled the other beautiful redhead into a tighter hug. "You look well, my child," she whispered. "I am so glad to see you thriving."

"I am well. Better than I have ever been," she agreed. "I assume you have been enjoying your new situation?"

"Every moment of it," Shanti agreed.

"You and Vibhi should visit us in Kerala before you leave. There is a lovely natural spring in the jungle nearby that you two will enjoy very much."

"I'm looking forward to it." Shanti hugged her again, and then she rejoined her husband, and Supriya refocused on Edmund.

"Shall we see who else is here, my love?"

"I can't imagine anyone I'd rather see than all of you," he replied.

"Then it's a good thing Neha has the best imagination of all of us," Supriya winked.

She took his hand and led him down a mossy path blanketed with sweet-scented violets, but instead of walking straight towards the gathering, she guided him into a maze marked by perfectly groomed hedges that were a good meter taller than Edmund's excessive height on both sides. His loving entourage followed.

Charlie fell back as he felt himself losing control of his excitement, and Kuveni materialized beside him and took his hand. He looked up at her, into her smiling face in the form of Kate Marriner (the form Edmund had believed was his estranged sister for the better part of the 20th century), and she gestured for him to remain silent.

As they turned the first corner of the maze, an elderly man who looked as if he was in his 70s stood in the middle of the path. Edmund looked to Supriya, who wouldn't give away anything. The man reached out his hand to Edmund.

"Colonel, it is a pleasure to see you again."

Edmund shook his hand, squinting to recognize him.

"Edmund Ridgeway-Jones, Colonel. The last time you saw me, I was just a boy. My mother was Lily Ridgeway. You saved her life on a steamer off the coast of Somalia in 1923, if I'm not mistaken?"

"Yes... yes, I did, but I didn't do it alone." He glanced back at the beautiful redhead, who smiled her support.

"Colonel, this is my family." Edmund's namesake turned to watch as a group of ten people, four adults and six children, approached from around the next bend of the maze. An elderly woman who looked very similar to him in age and features leaned on his arm as she reached out her hand to shake Edmund's. "You remember my sister, Eleanor Ridgeway-Jones? We played a wonderful game of cricket together the day you beat Cambridge in the intercollegiate championships of '47!"

"I remember it like it was yesterday," Edmund agreed. He shook the woman's hand, and then glanced behind them at the rest of the family who was watching the exchange with silent intrigue.

"These are my children, and their children, Colonel. We're all alive because of you," Edmund Ridgeway-Jones explained.

Edmund took in the group, looked back one more time at the beautiful redhead who stood beside Ellie smiling supportively, and finally, he let the meaning of the moment wash over him.

For two hundred years, every time someone had praised him for something he had done, he had berated himself for not doing more. He had let their positivity be twisted into self-castigation for his many haunting mistakes. But this time, for the first time in his life, he let himself fully and completely revel in the beautiful reality that despite whatever miracles he hadn't been able to accomplish, despite his various struggles against the darkness inside of him, despite the many unfinished tasks before him and the excruciating pain of his never-ending divine choices, he had done something, *many* things, in fact, that had mattered to a great many people. He had, with the help of his divine allies, saved the world from utter annihilation. And, long ago and far away, he had saved two little girls from some very villainous pirates.

Edmund smiled and began shaking the hands of his namesake's family, and with his change of heart, Supriya and the rest of his loving entourage cheered. Kuveni snapped her fingers, and fireworks exploded in the sky above them. From far off, the roar of an approving tiger mixed with the happy hoots and hollers from the larger gathering.

Edmund laughed. "Are they all following along?"

"They love you, my love. We all love you." Supriya pulled him into a kiss. "Shall we continue through the maze?"

He squeezed her hand, waved goodbye to the Ridgeway-Jones family, and let her guide him around several bends until they reached their next guest.

A very old man with only a few wisps of white hair on his bald, spotted head and large white cataracts clouding his squinting eyes sat on a stone bench with a cane propped up beside him.

"*Good on ya*, Colonel. You made it to your second station," he said cheerfully as they approached. He leaned heavily on his cane to stand up, and Edmund rushed forward to help him.

"Edmund Helmsworth," the man said with a thick Australian accent as he shook Edmund's hand. "My friends call me Ned. I believe you've already met me, but I wasn't even an ankle-biter yet!"

"Good lord…" Edmund murmured. "You are Oz and Yvie's son?"

"In the flesh!" he replied.

"Yes… we have met. I changed your diapers on many occasions, in fact."

The man laughed heartily. "I hope you won't hold it against me!"

"No… no, I won't hold it against you… But, Ned, we've met more than once. We've actually met many times."

"Really, when?!" Despite his aged weakness, the man was exuberant at the news.

"We met when we were at Oxford." Edmund prepared himself for a revelation he wasn't sure Ned was going to like. "Don't you remember me? The famous cricketer of Corpus Christi College?"

"You were *that* Edmund Marriner?" Ned sat back down on the bench, and Edmund took a seat beside him. "Strewth! We spent years drinking together down at the Oxford Arms! And you're telling me that the *whole* time, you knew I was your namesake?"

"I did."

"Bloody oath! That means that when we were trolling for sheilas, you knew exactly what the crowned jewels looked like!"

Edmund chuckled and relaxed at Ned's casual reaction. "I was quite sure they'd grown up as much as you did."

"You'd better believe it!"

Edmund helped Ned reposition his cane against the bench. "You can't imagine how tempted I was to tell you all of my secrets. Your parents were some of the best friends I'd ever had, and they knew more about me than I knew about myself."

"I wish you had. I would have been a bonza mate."

Edmund smiled. "I have no doubt. If I hadn't just had a particularly painful encounter after revealing too much to my college sweetheart, I probably would have told you everything. But, Ned, didn't you recognize me last year when my image was plastered across every television and newspaper? I look exactly the same as I did back at Oxford in '46."

"No, mate. I didn't recognize you. I haven't been able to see much of anything for about ten years."

Edmund glanced down at the cane as the implications dawned on him. "I'm sorry. I almost went blind myself back in the 1880s. It was one of the most unpleasant times in my life."

"No worries, mate. I'm ninety-four. Something had to go, and it might as well have been my eyes. At least it wasn't my bladder!"

He laughed heartily, and Edmund worked to hide his melancholy at the reminder of the mundane human plights so many of his loved ones had faced in their aged infirmity.

When he had gathered his wits, Edmund leaned in confidingly. "I'll tell you a little secret." Ned's ears perked up. "I met up with your parents on more than one occasion when they were visiting you from Perth. We went far outside of Oxford so you wouldn't stumble upon us at the pub. I haven't met a human before or since who could pace me on drink or joviality like your father could."

Ned sighed nostalgically. "I loved that man."

"So did I." Edmund paused as he momentarily debated his next revelation. "Your father asked me to look after you once he learned I was your mate. Do you remember that frosty night during Hilary term, when you won the drinking contest down at the Arms and then fell into the river on your stumbling journey home in the dark?"

"I almost drowned..." Ned whispered. "I couldn't get myself out of the water... It was too cold... and then... then I woke up in my bed in my pajamas as if nothing had happened. You saved me?"

"I did."

"Bloody oath, I might have died that night..."

Edmund squeezed his hand. "Well, there is no point in dwelling on the past. I popped down into the water and got you home safe and sound, and now here you are with another seventy years of wisdom under your belt."

"Thanks to you, mate." Ned pulled Edmund into a hug.

Edmund held on until he felt Ned shiver. "Sorry. I should have done something to warm myself up before this little journey down memory lane."

Kuveni snapped her fingers and left Charlie by Ellie's side to present Edmund with a steaming pot of tea.

"Ask and ye shall receive, my dear boy."

"Thank you, Kuveni." He drank down the entire pot in one Rakshasa gulp, and she took it back and dissolved it with a flick of her wrist. "I can't thank you enough for everything you've done for me over the years. I was just telling Mr. Montero…"

"My dear boy, you will have time to sing my praises later!" Kuveni interrupted him. "Lady Neha might explode from the strain of waiting for you to finish off your second station!"

"This isn't it? There's more?"

The beautiful redhead stepped forward and approached him. "Darling, I simply can't help but ask… Didn't you read Supriya's fourth manuscript for Ellie?"

"I did."

He glanced nervously towards Ellie and then to Supriya.

"Then, darling, do you know what it means that Ned is Yvie's son? After what Mr. Valov revealed to me about your mother when we were all in Australia together?"

"Good lord…" He glanced at Ned again. "We are related? Ned and I are related by blood?"

"Strewth," Ned murmured.

Edmund took a moment to process the implications, and then a wide grin spread across his face. He pulled Ned into another hug, and then he glanced over to Ellie. "It turns out you have another cousin!"

"Neha will have to get in line!" Ellie exclaimed.

"I have it on good authority that she hates waiting in line," Supriya laughed.

Edmund became serious. "Do you have a family, Ned? Are they waiting just around the bend?"

Ned sighed. "I had a wife once, many decades ago. We never got around to having any children. Work was always getting in the way."

"Ah yes. Your research. I almost stopped by in person to offer my congratulations after you made your breakthrough on the pneumonia vaccine, but I was back to being a spring chicken at the time."

"I remember your thoughtful letter. I still have it back home in Perth."

"I'm sorry you never knew the joys of family, Ned."

"Ah, I was alright. I did something that mattered to the whole world. How many other blokes can say the same?"

"Not enough, I suppose." Edmund became pensive.

The beautiful redhead took a seat on the other side of Ned. "I can see that the wheels are turning in Edmund's head, but we cannot have the birthday boy in a weakened aged state for the rest of his party. Would you like a second chance, Ned? In this life instead of the next?"

Edmund moved to argue with her, and then he held his tongue and waited for Ned's response.

"I... I suppose I'd never thought one lick about it. But there is no point in healing the cataracts of an old man. That is what you do now? You heal people with your hands? You should heal a child instead."

"That isn't how it works, Ned. There is no ledger." Edmund worked hard to push back the stress of his daily divine struggle.

The beautiful redhead rubbed her hands together until an eerie green glow emanated from her palms, and then she took his hands into hers. "We can do a great many things, Ned. I blessed your mother when she couldn't get pregnant back in 1923, and now I will bless you."

"If it fits your fancy... my lady?"

She smiled. "You may call me that if you wish. I am the Countess of Easton, after all."

She threw Edmund a sly glance, and then closed her eyes. With only one deep, purposeful breath, she finished her task.

"Whoa," Charlie whispered. "Wicked!"

She rolled her shoulders and reabsorbed the glowing power into her hands. Her green eyes flashed as she observed the results of her work.

Ned held his smooth hands out before him with wonder. His grey wisps of hair had been replaced by a thick mop of brown curls, his eyes had returned to their original blue, and his glowing pink cheeks reminded Edmund distinctly of his own. They now, as they had in 1946, looked like they could be first year Oxford roommates.

"I can't remember the last time I felt this good." Ned blinked several times as his eyes focused on Edmund. "Strewth. You really do look exactly the same as you did back then."

"I am not the only one, Ned."

Kuveni conjured a hand mirror and held it up before him. He gasped, and then ran his fingers through his thick, youthful hair.

"For the love of god..."

"Do not tell anyone that we can do this, Ned," Edmund said seriously. "It would throw the world into utter chaos if humans knew we could give them back their youth. We entrusted secrets this dangerous to your parents, and now we are entrusting them to you."

"Understood, mate."

"We'll talk to Hamish later tonight, and he'll get you all sorted with the paperwork to start your new life."

"Hamish?" Ned asked dazedly.

"He is our ally in the Secret Service. He has helped us with similar matters a few times now." Edmund took a long look at Ned, and then pulled him into a parting hug. "Welcome to the family."

Kuveni clapped approvingly, and another round of fireworks exploded in the air above them.

"Go." Ned urged Edmund up. "You have many more mates to meet, I reckon."

"I will catch up with you later," Edmund whispered.

"Come with us, Ned." Ellie pulled him into Edmund's entourage. "We'll introduce you to the rest of the family later."

Supriya took Edmund's hand and guided him once again into the maze. The entourage fell back, giving them a head start.

"This birthday is... it is a bit overwhelming," he admitted as they turned another bend and his heart fluttered in anticipation of their next meeting.

"But it isn't bad, is it?" Supriya asked.

"No... no, it isn't bad at all. It is just... it is too good. As if it isn't real at all. In two hundred years, I dreamed about so many things, but having all of you here with me, reconnecting with old friends and new family I never even knew I had... it is beyond my wildest imagination."

"I'm glad you approve."

Supriya enticed him into a kiss, and he gave into their moment of intimacy until their entourage caught up with them and cheered at the sight.

He pulled away as the heat of a red blush rushed into his cheeks.

"Shall we continue on?" Supriya asked.

Edmund nodded his agreement, and they returned to their course. His pulse only picked up as he noticed that their entourage was falling back again.

"My love, why are they giving us privacy?"

Supriya squeezed his hand and escorted him around another bend.

There, in front of a gently burbling fountain, stood a young priest dressed in Franciscan robes with jet black hair, rosy cheeks, and hazel eyes. His resemblance to Edmund could not be ignored, although he was over a foot shorter, and there was a harsh angularity to his features that Edmund's lacked. The priest held a rosary tight in his right hand as he forced himself to look at Edmund in the eye.

Edmund stopped, and Supriya felt him tense. "I did not expect to see you ever again."

The priest looked away. "I said things... things that I shouldn't have said. I have a demonic temper sometimes... a temper that I can't control, especially when provoked so thoroughly."

"You said things that you believed," Edmund countered. "And I learned long ago that there is no point in trying to change a mind that is so thoroughly entrenched in dogma."

The priest whispered a quiet prayer, and a familiar Yaksha, clad in his favorite traditional orange robes, donning his most ancient human form, the form of Saint Thomas the Apostle, materialized beside him.

"Tell him, my child," Thomas urged the priest. "Tell him what you came here to say."

The priest approached Edmund, and Supriya stepped back to give them their space. Edmund watched nervously but did not pull away as the priest took both of his hands.

"I forgive you," the priest whispered, staring straight at the ground.

Edmund glanced towards Thomas. "I have no interest in coerced declarations of forgiveness. I did what I did, and I have accepted the consequences. One's two hundredth birthday does not mean that all of his sins are absolved. You, more than anyone, should know that, Thomas."

Thomas did not let Edmund's stern tone faze him. He only waited patiently for the priest to continue.

The priest looked up into Edmund's eyes. "Father, I forgive you. For everything that you did, and everything that you didn't do. I have prayed constantly about all that came to pass on that fateful day, and it has taken me months to fully comprehend it. I admit that I am still confounded on many points, but I am clear about one thing: I forgive you."

Edmund glanced over to Supriya, who offered him a supportive smile, and then he gathered the priest into a gentle hug.

"I'm so sorry, my dearest Peter. I would have done everything differently if I'd known. I would have traveled to the ends of the earth to find you."

"I believe you," Peter whispered as he hugged him back.

Edmund gave into the rumbling emotions that he'd so skillfully kept under control, and he let his tears flow free. He held him, and they held each other for many minutes of catharsis, until the rustling of the entourage approaching disrupted their connection.

Edmund wiped his remaining violet tears back into his skin and cleared his throat. As the rest of the group turned the corner and entered the clearing, Edmund took in a deep, calming breath.

"Ellie, Charlie…" They approached him questioningly, as they knew him well enough to recognize his heightened emotional state. "I'd like you to meet Peter… your brother."

The priest looked up at Edmund as an expression of childlike excitement, a spitting image of Edmund's, washed over him.

He reached out and shook their hands, pausing for an extra-long moment on Ellie's. "You are just as cold as I am. I never imagined there were others who were so similar to me."

"It's been hours since I've had a cup of tea," she said self-consciously, working to hide her surprise at the shocking revelation. She had convinced herself many times now that she had finally learned the last of her father's deep dark secrets.

"I have always preferred hot milk myself," Peter admitted. "Tea was quite a luxury when I was a boy, but there was a dairy down the road from the monastery where I grew up."

"Dad?" Charlie asked nervously as he looked up at Peter's youthful face. "Is there something you needed to tell Mum?

Something else... you know... other than that you were an immortal alien god?"

Edmund chuckled. "There were many things I should have told your mother, Charlie. But Peter was born in 1841, if I'm not mistaken? A good century before your mother was even born."

Peter nodded his agreement.

"I didn't know about him until last year. But that is a story for another time. What matters is that he is here now... that is, assuming that you are planning on staying for the party?"

Peter looked up into his father's earnest eyes and smiled with genuine happiness for the first time in his life. "I would like that very much."

Edmund gathered him into another hug as an even more elaborate display of fireworks exploded in the sky above them.

"Surely that must be it?" Edmund asked. "What more could you possibly have to offer? I have everything I have ever wanted right here."

Supriya threw a knowing glance to the entourage. "We have one final stop, my love. We all worked together to make this happen. It took quite a bit of clever plotting and divine power to pull it together. Do you remember your riddle?"

"The wise men argue about whether man came first or god came first, but who came before both?"

"Do you have any final guesses?"

Edmund thought about it, and then shrugged his defeat. "I have absolutely no clue."

Supriya took his hand and led him one last time back into the maze. They wandered through the hedges, past more burbling fountains and empty stone benches, until they finally reached the center.

A rather plain brunette young woman, who looked as if she was in her late twenties, stood up from an old-fashioned ivory brocade chaise that looked strangely at home in the violet-carpeted clearing. She looked nervous as Supriya guided him to greet her.

"Edmund, this is Amélie de Paillette."

"*Enchantée*," she said as she reached out her hand.

He felt for any hint of Yakshini warmth or Rakshasa frigidity as he shook her hand, but she felt entirely human. His puzzlement only grew.

"Have we met? I'm sorry I don't have an airtight Rakshasa memory like most of the others do."

Amélie looked to Supriya.

"She doesn't speak English, my love."

Edmund switched into his perfect Rakshasa French, and after they exchanged a few polite niceties, they both returned their attention to Supriya.

"I do not understand. She agrees that we have never met."

"My love, Amélie is the living incarnation of your mother."

"She's what?"

"Your mother's soul resides deep within her just as so many of our former selves reside within us."

"My mother came before I was a god or a man... Good lord, are you sure?"

"I am positive."

"How on Earth did you find her?"

"Ask not how," Supriya smiled. "What is important is that Amélie is a fan of ours. She has agreed to let me guide your mother's consciousness to the surface so you two can meet."

"Do you really think it's possible?"

"I know it's possible, my love. Mélusine popped me back here last night while you were asleep, and we tested it out. The experience was positive for everyone. Now, would you like to meet your mother?"

Edmund nodded, too overwhelmed with emotion to say anything. Supriya guided them both back to the chaise, and sat down beside Amélie. She rubbed her hands together until the divine silver light of the Guardian of Memories emerged. She closed her eyes and placed her hand gently on Amélie's forehead. Amélie collapsed momentarily and then awoke with a start.

Supriya smiled. "Welcome back, Elise."

"I thought her name was Elizabeth," Edmund murmured.

Elise reached forward and yanked him into a hug. "*Mon dieu*, how beautiful my son is! Please, Edmund, call me *Maman*. Let me feel you in my arms!"

He squeezed her until he worried she might be struggling to breathe, and then he let her go. She kissed both of his rosy cheeks and then his forehead. She stroked his jaw and ran her fingers through his thick tufts of black hair.

"You look so much like my father. It is fitting, *mon fils*. He was a wonderful man too." She smiled wistfully. "I'm so glad you didn't take after your father. I was worried that you would be born with his black spikes and have to hide away with Kuveni until you could control them."

Edmund could not hide his shock at the revelation. "You saw my father in his demonic form? You knew he was a demon?"

She reached forward and stroked the soft skin behind his ear, and with a violent shiver, his demonic form engulfed him. He felt his black spikes emerge from his colorful skin, his ghoulish fangs erupt from his gums, and his claw-like fingernails burst forth from the tips of his fingers. He looked down at his unintended transition with horror.

"Look at me in the eye, *mon fils*. I want to see how beautiful you are in all of your forms." As he gazed at her self-consciously with his black eyes, she ran her soft fingers around the spikes on his face, gently tickling his patches of blue and green skin until he shivered again. "That trick worked on your father too. I often used it to calm him when his temper was out of control."

"You really are my mother," Edmund murmured. "You are the woman who gave birth to George IV's bastard demon child."

"*Mon fils*, you make it sound so horrible! So unloving! So dark! I gave birth to a beautiful divine child in a magical place devoid of suffering, surrounded by angels."

"I suppose there were angels there… in some sense… But I cannot believe that you didn't suffer. Please do not lie to me… *Maman*. I have drowned in lies for too long."

"Edmund, *mon chère fils*, the world is not always so dark. Saint Mélusine relieved my physical pain until the very end. The only suffering I endured was leaving you too soon. *Et voilà*, by the grace of God, here I am with my final prayer answered. Now I see the beautiful man you've become, and I have everything I ever wanted. It is far more than I ever deserved."

"I am not so beautiful," he protested. "Especially not like this."

"Oh how wrong you are, *mon fils*. But if you do not like being this way, release yourself. Return to the natural beauty God gave you."

He closed his eyes, took in a deep breath, and subverted his demonic form. He looked down at his human hands and sighed with relief. As he noticed her watching him with a loving smile, he couldn't hold back his emotions at the utterly unexpected truth that his mother loved him exactly as he was, and he gathered her into his arms and gave into his tears. She let him cry into her shoulder for many minutes.

"What is it, *mon fils*? Are these tears of joy or tears of sorrow?"

"I'm so sorry," he whispered.

"Sorry?" she asked. "Sorry for what, *mon chère fils*?"

"For killing you!" he exclaimed.

"*Non!*" She grabbed his hands, startling him with her strength. "*Non!* You will not be sorry for that. *Non, non, non.* Women have died since the beginning of time bringing their children into this world. You will not apologize for the agony nature imparts indiscriminately, or for the plight of humanity. *Tu comprends?*" She softened her tone. "*Mon fils*, you have the weight of the world on your shoulders. I can see it in your eyes. You feel such guilt for things that are not your fault. Tell your *maman* what you need to release yourself from your burden."

Edmund let a few more tears flow, and then he sucked in a deep, calming breath and absorbed his tears into his skin.

"It is necessary that I am my own harshest judge. It is not a state from which I should release myself."

"*Mais pourquoi?*"

He glanced over to Supriya as he debated what to tell her, but she only nodded encouragingly. "Do you know what I am, *Maman*? Do you know what this Amélie woman knows?"

"My last memory is holding you in my arms and naming you after my father and your father, *mon fils*. Beyond that, I know only what your wife and Mélusine told me when we met last night."

"Did she tell you that I am Lord Kalki? An incarnation of The Preserver of the Universe… of God?"

"Not in so many words, but I have always been a clever girl. Too clever for my own good sometimes. But, *mon fils*, doesn't God forgive? Or does He forgive everyone but Himself?"

"It isn't that simple."

"Perhaps sometimes it is."

Edmund became pensive. "Surely you must know that nothing is simple. You were… you were my father's mistress."

"Ah ha," she smiled knowingly. "And now we get to the questions. You must have so many questions, *mon fils*. And your wife tells me that after two hundred years, you are finally ready to know the truth."

He swallowed hard at the idea. "I suppose I am as ready as I'll ever be."

"Tell me, *mon fils*. Tell me what you want to know."

He grappled for a moment as a flood of unanswered questions bombarded him, until he let himself settle on the simplest one. "I thought your name was Elizabeth. Elizabeth Marriner."

She squeezed his hand encouragingly. "My real name was Elise Valentine Augustine Noëlle du Préille, Comtesse de Saint Cyr. My younger sister and I escaped the guillotine by hiding in empty wine barrels that were smuggled from Calais to Dover with the help of a few loyal servants. We were the only members of our family to survive, and we changed our names not long after we arrived in England."

"Why?"

"They were quite worried that our revolution might spread, and our names created problems we could avoid when we spoke the fluent English we'd learned from our English grandmother. We had already lost everything, why not our names as well?"

"I'm sorry."

"Why, *mon fils*? Why are you sorry for the ugliness of the world years before you were even born?"

"I am sorry for all suffering, *Maman*. It is my divine burden, and I have accepted it."

She sighed. "I could feel your greatness when you were growing inside of me, *mon fils*, and I could see the love in your eyes the moment you were born. I am so blessed to see the man you've become. You are just as I dreamed you would be. The light to counter your father's darkness."

Edmund shifted uncomfortably as he debated his next question.

"Don't be shy, *mon fils*. Ask me. Ask me why I loved your father."

"So you did love him? He did not... he did not force you?"

"No, *mon fils*. He did not force me. I shared his bed for years out of my own free will." She glanced to Supriya, and then readied herself for a revelation she'd never spoken out loud. "I was his wife, *mon fils*. We married in secret two years before you were born and told no one, not even Surpanakha. He performed the Rakshasa ceremony himself, and I played my role willingly."

Edmund let a sigh of relief morph into a grimace of confusion over the implications.

She recognized his struggle. "I did not love all of him, *mon fils,* but I loved enough. Enough to believe that I could temper his violence and protect humanity from his darkness, and I succeeded more often than I failed."

"So you knew the whole time? You knew he wasn't just the selfish Prince Regent?"

Elise laughed. *"Mais bien sûr!* I wasn't blind, *mon fils!* We met a few times before I was sure, but he was not particularly interested in hiding his true nature. The court was so terrified of him, they wouldn't have dared to stand in his way."

"And yet, you weren't afraid of him? A demon who had taken over the court of the King of England?"

"*Mon fils,* evil exists in many forms, human and demon alike. Was he worse than the humans who murdered my family? Who killed children and crippled old women as public sport without a hint of remorse?"

"But he was..." Edmund trailed off.

"He was what?" she coaxed.

"I should not tell you if you don't know."

"*Mon fils,* it is the Age of Truth, is it not? Your wife tells me that it is finally the beautiful era when everyone can be honest. Tell me."

"Before he was the Prince Regent... he was Robespierre." Edmund cringed as a look of horror blanketed her face. "I should not have told you."

She contemplated the idea for an excruciating minute of silence. "Robespierre was one man, *mon fils.* He did not break down the doors of our house and drag my mother and my brothers by the hair screaming and crying. He did not line them up in the center of Paris for execution, and he did not steal their wigs as a macabre token after the guillotine dropped. Humans did that. *Many* humans who enjoyed every minute of the suffering they were imparting.

656

He may have been the catalyst, but they were just as guilty as he was, and by loving him, by distracting him and giving him something else to do, I stopped the same darkness from plaguing England." She squeezed his hand. "I am glad you told me, *mon fils*. It means that my game was just as necessary to play as I thought it was."

"So you loved him to distract him from his evil scheming?"

Elise laughed. "I suppose you could put it that way. But I did love him, *mon fils*. It wouldn't have worked if I hadn't. Your father was arrogant and gluttonous and violent and petty, but he was not stupid. He was an excellent judge of character, and he knew I loved him. That is what kept me safe from his dark tendencies for so long."

"You were brave. He would have killed you if he'd thought for one moment you were manipulating him."

Elise shrugged. "I had nothing left to live for. It is easy to be fearless when you welcome death. But, *mon fils*, you must understand that the only beautiful moments of my life after I escaped the revolution happened because of your father... and because of you."

"I cannot fathom any beautiful moment anyone could have spent with him. Especially not a young, beautiful woman."

Elise smiled. "What makes you think I was beautiful?"

"Weren't you?"

"Yes. I was quite beautiful," she admitted. "Your father would not have found me interesting otherwise. But, *mon fils*, your father was very good to me. I saw a side of him that no one else could see, and we were both rewarded for it. There were moments when he could escape from himself—when we both almost believed that he was just a profligate human king."

"Kuveni and Mélusine thought that you believed he was George IV until the very end."

"As I said, *mon fils*, I was too clever for my own good sometimes. It was easier that way. It was easier than admitting that I'd fallen in love with the Devil himself."

Edmund paused to contemplate the avalanche of unexpected revelations.

"*Mon fils*, the world was burning back then. Good and evil, darkness and light, they were more subjective than they had ever been. My sister returned to France after the revolution and married a general in Napoleon's army. Together they marched across Europe murdering people just like us under the flag of democratic righteousness. It is only because Napoleon lost his final battle that he is not remembered as the liberator of Europe. Your father understood this ambiguity better than anyone, and he used it to his advantage. And in the end, your father was a better companion to me than that wicked general ever was to my sister. Your father treated me as if I were a treasure to be protected."

"One locks away the treasures he is protecting. Another word for treasure is prisoner."

"*Mon fils*, you mustn't think of me as a victim anymore. I was not any more of a victim than any other woman was at the time. We were all victims of our circumstances, and mine were better than most."

"It is more difficult a task than I'd like to admit," Edmund confessed. "For the last two years, since I met my father, I have often fantasized about rescuing you... About what I would have done to keep him from hurting you. Now I don't know what to think."

"You met him?"

Edmund looked away from her. "I killed him."

She stroked his cheek and nudged him back into looking at her. "I'm sorry, *mon fils*. I knew the day would come. I am so grateful to see that it has made you stronger."

"I do not understand. You knew I would kill my father?"

"The Rakshasa Oracle delivered a prophecy the morning after you were conceived. Kumbhakarna and Surpanakha forced me to leave your father that very night while he was distracted. I fought them at first because I knew it would ruin him, but then I realized it didn't matter. All that mattered was you—protecting you from him. I never saw your father again, but I knew that you would do what needed to be done. What no one else had been able to do. You would save the world from him."

"And yet you still loved him?"

"You must know by now that humans are utterly irrational."

"Yes... yes, I suppose I do."

"*Mon fils*, what more can I tell you? I loved him. I loved you. I loved Kuveni, and Mélusine, and Vibhishana. I even loved Kumbhakarna and Surpanakha. I suppose in the end, perhaps I was too loving of a person. But now I see the love in your eyes, even after two hundred years of suffering, and I cannot be happier that I was able to give you my light."

Edmund pulled her into a tight hug, and they held each other for many minutes.

"I love you, *mon fils*."

"I love you, *Maman*. Your light was the greatest gift anyone has ever given me. It saved me from him, and from myself."

"I know, *mon fils*. I know."

Edmund finally pulled away. "Stay for a few more minutes? I have some people I'd like you to meet."

"As you wish, *mon chère fils*. It is your birthday."

Edmund grinned and helped her up off of the chaise.

"Come along, you eavesdroppers. Show yourselves! Especially you, Neha," he called into the seemingly empty air.

Neha and Mélusine materialized beside them, while Kuveni guided the rest of his entourage into the clearing.

"*Maman*, I would like you to meet your grandchildren: Ellie, Charlie... and Peter."

She shook their hands and kissed their cheeks.

"Wicked," Charlie whispered. "You're really Dad's Mum?"

"For the moment," she agreed. "Until I return to my peaceful slumber, and Amélie takes back her rightful position."

"Slumber? Is that what being dead feels like?" Charlie asked matter-of-factly.

"It feels different to different people," Supriya interjected. "Perhaps we can discuss it later, when it isn't your father's birthday."

"*Mon fils,* I must ask…" Elise eyed the entourage, landing her attention on Supriya's dress and then his suit. "Has fashion really changed so little in two hundred years? It changed more in my lifetime than it did in yours!"

The group laughed, and with a subtle wiggle, Edmund presented his favorite well-fitted modern suit. Supriya followed his lead, switching into her favorite yellow sundress, and Neha skipped up beside them and morphed her costume into her favorite tight grey t-shirt and jeans.

"This is what we normally wear." He wiggled his suit into the relaxed linen pants and button-down shirt that he often wore in the tropics. "Neha orchestrated a fancy dress party for my birthday. I suppose we succeeded at dressing like it was the year I was born."

They all wiggled back into their costumes.

"How extraordinary," Elise said as she felt the cuff of his suit jacket. "Your father was never so skilled to switch clothing so quickly. He had to concentrate for many minutes on exactly what he wanted before he could produce it."

"I thought… I thought he was the greatest shapeshifter who ever lived."

Elise laughed. "He certainly wished that he was, and sometimes he even claimed that he was, but even he knew that his youngest brother was far better." She glanced at Vibhishana. "In that capacity, and almost every other."

"Grandma, are you staying for the cricket match?" Charlie asked excitedly. "It's Rakshasas versus Yakshas, with humans and gods on both sides!"

"Please, call me *grandmère, mon chère.*"

"*S'il vous plait, Grandmère!*" Charlie begged with his best impersonation of her French.

Elise laughed. "I'm not sure Amélie would be interested. She has been very obliging."

"She agreed to let you do what you wanted for the rest of the day, within reason, of course," Supriya explained.

"*Maman*, please join us," Edmund said as he gave into a wave of giddiness greater than any he had ever felt in his life.

"I don't know the rules."

"I can think of no greater pleasure than to teach them to you," Edmund offered.

"*On y va,*" she agreed.

"*On y va!*" Mélusine seconded.

Kuveni clapped her hands, and a grand finale of colorful fireworks exploded in the dusky sky. The hedges of the maze dissolved around them, and a large crowd of loving friends and family stood at the edge of the garden cheering on their victory.

Edmund gathered Supriya into his arms and dipped her into a passionate kiss. The crowd roared with approval.

"Happy birthday, my love," she whispered.

"It is the happiest," he declared.

As Neha skipped around them, readying herself to rally the crowd onto the cricket field, Edmund grabbed her arm and pulled her into the tightest hug they had ever shared.

"Thank you, Neha. I cannot thank you enough for giving me this day."

She squeezed him affectionately, giving into her own emotions momentarily before plastering her usual cheerful smile on her face and clearing her throat.

661

"All in a day's work, my lord." She winked. "Or perhaps a few days… with divine intervention."

"It was worth every moment," he reassured her. "At least it was to me."

She hugged him again. "It was worth it for everyone, Edmund. Absolutely everyone."

And so, as the warm April sun set in the brilliant pink sky over a cheering crowd of loving friends and family, the gods and their allies reveled in the many quiet triumphs of Lord Kalki's birthday surprise.

GLOSSARY OF HINDU REFERENCES

Hinduism, the world's oldest continuously practiced religion, is an exceptionally diverse collection of philosophies and rituals practiced by over one billion people globally. There is no single institution and no single written text that defines the 'rules' of Hinduism, and thus it varies widely in practice and belief across the world.

While there is a pantheon featuring a plethora of gods and goddesses with various regional names and stories, there are also numerous sects who worship Vishnu (Vaishnavism), Shiva (Shaivism), Shakti (Shaktism), and combinations/permutations of these major gods and goddesses, and their manifestations (including avatars), as representations of the one supreme being.

The vast and fascinating complexity of Hinduism cannot be captured in a short glossary, and it is not the author's intent to do so. This glossary is meant to give the uninitiated reader some basic context for references throughout the Ashley Mayers universe. Further research is recommended for those interested in digging deeper.

Agni (uh-**gnee**) – 'Fire' in Sanskrit, Agni is also the god of fire and the conveyor of sacrifices to the gods. It is Agni's role in the Hindu pantheon that is invariably linked with the many rituals, both daily and for special occasions, that require a *yajna*, or sacred fire.

Artha (**ahr**-tah) – One of the four aims of human life in Hindu philosophy, sometimes 'meaning, sense, or purpose,' *artha* generally focuses on the 'means to live the life you want,' including but not limited to wealth, career, and financial security. It can perhaps be thought of as 'why you do work.'

Asura/Asuri (ah-soo-ruh/ah-soo-ree) – Originally a term used to describe divine, powerful beings, good or bad, the term later came to represent primarily darker powered beings in Hinduism and is sometimes (but not always) synonymous with demons. Rakshasas are sometimes described as one type of *Asura*. *Asuri* is the feminine form of *Asura*.

Avatar (ah-vuh-tuhr) – In Hinduism, an avatar is a deliberate descent of a deity to Earth. The term is most commonly used to describe incarnations or manifestations of Vishnu, but has been used with other deities, including Shiva, Ganesh, and Shakti. The lists of avatars and consensus around them is dubious. Some sects believe that Shiva, as a formless entity, will never have an avatar, while others believe that Hanuman is an avatar of Shiva. The lists of Vishnu avatars range from ten to twenty-five avatars, and some characters in epics are referred to as 'partial' avatars, such as Rama's brother, Lakshmana, sometimes being considered 'one-quarter Vishnu.' One major thematic element throughout the Ashley Mayers universe explores what exactly it means (and doesn't mean) to be an avatar.

Ayodhya (ah-**yoh**-dyuh) – An ancient city located in Uttar Pradesh in Northern India that remains inhabited today, Ayodhya is considered to be the birthplace and ancient kingdom of Rama. In modern times, tragedy and controversy, fuelled by Hindu/Muslim animosity, have plagued the city after a violent uprising in 1992 that led to the destruction of the 16th c. Babri Mosque, which many people believed was built upon the site of Rama's original temple.

Bhoomi (**boo**-mee) – The embodiment/personification of 'Mother Earth.' Bhoomi is referred to as the mother of Sita, and at the end of *the Ramayana*, when Sita's suffering becomes unbearable, she returns to her 'mother,' being swallowed by the earth.

Ceylon (say-lon) – The historical, British colonial name of modern-day Sri Lanka, Ceylon is a key setting in *the Ramayana*, as the home of the Rakshasa king, Ravana, who kidnaps Sita and takes her back to Lanka to woo her (while she is imprisoned).

Chiranjivi (chee-ruhn-**jee**-vee) – Seven immortals in Hinduism who remain on Earth to lead humans in various paths of righteousness. In this series, we have two: Vibhishana, Hanuman.

Dasara (**Duh**-suh-ruh) – Otherwise known as *Dussera*, *Dushera*, or *Vijayadashami*, depending on the region and language, Dasara is a holiday at the end/culmination of Navaratri, the nine-night autumn festival devoted to the Goddess. Dasara traditions vary across India, ranging from sacred dances of Garba and Dandiya in the north, to a candlelight vigil and elephant parade in Mysore in the south, a city that considers itself the namesake of the Goddess in her defeat of the demon Mahishasura (sometimes referred to as *Mahishasura-Mardini* from the Sanskrit holy mantras). It coincides with the culmination of Durga Puja in Bengal, and always involves great cheer, festivities, and often fireworks and light shows.

Devi/Deva (deh-**vee**/deh-**vah**) – 'Heavenly' or 'divine' beings in Hinduism, *Devi* can be synonymous with 'god' or 'deity' but primarily refers to powerful beings who are 'good,' and can sometimes be contrasted with the 'evil' *Asura*. However, the designations of 'good' versus 'evil' are far less clearly defined in Hinduism compared to Judeo-Christian religions, and so, for example, Kartikeya, the god of war, is still considered a *Deva*. In Hinduism, an *Asura* can ascend and become a *Deva*, with Vibhishana being a prime example, demonstrating that birthright is less important than actions on Earth to define one's character and virtue.

664

Devi Mahatmya (deh-**vee** muh-**hat**-myuh) – The *Devi Mahatmya* is a religious text (from the *Markandeya Purana*, one of eighteen primary religious texts in Hinduism) devoted to the Great Goddess (Shakti). It recounts her manifestation on Earth in the warrior form of Durga to protect the innocent by defeating the shapeshifting buffalo demon Mahishasura, and her subsequent return of balance and virtue to the world. A text revered by Hindus across many sects, the *Devi Mahatmya* serves as a primary text for Shaktist Hindus, who believe that the Goddess is the Supreme Being. It serves as the inspiration for the festivals of Navaratri, Durga Puja, and Dasara/Vijayadashmi.

Dharma (**dahr**-muh) – One of the four aims of human life in Hindu philosophy, with many meanings, *dharma* is roughly translated as virtue, morality, righteousness, obligations, and correct conduct. The Hindu epics, *the Ramayana* and *the Mahabharata,* both demonstrate that there is often no single clear path to *dharma*, as various 'right' paths often conflict and need to be prioritized, with each difficult choice producing complicated consequences and satisfying drama.

Diwali (Dih-**vah**-lee) – Also known as Deepavali in many South Indian languages, Diwali is one of the most important festivals across Hindu tradition, and celebrates the triumph of light over darkness, knowledge over ignorance, and hope over despair. Based on the Hindu calendar, the festival of lights typically falls between mid-October and mid-November each year, and its observance dates back to ancient times. The rituals vary across the many cultures who celebrate the holiday, but it is generally consistent that people light candles and offer prayers to Lakshmi.

Durga (door-**gah**) – A principle form of the Goddess (Shakti), who manifests physically in many different forms depending on the task at hand, Durga is also called Maa Durga or the Holy Mother (not to be confused with the Christian/Catholic Holy Mother Mary). The primary hero of her own epic, the *Devi Mahatmya*, Durga is most famous as a warrior for justice who wields the power of the entire pantheon, coming to Earth with many arms and weapons to defeat the shapeshifting buffalo demon, Mahishasura. Her triumph in defeating an insidious, ever-changing manifestation of evil can be viewed as a model of perseverance that can be applied in everyday life. Every year her triumph is celebrated during the festivals of Navaratri ("Nine Nights," each celebrating a manifestation of the Goddess), Durga Puja (five nights celebrating her defeat of Mahishasura, primarily celebrated in Bengal), Dasara (the culmination of Navaratri celebrated across India), and Diwali (the Festival of Lights, celebrated across the Hindu world and by other related religions). As the Great Goddess, she is sometimes referred to interchangeably with Parvati, wife of Shiva, and she is sometimes said to manifest as Lakshmi and Saraswati in their roles as the primordial energy that animates the universe. Across most sects,

Durga is worshipped as the underlying creative, preservative, and destructive energy of the universe (Shakti), who exists as a formless entity always, and sometimes takes form within the gods or goddesses, to fulfill tasks on behalf of the universe.

Durga Puja (door-**gah** poo-ja) – A five-night festival primarily celebrated in Bengal, Durga Puja coincides with the festival of Navaratri in other parts of India, all in celebration of the Great Goddess (Shakti), manifested as Durga for her defeat of the shapeshifting demon Mahishasura. Known for its *pandals* (elaborate temporary altars to the Goddess), Durga Puja is celebrated with costume, dance, food, special rituals, and bright firecrackers, making the streets of Calcutta one of the liveliest (and most crowded) places in the world to experience the frenetic energy of the Devi in one of her most beloved forms.

Garuda (**guh**-roo-duh) – The 'mount' of Lord Vishnu, Garuda is a large bird, sometimes a humanoid bird, who flies Lord Vishnu around. Sometimes represented as a large phoenix, eagle, or kite, Garuda also exists in Buddhist mythology.

Hanuman (**hahn**-oo-mahn) – Rama's right-hand man and a beloved star of *the Ramayana*, Hanuman is a Vanara, a monkey-like humanoid race who fought by Rama's side in his attack against Ravana in Lanka. In *the Ramayana*, Hanuman uses his flying ability to track and eventually make contact with Sita while she is incarcerated by Ravana, but she refuses to go with him back to Rama. Various interpretations of this interaction range from it exemplifying Sita's purity through her refusal to be in another man's arms, even to be rescued, to a valid observation that had Sita agreed to go back to Rama with Hanuman, the entire war between Rama and Ravana might have been avoided. Hanuman is consistently referred to as one of the *Chiranjivi*, representing loyalty, courage and devotion.

Harihara (**hah**-ree-**hah**-ruh) – A combined form of Shiva and Vishnu (Transformation and Preservation), Harihara is sometimes used to explain/describe the complementary nature of the two gods as aspects of one supreme being. The symbolism evokes the necessary balance (and tug-of-war) between the two primary aspects of existence, each keeping the other in check.

Hiranyakashipu – (**hee**-ran-**yaak**-shih-poo) – A demon evil enough to warrant the Preserver of the Universe coming to Earth (as Narasimha, the fourth avatar of Vishnu), Hiranyakashipu gained a boon from Lord Brahma so that he couldn't be defeated by man or beast, thus requiring Lord Vishnu to take a more clever form, in his case, as a half-man, half-lion, to defeat him.

Lakshmi (**luhk**-shmee) – The female aspect of the Preserver of the Universe, often referred to as the goddess of prosperity (material and spiritual), and the wife of Lord Vishnu, Lakshmi (or Laxmi), is one of the principal goddesses of the *Tridevi*, or 'Trinity of Goddesses.' She is said to be the life-force of Lord Vishnu and is worshipped during the major festival of Diwali every autumn. As the wife of Rama, seventh avatar of Vishnu, Sita is an avatar of Lakshmi.

Kali (kuh-lee) – Hinduism's primary apocalyptic demon—not to be confused with Kali, a fierce incarnation of Shakti (spelled the same in English but not in Sanskrit)—this demon is often depicted with a dog's head. He is said to fan the flames of human greed, violence, and iniquity during *Kali Yuga* ('The Age of Vice'), an era that many Hindus believe describes the modern world. It is sometimes said that Ravana is an incarnation and/or devotee of the demon, Kali, and that Lord Vishnu will incarnate in his ultimate avatar form, Lord Kalki, to defeat Kali and bring the worlds into *Satya Yuga* ("The Age of Truth").

Kali/Kaali (Kah-lee) – A fierce incarnation of the female life-force of the Transformer of the Universe, Kaali (often spelled Kali in English, but too easily confused with the demon Kali), is one of the most misunderstood incarnations of the Goddess. Often referred to as the goddess of time, and represented with blue or black skin, her tongue out, standing on the dead body of her husband, Shiva, wearing a skull necklace and holding a severed, bloody head, she is often thought of as a ghoulish character by those who don't know any better. However, the symbolism of the imagery of her standing on Shiva's body is meant to represent that she is his life-force, and without her, he is lifeless. The life-force of change is fierce, and the ravages of time often frightening, which are two reasons why she is depicted in such a monstrous style. She is, however, a natural manifestation of the destruction required for our ever-changing universe to exist.

Kalki (**kuhl**-kee) – Lord Kalki, 'Destroyer of Filth,' the tenth and final avatar of Vishnu (the Preserver of the Universe), is believed to be the only avatar who has not already been on Earth. Legends tell of him being born in Shambhala, a mythical place of great spiritual power north of Tibet, a place of great interest to the sages when the stories were written, due to its association and proximity to the homeland of the invading Khans. While references to Lord Kalki can be conflicting, it is consistent in texts that Lord Kalki will come to Earth to defeat the demon, Kali, and restore balance and order, bringing humans back to the path of virtue, and ushering in the Age of Truth.

Mahagauri (Maa-huh-**gau**-ree) – A manifestation of Maa Durga (considered her eighth of nine manifestations by some sects), Mahagauri is worshipped on the eighth night of the festival of Navaratri in some parts of India. She is said to be "the fair one," with a fair complexion, who offers forgiveness and protection to all of her followers.

Mantra (mahn-truh) – Words or sounds, often repetitive, that are used in prayer.

Moksha (**mohk**-shuh) – One of the four aims of human life in Hindu philosophy, meaning 'release' or 'liberation,' *moksha* primarily refers to release from the reincarnation cycle of birth and death on Earth.

Naraka (nah-**rah**-kuh) – In Hinduism, Naraka, or the underworld (somewhat similar to Christian purgatory), is a temporary place for expiation of sins to be endured between a soul's mortal death and its return to Earth. There are many different forms of Naraka, each featuring colorful punishments that are related to a person's sins, such as murderers being eaten alive by Rakshasas. As positive and negative actions do not 'cancel each other out' in Hinduism, a soul can repent through their punishment in Naraka and enjoy the peace of *Svarga* (a heavenly place), both before their return to Earth.

Narasimha (**Nur**-sim-**haa**) – Regarded as the fourth avatar of Vishnu, Narasimha is a manifestation of the Preserver of the Universe who comes to Earth as a half-man, half-lion to defeat the demon Hiranyakashipu, who has immortality against "all men and beasts." He is considered a protector of the innocent and warrior for justice, as well as an example of one of Lord Vishnu's many clever responses to the inconvenient ancient boons held by his enemies.

Navaratri (Nuv-**rah**-tree) – Otherwise known as "Nine Nights," Navaratri is the primary festival of the Goddess and takes place at the beginning of autumn, typically three weeks before the festival of Diwali. Traditions and details of each night's symbolism differ across regions and sects, with fasting and the wearing of special colors to honor various manifestations of the Goddess being common across regions. In Gujarat, sacred dances known as Garba and Dandiya, enact Durga's battle and defeat of the demon Mahishasura.

Parvati (**pahr**-vuh-**tee**) – The wife of Shiva and one of the three chief goddesses of the *Tridevi* or 'Trinity of Goddesses,' Parvati is the benevolent female aspect of the Transformer of the Universe, and is often referred to as the goddess of power, love, fertility, and devotion. She is also sometimes referred to as an aspect or alternative name of Durga (the root form of creation, preservation, and annihilation), Shakti (the cosmic energy that underlies all life in the universe), and 'one thousand' other names/personas. In the Shaivism sects, Parvati is considered an inextricable force, without which, Shiva (and therefore God) would cease to exist, for it is her life-force that gives them both power and energy. Parvati is the benevolent form of Shiva's wife (a complementary aspect to the fierce form of Kali), and the mother of their two sons, Ganesh and Kartikeya.

Puja (**poo**-ja) – A prayer or offering, puja describes the manifestation of worship and reverence in Hinduism. Often involving offerings of light (candles or diyas), flowers, water, or food, along with prayers (often in the form of mantras), puja rituals are an important aspect of religious life for most practicing

668

Hindus, and are particularly common and elaborate on holy days, during festivals, and to celebrate major life events such as weddings, funerals, and baby-namings.

Rakshasa (**raahk**-shuh-suh) – Shapeshifting demons in Hindu mythology, Rakshasas have been referred to with various characteristics throughout Hindu and Buddhist literature. Ravana, Vibhishana, Surpanakha, and Kumbhakarna are Rakshasas in *the Ramayana*. Due to the varying (and often conflicting) representations of Rakshasas throughout the literature, this series has expanded on the mythological depictions with far greater detail than has been generally used in the past. While there has been a parallel drawn between some vampire representations and Rakshasas, they are not considered to be the same, in the mythology or in this series. The origin of Rakshasas on Venus was entirely invented by the author, upon the suggestion of Neha, as she was writing her own story.

Rama (**raah**-muh) – The main protagonist of *the Ramayana*, Rama is generally considered to be the seventh avatar of Vishnu. Often referred to as 'the ideal king' and 'the ideal husband,' despite the miserable ending of his wife, Rama is still a beloved figure in modern Hinduism. While there is significant debate about whether Rama should be considered infallible, this series explores the dichotomy between the divine and human aspects of his character, in line with major historical representations across the Hindu world, including the iconic version by the ancient Sanskrit poet Valmiki, that demonstrate his crooked path to virtue in great detail. The festival of Diwali, one of the most popular Hindu festivals celebrated by hundreds of millions of people every autumn, celebrates the triumph of light over darkness, as embodied by Durga's triumph over Mahishasura, and Rama's triumph over Ravana.

Ramayana, the (**raah**-mah-yuh-nuh) – One of the most well-known and beloved of the ancient Hindu Sanskrit epics, *the Ramayana* follows the many triumphs and tribulations of Rama, the seventh avatar of Vishnu, and Sita, his wife and the avatar of Lakshmi. While the epic covers a range of stories and characters, the primary conflict centers around Rama's battle with Ravana, the Rakshasa King of Lanka, after his capture and incarceration of Sita. While there are many versions of *the Ramayana* referenced across Southeast Asia including in India, Nepal, Thailand, Cambodia, and more, the most famous version is credited to the storyteller Valmiki. *The Ramayana* of Valmiki contains seven *kandas* or 'books.' The seven-book structure of *The Sita Chronicles* is meant to be a nod to the original epic.

Ravana (**raah**-vuh-nuh) – The main antagonist of *the Ramayana*, Ravana is the Rakshasa King of Lanka. He is said to be a devotee of Shiva, and to have received the 'nectar of immortality' as a boon from Lord Brahma that allows him to withstand any injury from any creature, other than a human. Lord Vishnu comes to Earth as the human, Rama, to take advantage of this epic loophole.

Sanskrit (sahn-skrit) – The primary sacred language of Hinduism, it has many forms and served as the foundation for many modern languages in Southeast Asia. Its role in spreading Indic culture throughout the region can generally be compared to Latin's role in disseminating and communicating literature, religion, and secular education throughout Europe for the two millennia spanning the Roman Empire to the end of the 18th century AD.

Saraswati (sah-ruh-svuh-**tee**) – The female aspect of the Creator of the Universe, Saraswati is also considered the goddess of knowledge, music, arts, learning, and wisdom. Saraswati is the wife of Brahma, and one of the principal goddesses of the *Tridevi*, or 'Trinity of Goddesses.'

Satya Yuga (saht-yuh **yoo**-guh) – 'The Age of Truth,' *Satya Yuga* is said to be the peaceful era that will return to Earth after the Preserver of the Universe vanquishes Kali, ending Kali Yuga (the 'Age of Vice').

Shakti (shuhk-tee) – The Great Goddess, the primordial cosmic energy of the universe, and the personification of the 'divine mother,' Shakti has many manifestations, including the *Tridevi*, Durga, Lakshmi, Saraswati, and Parvati. She is said to manifest on Earth as the embodiment of creative power and fertility, and of life itself. Some sects believe that Shakti is responsible for all creation and is the agent of all change, as it is her energy that animates everything in the universe, including the gods. In Shaktism and Shaivism, Shakti is worshipped as the animating energy of the Supreme Being.

Shiva (shih-vuh) – One of the primary deities of Hinduism, and one of the *Trimurti*, or 'Trinity of Gods,' Lord Shiva is considered to be 'the Destroyer,' 'the Transformer,' and 'the Regenerator.' He is represented by hundreds, possibly thousands, of different epithets. He is often represented as conflicting personas: He can be 'fierce' or 'benevolent,' and he is portrayed as a 'householder' with his wife, Parvati, and their sons, Ganesh and Kartikeya, but he is also portrayed as an ascetic yogi (chaste and focused on solitary prayer)— two lifestyles that are mutually exclusive in traditional Hindu society. Shiva's wife, Parvati (also referred to as Durga, Shakti, Kali, and many other names), is considered to be his life-force. In Valmiki's *Ramayana*, Ravana is a follower of Shiva, and Shiva is said to have given him a divine sword with the stipulation that if he uses his sword for unjust purposes, it will be returned to 'the three-eyed one' (Shiva himself). Shiva is often considered to be 'formless,' and it is common to worship him through the formless idol of a 'lingam' (internet image search recommended).

Sita (see-tuh) – The main female protagonist of *the Ramayana*, Sita is Rama's wife and an avatar of Lakshmi. Often referred to as 'the ideal wife' for her desire and ability to make the deepest personal sacrifices on behalf of her husband, Sita's tragic suicidal ending is controversial in modern academic discussions of the ancient epics.

Sugriva (soo-**gree**-vuh) – The king of the Vanaras (non-human intelligent primates who can fly), Sugriva's support is crucial to Rama's defeat of Ravana in *the Ramayana*. It is with Sugriva's army that Rama attacks Lanka. Many discussions around historical validity of *the Ramayana* have centered around the assertion that Rama led Sugriva's army over a formerly existing land bridge from mainland India to the island of Sri Lanka, as NASA images show that a series of lightly submerged sandbar islands do appear to have, at some point in the past, connected the two land masses.

Surpanakha (**soor**-puh-nuh-khuh) – The sister of Ravana, Vibhishana, and Kumbhakarna, Surpanakha is a primary female antagonist in *the Ramayana*. She is often considered the catalyst of the main events of *the Ramayana* (often taking the blame for Ravana's despicable actions). Surpanakha's story is also complex, as one of her primary scenes in the epic is when she falls in love with Rama. When she is rejected and humiliated by Rama, Rama's brother, Lakshmana, permanently maims her by cutting off her nose with a divine weapon. Surpanakha's hatred of Sita and her anger at Rama's rejection is a driving force of her character's antagonistic actions later in the story and in this series.

Tridevi (tree-**deh**-vee) – The 'Trinity of Goddesses': Saraswati ('the Creator'), Lakshmi ('the Preserver'), and Parvati, ('the Transformer'), serve as the female aspects and underlying energy of their male, godly counterpart husbands. Together they create balance between the three main aspects of existence. Each one individually, and the group as a whole, manifest Shakti's energy as is necessary to participate in worldly endeavors on behalf of the gods and goddesses, usually to support the cause of righteousness and restore balance.

Trimurti (tree-**moor**-tee) – The 'trinity' of Hindu gods: Brahma ('the Creator'), Vishnu ('the Preserver'), and Shiva ('the Destroyer' and 'the Transformer'). Together, the trinity complements each other, representing a descriptive model of various aspects of life on Earth.

Valmiki (**vahl**-mih-kee) – The most widely attributed author of *the Ramayana*, he is credited with inventing the poetic structure of epic Sanskrit literature, somewhat akin to Homer's role in codifying ancient Greek verse. In Valmiki's *Ramayana*, he participates as a character in his own work, being said to have taken Sita in after her trial by fire when Rama banished her to the jungle to raise their twin sons alone. Valmiki's own voiced admonishment of Rama's behaviour in the final chapters serves as a valuable, if controversial, reminder of the story's main point of demonstrating the complex and imperfect paths to *dharma* (virtue), along with its tragic consequences.

Vanara (**vaah**-nuh-ruh) – An ancient race of nonhuman, intelligent primates, the Vanaras are supporters of Rama and serve as his primary troops in his battle against Ravana. Sometimes referred to just as 'monkeys,' other times referred to as 'half-man, half-monkeys,' the literature is not consistent in its depiction of Vanaras. Hanuman and Sugriva are the most famous Vanaras, from their important roles in *the Ramayana*.

Varuna (vuh-**roo**-nuh) – The god of water and the celestial ocean, Varuna was the original chief god of the Vedic pantheon and later appeared throughout Sanskrit literature, primarily as the ruler of the sea. He plays a secondary role in *the Ramayana*, and is often referred to as a symbol of *rta*, an ancient vedic concept believed to encompass cosmic order and divine balance or justice.

Vibhishana (vee-**bhee**-shuh-nuh) – The youngest brother of the villain demon king, Ravana, Vibhishana is an important ally of Rama in *the Ramayana*. In *the Ramayana*, Vibhishana attempts to convince Ravana to return Sita to Rama, but his efforts are not successful. He then joins Rama and provides important intel that leads to Ravana's eventual defeat. Rama crowns Vibhishana the King of Lanka after Ravana is dead. Vibhishana's role in *the Ramayana* is a complex one, as he betrays his family and his race in order to follow a path he considers to be more dharmic. Still, there is no perfect path towards *dharma* (righteousness), and so, he is also considered a traitor. Vibhishana is one of the *Chiranjivi*, one of the seven immortals of Hinduism, who are said to remain on Earth to this day to guide humans on the path of righteousness.

Vishnu (**vihsh**-noo) – One of the primary deities of Hinduism, Lord Vishnu is considered to be 'the Preserver of the Universe.' Lord Vishnu is one of the *Trimurti*, or 'trinity' of Hindu gods, along with Brahma and Shiva. Together with his wife, Lakshmi (or Laxmi), who is considered his life-force, Lord Vishnu is mentioned throughout numerous Sanskrit texts and is worshipped as the supreme being by the Vaishnavist sects of Hindus. Rama is generally considered the seventh avatar of Vishnu among the *Dashavatara* ('ten avatars of Vishnu'). Some Hindu texts/sects refer to more avatars of Vishnu, including Mohini, a female avatar.

Vishrava (vihsh-**rah**-vuh) – The father of Ravana, Vibhishana, Kumbhakarna, and Surpanakha, he is described as a powerful rishi or 'seer.' He is said to have left his wife, Kaikesi, the mother of his four Rakshasa children, to return to his first wife after he became unhappy with Ravana's conduct.

Ya Devi Sarva Bhuteshu (**yah** deh-**vee** sar-vuh **bhoo**-teh-**shoo**) – The beginning of the *Devi Suktam*, one of the primary prayers/mantras to the Goddess (often sung in worship), these Sanskrit words celebrate the Goddess's embodiment of power, peace, knowledge, and many other necessary and beautiful aspects of existence in the universe, allowing the worshippers to feel the Shakti, or energy, of the Goddess within themselves, while bowing (figuratively or literally) to the greatness of all that is.

Yajna (yahg-nyuh) – 'Sacrifice, devotion, worship, or offering,' it refers to any ritual done in front of a sacred fire, often with mantras.

Yaksha/Yakshini (yahk-shuh / yahk-**shee**-nee) – A powerful nature spirit with shapeshifting abilities, generally considered to be the caretakers of Earth. The feminine form of a Yaksha is a Yakshini.

Yama (yah-muh) – The god of death, lord of justice, and the gatekeeper of the underworld, Yama is one of several deities who participates in the management of the afterlife. The gatekeeper of Naraka (roughly Hindu 'purgatory'), Yama is said to be one of the judges of human life/morality and 'the first mortal to have died.'

Pronunciation Key:

Rather than using the international phonetic alphabet that is not commonly used by the average reader, these pronunciation notes use references to common sounds in American English, more similar to a foreign language guide for casual travelers. Note that an "h" does not represent an aspiration in this transliteration; it is used to demonstrate various vowel sounds in English. Also note that the consonants have been simplified for an English speaker and do not fully represent the nuanced differences in the Sanskrit alphabet, such as aspirated v. non-aspirated consonants, that a native Hindi speaker would recognize.

Ah – as in "car" and "hard"
Aah – hold "ah" as in "car" and "hard" longer
Uh – as in "under" and "bus"
Ih – as in "in" and "interest"
Eh – as in "extra" and "**e**xcellent"
Oh – as in "over" and "ornate"
Ee – as in "cheese" and "beast," note that this does not indicate an elongation
Oo – as in "choose" and "I do," note that this does not indicate an elongation

This series is dedicated to the Goddess who resides in all of us. May she give us the energy, inspiration, and perseverance to triumph over all that holds us back, no matter what forms our enemies take. "We are told too often what we can't do." May we do it anyway. *Jai Mata Di.* ~Ashley Mayers

www.ingramcontent.com/pod-product-compliance
Lightning Source LLC
Chambersburg PA
CBHW030028030726
47500CB00001B/4